THE
SPIDER AND THE STONE

GLEN CRANEY

A
NOVEL
OF
SCOTLAND'S
BLACK DOUGLAS

 BRIGID'S FIRE PRESS

Published in the United States

FIRST EDITION (paperback)

Library of Congress Cataloging-in-Publication Data
Craney, Glen
The Spider and the Stone: A Novel of Scotland's Black Douglas/Glen Craney

ISBN 978-0-9816484-0-8

1. History-Fiction. 2. Historical Fiction. 3. Douglas, James (1286-1330)-Fiction.
4. Robert I, King of Scots (1274-1329)-Fiction. 5. Scotland-History-Robert I (1306-1329)-Fiction. 6. Scotland-History-James Douglas (1286-1330)-Fiction. 7. Scotland-History-War of Independence (1285-1371)-Fiction.

Brigid's Fire Press
www.brigidsfire.com

Chaucer Award
First-Place Category Historical Fiction

Foreword Magazine
Book-of-the-Year Finalist
Historical Fiction

indieBRAG Medallion Honoree

Wine is strong,
The King is stronger,
Women are strongest,
But Truth conquers all.

— lintel inscription
Rosslyn Chapel, Scotland

PROLOGUE

NORFOLK, ENGLAND
FEBRUARY, 1358

Lashed by a morning sleet storm, William Douglas paced with apprehension before the frozen earthworks of Castle Rising, an old royal mint so grim and neglected that it made London Tower seem hospitable. The clan patriarch of Lanarkshire warriors had survived English assaults on the bloody fields of Neville's Cross and Poitiers, but never had his fortitude lagged as it did now. He was homesick for Scotland, having served five months as a surety for the onerous Treaty of Berwick, a sacrifice required due to his rank as Earl of Douglas and his impending accession to the Earldom of Mar. He stole a glance over his shoulder at the East Anglian peat beds that lay north across the low broads. If he and his squire could break free of their English warden, they might reach the Borders and find refuge in Ettrick Forest, just as King Robert's mossers had done half a century ago.

He asked himself again: Why would the She-Wolf demand to meet *him?*

Did the brooding harridan wish to be entertained by his humiliation in defeat? No fellow Scot would shame him for shunning the task at hand, for inside that ice-corniced mausoleum prowled the most dangerous and reviled woman in all the Isles. Isabella of France, the hoary old queen mother of England, had been at various turns in her infamous existence an insatiable adulteress, a regicide and usurper of the throne, a changeling who wore armor into battle and perverted nature by making love like a man, a sorceress who had beguiled her own son by slithering into his bed at night, a necromancer who held séances with her beheaded—

The gate portcullis cranked up. A detail of English pikemen in hobnailed boots marched forth from the tower and trudged across the glazed boards.

Douglas sighed heavily, seeing his last chance to avoid the ordeal dashed. Led with his squire through an occulted archway, he searched the scratchings on the rampart stones for signs of Isabella's witchery. In her youth, the queen mother had gained a reputation for being a meddlesome princess in her father Philip's royal court in Paris, where she was said to have become privy to the heretical depravities of the Knights Templar. Bartered off to England as a marital bargaining chip in the conflict over Aquitaine, she had made good use of the cunning assassination methods perfected by those crusader monks. Her feckless husband, Edward Caernarvon, had duly earned his toll paid to Hell, but only a woman who consorted with demons could have arranged so heinous a death for a deposed king. When Isabella's first-born, Edward the Third, became old enough to climb atop the throne, he banished her from London, and she raged at the filial ingratitude by conjuring down the Black Death upon the Isles. Most believed that she had managed to survive these past twenty-seven years in this outpost only because she had long ago sold her soul to the Devil.

A forearm came roughly to the earl's chest, halting him. The sergeant of the guard opened a door and prodded Douglas and his squire into an austere room lit dimly by a solitary candle. Douglas heard the lock latch behind him. As his eyes adjusted to the dusty gloom, he spied a silver cross with *fleur-de-lis* flanges crowning a small altar at the far wall. That corner of the room shimmered with movement. A bent hag, shrouded in the brown habit of a religious, arose with difficulty from a kneeler in the slant shadows and shuffled toward him.

Douglas reached into his coin pouch and offered her a farthing, as was one's obligation when encountering a Poor Clare devoted to poverty. "Forgive us, *cailleach,* for interrupting your prayers. Would you inform the Queen Mother that William of Douglas awaits her summons?"

The nun kept staring over his shoulder at his squire.

Douglas feared she was senile. "Good woman, did you not hear me?"

The nun snatched the coin from his fingers. She held it under the candle's penumbra and traced a long nail over its raised face in profile.

Douglas cursed under his breath, suspecting that he had been led to the wrong chamber in a prank to entertain the garrison. "I am Douglas of—"

"I know who you are." The nun turned her evil eye again on his squire, who remained a step behind him. "Who is *this* man?"

"My second."

She returned the farthing. "I have scandals enough attached to my name. If Parliament were to learn that I accepted charity from a Scotsman, I would be led to the block on the next morn."

Douglas retreated a step, abashed at having mistaken the She-Wolf for a dotty anchorite. He surrendered a grudging bow to the shriveled womb that had given birth to his country's sworn enemy. "I beg your forgiveness."

Isabella smiled wanly as she took their wet cloaks and hung them on pegs. "You will have to wait your turn. There is a long line of men who seek God's intercession for my absolution." She extended a tremulous hand to invite them toward the cold hearth. "I would offer you wine worthy of your palate, but circumstances have denied me such provisions."

Perplexed by the welcome, Douglas considered the possibility that this frail woman might not be a bewitching harpy after all, but a victim of England's cruel imagination. He inspected her sparse quarters. Had she accepted this living martyrdom to draw the ire of the fickle English and deflect their challenges to her son's legitimacy? Yet she was still a Plantagenet by marriage, attached to the rapacious brood that was bent on crushing his country's independence, and he could not mask his hatred fueled by half a century of war. "We Scots are accustomed to being denied provisions. We have England to thank for that."

She nodded and sighed. "And yet, I can remember a time when your forefathers dined uninvited at many a table in Northumbria and Yorkshire." She studied his features. "You are kinsman to James Douglas."

He braced for the opprobrium *that* admission always elicited here in England. "My father, many years younger, was his half-brother."

"Your uncle was the most troublesome of the many trespassers who harried our northern shires." She squinted to peer over his shoulder again. "His skin was dark for a Scotsman, like that of your squire."

Born in the year of his famous uncle's death, the earl had often heard the Good Sir James's unusual coloring compared to that of a Castilian. "Aye, hence they called him the Black Douglas."

She waved off that explanation. "His dark countenance was not why he earned that wicked sobriquet. There is much you do not know about him."

He bristled at the suggestion that she was better informed about his clan's heritage. "May I inquire, madam, as to the purpose of this audience?"

Isabella lifted the clotted candle from the altar and drifted unsteadily toward the fireplace. She stooped, wincing to a knee, and held the precarious flame under a pile of green wood until it took the spark. "I am told the Canterbury scribes are filling their chronicles with calumny about your uncle."

Long inured to the Plantagenet industry of lies, Douglas shrugged with bitter resignation. "If paid handsomely enough, those monks would defame St. Peter himself."

Isabella stirred the fire, stalling for time as if debating his trustworthiness. Finally, she said, "I am the last mortal still drawing breath who knew James Douglas. I wish to have my say on his deeds before I die."

The earl set his jaw, incensed. Had he journeyed three days to this outback in the midst of winter merely to suffer a lecture on Westminster's version of Scot history? His tone turned raw. "I suppose you would have us believe that he ran from a match of arms against one of your tourney hotheads."

Isabella's wrinkled mouth pursed with faint amusement. "Lord Douglas feared no man. But there was one woman who daunted him severely."

A snort of disbelief puffed the air near the door.

Douglas turned and glared at his squire, chastising him for the indiscretion.

Isabella, smiling at their skepticism, arose with the earl's assistance and wrangled a chair nearer the fire. Gathering a shawl around her ankles, she sat and taunted the two men with a challenge. "If you Scots are as stout of heart as you always boast, surely you will not shrink from an old widow's tale."

The queen mother's claim of distant acquaintance with the Good Sir James intrigued Douglas, so he reluctantly agreed to hear her out. In truth, he had no choice, given the exigencies of his diplomatic commission. When Isabella motioned for him to bring up stools aside her, he complied, but his squire insisted on standing in the shadows behind him.

She stared for several moments at the crackling hearth. Then, she roused and, smearing the tip of the poker with charcoal, sketched a crude map of the Isles on the flagstone near her feet. "Long before you were born, your King Alexander died without siring an heir."

Douglas glanced back at his squire, wondering if he also found Isabella's voice now altered, almost otherworldly. Was the woman using her conjury to bring forth a spirit from beyond the veil?

Isabella tapped the floor with the poker to reclaim their attention. She scratched a mark on the southeastern region of her map to indicate the location of a port city at the eastern crease where Scotland and England met. "Four years before this century turned, your throne fell empty and the clans commenced scrapping for it like charnel dogs over a carcass. All the while, the Leopard of England stalked the Borders, sniffing blood and champing to pounce when the Lion of Caledonia fell lame from self-inflicted wounds."

The two men, beguiled by the strangeness of her bardic inflections, edged closer to better hear her.

"But one runt of a lad, inspired by a headstrong maid from Fife, would not sit prey for an easy clawing." Isabella stabbed at the crackling log as if gutting a combatant, forcing the earl to shield his eyes from the flying embers. She stared at the flames —was she scrying a memory vision?—and lowered her voice to a whisper taut with emotion. "Nay, sit prey Jamie Douglas would not. The stars had destined *him* to stalk the stalker."

ROLL OF
HONOR AND INFAMY

The Scots

James Douglas: *son of Wil Douglas*

Wil Douglas: *a rebel leader, nicknamed "the Hardi"*

Eleanor Douglas: *second wife of William Douglas*

Isabelle "Belle" MacDuff: *daughter of Ian MacDuff*

Ian MacDuff: *Earl of Fife and chieftain of Clan MacDuff*

Robert Bruce: *7th Lord of Annandale, grandson of the Competitor*

Robert Bruce the Competitor: *grandfather of Robert*

Gibbie Duncan: *childhood friend of James Douglas*

Elizabeth de Burgh: *daughter of the Earl of Ulster*

William Lamberton: *Bishop of St. Andrews*

Edward Bruce: *brother of Robert*

Thomas Bruce: *brother of Robert*

Nigel Bruce: *brother of Robert*

Mary Campbell: *sister of Robert Bruce*

Christian Seton: *sister of Robert Bruce*

Red Comyn: *patriarch of the Clan Comyn*

John "Cam" Comyn: *Lord of Badendoch, the son of Red*

John "Tabhann" Comyn: *Lord of Buchan, the nephew of Red*

Idonea Comyn: *widow of Red's eldest brother*

Thomas Dickson: *servant of William Douglas*

Christiana of the Isles: *leader of Clan Gamoran*

Angus Og MacDonald: *Lord of the Isles*

Dewar of Glendochart: *patriarch of the Culdee Church*

Ned Sween: *a Culdee monk, nicknamed "Sweenie the Wee-kneed"*

Murdoch, McKie and McClurg: *sons of the Galloway crone*

Thomas Randolph: *nephew of Robert Bruce, later Earl of Moray*

Sim Ledhouse: *A raider in the service of James Douglas*

William Sinclair: *Master of Scotland's Templar commandery*

The English

Edward I: *King of England, nicknamed "Longshanks"*

Edward Caernarvon: *son of Longshanks, he becomes Edward II*

Edward III: *son of Isabella of France*

Gilbert de Clare: *Earl of Gloucester, kinsman to the Bruces*

Robert Clifford: *officer in charge of the Scot Marches*

Aymer de Valence: *Earl of Pembroke, a commander in Scotland*

Robert Neville: *a knight known as "The Peacock of the North"*

Henry de Bohun: *a knight in the service of Edward II*

Thomas Lancaster: *Earl of Lancaster, a rival of Edward II*

Hugh Despenser: *second favourite of Edward II*

Roger Mortimer: *Isabella of France's paramour*

The French

Philip IV: *King of France, called "the Fair"*

Isabella of France: *daughter of Philip IV*

Piers Gaveston: *Caernarvon's Gascon favourite*

Giles d'Argentin: *a knight*

Abbot of Lagny: *a Dominican inquisitor*

Peter d'Aumont: *a Knight Templar from Auvergne*

Jeanne de Rouen: *a Cistercienne attached to the Knights Templar*

PART ONE
The Hammer Rises

1296–1307 A.D.

Dishonor was offered,
they refused;
Blood was upon the hair,
and from the harp
a sigh of sorrow.

— a Druid lament

ONE

Sooted by pillage smoke blown inland across the North Sea, hundreds of Scots—women, children, and feeble old men among them—dangled kicking and gagging from gallows that had been hastily erected below the burning spires of Berwick.

That morning, a shock force of English knights had launched the spring campaign of 1296 by cutting a swath of destruction into Scotland's largest port. Now, hours into the butchery, Yorkshire and Northumbrian *routiers* rampaged down the city's narrow wynds, stripping and rolling strangled inhabitants into the Tweed to clear the execution ropes for more victims. The river's blood-slicked currents swept this flotsam of misery and death toward the estuary on the coast, where the corpses eddied with the frenzied salmon driven harbor side by the poisonous spillage from torched merchant ships. Trapped in the motte tower at the center of the conflagration, a half-starved garrison of two hundred Scot knights could only watch from the ramparts and shout promises of vengeance at the English murderers below them.

On a distant hill overlooking the flaming walls, fourteen-year-old James Douglas collapsed to his knees and retched.

His two gray mastiff pups, Cull and Chullan, nipped at his heels as if to protest this shameful reaction to his first glimpse of war. Scoffing at rumors of widespread killings, he had convinced his best friend, Gibbie Duncan, to join him on the three-day run here from Douglasdale. But now he saw with his own eyes that the reports of a massacre were true. These English devils were burning and looting all that stood in their path east of the Selkirk Forest.

He fought for breath, wiping his mouth with his sleeve, and ran to catch up with Gibbie. A premature birth had left him sickly and slight from the start, but nature had compensated him with fierce agate eyes and straight black hair that he kept shorn short in the fashion of the Romans who had built the ancient stone wall south of his Lanarkshire home. He had heard the gossiped whispers: that his veins ran with the blood of a distant centurion and that his skin had darkened to the shade of lightly tanned leather when his mother, dying in childbirth, had screamed a pagan pact to bargain his survival.

Gibbie, a year younger but a head taller than James, rushed ahead and dropped to his knees on the brow of the next hill. He inched his eyes above the broom. Running a hand through his wild flaxen hair, he hissed through the gap where his front teeth should have been and pointed toward a column of mounted knights making fast for Berwick. "That's the English king!"

James staggered up the steep sandstone spur, refusing to believe it. "Edward Plantagenet wouldn't muddy his boots this far north."

Gibbie gnawed on a root tuber and spat his opinion of his friend's skepticism. "You think I don't know the royal pennon?"

James blinked away the sting of the smoke as he crouched atop the perch next to Gibbie. When his eyes had cleared, he looked down into the valley and saw that the lead rider of the armed column had freakishly long legs and wild white hair flowing to his shoulders. Gibbie was right—the English king *had* arrived from York. But it was another sight that tested James's unsettled belly again. The Plantagenet herald carried a standard with a fire-breathing monster reared on its hinds. Every Scot lad had been taught what the raising of the dragon meant: Berwick's defenders would be dealt with as traitors to the crown. His heart raced at the fearsome sight. These English knights who served King Edward the First rode chargers twice the size of Highland ponies and wore silver armour so resplendent that the old Roman road up from Sunderland now resembled a glittering snake. They seemed spawned from biblical giants of another race—and their Goliath was being hailed across Christendom with an ominous new title:

The Hammer of the Scots.

When the royal column disappeared over the far ridge, James clambered up to the limb of a sprawling oak for a better view of his father's defense of the Scot tower. Called "Le Hardi" in honor of his service to the Cross in Palestine, Wil Douglas had been recruited by the guardians of the realm to lead the insurrection against the English aggression. Sinewy and raw-boned, he stood a hand taller than most in his ranks and could still sling a log farther than any man in Lanarkshire. Yet a decade of fighting had aged him beyond his forty-two years; his eyes were ringed with smoky circles of fatigue and his thick chestnut shocks had receded to a band of grey tufts above the temples. He now slumped so severely from the weight of his hauberk that his torso appeared to have slipped the moorings of his spine. Although his crackling storytelling and bawdy jests used to be legendary across Scotland, James could not remember the last time he had heard his father laugh.

James searched the smoldering pines to the north. There was still no sign of the promised relief army from Stirling. Below the city's walls, on the banks of the Tweed, English soldiers guarded the lone bridge that led into the port. Swollen from the spring thaw, the river curved through the low dunes and came within a hundred yards of the tower before emptying into the sea. He feared that if the English were allowed to fire their catapult all night, his father's timbered keep would collapse before morning. If that happened, the road to the northern provinces would be thrown open. Weighing the risks, he drew a long breath and insisted, "We have to malafooster that stone thrower."

Gibbie chewed on his root. "Those scousers down there are thicker than a cloud of midges. How would we get into the camp unnoticed?"

James thought hard on that problem. He cocked his ear to the south. A minstrel's ditty wafted up in the breeze from the camp followers straggling behind the English army. Hatching an idea, he whistled an imitation of the tune as he pulled a penknife from his pocket and whittled a soft branch into a hollow flute with five holes. Satisfied with its pitch, he split off another limb and hurriedly carved three balls the size of crab apples. He threw the wooden balls at Gibbie. "How's your juggling?"

Gibbie lunged for the balls, but lost his hold on the limb and plummeted to the heather. Cursing, he arose and gathered up the balls, wondering what in hell's molasses his friend was up to now. He found James running toward the river armed with only a tune pipe and some cockeyed scheme. "Douglas, you bawheided choob! You're dafter'n an unbolt door on a windy day!"

As darkness fell, the two boys floated down river toward Berwick. Moving with the strong currents, they held their shirts and leggings above their heads while the pups paddled furiously behind them to keep up. After a half-hour of frigid swimming past the charred debris, they reached the banks below the tower and discovered that the English had advanced their lines to within a mere hundred paces from the walls. They dressed quickly, shaking the blood back to their toes.

James whispered a prayer to St. Ninian for protection, then nodded his readiness to Gibbie. He leapt over the embankment and marched into the English camp, playing the flute and singing:

"The pretty trees of Berwick
are hung with fruit so ripe."

Gibbie followed, juggling awkwardly while the pups howled.

The English soldiers sitting around the fires erupted with weapons drawn and searched the surrounding darkness for the source of the singing.

James, shaking with fear, forced himself to finish the song:
"Scots and dogs that deigned to pick
with their English lords a gripe."

The soldiers glared at the two ragged jesters—and burst into laughter.

Their merriment, however, was short-lived. A sullen-looking officer, clad in a black hammered breastplate and spiked gauntlets, marched through the ranks with a sinister gait that cowered the men to silence. He wore his long black hair lacquered back in a ducktail on his collar, and his liquorish mouth was coated with an evident distaste for all who fell under the inspection of his gimlet eyes. Glaring at the soldiers over a crooked nose notched by scars, he demanded, "Who halted the firing of this sling?"

Before the conscripts could hazard an answer, an older Englishman with reddish-blond hair and a finely trimmed beard cantered up on a sleek ebony horse. The three chevronels on his breastplate revealed him to be Gilbert de Clare, the Earl of Gloucester. "The men have been on the march for weeks, Clifford. Allow them this brief amusement."

Clifford.

James shot an alarmed glance at Gibbie. He had often heard his father curse the name of Robert Clifford, a mosstrooper granted seized Scot domains for serving as the Plantagenet watchdog here in the Borders. Although only in his mid-twenties, the English officer's hard, contemptuous features were so suffused with an urgency to inflict cruelty that he appeared to be much older.

Clifford refused the baron the courtesy of a direct look. "I am not leading a festival here."

Gloucester was quick to put the officer in his place. "You are not *leading* anything. His Highness commands this army. And I am his second in rank."

James was stunned to hear such insolence spoken to a nobleman. The English earl had a high forehead and pouchy, bloodshot eyes that gave him the weary look of a philosopher exiled into a world of crass thugs. Although married to the king's daughter, he was also kinsman to several prominent Scot nobles, a lineage that reportedly had cast him into disfavor in London. His counsel against this interference in Scotland's affairs had further strained his relationship with the king, and James suspected the wily Longshanks was testing Gloucester's loyalty by requiring him to accompany the army north.

Clifford's hand edged to his dagger. "You've dragged your heels since York."

Rankled, Gloucester straightened in the saddle. "You accuse me of treason?"

"Always one boot on each side of this border."

"Damn you, Clifford! Not in front of the men!"

Clifford turned laughing to the ranks. "So orders the cousin to the Bruces and Stewarts!"

Despite giving up thirty years in age, Gloucester leapt from his saddle and lunged at the mouthy officer. The two Englishmen clenched and grappled, but the bulk of their livery impeded their blows. A sergeant-at-arms finally broke them apart, and Gloucester surfaced from the fight clutching his chest. "I will have recourse for that slander! By the Cross, I will have—"

"My treasury!"

That shout, from behind them, had the silencing effect of an explosion.

Edward Plantagenet's wiry white locks fanned over his black velvet royal robe as he strode with long, loping steps toward the two scrapping men. The king stopped and, turning to a freckle-faced boy trailing behind him, remarked with a tone of deceptive benevolence, "I have spent half the coin of my realm to provision this army, Eddie. Can you tell me what it still lacks?"

The monarch's twelve-year-old heir, Prince Edward Caernarvon, stood cocooned in a miniature breastplate and armed with a sword half the length of regular issue. He carved a path through the downcast soldiers, who were forced to suffer his abuse. Looking up at his towering father, the boy offered a guess. "Archers?"

"Nay, I have a thousand Welsh bowmen."

The prince tried again. "Engines?"

The king's left lid drooped menacingly as he walked to the giant catapult and caressed its beams. This odd disparity of his eyes, one slack and the other sharp, gave the impression that two warring souls inhabited his body. When his lazy eye quivered, as it did now, a malevolent daemon seemed to take possession of him. "That surely cannot be the source of my troubles. This trebuchet has the longest range of any on the Isles."

The prince removed his small helmet, unleashing a mop of red hair. "I've guessed it now, father! You have no officers worthy of you!"

The king spun so swiftly on Clifford that the trailing royal attendants lurched into the muck. "From the mouth of a babe!"

Clifford kept his head bowed. "If Your Grace would assign command—"

The king lunged and pinned Clifford's neck to the trebuchet girding. "Why has that tower not been taken?"

Clifford gasped. "This man Douglas will not relent."

Shocked by the swift surge of violence, James watched the ranks. Although the soldiers kept their eyes down, Gloucester smiled coldly, clearly enjoying the insolent officer's comeuppance.

Finally, the earl interceded with a cool demeanor that suggested he held himself equal to the Plantagenet in both pedigree and intelligence. "These demonstrations of terror only stiffen the resolve of the Scots," he told the king. "Wil Douglas may be a firebrand, but he has grievances."

The king shoved Clifford aside and closed fast on Gloucester. "Grievances? These Scots beg me to arbitrate their disputes! And this is how they show their gratitude? I did not betroth you to my daughter, sir, to suffer your insipid lectures on statecraft!"

James saw Gloucester redden. The baron, however, had no choice but to swallow the affront. Gloucester was one of the few men alive whose memory reached into those tumultuous decades after the English king's grandfather had been brought to heel at Runnymede in 1215. Yet this Edward now ruled as if the Magna Carta had never been signed. When, months earlier, the Scot nobles had petitioned Edward to arbitrate their dispute over their empty throne, he had twisted the request into a pretext for annexing the kingdom to his own.

"Your Highness," Clifford interjected, searching the camp as if desperate for a diversion to lighten the king's mood. "Why not demonstrate to the rebels how little worried we are by their defiance? A few verses by this rhymester and his juggler will raise our spirits."

Hearing *that* offer, James swallowed hard and hunted for an opening to the river. His plan had been to deceive a few conscripts into letting him sleep close enough to set the engine afire during the night, not to give a royal performance.

Clifford snapped his fingers for James and Gibbie to step up on the quick.

Given no choice, James cleared his throat while searching for a new verse. Finally, he sang:

"By Longshanks he is known."

Groans from the ranks revealed too late that the king's nickname was never spoken in his presence. Yet James forced himself to continue, fearing that hesitation would prove more disastrous:

"From Wales to far-off France,
For his boots reach long,
And his step be strong
The better upon …"

He racked his brain for a finale.

"… their necks to dance."

An uneasy hush fell over the men—until the king gave up a hearty laugh.

Relieved, James offered a half-bow. When he arose, he saw, in the clearing just beyond the tents, a band of captive Berwick residents being herded toward the gallows. The poor wretches trudged across the camp in a wavering line of misery, their battered heads slung in despair. An old woman in the condemned group turned and screamed something at him in Gaelic. He took a step to go her aid, but caught himself and looked away.

Longshanks and his officers were now trading jests, oblivious to the next batch of victims being driven to the ropes. Prince Edward, however, was quiet and observant, and his gaze came to rest heavily on James.

James turned, too late, to see suspicion in the prince's eyes. He feared the English boy had detected his consternation about the hangings.

"From where do you hail, jester?" the prince asked.

James enunciated the name of a Yorkshire town in his best imitation of the way the English inhabitants of that region spoke. "Knaresborough."

"Knaresborough, *my lord*. You address the future king of England."

James lowered his head. "Forgive me, my lord."

The prince turned toward Gibbie. "And you?"

Gibbie gave the same answer as James, but his Lanarkshire twang was much too evident, causing the prince's eyes to narrow.

Young Edward tugged at the king's sleeve. In a childish voice that James realized was artifice, the prince asked, "Father, why does this boy talk so queerly?"

The king only then noticed that the hoisted woman's screams of "Douglas" mixed with Gaelic seemed to be aimed at James.

James sensed the danger of the discovery. He nodded for Gibbie to start singing another ballad to distract the king. He joined in, and soon they were both bellowing like drunkards and drawing laughter again from the men.

Yet this time Longshanks was not fooled. The king took a step closer toward the gallows. Narrowing his eyes like a hawk, he answered his son's question. "Perhaps we should inquire, Eddie."

Clifford understood at once what his liege was contemplating. The officer prodded James and Gibbie toward the gallows.

Heart pounding, James cursed silently each time Clifford slapped him on the back of the head. Without turning to give away his plan, he stole a conspiring glance at Gibbie and searched the perimeter of the camp for the nearest path of escape. Clifford forced him to climb the steps, and when he resisted, the officer grabbed him by the shirt and dragged him up.

The dangling Scot woman was ordered dropped from the beam. Revived, she looked up and saw James's terrified face staring down at her. She tried to avert her eyes, until Clifford ordered her lifted again. Unable to stand by while she suffered, James broke from Clifford's clutches and rushed up to support her legs, but the henchman corralled him back to the boards.

Clifford kicked James, stepping over him, and raised a gloved hand to clamp the woman's raw throat. "Your life for a name."

Motivated with another yank of the rope, the half-dead woman rasped, "The Hardi's son! Lord, forgive me!"

From below the gallows, Longshanks watched this exchange play out. Now even more intrigued, he turned toward the tower to compare James's features with those of the Scot commander on the ramparts.

Helpless on his hands and knees, James looked longingly toward his father, who was too far away to discern in the darkness what was causing the commotion in the English camp. In a surge of desperation, James leapt from the gallows platform and Gibbie dived after him. Splattered in the mud, the two boys scrambled to their feet and darted for the river, but the soldiers pounced on them near the banks and dragged them back to the camp.

Pummeled with clods of mud, James looked up over his elbow in time to see the skeleton of the great catapult being ratcheted for another launch. A stone was sent crashing into the motte tower.

Longshanks's laugh punctuated the whine of the arm's recoil.

At dawn on the next morning, Wil Douglas, renewed with hope by the cessation of the bombardment, peered over the battered ramparts of his motte tower. In the light of the rising sun, he saw for the first time that the English lines, supported by the catapult, had closed to within fifty yards during the night. Yet that was not what caused his face to drain.

James and Gibbie stood on the siege engine with their necks noosed.

Longshanks rode closer to the tower to enjoy the Scot commander's reaction. "Surrender, Douglas, and your garrison will be spared!" Resist, and your son will hang! I am told he's your only child! You should have spent less time inciting treason and more nights bedding that Northumbrian whore of yours!"

James could not bear to look at his father. His reckless disobedience of the order to remain in Douglasdale had placed the garrison in even greater peril. After a brittle silence, he heard the clang of swords dropping to the allure boards. Moments later, the gates cranked open. His father and the half-starved Scot knights walked out unarmed.

The English soldiers moved in and descended on them with fists and pikes.

Bloodied, Wil Douglas was forced to kneel before the English king. "Do what you will to me. Release my son."

Longshanks ordered the noose lifted from James's throat. "I am merciful."

"And the other lad," Wil Douglas demanded.

Longshanks shook his head and grinned. "For *him*, another exchange must be negotiated." On the king's command, the soldiers dragged up the elder Douglas to take James's place on the beam.

Gloucester lashed up on his horse to confront the king. "My lord, you gave your word that the garrison would not be harmed."

Longshanks turned away from the earl. "I said nothing of its leader."

"This is sharp practice not worthy of your Grace."

The king spun on the baron and shouted, "Hold your tongue! Or by the Cross I will have you remanded to York for treason!"

Gloucester surveyed the troops for support. But he found no protest in their eyes, only blood lust for the delay and casualties the Scots had cost them.

Having gained the baron's grudging silence, Longshanks stood in his stirrups to be heard by all of the Scot prisoners. "By divine ordain, we English are your brothers! Holy Mother Church has called on me to rid you of your pagan scrapping! The decision is yours this day! Will you accept the sovereign benevolence of England, or God's retribution?" He looked down and smiled at James, who had been forced to his knees. "You will be the first to make the choice, lad. Which shall it be? Comrade or clan?"

James suddenly understood the sinister strategy that Longshanks had devised to steal Scotland: By stoking the ancient enmities between the clans, the king intended to prevent them from uniting. James could only watch in horror as the Scot knights, lined up against the wall, tried to rush the gallows and save his father, but they were driven back.

Wil Douglas struggled against the rope. "Leave the lad out of this!"

Longshanks yanked the cord at James's waist. "Choose, or both will die."

Gibbie shook his head in a plea for James not to break.

Longshanks dismounted and forced James to confront the two persons he loved most. "If you commend your father to Hell, lad, you will inherit his lands as my vassal. Yet if you turn against your fellow conspirator up there, you will be shunned as a turncoat. 'There goes Douglas,' your countrymen will curse under their breaths. 'He gave up his mate to save his papa's neck.'"

Weak in the legs, James wanted to die rather than make the choice.

Longshanks laughed at his anguish. "Either way, my golden-tongued fool, you will be of no consequence to Scotland from—"

Gibbie leapt from the beam.

Wil Douglas thrust out his leg to stop the boy—he was too late.

James rushed to climb the beams and lift Gibbie's legs, but the English soldiers held him back.

"Save him, damn you!" Longshanks shouted at his officers.

Clifford scaled the scaffolding.

Gibbie, gagging, kicked away the officer's reaching hands. Twirling in the ember-choked wind, he looked down at James with bulging eyes, desperate to communicate a dying wish.

The English officer finally reached the top beam and hacked at the rope with his blade. Gibbie fell limp to the mud. Clifford leapt down and straddled the body. Finding no pulse, he cursed and slung aside Gibbie's lifeless arm.

After a stretch of stunned silence, Gloucester rode up with his blade drawn and severed the rope restraining Wil Douglas. The earl ordered the sergeant at arms, "Take this man to the dungeon with the rest of the garrison. Hold him prisoner there until further order."

The sergeant looked for royal confirmation of the command.

Longshanks quivered with rage at the brazen challenge. But seeing his troops nod with grudging admiration for the Scot boy's brave martyrdom, the king chose to leave the confrontation with Gloucester for another day and spurred north while the prisoners were herded away.

Prince Edward, on his pony, followed his father and spat on Gibbie's body when he passed over it.

As the pups tugged at Gibbie's sleeve, James knelt aside his dead friend and heaved with choking breaths. With the Yorkshire conscripts smirking over him, he silently vowed that no Englishman would ever again see his tears.

TWO

Fourteen-year-old Isabelle MacDuff slacked her reins to take mercy on her garron as it fought for footing across the rough headlands above the Firth of Forth. Sensing a dark chill of danger, she looked toward the fore of the mounted column and saw her father, Ian, and her brothers signing their breasts in mournful silence. Despite her fear of heights, she risked a glance over the cliffs to discover what they had passed.

Just then the fog thinned, revealing a circled cross of stone that had been erected on the ragged dunes below her. Truly, she thought, Kinghorn had to be the saddest place in all of Scotland. Eleven years had passed since King Alexander, full of drink and hot to share the bed of his queen at Methil up the coast, had galloped past these crags during the worst storm in memory. The MacDuffs had hosted the monarch in Fife on that eve of March 18, 1285, a date all Scots had come to fear. Several years earlier, a hermit's apparition had appeared in the royal court to warn of a future disaster. When the foretold night finally arrived, her father had begged Alexander to remain at Dunfermline and sleep off the effects of the feast. But the king, an impatient and stubborn Celt, had dismissed the ghost sighting as a foolish superstition.

The next morning, Alexander's body had been found washed ashore here.

She studied her father's slumped shoulders and tried to divine his worries. Muscular and stout, he had a round head that nurtured only a few scrubs of once-reddish hair turned the color of straw with age. And like all full-blooded MacDuff men, he possessed the distinctive family lineament: wide-set eyes with bushy brows that merged over the bridge of a thick nose. Her male ancestors had been so proud of this fearsome feature that for centuries they had left open notches on their helmets to warn their foes that they were about to die at the hands of the legendary clan.

As if sensing her scrutiny, her father turned in the saddle and shouted at her. "Keep up, Belle! The nag will scaur if it falls behind!"

Angling her garron away from the slippery cliffs, she whispered a prayer for Alexander's soul. Why had God taken their king at such an inauspicious time? Was it truly in retribution for his heretical attachment to the old pagan ways? If so, why were so many people required to suffer for the sins of one man? One tragedy was not baneful enough, it seemed, for Alexander's lone surviving heir and granddaughter, the infant Maid of Norway, had met her own miserable death a few months later on a capsized galley near Orkney. That disaster left the clans quarreling for the empty throne, and on this journey south from Fife, she had seen firsthand the calamitous results: Ancient oaks stood split and charred, sheep carcasses lay rotting in the fields, and beggars lined the roads. In the six months since the loss of Berwick and its seventeen thousand citizens, the English invaders had turned Scotland black with desolation.

When news of the massacre reached Fife, she had asked her father why the other clans did not go to the aid of Wil Douglas when they still had the chance to turn back the English. *There be only one creature a Scotsman despises more than an Englishman*, he had told her. *That be another Scotsman.*

The path west turned inland toward a shadow-streaked glen, and the sun threatened to disappear over Ben Cleuch. Vowing to chase these melancholic thoughts, she gathered her long black hair around her neck and tightened her cloak against the rising sea winds. She was grateful at least that one of her prayers had been answered: By this time on the morrow, at the annual Michaelmas gathering of the clans at Scone, she would attempt to sneak a glimpse of the fabled Stone of Destiny.

She had always been enthralled by stories of the *Lia Fail*, the name given to the Stone by the Highland monks who still spoke the Gaelic. Brought to Ireland by the ancient Israelites and ferried across the sea by the first kings of Scotland, the sacred relic possessed the gift of prophecy and was said to scream its blessing when touched by the true king. Her clan, the oldest of them all, had for centuries performed its exclusive privilege atop the Stone: The laying of the crown upon the head of a new monarch.

No MacDuff, no King!

That was the warning spoken as the first words to every babe delivered of a MacDuff womb.

She hadn't slept for two nights, exhilarated by the chance to finally visit the venerated Mound of Credulity, where divine sanction was bestowed upon royal power. Had the Stone truly been the pillow used by the biblical Jacob to rest his head while he dreamed of the Ladder to Heaven? It was said that no other rock of the same texture and composition existed. Would its black sheen still be stained with the blood of the Canaanites? She held fast to a reassuring faith that England would never subjugate Scotland so long as the kingdom possessed the most powerful talisman of protection in all of Christendom.

Wearied of her obsession, her brothers constantly taunted that she would never hear the Stone speak. Only men, they enjoyed reminding her, were allowed within the confines of Scone Abbey, where the Stone was kept under guard on a wooden pedestal before the high altar. Inconsolable after learning of the ban, she had prayed for months to St. Bride, patron saint of courageous women, whose nuns tended the eternal flame in Ireland and threatened damnation on any man who stole a gaze at its sacred light.

Then, nearly a year ago, on her birthday, an old bard had appeared under her window in St. Andrews to deliver a message: *One day you shall hear the deafening shriek of the Heaven Stone.* She had protested that such a miracle would require her to be in the presence of a monarch during his coronation. How could she ever manage such a feat? He had offered her only an enigmatic riddle in reassurance: *The Stone comes to those who serve it.* Ever since that night, she had kept her promise to the bard never to speak of the revelation. After all, to be blessed with an oracle by a Highland poet was a mark of solemn fate, and of all the MacDuffs living and dead, only she had been so honored.

Her garron neighed sharply in warning. Caught up in her musings, she only then realized that her father had not turned the column north at Inverkeithing, but was continuing west along the coastal route. She caught him glancing back at her, as if expecting a reaction. She cantered closer and asked him, "Do we go to Scone by Stirling?" When he remained defiantly silent, she persisted. "Father?"

Finally, he admitted, "We are not going to Scone."

"Not Scone? Where then are the clans to meet?"

"Douglasdale."

She stared at her father, unable to comprehend the change of plans. "The South? But the clans have always met at Scone!" She leapt from her pony and circled his horse in a fit of despair. Her outburst threw the column into disarray. "You have deceived me!"

Ian dismounted. "I warned you to chase this foolishness from your head!" Taking her by the shoulders, he shook her to silence, then gazed sadly toward the north, revealing that he was also distraught over this breach of the ancient tradition. "None of us will see the Stone this year. Perhaps never again."

She was stricken. "But why?"

"The Stone is not on Moot Hill." Driven by her demanding glare, Ian finally explained, "Edward Longshanks has taken the Stone to London. The monks at Perth gave it up without a whimper. Those tonsured cowards expect us to fight their wars, but they would betray Christ Himself before risking their own necks. The English king keeps it under his throne in Westminster and now boasts that, by our own laws, he is master of Scotland."

"The Stone screamed in his presence?"

He would not look at her directly. "There were screams enough … from London Tower."

Biting on her sleeve to stifle a sob, she imagined to her horror how the English tyrant must have kicked and abused the Stone, torturing it like a prisoner on the rack to extract its secrets. "Edward Longshanks cannot become king of Scotland! Not without the Stone's affirmation! You told me so!"

Her father's eyes hooded with shame as he gazed at the distant banners of an English occupation garrison fluttering over Stirling Castle to the west. "That tale was just a priest's deceit to gain donations for a new abbey."

She thrashed at him in protest. "The Stone is true!"

Ian captured her wrists until she relented. "I stood witness at Alexander's coronation! I tell you there was no scream! It is high time you gave up these foolish fantasies!" He turned away and looked grimly toward Stirling Bridge, where all of Scotland's troubles eventually crossed.

Crestfallen, she coughed back tears. "Can we go to Scone to see where the Stone once rested, at least?"

Her father shook his head. "I'll not lay eyes on the sacred mound so gutted and defiled."

She fell to her knees, undone. To lose a precious dream was anguish enough, but to have it renewed upon one's heart only to be dashed a second time was a cruelty that she could not fathom. The bard's prophecy had been nothing more than a soothsayer's ruse. All faith drained from her, and she vowed never again to believe in a God who would allow the perpetuation of such a falsehood. She looked up at her father, who had remounted, and called out to him. "Why then have you brought me on this journey if not to see the Destiny Stone?"

As he road off, he answered her without turning, "You'll meet *your* destiny soon enough!"

Snapping their reins to renew their journey, her brothers glanced back at her with knowing grins.

CHREE

Belle and the MacDuffs were greeted by hostile stares from the other clans, who had gathered under an expanse of tall oaks in a sheltered Lanarkshire vale. On her journey south, she had overheard her father warn that such a large congregation of armed men threatened to draw retaliation from the English garrison at Carlisle. But Wil Douglas, the rebel leader who had recently bribed his release from Berwick's dungeon, knew Edward Longshanks's scheming mind better than most, and he had convinced the guardians that less suspicion would be aroused if they held their secret meeting here in the South, disguised as the annual harvest celebration. It was for this reason that her father and his ally, Red Comyn, a claimant to the throne, had reluctantly agreed to cross into the shire of the despised Douglases, the clan that had been their enemy for centuries.

As her father and brothers rode through the encampment with their chins in the air, she hung back several lengths, the only protest she could muster against her contrived presence here. She saw Wil Douglas waiting for their arrival at the tower of his castle with his second wife, the former Eleanor de Louvain, a frail Northumbrian sparrow who had fallen in love with him after he had taken her hostage during a raid on Jedburgh. She felt sorry for the Douglas chieftain's new wife, for she was rumored to have no friends, disowned by her Northumbrian kin as a traitor and shunned by distrustful Scots.

She scanned the bleak environs and shook her head, unimpressed. These endless meadows, broken only by an occasional rocky eruption, resembled Yorkshire more than the northern Scot provinces. Huts slathered with pitch circled the tower like clusters of barnacles, and the curtain wall looked to have been razed and rebuilt so many times that its patchwork masonry brought to mind a cheap quilt. On a barren hillock to the west stood a sleepy village of twenty mud-joisted cabins. The Douglas Water, a rusty creek barely deep enough to sustain a small school of salmon, meandered past the only redeeming feature in this forgettable place: a small kirk dedicated to St. Bride.

Dismounting without an offer of assistance, she walked unescorted through the camp. Everyone was talking about the war, laying blame for the loss of Berwick, and she found it nigh impossible to follow these swirling tempests and feuds. But there was one reality she understood all too clearly: That despicable English king with the odd nickname had ruined her dream of seeing the Stone of Destiny, and she would very much like to curse the ogre to his face.

She was about to rehearse the precise wording of that condemnation when a blast from a ram horn disrupted the clans from their ale-fueled arguments. As if struck by madness, the men ran howling toward the south gate. She was swept up in their rush and deposited in an open field where twenty boys, including her two youngest brothers, crouched at the ready with axes in their hands. Barefoot and naked to their waists, they had formed up what appeared to be a battle line. Breathless, she exclaimed, "Are the English upon us?"

A tall, shaggy Bute man standing next to her spewed his mouthful of ale. "English? Are you a peat brick shy of a decent fire, lass? The lads are running for the Dun Eadainn Ax."

The rube spoke with such a thick tongue that she had to ask him to repeat his explanation. Disgusted with her ignorance of the northern Gaelic, he peppered his translation with enough Scot words that she finally took his meaning. "They'll catch their deaths in this cold! Just for a tool?"

The inebriated Highlander swooped over her again, dowsing her in spittle. "A tool, you say? A talisman of miracles it is, holy as the Rood itself! Brought across the sea by Fergus and buried under the great Arthur's throne on Eadainn Fort Hill!" He cursed her ignorance with a wild swipe at the air. "Go clean the trestles! This is no business for a mush-headed filly anyway."

She looked around and saw that the other women had retired to the tower, no doubt to warble about wool spinning or the latest in fashion from the Continent. Not interested in such trivialities, she ignored the command to join them and pushed deeper through the throng of men to find out what was so important about this race. At the starting line, she found the young competitors elbowing for the best position. She risked another question to the hairy drunkard who had just tried to banish her. "Which one's the fastest?"

The Bute man huffed, resigned to her persistence. "Put your purse on the carrot-headed one with the idle eye. He's half blind, but don't let that fool you. He's as ornery as his old man. John Comyn's his name. Everyone calls him 'Cam' because of the crooked way he ganders."

Hearing his name, Cam Comyn looked up from his three-pointed stance and startled Belle with a buck-toothed grin. His lazy eye trailed off, causing her to look toward its unintended direction. He regained her attention by flexing his scrawny biceps in her face.

She was astonished that anyone might suppose such boorishness remotely impressive. Sniffling and blowing snot, the clod possessed the vapid stare and twittering movements of a dullard. Indeed, a more repugnant creature she could not imagine—until the taller boy next to him turned toward her. That one possessed severe Nordic features with dirty sandy hair and slant narrow eyes. His high pale cheekbones were pocked from the pox and his bridged nose resembled the jutting prow of a galley. She had seen gargoyles more pleasing to look upon.

The Bute man poked her shoulder in a taunt. "Then again, there's his cousin, John Comyn of Buchan. He's more balm for the eyes, eh lass?"

"I thought you said the other one was John Comyn?"

"The whole brood goes by that name. Mayhaps those are the only two words they can all scribble." The Highlander's huge girth rippled from his laughter. "Tabhann is what they call the taller lad to keep the two scarecrows straight. You wouldn't know what that name means, would you now, being a right learned Fife lady and all. Tabhann is Gaelic for a dog's bark." He unleashed a volley of ferocious yelps. "Do you catch it, lass? His bark be worse than his bite!"

With her ears ringing, she tried to escape the converging huddle of men, but Tabhann Comyn cut off her path. She forced another opening with her elbows and took off on a dash, dodging the laughing clansmen—only to whipsaw like a newborn colt into a short, bare-chested competitor.

The clansmen howled with laughter at her skittishness.

Blinded by embarrassment, she was pulled to her feet by the boy she had just head-rammed.

"Here's a fine turn," the boy announced with a slight lisp. "For once, a lassie running *to* me." Just as swiftly, he turned his attention back to the race and fixed his eyes on the only high ground within sight, a distant crag overgrown with trees and circled by a narrow path.

She couldn't be certain what unnerved her more: this tadpole's smirking quip, or his ability to put her out of his mind so easily. As if reading her thoughts, he turned again and winked. She recoiled with a bounce of her chin. *Who is this infuriating lad?* Such preening confidence was unnatural in one so slight. She caught herself staring at him with a blushing smile.

Tabhann crumpled her new admirer with a fist to his ribs. "Leave her be."

A second blast of the horn shot the runners off in a whirl of mud and grass. Tabhann took off with them, turning to laugh at his victim, who was still on his knees and gasping for air.

Belle ran to the injured boy and lifted him to his feet. Her act of mercy miraculously revived him, and although his head barely reached her chin, he lifted to his toes and kissed her on the lips. She shut her eyes in shock. When she reopened them seconds later, she discovered that he had shot off like a hare. She was allowed no time to either enjoy or despise the moment—her arm was nearly yanked from her shoulder.

Her father dragged her away. "Stay clear of the Douglases!"

Roughly handled, she glanced back at the last runner—*that* faint sliver of bone and flesh was the son of Wil Douglas? "I only asked if he was hurt!"

"And shamed your own kin!"

"Are the Douglases not Scots?"

Her father answered her with a slap that stung like flung ice. "Black stain of Original Sin, you are!" he shouted. "Damnable jeeger of me whole brood!"

She stifled a cry. The blow hadn't hurt half as much as the judging gawks of the clansmen around her. Tall, with thick dusky hair and a copper complexion, she was again made aware that she looked nothing like her stout father and choleric brothers with their flaming red scalps and freckled, liverish skin. They treated her like a bastard child, so much so that she often fantasized that she had been stolen at birth from another country. It was near to the truth, for her father never tired of shaming her with the story of how the first MacDuffs had arrived with the Gaels to subdue the darker Pict savages who painted their bodies with pagan tattoos and sacrificed children to appease the gods of their warrior queens. She was forever being reminded that her deceased mother had come from those same witch-hatched natives.

Wiping the sting from her cheek, she stole another glance at the competitors running off. The Douglas boy, she realized, was dunned with the same tawny complexion. She wondered if he also suffered taunts of being sired from the Black Danaan, a race of foreigners said to have arrived on the Isles from Iberia.

Shrugging off that mystery, she looked up and caught Red Comyn watching her humiliation with unabashed relish. Thickset and looming, this awful man who claimed title to the Scot crown had a ruddy face overgrown with an unkempt flaming beard, and he took in all that passed with the cold eyes of a mountain cat. But there was no stealth of movement about him; he walked with a lumbering step and was always heard before seen, wheezing and heaving with each breath, as if unable to summon sufficient air through his trefoil nose webbed with fine blue lines. Most who encountered him for the first time mistook this odd mannerism for derisive snorts.

Red chortled. "You could have used another son, eh MacDuff? But she serves your purpose nigh."

Ian forced a leg of roasted rabbit into Belle's hand. "Put some meat on that scrawny frame! Red's kinsman won't beseek a bag of bones for a wife!"

She stared gape-mouthed at her father. "I am to be … married off?"

"Did ye think I brought you here for idleness?" he said with a snarl. "You're a woman now. That's what you're always telling me. Bonnie chance it is that Red here and his roosters take a fancy to you."

Red dug his greasy hand into her hair as if planting a claim. "You're not too fine for us, are you now, lass?"

She tried to fight him off. "I'd rather die!"

Her father cocked his fist at her again. "I'll damn well grant the wish!"

She flinched, but this time she felt nothing.

A loud collective roar caused her to open her eyes. Wil Douglas had rammed her father into a tree. Stoked by the prospect of a fight, the clansmen cheered the two brawlers on. Forgotten in the melee, she stalked the scrum and silently urged the Douglas chieftain to deal her father a painful lesson.

The elder Douglas heaved Ian onto his back. "Take a hand to that lass again and I'll make certain you never sire another miserable MacDuff!"

Red Comyn dragged Wil Douglas off of Ian. "We've had enough of your meddling! You lost Berwick! But you had no trouble saving your own hide!"

The Douglas chieftain raised his fist. "Berwick fell because you—"

"That's Jamie Douglas in the fore!"

Alerted by that shout of disbelief, the clansmen turned to see the puniest of the competitors leading the pack down the slope at the halfway point.

Belle took advantage of the distraction to get away from her father and the Comyn chieftain. She rushed to the edge of the camp and saw young Douglas pull several paces ahead of the other boys. He was almost flying across the rocks while carrying an ax half as heavy as his own weight.

A MacDonald man drained his tankard and chased the gulp with a gibe at the Comyns. "Red, when's the last time one of your brood lost the race?"

Before Red could recover from the shock, Wil Douglas answered for him, "When I outpaced him on Ben Nevis thirty years ago."

The clansmen cackled and thumped forearms—all but the Comyns and MacDuffs, who stood glaring in stupefied silence at the approaching runners.

While the others rushed to gather at the finish line, Belle saw Red Comyn nod furtively to her eldest brother, who acknowledged the mysterious signal and slithered off. The Comyn chieftain pointed a finger at her in warning that she'd best not reveal what she had just witnessed. She turned back toward the crag in time to see the Douglas boy disappear into the thick oaks.

h is calves threatened to cramp, but James drove on through the swirling patches of low fog and blinding glints of light. Having run this route a hundred times, he knew the last stretch would be the most difficult, a steep descent down loose rocks followed by the long kick over the flat valley. But he had never risked a sprint so early in a race, and now his sides felt as if they were going to split. Would he have enough strength left for the straightaway?

He heard the yells of the other runners several lengths behind.

The black raven that had followed him from the start circled and led him on. Another turn, and he arrived at the final target: an image of a dragon painted on an ancient oak. Should he waste precious seconds to cross the ravine and impale his ax at close range? If he threw it on the run and missed, the ax might tumble into the gorge, and he'd be disqualified. Without slowing, he drew a deep breath and let the ax fly.

The weapon hurdled across the ravine and held its bite on the dragon. He laughed, now certain of victory. Those nearsighted Comyns couldn't hit a church door from the top step. He thought about stopping to enjoy their shocked discovery, but took off for the brow of the crag where the path descended to open ground and—

His feet gave out from under him.

Tumbling headfirst to the rocks, he felt a sharp pain swell up in his nose. Groggy, he reached up and found a wet gash on his forehead. He climbed to his knees and, looking around with watering eyes, saw a rope pulled across the path. Distant laughter was followed by the pounding of approaching feet. He tried to stand, but his ankles buckled. A heel slammed into his ribs, and he rolled across the ground fighting for breath. He looked up and saw Tabhann pressing a foot against his chest.

"We heard how you gave up Gib Duncan to save your old man."

Another thump sent him rolling toward the cliff.

Tabhann threw his ax and hit his mark on the tree. Laughing, he took off down the crag while the other runners came behind him, abusing James with kicks as they ran past and fired their axes. James slid down the scarp and broke his fall by catching a briar. The raven perched on a rock and watched impassively while he clung to the branch. He blinked the sweat from his eyes. Was he visioning from the pain?

The raven dipped its beak and shape-shifted into a woman draped in black robes. Wielding a sickle, she had wild hair the shade of fresh-drawn blood, and her skin was so white that she looked anemic. She glared at him with dilating, almond-shaped eyes as green as a Galloway hillock after a rainstorm.

He hadn't felt such chilling fear since Gibbie jumped to his death. Then he remembered—he had seen this hag once before, when he was bedridden years ago with the weakness in his lungs. His stepmother had screamed her name: Morgainne, the Raven Goddess of Death. He cried out to her, "Help me!"

The goddess was unmoved. "I tolled your crossing once."

He looked down at the sharp rocks below. "I don't want to die!"

"Come now, what follows after this life is not as horrid as you mortals make it to be." The goddess snapped her sleeves and conjured up a vision of Gibbie against the roiling clouds. At her stern nod, Gibbie's apparition reached forth and begged James to come to the other side.

When the goddess turned to await his decision, James saw Gibbie shake his head in warning. He felt his grip slipping. "I'll do anything!"

"You barter with *me*? You who could not fight off that pack of pups?"

"To Hell with you, then!" He closed his eyes and braced for a fatal fall.

Morgainne weighed his plea. "Impertinence, even in as I draw nigh. That is rare enough. … The cost shall be two souls for the salvation of one. Of my choosing. At my time. Until then, you serve me."

Before James could protest the bargain, the death goddess melded back into the raven and flew off. The branch's roots ripped from the cliff, and he fell down the long jag of rocks. When he finally came to a stop at the base of the pog, he groaned and flexed his arms and legs. Miraculously, he had suffered just a few scrapes.

A roar of discovery rumbled across the valley.

Seeing the first runners emerge from the woods, and now only five hundred paces away, the clansmen rushed to the finish line.

Belle elbowed her way into the human funnel that would soon engulf the runners. In the distance, she saw Tabhann leading the pack with a confident pace. He pumped his fists in celebration as he outpaced the others by several lengths, easing his way down the winding path on the last half-mile sprint across the heather. She narrowed her eyes in disbelief. The Douglas boy was nowhere to be found. She turned on Red Comyn with an accusing glare, but he just smirked and slapped the backs of the confused clansmen.

"All's right with the world again, lads," Red announced with a sinister grin.

Disappointed that an upset was not to be witnessed, the clansmen retreated to the ale casks to replenish their mugs and rejoin their war arguments.

But Belle held back. She glanced over her shoulder, and from the corner of her eye, she saw something stagger from the brush on the heights. Young Douglas, bleeding and heaving, was running toward the camp as if his life depended on every stride. She rushed beyond the finish line and yelled, "Come on!"

The departing men spun back. Red Comyn shoved his way to the front and bellowed at Tabhann, who had slowed his approach to a victory jog.

Tabhann risked a glance over his shoulder and then forced his legs into an unexpected trial. The Douglas lad was still running, even after his beating.

And he was gaining ground.

Their excitement ignited again, the clansmen jostled back to their positions on the finish line and haggled over last-minute wagers.

A hundred paces from the waiting scrum, Tabhann's legs buckled.

James caught up with him and returned the elbow he'd received at the start of the race. Nose and nose they came, careening, their neck veins bulging and their faces crimson. The clansmen tightened the finish rope.

James thrust a hip into Tabhann's side and lunged across the line first.

Tabhann crawled in second, yelling and cursing as Red kicked at him like a butcher driving a hog to the slaughter pen. One by one, Cam and the other boys staggered across the line behind him.

Risking her father's wrath again, Belle ran to the collapsed Douglas boy and cradled his head in her lap. Could this really be the same carefree lad who had kissed her at the start of the race?

The rules judge—a local priest from St. Bride's kirk—mounted a Shetland pony and cantered off toward the pog to confirm the accuracy of the ax throws against the dragon mark on the tree across the ravine. The clansmen waited in tense silence for his signal. When the priest whistled to verify that James had indeed hit his mark, they erupted again in raucous celebration.

Enraged, Red Comyn fought a path through the cheering throngs to challenge Wil Douglas. "There's devilry in this!"

"Aye, by your doing," the elder Douglas said. "Hand it over."

Red felt for his dagger, but several of the clansmen countered his threat by drawing their weapons. Finding no allies for his protest, the chieftain could only nod angrily for his kinsmen to bring up a packhorse. He reached into his saddlebag and pulled out Scotland's most coveted prize, a rusted ax featuring a handle carved with the names of past winners. He slung the Dun Eaddain ax at James's feet. "You won't have it long." He led his kinsmen in a huffing march from the camp. "Our business in this pigsty is done."

"The Guardians meet here on the morrow," Wil Douglas reminded his old rival. "Attend, or lose your vote."

As the jubilant clansmen hoisted James onto their shoulders and carried him across the field, Red slapped the back of Tabhann's head in punishment and hurried his family away, muttering threats under his breath.

Caught in her father's grasp, Belle was forced to leave with the Comyns. She risked a glance back at the celebration and saw James waving.

Was he trying to say something to her?

FOUR

As her garron clopped onto the narrow wooden bridge that crossed the River Clyde, Belle swallowed her fear and reined closer to the railing. Praying the currents would be swift enough to sweep her away, she slipped her toes from the stirrups and—

A hand reach out from behind her and captured her arm.

"Steady there, lass," Red Comyn said. "We wouldn't want to lose you."

Disconsolate, she slumped over the saddle, her last chance to escape thwarted. The Comyn chieftain now sensed her desperation and would likely keep her under guard when they arrived at Kilbride, his southernmost fortress.

Red drew a deep, satisfied breath as he led her pony across the bridge and onto Comyn land. "That Douglas stench is nearly gone us, eh?" After glaring a warning at her against scheming more such foolishness, he rejoined her father at the head of the column to renew their negotiations over her dowry.

She choked back tears. Within the week, she would be bound forever to this detestable clan. Resigned to her fate, she resolved to learn all that she could about the two Comyn boys who rode several lengths ahead. Only a study of these men who would rule her, and the manipulation of their weaknesses, might offer her hope for a tolerable existence. But whom could she consult in confidence? She scanned the wind-burnt faces of the Comyn womenfolk bringing up the rear of the train. One old hag, so listless that she appeared on the brink of tumbling from her mule, seemed the most harmless of the lot. When a bevy of quail distracted the men ahead, she slowed her pony to gain some distance from the others. Then, she came aside the wizened woman and attempted to make conversation. "My lady, are you chilled? I have a spare cloak in my roll here that you are welcome to use."

The crone peered out from her frayed shawl with a suspicious eye, astonished that anyone would care a whit about her condition. "And you be?"

"Isabelle MacDuff of Fife."

The woman bared her gums and screeched a throaty cackle. "Another one tossed into the boiling pot!"

Belle suspected that the poor woman had slid past the borders of sanity. To test that possibility, she decided to answer her babbling with equivalent nonsense. Loosening the shawl from her neck despite the stiff headwind, she observed, "Boil indeed. A day this hot would cause Hell to complain."

The woman inched her mole-tipped nose out a bit farther, until discovering that her ruse of playing senile had been exposed. She retreated into her shawl muttering a flurry of Gaelic curses. Moments later, her crinkled face reappeared like a turtle's head from a shell, and she nodded with grudging admiration. "You play the actor better than you jump the rail. I can see those questions burning a hole in that pretty little head. Out with them, then."

Belle was stunned to discover that the crone had somehow divined her intent to escape on the bridge. Yet her clairvoyance was at best undependable, for she had fallen for the nonsense trap. Careful not to glance at the Comyn boys, Belle silently asked herself which of the two cretins she would be forced to—

"The cousin," the crone answered before Belle had even finished her thought. "Red will save his depraved son as bait for bigger fish."

Belle grimaced as she watched Tabhann whipping the bloodied flanks of his horse. She could not bear the thought of sharing his bed. Cam was uncouth, but at least he was too stupid to be capable of intrigue. Tabhann, on the other hand, seemed malevolent and conniving, having perfected the art of exploiting the weaknesses of those around him with cruel efficiency.

"Now who's looking sickly," the crone sniggered.

"Why me?"

Disgusted by Belle's cry of self-pity, the crone shot a wad of bile over her hackney's nose. "Only foolish virgins wail on so. Come now, lass. Think of a chessboard. What strikes you apt about that plain of strategy?"

Belle now regretted her decision to make conversation. Hoping to find a graceful excuse to beg off, she blurted the only answer that came to mind. "It has two colors, but what is—"

"How is it arranged?"

"In squares. Still, I do not see what this has to do with my question?"

"Blessed me, but aren't you the clever one!"

Angered at being the brunt of a joke that she didn't even understand, Belle whipped her hood over her head and prepared to leave the old bat to stew in her bile.

The crone captured her hand to delay her. "Forgive me. I've lost all manners. It's been months since I've held discourse with anyone. I tend to rail against the spirits when …" She pursed her lips, having nearly revealed some dark secret.

"Then I would then have you address me directly," Belle insisted. "If I am to be cast into this despicable betrothal, I must know what awaits me."

"Directness is not always the best choice. Forget ye that direct is the path of the ax upon the neck? You must learn to look sideways and speak in shrouded ways." The crone glowered at the Comyn boys ahead, as if conjuring up a fitting spell for their demise. "Scotland is the chessboard, and each clan a square. None be the same color as that upon its borders, aye?"

Belle nodded slightly, uncertain where all of this chess talk was leading.

"If the red squares were all in the north and the black in the south, peace would be granted us." The woman spat again through her toothless gums in a gesture of malediction. "But the Almighty in His inscrutable wisdom has determined it not to be. And we suffer for it." Finding Belle too baffled to form a question, the woman shook her head, frustrated at her failure to communicate the critical point. "Think of the Comyns and their domains as the red squares."

"And the black?"

"The Bruces."

Belle had heard only passing references to that Southern clan. "The Bruces of England?"

"Of Scotland, as well. That clan holds fiefs on both sides of the border. The eldest, Bruce the Competitor, was King Alexander's fealt comrade. He's now even longer in the tooth than me."

"The Competitor claims the throne against Red?"

The crone nodded. "The two are like cats in a sack."

Belle waited to hear the significance of that observation. "Aye, and … ?"

"Edward Longshanks pulls the drawstring."

Belle failed to see what relevance all of this political intrigue bore upon *her* problem. In two days, her father would depart for Fife, leaving her at the mercy of the Comyns. Would she ever see St. Andrews again? What would become of her diary? She had left it in her bedchamber under lock. Nothing would prevent her brothers from prying it open and—

The crone snapped two bony fingers to regain Belle's wandering attention. "The destiny of the branch can be read in the roots. The time of both the Competitor and the Red is fast passing. Old Bruce's feckless son has turned recluse in Norway. It is the grandson, Robert, who was born under auspicious stars. I have scryed his future in the black glass. He will vie for the throne against Red's pups. Only a malevolent aspect with Saturnia can keep him from his fate. Melancholy will be his crown of thorns. But the English king has seers, too, and he will try to keep young Bruce under his spell in London."

Belle's head was pounding from trying to follow the woman's strange manner of speech. She watched, confused, as the crone played imaginary chess moves upon the pommel of her saddle, tossing aside invisible knights and queens with building vehemence.

"The Bruces and the Comyns scheme to checkmate each other," the crone explained in a running commentary. "For every Bruce castle, you will find a Comyn keep in the next square. To win the kingship, a Bruce must leap a Comyn and a Comyn must leap a Bruce."

At her wits' end, Belle finally went off like a steam cork. "But what does any of this have to do with me?"

The other women riding just ahead turned at her loud burst of exasperation.

The crone recoiled into her hood, feigning lack of interest. When the women were finally disarmed of their suspicions, she turned and glared at Belle for the dangerous indiscretion. Lowering her voice in a signal for her young companion to do the same, she revealed, "Fife is the last square. And you are the final piece protecting the king. Ready to be jumped?"

Belle's face twisted at the crude sexual innuendo.

"There are two branches of the clan. The Red is patriarch of the Badenoch line. He governs all Comyn lands. His cousin Tabhann will become the Earl of Buchan and Red's most powerful vassal. The Comyns are conniving to surround the Bruces by arranging bonds with the earls of Strathearn, Angus, Dunbar, Ross and Balliol."

"What about Fife?"

"Only the allegiance of your father's domains is left to be bargained off. Both the Red and the Competitor were distantly related to King Alexander. Bruce is a generation closer, so he holds the truer claim to the throne, if only by the breadth of a bald priest's hair. But Ian MacDuff is a clever player of the game. He has held off both the Bruces and the Comyns until the stakes have risen."

"What stakes?"

The old woman gaped her toothless gums, astonished at Belle's ignorance of her father's motives. "Can ye not see the nose on your own face, child? When the Comyns have you, they will have the crown in their grasp."

The ancient clan motto—*No MacDuff, no King!*—rang like a judge's sentence in Belle's head. Only now did she understand the full extent of her father's plotting during these past months. She quickly calculated the line of succession of the Comyn clan. After Red, Cam would be first in line, then Tabhann. If Tabhann survived Cam, she might one day be queen. And she would not put it past Tabhann to speed the matter by allowing Cam to encounter some accident. "Why does Red not betroth me to Cam?"

"He hopes Longshanks will sire another daughter."

After an agonized silence, Belle whimpered, "What am I to do?"

The crone scoffed at her lament. "Does the rook command the player? Of course not! You'll wait to be played like the pawn you were born to be."

Again, the other women in the column turned with disapproving glances. This time, wearied of playing the imbecile to their gossip mongering, the crone twirled her middle finger at them, mocking the conjuring ritual of a witch. Horrified, the women increased their distance and crossed themselves to ward off the evil influences.

Belle couldn't help but admire the old bag. She might be crude and queer, but her defiance was refreshing. "What may I call you?"

The crone hesitated, as if at a momentary loss. "Idonea ... I'd near forgotten my own name. It's been so long since anyone has inquired."

"Why do the others treat you like a leper?"

Idonea set her eyes coldly on a distant memory. "I too was once meant to be a queen. Forty years ago, I was married off to the Red's eldest brother. Three weeks after the wedding, my husband got himself hacked to death in a haggle over ten heifers." She screwed her face into a stony indifference. "There is nothing more useless in this country than a woman who has lost her man."

Belle tried to imagine a crown on the widow's grey head. "Still, the Red keeps you in his household. Is that not better than a cold nunnery?"

Idonea snorted at the suggestion that the Comyn chieftain might possess a shiver of compassion. "He threw me into the tower at Dundarg to make certain I didn't take my womb to another clan. Only when I turned fallow did he unlock the door."

"But if you are no use to him now?"

"He thinks I gained the power to blacken fates during my time in the darkness. Else, he would have turned me out to the moors long ago. The Comyns shun me, but they daren't harm me. Small blessing. None of them is worth the breath of a word exchanged."

"Did you?"

"Did I what, child?"

"Gain the power to blacken fates?"

Idonea turned toward the tawny belt of dusk that hung over the distant Western Isles, where the magic of the ancients was still practiced despite Rome's threats. With a heavy sigh, she counseled, "When one is shut away for half of one's life, one discovers that others beyond the veil walk with you. But what truly matters, lass, what your survival will depend upon ... You must make those whoresons *believe* that you command the spirits."

Belle was certain from her father's evasive manner that he had agreed to the terms of the marital contract and was delaying telling her of its ratification until after the secret meeting of the guardians. Earlier that morning, after locking her in a room in Kilbride's tower, he had gone to Dumfries with the Comyns, no doubt to have the document sealed by the magistrate. Red had left orders for her brothers to keep her inside the castle. But when she complained that the lads reeked horribly, they retaliated by demanding that she wash their laundry at the river. She had put up a strenuous protest, arguing that such a menial task was not befitting a MacDuff princess. The simpletons had taken the bait, shoving her out of the castle with the loaded basket.

She treasured this rare moment of solitude, her first in nearly a week. As she walked the forested path with arrows of light shooting through the low autumn mist, she fantasized about escaping. It might take hours in this thick fog for her brothers to find her tracks. But how would she feed herself? Winter was approaching, and no village owing vassalage to the Comyns would take her in. She might seek refuge in a convent, but the nuns would likely ransom her for an endowment. Despite her troubles, she began to feel lighter, as if she might levitate even. If only Our Lord would transport her to Heaven like the Virgin and take her away from these problems.

A rustling startled her.

She stifled a shriek. Twenty paces away, a young roe had staggered into a tree. The creature rebounded, bloodied from the bark, and struck another trunk, repeating the strange ritual over and again. She saw that its hide was splotched with raw patches from neck to tail. Although winter was approaching, the animal was molting, and a bulbous mass of flesh and soft bone striated with veins had grown down from its forehead to blind its eyes. She had heard the witches who plied the craft of *da-shealladh*, the Second Sight, call such rare creatures "wiggers." Abandoned by its herd, the poor thing was caked with dried blood, having been attacked and castrated by wild dogs while its antlers were in velvet.

The appearance of a wigger was deemed a dolorous omen. Yet she approached the blind roe and, capturing its battered head, offered it some of the berries that she had brought for lunch. As the roe whimpered in gratitude, she whispered to its ear, "St. Bride will heal you." With that blessing received, the roe scampered off into the grove.

Shaken by the encounter, she walked on until she reached the river's bank. She pulled the basket off her back and turned it over on the pounding rocks.

The basket was empty.

Bewildered, she reexamined her route and saw a saffron shirt hanging from a branch. How did *that* happen? Across the glen, steam ascended eerily from the cold water heated by the hidden sun. Had she stumbled into a sacred domain of the roguish Little People? She retraced her steps through the mists and found blouses and leggings dotting the trees like blossoms.

A loud splash broke the calm.

She turned toward an offshoot of the Clyde and saw circles of ripples expanding. A hand broke surfaced, as if the Lady of the Lake was offering up Excalibur. She screamed—the fist held one of her intimate garments.

A dark face—with an insufferable smirk—followed the hand up from the water. "Looking for this?"

Her jaw dropped. The Douglas boy had been stalking her all this time, stealing the laundry piece by piece. Infuriated, she knelt with the stillness of a hunter and scooped a handful of rocks. When he swam closer, she demonstrated how fast a Fife maid could launch missiles. His puckish grin vanished as he dove into the water to avoid being brained. Each time he surfaced, she sent him down again. But this time, his head did not reappear. Only a few bubbles percolated as the ripples settled.

I've drowned him!

She rushed into the water, splashing to find him as her skirt floated to her waist. Thwarted by its buoyancy, she ripped it off, leaving her in linen under-leggings. She drew a deep breath and dived under, but the water was too murky. She prepared to give up the attempt—

A water creature clamped on her legs.

Her scream died to a gurgle as the beast's claws pulled her under. The scaly monster had devoured the Douglas boy and was now about to swallow her! She fought to the surface, but the serpent dragged her under again. Finally, struggling mightily, she managed to raise her chin above the water. Smelling blood, she closed her eyes for fear of seeing his detached limbs. The creature released its grip, and she risked a look behind her.

A mischievous grin hovered just a breath away from her nose.

Before she could retreat, the Douglas boy pressed his lips to hers. A rush of panic and pleasure swept over her. And then, the strangest of thoughts came to her: *Will I ever be kissed without danger as its companion?* Her first had been in full view of the clans, followed by her father's punishing hand. This boy had thoroughly enjoyed that conquest, while she had been forced to suffer the consequences. This second kiss had been equally unacceptable.

I will be smouriched my way. She dove into his arms. *Let's see how he likes that!*

She pressed her soaked bosom to his chest and demonstrated a proper Fife bussing on him—long, languorous and soft. In the midst of the lesson, she made a disconcerting discovery: he was wearing not a stitch of clothing.

She pushed him away, but he swam toward her, eager for another embrace. She thrust his head into the water and paddled for the bank, kicking away his pawing hands. Dripping wet, she scampered out with her backside revealed by the clinging linens.

"Come back in!" he shouted as he took a step closer, the water dropping to his waist. "Or I'll come out."

"Don't you dare! Put your things on!"

"I seem to have lost them."

She covered her eyes and, after several groping lunges, retrieved the nearest item of scattered laundry, a nightgown. She wrapped it around a stone and threw it at him.

He slipped the frilly chemise over his head and walked out of the water resembling some mythical half-lad, half-lassie.

Her anger melted into a rolling laugh, the first she had enjoyed since leaving Fife. "You've got hazel nuts rattling in that skull of yours!"

While he sunned on a rock, she hopped from tree to tree to recover the laundry. She finally gave up the doomed effort and returned in mock brooding. She plopped upon the large boulder next to him and squeezed the water from her long black hair back, whipping it deftly to ensure that his face suffered a lashing. She turned to find him staring at her wet bodice.

"I'm thinking I didn't get all of my rewards for winning the race."

She caressed his head, bringing his eyes closer to the object of their lustful gaze—and pushed him into the water. "My father was right! You Douglases *are* full of yourselves."

James bobbed up spewing. He was about to retaliate by dragging her back in with him, but suddenly he doubled over, his breath stolen by the pain from the injuries he had suffered during the race.

Alarmed, she helped him back to the boulder and examined his bruised ribs. As she tended to him, he brought her to his embrace, and she put up a weak struggle, warning, "If we get caught …"

He rested her head on his chest and stroked her long hair. "They already showed they can't run fast enough to catch me."

She leapt to her feet, nearly head-butting his chin. "You're as crouse as a new washed louse! What woman would marry *you?*"

He tickled her sides until she relented by sliding into his embrace again. "So, you've been thinking about marrying me?"

Angered by his presumption and her own reckless indiscretion, she fought to escape his grasp. "You need some sisters to show you how to court."

"You were pulling for me yesterday."

"I certainly was not!"

"Aye, you were."

"What if I was?" She turned serious, fending off his tickling. "There's something you should know. ... My father intends me to marry Tabhann Comyn."

His flirting grin turned upside down. "They'll have me to deal with first!"

"Red Comyn says I'll be a queen."

"That's a fool's hope! The Bruces hold the true right to the throne."

Peeved by his curt dismissal of her possible royal ascent, she said, "I'm told the Bruces would sell us out to the English."

"The Comyns have already addled your head with their lies."

"And what do you know about it?" she demanded.

"My father is loyal to the Bruces. If Scotland is to be saved, it will be by the Bruces, not those Comyn traitors."

She set her teeth; here was another man, just like her father and brothers, lecturing her on matters deemed too complicated for her to understand. "If you're so clever, then tell me why Robert Bruce is held in such fondness by Edward Longshanks?" She waited for a rebuttal to that troubling point, but he could offer her none. The Bruce clan's service to the English king, and young Robert's schooling in London in particular, caused all Scots consternation, she knew. Yet this Douglas lad apparently labored under the delusion that his father would never become allied to a clan that might betray Scotland. She had witnessed enough treachery in her own family to question such guilelessness. She was about to tell him so when she heard distant shouts. She quickly gathered up her basket. "I have to go."

"I'll make you queen of Castle Douglas."

"I don't want to be queen of anything!"

"We'll jump a galley to Dublin."

"And do what? Starve? A man can make his own destiny. A woman is bound by the dictates of others."

"I can provide for you. I'm to inherit all of this land."

"As a Scot? Or as an English vassal of the Bruces?"

"A lassie's head shouldn't be filled with concerns about statecraft." He stole another kiss. "You're meant for other things."

This time, she shoved him away, incensed that he had dismissed her views so flippantly. "You're no different than the Comyns!" Unable to find the words sufficient to vent all the rage that had built up inside her these past days, she retreated up the path toward the castle, crying and yanking down the laundry from the branches as she ran.

"A week from this night!" he yelled at her. "Meet me here!"

When out of his sight, Belle stopped running and crumpled to the ground, torn with confused emotions. This Douglas boy was infuriating, but he possessed a strange hold on her. She looked down and saw a smooth rock in the shape of a heart, with a tiny hole eroded by water through its center. The old folk called such sculpted rocks elf cups, for fairies left them as omens of fated love. *Rely upon shrouded images that are not direct*—wasn't that what the crone had told her?

She picked up the heart-stone and heaved it through the mists. *That* would be his answer. If his feelings for her were true, the Little People would help him find it.

James heard a muffled whistling through the fog. He dived just in time to avoid being brained by a stone that splashed the water. He looked down at the ripples and saw a heart-shaped stone floating back toward him with the current.

Had the heavens dropped it on him?

He fished the stone out and studied it. Gathering his clothes on the bank, he quickly dressed and, pulling a leather cord from his leggings, threaded the stone and hung it around his neck. He scampered to a nearby oak and retrieved the crude flute that he had hidden with his prized ax. He played a few notes and sang an old ballad that his stepmother had taught him:

> "On Raglan Road on an August day
> I saw her first and knew
> That her dark hair would weave a snare
> That I might one day rue.
> I saw the danger yet I walked
> Along the enchanted way
> And I said, 'Let grief be a fallen leaf
> At the dawning of the day."

Falling leaves showered him with a warning that the season would soon turn cold and dark. He waited, hoping for Belle's response, but the glen remained silent. "A week hence, we meet here again!" he called out through the mists. "If you say nothing, it's a promise!"

Only the cackaws in the treetops answered him.

Racing the sun in a dash for home, he slowed his approach as he came upon a dark tunnel called Ninian's Faint. This winding shepherd's path bordered by steep limestone scarps was the last difficult stretch before the Lanark hills opened up into the wide vales of Douglasdale. Above him, a precarious ridge of cracked rocks crowned the notorious ravine.

His father had once told him how the Druids of old believed that malignant spirits congregated in these swires. Legend had it that St. Ninian proved Christ's superiority over the tree-hung god of the ancients by walking the scree alone at night. The saint never revealed the trials he had suffered here, but it was said he always marked the anniversary of his feat with a resounding sermon on Our Lord's temptations in the Judean desert.

The light was fading fast, and to go around the cranny would delay him an hour. Cull and Chullan held back, but he whistled them up and walked into the defile, turning sideways to avoid the jagged corners. After several minutes, the ravine splayed open toward the low sun. He shielded his eyes and turned toward a fleeting sweep of shadows.

The pups yelped a warning—seconds before a rock hammered his forehead.

"I thought I told you to stay away from her."

Hearing that voice distantly, he reached to his scalp and felt blood oozing down his brow. Dazed, he lifted to his knees and forced his eyes to focus.

Tabhann, twirling Belle's nightgown, stood over him.

Cam and the MacDuff brothers were with Tabhann, seven in all.

He cursed his carelessness. He had fallen for the oldest Highland trick, the ambush in an enclosed pass. He glanced over his shoulder and saw one of the MacDuffs, armed with a rod, blocking the defile to his rear. Firming his grip on the ax, he vowed to take a couple of them down with him, and Tabhann would be the first. He charged at the oldest Comyn, but his blow was glancing and the ax slid from his hand. Tabhann and his mates took turns pummeling him. He slowly slipped into blackness—until a rustling shook the brush above him. Bloodied, he revived and rolled to his knees.

Tabhann and his gang were staring up at the bluff, where an older boy sat mounted on white steed as sleek and fine as a racehorse. The rider was attired in the saffron regalia of noble birth and had a square jaw and a broad, noble forehead.

"Keep moving," Tabhann warned the traveler. "This is none of your concern."

The rider ignored the order and edged his horse down into the ravine. His dark blue eyes, lustrous but sensitive to light, swam with an aqueous film that gave him a pained expression. He looked around the swale in mock confusion. "Am I not in Scotland?"

Cam balled his fists. "Are you brain addled?"

"Maybe he can't hear," Tabhann suggested, "with all those baubles jangling from his shirt."

The traveler dismounted and sniffed the air. "I can certainly smell Comyn dung, so this must be Scotland." He came nose to nose with Tabhann. "And that makes it my concern. … Because I'm your future king."

Tabhann darkened, suddenly recognizing the stranger. "Robert Bruce." He spat, as if to void his mouth of a foul taste. "English scum. I'll go to the grave before I see you crowned."

Bruce leaned down to wipe Tabhann's spittle from his boots. "Let's get a start on it, then." He came back up with a cross hook that sent Tabhann airborne.

Cam rushed to his cousin's aid, but Bruce buckled him with a forearm. The MacDuff brothers dove into the fray, and Bruce parried their charges like a trained swordsman, but the force of their numbers soon overwhelmed him.

Forgotten in the melee, James climbed from his knees and leapt on Tabhann's back, riding him face first into the prickly gorse. Recovering to his feet, James fought his way out of the scrum and came back to back with Bruce. Surrounded, he whispered to his new comrade, "They got us in fists."

Bruce wiped a trickle of blood from the corner of his mouth. "Aye, but we got them in wits. Two to none, by my count."

The Comyns and MacDuffs puffed like bulls as they closed ranks for another charge. James saw his ax and dived for its handle, but Tabhann denied him with an elbow. Pinned, James slung the ax inches from Tabhann's reach.

Chullan pounced on the weapon and dragged it to Bruce.

Rewarding the pup with a pat, Bruce whipped the weapon around his head so deftly that the Comyns and MacDuffs were momentarily stunned into inaction. "This has a fine heft."

Still under Tabhann's weight, James grunted, "Don't get too attached!"

Tabhann kicked James aside to charge at Bruce.

Bruce hurled the ax at Tabhann's jaw. Stunned with a gash from the glancing blow, Tabhann staggered back. One by one, the Comyns and MacDuffs scampered off. Tabhann, the last to retreat, shouted promises of revenge.

Wincing from his bruises, James leveraged gingerly to a knee and offered his hand to his rescuer in gratitude. "I owe you one."

Bruce picked up the ax again and held its handle toward the fading sun to examine the name on the last inscription. "You're Wil Douglas's son?"

"Aye."

Bruce firmed their handshake. "Good timing. You can show me the way to Castle Douglas. I'm to meet my grandfather there this night." He had a quick, expressive mouth and a sonorous voice that betrayed a dissonant hint of self-doubt. His smile was never fully committed, but remained in conflict with some inner sentinel against hubris. "So, was it over a lass or an insult?"

James stretched his arms to check for damage. "How did you know?"

Bruce retrieved his skittish horse and palmed its nostrils to soothe its nerves. "Do we Scots fight over anything else?" He winced from a thigh bruise as he tried to mount.

James helped him to the stirrups. "The lass I love holds *you* to be no Scots-man at all."

Offended by the questioning of his loyalty, Bruce repulsed the assistance. "My father's ancestors came to this isle with the Conqueror, as did yours, Douglas. You and I are half-bred from Norman stock."

"So, does she speak true?"

Sighing, Bruce hung his head with a sadness that seemed passing strange for one so blessed in fortune and features. He muttered to himself, "What is a Scot? A Norman? A Dane? A Pict? An Irishman who swims?"

James had always assumed that the cut of a Scotsman was readily evident. Now, he wasn't so sure. As he led Bruce's horse up the ravine, he pondered the question at length, and finally he offered, "Any man who fights the English. There's a bloodline good enough for me."

Bruce smiled ruefully, amused to find that James had been wrestling with what had been offered as a mere rhetorical comment. "The French may take issue with you. ... Perhaps a Scotsman must be made, not born."

James enjoyed a laugh at his own expense. Despite Belle's doubts about the Bruce clan, he liked this Robert Bruce. She might dismiss the Bruces as Longshanks's lackeys, but no true Englishman would have risked his life here in the Lanarkshire wilds to help a foreigner. Perhaps the Almighty had intended the future Lord of Annandale to spend his youth in England for some greater purpose. After all, as James's father had once told him, the wolf must first sleep with the lamb to gain its trust.

FIVE

That night, James and Robert Bruce slipped unnoticed into the shadowed periphery of Castle Douglas's great hall, where the chieftains of the realm, meeting in secret to decide how best to confront the English occupation, were arguing over the latest dire news: Longshanks had thrown John Balliol into London Tower on charges of financial malfeasance.

Months earlier, the English king had appointed the incompetent Balliol as puppet ruler of Scotland, but that cynical act was now exposed as a clever ploy to force the Holy See and the royal courts across the Channel to concede that the clans were incapable of governing themselves. Each man present had cast his lot with the Comyns or the Bruces in the ruinous struggle for the throne, and now none could travel across their ravaged shires without suffering accusations of greed and betrayal.

Red Comyn, Ian MacDuff, and John of Lorne, the patriarch of the MacDougall clan, sat on one side of a long trestle table, accompanied by five lesser nobles from the North. Across from them sat James's father and his ally, Robert's grandfather, old Bruce the Competitor. With his long white hair oiled and gathered in a tail, the Competitor appeared exactly as a king should, James thought, and though crippled by a mysterious ailment that ate at his skin, he still retained a quickness of gesture and met all with a righteous jaw.

William Lamberton, the Bishop of St. Andrews, stood at the head of the table, looking out of place among these crusty warriors. The cherubic cleric's fleshy jowls were sprinkled with the hue of crushed pomegranates, and his healthy girt begged for one button more to be loosed above the waist cord. A thicket of dark tangled hair had merged with the overgrowth of his peppered beard to give his face the appearance of being framed by a molted yuletide wreath. A natural diplomat born with a dogged optimism, he was cherished by all Scots for his disarming cheerfulness and lust for life's pleasures, be they a hearty repast or a bawdy yarn.

Yet the bishop's sanguine disposition was being tested this night. Folding his hands in a gesture of spiritual authority, he pleaded for these bitter adversaries to set aside their grievances for the good of the country. "My lords, now is the time to strike. My informants tell me that Longshanks has returned to London."

Red Comyn twirled his ivory-hilted knife against the table, skeptically weighing that bit of surveillance. "Clifford remains camped at Jedburgh."

Lamberton abandoned his post of neutrality and moved toward Red with outstretched hands. "Longshanks has siphoned off troops to Brittany to fight the French. If we rise up now—"

Red Comyn stabbed his dagger into the boards. "Aye, priest, easy for you to call the muster! When the blood flows, you retreat to your cloister!"

Old Bruce the Competitor pressed to his unsteady feet. With a trembling hand, he extracted the dagger, slid its blade into a crack, and snapped it at the hilt to demonstrate he still possessed strength enough to command respect. "I'll not hear the Bishop slandered! He is more patriot than any Comyn!"

"He preaches your cause as the gospel!" Red snarled at his old rival. "His donation plate is kept so perpetually filled by Bruce emoluments that it's oft mistook for the cauldron of Bran."

The Competitor shaded purple, unable to summon words to vent his rage.

Seeing the elder Bruce thwarted by the mental slog of age, Wil Douglas eased him back to his chair. Then, Wil turned to the bishop and asked the question that was on all of their minds. "What makes you believe another rebellion will succeed when all the others have failed?"

Lamberton pulled a chalk numb from his pocket and traced a crude map of Scotland on the table, circling the area representing the Tweed Valley. "The Marches are laid waste from Berwick to Stirling. If we draw the English north of Perth, we'll stretch their lines of provision to the breaking point. Another month, and they'll be starving."

"We're already starving," Ian MacDuff reminded the cleric. "Another month, and Longshanks won't have to war on us. We'll all be dead of famine."

Even from his distant vantage in the far corner, James could see that the bishop's strategy would lead the English advance through Lanarkshire and his father's domains. As always, the South would suffer the brunt of the war and pillaging, while the North—much of it Comyn country—would remain unscathed. In the past, he had heard his father express doubts that Longshanks would fall for such a ruse. But Lamberton was an old family friend, and he knew that his father had promised not to speak out against the bishop's proposal until all the guardians had been given the chance to vote on it.

Red pressed the wily bishop for more details on his plan. "And who would you have command this new army of uprising?"

Lamberton walked to the hearth to stir the fire. With his back turned, he said in a near whisper, as if to blunt its impact, "William Wallace."

Hearing that, James traded a hopeful glance with Robert. Wallace, the rebel son of Alan Wallace, a noble from Elderslie, had continued to fight with hit-and-run tactics long after the other chieftains had surrendered. He was fast becoming a hero to every Scot boy from Melrose to Aberdeen.

Yet these hard-boiled chieftains around the table reacted as if they had not heard the bishop correctly. Finally, Red Comyn repulsed the nomination with a loud snort. "Wallace is nothing more than a sheep herder turned brigand."

Ian MacDuff agreed. "The man couldn't lead a mule to a trough."

Lamberton lunged and pounded the boards so hard that several empty tankards were sent flying. "He leads well enough while you sit here idle! He has a thousand men in the Selkirk! Join him and ten thousand more will follow!"

The bishop's anger was a revelation to James. Beneath the cleric's façade of Christian meekness lurked a fighter no less fierce than any of these men.

Red snickered to MacDuff, "The Church now does the bidding of outlaws."

"I do my own bidding," boomed a voice at the door.

The men turned, reaching for their weapons.

At the threshold stood the largest man that James had ever laid eyes upon. Two hands taller than six feet, he wore his hair braided and draped over his broad shoulders and carried across his back a broadsword that was a third longer than standard length. Lines of rage had been scored into his face, and his protruding marbled eyes, hooded with lids bruised ruddy from weariness, amplified his looming presence. Alerted by a keen sense of all that moved around him, the intruder turned toward the shadows in the corner, giving away the presence of the two boys with his held gaze.

James glanced worriedly at his father, expecting to be scolded for listening.

Finding James staring raptly at his sword, the stranger offered it for his inspection, and then asked the elder Douglas, "Your stripling, Wil?"

"Aye." Wil made no attempt to hide his disapproval at the intruder's brazen act of appearing at the meeting uninvited. "Jamie, meet William Wallace."

Wallace nearly crushed James's hand with his clasp. "You're the lad who won the ax this year." He glared at the chieftains, as if to emphasize that his next admonition was also intended for them. "With honor comes duty."

Unable to lift the heavy broadsword, James slid its tip across the floor and offered it to Robert for his admiration. But the Competitor, glaring, denied his grandson the opportunity to test it.

"Off to bed with you, lads," Wil Douglas ordered.

James saw Robert grimace, as if silently protesting that he was too old to be called a lad, let alone be told when to turn in.

"Let them stay," Wallace said. "They should hear what I have to say." As the boys hurried to the table before their elders could countermand that suggestion, Wallace paced the room. Finally, he stopped and reminded them all, "My woman was garroted for staving off the advances of an Englishman."

James nodded with empathy for Wallace's heartbreak, but the Northern chieftains merely smirked and huffed with impatience. James knew that they had all suffered similar losses; such mournful tales of murdered kinsmen and confiscated lands drew little sympathy in Scotland these days.

Sensing the futility in that appeal, Wallace retreated from sentiment and resorted to baser interests. "Longshanks would declare it a felony for our women to marry us. If the English are allowed to steal our womenfolk, the blood of our ancestry will be forever poisoned."

"Then go on and fight the English, hotfoot," Red said. "We'll give you a week's provision and endow a Mass for your success."

Wallace hovered over the seated chieftain. "You think me a fool, Comyn. But I'm clever enough to know that I cannot win this war alone. If Scotland is to be free of the English yoke, I must have all of you with me. The Comyns, the MacDuffs, the Douglases"—he turned sharply to the Competitor—"and the Bruces."

The Competitor was not accustomed to being called out, particularly by a man of such inconsequential rank. He clenched his pocked jaw defiantly and glared at his grandson, as if to inoculate Robert against such high-sounding harangues. "If sermons won battles," he muttered, "Christ would never have been nailed to the Cross."

Wallace and the other clansmen waited for an answer from Red Comyn, who controlled the most castles and troops.

Red allowed the tense silence extend, savoring his position as linchpin for bringing the majority of the clansmen to the rebellion. At last, he said, "I will draw my sword. ... But only if Bruce recognizes my right to the kingship."

"You have no right!" the Competitor shouted.

Lamberton tried to render stillborn the argument that they all had endured a thousand times. "I pray you! At least give Wallace a hearing!"

In the midst of these hurled recriminations, the Competitor clutched his chest and lurched backwards. Robert broke his frail grandfather's fall and eased him back to the bench. The Competitor finally mustered enough strength to answer Wallace in a barely audible rasp. "Edward will put down this insurrection and turn Stirling into another Berwick."

"Bruce should know," Red quipped loud enough for even the Competitor to hear. "His pups have been weaned on the Plantagenet teats."

The clansmen erupted again with shouts and accusations.

Wallace slammed the flat of his broadsword against the table, silencing them. "If this be the example of your stewardship, then English rule can be no worse!" He slid the sword down the table toward Wil. "My brother served in your ranks at Berwick, Douglas. This blade was all that came back from him. You saw firsthand what permanent English dominion would mean for us."

James saw his father steal a nettled glance at him, as if unsure what to do.

Wallace circled the table, glaring at each chieftain as he passed. "Yet here you sit, quarreling over whose wrinkled ass best fits the throne. You'll be kings, for certain. The lot of you. Kings of gutted castles and scorched moorlands, if you persist in this bickering."

Red dipped his dagger's point in the candle grease and drew a line through the bishop's map toward Annandale, the disputed land fought over with the Bruces for decades. He aimed the dagger at the Competitor. "If *this* snake remains on my borders, I'll not move my forces."

Wallace turned to the Competitor. "Bruce, will you take up the cause? If not for me, for the legacy of your grandson here?"

The men hung on the Competitor's reply. If he joined the rebellion, they would all be forced to follow to avoid losing face.

"I'll not send my flesh and blood to die for your folly," old Bruce said.

Denied, Wallace looked to Wil Douglas, his last hope. "Hardi, you once fought to the very walls of Jerusalem. Will you not stand aside me in this crusade against the Devil?"

A loud report cracked in the hearth, and Wil stared at the embers, as if questioning whether the heavens had just sent him a warning. Troubled, he turned back with deadened eyes toward Wallace … and shook his head.

Wallace burned into memory the faces of those who had abandoned him. He tried to dredge up another indictment of their cowardice, but then waved it off as not worth the effort. Seeing the ax in James's grasp, he dropped to a knee and ran his fingers across its lacquered handle. "Why did you run that race, lad?"

James proudly displayed his prize. "For this."

Wallace tested the weight of the ax, a mere kitchen cleaver in his massive hands. "Nay, you ran it because your old man ran it forty years ago. Just as his old man ran it before him. I remember that day, by Christ, a cold morning it was. The winds were howling down Ben Nevis louder than the ghosts of the damned. Your father thrashed me sound, he did, and Red there, too." He paused, allowing the ideals of youth to return to these failed memories, and then stared at Wil Douglas while continuing to address James, "You ran the race, lad, like all of us did, because you're a Scotsman." He slammed down the ax and split the boards. "And if Edward Longshanks has his way, you'll be the last of us to run it!"

Wil Douglas erupted to his feet at the insult.

Wallace leaned to James's ear, intimating that his young admirer was the only person present worthy of his confidence. "Remember this night, lad. Remember to rise above the pettiness of greedy old fools." He pushed the table over in a fury, sending several of the men tumbling. Before the chieftains could draw their daggers in retaliation, he slung his broadsword over his shoulder and walked toward the door.

"Wallace!" Wil Douglas shouted.

The rebel leader turned with his gnarled fists balled for a fight.

Wil Douglas extracted the ax from the trestle boards and marched toward the man who had just called him out. Bishop Lamberton tried to intercede, but the elder Douglas, eyes afire, pushed the cleric aside.

Wallace stood before his old comrade, bracing for a blow.

Wil Douglas quivered with raw emotion as he raised the ax—and tossed it to James. He reached for Wallace's hand, changing his mind, and said with little enthusiasm, "I am with you."

A gasp of dismay filled the room.

James saw Robert look to his grandfather, silently begging him to join Wallace and avenge their clan's good name. But the Competitor answered his grandson with a contemptuous hiss.

The next morning, the clanging of a hammer against an anvil roused James from a fitful sleep. He found Robert, already dressed, sitting on his cot and staring into the pre-dawn darkness. Neither had managed to gain much rest. After the exhilaration of the night's meeting had faded, James remembered the oath that his father had given to the English as a condition for his release from Berwick's dungeon. If captured again, his father would face imprisonment or execution. Robert, however, had lain awake for a different reason. Although his grandfather had repeatedly explained to him the necessity of pitting clan against clan, he felt humiliated by the decision to put their personal interests before those of Scotland.

The boys descended the stairs to the armory and found James's father honing his weapons and his servant Dickson testing the straps on the livery.

"You leave this morning?" James asked.

"Wallace intends to reach Selkirk by nightfall."

James's voice cracked with emotion. "I want to go with you."

"Heed me on this! I'll not have you disobey me again as you did at ..." Wil cut himself short, regretting the outburst.

James choked up. His father had never spoken to him of Gibbie's death, for the tragedy at Berwick was still too painful for them both.

Robert made a move to leave them alone.

"Rob, lad, stay." Wil ran an oilcloth down the broadsword that he had carried for decades. "Sit you both down here, aside me."

Handed the hallowed weapon that had drawn infidel blood, Robert marveled at its workmanship. James nodded for him to test it, but Robert, eyes downcast, returned the blade, considering himself unworthy.

Wil braced Robert with an arm to his shoulder. "Your grandfather is a great man, Rob." Seeing the boy tear up with doubt, the elder Douglas asked him, "Has he told you of our campaigns in the Holy Land?" When Robert shook his head, Wil leaned against the blackened stones that he had mortared with his own hands. His gaze turned distant as Dickson came to his side; the elderly servant's role in confirming the details of his master's stories was time-honored. He primed Dickson for the setting. "Was it not the siege of Acre, Tom?"

Dickson stiffened his creaking bones to attention, as if they were back again in Palestine facing the Moorish ramparts. "A sweltering day it was, my lord. Fit not for any loch-loving Scotsman."

Wil swept his hand across an imaginary range of parapets. "We weren't much older than you, Rob. Walls thrice the height of this tower. And mangonels. Christ as my witness, heinous machines with devious workings the likes I hope never to see again. But on we came. The infidels heaved cauldrons of boiling pitch on us and launched arrows so thick that the sun was blotted."

James and Robert, enthralled, held their breaths.

"Your grandfather and the Earl of Carrick led our advance," Wil said. "And on our flank stood the knights of the Red Cross."

James dropped to his knees in anticipation. "Templars?"

Wil's eyes blazed upon the ladders thrown against the walls of Acre. "God-fearing monks trained to kill the Devil himself. But none fought with more courage than Bruce the Competitor. Aye, Scotland carried itself proud that day." Flinching from the memory of a blow, Wil clenched Robert's wrist, as if to insist what next he would reveal must be felt in the flesh. "Carrick died a hero's death, Rob. With his last breath, he bade your grandfather sail for Ireland to assure Dame Carrick that he had gained the Lord's salvation."

"Grandpa fulfilled the oath?" Robert asked hopefully.

Wil nodded wistfully. "And your grandfather fell in love with Carrick's widow the moment he laid eyes on her. There was grief, to be sure, but the Almighty had a greater purpose in mind." He smiled as he looked into Robert's liquid eyes. "Carrick's widow became your grandmother. You and Jamie both run with the maternal blood of those who first walked this Isle. Your grandfather is no coward. You must never think it so." Pulled back to the present by a neighing in the stables, Wil looked up to see his servant slumped with nostalgia. "Tom, tell them what we learned in those days bygone"

Old Dickson had to clear a lump in his throat. "There be nothing stronger than a man's bond with his comrade in battle."

Wil grasped Dickson's forearm to honor again their unshakable brotherhood, forged under fire. "Aye, nothing. Forget it not, lads. Nothing stronger."

The tale had accomplished the intended effect of raising Robert's spirits, but it had also saddened James, who was now even more convinced that he had let down Gibbie, his only true friend.

Seeing his son so distressed, Wil finally summoned the courage to discuss the subject that he had avoided for too long. "Jamie, you were given no choice at Berwick. Gibbie died for Scotland. Many have suffered the same fate. Many others will. You mustn't let this fester in you."

At the door, William Wallace, listening in the shadows, revealed his presence. "Wil, we'd best cross before first light."

The half-blind Dickson left his master's side and returned from the stables with two saddled mounts. "I've packed enough meal for a fortnight."

Wil Douglas grasped his servant's shoulders to soften the news. "Thomas, you have been with me in every battle since my father gained his heavenly reward. But this time, I need you here." He broke away with difficulty and walked out with Wallace. Near the door, he saw the Dun Eadainn ax hanging on its tenders. He took the relic down from its display and smiled sadly, as if recounting the many memories it had brought him through the years.

"Take it with you," James begged.

Wil replaced the ax on its hooks. "It's yours now. Keep watch on your stepmother. I'll be home when the troubles are over."

In the bailey, Wallace mounted and, with one foot in the stirrup, stared down at James and Robert, as if attempting to divine their future. Whatever he saw in them, he chose not to share it, but instead slung his massive broadsword over his shoulder and rode off with the elder Douglas.

Until that moment, James had held in check all the shame and pain that had welled up in his heart since Gibbie's death. Now, as his father departed for battle yet again without him, he fell to his knees, inconsolable and ashamed that Robert was witnessing his unmanly display.

Yet Robert was weighed down by his own humiliation. Watching his grandfather in the bailey prepare the horses for their return north to Turnberry, he lifted James from his knees. "I intend to take the Cross one day. I'd be honored to have you by my side when I do."

"You'll not want me," James protested.

Refusing to be denied, Robert offered his hand to seal the promise, just as James's father had done with Wallace during the meeting that night. Going off on crusade to the Holy Land would now become the driving purpose of their lives. If they couldn't go fight for Scotland, at least they would one day gain glory on the sands walked by Christ. "To the Tomb of our Lord together," Robert vowed. "No Moor will ever stop a Bruce and a Douglas."

James firmed his clench. "An oath it is."

After a week had passed with no word from his father, James was torn between his duty to guard the tower and his promise to meet Belle. All had been quiet, and the English were reported more than a two-days march away. He was confident that he could make it back before dusk.

When midnight came, he cracked the door to his stepmother's bedchamber. Finding her asleep, he slithered out the tower and tiptoed past the slumbering Dickson. He pocketed his homemade flute, threw the Dun Eaddain ax over his shoulder, and rappelled down the wall on the rope he had hidden in a barrel.

He ran as fast as his sore ribs allowed. After several hours, he reached Kilbride just as the sun broke over the tawny Lanarkshire horizon and revealed the tips of the Comyn towers. Eager for another kiss, he rushed breathless into the thicket near the river.

Belle wasn't there.

Caressing the heart-stone hanging from his neck, he asked the sprites for a sign. Why hadn't she come? If he went near the castle, he would risk an arrest for trespassing. ... He saw no smoke rising from the turrets.

Alarmed, he raced along the riverbank. As he neared the moors north of Kilbride, he heard the faint braying of horses. He scampered up to the brow of the next hill and gazed down at the trail.

The Comyns were riding north—and Belle was with them.

The path doubled back for nearly a league to avoid the high ground. If he hurried, he might catch them at the bend. He kept out of sight as he dashed along the ridge that ran parallel to the route on the far side of the valley. Maneuvering in this blind swire prevented him from gauging the speed of their advance, so he would have to guess when to make his move.

After several more lengths, he clambered up a rocky upthrow where two scrub-covered humps funneled the path into a defile. He pressed his ear to the ground and heard the distant thumps of hooves. Belle was on the sixth horse, he remembered, with Red in the lead. If he timed his jump, he could be away with her before the bastards knew she was gone.

He counted off ten seconds—two for each horse—and scaled the hillock.

He had guessed right. Belle was riding a few paces ahead, with Cam on her far side. He ran for her.

She turned, hearing footsteps, and shook her head for him to go back.

He ignored her and, reaching the horse at last, knocked Cam from the saddle. Mounting behind her, he lashed the garron into a tight turn, and when they reached a clearing, he kicked the garron in gallop toward Douglasdale. She tried to look back, but he kept her head facing forward. He glanced over his shoulder and saw Red still riding north, unaware of the ambush. Cam lay on the ground, stunned. He laughed and congratulated himself on outsmarting the fools.

Belle finally regained her breath. "Jamie, no!"

He covered her face with her shawl to muffle her shouts. Headstrong lass! He had saved her from the clutches of the Comyns, and here she was criticizing his horsemanship.

She struggled against his restraint. "Go back!"

A sharp blow hammered the back of his head, driving it into her shoulder.

He regained consciousness on the ground—with Tabhann, on a horse, circling him. He cursed himself for failing to anticipate that Red would station a rider far in the column's rear. Several paces away, he saw Belle struggling to regain control of her spooked pony. He shouted at her, "Run!"

Tabhann whipped his mount to and fro, debating whether to ride him down or prevent Belle from escaping.

Belle circled her garron and came rushing back toward them.

James reached behind his back for the ax, but it was gone. He must have lost it on the run. He shouted at Belle again, "Go back!"

Tabhann thundered down the ridge and careened into James. Rolling from the painful blow, James struggled to his knees and looked up to see the Comyns galloping back toward him. Tabhann dismounted and found the ax in the high grass. He raised the weapon over James's head for the finishing blow.

"Tabhann!" Belle screamed. "Leave him! There may be more!"

James froze in confusion. *She is warning Tabhann?*

Grinning at Belle's altered allegiance, Tabhann leapt on the pony behind her and rode north to catch up with his kinsmen.

James rushed after them—until Red came storming back over the ridge.

The chieftain drove him across the heather on his hands and knees. "You're on my ground now, Douglas!" He pulled Cam to his saddle and rode north to catch up with Tabhann. "Come near that lass again and I'll show you Comyn justice!"

On the horizon, Tabhann circled back and waved the stolen ax over Belle's head in a taunt.

James limped home, trying to make sense of Belle's betrayal. Why hadn't she escaped with him when she had the chance? Had she pitted him against the Comyns all along just to curry their favor? He clutched at the heart-stone pounding at his chest, wondering if its message had just a figment of his imagination. Before he could come up with an answer to those questions, an acrid rush of smoke attacked his nostrils. He rushed toward the spine of a braeside that descended into Douglasdale. An orange glow flickered through the leafless birches above the night's horizon.

Castle Douglas was engulfed in flames.

With his vantage obscured by the billowing smoke, he dived into the Douglas Water and swam furiously for the far side. When he surfaced, twenty English troopers on horse surrounded him. He tried to retreat to the far bank, but the soldiers flushed him out, lashing him with whips and laughing as he bobbed and dived to avoid drowning. He fought and kicked at the hooves of an English mosstrooper's horse, trying to stave off its thumps.

"Have you men been fishing again?" asked the mounted officer prodding him from the water. "This minnow is so puny you ought to throw it back."

James shivered with doubled fear. He had never forgotten that haughty Herefordshire tongue that sounded so Welsh—it belonged to Robert Clifford, Longshanks's cutthroat who had presided over Gibbie's death at Berwick.

Clifford dismounted and dragged up Eleanor Douglas from the middle of a scrum that was abusing her with taunts and snaps of their reins. He clamped her chin and forced her to look at James, who was still on his hands and knees. "Is this who you've been looking for?"

Eleanor averted her eyes. "I don't know this lad."

Clifford pressed a heel against James's neck to inspect his face more closely.

"My father rides here within the hour!" James blurted as his head was being crushed against the ground. "You'll pay for this!" From an angle, he saw his stepmother close her eyes in anguish, and realized too late from her slumped reaction that she had been trying to hide his identity from the English. He had given himself away by his sheer rage.

His memory of Berwick revived, Clifford grinned and signaled for his troopers on the walls to drag out another prisoner. "He beat you to us."

Bloodied and half-conscious from a beating, Wil Douglas was hauled through the gate. He looked up in despair to find that James had again disobeyed his order to remain home.

Clifford enjoyed watching their mutual humiliation. "This castle is forfeited to England. Its lord, a traitor, will be delivered to London Tower."

James fought to escape his captors. "You won't take him!"

Clifford throttled his neck. "Do you know where William Wallace hides?"

When James shook his head, Clifford threw him to the ground and ordered his troopers, "Release the old man. Take the lad instead."

"No!" Wil Douglas shouted.

James tried to rush to his father, but he was held back.

Laughing, Clifford slapped Wil to his knees. "He's a damn nuisance to you, Douglas. Why not be rid of him?"

Glaring a warning at James to remain silent, Wil pleaded with Clifford, "Take me. That is the law."

Clifford strode before his bemused troopers. "The outlaw quotes us the law!"

"These Scots breed like rats," a sergeant warned. "If we don't root out the whole brood, the young ones will come back to bite us. Let me string up the whelp."

Clifford stared at James for a dangerous moment—and kicked him aside. "This one doesn't even have babe teeth yet. He won't nip at us. We hung his better half at Berwick."

The sergeant didn't look convinced by that prediction. "I've seen rats maul a hound in these parts."

Clifford waved off the warning as he mounted again. "Leave the culls to breed. Soon enough, they'll all be runts like him."

James crawled to his father. "I'm sorry!"

On his knees, Wil grasped his son's head with bloodied hands and whispered to his ear, "Your stepmother is with child." He pressed so hard in desperation to impart the importance of what he would next say that James nearly screamed from the pain. Looking deep into his son's frantic eyes, Wil ordered him, "Remember, you are a Douglas. You bend to none but God and your conscience."

James fought back his tears, determined to honor his vow made over Gibbie's body at Berwick, never to let the English see him weaken again.

As her husband was dragged away, Eleanor was prodded toward the burning tower, so near to the flames that she was forced to shield her face from the searing heat.

"You and the lad may stay with these walls," Clifford said. "Or what remains of them after they've cooled. Henceforth, all rents from this domain will be paid to me."

"Winter will soon be on us!" Eleanor cried, falling to her knees to beg. "How will we find food?"

Clifford laughed over his shoulder. "You heathens are an enterprising tribe. You always seem to manage."

six

The winter of 1298 brought down the worst storm in memory from the Highlands, piling snow high against Castle Douglas. Robert Clifford had burned the hunting groves for fuel that fall, scaring off all wildlife except a few grouse, and the granaries had long since been emptied. Eleanor Douglas, too weak to nurse, had sent her new babe, Archibald, off to live with her husband's kin in the north. And without even a crib of fodder left, many of the villagers had been forced to abandon Lanarkshire to beg for food on the streets of Carlisle or Stirling.

Wasted to the bone, James trudged back through the vast drifts toward the desolate tower and its crumbling roof, which now sheltered only a small section of the floor. Earlier that morning, leaving his stepmother wheezing aside the cold hearth and old Dickson nearly frozen at his post near the door, he had plodded outside, barely able to stand, hoping to snare anything that moved. Returning now empty-handed, he kicked open the iced door and staggered inside the fireless keep. He found Bishop Lamberton helping his stepmother sip from a gourd of cold gruel.

Seeing him, Eleanor struggled to her feet and drew a painful breath. "Jamie, ready the horse."

James was so dizzy that he had to find the wall for support. Recovering his balance, he muttered the same promise he had made a hundred times. "Father will return soon."

Eleanor shook her head to negate that hope. "The bishop here has generously agreed to take you in."

Lamberton reached into his belt pouch and brought forth a sliver of rabbit jerky. "Come, lad. It's for the best."

James shunted aside the offer, undone by his stepmother's loss of faith in his ability to care for her. "You'd have me give up our home?"

"I'd have you live! There is nothing left for you here."

Anxious to depart before the English patrols arrived, the bishop gathered up some of James's ratty clothes strewn across the floor and packed them in his knapsack. "I need a notary, lad. I'm told you're adept with the script."

James resisted his attempt to lead him away. "I want to fight with Wallace!"

Lamberton monitored the flapping oilcloth on the window for sounds of the dogs barking outside. "You must cast that nonsense from your head."

"He was good enough for my father!"

"And for me, once," Lamberton lamented, his voice trailing off in despair. "But we were all betrayed by our hearts."

James turned on his stepmother, trying to find some sign of fight left in her. Four months had passed with no word from his father or Belle, true. Yet Eleanor had been the one who had firmed his father's conviction when he doubted the wisdom of joining Wallace. She had even sent Hugh, her own eldest son by her first marriage, to take up with the rebel army. Now, she turned away from him, the last reserve of her resolve spent.

Lamberton spoke what she could not. "Steady yourself, lad. ... There is droch news from Falkirk."

"Wallace?"

"Defeated in battle."

James refused to believe the claim, until—

"Hugh!" Eleanor broke into tears of grief. "His body ... found mutilated."

Informed of his stepbrother's death, James glared at her in accusation. How long had she known of Wallace's defeat? She had tried to take the place of his deceased mother, Elizabeth Stewart, but he had never been able to forgive her for her English origins. Now, despite her losses, he turned a cold shoulder on her and, though fearing the answer, asked the bishop, "Wallace ... is he dead, as well?"

Lamberton shook his head. "It was a near-run scrape. I begged him to take to the forest and wait for better ground. A prideful belief in his own invincibility blinded him. He formed up in the open fields against the English knights."

"Where is he now?"

"In the Selkirk, with what remains of his force. The North is open for plunder. My own lands in Kirkliston are aflame."

"Wallace will fight again!"

Eleanor reached for his hand to calm him. "Jamie ... Ian MacDuff was also killed in the retreat."

James stared at the bishop, trying to make sense of what *that* welcome news might bode for his future. Then, suddenly roused from his torpor, he shook the snow from his cloak, determined to start out again and find Belle.

Eleanor blocked his path to the door. "I know you having feelings for the MacDuff lass. But her brother will now lead the clan, and he is no friend to us. The Comyns are in league with the MacDuffs. You must forget her. She'll bring you nothing but trouble."

His vision tunneled from hunger and confusion. His expectation of Wallace's victory and of marrying Belle during the peace that would follow was all that had kept him going. Inconsolable, he slid to his haunches.

Lamberton brought him back to his feet. "Come, lad. Serve as my scribe and learn the ways of statesmen. You may one day find the knowledge useful."

Lamberton led James on horse down the old Roman road that skirted the royal hunting park south of Stirling Castle, the legendary keep that guarded the main passage to the northern provinces. Clifford had set a toll station on the King's Table, a circular plateau at the base of the crag where the great Arthur had once gathered his Grail knights, and English soldiers were hassling a long line of weary Scots, forcing them to pay an exorbitant tax to suffer the indignity of crossing Stirling Bridge and pass a macabre gallery of heads severed from those defenders butchered at Falkirk.

The bishop slowed their approach, and when the guards were distracted with abusing the waiting Scots ahead, he reined off the road into a thicket.

Aghast at the trespass, James resisted. "They'll hang us for poaching."

Lamberton signaled for him to follow on the quick, so James reluctantly obeyed. They gained the cover of the trees, and the bishop cocked his ear to make certain their detour had been accomplished without detection. The snowdrifts off the pike were too difficult for the horses to navigate, so the cleric dismounted and walked his mount along a frozen creek, the only path through this remnant of the ancient Caledonian Forest. Assured at last that they had not been followed, he revealed at last, "We are not going to St. Andrews."

James held back, angered at being deceived. "The Hell you say!"

The bishop tromped on through the snow. "A galley awaits us in Argyll."

"The Isles? Why did you lie to me?"

"Let this be your first lesson. Reveal your plans to no one, not even your closest comrade. The English have ways of forcing one to betray his loyalty."

"I'll not hide atop the peaks like some vagabond!"

"We sail from the Isles for Paris on the fortnight. France is our only hope to stop Longshanks."

"What if the English discover you've left the country?"

"By law, I answer only to the Church. But I do not intend to test the immunity afforded me as a diplomat. We will sail from the west, out of reach of their ships in the Channel. And there is a landmark on our route that I wish you to see."

uring their weeklong journey up the west coast, James found the bishop to be a mysterious, elusive man with many pagan quirks. Lamberton neither honored the Sabbath nor offered prayers in the traditional offices of a cleric, but rode with the wary gaze of a soldier, scouting each ridge and zigzagging between copses for cover. One morning, passing a Benedictine abbey near Turnberry, the cleric shot a wicked eye at its crooked Roman cross, denying it the traditional signing. Yet the most queer of all his rituals was a penchant for stopping under ancient oaks and pronouncing Gaelic blessings.

They had engaged in only desultory conversation until, reaching the Glen of Kilmartin at approaching dusk, they came upon a low bogland bordered by the purple hills and flooding waters of Loch Crinan. A giant fist of gray rock broke through a valley that had been turned into a glade by the melted snow. In the fields around this strange crag, peat harvesters had unearthed a dozen granite dolmens, all set in a circle.

Spying the imposing mount, the bishop lashed into a gallop as if greeting an old friend. He dismounted at the foot of the crag and waddled up a winding path, signaling for James to follow. Heaving from the exertion, the bishop finally staggered to the summit and dropped himself on a boulder. After regaining his breath, he ordered his new charge, "Tell me what you see."

Gazing into the west, James shielded his eyes from the low sun. He could just make out the white foam of the Irish Sea through the mists. "I see the end of Scotland."

"Nay, you see the *beginning* of Scotland."

Perplexed by that suggestion, James looked down at his feet and saw that he was standing on an oblong slab the breadth of a shield. On its face, streaked with deep fissures channeled by rainwater, had been carved a drawing of a wild boar next to a worn footprint a knuckle in depth.

Lamberton raised his hands over the crag as if offering a benediction. "A thousand years ago, our first kings were inaugurated here. A great race of men brought the Stone of Destiny from Ireland to this very spot."

James leapt off the sacred rock, afraid that he had just committed a sacrilege. "How did a bunch of sorry Irishmen get their hands on the Stone?"

"The Sons of Light were not Irish by birth," the bishop explained. "They came from the East and taught the mysteries of civilization to many nations before settling in Ulster. They knew from their study of the stars that a great flood would soon inundate the world."

"Drunken Ulstermen," James scoffed.

The bishop smiled knowingly. "Drunk with wisdom. The Sons divined by second sight that only those dolmens down in that vale down there would survive the coming deluge. When the Druids arrived here from the mainland, many years later, they heard the stones whispering the prophecy."

James ran a hand across the wrinkled rock, trying to imagine the Stone of Destiny resting on its base. "You've heard the Stone speak?" When the bishop did not answer him, he became more intrigued. He knelt and pressed his palm into the ancient footstep. "This is why you brought me here? To see a pile of old slags?"

"Your education is now my duty. If you wish to help me save Scotland, you must know what is truly at stake. William Wallace is a good man, but he has no understanding of the shrouded reason we must fight this war."

James gazed south past the shimmering waters of Loch Fynne, unable to make sense of it all. Longshanks had already stolen the Stone of Destiny. How long would it be before he pilfered these sacred menhirs, as well? "It's clear to me why we're fighting. To drive out the English."

Lamberton sized up his new student, as if judging whether he was capable of keeping a confidence. Deeming the risk worth the price, the cleric asked him, "You have heard of the Culdees?"

"The wizards who cower in the Highlands?"

Lamberton bristled at that slander spread by the Roman monks. "The Culdees are not pagan soothsayers. They are descendants of the first saints in this land, disciples who brought Christ's teachings back to these shores long before the conniving Italians had ever heard an Apostle's sermon."

"Back here? What do you mean?"

"Our Lord came to this land as a young man."

"Why?"

"To study with the Druids. Christianity was not brought to this Isle. It was *born* here." Seeing James frown skeptically, the bishop persisted. "Do you know the name of the Druid god?" He did not wait for an answer. "Hesus. The name meant 'He who survived death upon a tree'"

"I thought St. Patrick brought the Holy Word."

The bishop scowled to belie that myth. "Rome claims to be the ordained ruler over all Christians, but the Culdees knew the truth. Their lineage reached back to the first believers in Jerusalem. When the missionaries from the Roman abbeys in France crossed the Channel, they discovered that the Culdees had been teaching Christ's message for centuries. Rome tried to destroy the Culdees, but some of them survived by hiding in the caves and forests."

James regarded him with renewed intrigue. "How do *you* know this?"

After a hesitation, Lamberton revealed, "I am one of them."

James's jaw dropped.

Lamberton smiled with cold revenge on his lips as he gazed across the sacred horizon. "Aye, I wear the robes of the Roman church. I have no choice. But I carry on the Culdee fight to preserve God's truth. That cause and Scotland's freedom are bound together. Until our countrymen understand this, we will never be rid of our slavery to the Pope or to England. For now, it is a war that must be fought in the shadows."

James wondered if this bishop had gone bampot in the head. "I still don't see what this church dispute has to do with our rebellion."

"There is always a deeper principle at stake than the one told the common soldier. Scotland is the last refuge of a much older faith, one that knows all men to be gods in the example of Christ the teacher."

"That's blasphemy!"

"Did Our Lord not promise that we would perform miracles even greater than His? Did He not say that we would only find Heaven by asking and seeking? His was not a command for blind allegiance to dogma, but a quest for one's own truth."

Confused, James shook his head. "And that is why England seeks to conquer us? To suppress Christ's true teachings?"

The bishop rubbed his fists to ease the aching ague that had twisted his meaty fingers. "Longshanks lusts for dominion over France. He will do the pope's bidding so long as Rome wields the balance in diplomacy. If we are to survive, and the true Church of Scotland is to survive with us, we must find a king with the heart of Wallace and the wiles of Edward Plantagenet."

"What man could manage all of that?"

The bishop stood from his sitting and, with a tight-lipped smile that suggested he indeed had a candidate in mind, began walking back down the crag.

Left alone on the summit with no answer to his inquiry, James removed his boots and stood barefoot on the altar where the soothsayers of those Sons of Light had once uttered their oracles. He bent down to kiss the etching of the boar, the ancient Scot symbol of sacrifice and courage. There was so much about the future he desperately wanted to know. When would his father return home? Would Scotland survive this war with England? If he agreed to sail with the bishop across the Channel to France, would he ever see Douglasdale again? And whom did the bishop have in mind for their new king?

Yet one question above all others burned in his heart.

He leaned to the altar and whispered the plea for a divination, "Did Belle ever love me?"

He waited for an answer, but he heard only the wind whistling through the dolmens in the glen below him.

SEVEN

donea Comyn slipped unnoticed into the chapel of Dundarg castle, a dismal old keep that guarded the cliffs of Aberdour Bay on the northern border of Comyn country. Approaching the altar with trepidation, she interrupted Belle's morning prayers. "Child, your father ..."

Belle opened her eyes, her heart sinking. "Has he returned so soon?"

"He is dead."

She felt neither shock nor grief, only a disturbing elation. By God's grace, her father had delayed her betrothal to Tabhann that spring to rush south and join William Wallace's army. Yet his procrastination in bartering her off to the Comyns had nothing to do with paternal compassion. Wallace's stunning victory at Stirling Bridge had so weakened Red Comyn's claim to the throne that some of their countrymen had called for the new rebel leader to be named Protector of Scotland. Cunning as always, her father had decided to delay the marriage until the shift of clan power played out, leaving her in the custody of the Comyns with the promise that her dowry would be paid and the bonding formalized at the end of the summer campaign.

"There was a battle at Falkirk," Idonea said. "Wallace has been routed."

Belle erupted from her kneeler. "And my brother?"

"His body was not found. But if he had been captured, there would be a ransom demand. I have heard talk ..." The widow ground her rotted molars when, as now, she became agitated, producing a sound similar to that of rats gnawing on wood. "Longshanks personally commanded the English army. There are some who say Red held back his forces to save his own neck."

Belle hesitated before asking her next question, fearful the widow would only scold her again for still pining for the lad from Lanarkshire. "Is there word of the Douglases?"

Idonea grinned grimly at Belle's concern for the welfare of her clan's enemy over her father's demise "The Hardi has been taken to London Tower."

Belle grasped the chancel railing for support. Knowing all too well what horrors awaited Jamie's father in that devil's pit, she offered up a prayer for the gallant Crusader who had come to her defense in Douglasdale.

God forbid, was Jamie among the captured or killed?

It would have been just like him to run off to join the rebels. She had heard nothing from him since that day he had tried to save her in Kilbride, and even if he were still alive, he had likely sworn off all feelings for her, convinced that she had betrayed him. She had written him letters explaining that she went with the Comyns to prevent them from murdering him, but her correspondence was always intercepted, and she had paid the price with beatings. She knew she should be distraught over her father's death. Yet all she could now think about was Jamie. If the Comyns ever caught her speaking his name again, even in her sleep, they would flog every ounce of blood from—

Alarums in the bailey broke the morning calm.

She shuddered with a sudden thought: If Wallace's army was crushed and scattered, nothing now stood between the English army and Fife.

As if reading her mind, Idonea retracted the fabric screen that covered the window, offering a vantage into the valley. "Longshanks has wasted no time."

Belle hurried to the slit and saw Red and his kinsmen, caked with the mud of battle, galloping through the gate, chased by a hail of arrows. She rushed from the chapel and climbed to the top floor. Below her, on the moors, hundreds of English besiegers were surging toward the ramparts.

Following her, Idonea shouted with diabolical glee, "Rabbits in the skillet!"

Belle was stunned to hear the widow reveling in the spectacle of disaster, apparently not the least concerned that they were also trapped. Idonea seemed to harbor such a fervent death wish that she would gladly give up her life to see the Comyns dragged to perdition with her.

"This time the Hammer won't stop until he reaches the Isles!"

Belle abandoned the callous widow to her manic ranting and ran down the stairs of the tower. In the bailey, she found Red running about the grounds like a madman, trying to set his outmanned defenses.

Red saw her at the entry. "Get back inside!"

Belle stood her ground. "I know what you did to Wallace!"

The chieftain took a threatening step toward her. "I'll rip that sassing tongue from your throat!"

"Longshanks will have yours first!" Idonea shouted down from the tower.

Withered by the hag's witching eye, Red took out his frustration by slapping the nearest of his soldiers toward the ramparts. As the screech of the approaching English siege gun grew louder, he paced and slashed at the ground with his broadsword, as if the very earth under his feet had betrayed him.

From the allures, Cam warned his uncle, "We can't hold them off!"

Tabhann pulled Red aside. "We don't want another Caeverlock. Longshanks executed every defender in that keep for the trouble they caused him."

"But he knows we took up with Wallace."

"We can negotiate terms," Tabhann insisted. "Clifford will never find Wallace in the Selkirk, and Longshanks knows it. Offer to set up a meeting with Wallace. No one will suspect us."

Red pulled at his own beard. "If the clans discovered we gave him up ..."

"Wallace is finished," Tabhann promised. "If we don't settle a pact with the English here, Bruce will take the advantage and move against us."

Red and his kinsmen rode out from Dundarg's gate under a flag of parlay, and Clifford led them into the English camp, passing under the shadow of a trebuchet whose arm had been cut whole from the tallest fir found in Brittany and ferried across the Channel. Escorted into the royal pavilion, the Comyns were forced to wait in silence as Longshanks bandied with the ladies of his court and tasted an array of appetizers prepared for his approval.

At last, Clifford brought an end to their humiliating penance. "My lord, the Earls of Buchan and Badendoch beg an audience."

Longshanks turned in mock surprise. "Whom did you say?"

Clifford shoved Red forward. "These Scot defenders who put up a valiant defense for all of an hour."

Longshanks spat a slither of lime rind and held out his flagon to an attendant for refilling. "Make haste, Comyn. I haven't all day."

Red tried to affect confidence. "I have come to discuss terms."

The king flung his flagon at Red's forehead. "You dare speak to *me* of terms?"

Red staggered on his heels, his brow wet with wine and trickling blood. Spurred on by Tabhann's pressing hand to his back, the chieftain mumbled, "I can offer you Wallace."

"You *will* provide me with that miscreant. Within the month."

"In return—"

"You and those wretched varlets you call vassals will swear fealty to me."

Longshanks dismissed the ladies from his presence and ordered up another flagon of wine. He fingered the cup ominously while circling the trembling Scot chieftain. At his nod, Clifford pressed the Comyns to their knees.

Fearful of being cold-cocked again, Red flinched as Longshanks passed behind him. "By your grace, when this deed is done, I trust my kinsmen and I shall retain our other castles."

Longshanks coughed up a ball of phlegm and shot it through his puckered lips at Red's battered face. "I'd sooner have castrated dogs guard them."

Streaked in spittle, Red glanced with alarm at Tabhann, who had edged away, leaving the chieftain more exposed. Red pleaded with the king, "My lord does remember that I am the ranking noble in this realm?"

Longshanks snatched a letter from the grasp of a French envoy who stood in the corner. He handed the document to Red to read. "Evidently you've not heard the latest news from Paris. The Flemish have smacked Philip about quite roughly." He asked Clifford, "Where was it he met his comeuppance?"

"Coutrai, my lord."

"Undone by burghers armed with brooms!"

From the corner of his stinging eye, Red saw the Capetian diplomat seething at the king's exultation over France's recent misfortune. Yet the envoy was wise enough to play the part required by his circumstance, for all foreign dignitaries to the Plantagenet court knew that the monarch had once flailed his own servant so horribly in a fit of rage that Parliament had ordered royal damages paid to the victim's family.

Longshanks came shadowing over the kneeling chieftain. "So, as even you can see, Comyn, Philip and his craven toadies have wasted little time in suing for peace. I fear your meddling friends across the Channel will no longer be supplying you with arms and funds. And, as a result, I am now freed to put down these Border uprisings once and for all. Perhaps you will wish to reconsider your terms to, shall we say, leaving your heads attached to your shoulders?"

Red realized that he had severely miscalculated in trusting Tabhann's advice to demand terms. "My lord, we ask that you accept surrender of this castle under the protocols of war."

"I think not."

Red's eyes bulged. "You refuse our surrender?"

Longshanks strode out of the tent, and his guards prodded the twittering Comyns through the flaps toward the new English trebuchet, so recently hewn that it still had the scent of the mill. The king caressed its riggings like an executioner examining the sinews of a condemned man's neck, all the while forcing the Comyns to take the full measure of the contraption's enormity. "I've named it War Wolf. I've been promised that it will launch a stone the size of a horse. Do you know how much it cost me?"

Red's answer could barely be heard. "No, my lord."

"Ten thousand pounds."

"There is no need of it," Red pleaded. "The castle is yours if you will—"

Longshanks thumped the chieftain's scabrous forehead with the heel of his palm to demand silence. "I did not sail this gun down the Thames and up the coast, dismantle and drag it through two hundred miles of Scotland shit, only to haul it back without being fired!"

"You surely cannot mean—"

"Escort our esteemed combatants back to their tower," the king ordered Clifford. "Supply them with a case of wine. I would have them enjoy a night they shan't soon forget."

Red could not force his legs to move—until Clifford's forearm to the chieftain's chin provided the motivation.

At dusk, the tolling of Dundarg's bells was followed by a fireworks display worthy of London fete. Several minutes later, the sky fell silent, and the War Wolf went into action. All that night, Belle and the women cowered under pews in the chapel while Longshanks's trebuchet launched a whistling missile every fifteen minutes through the walls and roofs, crumbling them as if threading rotten kindling.

When morning finally broke, the firing ceased.

Belle opened the chapel door and found the bailey littered with debris and the walls smashed. Red and his defenders cowered behind the piles, too frightened to raise their heads.

Clifford rode through the gate and drove the Comyn men from their holes with the flat of his blade. "The king humbly requests your presence for the taking of an oath."

Shaken to the quick by the night's ordeal, Red led his frazzled defenders and the women to a field below the walls. He found Longshanks ensconced atop a platform with his entourage, breakfasting on currants and pastries.

"Comyn!" the king shouted. "What think you of my new sling? If this slag dump can be brought down so soon, think of what it will do to those insolent French bastides in Normandy." He slapped the back of the grim-faced Parisian envoy at his side. "*Monsieur*, do make certain to include in your report to Philip that the razing of this Scot tower took only eight hours."

Clifford forced Red to his knees, along with Tabhann and Cam. The Scots were now grateful to have escaped the bombardment with their lives, though they would henceforth be required to do the bidding of the English crown.

Belle was the last of the Comyns to remain standing, but finally she also descended. At last, she had come face to face with the fiend who had stolen her precious Destiny Stone. She held a bitter glare on the king, silently mouthing a curse. She took heart at the lone bright prospect to this entire sorry affair: At least her father's death had released her from the marital bond.

While the Comyn men mealy-mouthed their oaths, Longshanks strode among them, tapping a carving knife against his thigh. "Rattray, Slains, Banff, all will be delivered within the week," he ordered. "I shall install my headquarters at Lochindorb. See to its provisioning."

Tabhann stole a calculating glance at Belle, then he crawled toward the king and begged, "My lord, may we look to you for the administration of law in our provinces?"

The king laughed. "If I'm not mistaken, you've just had a sampling of it."

Tabhann bowed his head even lower to accept the brunt of the jibe. "There is a legal matter that I would submit to your adjudication."

Longshanks settled into his chair, his stretching legs hanging over the edge of the raised platform. "The common law is my passion. I would see it applied with all due alacrity. Is the other claimant present?"

"Aye, my lord," Tabhann said. "I am betrothed to Isabelle MacDuff, the daughter of the Earl of MacDuff."

The king asked Clifford, "Did we not dispose of a rebel named MacDuff?"

Clifford nodded. "With no small help from these stalwart Scots. They held back their forces at Falkirk when we advanced."

Longshanks grinned wickedly at the feckless Comyns. "I must keep that equitable action in mind when I render my decision."

Tabhann stammered, "I ask the marital contract be enforced *post mortem*."

Caught unprepared by Tabhann's ploy, Belle looked desperately to Idonea, who tried to calm her with a cautioning glare.

The king searched the kneeling Scots. "Where is this woman?" Seeing Belle glare at Tabhann as she slowly arose from her knees, the king ordered her, "Come here. Let us have a look."

Nodded forward by Idonea, Belle took several guarded steps toward the king. As she did, she looked around the pavilion for the coronation relic, suspecting the ogre was vain enough to travel with it.

Longshanks caught the silent exchange between the two women, He asked Belle, "Does the Earl of Buchan speak true?"

"I am betrothed against my will."

Tabhann tried to shout over her. "MacDuff agreed to the terms!"

Longshanks silenced Tabhann with a pointed finger. "This is easily settled. Produce the contract signed by her father."

Tabhann dodged and shifted. "The woman's father promised that the deed would be accomplished on his return. Surely my lord sees the injustice of allowing this pact to lapse."

The king turned his hawkish eye on her again. "What say you to this, woman?"

Belle tried to quell her shaking. "If my father is dead, am I not emancipated from his reach in the grave? No woman should be bound to a marriage arranged by one not her kinsman."

"An agreement in principle!" Tabhann cried. "Her father's desire was to see it enforced!"

From the rear of the kneeling gaggle of Scots, Idonea shouted, "Not after you Comyns abandoned him in battle!"

Red tried to cower the widow to silence. "Give that woman no heed, my lord! She communes with the Devil!"

Longshanks swept his narrowing gaze over the prostrate brood, until his hard eyes fell upon the widowed hag. "I'll not have witchery in my presence."

Idonea remained unbowed. "Aye, but you'll have lies and treachery. Would the wise King of England trust the word of scoundrels who betray their own countrymen?"

Longshanks sank into his chair, unsettled by that point.

Out of earshot of the Scots, Clifford whispered to the king, "My lord, there may be an advantage to us in the enforcement of this marriage."

"How so?"

"If we weaken these Comyns too severely, the Bruces may turn against us and try for the throne. Is it not wise to let the cat guard the rat and the dog guard the cat?"

"How would the disposition in marriage of this filly gain us Scotland?"

"These tribes adhere to a quaint practice," Clifford whispered. "The clan MacDuff must crown their king. When this woman's brothers are captured and hanged, she will become the head of her brood. Attach her to these Comyns, who shall remain under your thumb, and a Bruce will never wear the crown."

Longshanks waved the officer aside and studied Belle as if testing her mettle. "You have sufficient reason to protest this marriage, my lady?"

"My heart is given to another," Belle said.

Longshanks reacted as if he had not heard her correctly. "Are you under the impression that your *heart* is of concern to me?"

Belle stood steadfast, even though her blood was racing. "If my lord will not honor a lady's devotion, I pray you will enforce God's justice. None here has cited precedent that would require my marriage to this man."

Longshanks tapped the armrest, deliberating while he watched Idonea. After several tense moments, he smiled at Belle and announced, "I find nothing in the law that requires this lady to marry against her will."

Belle released a held breath. Had she misjudged this English king?

The next morning, Belle awoke alone in the battered chapel. Finding the castle deserted, she hurried to the ramparts and saw Longshanks and the Comyns enjoying repast on a raised dais overlooking the dunes. Below them, on the beach, Idonea stood tied to a stake. Water engulfed the widow's feet, with each wave rising inches higher. High tide would submerge her within the hour.

Numb with terror, Belle ran from the tower and climbed to the king's platform. "My lord, what has she done?"

Longshanks affected surprise at her arrival. "Ah, our little jurist! She who would have us apply the legal maxims to the letter. You see, my lady, inspired by your example, I consulted my judiciary on the matter. Do you know what I discovered? The statutes require a woman suspected of witchery to be subjected to an ordeal. Stickler for the law as you are, I am certain you agree that I had no choice."

Belle broke through the cordon of guards and rushed to the beach.

Idonea warned her back as the water surged to the widow's waist. "Leave me, child! It will be a blessed release!"

Belle pulled at her hair, desperate to stop the grisly execution. She ran back to Longshanks and fell to her knees, crying, "I beg of you, my lord! This woman has shown me great kindness."

Longshanks casually stabbed another helping of mincemeat with his knife. After several chomps on the morsel, he mumbled with a full mouth, "It is out of my hands." He stole a quick glance at Belle to assess her reaction.

Stricken by the trickery, Belle saw Tabhann grinning at her predicament. Only then did she piece together the conspiracy that these craven men had concocted overnight at her expense. She would have to agree to the marriage with Tabhann to save Idonea from drowning. The rough waves surged to the widow's neck and forced her to cough up salt water. Finally, she cried, "I will submit!"

Longshanks kept his gaze fixed on the sea's horizon. "I would never force a lady to troth against her heart."

Belle heard Idonea spitting water and gasping for air. Sick with despair, she capitulated to the king and folded her hands. "I wish to marry him!"

Tabhann chortled at the fruits of his connivance, until the king withered him to silence with a threatening glare.

A ray of the sun broke through the clouds, and Longshanks seized the opportunity. "A sign! The accused has been exonerated by the saints."

In no hurry, the English soldiers sauntered down to beach and reached the stake as the waves submerged Idonea's head. They cut the widow free and dragged her half-conscious to the dunes.

As Idonea slowly revived spitting sea wash, the king speared a slither of salmon from his plate and held it aloft on his knife to cool in the breeze. "We must never fail to enforce the law. It is all that separates us from the savages."

eight

A bloodcurdling scream pierced the din of Parisian commerce on the Ile de Cite. James looked up at Notre Dame's south tower and saw what appeared to be a living skeleton in rags falling from a rope that had been hoisted from the tollhouse at St. Michael's Bridge. Apparently hoping to speed his death, the airborne man pressed his arms to his sides and crashed to the stones with a sickening thud. Yet the crowds congregating around the markets near the cathedral's portico continued about their business as if nothing more than a dead pigeon had dropped from the sky.

Shaken by what he had just witnessed, James looked to Lamberton for an explanation, but the bishop kept hurrying him toward the shady oaks on the Pont Neuf to escape the oppressive summer heat. Finally finding a breeze, the cleric wiped beads of sweat from his forehead with a kerchief and said, "Once a month, King Philip offers a criminal the choice of walking the rope to freedom or suffering the noose. He holds these spectacles to distract his subjects from the bread riots."

James put a sleeve to his nose, trying not to retch. Each day he spent in this noisome city made him more homesick for Scotland. The stench from the urine and the piles of refuse thrown from the windows were nauseating enough, but now this cruel execution had roiled his stomach even more. The blighted wheat harvest on the Continent had been the worst in thirty years, drawing thousands of starving refugees from the far provinces to Paris like flies over a carcass. As if color and entertainment alone could obliterate their misery, the French king had ordered shops hung with banners of blue and gold cloth, the fountains filled with red Claret, and choirs of white-garbed virgins to sing melodies in the parks to drown out the cries of the beggars.

The bishop took him by the arm again, and together they plowed a path through the perfumed crowds until, at last, they reached the gilded gates of the royal palace. James had been looking forward to their long-awaited audience, if only because it promised a rare escape from these putrid hordes. Strategically situated downwind from the markets and charnel houses, the palace grounds were surrounded by gardens designed to throw up a cordon of fragrance.

Admitted into the outer courtyard, he and the bishop were engulfed by a sea of courtiers, ladies-in-waiting, minstrels, diplomats, clerics, knights, and earls, all clamoring to gain the ear of the chamberlain who manned the public entry into the great hall. After an hour's wait, they were finally summoned into the presence of King Philip, who was known as "the Fair," not in honor of his compassion, which was non-existent, but because of his pallid complexion and imbecilic stare, which made him look like a wax statue.

Over the hum of a hundred conversations, a herald blew his horn and announced, "The Bishop of St. Andrews!"

James stepped forward with the bishop and caught his first glimpse of the king, who sat in the center of the chamber, oblivious to the tumult swirling around him. He had been warned not to show surprise or betray amusement at the monarch's strange behavior. A month earlier, the Archbishop of Pamiers had compared Philip to an owl, beautiful to gaze upon but otherwise a useless bird. When the injudicious remark found its way back to the court, the cleric had been racked and beheaded for the indiscretion.

Philip was indeed an oddity, but James was more intrigued by the maiden who sat at the fatuous monarch's right hand. With long blonde curls and delicate seashells for ears, she was smartly attired in an embroidered bodice of forest green silk that highlighted her blossoming bosom.

Detecting his interest, Lamberton whispered across his shoulder, "Isabella, his daughter. So they say."

He well understood the doubt regarding her paternity. The king's sluggish introversion was exposed in sharp relief by the quick expressions and attentiveness of this precocious lass whose striking cobalt eyes took in all that moved. Her delicate nose tipped up just slightly, and her upper lip formed a perfect Cupid's bow. If Philip was an owl, his daughter was a beautiful white hawk, breathtaking to gaze upon, but also a predator.

The princess turned on him with a provocative smile. Averting his admiring gaze too late, he shifted uncomfortably under her bemused inspection. During these past months in France, he had grown into a chiseled young man, and although he was still shorter than most his age, his dark features, often mistaken for those of a Castilian, were so exotic and unusual here that they caused even the worldly Parisian ladies to turn at his passing.

The princess whispered to her father's ear, and the king swiveled and stared quizzically at the two Scots, as if questioning how they had suddenly materialized before him.

Lamberton bowed. "Sire, it is an honor."

Phillip's powdered cheeks flushed with irritation. When his daughter again whispered the identity of the man giving homage, the king blinked to revive his dormant brain and finally made the connection. "What news have you of this rabble uprising in your land, priest? I'll not allow your Highland squabbles to spoil my daughter's future with the Prince of Wales."

Stunned, James interrogated the princess with a glare of accusation. *You are to be condemned one day to the bed of Edward Caernervon?*

Isabella quickly cast her eyes down; her expressions were as fleeting as the light filtered through St. Chapelle's miraculous windows. When she glanced up again at him, she had been transfigured by a haunting sadness.

Lamberton risked a cautious step forward. "Excellency, we seek only to defend our borders. The English abuse us beyond all Christian civility. I trust France will not turn its back on its staunchest ally."

As Philip tapped his curled shoe, annoyed at being required to discuss matters of state, a tall Dominican monk with sallow skin and a cadaverous face emerged from the royal retinue and came to the monarch's rescue. "France deals only with sovereign nations," the monk said. "Scotland and its mission church must submit to England, as England submits to France."

"We have not been introduced," Lamberton said coldly.

The Dominican's upper lip protruded over a half-moon overbite, making him appear incapable of a smile, and the skin hanging from his neck resembled the leather on the worn copy of Scripture he carried in his scabrous hand. Yet the strangest aspect of his houndish countenance was its bicameral division; the left side of his face seemed frozen, refusing to participate in the expression of its mirror counterpart, a peculiarity that gave the impression his soul was perpetually at war with his flesh. "I am Diredonne, Abbot of Lagny," he said haughtily. "Papal legate to the House of Capet."

Alarmed, Lamberton tried to simulate indifference as he inquired of the king, "Your lordship now feels the need to maintain an inquisitor?"

Philip was too distracted by the minstrels to hear the question.

The Dominican seized the opportunity to press his advantage. "The Tribunal of Whitby long ago brought the Church of Scotland under the authority of the Holy Father. I trust our wayward mission daughter has not relapsed into its old heresy of claiming independence from the chair of Peter."

Lamberton's jowls flamed. "We are all children of equal worth in God's eyes."

"Yes, but children spared the rod of discipline tend to stray from the guidance of their elder and wiser siblings."

"I would remind my brother in Christ that Scotland has produced Britain's only saint canonized by Rome, the venerable Margaret." Lamberton waited for the traditional signing required at the utterance of a saint's name, and when the inquisitor finally relinquished the half-hearted gesture, the bishop drove his minor but satisfying score to the hilt. "I regret that England has only locally proclaimed saints, the Confessor and Beckett. If Rome is the arbiter of all holiness, then God's grace has been dispensed in greater measure upon my country."

The Dominican's moist upper lip quivered.

Isabella interrupted their theological disputation. "Bishop, your scribe here. Is he mute, or merely rude?"

Lamberton was taken aback, not just by the nature of the inquiry, but also because the king's daughter spoke the Anglo-Norman so well. "Apologies, my lady. This is James of Douglasdale."

Isabella turned to her father, who was keeping time to the music with his feet. "Why does Douglasdale ring familiar, *Père*?" When the king persisted in scanning the hall for a diversion, the princess answered her own question. "Of course! I do now remember some correspondence from my betrothed about a border chateau added to his inheritance. I think he has placed it in the care of one of his father's vassals." She narrowed her eyes in a taunt at James. "Perhaps I shall have a summer palace built there."

Lamberton clamped James's elbow to check his temper before he said something they would both regret. "We have imposed too long upon the patience of His Highness."

Philip had long since dismissed the two Scots from his attention, but Isabella arched her thin eyebrows, as if making another last attempt to incite an outburst from James as he departed.

The bishop bowed and backed away. Out of royal earshot, he pulled James into the anonymity of the waiting throngs. "I have one more piece of business to conduct here before we leave."

James paced like a caged fox. "Did you hear that warbling strumpet?"

Lamberton muttered a curse at the inquisitor protecting his position at the king's side. "Aye, we both ate from humble pie. But now is not the time for retribution." From across the chamber, the bishop saw a knight adorned in a coarse white mantle with a splayed red cross on his shoulder. Catching the knight's eye, he nodded furtively, and then ordered James, "Remain here until I return. Make yourself inconspicuous."

Waiting until a jester distracted the court with an acrobatic leap, the bishop followed the white-robed knight, undetected, into a private compartment.

Left alone, James retreated to a corner of the hall and rehearsed again the cruel manner in which he would one day deal with Robert Clifford, preferably with that upstart French princess present. His black reverie of revenge was interrupted when the musicians struck up a lively prelude and the floor cleared in

preparation for a *pas de deux*. The ladies paired off with knights in two lines, face
to face with their partners. These French peacocks and hens began stalking each
other and fluttering away in a ritual that seemed designed to frustrate the men
and show off the women.

Halfway through the *Pas*, he found himself surrounded by a well-endowed
demoiselle and two giggling accomplices. The French lasses pleaded with him
to enter the dance, but he resisted. Not to be denied, one of them interlocked
her arms with his to demonstrate the steps. He made a half-hearted attempt to
imitate the pattern and stumbled badly. His misadventure drew more young
ladies to his aid, until he was trapped in the middle of a cackling bevy of fluttering fans. Suddenly the music stopped in mid-chord, leaving him the only
one in fractured motion.

Princess Isabella split the rows of dancers. With all eyes following her, she
offered her hand to James. "You've never danced the *Pas?*"

The displaced *femmes* shot glares of envy at the princess as they backed away
with perfunctory bows, leaving him no choice but to accept Isabella's invitation. She demonstrated a series of intricate steps, and he awkwardly tried to
follow her lead, but this infernal dance was a maddening test of subtlety and
restraint, nothing like the Scot reels that gained momentum and emotion with
each stanza.

The courtiers monitored his halting progress with smirks and whispers. He
attempted another spin and landed on his backside. Isabella laughed as she
helped him to his feet. He tried again, this time with more success, and soon he
was floating with her across the floor. Her mint-laced breath filled him with a
tingling as she led him through the gauntlet of dancers.

Isabella whispered to his ear, "Say nothing of import to anyone here. There
are those who would see the interests of your country thwarted." She directed
his glance toward the Dominican inquisitor. "That malignant friar will use
any loose utterance to further his designs."

He realized that he had misjudged her. She had spoken of Douglasdale
during the audience not to be cruel, but to quell the inquisitor's suspicions
regarding her loyalties to her future father-in-law. He squeezed her hand in
gratitude for the warning, and spun her in a dazzling pirouette.

"You are a natural," she gasped.

"And you are a *tres* bonnie teacher."

Isabella glowed, delighted by his unintentional cobbling of Lowland Scot
and French. "Dancing is not my only subject of instruction."

Before he could decipher her meaning, she curtsied and spun off to another
partner, a tall French knight with a weathered but handsome face creased by

scars. He cursed under his breath. The infuriating princess had spiked his ardor only to abandon him. *Damn all lasses anyway! Inconstant creatures! All designed to destroy me!*

Returned from his private meeting with the robed knight, Lamberton had been watching the performance from the periphery. He finally caught James's eye and nodded sternly for him to join his departure. Passing through the cordoned entrance, the cleric chided his charge with a whispered aside, "Remind me never again to advise you to remain inconspicuous."

"I did nothing but obey that princess's command."

Lamberton glanced back at Isabella. "Aye, I am discovering that you have a remarkable talent for drawing the notice of those in high station."

Still in the arms of the French knight, she was casting provocative glances at James. She countered the bishop's scowl with a lording smile of conquest.

Vexed by her inexplicable interest in his young companion, the bishop hurried their escape from the palace and warned under his breath, "That lass is too clever for her age. Consider yourself fortunate that she will have forgotten about you by the time you leave her sight."

A week later, the door to James's small cell in diplomatic lodging at the Hotel de Ville creaked open. Lying naked in the oppressive night heat, he tensed and reached under the bedding for his dagger to fight off the intruder.

The flame of a candle approached, and Princess Isabella came into the penumbra of the light. Stunned, he dropped the dagger clanging to the stones. She let her scarlet robe fall to the floor, revealing a diaphanous gown. Speechless, he pulled the blanket up to his chin. How had she gotten a key?

She sat on the bed and ran her hand across his stubbled jaw. Her exploration migrated to the ridges of his muscled torso and threatened to descend below his abdomen.

He tried not to look at her. "My lady … "

Smiling at his quaint modesty, she pressed a finger to his lips to gain his silence. She untied the drawstring of her blouse and slid it from her shoulders.

He pulled her closer, desperate to kiss her. Heart pounding, he brushed her cheeks and felt her sweet breath as he captured her arms above her head to admire the fullness of her breasts. He nuzzled them tenderly with his tongue and returned to waiting lips for another kiss—Belle's face stared down at him.

He pulled away and turned aside.

"Do I not please you?"

"I am promised to another."

She led his hand back to her taut nipple. "We are all promised to another."

He pulled his hand back and struggled to avert his eyes.

When he did not weaken, the princess covered herself and plopped cross-legged at the foot of his bed. She slapped his sternum playfully with her heel. "Silly *jeune homme*. Tell me about her, then, if you must."

He gazed through the window toward the Seine, recalling that day in Kilbride when Belle's long hair had hung dripping down her slender neck. "She's the most bonnie lass in all Scotland. Eyes blacker than a Highland night, and what a temper! Skittish as a colt and just as fast. God, what beauty!"

Isabella allowed her blouse to slide farther down her shoulders. "More beautiful than *moi*?"

He failed to even notice. "Aye, more fetching than—"

She punished his stomach with a sharp kick. "You are an *imbécile* when it comes to *femmes*!" She gathered up her cloak and turned to leave.

He captured her wrist to delay her a moment more. "So I've been told. You are both beyond any man's dreams. It is so strange. You and Belle share a name. And the way you look at me, it is as if you also share a soul."

She shot him a sideways glance of suspicion. "Your dancing improves. ... Are you betrothed?"

He sank, dejected. "Her father schemes to wed her off to another clan."

Isabella ran her hand through his thick hair. "Then you must forget her."

"She will wait for me. I know she ..." He fell silent, stopped short by the memory of her riding off with Tabhann that day in Kilbride.

"Has she told you that she loves you?"

He hesitated. "Not in those words."

"Then we are not so much alike. If I loved a man, I would use those words *exactement*."

Incensed by her skepticism, he bolted up. "And I suppose you've whispered many a honeyed verse into Caernervon's ear!"

The princess turned away in hurt.

He embraced her, apologetic, uncertain how to comfort her. In that moment, with her angelic face strafed by pain, she seemed much older than her tender fifteen years.

"My father requires peace with England. I am to be his means to attain it."

He reached into the crease of her untressed nightgown and examined a locket that hung from a gold chain. Before she could deny him, he opened its casing and found the imprint of a knight's heraldry. "So, I am not the only one who pines away."

She snapped the locket shut. "My father sent him away to the Flemish war."

"Coutrai?"

She answered him with a rush of tears.

Her lover, he realized, had been one of the hundreds of knights killed at the Battle of the Two Hundred Golden Spurs, a disaster from which Philip's army had yet to recover. "And now you've agreed to suffer the rest of your life with a man you'll come to despise?"

"You seem to know a great deal about my future husband!"

He looked off into the distance, stung by the dark memories of Berwick. "Aye, I have laid eyes upon Edward Caernervon. And I would give the little I own to do so again." His grip on her arm had tightened so fiercely that she winced. He gently rubbed away the welt. "Listen to me. You must refuse this marriage. It will bring you only sorrow."

Sighing, the princess rested her head on his chest. "'Refuse' is not a word in the lexicon of my sex."

"If you *are* forced into this arrangement," he said with determination, "I promise I will one day make you a widow."

She greeted that naïve boast with a forlorn smile of resignation. "All of us, sooner or later, must give up the vanities of romance."

He would not have believed a lass so young could turn so coldly cynical. "I'll never stop loving Belle. Even if she …" He could not finish the thought.

She kissed his forehead. "If you will not accept my charms, at least take my counsel. Should you truly intend to abide by such a foolish pledge, you must never become caught in the orbit of a king." She arose from the bed and gifted him with one last glimpse of her ravishing figure. Stoked, he reached to bring her back, but she repulsed his hand and whipped her cloak to cover herself. "Ah, but you are promised to another." She blew out the candle and vanished into the darkness.

Frustrated, he fell back into the bed.

Moments later, he heard the door crack open again.

In the darkness, Isabella's voice warned, "This lady you love will pay dearly for your *haute* principles, James Douglas. Men make oaths. And we women suffer the consequences."

NINE

Two months after their royal audience, Bishop Lamberton slipped unannounced into James's sleeping cell late at night and tossed him a black robe. Warned by a finger to the lips not to speak, James put on the religious garb and followed the bishop down the back steps of the Hotel de Ville to the deserted Paris streets near the Grand Pont. Wherever they were going, disguised as friars, they were taking a circuitous route, backtracking to the same shadowy corners that they had passed minutes before. Satisfied at last that they had not been followed, Lamberton hurried him toward a winding staircase that led down to the banks of the Seine. An oarsman helped them aboard a small fishing boat and then rowed them up a pitch-dark canal that flowed past the walls toward the northern outskirts.

An hour later, they disembarked at the port of an isolated fortress whose most prominent feature was a central chapel built in the shape of an octagon. The thick oaken gates of the compound screeched open, and into the slant light walked the elderly knight who had met privately with the bishop at the palace. One of the rampart tapers flared, revealing the full extent of the environs. They were standing inside the Paris Temple, the most heavily guarded sanctuary on the Continent.

Five monks, draped in white burrel mantles blazoned on their right shoulders with the red *cross-pattée,* stepped out from the recesses behind the columns and came aside their leader. These celibate initiates of the Order of the Poor Knights of Christ, commonly called Knights Templar, could have been mistaken for Old Testament warriors. Every aspect of their training and appearance had been prescribed for advantage in battle; they sheared their hair to prevent it from being grasped by enemies and grew their beards wild because the Moslems considered a smooth face a sign of effeminacy.

James looked around for the chests of gold that he had heard tales about, but the vaulted chamber appeared empty and austere. The Temple maintained hundreds of commanderies across Christendom, and this fortress served as its headquarters. After their loss of Palestine to Saladin, the Templars had turned to the pursuit of commerce and—rumor had it—to esoteric practices such as alchemy and magic. By dominating the Mediterranean trade routes and offering banking services to the courts, they had also grown wealthier than any monarch, even the rapacious Philip.

The eldest knight locked the massive doors. "I ordered you to come alone."

Lamberton signaled for James to descend to a reverent knee. "The lad is in my trust. He is the son of William Douglas the Hardi."

The grand master eased his defiant stance and brought James back to his feet. "I am Gerard de Villiers. I fought with your father at Acre. Is he well?"

James's throat tightened. "He rots in London Tower."

One of the hooded monks behind the grand master closed in on them with a threatening glower. "At least he lives. That is more than can be said for our brothers you Scots murdered at Falkirk."

James fought against Lamberton's restraint, hot to charge the mouthy monk. "I'll have your name before I send you to Hell!"

Challenging them with a better look at his scarred face, the monk retracted his cowl with a finger shorn at the lowest knuckle, a remnant from Moslem torture. Cursed with brooding eyes and a turtle mouth, he held the rigid imperiousness of a man who had little use for Christian charity and meekness. "Peter d'Aumont. Burn that name to memory. If you should ever cross into Auvergne, you will receive a different welcome."

James saw the bishop grimace with regret at hearing the Falkirk calamity invoked. In that battle, the London Temple had broken its vow of neutrality by joining Longshanks to help defeat Wallace. Two English Templars, Brian de Jay and Alan Froumant, had been killed in the final charge.

Deflecting d'Aumont's threat, Lamberton tried to convince the grand master to see the matter in a different light. "Edward Plantagenet uses your Order for his own designs."

"The English king is our benefactor. Our brothers across the Channel took up arms with him for a Christian cause."

"Against fellow Christians," James reminded him.

"The boy has a loose tongue," de Villiers said.

"An inheritance of his lineage," Lamberton admitted. "As is his compulsion to speak the truth."

"If Philip's spies discover that you have come here without his sanction," de Villiers warned, "you will never leave Paris alive. I agreed to this meeting only because of Scotland's service in Palestine. Now, then, what is this proposal of such urgency that you would have us consider?"

Lamberton glanced with concern at the other monks. He had hoped to prosecute his cause in private with the grand master, but he saw that he would have to risk that their lips remained sealed. "Philip sues for peace with England to purchase time to rebuild his army. If the treaty is signed, Longshanks will be free to recall his forces from France and send them against us."

"We will offer a Mass for the salvation of your soul."

The bishop let that snide dismissal pass. "We need arms and financing."

De Villiers repulsed the bishop's brazen request with a punishing glare. "Why should we care who wins your war with England? A cellar of rats would be a preferred venue to your country. You Scots have brought on your troubles with your incessant bickering. You cannot even agree on a king."

Lamberton fingered the onyx crucifix hanging at de Villiers's breast. "By whose authority do you serve?"

D'Aumont answered for his superior. "Christ and the Blessed Virgin."

"And yet your charter requires that you answer only to the pope."

D'Aumont bristled. "The Holy Father is Christ's vicar on earth. Have you marcher heathens forgotten that?"

Lamberton walked to a lancet window and studied the distant torches of the royal palace to assess how difficult it would be for Philip's army to storm this fortress. "If the pope *is* Christ's vicar, why then does he wander France as a nomad under the king's thumb? Philip taxes the clergy to finance his wars, but Clement raises not a whimper of protest. Our Lord's Kingdom seems more and more of this world."

"The Temple is not taxed," d'Aumont said. "What impositions other orders accept are of no concern to us."

"Your treasury dwarfs Philip's coffers," Lamberton said. "He ransacked the Lateran in search of gold. Why would he think twice about gutting the Temple treasury in his own city?"

D'Aumont shared a sardonic laugh with his cloaked brothers. "The Scots send us lunatics and orphans for envoys!"

Despite their professions of indifference, James sensed that these monks were also concerned by the growing power of the Dominicans, just as the bishop had surmised. That day at the palace had made it all too evident, even to this powerful grand master, that the inquisitor Lagny had wormed his way into the inner circles of the Capetian court.

"The Keys of St. Peter are now kept locked in Philip's privy chamber," the bishop reminded the Templars. "One monastic order, and only one, has positioned itself to gain their possession. And it is not the Temple."

De Villiers narrowed his glare. "Reckless talk like that could get you a seat before an Inquisition tribunal."

Lamberton allowed the ensuing tense silence to extend, underscoring the gravity of what he next asked. "Why do you suppose every conqueror since Caesar has tried to subjugate my country?"

D'Aumont snorted. "You have a few monasteries worth plundering."

Lamberton waited for the derisive laughter to fade, then nodded and surrendered an enigmatic concession. "It is true that we Scots possess little of material value. And yet, we hold a priceless treasure."

Intrigued, de Villiers drew closer, waiting for the revelation.

Lamberton smiled knowingly at James to confirm how easily his trap had snared its prey. "You see, lad, these Poor Monks of Christ are not content to await Heaven. They hoard earthly lucre, but what they truly lust for is secret knowledge of God's power. An odd vice for holy men sworn to obey the Holy Father and reject all things of this world."

"Our Lord admonished us to seek!" d'Aumont shouted.

Lamberton met the Auvergne monk's loud indignation with calm assurance. "Aye, and no doubt you have found."

James took the bishop's oblique answer as a barbed reference to rumors of clandestine Templar diggings in the Holy Land, excavations that had revealed certain practices and travels of Our Lord that might prove embarrassing for Rome—or wherever the French pope was resting his head these nights.

Having just demonstrated that he was not some guileless Highland priest, Lamberton drew de Villiers aside and lowered his voice in an attempt at conciliation. "You and I, Gerard, are pilgrims set upon the same quest. I now require your aid. One day you may seek mine."

Overhearing the prediction, d'Aumont hissed contempt. "A soothsayer in Christian garb! What say you, prophet? Shall I dine on venison or pheasant this night?" He closed on Lamberton with threat. "I will offer *you* a prophecy, you Druid bag of wind. The Channel will turn to wine before the Temple looks to Scotland for salvation."

The monks laughed coarsely—until de Villiers glared them to silence.

Lamberton nodded at James to indicate that they had suffered enough insults for one night. The bishop made a move to leave, but the Templar master delayed him with a hand to his arm.

"This Stone that holds such fame in your country. You have seen it?"

Lamberton affected surprise at the grand master's interest. "Many times, before it was stolen by ... what was it you call him? Your *benefactor?*"

De Villiers weighed his next inquiry carefully. "Do you believe it to be the pillar on which Jacob rested his head while dreaming of the ladder to Heaven?"

Lamberton probed for the real reason why the grand master was so interested in the Stone. "Is that what you have been told?"

Before answering him, de Villiers dismissed his monks from the chamber. D'Aumont hung back, but finally he too was chased by his superior's glare.

Alone with the two Scots, the grand master retreated to the hearth and ran his finger across the joints of its arch. "In Palestine, I heard Arab prisoners speak of a legendary basalt stone that held the Ark of the Covenant in Solomon's Temple. They claimed the stone became suffused with miraculous powers from its proximity to the Ark." With a calculated casualness, he turned to the bishop and inquired, "Of what shade and texture is this Destiny Stone of yours?"

"My memory fails me on that point."

"No doubt your memory could be revived."

"I grow more forgetful each day," Lamberton said in a veiled warning. "My feeble mind may soon fail me completely unless my country finds assistance in its cause for freedom."

The Templar master was vexed by the bishop's refusal to be more forthcoming. "Perhaps I should go to Westminster and see this Stone for myself."

Ushering James to his side, Lamberton drew his hood over his head and reached for the door ring. "I've no doubt you already have."

The next day, James followed Lamberton across the tourney fields north of Notre Dame, where they came upon a bizarre scene: A knight stood waist-deep in a pit, dug just wide enough to allow him to swivel while a dozen opponents took turns attacking him. After dispensing with the last of his challengers, the half-buried showman threw off his helmet, revealing flowing blonde hair, a trimmed beard, and a narrow face creased with scars.

James bit off a mumbled curse of recognition. This French courtier planted in the ground like a cranebill was none other than the knave in whose arms Isabella had escaped during the dance at the royal palace. Broad-shouldered and impressive for a knight in his early forties, he could have stepped out of a Grail legend. Yet there was a sad wisdom in his soft sapphire eyes that transfused him with an emanation of timelessness.

The knight twirled his sword to taunt his demoralized attackers. "Shall I burrow to my chin and fight you with my teeth? Saints of Christ! This is what passes for the king's champions? I've met blinded Moors with more skill! Come on! I'm twice the age of you sucklings!"

Finding none of his students willing to risk a second foray, the Frenchman spotted the two Scots watching the lesson. He flung his sword at James's feet and shouted, "I have heard of your brave Wallace, *jeune homme!* Show these cockerels the purpose of a blade!"

James waited for Lamberton to explain this insanity, but the bishop merely nodded for him to pick up the sword.

"I haven't all day! Give me a run!"

Disgusted by this charade at his expense, James threw the weapon aside.

The knight kept taunting him. "That's a Scottie for you! They showed the cracks of their *derrieres* at Falkirk, *aussi!*"

James lunged for the sword and charged at the slandering Frenchman.

The knight, though restricted to moving his upper torso only, ducked deftly and whipped his mailed forearm into James's shin, collapsing him. Before James could make sense of what had happened, the knight captured the end of the blade, snagged his collar with its hand guard, and dragged him to his smirking face. "So what they say is *véritable*. A Scottie always leaps before he thinks."

Lamberton pulled James to his feet just in time to cause his punch to land short. "Jamie, meet Sir Giles d'Argentin. He's the only knight to have unhorsed Longshanks in a tournament."

The grinning Frenchman climbed from his hole and offered his hand.

James, still smarting from the clap to his shin, refused it.

"I meant no insult, *monsieur*. Fight with your eyes, not your ears. The bishop tells me you hail from fine warrior stock."

James spun on the bishop. "You planned this?"

Lamberton shared a conspiratorial smile with the French knight as he dusted off James's shirt. "Lord d'Argentin has agreed to take you into his training."

James rubbed his bruise. "I can do well enough on my own."

"Aye," Lamberton said. "Well enough to get your head lopped off."

"Let's see what you *can* do, shall we?" The instructor scanned his eager students and then called out, "Rouen!"

A helmeted student, shorter than the others, stepped forward.

D'Argentin ordered up a helmet, padded gambeson vest, and broadsword for James. "There you are, Scottie. *Alors*, show us your *dextérité* with the blade."

James reluctantly put on the gear and tested the weapon; it was lighter and had more torque than those forged in Scotland. The student confronting him held his sword vertical to protect his torso. He accepted that he was shorter than most Parisian men his age, but he was a head taller than this opponent, and he was confident he'd have no problem thumping the pipsqueak.

They circled each other, neither willing to make the first move.

D'Argentin cried, "This hole will be my grave before you strike!"

Fed up with the ridicule, James rushed at his opponent's exposed leg, but the student whipsawed his blade and pinned his sword hand against his thigh.

"Unclench!" the instructor shouted.

Shoved away, James stumbled to the ground. He erupted to his feet again and lunged wildly, but was sent sprawling from his own momentum. He looked up to find his opponent offering his sword in surrender. He laughed at seeing the pampered Parisian already worn down. Typical Frank—all *élan*, no stamina. He dropped his weapon and swaggered up to accept the concession. When the extended handle was nearly in his reach, the student retracted the blade and buffeted him on the head with its knob.

He came back to mindfulness convinced that he was suffering from a concussion hallucination: Above him hovered the vision of a comely female face, framed by short auburn hair cut like a man's shocks. He heard d'Argentin's distant voice echoing in his head. *Are you still with us, Scottie?* He managed to stand, only to be sent to his knees again—this time by confusion—as his opponent removed his helmet.

Not a man, but a lass stared down at him with the same long-lashed eyes and pert red lips that he had just banished from his bollixed brain.

Lamberton and the students cackled at his gawk of surprise.

D'Argentin consoled him with a hand to his shoulder. "Head high, Scottie. She has bested most of them here."

The armoured maiden offered to assist him to his feet. "My name is Jeanne. You are not injured, I hope."

James repulsed her reach and, angrily yanking off his helmet, searched for cuts. Did the scheming wench deem herself immune from all rules of chivalry? He protested, "You presented your sword in surrender!"

D'Argentin stole James's sword by its cutting end and jabbed him with the hilt knob to demonstrate the famous Murder Stroke. "Count yourself fortunate that she did not separate your hollow skull from your shoulders, *monsieur*. A spoken confirmation must accompany a concession."

"Sharp practice! You Franks are full of deceit!"

D'Argentin kept poking him. "And the charnel fields are fertilized with the rot of dupes like you. Tell us, what is the purpose of combat?"

"To gain the field with honor."

"*Cela est absurde!* Do you think the Moors and Flemish care about our honor? Two hundred of our chevaliers drowned in their precious honor at Coutrai." D'Argentin circled him, lecturing and prodding. "First maxim. Know your weapon. What is the most dangerous part of the broadsword?"

"The blade," James muttered. "Any idiot would know that."

D'Argentin wailed him with the knob and sent him curling into a ball. "The hilt, you Highland *bouffon!* The hilt! Why?"

When James shrugged, clueless, Jeanne volunteered an answer for him, rubbing in his humiliation. "The forging is strongest at the grip."

After being dragged through the mud, James recovered to his feet and checked his scalp for blood. Glaring at the duplicitous Amazon, he retrieved his blade and retreated a step, watching for her next underhanded ploy.

"Cross guard!" the instructor ordered.

Jeanne raised her hands to her face and turned the blade's point down. James saw an opening and attacked, but the lass rotated the blade and spun his sword from his grasp.

D'Argentin flew into a prancing fit. "Keep low, Scottie! And spread your hands!" He pushed James aside and took the position confronting Jeanne. With a series of quick maneuvers, the instructor sent his female student backtracking. "Offense and defense at the same time! Every stroke sets up three thrusts hence! Advance with the foot on the same side as your sword hand! Four openings!" He punctuated each shout with a sharp blow. "Shoulder *droite!*" Thump! "Shoulder *sinistral!*" Thwack! "Leg *droite!*" Thump! "Leg *sinistral!*" The knight's final smote alighted Jeanne on her backside.

James thoroughly enjoyed that *dénouement*—until he found d'Argentin's blade aimed at the space between his brows.

"Does he show promise?"

That sweet voice drove the French students and instructor to their knees.

James escaped from the blade's threat to find Princess Isabella standing on the bluff above the dueling field, a few steps away. How long had she been watching his embarrassing comeuppance at the hands of this sword-wielding girl? Accompanying her was the same retinue of ladies who had been at the palace during the dance. They batted their eyelashes at him and flapped their fans like geese wings.

D'Argentin arose from bent knee and straightened his spine, trying to make his aging frame appear taller. "My lady, you honor us with your unexpected presence."

"I wished to take one last stroll along the river."

Lamberton came forward and, kissing her hand, led her down the bluff. "Surely you will have many more."

That expressed hope chased Isabella's smile. "I leave for England on the morrow to meet my future husband." She stole a furtive glance at James to emphasize that this encounter was no coincidence. "I know not when I shall return."

Lamberton searched for words of solace. "You will be dearly missed. We can only pray that France's temporary loss will be England's education."

Isabella came nearer to James and feigned an attempt at recognition. "Your scribe, if I recall, Bishop? Odd training for one meant for the monastery."

The students stifled smirks and chuckles—all but Jeanne, who held a nettled frown, as if detecting more than just a passing interest from the princess in that observation.

James shot a lording glare at the jealous French girl who was gripping and regripping her sword, apparently pining for a rematch. Now *she* knew what it felt like to be on *her* heels. Prodded to courtesy by the bishop, he turned from his irked opponent and offered a kiss to Isabella's wrist. While bent, he stole another brandish, sideways glance at Jeanne, but quickly lost his smirk, remembering that this might be his last opportunity to speak to Isabella, perhaps forever. He could never reveal their unlikely friendship. During their many secret but platonic trysts, the princess had made great strides in educating him in the ways of a gentleman, including giving him instruction in the French language and the lute.

Isabella remained in his gaze too long for propriety. Daubing a tear, she looked to the sun to ascribe blame for the irritation and reluctantly broke off their silent exchange. She began walking toward the palace, but then turned back. "Lord d'Argentin, you did not answer me."

"My lady?"

"Does our transplanted Scot here show promise?"

D'Argentin regarded James with suspicion, questioning why the princess would take interest in a lowly foreign squire. "Too soon to know."

Isabella stole a last glance of regret at James, her effort at flirtation dying with a sigh of resignation. Trying to mask the emotion in her voice, she gamely advised the instructing knight, one of her many admirers: "Then you must not divulge *all* of our secrets to him, no?"

TEN

Belle followed the Comyn men up the puddled steps of Berwick Castle and looked down upon the rows and rows of new rooftops gabled in the London fashion. Married off two months ago to Tabhann, she had thought nothing could exceed that misery; but now, witnessing the tribulations of her fellow Scots here in the Borders, she felt her heart breaking again.

Almost nothing remained of the port that she remembered from her first visit here as a child. The English had built thick curtain walls to the banks of the Tweed for protection against raids, and the adjacent burgh, transformed into a bastide with its own formidable ramparts, had been repopulated with Yorkshiremen whose forges now hummed with military preparations. Beyond the gate lay grassy mounds over the mass graves of those massacred here nine years ago, the only reminder left to bear witness to Longshanks's brutality.

The guards herded the Comyns and her into a waiting line of five hundred Scot nobles who had been summoned, under the penalty of treason, to appear and swear loyalty to the Plantagenet crown. Forced to stand in the rain for an hour, they were finally admitted into the shelter of the great hall. Near a raging hearth, Longshanks sat on a raised platform watching the arrivals as Robert Clifford roughly check them for weapons. Accompanying the king were his son, Edward Caernervon, and his Privy Council, which included the Earl of Gloucester, Hugh Cressingham, the Treasurer of the Realm, and William Ormsby, the English-appointed Chief Justiciar for Scotland.

Belle scanned the hall and saw an unfamiliar face on the dais. At Caernervon's side sat a slender, sable-haired knight who playfully nudged the prince while whispering jests at the expense of her forlorn countrymen. Raffishly coiffed with curls and trimmed beard glossed to a point, the brazen churl wore an outlandish tunic of crimson silk sewn lavishly with sparkling gemstones. Watching him preen without shame, she suspected the man, so untutored as he was in the virtue of Christian modesty, to be none other than the notorious Piers Gaveston, a Gascon dandy whose tongue was said to be as cutting as his sword. There was something so unnatural about his mincing presentment that she was at the same time repulsed and incapable of diverting her gaze.

Caernervon's future wife, Isabella, sitting on the prince's left, also witnessed the Gascon's risqué conduct. She turned toward Belle with a pointed glance of sickened anguish so shocking in its familiarity that Belle could not shake the absurd feeling that the princess somehow knew her intimately.

Shoved toward the swearing stand, Red Comyn discovered the Bruces standing in the fore of the procession. Enraged by what he perceived as an end-run around his right to the throne, the chieftain attempted to elbow his way ahead of them. "The Comyns must be heard first!"

Clifford buffeted Red's yapping jaw with the back of his hand, sending the chieftain reeling. Laughing, the officer regaled the king, "They trample themselves to kiss your ring, my lord!"

A groan of humiliation rose up from the Scots—from all, that is, but the Bruces, who nodded with satisfaction at seeing Red Comyn receive such a bruising welcome. Old Bruce the Competitor, tottering and disoriented, was supported at the elbows by five grandsons so varied in features and temperament that none would have guessed them to be kin. Wrapped in the black robe of a Cambridge scholar, Alexander Bruce was the shortest and fairest of the brood, with his soft, delicate lines and smooth skin protected by days spent in libraries. Edward Bruce, the second eldest, was stout, edgy, constantly in motion, pushing always, his sienna hair as wild and raging as his smoldering hazel eyes. Unlike their older siblings, twins Thomas and Nigel had inherited the optimistic nature of their Irish mother, and even in this hour of confrontation and discord, they traded broad, hail-thee-well grins with comrades.

Yet it was Robert Bruce whose firm stance and determined brow made clear that he now governed the clan. Although an accomplished knight well into his twenties, he was rumored to prefer the comforts of the English court to the demands of his Scottish rank. His entrance had been met with icy glares from his fellow countrymen, for there was talk that he had tarried in bringing up his troops to aid Wallace at Falkirk. But that was just slander, Belle knew, spread by the Comyns to shunt responsibility for their own malfeasance.

Longshanks ignored Red's protests and offered his jewel-spangled hand to the lady accompanying the eldest Bruce brother. "Dearest Liz. I'll never forgive Rob for stealing you from my court. I trust marriage is agreeable?"

The former Elizabeth de Burgh, daughter of one of Longshanks's most valued allies, the Earl of Ulster, curtsied stiffly, allowing her strawberry blonde curls to fall over a green bodice that had been expertly tapered to announce her ample bosom. "It is all I dreamed of and more, Sire."

Belle found Robert's choice for his second wife troubling. His first, the Scot daughter of the Earl of Mar, had died two years ago in childbirth, leaving him a weakly daughter, Marjorie. Robert had remarried into high nobility, true, but she would have preferred another Scot lady, and one a bit less arrogant. Elizabeth was tall, freckled, and big-boned; every inch of her impressive frame, which tended toward a meaty fleshiness, was cast in vibrant shades of red. She could have been one of those fire-haired warrior queens who once ruled from the sacred mound of Tara. And yet, there was none of that Irish acceptance of fate's inevitable damnation in her temperament. Raised in the rarefied air of the London court, Elizabeth reportedly insisted on the finest of accommodations and was said to despise the brutish journeys across the Ulster moorlands to visit the Irish holdings of her father.

Longshanks draped his vulture-winged arms across the shoulders of Robert and Edward Bruce. "Ah, lads, I had no doubt you'd rush to my side. Children, Rob! Has it not been a year? And still our lovely Liz has not bloomed? Delay much longer, and I'll suspect you of being distracted from your husbandly duties." He playfully slapped the back of Edward's head, each tap more forceful. "And you, Eddie? Not a word since you took leave from my household?"

Damned from birth with a face that never camouflaged a thought, Edward Bruce tried to protest, "That arrangement was not by my—"

Robert silenced his impulsive brother with pinch to the nape of his neck in what only appeared to be sibling affection. As if to gain a distance from the taint of his fellow defeated Scots, Robert made it a point to speak the London dialect that he had learned as a boy in the Plantagenet court. "I have been occupied by troubles in our Galloway domains, my lord. Comyn and his outlaws harass me without cease. If you would recognize my right to the kingship—"

"I pay your debts!" Longshanks screamed, suddenly turning apoplectic. "Do you now expect me to buy you a kingdom?"

Robert was driven onto his heels by the swift alteration in the king's mood. "My lord, I have been a loyal vassal—"

"Loyal to my overly generous purse!" Longshanks shouted so shrilly that his hounds sprawled near the hearth erupted with howling. He contemptuously surveyed the slump-shouldered Scots. "He who rids himself of shit does good business."

A wave of muttering rippled through the scowling Scots.

Seeing the Competitor baring his toothless gums in a half-snarl, the king settled into his chair and ordered old Bruce to the base of the dais. "I shall hear it from you first, Lord Annandale."

Robert tried to mitigate the king's ire by stepping in front of his grandfather, but Clifford forced the Competitor to the fore. Shaking with the palsy, old Bruce shuffled pitifully to the dais, begrudged a difficult collapse to his knee, and mumbled the oath. Having swallowed his enforced dose of shame, he glared his grandsons to their prostrations.

Robert was the last to descend.

The English barons eased their martial stances, placated with this, the most significant of the many debasements that would follow that morning.

The Earl of Gloucester, cousin to the Bruces, assisted the Competitor back to his feet. Deprived of his dream to become king of Scotland, the Bruce patriarch could only offer him a browbeaten nod in gratitude for the kindness.

Amused by their groveling prostrations, Longshanks turned next to Red Comyn. "You should be quite accomplished at this exercise, Comyn. God knows, you've practiced giving oath to me so many times, we've lost count."

The chieftain, still woozy from Clifford's blow, stumbled to his knees. "My lord, as always, the Comyns shall keep true with you. May I present my son, the Lord of Badendoch, and my nephew, the Lord of Buchan."

While Tabhann and Cam mealy-mouthed their oaths, Longshanks squinted beyond their shoulders and found Belle still standing. Seeing her shove away Red's hand when he tried to pull her down, the king mulled this rare demonstration of defiance. "Your men have barked, Comyn. It seems your women will not. I'm not surprised. My houndsmen tell me the orneriest bitches always mate with the puniest males. A law of nature."

Red labored under the delusion that Belle, not he, had been insulted. "You will remember her, my lord. At your behest, she is the wife of my nephew."

"Her father's skull still hangs from Stirling Bridge," Clifford reminded the king. "The son of MacDuff continues to prosecute his banditry in the Selkirk."

Longshanks did not receive the reaction that he had expected from the mention of Ian MacDuff's death. Instead, he found Belle distracted by the block of limestone resting below his feet. "Do you recognize it, my lady?"

"No, my lord."

"Of course not. What was I thinking, asking such a question? Your crass traditions denied you the right to remain in its presence. I am your liberator. Gaze on it to your heart's desire. I believe you call it your Stone of Destiny."

Belle stared dumbfounded at the crude lump. Iron rings had been driven into its sides so that it could be carried like a lump of rock salt. Could this disappointing chunk of common quarry truly be the Stone of Miracles? When it slowly dawned on her what base treatment it had suffered in captivity, she stumbled from faintness and nearly fell.

Robert Bruce rushed to her with an arm for support. She saw from Robert's ashen expression that he shared her distress. She had refused to believe her father's insistence that the relic held no special powers, but here the Stone sat before her, a silent witness to Scotland's humiliation, impotent as the craven men who stood around her.

Longshanks enjoyed her torment. "Tell me, Lady Buchan. Is it true the Stone must scream before one can be accepted as your king?" When she did not answer him, he slammed his heel into the block and sent a chip flying from its corner. "Did you hear it scream?"

Belle rushed forward to salvage the shard, but the guards drove her back.

Longshanks jumped to his feet, ricocheting his chair. "I asked if you heard it scream!" He drove his heel into the Stone's soft limestone again.

Many of the Scots turned away, unable to watch the sacrilege. Finally, Robert Bruce put a stop to the abuse. "We heard it, Sire."

Satisfied with that concession, Longshanks strode with loping steps to the table that held the Ragman Rolls, the derisive title given to the shameful oath documents. "Afford me obedience, and you will live in peace. Deny me, and you will suffer the same fate as this city that chose defiance nine years ago."

Rousing from his whispers with Gaveston, Caernervon pointed out two hooded men who stood at the entrance. "Father, not all the dogs have yelped."

The Scots parted to make a path for two unidentified arrivals.

One of the newcomers lowered his cowl. "In accord with your command, my lord, I present myself, along with my clerk."

There was a rumble of surprise, and then an explosion of excitement. The Scots, who had long prayed for the return of their beloved Bishop Lamberton, rushed up to be the first to gain the cleric's hand and welcome him home.

In the scramble, Belle was shoved aside, denied a clear view.

Longshanks motioned up the Scot cleric. "We feared you'd fallen prisoner to the French." He scrutinized the young man accompanying Lamberton and turned to Clifford for some indication, but the officer could only shrug to indicate his own lack of recognition.

With a hesitation, Lamberton revealed, "James Douglas, Sire, of—"

"Castle Douglas!" James yanked down his hood in defiance. "Your shireman stole my home and abducted my father."

Belle gasped. She jumped repeatedly, but she could not see over the shoulders of the men in front of her. His lisping voice sounded different. Had he picked up a hint of a French accent?

His memory revived, Clifford told the king, "My lord remembers the felon William Douglas." He checked James for weapons. "Give oath to His Excellency, and the crimes of your father will not be held against you."

James repulsed the officer's hands. "I will first speak with my father."

"That may prove bit difficult." Clifford said, sharing a grin with Longshanks. "Unless you can commune with the dead."

James's legs threatened to give way. He turned in disbelief to the bishop, begging for a denial that it could be possible, but the cleric's stricken look confirmed the worst.

The guards took a step toward him, expecting violence. Faint with grief, James only then saw Princess Isabella sitting at the end of the dais, secluded in the flickering shadows. In these few weeks she had been in England on her visit, she had so aged and altered in appearance that he was required to take a second glance. Her cheeks were hollow and her once-sparkling blue eyes, swollen from nights of weeping, pleaded for him to remain strong.

Detecting the exchange, Caernervon glared at his future wife in accusation. Isabella looked toward Gaveston in a stinging reminder that the prince held no standing to levy a charge of indiscretion at her.

The Scots in the receiving line stood stunned at the news of Wil Douglas's death. None held any illusions about the grisly manner in which he had been dealt with in the Tower. Propelled by a great wave of indignation, they erupted in a maelstrom of angry shouts and promises of vengeance.

Caught up in the jostling, Belle became separated from the Comyns. She was shoved from the chamber by the guards as they maneuvered with pikes flashing to abort the uprising. She screamed for James, but her calls were drowned out.

Bishop Lamberton removed his riding cloak to reveal his clerical garb in a reminder to the king that he still wielded divine authority. "William Douglas was to be held under the protection of Christian law."

"He succumbed of natural causes," Clifford said.

James rushed at the officer. "Murderer!"

Clifford met him with the point of his dagger. "Swear."

"I'll swear nothing but vengeance!"

The Scots mouthed threats as they moved toward the guards.

Denied a full sweep of his weapon, Clifford wrestled James toward a side portal to use him as a shield.

"Release him!" Longshanks ordered.

The privy councilors were shocked by the command.

But Longshanks moved to abort the growing mutiny that was about to forfeit all that he had accomplished in breaking the spirit of the Scots. "The lad grieves for his father, as would any son. My justice is tempered by mercy."

The Scots broke into quarrels, some demanding retribution for the murder, others whispering their preferences for the surety of Plantagenet governance over the anarchy of more clan bickering over the throne in Dunfermline. Offered this unexpected reprieve, Lamberton hurried James toward the doors before Longshanks could change his mind.

James shook off the bishop's restraint long enough to accost Robert Bruce with a glare of accusation for giving the traitor's oath. Robert turned away to deflect his old friend's silent indictment. Lamberton was about to shove James outside when—

"Bishop!" Longshanks called out from the dais. "I hold a feast this eve to celebrate our union. I hope to see you in attendance."

James felt the bishop's grip on his arm tighten. With his back still turned, Lamberton silently mouthed a curse.

Princess Isabella escaped the afternoon's tedious oath ceremony with her usual excuse of feeling feverish. Despondent and homesick, she walked aimlessly through the dark halls of the tower until she found an abandoned storage room. Sneaking inside, she slumped into a corner and began sobbing, distraught over her bleak future. She heard a voice and, crawling closer, discovered that the door to an adjacent room had been left ajar.

She peeked through the crack and saw her husband sitting on his bed with a board on his lap that supported a wood model of a miniature waterfall on the steps of Westminster Abbey. He had designed this engineering feature to cool the summer breeze for pilgrims who would offer up prayers on his behalf in gratitude. Although the prince had reached the age of majority, he dreamed not of kingdoms, riches, or crusades, but, strangely, of rushing water. Since childhood, he had been fascinated by canals, aqueducts, moats, fountains, sewers, and, in particular, the new toilet devices that flushed offal away with only a pull of a cord. Many in the court even suspected him of drinking enormous quantities of liquids merely to prolong the enjoyment of urination.

As the prince poured a rippling stream of red Claret from a goblet down the tiny steps of his model Abbey, a drop of rain plopped against his head. He looked up to inspect the ceiling, but he found no leak.

Seconds later, another droplet plunked him.

Exasperated, he threw the goblet at the timbers. "Damn these Scots! Can they not construct a simple roof?"

He shoved the bed closer to the hearth and returned to his fantasy world, meticulously fastening a belfry to his tiny Abbey tower.

Swish! Splat!

That was not a drop, by God, but a gush of cold water!

Before the prince could recover, a flagon from behind the headboard poured its remnants down the bridge of his nose. Piers Gaveston appeared above him, unleashing a howl of roguish delight at having fooled his gullible lover.

"Miscreant!" the prince cried, spewing water. "I should have you hanged!"

Gaveston leapt over the headboard and straddled Caernervon's chest. "I am already hung quite admirably. Admit it, or I shall have to prove it again."

Caernervon nervously regarded the door. "Not here."

Gaveston feigned hurt. "You no longer love me?"

Through the cracked door, Isabella looked on as Caernervon brought Gaveston into his arms. The prince could not resist this flamboyant Gascon who, even by Longshanks's grudging admission, was the most promising knight in the royal service. Still, the English barons made no secret of their concern over her future husband's deepening bond with this favourite, for Gaveston's greatest talent had proven not to be his skill in battle, but his uncanny ability to infiltrate the highest echelons of the royal court.

She had been told in confidence by the prince's former nursemaid that Edward had never fully recovered from the death of his doting mother, Joan of Aquitane, who had raised him while the king was off campaigning in Wales and Scotland. The prince had early on shown a promise of maturation, even donning custom-made armor at Berwick while mimicking his father's orders. But by his fifteenth year, he had turned inward, suffering debilitating spells of lost resolve and unfounded suspicions against others. The only reason that the king endured Gaveston's presence was his hope that the Gascon's superb fighting skills and preening confidence would take root in his son.

Gaveston pecked at the prince's lips. "It has been hours since you've shown me affection. Don't I deserve a reward for enduring those foul-smelling savages out there?" His whimsy merely served to provoke Caernervon's insecurities.

The prince firmed their embrace. "I would go insane without you."

Gaveston puffed his chest in mockery. "Did you see old Gloucester strutting out there like a constipated rooster? And that gasbag Clifford must soon take a wife. I'd challenge him to swordplay, but he is wound so tight in the tethers that one prick might explode him like a dropped melon."

Edward retreated to a distant glare of revenge. "They'll all be gone when I am king! They treat me as if I am a leper!"

Gaveston whimpered into Caernervon's ear. "And what shall become of me, Poppy? Will I be an earl? Of Gloucester, perhaps. But then I would have to take in that old fart's leggings."

"They will pay! The Tower's not large enough to hold—"

The front doors flew open—Longshanks strode into the room.

Gaveston scrambled half-naked from the bed and fell to his knees. "My lord, the prince and I were debating the advantages of the mace in close quarters."

The king kicked Gaveston aside and came towering over his son. "Where is that French kitten who will be given the dubious duty of producing your heir?"

The prince puffed up his pillows behind him and returned to the task of arranging his Westminster toy model. "How should I know?"

Longshanks cleaved the toy board in half with his fist.

Horrified, young Edward howled and rushed from the bed to retrieve the pieces of his destroyed craftwork. "You allow that upstart Scot to spit in your face! And now you abuse *me*?"

In the next room, Isabella snuggled closer to the side door to better hear. She accidentally nudged the rusty hinge.

Longshanks glanced toward the noise, but fortunately, for Isabella, his son's rant distracted him again. The king turned on Gaveston and slammed his boot toe into the Gascon's buttocks. "Get out!"

Gaveston tried to incite the prince with a glare to stand up to the old man, but Caernervon was too distraught with salvaging his balsawood fragments. Denied a confrontation, the Gascon could only rush from the room in a huff.

The door recoiled against Isabella. Curled in the corner, she hurriedly rolled away, opened a book, and feigned reading.

Gaveston stared down at the French princess, debating whether to reveal her lurking. He settled for throttling her neck and whispering with a hiss, "Speak a word of what you just heard, you conniving Paris whore, and I'll make a bookmark out of that wagging tongue of yours."

Isabella squirmed and fought against his digging fingers until Gaveston, glancing back to make certain the king had not followed him, finally released her with a flick of his wrist and marched from the room through another door. She rolled to her stomach and stifled coughs, trying desperately not to alert the king and her husband of her eavesdropping. At last, recovering her breath, she risked crawling toward the cracked door again.

The king was so angry that, thankfully, he had not heard the commotion of the Gascon stumbling over her. Longshanks paced in a tightening spiral of frustration, his white mane whipping around his head like cat-o-nine tails. "Watch my actions, not my words. Do you think I place a whit of faith in their groveling?"

Caernervon slowly lowered his arms to test the easing of his father's rage. "Why then must we waste time with such nonsense?"

Longshanks gazed through the window at the bridge over the Tweed, where the Scots were being dispatched after their oath signing. "I wanted to look into their eyes, mark their manner. That sprig Douglas was the only one foolish enough to speak what the others were thinking."

"If I were you, I'd throw him in a pit before he causes more trouble."

Longshanks turned slowly. "What did you say?"

"I said if I were you—"

"You are *not* me. You've made that evident enough."

"Hang him, father. Make an example of him."

"Nay, I've cuffed enough Scot ears for one day. I have other plans for the Douglas cub. The Bruce litter is the one we must keep closely surveilled. Did you notice young Robert?"

"I don't fancy him."

Through the door crack, Isabella saw Longshanks lift his son by the collar and pin him against the wall.

"I swear your mother was inseminated by a head-shorn incubus from the dregs of Limbus!" the king shouted. "Witless dolt! Listen to me! When Douglas refused the oath, Bruce had a wan look about him."

Toes dangling, Caernervon pipped, "A wan look?"

"Of treason. ... Never forget what I am about to tell you, Eddie. We must at all cost keep these Scots clawing at their own throats. Else they will come at ours." Longshanks dropped the prince like a sack of coal and marched out—but not before glancing at the cracked door to the anteroom.

T he discovery that he had been responsible for his father's death was too much for James to endure. That afternoon, after the humiliating oath ceremony, he had vowed to regain Douglasdale, or die trying. With his few coins saved up from Paris, he had purchased a half-lame horse in the Berwick market and had headed west.

Now, as he lashed the nag west across the hills of Lanark, he turned to find another rider galloping for him, hard in chase.

Clifford had wasted no time in coming after him.

He drove the old horse to its breaking point, but the Englishman was gaining ground. He drew his dagger, and when Clifford came neck to neck, he jumped the officer. He dragged him to the ground and raised his weapon for the kill—

His attacker threw off his helmet.

Not Clifford, but Robert Bruce lay under him.

Stunned, James tossed aside the dagger and ripped open his own shirt for a target. "Longshanks sends you to do his butchering? Have at it, then!"

Robert climbed to his feet. "You left before—"

"Before what? Before I could sell out my country, like you did?"

Robert jerked as if slapped. "That oath means nothing."

"I know well enough what *your* word means."

"I am sorry for your father. And for your lady." Robert was perplexed by James's look of confusion. "Did you not see her?"

"Belle ... was in Berwick?"

"Aye, she was close enough to touch you."

He racked his memory of the faces in the hall that morning. "What was *she* doing there?"

Robert retreated a step, unprepared to be the deliverer of this news. "I thought word had been sent to you. She was married last spring to Tabhann Comyn."

His throat seized. In one disastrous day, he had learned his father was dead, the girl he loved had spurned him, and the man he thought was his friend had handed over Scotland to the English. Now, he was even more desolated, if that were possible. "You rode all this way to tell me that? It must give you great pleasure."

"I came to convince you to return to Berwick."

James whistled for his horse. "I've suffered enough English insults."

Robert captured his arm. "We bide our time."

He shook off Robert's hand and climbed to his stirrups. "Until what? Until Longshanks has garrisons posted in every town? You are destined to be our next king, God help us! Instead of acting the part, you stand idle."

"My position is not that simple."

"You took a wife from Longshanks's court. And Belle is a traitor as well."

"A traitor to what?"

"To my heart. But she was right about one thing. A leg on each side of the border will always be *your* position."

Robert yanked the reins so violently that James's horse reared. "Run, then! Isn't that what the great runner always does when the heat is on? You ran from Berwick! You ran from Douglasdale! You ran from your woman! You ran from Scotland! Now you run from me! I wouldn't have you at my side!" He slapped the steed's nostrils and caused it to snort and buck.

When James had finally regained control of his horse, he turned and found Robert galloping back south.

eleven

That evening, the Scot nobles returned to Berwick's great hall to find its rafters decked with the finest banners of yellow and blue silk that the English quartermaster could requisition on short notice so far north of York. Thick weaves of ivy and rhododendrons filled the chamber with soothing fragrances reminiscent of a Yuletide feast, and minstrels danced around white-bloused scullions balancing wine casks on their shoulders. At the royal table, Longshanks, showing off a new burgundy tabard gifted him by his English subjects resettled in Berwick, seemed bent on eradicating all enmity between the two kingdoms with an assault of color and music alone.

Yet Belle and her fellow Scots were not deceived by this enforced hospitality. They mingled cautiously, monitoring their own countrymen with as much suspicion as their hosts. She found the scene surreal: Hard-bitten men who had clashed on the battlefield now exchanged pleasantries as if the Berwick massacre had never occurred. Studying the cagey English monarch, she was reminded of an old Fife adage: Invite your enemies to dinner, and by the manner of their eating shall you discover the temper of their sword.

She looked toward the far corner of the hall and saw Robert Bruce, resplendently attired in a blue-green shirt dyed from the snails found only on the coast of his Turnberry birthplace. He stood apart from the others, brooding and shifting restlessly. After concocting an excuse to escape from Tabhann, she approached the oldest Bruce brother with no small trepidation. "Sir, we have never been introduced. I am Isabelle Comyn."

Grateful as he seemed for a respite from his private burdens, Robert could not fully divert his attention from his enemies around him. His face grew increasingly drawn as he watched the Comyns strut across the chamber like a bevy of peacocks. Finding him preoccupied with thoughts of revenge, she made an effort to retreat, but he roused from his distractions and apologized for his rudeness by kissing her hand. "I prefer to think of you as a MacDuff still."

She blushed. "I was warned of your charming ways. It is said that you know the straightest path to a lady's heart." After a hesitation, she observed, "It may not be my place, but you seem troubled."

Robert's smile vanished. "I wager the same man troubles the both of us."

"I cannot believe my husband costs you sleepless nights."

He stared at her with mouth agape, aghast that anyone would think him remotely discomfited by Tabhann Comyn. "I meant Jamie Douglas."

Stunned, she drew him away from the crowd. "You know about us?"

Robert nodded with a taut jaw. "He told me of you years ago. A pig-headed fool he is! Plagued by a temper so foul that the Devil himself could light Hell with its sparks!" He found her suppressing a chuckle. "Do I amuse you?"

"I'm sorry." She lowered her eyes in feigned penance and stole a sheepish glance up at him. "It's just ... I have heard the same said of you."

Robert was about to defend himself, but in a rare moment of self-reflection, nodded ruefully, accepting the charge as justified.

She searched the chamber again. "Do you know if Jamie will be here?"

He shook his head. "He'll not step foot in Berwick again, at least not unarmed." Seeing that his prediction had saddened her, he placed her hand between his palms as if to bring warmth to her distressed heart. "We must dismiss him from our thoughts this night."

The music stopped.

Longshanks had finished his repast and was stretching his limbs like a bear coming out of hibernation. "A *pas de deux!* At once!" Invigorated by the wine, he leapt from the dais and stalked the floor to snare a partner. Finding no ladies bold enough to risk his judgment, he drafted his future daughter-in-law, who had adjusted her veil, too late, in an attempt to avoid his eyes.

Caernervon gladly shoved Isabella toward the floor, eager to turn his full attention to Gaveston.

The king led the princess to the middle of two columns of English dancers that had faced off with their partners in preparation for the opening sequence.

The minstrels struck up a restrained tune that sounded shrill and lifeless to Belle's ear. Several of the Scots reluctantly joined in, seeing that political expediency required yet another debasement. While the English dancers twirled gracefully and halted at the appropriate breaks, the Scots lurched and staggered, unsure of the steps. On the sidelines, Clifford and the royal retainers made no attempt to hide their amusement at the ineptitude of their conscripted guests.

Not to be outdone in this ritual of rank, Tabhann insisted that Belle accompany him into the dance. She had no choice but to acquiesce, even though her unadorned green gown with its frayed hems made her stand out sorely aside the rich appointments of the English ladies. As the *pas* progressed, the women of both realms were segregated to one side, and she found herself shuffled next to Isabella of France.

Isabella whispered to her, "I am told we share something."

Belle turned abruptly, stunned that the French princess would deign to speak to her. "I'm sorry, my lady?"

Maintaining a straightforward gaze—an admonition that Belle should do the same—the princess nodded slightly with the beat, a sophisticated court trick to camouflage the object of one's attention. With the tight-lipped skill of a ventriloquist, she explained, "A name. I am Isabella. I suppose that might be called Isabelle in your land?"

"I know not."

The princess spun on the high note and bowed with the gracefulness of a swan. "I was intrigued this afternoon by one of your countrymen. … Douglas, I believe was his name."

Thrown off her count, Belle discovered that she was the only dancer still upright. Embarrassed by the misstep, she became even more disconcerted at finding Tabhann five partners down the line and fast approaching.

"Do you know this man Douglas?"

Belle tried to follow the princess's lead while fixing her eyes straight ahead. "I have met him, aye."

Isabella demonstrated the perfected art of keeping time to the music while carrying on a conversation. She pirouetted and returned to the precise angle at which she had started. "Does he always insult kings?"

Blindsided by that barb, Belle abandoned all effort to remain inconspicuous. "Does *your* newly-adopted king always insult Scots?" She turned and saw several of the ladies glancing over at her. *Be damned with them all! And be damned with this meddlesome French coquette!*

The French princess seemed not the least unnerved. Having gleaned the confirmation of Belle's true feelings, Isabella captured the countess's wrist and, for the first time during the dance, looked directly at her. "I should pity the lady who wins the heart of such an unruly man."

Belle put on an unconvincing nonchalance. Lost in these nonsensical steps, she curtsied awkwardly and excused herself from the dance before she broke down completely. She dashed from the floor—and ran headfirst into James. She gasped—had he been standing there watching their exchange?

The dancing stopped in mid-pass as the participants stirred with whispers of surprise. James walked past her without even a nod of recognition and, bowing to Princess Isabella, petitioned the Frenchwoman's hand.

The princess shot an alarmed glance at Longshanks, who, preoccupied with Elizabeth Bruce's well-buttressed bosom, remained unaware of James's return.

Before Clifford could intervene, James took the startled princess into the line—just as she had done to him in Paris—and signaled for the musicians to resume. The dancers, uncertain how to respond, slowly returned to their positions and found their beats again. Both the English and Scots watched in disbelief as James moved the princess deftly across the floor, excelling every man present in dexterity and grace. When the unlikely twosome passed Longshanks, Elizabeth Bruce distracted her wine-addled partner by whispering a salacious bit of gossip into his ear.

The princess, relieved that the threat of immediate danger had passed, surrendered to James's lead. Not since Paris had she felt such strength. She closed her eyes and whispered, "You have become a man."

He spun her to face Caernervon, who was nudging Piers Gaveston in playful banter. "And you are in practice to become an ornament."

Insulted, the princess struggled to escape his accusatory grasp, but he tamed her into submission. Try as she might, she could not remain angry at him. "That was foolish of you today," she whispered. "I would not have you lose your head, even if there is debate whether anything resides in it."

"But you *would* have me lose my country."

She saw the Countess of Buchan standing alone in the corner, humiliated by being forced to watch their dance. She looked for Robert Bruce and, finding him on the far side of the *pas* line, nodded him to the task. Taking her intent, Robert captured Belle's hand and brought her into the swirling columns.

James retaliated by pulling Isabella closer to his side.

Seeing that she had become a pawn in this escalating encounter, Isabella whispered to his ear, "The lady still loves you."

"How would you know?"

She squeezed his hand to calm him. "Do you remember what I told you about vows and empty words? It is her heart that matters."

"In my country, men die for words."

She stomped on his arch, making it appear to be an accident. "I've yet to decide whether you are even worthy of her. Dance with her this night, or you shall regret it the rest of your life."

The music paused to signal the change of partners, and James took the opportunity to bend down and examine the damage to his foot. Feeling the princess tug his arm, he came upright to discover that Isabella had schemed to position him next to Belle and Robert.

The princess captured Belle's hand before she could escape. "You cannot guess whom I have found. Did you not tell me you once knew this gentleman?"

Flustered, Belle could not bring herself to look at James. "I should think he does not remember me."

The princess tapped her toe dangerously near James's aching arch. "A man who could forget such beauty would have to be blind or severely damaged in the head." She glared at Robert in a silent petition for him to join her match-making. "Would you not agree, Lord Bruce?"

Robert was about to unleash a torrent of invective at James when the princess flitted him off to the floor with her. Left together, James and Belle were swept into the vortex of dancers.

Several moments passed before Tabhann became aware of the gossip being directed at his wife. Enraged, he threaded his way toward Belle. From across the room, the princess gained Elizabeth Bruce's attention again and nodded her to the rescue. Taking the cue, Robert's wife extricated herself from Longshanks's groping in time to intercept Tabhann. She reroute the Scotsman to the floor before he could come within shouting distance of Belle and James.

James's angry lead unsettled Belle. He gave her not even a glance, but moved so expertly that she questioned whether he could be the same rough-hewn boy who had clumsily wooed her that day at the river. Soon she was floating in his firm embrace. "You put me to shame," she whispered, breathless.

He executed a harsh turn. "You do well enough at that on your own."

"I tried to send word."

"Word of what? That you preferred a Comyn to a disinherited beggar?"

"I don't love Tabhann."

"Of course you don't. That's why you married him."

"You must believe me—"

"Believe you? It matters nothing now."

She clutched his hand in pleading. "Jamie, don't say that."

"Damn these London manners!" He glared at the other dancers in the hall. "Don't you see what Longshanks is doing? He's trying to turn us into English sycophants with these pacifying, blood-thinning chorales meant for children!"

The *pas* ended and the dancers began to disperse, but Belle clung to James's arm, begging for a chance to finish her explanation.

He brushed off her hold. Marching to the center of the floor, he stole a lute from an astonished musician and began churning out a rousing reel. High-stepping to the Gaelic tune, he confronted his fellow Scots, challenging them to turn back the English ploy to destroy their traditions. One by one, the clansmen became caught up in the emotion of this veiled martial call. They entered the circle, arm in arm, pounding the floor as if marching to battle.

Playing each stanza faster until the timbers shook from the attack of boots, James strutted toward Robert and taunted him to join in.

Angered by the reckless bluster, Robert shoved him away.

Clifford moved to quash the blatant act of defiance—until Princess Isabella rushed in to join the reel. She laughed and clapped, defusing the tension, and the king, monitoring the movements as if the floor were a field of battle, motioned Clifford to back off.

Belle could only stand by and watch as James danced toward Clifford in a challenge. The necklace holding the elf-stone flew from the crease of his shirt and hung at his breastbone. She was stunned. *He still wears it.*

A horn's blast brought the reel to a jolting halt, and before she could speak to James again, Longshanks came loping across the floor. The Scots fell silent, retreating to the reality of their plight.

Satisfied that the brief defiance had been aborted, Longshanks downplayed the veiled act of insurrection. "Well done! An entertaining example of your quaint customs. It is heartening to see how far we have come from the cave and the hut." He smiled with more than just a hint of threat at James, who was still heaving from his exertion. "This competition of feet has given me an idea. Shall we continue with the theme? On the morrow after next, I will hold a joust! A most agreeable benefice shall be awarded to the victor."

The English barons traded alarmed glances at the prospect of allowing the Scots access to arms, if only tourney lances. Clifford tried to convince the king to change his mind, but Longshanks dismissed the counsel and refilled his goblet in preparation to retire to his quarters. Reaching the door, the king turned back and shot a quick grin at Robert, then announced to all in the hall: "To make it interesting, let's have it Scots against my English knights, shall we?"

Robert nearly ran James over as he stormed out of the hall.

The morning of the tourney brought clouds as dark as the faces of the hundreds of Scots who had gathered along the rails below the royal pavilion. News of the tournament had reached Stirling and Newcastle, and commoners from both sides of the border had rushed to Berwick to witness the rare contest. Yet none could have dreamed of what now appeared over the horizon from the south.

A column of ten knights rode up in tight formation under the Beausant emblem of the Knights Templar. The standard, a solid black square set atop a solid white square, symbolized the eternal battle between God and Satan and was kept perpetually unfurled with tethered rods to be seen as a rallying point in battle. Having long ago abandoned the austere practice of riding double, the Templars came trotting haughtily into the lists on large destriers wrapped in lustrous caparisons of white and blood red.

Lamberton rushed forward to confront the monk leading the mounted column. "This contest does not involve the Almighty."

The Templar removed his helmet. "Then why are *you* here, Bishop?"

Lamberton was shocked to discover that he was speaking to an old comrade. William Sinclair of Roslin was a descendant of crusaders rumored to have discovered the Holy Grail on their sojourns in the East. The clan Sinclair, whose nomen meant Holy Light, had built the only Temple preceptory in Scotland at Ballentradoch, a forested glen south of Edinburgh. "Wil, by Christ! You cannot mean to take up arms against your own?"

"I was ordered to come."

"By the Master of London Temple. Your allegiance lies with Scotland."

"Out of our way, priest!" warned one of the Templars riding behind Sinclair.

Lamberton had thought the day could not turn more foreboding, but he was proven wrong when the surly knight who had just shouted at him removed his helmet and revealed himself to be Peter d'Aumont, the Auvergne preceptor who had hurled threats of retaliation at him during their covert Paris rendezvous. Had d'Aumont crossed the Channel to expose their clandestine meeting to Longshanks? Why else would the king have sent for these Templars if not to force a public demonstration of their loyalty? The bishop was forced to give way as d'Aumont led his arrogant monks toward the royal viewing box.

Longshanks licked his teeth, eagerly anticipating the competition. "Poor Knights of Christ! You must be famished from your journey! We know how dutifully you fast in imitation of Our Lord!" His dripping sarcasm drew derisive laughter, for all knew that these despised monks were never ill fed, let alone poor. In fact, jokes and curses were often aimed at the holier-than-thou Templars, who insisted on remaining secluded behind their commandery walls, except to come out and harass the local inhabitants for tithes or to show off their swordplay. He winked at his councilors as he waved the monks up. "I laid wager that you would join us. Templars always choose the winning side, eh?"

Torn by conflicting allegiances, Sinclair shifted restlessly in his saddle. But d'Aumont suffered no such qualms as he cantered across the lists and scowled at the Scots who had killed his brethren at Falkirk. The crowds jeered and pushed against the railings to gain a better view of the overbearing monks.

Longshanks surveyed the reluctant northern nobles who stood arrayed below his stand. "Who contests for Scotland?"

The Scots murmured among themselves. They had not counted on confronting these ruthless crusaders. After a hesitation, Red Comyn stepped forward with Tabhann and Cam. Neil Campbell, who was married to one of the Bruce sisters, also took up the challenge. Edward Bruce itched to join the team, but Robert forced his hothead brother to remain uncommitted.

"Only four?" Longshanks asked in reproach.

Seeing no other volunteers come forward, Lamberton signaled for James to step up and fill the final slot.

"Five a side, then." Longshanks's eyes twinkled with mischief as he motioned forward Sinclair. "Who from the Temple shall represent us?"

"Brother d'Aumont and I accept." Sinclair spoke with no enthusiasm, making clear that the king's order to participate was not voluntary.

"Even with Clifford and Gloucester, we are still one short." Longshanks turned to the Bruce clan. "Rob, I've never known you to pass up a tourney."

Robert saw now that the king had concocted this challenge of lances to force his hand, testing his allegiance in full view of his fellow countrymen. He glanced at his feeble grandfather, desperate for his guidance, but the old Competitor was too befuddled by the bustle around him. Tarrying while trying to think of a way to avoid the call, Robert tried to find refuge in false modesty. "My lord, there are others here more worthy. Lord Gaveston is accomplished."

"Nonsense!" Longshanks climbed to his viewing seat on the pavilion and slapped his hands to commence the tournament. "Don't think I haven't heard the talk, Rob. Some are trumpeting you as the most skilled knight west of Constantinople—behind d'Argentin and me, of course. If not for this infernal gout, I'd be out there myself. Now, to the task, lad! Give us a show."

Gloucester drew his cousin aside. "You needn't do this. Claim injury."

But Robert knew that refusal was not an option. He slammed his visor and joined the English combatants on the north end, fixing a withering glare on James in the distance for having fomented this trouble for him.

While the Comyns prepared their ponies with blinders, James chose a set of rusted armour from the pitiful array of choices offered by the quartermaster.

Tabhann, laughing, forced a lance into James's hands. "When this is finished, Douglas, why don't you swim back to France and take up again with those Parisian sodomites."

James shoved the offered weapon aside and found one to his own liking. "So you'll be free to make treasonous deals with Longshanks?"

Red restrained Tabhann from throwing a fist. "It's the English we're fighting this hour. We'll take care of him later."

James put one foot in the stirrup. "I want Clifford."

Red smirked. "We've decided you'll take the Bruce."

Mounting to wait his turn, James looked to Campbell for support in his protest, but the Comyns outranked the Bruce kinsman, and Campbell could only shrug, powerless to overrule the decision.

Red grinned at his own cleverness as he took the first position in the lists to face off against the Templar Sinclair. Both riders circled their skittish mounts, and when the horn blasted, Red charged through the low mist screaming Gaelic curses. He collided with the Templar in a din of skidding violence and was catapulted to the ground. The Comyn men rushed over the rails to examine Red. Relieved to find him only dazed, they dragged him from the muck. The victorious Sinclair returned to his post, accepting with indifference both the English accolades and the Scot hoots.

On the pavilion, Longshanks chortled while warming his hands over a cauldron of burning coals. He noticed that Princess Isabella did not share his enthusiasm for the initial English victory. "I do hope you'll write of that result in your letters to your vapid father. Be certain to describe every detail. Perhaps he will be less inclined to foment alliances with these Scots behind my back."

The princess looked toward the far end of the pavilion, where her future husband was cavorting with Gaveston in a game of chess. Trained in the French art of the subtle *riposte*, she asked the king, "Does your son not partake of the joust?" When that question chased the monarch's biting humor just as she intended, she answered her own question with mock innocence. "No, I am learning that he prefers more delicate pursuits."

Distempered by that observation, Longshanks demanded more warmed ale and turned back to the lists in time to see Neil Campbell draw the assignment against Gloucester. Gaining a step on the horn, Campbell charged and hugged his steed's neck to avoid offering an easy target. A few paces from impact, Campbell leaned toward the right and thrust his lance across his body to catch Gloucester by surprise. Both lances shattered and rained black shards across the slate sky. Gloucester wavered, finally slipping from the saddle. Bleeding from a shoulder gash but still horsed, Campbell returned unsteadily to a greeting of thunderous Scot cheers.

On the pavilion, Isabella leaned over to receive the king's assessment of that loss, but he pointedly ignored her.

At the English end in the lists, Clifford snorted with satisfaction at seeing Gloucester thrown. Yet the officer's mood soured when Cam Comyn drove d'Aumont from his destrier with an unorthodox smote, slamming the Templar sideways with the lance rather than using its tip.

D'Aumont rushed limping on foot to the pavilion to cry foul, but Longshanks was so confident in the superiority of his two remaining knights that he waved off the protest; this loser was a Frenchman and a Templar, after all, and his defeat had been a rousing crowd-pleaser with both sides.

Before mounting for the fourth run, Clifford slammed his mailed forearm into Robert's chest, a ritual designed to prepare one's comrade for the coming jolt. The blow, more forceful than necessary, caught Robert by surprise and caused him to stumble. Clifford laughed as Robert lurched to recover his balance under his heavy hauberk. "Gloucester was meant for the monastery," he said as he rode to the launch position. "Gird up, Bruce. We need to teach these Highland root grubbers a lesson before they gain the notion that they can stand on a field with us. I dealt with the half-wit father of that Douglas polecat. He'll come at you wild and uneven."

At the Scot end of the lists, Tabhann waited for the horn, nervously rubbing the length of his lance handle. At last, the blast shook the skies. Wrapped in black and silver, Clifford's charger came snorting toward the climax with such pounding fury that it resembled a fire-breathing monster. Near the collision, Clifford deftly shifted across his pommel to avoid Tabhann's lance. Tabhann took the impact in his gut and landed so violently that he tumbled across the ground like a wind-driven pinecone. The exuberant English peasants pelted Tabhann with rotten apples.

Delighted by Clifford's triumph, Longshanks needled Isabella, "You must concede that in the art of theatrics, we English do excel you French. Look at the *dénouement* that I have arranged for your delight."

As James and Robert prepared for the last encounter of the day, which would determine the contest, the princess scanned the throngs pressed against the rails and saw Belle wrapped in a tattered cloak, shivering and white with fear. "My lord, your chivalry exceeds your love of play-acting, I trust?"

Longshanks was annoyed at being distracted from the preparations for the last run of the day. "What say you?"

Isabella pointed to the crowd. "I fear that poor lady down there is nearly frozen from the wind. May we invite her to the protection of our canopy?"

Longshanks squinted at the shivering woman. "Is she not a Scot?"

"She is, my lord."

"Then my advice to you, little one, is to leave the governance of my realm to me and attend to making yourself desirable to my son."

"Sire, I was only—"

"And remind me to have that side door in your bedchamber greased. I'm told it has an annoying creak."

Informed that the king knew of her lurking in the anteroom, Isabella tried to dissemble her alarm. Had he also become aware of her other covert activities, such as sending coded messages to Paris about troop movements and gathering surveillance about his health from the court physicians? She looked down at the list rails and saw that the spectators had become so desperate to witness this last meet that their surge had caused the plankings to give way. The guards had to drive them back across the boundaries with pike thrusts.

At the far end, James waited for Robert to make the first move.

Robert was desperate to avoid the confrontation, but he knew delay would only sharpen Longshanks's doubts about his loyalty. With a resigned heave of disgust, he took to the stirrups and accepted his lance.

As James lowered his helmet and came to the position, Belle fell to her knees, praying that neither man would be injured.

The horn sounded, and Robert exploded in a fast start. His ponderous stallion had been foiled to match its master both in breadth of stature and explosive temper.

James spurred his outsized pony toward the confrontation. Down the stretch, Robert lowered his lance, steadying its point. Nearing the collision, James reined to a dangerous halt—and threw his lance to the ground.

Robert reined up, lurching sideways in a violent halting maneuver that threatened to fracture his stallion's front legs. He finally regained control of the testy horse and circled James in an attempt to understand what had just happened. "In God's name! Up with you!"

James refused to move. "I'll not break lances on the helm of another Scot for the amusement of Englishmen."

Robert glanced at the pavilion and saw Longshanks pacing in agitation. He removed his helmet and muttered through set teeth, "Pick it up, damn you! We'll be the laughingstock of all England."

"I don't see Longshanks laughing."

Before Robert could stop him, James rode to the pavilion and sat stoically before the English king, scanning the cold faces of his countrymen who had crowded up on both sides of the lists below the raised platform. The Scots at the rails stood silent, waiting to hear an explanation for his refusal to take on the Bruce. He glared at them, disgusted at their inconstancy. How many of them had come to his father's aid at Berwick? Robert had now shown his true colors as well, accepting the draft onto the English team rather than standing up for his mother's ancient Celt lineage. He stole a bitter glance at Belle, who knelt shivering aside Tabhann, tending to his gut wound. She looked up at him with pleading eyes, but he knew the truth. She had also rejected him to further the interests of her clan in the hope of becoming queen. Denied a decision on the tournament, even his fellow Scots began pelting him with debris.

Traitors, all of them. To the man … and woman.

Longshanks paced in front of his viewing chair, furious that his scheme to force Robert's hand and turn him against his fellow Scots had been thwarted. He shouted at James, "You pimple-assed puke! I would have returned your father's castle had you won the day."

James knew better. He fixed his glare on Princess Isabella as he answered the king, "Then you would have merely given me what I already own." He turned and lashed his pony across the field.

Longshanks restrained Clifford from making the arrest.

The officer could only look on in disbelief as James, for the second time in as many days, was allowed to depart Berwick with impunity.

James galloped through the lists, and this time it was Robert who was forced to give way.

twelve

A roar clamoring up from the banks of the Thames rattled the stained-glass windows of Westminster Hall, and the lords of the English Parliament, fearful that another bread riot had broken out in the city, adjourned their plenary session to take up their arms in the cloakroom. Bishop Lamberton, swept up in the rush from his diplomatic station in the rear benches, elbowed his way to the doors. His heart sank at what he saw.

A London mob was parading William Wallace, half-naked on a nag, down the Strand. Crowned with a laurel wreath to mock his injudicious boast at Stirling Bridge that he would one day wear the English crown, the once-indefatigable Scot warrior had aged terribly during his seven years on the run. His massive frame was now gaunt and his long hair had thinned to a pitiful mane.

The bishop fought a path through the jeering throngs. "Wallace!"

Heartened to hear a brogue, Wallace turned and found the only friendly face in the rabble.

"Who betrayed you, Wil?"

Wallace hung his head, ashamed at having let down the bishop in his command of their insurrection forces. He growled the revelation hoarsely, his throat strafed from thirst. "Mentheith!

Paling with rage, Lamberton now counted it a blessing that he had left young Douglas in Scotland, sparing him this shameful spectacle. Driven back by a volley of hurled rocks, he cursed the treachery of Sir John de Mentheith, the keeper of Dumbarton Castle and one of Red Comyn's vassals. The bishop slipped behind the barricades and hurried alone through a back alley toward Westminster Hall. Reaching its doors again, he demanded reentry by invoking the ecclesiastical authority of his onyx crucifix.

Inside the chaotic courtroom, Peter Mallorie, the king's chief justiciar, sat perched on the bench surrounded by jurists chosen from the usual slate of petty barons whose allegiance had been purchased by the Plantagenets. Shackled and half-starved from the forced ride south, Wallace was dragged to the docks and manacled with chains like a caged beast.

Mallorie could barely be heard above the tumult. "You, William Wallace of Renfrew, are charged with high treason!"

Roughly handled by the bloodthirsty rabble, Lamberton surged against the bar and shouted at the justices arrayed above him, "The accused must be permitted an advocate!"

Mallorie ignored the point of order and hurriedly read out the indictment. "A runaway from righteousness! A robber! A committer of sacrilege! An arsonist and a murderer more cruel than Herod and more debauched than Nero!"

Wallace heaved with each difficult breath. "The victim robs the robber?"

Mallorie pointed at him in threat. "The prisoner shall be silenced!"

"My woman!" Wallace fought the restraints. "Ravished and murdered!"

A gang of dockworkers and tavern thugs, paid by the king's henchmen to make certain the jurists did not lose resolve, shouted rehearsed calls for the death sentence, drowning out the few scattered protests. Lamberton saw that these judicial shills were determined to hold a sham trial without calling witnesses. While in London these past months attempting to negotiate a truce, he had told all who would listen that the High Sheriff of Lanark, William de Heselrig, had murdered Wallace's wife, and only then had Wallace retaliated by killing the English officer. More than a few Londoners were sympathetic to the grievance. Wallace had, after all, harassed mostly Northumbrians, deemed by Londoners to be only a hair less savage than Scots. Moreover, Wallace's arrest set a troublesome precedent; duly elected as a Guardian of Scotland, he was entitled to the protection of an ecclesiastic law that banned the execution of heads of state without arbitration by the Holy Father.

Wallace denied the charge. "I swore no homage to Edward Plantagenet!"

Lamberton shook his head to warn him that such claims, though justifiable, would only inflame sentiment for his execution. He knew that all now rested on Wallace's standing as a former governor of Scotland.

Regaining a semblance of order, Mallorie shouted from the bench, "At Stirling, you did slay Hugh Cressingham and six hundred troops by stealth, seducing them into your snares like criminals in the night! At Dunbar, also, and at Falkirk, murder was committed!"

His infamous temper sparked, Wallace roared at his accuser. "Does your King commit a crime when he takes the field to fight the French? If I am charged with waging war for my country's freedom, then I stand guilty as accused!"

"He confesses!" one of the bench barons shouted.

Wallace rattled his chains at the bribed justiciar. "Aye, I have slain Englishmen! And I have stormed castles unjustly claimed by your King! If I have done injury to the houses of religion, I repent. But Edward of England has committed the same acts upon ours!"

Mallorie sped his notary to ink the quill. "The accused affirms his guilt!"

Lamberton shouted over the hooting. "Of rightful conflict only! He must be dealt with as a prisoner of war!" Ignored by the bench, he pleaded with Wallace, "Demand to be represented by a Guardian! That will gain delay!"

But Wallace merely slumped in defeat. Delivered up as a scapegoat by his own countrymen, he had no more fight left in him. He shook his head at Lamberton. "Save yourself, Bishop. Tell the lads I did my best."

Lamberton, helpless to thwart the inevitable outcome, stared incredulously at his old friend as the swarming scum shoved him to the rear.

On the bench, Mallorie stood to be heard. "The prisoner shall be dragged to Smithfield and hanged until unconsciousness, cut down and revived, castrated, disemboweled, his entrails burnt before his eyes, quartered and decapitated. His head shall be displayed on Tower Bridge and his limbs exposed to public view. What remains of his corpse shall be mutilated and burnt."

When the crowd hushed to hear the prisoner's reaction, Wallace straightened and spoke in an unwavering voice. "My suffering will last but minutes. England's torment will endure until the last Scot draws breath."

Lamberton vowed to remain with his old comrade to the end. As a churchman, he knew that the torment of such a brutal execution was designed to be both physical and spiritual. Holy Church held that no mortal could gain Heaven unless buried in blessed ground with body intact, a doctrine promulgated to justify the superstition that all flesh would arise on Judgment Day. Those dissolute cardinals in the Curia could not fathom angels traipsing all over the world to gather up missing arms and severed heads, so they had embraced the inane dogma that the mutilated would be denied the Resurrection.

Damn their prideful souls!

That afternoon, as a mule dragged Wallace the five miles to Smithfield, Lamberton walked behind the grisly procession and petitioned a miracle for Scotland, whose survival now seemed more doubtful than ever. He also begged forgiveness for having so callously dismissed Wallace to young Douglas after the Falkirk defeat. Unlike the Bruces and Comyns, Wallace had cared not for lands or titles. His lone cause had been Scotland's honor.

When, five hours later, the executioner raised his ax for the last time, a blood-covered Wallace turned to Lamberton and screamed, "Scotland free!"

His head bounded from the gallows with his eyes willed open in defiance.

He had fought the whoresons to the very end.

At that moment, Lamberton was gifted with his miracle. He now understood what he had required to win this war with England: Not treaties with the

French, or armaments, not even a new king. No, on this day Longshanks had unwittingly delivered up the most potent weapon for Scotland's arsenal.

A martyr.

E dward Caernervon stepped warily into the royal bedchamber at York and covered his mouth to stifle the acrid stench of flesh rot. Tar pitch had been lathered across the walls to capture the invisible humors, and on the bedside table sat a silver bowl with bloodletting instruments.

Blessed accoutrements of death.

Summoned north from his hunting excursion with Gaveston, he had been promised that his father, delirious with rheumatic fever, was near the end. He had ruined two horses in his haste to arrive in time to witness the glorious last breath, stopping only to send orders to London to have his coronation robe spun and his wedding to that French bitch arranged.

Now, as he inched closer to the bed, he signed his breast in renewed hope. Below him lay the king, horribly blotched and immobilized between two pig's bladders filled with ice, his prodigious legs elevated with pulleys to drain the malignant fluids into his bowels. Desperate for a confirmation, the prince perked his ear to hear the whispers around the room. He had been disappointed too many times, but the sullen faces of the physicians suggested that this indeed was the hour of his ascension to the throne.

Sensing a hovering presence, Longshanks opened his eyes. "The Borders?"

Caernervon passed a hand across the scabbed face to test his father's sight. "You should never have let that scofflaw Scot go free."

Longshanks beckoned his son nearer with a turn of his shaking hand. "My hearing is weak." When Caernervon leaned down to repeat his admonishment, the king erupted from his pillow and snared his son's collar with a choking hold. "By God, I will take you with me to Hell before I leave England to your folly! I did not ask your counsel! Answer me!"

Caernervon shrieked as if bitten by an asp. "I've not been in the North!"

The king reeled back with a choking spasm. The physicians rushed up flashing their scalpels, but he repulsed them with wild swipes.

Caernervon was horrified. His arrival had only served to revive the old man.

Longshanks rasped, "You think I don't know where you've been?"

"Why was I ordered here if you are not—"

"Your incompetence is the best medicine at my disposal!" The king dug his cracked fingers into the melting slabs of ice and brought a handful to his burning forehead. "You said I should not have let someone go."

"That day at Berwick, when the Douglas cur refused to joust the Bruce. His defiance has emboldened the heathens, from what I hear."

"From what *you* hear? You gather your reconnaissance from where? Those sodomite brothels in London?"

From the shadows, Clifford stepped forward with caution and reported, "I fear the Prince speaks true, my lord. My spies in Lanark report that Robert Bruce has inherited his grandfather's lust for the Scot throne. And there is talk about that the Border rebels are being stirred up again by this son of the Douglas traitor that we disposed of in London Tower."

Longshanks gargled lemon water and spewed it across the room, dousing his attendants in a shower of disease. "Then we must call Bruce's bluff before he gains strength."

"Father, grant me command of the army. I will bring Robert Bruce back in chains and raise his head next to Wallace's on London Bridge."

The king sucked furiously on a chunk of ice to soothe his throat. When that remedy proved only temporary in its relief, he threw the bowl of frozen shards against the wall, ricocheting it contents off the heads of his retinue. "Appoint him sheriff of Lanark."

The prince whined, "Why would I want to be in charge of that swine sty?"

Longshanks searched for anything in reach that would serve as a cudgel. "Not you! Clodplate! Bruce! Appoint Bruce!"

Caernervon insisted to the physicians, "He is delirious."

Longshanks struggled and grunted until he finally managed to lever his elbows. "When Bruce accepts the commission, send an order under my seal for him to raze Castle Douglas."

Clifford had been enjoying the prince's torment, but now, finding his own interests at risk, he protested weakly, "My lord will recall that Douglasdale was granted to me for services rendered to the realm."

The king's fevered eyes blazed. "And you, sirrah, will recall that you keep your commission and your head at my pleasure!"

Chastened, Clifford bowed. "Shall I deliver the order to Bruce?"

Gulping another difficult breath, Longshanks gasped, "Nay, send a courier. I have another task for you. Where are Red Comyn and his brood of grass snakes nesting these days?"

"Near Dumfries, by last report."

Longshanks sopped streams of the fever sweat from his forehead. "Young Bruce will not be any easy carp to hook. The Competitor will make certain of that. While we keep those two cornered, we'll slip a second line into the water." Wearied from the exertion, the king waved Clifford and the physicians from the room. The prince hurried to take his leave with them, but Longshanks captured his son's wrist and, pulling him down to the bed, caressed the back of his balding head. "Eddie, is there something more you wish to tell me?"

"More?"

The king clamped the nape of Edward's trembling neck. "I am told you and Gaveston broke into the Bishop of Coventry's park and poached his deer."

The prince yelped, his chin stretched to its limit. "What does that matter? His grounds are subject to royal inspection."

Longshanks kicked his legs from their restraining straps, knocking the ice bladders across the floor. He flailed tottering to his feet and dragged the prince toward the door. "Where the Devil are my councilors? Planning my funeral?" When Gloucester and the guards burst into the chamber, the king shouted, "Remove this reprobate from England!"

Horrified, Caernervon slid to his knees. "You cannot exile me!"

Longshanks stomped and thrashed with his heels, trying to beat his son senseless, but the fever's blurring prevented him from finding his target. "No more funds to him, by Christ! And see to it that Gascon coxcomb is also sent across the Channel! The Rhineland's not far enough!"

Caernervon cried. "Not Piers!"

Longshanks ripped off his soaked nightshirt and drove the prince on all fours toward the door by urinating on his back. "I'll piss on your grave before I see you squander all I've gained! Out, damn you! A daughter would have had more balls! A blade, damn it! Bring me a sword!"

Saturated in piss, Caernervon crawled sobbing over the ice. "I *will* be king! There is nothing you can do to stop it!" He found a boot and hurled it. "If I am malformed, it is from your seed!"

Longshanks took the plated toe of the boot against his nose. Now even more livid, he charged blindly and nearly had the prince in his grasp when he staggered, coughing up gobs of clotted blood.

Caernervon, aghast at finding his shirt splattered, escaped the room.

"God help us," the king muttered as Gloucester assisted him back to the bed. "If the branch grows so perverse when green, what crooked form will it take when seasoned?"

Still on his knees just outside the door, Caernervon prayed the old man would choke on the purging of his lungs.

Rowed in a bark toward the canal entrance of Lochmaben Castle, Robert Bruce sat captured in thought, beset by a thousand memories. Impatient with the pace, he leapt into the loch and waded toward the mist-shrouded banks where his grandfather had taught him to hunt and fish as a boy. Reaching high ground, he ran to the ancient Bruce stronghold that guarded the Solway Firth and raced up the steps. At the door to the last room, he hesitated and took a deep breath, then forced himself to enter.

The Competitor lay on his deathbed, surrounded by many of his old comrades, including James the Stewart and Bishop Lamberton. The cleric gripped Robert's shoulder for courage and, finishing the last rites, led the others out.

Robert grasped his grandfather's frail hand, choking off a cough in grief.

"Robbie … lad, is that you?"

Robert finally found his voice. "Aye, grandpa."

Stirring, the Competitor drew back the blanket to reveal their clan's ceremonial broadsword at his side. "It is yours now. You must gain what I could not."

Robert turned to hide tears. "I'm not ready."

"You *are* ready."

"Wallace is dead."

"Wallace was your Baptist. He was sent to prepare your way."

"I fear Longshanks suspects our plan."

The Competitor pursed his lips to beg for water, and when his thirst was slaked, he drew a long sigh and warned, "Longshanks won't long survive me. You must remain uncommitted until his wastrel son gains the throne."

"And if I my hand is forced?"

"Time is your ally," the Competitor counseled. "Longshanks knows he must bring the game to a head soon. Do not fall for his trap."

"Caernervon may be irresolute, but Lancaster and the earls are not."

"The English lords are drained dry by these wars. Play upon their enmity with the Plantagenets. Divide them, as they have divided us. Learn whom you can trust amongst our own. Earn their loyalty and never betray it."

Robert tried to think of whom he could rally to his side. "There is Edward, but Nigel and Tom are too young, and Alex is only a gownsman. I know of no one else I can call upon."

"The Hardi's son?"

"He now holds me in low esteem."

"No truer Scot than Wil Douglas ever drew breath. Go to the lad and make amends." The Competitor clutched desperately at his grandson's arm. "Rob, there is a matter that I have too long held from you."

"You must rest."

Old Bruce became more agitated. "Hear me on this! Decades ago, your great-great uncle committed an act of despicable judgment that has long plagued our clan. A holy hermit named Malachy came to this keep and asked for boarding. That night he was fed well enough, but during the meal, he learned that a robber was to be hanged before dawn. He begged our kinsman to spare the felon's life in an example of Christ's mercy. Our forefather granted him the pardon. But the next morning, the hermit found the criminal dangling from a tree, in breach of the promise."

The bizarre tale caused Robert to suspect that the fever was ravaging his grandfather's mind.

"The hermit was declared a saint! He placed a curse on us!"

Robert eased him back to the cot. "No saint would seek such vengeance."

The old man's swollen eyes were livid with fear. "That year a flood destroyed our castle at Annan. We have been denied the throne because of the saint's anger. Robbie, I fear for my salvation ... for the salvation of us all."

Robert had never witnessed such weakness in him. "You took the Cross, grandpa. God will welcome you into His arms."

"You must gain forgiveness for us, Rob. Promise me!"

"How?"

Weeping like a child, the Competitor tried to reveal the penance required, but his lips froze.

Robert had heard only one word of the request: *Jerusalem.*

The next morning, the Bruce brothers carried the Competitor's casket to the clan necropolis overlooking the loch. Lamberton offered a few words in eulogy, which went unheard by Robert, lost in troubled thought. The diggers were about to shovel the black Galloway loam into the grave when a courier rode up and threw a packet into the burial pit, then sped off. Robert climbed into the grave and broke open the letter's royal seal. He turned ashen as he read its contents. Looking down at the coffin, he would have given all he had inherited to ask his grandfather just one more question.

Accompanied by the thirty English troopers placed at his command, Robert slowed his approach into Douglasdale and tried to think of a way to avoid the dilemma that Longshanks had devised by appointing him sheriff of Lanarkshire. As he and his small command spurred across the Douglas water, the ruins of the once proud tower stopped him short. A heap of neglected stone was overgrown with thistles and brush. Why had Longshanks ordered him to raze Castle Douglas if it offered no refuge for resistance? He turned to Clifford, who had been constantly at his side pestering him during the journey, and remarked dryly, "You've kept it up in fine fashion."

"The rents pay my gaming losses," Clifford quipped with a grin. "But the confines, I am told, are still infested with a few rats."

Screams came from the village, a quarter-mile away.

Robert cantered closer and saw six of Clifford's men rounding up the inhabitants for hanging. "I gave no order to gather prisoners."

Clifford signaled for troopers with torches and grappling hooks to surround the castle. "You'll see their usefulness soon enough. Issue the command."

Robert rode up to one of the noosed Scots. "Sir, do I know you?"

The half-blind man turned toward his voice. "Thomas Dickson is my name."

The color drained from Robert's cheeks. He affected indifference to avoid revealing the identity of the man who had served as Wil Douglas's attendant. "I am mistaken. I thought you were—" An arrow whizzed by his ear.

"You *are* mistaken."

Robert looked up at the tower to find the source of that indictment.

On the wall, James stood with his bow reloaded. "Mistaken for a Scotsman by all who thought you one. This time, I *will* fight you."

Robert now understood, too late, that Longshanks had set a trap for him, just as his grandfather had warned. He had assumed James was in Fife, under the watchful eye of Bishop Lamberton. He swung around in the saddle and demanded of Clifford, "Why was I not told James Douglas held this keep?"

Clifford reined a few steps back for safety's sake while enjoying Robert's consternation. "The new sheriff of Lanark needs to improve his surveillance."

Robert pulled the royal order from his saddlebag and read it again. Razing the castle was its sole directive, couched in the usual language allowing discretion for unforeseen circumstances. He rode to the walls and pleaded with James, "I would have a word with you in private."

Clifford lashed up to intercept him. "No negotiations, Bruce! You'll be the one swinging if delay is your method!"

Ignoring the officer's threat, Robert dismounted and hung his buckler on the pommel to indicate his peaceful intention.

James debated the request, then motioned him past the portcullis and led his old friend in silence through the shambled castle.

Robert turned a corner and found the ghostly specter of Eleanor Douglas lying near a sputtering fire. Cull and Chullan, now long-nosed mastiffs, snarled at him when he reached for the widow's hand. She crawled away, screaming and fighting off his attempts to assist her to her feet. He realized to his horror that the poor woman had mistaken him for one of Clifford's henchmen. He had barely managed to hold up under the pressure, and now this discovery of the suffering his own unwitting complicity had inflicted on James's family was too much to bear. He dropped his hands to his knees, fighting back the emotion. "Jamie, they've given me no choice."

James led him through the ruins into the old armory where they had vowed their friendship years ago. "I surrendered this castle to the English once. I'll not do it again."

"Clifford will string up the villagers if you resist. Give me governance of the tower. I will see you and your stepmother escorted away under safe conduct."

"To where? An English dungeon?"

Having not slept for nights, Robert half-staggered to the window and looked down at the approach to the tower. He gripped the stone sill while he watched Clifford abuse Dickson, pinning a target on the old servant's shirt for a rock-throwing contest. "We could escape from the north wall. We'd be away before Clifford discovered us. Sail for the Holy Land, like we once said we would."

"If it is God's enemy you wish to fight, the Devil has come to you."

Robert lowered to a perch stone to rest his legs. A moment passed before he remembered that this was the same block on which he had sat listening to Wil Douglas tell stories of his grandfather's glory in the Levant. He could not bear to look at James. "You heard what they did to Wallace?" When James turned aside, Robert persisted in trying to draw him out, even though he knew that James's father had likely suffered similar torture in London Tower. "Do you ever think about what Wallace endured? The bishop said the man never cried out. I don't have that kind of strength."

James kicked at the dying embers in the hearth. "Do you believe we live but once?"

Robert lifted his head-slung gaze from the ground, annoyed to find that his old friend still had the infuriating knack for going off on wild tangents. "Of course I do. The churchmen say we lie fallow until the Day of Judgment, when all unstained souls shall be raised."

"The Culdees say different."

"You give credence to the ravings of those madmen?"

"The Highland hermits may know more than you give them credit."

Robert huffed. "I have no time for a discussion of theology, damn you!"

James drew a circle on the wall with a shard of stone. "What if we return to this world again and again? What if all that the priests have taught us is a lie?"

Robert stood to pace. "Jamie, for the love of Christ."

James held a distant look, full of premonition. "The old ones are all dying off. They came into this world together. Now they're leaving together. My father. Your grandfather, Fraser, Moray, Wallace ... and soon Longshanks."

"What in Finian's name are you driving at?"

"The war is being passed on to us. To know our fate, the Culdees say we need only look to the character of our enemies."

"You mean ... Caernervon?"

James carried his sword to a whetstone set up near the wall. As he sharpened the blade, he watched Clifford through an archer slit in the wall. Bored with tormenting Dickson, the English officer and his mossers were now practicing for the razing of the tower by throwing their hooks into the trees and pulling down the limbs that he had climbed as a boy. "I can't bring myself to believe that we were born to bow down to the likes of Caernervon and Clifford. Our time is at hand."

Robert shook his head, dismayed by James's heretical musings and weakness for the nonsense of the old ways about reincarnation and the circling of time. He himself was a religious man, not given to questioning the Church or dabbling in pagan mysticism. After near a minute of anguished debate, he stood and departed without another word.

James took up the sword and followed him through the gate.

Outside the walls, Robert retrieved his mount and ordered Clifford, "Bring up two horses."

"Horses?" Clifford protested. "What in Hell's name do you intend?"

Levering to his saddle, Robert announced to the soldiers and townsfolk, "This tower presents no danger to England. It is apparent to me that the king has been misinformed."

Clifford captured Robert's reins to restrain him. "This is treason!"

Robert drew his blade. "Slander me again, Clifford, and one of those stones will mark your grave."

Clifford tried to stare him down, to no avail. Finally, he chose not to press the confrontation and angrily signaled for his sergeant to deliver the horses.

Robert fixed a pleading glare on James while he finished declaring his judicial decision on the matter. "I will take the inhabitants of this castle into my custody until the king sends more instructions." He knew he was testing the limits of James's trust; if cast into the same predicament, he would never surrender Lochmaben. And even if James submitted, the odds were long that he could keep him out of an English prison. But one thing was certain: If James resisted, all hope of a Bruce ascending to the throne would be forever dashed.

James retreated into the tower and slammed the gate. Amused by James's refusal to heed Bruce's request, Clifford signaled for his mosstroopers to surround the walls and commence pulling down the topmost stones.

Robert dropped his head in defeat. As the grappling hooks flew over the ramparts, he turned away, unwilling to witness the tower's destruction.

The gates swung open again.

James walked out with his stepmother on his arm. He lifted Eleanor onto one of the horses and whispered orders to his two mastiffs to remain at the tower until he returned. He mounted, refusing to look at Robert, and waited to be led away, just as his father had been arrested and taken into exile by Englishmen under the shadows of this same tower.

chiRceen

A thudding of hooves entering the bailey of Dalswinton Castle woke Belle in the middle of the night. She hurried from her bed in the upper reach of the tower and peeked down through the crack between the window coverings at a gathering of shadows near the stable.

Was that Robert Clifford with an unmarked escort?

Why had the Marcher officer traveled here under the cover of darkness on the eve of Whitsun Sunday? This cold keep in the southwestern reaches of Scotland, one of several defensive posts held by her husband and Red Comyn for Longshanks, possessed no military significance for the English occupation forces, at least none that she knew about. She hurried to the offal chute in the privy closet adjacent to her bedchamber, which sat directly above the great hall. Placing her ear to the floor, she heard Red Comyn and her husband greet Clifford warmly and lead him into the hall below, as if having expected his arrival.

Red's voice shrilled in disappointment. "The tower still stands? What about Douglas?"

"Taken prisoner."

"Fill the man's flagon!" Tabhann cried, apparently to Cam. "At least we'll drink to that whoreson rotting away in Berwick's dungeon."

"He's not in Berwick," Clifford said. "Bruce placed him under the watch of your bishop in St. Andrews."

"That is clear artifice!" Red protested. "Bruce must be arrested for treason!"

"Gloucester convinced the king to give Bruce a hearing first."

Tabhann sounded agitated. "Gloucester plays both sides!"

Clifford lowered his voice, forcing her to strain to hear his next words. "All the more reason our plan must not fail."

"We are to meet Bruce at Stirling in a week hence," Red said. "But what if Gloucester—"

"Gloucester knows nothing of this," Clifford assured them. "It must be in writing. Send it to London by a courier you trust."

"Even if Bruce agrees," Tabhann warned, "you'll not draw him south of the Borders. He'll be wary after eluding our first trap."

"His ambition will bring him," Clifford promised. "As would yours."

After a long silence, Red and Tabhann laughed crudely and clanged flagons.

An hour before dawn, Belle heard Tabhann, drunken and singing incoherently, stagger up the stairwell. When the door flew open, she sat up in the bed, hopeful he might inadvertently divulge more details about the mysterious discussion she had overheard earlier that night.

Tabhann floundered in the dark toward the closets. He flung armfuls of clothes across the floor in search of his riding cloak.

"You are leaving?" she asked him from the shadows.

Startled, Tabhann rammed his forehead into the closet door. "Damn you, woman! Since when did you become so interested in my goings?"

She climbed from the bed and rubbed the bump above his brow. "If it is to be long, I would have you miss me."

Tabhann studied her with a wobbly glare, unaccustomed to such advances. He dragged her to the window to scrutinize her smiling face in the light of the moon. When she untied her chemise, he attacked her nipple, drawing a wince from the burn of his beard. Stoked, he clumsily began loosening his leggings. "I'll be king soon enough. Maybe I *should* seed my heir."

While he tore off her gown, she tried to make sense of his drunken blathering. Both Red and Cam preceded him in the succession. What had Clifford revealed to make Tabhann believe he would inherit the throne? Crushed under his weight, she grunted, "You mean … after your cousin."

He pried her legs apart. "What say you?"

"Cam … he is in line."

Tabhann was inside her, thrusting hard. "I'll take care of Cam in good time."

"But the Bruce—" She heard the swish of his hand, too late. Her face burned from the blow. Before she could regain her breath, he began riding her so violently that she feared she might vomit. Blessedly, his heaves slowed and his glazed eyes fluttered closed. His chin fell to the pillow, narrowly missing her chin. With difficulty, she rolled him over and cupped his groin to revive him. "When will I be queen?"

Rousing, he mumbled, "Bruce signs. Scotland is ours."

She stroked him harder, trying to pry more details. "He relinquishes his claim?"

"And his head from his shoulders, soon enough! Aye, woman, don't stop!"

She tensed with alarm. Robert was in danger—that much she suspected, for Clifford had intimated something earlier that night about baiting the Lord of Annandale to London.

A neighing came from the stables. The horses were being saddled. Was Clifford leaving before dawn? If Jamie *was* under guard in St. Andrews, she had to find a way to warn Robert directly. She escaped the bed and covered herself with the sheet. "I nearly forgot."

Tabhann tumbled to the floor. Thrashing to find her in the darkness, he growled, "Damn you! Come back here!"

At the window, she saw Clifford bridling his horse near the gate. She turned to Tabhann, who still was on his hands and knees, bobbing with the prospects of retching. "The English princess gave me a set of brass candle holders when we were in Berwick last. I must reciprocate the gift. It would not do for the future king of Scotland to be gossiped an ingrate."

"What in God's name are you bleating about?"

She searched the closet blindly for anything to write a message on, but then decided that would be too risky. Clifford might inspect it. Defeated, she reached to the top shelf for another chemise to wear back to bed and pricked her finger. Her hand was bleeding from a cut. In a fit of anger, she reached for the offending object and pulled out a pair of rusted spurs that Tabhann had left under her linens. She turned to heave the damnable things out the window—

She stopped, and stared at the spurs.

Tabhann crawled toward her in the darkness. "Where the Hell are you?"

She hid the spurs behind her back. "I will ask the Englishman to deliver our gift. Does he leave this hour?"

"Clifford? Aye, but how do you know of ..."

"I won't be long. Will you stay awake for me?" Her question went unanswered. He was now snoring, spread-eagled on the floor.

Releasing a breath in relief, she wrapped the spurs in a lambskin cloth, drew two coins from her purse, and inserted them into the package.

Robert tried to hide his disappointment as Longshanks arose from a table in Westminster Palace and welcomed him with a bear hug. The reports of the king's impending death were clearly unfounded. Inexplicably, the old man's grip felt stronger than when they had last been together.

"Rob, lad! I trust the journey was uneventful?"

Nervous, Robert looked around the chamber. A week had passed since Whitsun Sunday, but the beams were still strung with the trappings of the recent feast. His cousin Gloucester and Isabella of France nodded to him from the far end of the dining table. Their presence, and Longshanks's jovial mood, eased his worries. After much agonized debate, and despite Elizabeth's fear that something was amiss, he had decided to answer the royal summons. His wife often rattled on about her Irish intuitions, but she little understood the demands of his situation. As the newly appointed sheriff of Lanark, he could not refuse to explain his decision to leave Castle Douglas standing. The best method for taming a lion, he had assured her, was to place one's head firmly within its jaws.

He also needed to buy time. Earlier that week, fortune had smiled on him from an unexpected source: Red Comyn had come to him with an offer to heal the divisions that prevented Scotland from throwing off the English yoke. If he agreed to transfer title to all lands disputed between them, Red promised to give up his claim to the throne. The bargain was costly and fraught with risk, but he was determined to avenge his grandfather's failure to gain the crown. He had accepted the arrangement with the caveat that Red would not publicly announce it until his return to Scotland. If he could allay Longshanks's suspicions a few more months, he would be able to muster his forces, consolidate the support of the Comyn vassals, and prepare the country's defenses.

Longshanks led him to a table spread with slices of roast lamb and candied ginger. "Come, Rob, it's been too long. How is my Liz?"

"I fear she misses the gaiety of your court."

"You must bring her to us more often."

"My liege, the Douglas tower ..."

Longshanks waved off that subject and commanded more wine. "No business this night, Rob. Slake your thirst. I've just received a new shipment of claret from Brittany. I think you'll find it to your liking. Don't you agree, Gloucester?"

Gloucester appeared lost in sullen thought. "I've not sampled it."

Longshanks harrumphed in disgust. "Ah yes, the Earl of Sobriety. I could find a more entertaining dinner companion in a monastery of deaf-mutes."

Despite the king's apparent lack of interest in the Douglasdale affair, Robert was determined to resolve the issue without further delay. "I'd not have you think that I disregarded your wishes."

Longshanks dug his teeth into a leg of lamb and spat out a chaw of gristle. "You took the Douglas rebel prisoner, I am told."

Robert was relieved to find the monarch amenable to his decision. "I placed him under the bond of the Bishop of St. Andrews until I received further instructions from you. I have a grievance to lodge against Robert Clifford. The man abused me with slanders and threats."

Longshanks did not miss a bite. "Clifford is long on action, short on brains. Good thinking on the tower. We may need it as a staging base. I was too vague in my orders. If only I had more men like you who could take the initiative.

Well, eat up, Rob. You don't think we'd poison you, do you?" Nearly choking from laughter at his own jibe, he turned to Gloucester for confirmation of its wit, but the earl did not share in the merriment.

Isabella came to Robert's assistance. "Your Highness, Lord Bruce has endured a long journey. Perhaps he wishes to retire for the night."

Robert nodded to her in gratitude for the excuse to depart before the king's temper could turn sour.

Longshanks waved him off to the door. "By Christ, Rob, you're becoming an old man! What was it? Seven days ride from Lochmaben? Hah! I've made that route in half the time. Off to bed with you, then! I'd not send a sapped husband back to Liz!"

Robert bowed and quickly took his leave.

"Sleep well," the king said. "We have much to discuss in the morn."

After Robert departed, Clifford entered the dining hall from a side door and whispered to Longshanks, who nodded grimly and impaled his carving knife into the table.

Dismissed, Clifford turned to depart. Then, remembering another task, he opened his courier bag and presented a small bundle to Isabella. "I was asked to deliver this to you. Something about candle holders."

Perplexed, Isabella began to open the parcel. "From whom?"

"The Countess of Buchan."

Too abruptly for discretion, Isabella stopped untying the package. When Clifford tarried to observe its contents, she feigned disgust and flung the bundle aside. "Do these Highland peasants really think I'd have their crude ornaments cluttering my compartments?"

Clifford mulled her indignation, then shrugged and took his leave.

Isabella bowed to the departing king who, enervated from the artful performance of good health that he had staged for Robert's benefit, required the assistance of two servants to carry him to his bedchamber. When Longshanks was near the door, she lowered the package to her lap and unwrapped the lambskin below the linen covering on the table. Two coins and a pair of spurs fell out and clanged to the floor. She kicked them under the folds of her kirtle.

The king turned toward the noise, and the princess displayed a dropped knife as evidence of her clumsiness. He shook his head and ordered the servants to continue escorting him from the room, muttering something under his breath about how the French cow was more trouble than she was worth.

Isabella watched as Gloucester, burdened by troubled thought, lingered a few steps behind the king. She could not fathom why the Scotswoman had sent these items to her. And why had Clifford been at the castle of the Comyns?

She noticed a smudge near a folded corner of the lambskin. The word "Bruce" had been scrawled in a harried script.

Spurs … Coins … the king of England … Bruce.

There was only one person she dared consult. "Lord Gloucester, a word?"

The earl, annoyed by the delay to his night of rest, threaded back through the scullions who were cleaning the tables. "Yes, my lady."

Isabella waited until the servants returned to the kitchen. Then, she lifted the hem of her kirtle to reveal the spurs and coins. "These were sent to me by the Countess of Buchan. I know not why."

Gloucester's eyes widened. "Where is my cousin lodged?"

"On the third floor of the north tower."

He slipped the contents of the package under his cloak. "Say nothing of this to anyone."

ours later, a knock at the door woke Robert. Groggy and in his night-shirt, he rose from the bed and found the royal keeper of the wardrobe holding a silver platter crowned by a large warming bowl. "From Lord Gloucester, sir. He was concerned that you did not partake of dinner."

Robert rubbed the sleep from his eyes. "What hour is it?"

"Half past matins."

Robert moved to slam the door. "Advise the earl that I do not appreciate his nocturnal pranks."

"He said I should tell you it was cooked by the French princess."

"Cooked by the princess my ass! Give me the damn thing, then. By the Rood, he will pay for this horseplay!" Robert lifted the cover from the platter. "What in God's name …" He stared at the dish under the warming bowl.

While the court official waited to be dismissed, Robert stood with his back to the door, examining the spurs and the coins imprinted with Longshanks's profile. He kept the platter hidden from the Keeper's view as he tried to make sense of this delivery. Spurs were a common Highland symbol for flight, often sent when written messages were too dangerous. But how could the French princess have known their meaning? And what was he to make of the pennies? Were they meant as Judas gold, the Biblical symbols of betrayal? He was so tired from the journey and strained by the events in Douglasdale that he feared his mind was playing tricks with his judgment.

Did Longshanks intend to murder him this night?

Pale with alarm, he told Gloucester's messenger, "Send my thanks to the earl and the princess." The tremor in his voice threatened to betray his fear, but he asked anyway, "Are the guards still posted on the steps below?"

"Yes, my lord."

Robert gave the man more coins. "Bring them a small cask of your best wine. And one for yourself."

The functionary bowed and departed, and Robert locked the door. Praying the wine would keep the guards distracted, he pulled a torch from its moorings, extinguished its flame, and thrust its handle through the slots. He threw off his nightshirt and dressed quickly, pulling on his boots as he searched the room.

One window.

Finding no other means of escape, he crawled onto a ledge that hovered several stories above the moat. With difficulty, he reached a crenellation and pulled himself over the wall. After the constables passed by on their rounds, he scampered to the roof and rushed down the stairs to the stables.

During his four days of hard riding north, Robert had avoided displaying his herald for fear of alerting the local sheriffs who would have been alerted of his escape from London. Now, as he approached the hills of Northumbria and the old Roman wall that ran from the east coast to Carlisle, he wondered again if he had misconstrued the spurs and coins that Gloucester had delivered to him. Could Longshanks truly have conspired an attempt on his life? If so, why had the king not confronted him that night, when he'd had the chance? Perhaps Gloucester had simply overreacted to some harmless jest.

None of that mattered now. His absconding would be seen as clear evidence of his treason. He had failed to heed his grandfather's warning. If he *was* wrong about Gloucester's message, he had played his hand too soon.

Hearing the distant thud of hooves, he shielded his eyes from the morning's slant light and saw a man riding fast toward him from the north. He had passed a hundred such travelers without incident. Still, to be safe, he slid his hand to the dagger under his cloak. His heart quickened—the man's banner bore the Comyn herald. What would a Comyn man be doing south of the Borders?

He shouted, "Stop, I say!"

The rider ignored the command and increased his speed.

He flashed his dagger. "Did you not hear me?"

The rider angled in a search for some means of avoiding the confrontation. When he tried to dash past, Robert caught up with the knave and buffeted him from his saddle. He leapt down and ripped off the man's hood to expose his face. "I'll have your name or your life."

"Brechin."

That revelation rang ominous to Robert's ear. The Brechins, an Angus clan allied with the Comyns, had been one of the first Scots to rush to Longshanks's side during the invasion of 1296. "What purpose does Brechin of Comyn service have in England?"

"Deal basely with me, and you will answer to the king!"

Robert pressed his blade against Brechin's throat. "And which king would that be?"

"The rightful king of Scotland. What business is it of yours, Englishman?"

"I report to Edward Plantagenet," Robert said, lying to smoke him out.

"Then you'd do well to escort me to him without delay. I have a communication for him from Red Comyn."

Robert emptied the courier's bag and found a letter pressed with the Comyn seal. He slit open the correspondence and read it:

> To His Royal Highness,
>
> The deed is done. Enclosed find the indenture bearing Bruce's attestation. At this hour, I muster men to take command of the Bruce castles in Turnberry, Kildrummy, and Lochmaben. By the time you receive this, I trust you will have sent the traitor to join the Competitor in Hell.
>
> Your servant, Comyn the Red, Lord of Badendoch

Seething at the betrayal, Robert opened his cloak to reveal a silver brooch studded with crystal.

Brechin stared wide-eyed at the famous Bruce reliquary that contained the bone fragments of the first saints on Iona.

Robert gave him a choice. "Your last breath, or your altered allegiance."

Brechin refused to be cowed. "I serve Scotland, not you."

Robert itched to run the traitor through, but he held back. "Two weeks ago, Red Comyn offered me the throne in exchange for my lands."

"I knew nothing of this."

"Where will I find the treacherous whoreson?"

After a hesitation, Brechin revealed, "He litigates a case in Dumfries."

Robert dragged the Comyn vassal back to his horse. "Ride to St. Andrews with all speed and tell Bishop Lamberton that I am in swift need of our mutual friend. Then make haste to Dumfries and advise Comyn that you have made good your delivery to London. Fail me on this, and nary a rabbit hole north of the Tweed will offer you refuge from my wrath."

FOURTEEN

orn with indecision, Robert had been pacing for nearly an hour across the highest hill above Dumfries, the site of numerous clan skirmishes with the Comyns over the centuries. Jangled from no sleep for three nights, he was having trouble keeping his thoughts clear. His reconnaissance that morning had confirmed that Red Comyn was lodging in Greyfriars Abbey, just outside the town, and that the market craw-roads were thick with the chieftain's armed men. Fearing his twin brothers, Nigel and Thomas, would gainsay his plan before he could prosecute it, he had delayed telling them the reason for his hasty summons of them from Lochmaben with instructions to bring vassals Christopher Seton, James Lindsay, and Roger Kirkpatrick. He shoved the nearest twin toward a waiting horse. "Tom, off with you to that ridge again."

"You sent me up there fifteen minutes ago," Thomas Bruce grumbled. "Who is it you expect me to find?"

"Jamie Douglas."

Thomas stared gape-jawed at him. "After you arrested him and gave up his tower? We'll see Wallace's ghost come join us first."

Robert bit off another flurry of curses at David Brechin, the Comyn turncoat he had intercepted on the rush back from London. By his calculation, Brechin should have reached St. Andrews two days ago. He wouldn't consider the possibility that James had refused to come to his aid. If, as he suspected, Brechin had violated his oath by telling Red of their encounter in Yorkshire, the Comyns would be lying in wait. Riding into Dumfries with only six men would be a dangerous gamble. Yet putting off the confrontation would only allow Red to escape east and combine his forces with Clifford at Berwick.

"Whatever it is you intend," Nigel insisted, "let's have at it. Else Tom and I are going home."

Robert shook his head, stung by the bitter hand that fate had dealt him. If he could not command obedience from his own brothers, how could he expect to rule a country? Edward, next in seniority, had always been the enforcer of clan solidarity, but he had chosen an inauspicious time to be away in Hartlepool retrieving a shipment of wheat. Kicking at the dirt to vent his anger, Robert motioned the others to their horses, and then climbed to his saddle. He glanced longingly at the northern horizon one more time. Seeing no sign of James, he led his paltry troop, disguised in hoods, down into the Galloway valley.

A half-hour later, the Bruces arrived at Greyfriars Abbey, and Robert dismounted, signaling for his men to guard the approach. Walking to the monastery's door, he pulled the cowl further over his head to obscure his face, and banged the clapper.

A friar opened the whispering slot. "Full for the evening."

Robert thrust his arm through the aperture to prevent the friar from ignoring him. "Advise Lord Comyn that Brechin brings news from London." He retracted his arm, and the waddling friar slammed the slot shut.

Minutes later, the friar returned, opened the gate, and allowed Robert to enter the outer courtyard. "Comyn says you are to wait here until the Abbot finishes a private Mass for him."

Unable to shake the pesky Franciscan, Robert reluctantly took a seat on a bench and searched for a way to enter the chapel unnoticed. Red's troopers, he feared, would be returning any moment now for the end of the Mass. He rubbed his stomach to feign hunger. "Might you spare some bread?"

The friar kept his eyes fixed on his navel. "There is a tavern down the street."

Robert restrained his urge to throttle the stingy oaf. Fast running out of time, he decided to try a different tactic. "My liege intends to grant a benefice to honor the many rewards that God has granted him. There's enough coin in my saddlebag to build a new church." He leaned toward the friar, as if to whisper a confidence. "You must not tell your abbot, but the Red has narrowed it down to this abbey or Jedburgh." He stood to depart. "Perhaps I will return later."

The friar, his beady eyes flaming with gold lust, grasped Robert's arm to delay him. "Thieves lurk about in these parts. I'd best take your treasury to the chapter house for safe keeping."

When the tonsured lout hurried past the abbey's entrance to retrieve the donation, Robert slipped inside the cloisters and fell in with a cadre of ascetic brothers who were ambulating in a circle, deep in prayer. He counted three Comyn men guarding the chapel. After a second pass around the courtyard, he disappeared unnoticed into a vestibule and found a vestment frock and a chalice. Trading in his riding cloak for the vestment, he hid the chalice under his sleeves and reentered the cloisters. He merged again into the circulating herd of meditating friars whose eyes were trained inward. Approaching the chapel, he brought out the chalice and bowed his head, waiting to be allowed entry.

The guards, thinking he was delivering the Eucharist, waved him inside. The door closed, and Robert clicked the bolt behind him. Red Comyn, the only congregant present, knelt on the front pew. The abbot was about to offer the benediction when he stopped, seeing the dim outlines of a hooded figure standing near the baptismal font.

Alerted by the abbot's distraction, Red turned and squinted through the haze of incense toward the door. "Brechin? I told the monk to have you wait." He arose from the kneeler, his eyes full of hope. "The deed ... it is done?"

Robert retracted his hood and stepped into the light. "Not quite."

Red's eyes bulged. He couldn't fathom how the friar had mistaken Robert for the shorter Brechin. "Bruce ... I was told you were in London."

Robert walked slowly down the aisle, reassured by the discovery that Brechin had not double-crossed him. "I was nearly to York before I realized that I failed to obtain your signature on our agreement."

"What say you? I executed it, by Christ! My own copy bears the mark."

Robert reached into his hauberk, pulled out a folded parchment, and laid it across the altar lintel. "Sign it, and I will leave you to your prayers."

Annoyed at the interruption, Red drew a quill from an inkwell near the baptismal and smoothed out the document to find the empty space for the signature. "There it is, clear as ..." He reread the last line—*not* of their agreement, but of his secret letter to Longshanks. "Where did you get this?"

Robert came up fast to deny him a reach for his weapon. "Lying knave!"

The abbot fluttered his cassock sleeves in protest against the sacrilege. "This is a house of God!"

Robert shoved Red toward the altar. "Nay, a viper's nest!"

"Off me, Bruce!"

"You schemed my death!"

Red turned to call his guards, but he fell silent when Robert opened his stolen frock to reveal a dagger at his belt. Unnerved by the crazed look in Robert's eyes, Red raised his hands in a gesture of concession. "Take the throne! Keep your damn lands as well!"

"In writing. And you will read it aloud in the town square."

Cornered, Red reluctantly began inscribing the terms of the devolution. When the quill ran dry, he dipped it into the ink well. He hovered the stylus over the parchment—and drove the quill's point at Robert's eyes.

Robert swerved to parry the attack, but the quill impaled his hand and splattered ink across his face. Blinded, he cried out and he clung to Red's shoulders. Red threw Robert to the floor and ran for the sacristy door. Robert captured Red's leg and held fast, his eyes burning so horribly that he feared he was losing his sight. He released Red's ankle and staggered to his feet while swinging his fists. Red tried to run past him, but he drove a shoulder into the chieftain's chin and heaved him back against the altar.

The abbot saw the dagger at Robert's belt. "No weapons here!"

Robert heard the cleric's shout as a warning that Red had drawn his blade. He pulled his dagger and rammed it into Red's chest.

Red looked down in disbelief at the hilt buried to his sternum. Blood trickled from the chieftain's hands onto the altar linens. He slid to his knees and struggled to extract the weapon from his gut.

Robert furiously rubbed his bloodshot eyes to regain sight. Horrified at what he had done, he looked to the abbot for absolution. "God's mercy! I did not mean to …"

The abbot pointed to the crucifix above the altar as if calling on Christ for a witness. "Mortal sin! Hellfire will be your justice!"

Red collapsed unconscious, his stomach gashed.

Robert fled to the sacristy and ran through the cloisters. The friars walking in prayer stared at him in horror, as if confronting a black-splotched demon.

The Comyn guards rammed open the chapel door and discovered Red lying in a pool of blood. "Bruce!" they shouted. "Take the Bruce!"

Robert escaped the lunges of the startled Franciscans and scaled the abbey walls. He dived head over heels and landed in the alley between the monastery and the tithe barn.

Nigel Bruce found his brother, bloodied and dazed, hiding on his haunches in a corner of a cattle pen. "Rob, what in God's name has happened to you?"

"I fear … I've killed him."

Nigel backed away a step. "Comyn? In a sanctuary?"

Robert stared at his own bloodied hands. "I am lost."

The other Bruce men came running up they alley, but they were driven back by the mob pouring down the other end.

Kirkpatrick drew his sword to slow the attackers. "Get him out of here!"

Robert was in shock, unable to move.

Kirkpatrick dragged him to a stabled horse. Slapping at the mount's flanks, he sped Robert off with his brothers through the barn toward the outskirts of the village. "If Comyn lives, he'll turn this deed to his advantage! Lindsay and I will make certain the deed is done!"

Robert and his brothers had remained crouched for three hours behind a copse on the lookout hill above Dumfries. With no sign of Lindsay and Kirkpatrick, they feared the two men had been captured.

Now, a lone horseman galloped in from the west, with the afternoon sun sinking from its apex behind him. Robert knew that the Comyn loyalists in Dumfries would be sending word of the murder to Dalswinton to marshal reinforcements. If the messenger got through, he and his brothers would be doomed. Still splattered with Red Comyn's blood, he signaled his brothers to hide in the ravine while he climbed a tree that hovered over the road. When the rider passed under its branches, he pounced and knocked him from his saddle.

Thomas and Nigel came running and aimed their blades at the intruder. Robert leapt to his feet with dagger drawn, ready to drive it home.

The downed rider rolled over and shook his head in accusation. "Castle razing, and now highway banditry? Can't you Bruces find honest employment?"

Grinning for the first time in days, Robert raised James and embraced him. Then, he shoved his friend away in hot anger. "You took your damn time!"

James rubbed his smarting scalp. "I wanted to see a little of the countryside first." With biting emphasis, he added, "There's not much scenery in a jail."

Robert was about to protest that indictment as undeserved when Kirkpatrick and Lindsay came galloping over the ridge. The two men reined up and fell exhausted from their saddles.

Kirkpatrick heaved for breath. "A near thing ... but done."

Robert stood paralyzed by his vassal's confirmation of Red's death. All his life he had yearned to be rid of his clan's most hated enemy. Yet during these past hours, he had prayed for Red's survival, fearful the clans would raise the dead Comyn chieftain up as a martyr and dismiss his traitorous letter to Longshanks as a forgery. He knew that Tabhann and Cam would now cite the murder as justification for their right to the throne.

James glanced around. Finding himself surrounded by men slumped in silent despond, he demanded, "Is somebody going to tell me what all this head-slinking skullduggery is about?"

Robert could not look him in the eyes. "I killed Red Comyn." He turned away in despair. "It is the end of me."

James slammed his fist into his palm, celebrating his old enemy's fitting demise. "No! A beginning, Rob! If you will seize it!"

Deafened by his own self-pitying lament, Robert kept muttering to himself. "The murder of a Guardian under the king's peace on holy ground."

James grasped Robert's shoulders to instill him with resolve. "Where are Red's kinsmen?"

Robert remembered that same manic grin from the day the Comyns had surrounded them as boys in Douglasdale. "At Sweetheart Abbey, by last report. But what does—"

"Up with you!"

"To go where?"

James leapt on his horse and pointed the Bruce brothers to their saddles. Grinning wild-eyed, he shouted at Robert, "To see you become a king!"

Pelted by a cold rainstorm, James led the Bruces to the walls of Dalswinton Castle, the Comyn bolthole that sat two leagues north of Dumfries. He called up to the tower, "The Bruce would speak with Red Comyn!"

The sergeant of the keep peered over the rampart. "Comyn attends the bench in Dumfries."

"That is base hospitality!" Dripping wet, James trotted along the walls feigning outrage. "He was to meet us here! By God, we will take our counsel with the Earl of Badendoch, then!"

"At Sweetheart. With his cousin, Lord Buchan."

Slipping a hidden smile at Robert to confirm their good fortune, James shouted up at the sergeant, "Well then, that means you must be in charge! The Bruce is in peace with Comyn! You have been advised, of course!" When the sergeant met that news with a look of skepticism, James barked at him, "Am I required to produce the bond while we stand out here to catch our deaths? There will be Hell to pay if my liege is forced to seek shelter at Roslin!"

The sergeant finally ordered the gates opened. Robert lunged his horse forward, too eager to enter, until James captured his reins to prevent him from creating suspicion. Once inside, James surveyed the walls and saw that ten men defended the keep. He nodded the Bruce brothers to the left and Kirkpatrick and Lindsay to the right.

"You are in luck!" The sergeant on the ramparts pointed toward the southern moorlands. "My liege returns."

Swallowing a curse, James cracked open the gate. Two hills away, Tabhann and Cam led thirty riders on a forced pace toward the castle. If the portcullis were dropped, he and the Bruces would be trapped. Yet if they allowed the keep to remain manned, the Comyns would retain a crucial base from which to harass Lochmaben. He shouted at the sergeant, "The Bruce shall ride forth to greet the Comyns! And I shall announce our arrival to those inside the tower!"

The sergeant hesitated, debating the unconventional protocol, but finally he nodded his agreement. Robert and his brothers had no choice but to trust James's instincts, and they cantered toward the gate.

James sidled up aside Robert and whispered, "I'll meet you at Stirling."

"I'll not go without you."

"Get out!" James muttered while smiling at the sergeant. "Now!"

Robert and his men kept good formation as they rode out of the castle, as if to greet the approaching Comyns. A quarter-league away, Tabhann and Cam halted to discern the identity of the distant riders. Robert maintained a gentle canter—until wheeling ninety degrees and spurring north with his men.

Tabhann, suddenly recognizing the Bruces, lashed to the chase.

While the guards on the walls were distracted, James retreated on his horse into the inner tower. He climbed the central staircase, scraping the lacquered floorboards with his mount's shoed hooves. Reaching the second floor of the great hall, he unloosed a torch from the wall to set fire to the tapestries, and soon the hall was engulfed in billowing smoke. He reined the spooked horse back toward the stairs and, turning to make certain the flames had taken, saw a flash of metal above the hearth.

The Dun Eaddain Ax.

Determined to regain his boyhood prize, he drove the balking horse back into the inferno. Choked by the smoke, he pressed his sleeve against his nose and searched the hot stones for the relic that Tabhann had stolen. At last he found its handle and pulled the ax from the moorings. His horse buckled in a panic, nearly overcome by the heat. As he reined back toward the staircase, he heard a shout through the smoke—

"Idonea!"

That voice sent a shudder down his spine. Was his mind playing tricks? No, it couldn't be. The Comyns would never risk bringing Belle this far south.

"Where are you?" screamed a woman from deep within the smoke.

His throat was too strafed to call out. One of the Comyn guards broke through flames, but he kicked the man back into the inferno. The smoke prevented him from finding the staircase. Losing consciousness, he saw a faint beam of light streaming through the haze. The golden particles formed an image of the Virgin Mary. Her radiant halo pulsed with hues that transformed from a cold indigo to the incandescent orange of the sun. The Virgin stood beckoning him toward her with outstretched hands.

Was this the hour of his death?

He crossed his breast, grateful at least that the Blessed Mother, not the raven goddess Morgainne, had come to escort him to his Judgment. The blackness became peaceful and … the frightened horse charged toward the holy light. He hugged the animal's sweating neck and recoiled from a jaw-jarring impact.

A loud shattering rang out like the singing of angels.

A rush of wind assaulted his face—he was airborne.

He came to his wits sprawled on the bailey grounds. A few paces away, his horse writhed with a fractured leg. He looked up to the tower and saw that he had just crashed through a stain-glass window bearing the image of the Blessed Mother.

Tabhann leaned out the broken window. "Close the gate!"

Recovering his jarred sight, he discovered that the Comyns had returned to the castle after giving up their chase of the Bruces. Ax still in hand, he mounted the nearest pony and dashed for the portcullis. He saw that he wouldn't make it through in time, so he leapt off the pony and slapped it toward the lowering spikes.

The guard was forced to abandon the crank to draw his sword.

James dodged the blow and swung his ax.

The guard looked down in disbelief—at his severed arm.

Twenty Comyn men rushed down the tower, angling to surround him. He clambered up the ramparts and jumped over, a second before a volley of arrows zinged overhead.

The pony was waiting for him.

Tabhann held a sword at the throat of the sergeant who had been duped into allowing the Bruces to enter the castle. "Who did this?"

The sergeant's wobbly knees buckled him to the floor. "The Devil himself, by the blackness of his skin."

Tabhann's searching gaze swept toward the mantle above the hearth. The brackets that held the ax were empty. He kicked at the sergeant in hot anger.

Belle, dusted with smoke residue, ran into the great hall and found her husband with buckets in his hands, inspecting the fire damage. Before she could speak, Cam staggered up the staircase clutching a letter.

"He's dead!"

Jubilant, Tabhann embraced his cousin. "We are finally rid of Douglas?"

Belle collapsed to her knees at hearing the news of—

"My father!" Cam cried. "Bruce murdered my father!"

Belle sank in relief. It was not James who had been killed, after all.

Disgusted, Tabhann threw open a window to air out the chamber. The smoke slowly cleared, revealing Idonea's charred body under the mouth of the chimney. He kicked the widow's corpse aside and muttered as he walked out, "At least the day hasn't been a total loss."

Belle rushed to the crone and unclenched her rigored fist. A shard dropped from the dead widow's hand. In her last moments of life, Idonea had pressed her face to the flue in a frantic search for air. Belle covered the ghastly burned body with a blanket and, grief-stricken, prepared to leave when she saw a message scribbled on the stones above the hearth.

No MacDuff, no King.

Not even Bishop Lamberton's arrival with Elizabeth Bruce could lift the black cloud of despair that had descended on their new king. Robert sat slumped in a corner of the abbot's quarters in Scone Abbey, the exhilaration of the past days replaced by a grim realization that half of Scotland now condemned him as a usurper. With James's aid, he had crossed Stirling Bridge before the Comyns could prevent his escape and, rushing to this ancient site of coronations, had seized the crown. But the hasty ritual held the day of his arrival had fallen flat, and on this night, the clansmen were gathered in the nave to hear his justification for the brazen act.

Elizabeth could no longer stand by in silence and watch her husband spiral deeper into his pit of melancholy. "It is easy enough to be king of summer, Robert! But persist in this morose pity, and king of winter you will never be!"

He repulsed her reaching hand. "Now *you* turn against me, woman?"

James came to Elizabeth's defense. "You've turned against yourself. Confront the clans in this unseemly gloom and they will also turn against you."

Robert glowered at him. "I have you to blame for this."

James bristled at the charge. "I advised you to be resolved. I'd rather be certain than right. You've always preferred to be right and never certain."

Robert hung his head, too distraught to offer a rebuttal.

The bishop signaled for James and Elizabeth to give him privacy with the king. Led by James from the chapel, Elizabeth began weeping, fearful of what now awaited the consort of an irresolute traitor to England. When he was alone with Robert, Lamberton dragged a chair near the hearth and donned his purple stole. "I will hear your confession."

Robert turned aside. "It is no use. I am doomed to Hell's fires. No monarch can survive a papal interdict for murder. Clement will order every priest in Scotland to withhold the sacraments."

"The pope does not dictate who rules Scotland."

"And God? What of His judgment?"

The bishop perfunctorily signed his breast and muttered the necessary incantations, not revealing to Robert that he despised this Roman abomination of mandatory annual confession, which had no precedent in Scriptures. "Allow me to worry about the Almighty's judgment. What sins have you committed?"

Robert's eyes flooded with self-reproach. "I have lusted for power."

"Go on."

"And nurtured a burning hatred for the Comyns."

"A righteous hatred."

"Murder on holy ground."

Lamberton lifted Robert's chin to demand his reluctant gaze. "Did Christ not commit violence upon the money changers in the Temple?"

"Aye, but …"

"The English and their Judases prey upon our land. You have overturned their usury tables. You will drive them from our temples."

"Can I be so easily forgiven for Red Comyn's death?"

"God alone is the arbiter of men's souls. But this I can promise you. I will stand with you on the Day of Judgment and contend against St. Peter himself to prove that you have acted with God's blessing. For your penance, you must, for the remainder of your life, abide by two oaths. First, you will never accept papal tyranny over Scotland."

"And if I have no choice?"

Lamberton placed a hand on Robert's head. "I will see to it that you do."

Robert thought hard on that promise. Before committing, he asked to hear the condition that he was required to accept.

Lamberton fixed a fearsome glare on his royal penitent. "Never again doubt that you are our rightful king."

Robert flinched from the piercing inspection of his soul. Yet the cleric had uttered that last assurance with such spiritual certitude that, for the first time, he felt instilled with the conviction that his destiny was indeed preordained. He kissed the bishop's ring in gratitude and arose with a deep breath of renewal. Whispering a prayer to seal his confession, he arose, lifting his shoulders, and walked into the abbey's nave. Six hundred nobles stared up at him in harsh accusation. He waited until their murmurs dissipated. Then, he shouted, "I will avenge the murder of Wallace! And I will see you free of English tyranny!"

The lairds were stunned by his transformation. This self-proclaimed king held none of his usual shiftiness of glance or look of wishing to be elsewhere. They had expected to hear another rambling legal brief in defense of his seizing the throne, but instead he had greeted them with a ringing call to action the likes of which had not been heard in this chamber since Wallace. Recovering from a stupefied silence, they erupted in cheers and stomping.

Drawn by the clamor, James rushed into the nave. Robert greeted him with a smile begging his forgiveness.

From the sacristy, Lamberton watched their reconciliation with pride. When the acclamation reached a crescendo, the cleric pulled a cord and unfurled the royal standard from its perch over the clerestory.

The clansmen gasped, and not a few wiped tears, for they had not seen the hallowed banner in twenty years, not since it had been ceremoniously withdrawn from view after King Alexander's death.

"You crown a murderer!"

That shout—from the rear of the nave—disrupted the veneration. At the doors stood Ian MacDuff, the outlaw son of the chieftain who had been killed at Falkirk. Young MacDuff swaggered down the aisle and lifted Robert's hand into the air. "Still stained with Comyn blood!"

Robert yanked his hand back and tried to stammer a defense.

Before Robert could finish a sentence, James lunged forward and drove MacDuff against the rood screen. "Your blood will stain mine!" As the clansmen erupted in heated arguments, James elbowed MacDuff aside and jumped atop a stall to be heard. "Comyn's death was self-defense!"

"What did you expect a Douglas to say?" MacDuff countered.

"Longshanks wants Bruce dead!" James reminded the clansmen. "Does that not tell you who should lead us?"

MacDuff raised his arms for silence. "It matters not! Have you forgotten?"

"Forgotten what?" asked one of the men.

MacDuff snarled an evil grin. "The Destiny Stone remains in Westminster."

The clansmen deflated, cruelly reminded that no coronation could take place without the holy relic. They turned to Lamberton for his opinion on the legality of that ancient impediment.

"MacDuff speaks true," the bishop conceded. "No king can rule without the scream."

Robert slacked his jaw at the bishop's inexplicable betrayal.

MacDuff reached into his pocket and threw a few coins across the floor of the nave. "Drinks for you lads! I'd not have you waste a journey." With his defeat of the Bruces confirmed, he strode confidently toward the rear entry and reached for the bolt on the latch—

The doors opened, seemingly of their own accord.

Six Culdee monks carried in a wooden box half the size of a casket. On Lamberton's command, they lowered the casement and pried open its lid. The clansmen gathered around the box and saw that it held a stone of black basalt whose shape was more a pillar than a block. Polished to a gleam, it was intricately carved with ancient symbols such as triangles and spirals that merged and danced in waves as if animated with an ineffable energy. The reflection from the candles sparkled and multiplied off its brilliant sheen. Confused by this delivery, the clansmen turned to the bishop for an explanation.

Eyes glinting with mischief, Lamberton asked them, "Did you really think I'd let the English take it?"

One by one, the men leaned over the casket to take a second look. Many were too young to have seen the Stone of Destiny and had only heard it described as a chunk of pale red sandstone drilled with holes. Some of the men fell to their knees, others scrambled to caress the precious talisman.

As a low buzz of excitement escalated into cries of unabashed joy, Lamberton nodded to James in sheepish contrition. Raising his voice so that all could hear, the bishop explained how, during the English invasion of Perth in 1296, he had directed the Culdees of Glen Dochart, under an oath of secrecy, to remove the true Stone across the Firth of Tay to a cave on Dunsinnan Hill, near the crumbling castle of old King Macbeth. In its stead, he had ordered a cornerstone from an abandoned kirk be carved with a few meaningless glyphs and placed below Scone's altar. When Longshanks and his soldiers marched into the Abbey that tragic day, the Culdees had put up a spirited defense of the forgery.

The clansmen stomped their boots in admiration for the clever ruse.

"A sign!" James shouted. "God saved the Stone of Destiny for the Bruce!"

Ian MacDuff stood motionless, unable to believe this sudden turn of events. As the delirious clansmen pushed past him to touch the relic, he fought his way down the aisle to confront Robert again. "Aye, you may have the Stone Fatal! But you still lack a MacDuff! My clan must give the oath! It is the law!"

This time, Lamberton's consternation was genuine. In the excitement, he had forgotten the second condition for installing a new king.

MacDuff came nose to nose with Robert and taunted him with the shibboleth that would doom his royal ambitions. "No MacDuff—"

"No King!"

MacDuff spun to accost the scoundrel who had stolen his thunder.

At the opened doors, surrounded in an eerie haze of steam, stood a hooded woman draped under a cloak muddied from a forced ride.

The men were aghast at this violation of the ancient prohibition against women entering the presence of the Stone.

James took a step closer to aid his sight in the nave's dim light. *It cannot be.* Even if Tabhann *had* allowed Belle to come south from Dundarg, a journey this far on horseback in such short time in harsh weather would have been nearly impossible. His chest tightened with a foreboding. Had the voice he heard at Dalswinton been hers in the flesh, and not his imagination? Had she died in the conflagration, only to come back now in the ghost?

But this was no shade that now strode down the aisle.

Belle repulsed her brother's attempt to block her from the Stone. Tears streamed down her cheeks as she lowered to her knees and ran her hands across the ridges of hieroglyphics that circled the basalt. The blessed talisman appeared exactly as she had seen it in her dreams—noble, defiant, and mysterious. Ten years ago at Kinghorn, her father had banished her heart's desire, but she had never given up hope. The lead-cased windows flashed from a streak of lighting, and a shattering scream came from Moot Hill, a hundred paces to the north. The clansmen shuddered from the unworldly sound. She looked up and saw a golden nimbus swirling around Robert's head.

The sign.

She kissed the Stone and retraced her steps down the aisle. Reaching the rear doors, she turned back. With her face aglow, she shouted at the men, "This night, a MacDuff stands for the Bruce!"

She threw open the doors and marched out into the driving rain.

The clansmen were too stunned to move.

James rushed Robert to the doors before the others could fathom what was happening. Lamberton, signaling the Culdee monks to retrieve the Stone, hurried them to follow.

Only when Robert had been whisked from the Abbey did those who remained behind divine the unthinkable act that Belle was preparing to perform. They rushed from the abbey, jostling and elbowing to be the first to reach the mound where kings had been inaugurated as far back as memory could attest.

As Belle led the soaked procession to Moot Hill, she smiled at the irony in God's inscrutable ways. In times of old, before the Roman missionaries banished women from their spiritual authority, men had followed Pict queens up this same path. She reached the grassy apex and turned her face toward the attacking rain to invoke the spirits of those holy women who had come before her. Extending her hand, she called for the slender band of hammered gold that the bishop kept under his cloak. She stood behind the Stone and, waiting, held the crown aloft.

Still flustered by her miraculous arrival, James climbed closer to her and whispered, "You would do this for him?"

"I do this for you."

"You're putting your life in danger."

"By this, I would make it right between us."

James backed away, allowing Lamberton to escort Robert to the Stone seat.

Belle pressed her womb against Robert's back to steady against the wind.

Robert felt her shivering against him. "My lady, you are cold."

"No, my lord," Belle whispered. "I tremble because I have, at last, come to know the purpose of my life."

Ian MacDuff fought his way up the hill to the fore of the gathered ranks. "Woman, I forbid this! You will not betray your clan and husband!"

Belle shook so fiercely from a rage fed by a life of bending to men's threats and violence that she feared she might drop the crown. "What is a clan without a country? As for my husband, you and my father forced the Comyns upon me for your own gain!"

"You are no longer my sister!"

Her reply shook the heavens. "I was *never* your sister in heart!"

Enraged by her defiance, Ian drew his sword.

James unsheathed his weapon to counter the attempt to stop the coronation.

With the zing of blades sounding all around her, Belle lowered the crown onto Robert's head. "Robert Bruce, a MacDuff crowns thee King of Scotland."

The northern lights flashed through the rain clouds across the night's horizon, and thunder crashed across the moors.

Robert was struck momentarily speechless by Belle's bold act. Only now did he fully comprehend the sacrifices that she and James had accepted to see him reach this summit. He nodded a concession to Lamberton, who had been proven prescient in his insistence that the ghosts of the ancients would come to Scotland's aid. Then, he stood for the first time as King Robert the First of Scotland and raised the hands of Belle and the bishop to the heavens, affirming that it was a Pict princess and a secret Culdee, not a Roman pope, who had helped bring him to this hour of his destiny. "Spread the word!" he shouted. "This night, I call a wapinshaw! All able-bodied men shall report to Stirling within the week. Armed and provisioned for war!"

FIFTEEN

Seated with the other ladies of the royal retinue, Isabella of France peered over the railing of the clerestory balcony above London Temple and shook her head in disgust as she watched three hundred esquires, the pampered progeny of England's nobility, trample one another in a drunken stampede to reach the dais in the crowded nave below.

Attired in ceremonial robes, Longshanks limped into the octagonal church of the Knights Templar and tapped the shoulders of the kneeling Caernervon with the sword that he had used to subjugate Wales. Two months after receiving news of Robert Bruce's coronation, the ailing monarch had decided to initiate the largest class of knights in the history of the realm for another invasion of Scotland. He had also recalled his son from exile on the Continent to join in receiving the collective knighthood, an act of clemency that she had greeted with great chagrin, for Caernervon's absence had given her an excuse to return to France that spring. With her fiancé's return to England, she too had been called back to London for yet another visit, this time ostensibly to choose the maids who would serve as her attendants here when she was finally married. In truth, she knew the real reason for this enforced invitation was that Longshanks did not trust her father to comply with the terms of the marital treaty.

Aside from the king, the only sober men in attendance were the involuntary hosts of the ceremony, including Peter d'Aumont, the Auvergne crusader monk. The Templars maintained a marked distance from the debauched initiates, forced to stand by and watch their hallowed sanctuary be fouled. Longshanks had commandeered their headquarters on the excuse that Westminster was not large enough to hold the proceedings, but Isabella knew that the king was merely testing the loyalty of the Temple before he departed for York.

The Bishop of Canterbury tried to stammer an invocation, but the inebriated roars drowned out his oration, and the feeble cleric gave up his effort.

Outraged by the sacrilegious conduct of the initiates, the old king stumbled down into the midst of the startled esquires and flailed his long arms at them like cudgels. "By Christ, I will have silence!"

The debauched esquires floundered heaving and retching to their knees.

When the king had finally regained what passed for decorum, he commanded the doors be opened, and retainers carried in gold platters laden with white swans tethered under chains of gold.

"Before God and these swans," Longshanks announced. "I swear to avenge the death of John Comyn! I welcomed Robert Bruce into my household! And he repays me with treachery!"

"To war!" the esquires warbled. "Scotland must heel!"

Longshanks was flushed with renewed vigor, having miraculously risen from his deathbed with the anticipation of another military campaign. "We have temporized with these heathens long enough! I will raise the largest army ever assembled on this Isle! The garrisons at Carlisle and Berwick are being provisioned! I have assigned command of the western advance to my son, with Henry Percy at his service! And I shall take personal command of our eastern advance!"

Cued to his grand moment, Caernervon staggered to his feet, belching from the wine. "I swear by all I hold sacred that I shall not sleep two nights in the same bed until I bring Bruce's head back to London on a pike!"

A cad quipped an aside to another esquire, "Easily done, considering Eddie hasn't slept in the same bed twice since he sprouted whiskers."

The tottering king, too deaf to hear the jests directed at his son, called forward the esquires to receive their knighthoods. At his signal, the scullions released the chains on the platters, and the swans took flight with a loud flapping, unleashing their droppings on the assembly.

Caernervon prattled on while the esquires slipped and fell on the bird dung in their rush to be knighted. "I am your Arthur, my good knights! And you are my Round Table!"

"To the tables!" the new knights shouted, elbowing for the doors.

As the other female observers on the balcony descended the stairs to cross the grounds and join the Westminster feast, Isabella was left forgotten on her perch high above the main floor. Grateful for this respite from the three-day debauch, she decided to linger a while longer.

After a few minutes of rare quietude, she reluctantly raised her head above the banister in preparation to leave. Below her, in the empty nave, she saw a tall monk lurking in the shadows near the rear of the church. She ducked to avoid being seen, fearful that the cleric would report her transgression of the Templar bylaw against women remaining alone in the sanctuary. She risked another peek and only then recognized him to be the Abbot of Lagny, the cold fish who had served as papal prelate in her father's court in Paris.

What was *he* doing here in England?

Watching through the banister's brocade, she saw Caernervon double back into the sanctuary from a side door. Her husband slithered aside to the monk and asked in a frantic voice, "Is there word from Gaveston?"

The Dominican glanced around the nave, making certain they were alone. "We have lodged him in Bon-Repos abbey in Brittany. As near the Channel as prudence allows."

"He knows of my plan?"

The Dominican hesitated. "The king's health appears to have steadied."

"This Scotland campaign will put an end to him," Caernervon promised. "Tell me of Piers. I cannot bear his absence."

The Dominican lowered his voice, forcing Isabella to place an ear to the floorboards. "I am uncertain how much longer I shall be able to serve as intermediary for your correspondence."

"What do you mean?"

"You are aware of Gaveston's ... inclinations?"

"Tell me he has not taken another favourite!"

The Dominican tried to calm the excitable prince. "I have learned that his mother was burned for Albigensee witchery."

"You would damn him for his mother's sins?"

"There are rumors that the Gascon is proficient in the black arts. I only advise you of these matters for your protection."

"I cannot lose communication with him." The prince turned calculating in his tone. "What is it you want? Gold? A bishop's ring?"

The Dominican folded his hands in a gesture of piety, affecting dismay at such an offer. "Perhaps I should take up the matter with your father."

"I will be king within the year."

When their voices trailed off, Isabella crawled along the boards to follow their movement.

"King Philip has been presented disturbing information," the Dominican reported. "The Temple in France is rife with heresy. We suspect the commanderies here in England are also infected. The Holy Father is examining the evidence as we speak."

"The Templars? Heretics? That is absurd!"

"I too dismissed the possibility," the Dominican said, "until I was presented with the testimonies of the monks arrested and brought to Chinon."

Caernervon's voice turned suspicious. "The French king has never given a whit about theology." His voice suddenly leapt an octave with discovery. "The

Temple's treasury would be a windfall for him. And you Dominicans would be rid of a rival order."

"My lord does me an injustice."

"What does any of this have to do with me?" Caernervon demanded.

The Dominican bowed, hiding an astringent smile. "I wish only to keep you informed of possible traitors in your midst. I will continue to strive to serve His Excellency in all ways. All I ask in return is that you remember me in your prayers."

As the two men slipped out of the sanctuary, Isabella finally felt safe enough to release a held breath.

sixteen

As an English column rode out from Perth castle under a flag of parlay, James inched his fingers toward the sword at his side.

Mounted next to him, Robert reached over to restrain his arm.

Bridling at being forced to stand down, James suspected that Robert still held out hope that Longshanks would recognize his right to the Scottish throne in exchange for another oath of fealty. But that was a fool's fancy, he knew, for the response to their call to arms at Scone had been disheartening. The clans, cowed by the arrival of English galleys near Carlisle, had sent only a tenth of their wapinshaw allotment, a setback that Clifford's spies certainly would have reported to London. He had pleaded for a quick attack on Perth before the main English army could come north, but Robert had temporized for two weeks, citing every excuse from a lack of siege guns to his expectation of more reinforcements from Carrick.

"Keep rein on that temper, Jamie. There is no harm in hearing what Pembroke has to say."

"Do you forget that he is kin to the Comyns?"

"Pembroke is an honorable man."

"An *English* man. And one who takes counsel from that scar-faced cur."

"He will hold Clifford in check, as I must hold you."

James set his jaw in protest as Robert moved his steed several lengths away to draw him out of earshot of their five hundred volunteers.

"The men watch my every move," Robert reminded him under his breath. "I cannot have you always questioning my decisions."

James looked over his shoulder at their thin ranks. These few who had joined them were hard-bitten veterans of the Wallace campaigns, aged from years on the run but still itching to give battle. Their uncertain glances betrayed their doubt that Robert had the mettle to hold the crown that he had so impetuously grasped. Each of these patriots had lost a brother or father to Clifford's terrors.

Simon Fraser, the grizzled bear of a man who had fought on Stirling Bridge, was the eldest. And at his side, as always, stood ancient Alexander Scrymgeour, the tall, sloe-eyed standard-bearer whose family had long held the honor of carrying the royal banner. The last member of this triumvirate of nobility was the Earl of Atholl, the rotund castellan of the northern Bruce keep at Kildrummy, affectionately called the "Falls of Atholl" because he sweated so profusely even in winter. Accompanying these lairds stood several men in their service, including Christopher Seton and Robert's young nephew, Thomas Randolph.

The rumbling of a second column riding up from the south stirred him from his troubled contemplation. He reconnoitered the new arrivals and found Edward Bruce escorting in not the promised force of two thousand, but a paltry party of thirty that included Bishop Lamberton and several cloaked women. Lashing up to confront Edward, he searched the horizon behind the riders. "Have you ridden ahead of the main force?"

Edward Bruce ignored him, insisting on speaking to Robert first.

Slowly it dawned on James that the hotheaded Bruce brother had failed to convince even Robert's vassals in Carrick and Annandale to take up the cause. He rode to the rear of the entourage and discovered the hooded women to be Elizabeth Bruce and her court, which included Robert's married sisters, Mary and Christine, and Robert's daughter, Marjorie. He did not recognize the last lady in the queen's retinue—until she shed her cowl.

His face hardened. Why in God's name had Edward brought *her* here?

He thought Belle had long since returned to Dalswinton. She met his glare with her own quizzical glance, until he broke off their silent sparring. Did she expect a warm greeting after abandoning him for Tabhann Comyn? She had crowned Robert, but she remained married to his sworn enemy. He turned from her and cracked at Edward, "Perhaps you'll arm the women. Ah, but that is well nigh impossible, since you've also failed to bring more weapons."

Edward dismounted in a red heat, champing for a fight. Eager to accommodate, James leapt from his horse and drove a shoulder into his chest. Wrestling Edward to the ground, he was about to land a fist when Lamberton reined up to break them apart.

"Enough! You only embolden the English with this scrapping!"

On the far ridge, Pembroke—so pale that Piers Gaveston had nicknamed him Joseph the Jew—sat with a bemused smile while watching the Scots bicker. Finally, tiring of the entertainment, the English earl led his officers forward and met Robert with a look of affected insouciance, as if he deemed this entire exercise beneath him. "Surrender, Bruce, and I will treat you with mercy."

Remounting, James rode up to remind Pembroke, "You speak to a king!"

Clifford snorted at that conceit—until James's blade came zinging to his chest. He brushed it aside with his forearm. "You will pay for that, Douglas!"

"It is *your* account that is overdue!"

While the two men hurled recriminations, Pembroke sat in the saddle casually examining his fingernails. He glanced over at Robert again and remarked dryly, "A king, it seems, who does not honor a flag of truce."

Shamed at being called out for a breach of chivalry, Robert signaled for James to break off the confrontation. He asked Pembroke, "Where are the Comyns?"

"In Perth," Pembroke said. "I have their word there will be no reprisals."

While Robert debated the offer, James studied the reaction of the volunteers. Although outnumbered, they showed no stomach for capitulating to the treacherous Comyns. This low ground below Perth was ideal terrain for the larger English horses, all the more reason to question why Pembroke had delayed delivering his demand for submission until so late in the day.

"We will afford you an hour to mass," Robert said, testing the earl's resolve to fight. "This field is as good as any."

For the first time, Pembroke's hooded eyes flashed surprise. "Don't be foolish, Bruce. We have twice your number in infantry."

James blustered at him, "You'd best return to England and look after your estates. I hear Caernervon is shopping for a manor to gift his favourite."

With a supercilious smirk, Pembroke played his trump card. "The Holy Father has excommunicated you, Bruce, and all who join in this insurrection. The anathema has been pronounced from every pulpit in England."

Lamberton slapped his pony to Robert's side to afford him time to regain his composure. "Longshanks must have put quite a dent in his treasury with that purchase. What does the pope charge for an excommunication these days? A week's worth of feasting at Avignon? Let Clement come to St. Andrews, if Philip will allow him out of his sight. There he will receive a different account of who merits the Almighty's wrath."

"Blasphemous priest!" Clifford shouted.

Ignoring the bishop's taunt, Pembroke insisted on addressing Robert only, as if they were both hampered by the crassness of the inferior men who served them. "The sun will set soon, Bruce. Give me your word that you'll not abscond during the night, and we will engage you in seemly order in the morning."

Looking relieved—too much so, for James's preference—Robert asked the earl, "The dragon will be lowered?"

Pembroke nodded his assent to the condition that all combatants would be protected under Christian rules of engagement.

James sensed that something was amiss. "Rob, a word with you."

Robert displayed a flash of anger at being addressed so informally in the presence of the English. He requested a moment to confer with his officers.

As the Scots rode off, Pembroke muttered to Clifford, "Officers. His exchequer must be that halfwit with the sheep's bladder on his pike."

James led Robert and his councilors to a near hill. He turned and studied the English contingent from afar. "They're using this truce to judge our strength."

Robert circled his horse in a tight radius, his ritual when nervous. "More of our men may arrive by morning. We'll face the low sun if we fight now."

"They won't follow us to the Isles."

"Whose side are you on, Douglas?" Edward demanded. "I say we give them the blade on the morrow and end this now."

"They hold the high ground," James reminded Robert.

Edward was itching to finish their interrupted brawl. "My brother is king—"

"Then stop heckling him to act like some sow-headed clan lord!" James turned from Edward and grasped Robert's pommel to drive home his plea. "We should draw them deeper into the Highlands. Let them starve crawling home."

Rubbed raw by the tepid response to his muster, Robert now reacted harshly to any slight that even smacked of betrayal. "You've swiftly enough turned colors. An hour ago you were as hotfoot as Eddie to attack."

"Clifford is up to some mischief," James insisted. "Each passing day we keep the Comyns pinned behind those walls is a day closer to Longshanks's death."

Robert chewed nervously at his lower lip. "Aye, and every day that passes, another clan deserts me."

James could not deny that sobering truth. Perhaps, for once, Robert was making a decision with a long-term strategy in mind. A retreat on the brink of their first battle might be tactically wise, but it could also destroy what little trust the clans still held in him, to say nothing of his own faltering confidence. To prevent the Comyns from turning the entire country against them, these Bruces needed a victory, and soon. Feeling Robert's waiting stare, he reluctantly nodded his assent to reassembling on this field for battle in the morning.

Having gained a consensus, Robert led his officers back to waiting English and agreed to their proposed terms of engagement.

Pembroke betrayed no relief or surprise, but merely reined around to retire into the city. As he cantered past the Scot ladies, he bowed his head with an affectation of courtesy to Elizabeth Bruce. "Your father sends his regards."

There was threat enough in that message, James knew. The Earl of Ulster was being hard pressed by Longshanks to recall his daughter from Robert's side and recruit an army of Irishmen for the invasion of Scotland.

While Elizabeth stammered for a response, Clifford tried to place Belle's face. "You are the Countess of Buchan, if memory serves."

Belle calmed her garron, spooked by the proximity of the officer's bullying horse. "Your memory serves you better than your honor."

Clifford smiled thinly at the insult. "The Bishop of Canterbury would have you remember, woman, that your abandonment of the marital bond is yet another reason for *your* excommunication."

Those Scots on foot closed ranks in support around the Lass of Scone, the name that the bards had given Belle for her courage in crowning Robert.

Remembering how Robert had become distraught over the threat of eternal damnation, Belle sidled her pony closer to the English party and answered Clifford, loud enough for all to hear, "You may advise the archbishop, sir, that I'd sooner follow a king of Scots to Hell than an English king to Heaven. But I'll lose no sleep worrying over ever confronting that choice. The odds of Edward Plantagenet passing St. Peter's gate are as long as those for finding his son in bed with a satisfied wife."

The Scots howled and beat their shields at her crackling put-down.

Clifford's lips quivered. "A wicked tongue on a woman is a facile skill. You are fortunate to be spared the rectification of battle."

Belle met him glare for glare. "No, it is you, sir, who is fortunate. If I *were* a man, the day to follow would be your last."

Clifford tried to summon a reply to her impudence, but finding no words sufficient, he spurred to catch up with Pembroke, driven by catcalls.

As the Scots cheered Belle's mettle, James saw that Robert had sunk deeper into despair. He rode to the women and faced their ponies toward their sulking king. "What say you, ladies? Will you still ride with this crown-toting devil?"

Belle was a ready conspirator. "Aye, and fight St. George's legions for it if need be. But surely this cannot be Hell's keeper who sits before us. I have it on good authority that the real Satan has freakish legs stretched to keep his royal baubles from being singed by the flames. I'm also told that long shanks make good cooking over a hot spit!"

The men roared and stomped about, imitating the English king's loping gait.

Try as he might, Robert could not suppress a grin at that crack.

Simon Fraser tossed a dagger to their new Amazon, and Belle, catching the weapon, smirked at James to match that feat. He grinned back at her, his anger melted by this, her second courageous act to bolster their new king.

The old MacDuff sass had returned.

That night, the Scots pulled back from Perth and bivouacked in a tree-lined vale near the abandoned castle of Methven, less than a league from the next day's designated field of battle. Robert refused to take shelter in the tower and instead placed his bedroll along side those of his men.

He had intended for his brother Nigel to escort the women to Kildrummy that night, but Elizabeth had convinced him to delay their departure until a few hours before dawn.

Belle sat on the outskirts of the camp, feeling out of place, a Comyn woman among these Bruces. After turning against her brother and husband, she'd had nowhere to call home, until Elizabeth Bruce had asked her to join her court as a lady in waiting. Seeing the new queen traveling without a servant, she had gratefully accepted the offer, cheerfully taking up the tasks of attending to the royal meals and laundry despite her noble station.

Now, finding the men preoccupied with tending to their weapons, she threw a bundle of soiled clothes over her shoulder and walked alone toward a nearby stream to wash them. It was one of those clear midsummer eves when dusk cast a shimmering hue and danced with shadows. At the banks, she sat on a boulder and reached into her bundle.

The basket was empty.

She was about to bite off a choice Fife curse when she heard singing:

"On moonlit moor in November
We tripped lightly along the ledge
Of the deep ravine where can be seen
The true worth of passion's pledge…

She thought the tune sounded vaguely familiar.

"The Queen of Hearts still making tarts
And I not making hay.
Oh I loved too much and by such,
Is happiness thrown away. …"

She stalked the voice, but the nearer she came to it, the more it receded. Were the Little People serenading her? No mortal could conjure such unnatural glamourie, for the voice became fainter, then stronger, as if the singer was able to fly around her:

"I gave her gifts of the mind,
I gave her the secret sign,
That's known to the one who has seen
The true gods of sound and tone.
And word and tint, I did not stint
For I gave her poems to say.
And with her own name there,
And her long dark hair
Like clouds over the fields of May."

The singing finally faded, causing a heavy sadness to strike at her heart. Forced to return to the real world, she walked back along the stream and heard something flapping above her. One of the queen's undergarments was hanging on a branch. Farther upstream, she saw another dangling blouse, and then another. She scurried to gather them before anyone in the camp saw them. She reached up for the last garment—and arms grabbed her waist from behind. She tried to shout a warning that the English were attacking, but a hand stifled her mouth.

"You still fall for it."

Heaving with fright, she turned and found James rollicking with laughter. He had repeated the prank he first played on her in Lanark years ago. She pushed him away, feeling the firmness of his chest, and huffed off.

"Belle, I did not mean to …"

She flushed with indignation, but her heart raced from a disturbing elation. Pulled by conflicting emotions, she stole the crude mandolin he was carrying.

Astonished by the brazen theft, James tried to retrieve the instrument.

She turned a shoulder on him to deny the attempt, and then pushed him into the stream. "And *you* still fall for that!"

James landed with a thudding splash, and went under.

When his head bobbed up, Belle loaded a handful of rocks and sent him back down. After she had spent her rounds, the water slowly calmed, broken only by the soft rippling of the undercurrent. Alarmed, she began stripping off her cloak to go in for him. But then, she remembered his old trick, and held back. She had wised up since those days when he declared her the most gullible lassie in Scotland.

Submerged for nearly a minute, James sprang up holding his nose, expecting to find her frantically searching for him. She was nowhere in sight. Had she run off in anger? He felt a sharp pang of regret. She was a woman now, and a married one at that. She likely thought him immature and shallow. Things could never be the same as before, he realized. Too much had happened to darken their lives. Chastened, he prepared to walk out from the stream and return to camp—

His feet were pulled down into a whirlpool.

He struggled for breath as his head went under again. He was drowning in the jaws of a loch creature, and no one would know! He fought to the surface gulping air. His head shot forward, buffeted by a sharp cuff behind the ear.

Belle had thumped him with the Aberdeen Sweetie, a thumb flick used by Highland wives on their lazy husbands.

"Are you trying to kill me before Clifford gets his chance?" he sputtered.

She resurfaced a few feet from his reach and, sticking out her tongue, splashed water into his face. "Oh my! If you were to give up the ghost, the Parisian courtesans would fill the Seine with their tears."

"That was not my doing! The Bishop forced me to go!"

She backstroked away, arching her wet bosom. "And did the Bishop also force you to make puppy eyes at that French tart?"

He swam after her. "And what about you? It wasn't me who went off and married—" He stopped himself, too late.

She hurried to the bank and wrapped herself in one of the hanging garments. "Go off?" she cried. "You don't know anything, Jamie Douglas! Not a word from you! What was I to do? Run away? I couldn't just board a ship and sail from my suffering like you! A woman's love means nothing in this world."

"You speak of love?"

She plopped onto a rock, dropping her head to her hands to hide her sobbing.

James crawled to the bank. "Why didn't you tell me?"

She tore at his collar, ripping off two buttons and extracting the cord from around his neck to display the heart-stone. "What did you think this meant? Are all men so thick-headed that they cannot understand such things?"

"I kept it, didn't I?"

She was stunned. His coldness at Berwick, she realized, had been only a front to hide his injured heart. How foolishly blind she had been. She couldn't look at him for fear of suffering his judgment.

He gently captured her shoulders, but she drew away. How could he want her after she had been with Tabhann?

He pulled her to the dewy grass, hiding her from view of the camp on the far banks, and wiped tears from her cheeks. Their lips met, and they kissed savagely. She wrapped her legs around his waist. Slowly, threateningly, he caressed the flaps of her necking while examining the mayhem that she had inflicted upon his saffron shirt. With a grin of anticipation, he ripped apart the fastenings on her blouse in retaliation.

A rush of air swept down the valley of her exposed chest. She pushed him on his back and waited for him to finish disrobing her.

He lay transfixed by the ripped blouse that tenuously held her breasts in check. She reached behind her neck, untied the blouse for him, and slid it from her shoulders. She rested her hands at the sides of his head and hovered inches from his gaze. Mocking him with an exaggerated French accent, she purred seductively, "*Mon dieu!* Have you never seen the Highlands, *monsieur?*"

He rolled her onto her back and pinned her arms behind her head. "Bonnie as Ben Bulben they are, *that* I cannot deny." His tongue trailed down her neck and made the slow pilgrimage toward her navel. "Stirling Bridge, the gate to all worth having." As he moved deeper down into the borderlands, he blessed each landmark on her ravishing dark body with a kiss. "The Highlands are fine, *mademoiselle,* but I'm partial to the lush vales of the south."

Shuddering, she was about to cry out when he silenced her with another hard kiss. He fumbled to remove his leggings, and she assisted him until he was freed and atop her. She surrendered to him with tears of bitter joy. After all those nights under Tabhann, she feared she could never feel this way. She wanted to lose herself in this moment, never let it end—

"No!"

Startled by his shout, she opened her eyes.

He sat trembling, gazing up into the darkness.

"Jamie, what's wrong?"

He had not heard her question. A raven sat perched on a nearby limb. After staring down at him for several moments, the black harbinger blinked and fluttered away, causing him to shudder. Eight years had passed since the goddess Morgainne had demanded two souls for his survival. Until this moment, he had forgotten about the pact made during his boyhood race. He could not possibly tell Belle of the bargain forced on him that day. She would never believe him, or worse, think him deranged.

"Am I not pleasing to you?" she asked.

James rolled aside her and drew his knees to his chin. "Too much so."

She wrapped herself in his cloak and knelt waiting for an explanation, but he could not look at her. She gathered him into her arms and stroked his chest. Somewhere in the darkness, the raven cawed like a mother protecting its nest. That eerie sound caused her to think of the stories told by the old women in Fife about the raven Valkyries that flew over the camps on the night before a battle to choose their next victims. She had always wondered why only the female ravens were held to be omens of death. Probably because men blamed women for all of their troubles.

The playful voice of a girl roused Belle from the memories. Across the stream, she saw Robert sitting near a fire with Elizabeth and his ten-year-old daughter, Marjorie, who was trying to engage her parents in a game of dice. Belle sighed, empathizing with the poor girl who had no sisters with whom to frolic. "Robert seems changed since Scone."

"We've all changed."

"Not you." She wrung her soaked blouse over his head as evidence.

Instead of rising to her bait as he used to do, James turned reflective. "Maybe a king can't have a friend. There's a distance between us now. He has a family. That will change a man."

"Do you think about children?" She regretted that question as soon as she spoke it. Yet, seeing that he did not flinch from it, she risked snuggling closer. "How many?"

"Ten would fill a castle, no?"

"Does Castle Douglas still stand?"

"Last time I saw it, the walls were near collapsing."

She rested her head on his chest and gazed up at the clear sky. "Remember the night we spent looking for your star?"

He pointed out their favourite constellation. "There it is."

"Tell me the story again."

"I told you stories?" James was driven to the tale by a sharp elbow to his ribs. "St. Columba, like all Irishmen, loved words. Especially those spoken from his own mouth."

"Are you sure you're not Irish?"

"Will you hear the tale or not?" Only when she surrendered a nod of contrition did he agree to continue. "Many centuries ago, there existed just one copy of the Holy Gospels in all Ireland. Ulstermen are a strange breed, believing as they do that a book carries magical powers. So, St. Finian, the owner of this precious tome, forbade all from looking upon its pages lest their thaumaturgy be stolen. One night, Columba hid inside Finian's abbey and copied the Gospels. The next morning, Finian sensed with his vision powers that the book's magic had disappeared." Suspecting her of enjoying his embrace more than the story, he paused to test her attention.

"Well? What did Finian do?"

"A bard has to be paid." Compensated with another kiss, he revealed, "Finian offered a prize to any who could recite the twelve Apostles in order."

"Columba didn't fall for that, did he?"

"Aye, he did. Columba admitted the theft, and he was set off to sea in a hollowed trunk and ordered not to set foot on land until Ireland disappeared from his sight." He angled her head toward the west. "While the saint rowed, he kept watch on that star until he landed at Iona."

"On our Scotland."

He nodded. "And every night for the rest of his life, Columba would gaze upon that star. He knew it'd be the closest he'd ever again come to seeing home." Seeing that the story had cast Belle into a melancholic silence, he stroked her long dark hair, tangled and frazzled by the night air. "You needn't worry, Belle. You've found your home now. And you'll never be forced to leave again."

"Tabhann will come for me."

"Coming and getting are two different things. I'll not leave you again. And you must promise you'll never leave me." He moved in for another kiss, but she turned aside, trying to swallow the knot of emotion in her throat.

"Have you forgotten that I'm a married woman?"

"You're not married in God's eyes."

"So now you see what God sees, do you?"

"No loving God would perpetually tie you to that rank excuse of a man."

A chilling call broke their embrace. … The raven had returned.

James threw a stone to chase off the death goddess. He tightened his arms around Belle in defiance of the raven's warning. "I intend to wed you, Isabelle MacDuff. And you best be preparing yourself for those ten children."

Her eyes flooded. In moments of foolish revelry, she had dreamed of hearing those very words. Yet she could not allow herself to believe that such a thing was possible. "No priest would ever join a bonded woman and an unchurched rebel."

The raven cawed again, as if to mock that hope.

James looked up at Columba's star. Did the Almighty revel in the perverse sufferings of mortals? Why would He take Belle and marry her off to Tabhann, only to bring her to him again for this fleeting hour? In what cracked world would such a cruelty be abided? He leapt to his feet and threw on his leggings. "I'll wager you a life of washing my laundry that I can find a priest who will."

"Wash your own—"

He nearly yanked her arm from its socket as he dragged her through the woods toward the camp, giving her barely enough time to fix her clothing. He sloshed with her hand-in-hand across the stream and rushed her to the ridge where the others in the camp were congregated. He roused Robert from his blanket and, bending to catch his breath, said, "I'd ask a boon of you."

Robert was perplexed by his agitation. "You've earned a hundred."

The other men, awakened by the commotion, arose from their bivouacs and drew around James to learn the reason for the excitement.

"The hand of this lady in matrimony," James told Robert. "You're the king now, *regnum* father to us all. And my *anam* friend."

Robert was about to laugh, until he saw that James was serious in the request. He signaled for old Fraser to wake the snoring bishop.

Escorted to the king like a groggy condemned man, Lamberton grumbled, "There'd best be a bonnie good reason for this rough summons."

Robert spun the plump cleric to face James and Belle. "It's high time you earned your keep, Bishop."

James stifled a grin, knowing that Lamberton was expecting to hear another of the endless disputes that he was always being required to arbitrate in this army. Being the most learned man in Scotland, the cleric was constantly called upon to resolve wagers ranging from the length of Edward Plantagenet's femur to the theological explanation of why salmon swam upstream.

"Well?" the bishop demanded, growing impatient.

"I say you can perform miracles," James said. "But this lady here doubts my faith in you."

Lamberton waved off the challenge. "This lass is the miracle worker, not me. She shape-shifted our London dandy here into a king. Nothing I could conjure would match that feat. Pay her what you owe her and leave me to return to my dreams."

"Turn back time," James begged his old mentor. "Make us man and wife, and your sainthood will be assured."

The bishop studied Belle. "This is your wish, my lady?"

She cast her eyes down in shame. How many nights had she cried herself to sleep pining to be Jamie's wife? Yet she knew Tabhann would never stand for it. If she went through with this ceremony, the Comyns would exact a fearsome revenge. How could she be so selfish? Did Jamie truly expect her to jeopardize Robert's kingship by igniting another clan war, all for her love for him? She reluctantly reminded the bishop, "I am bound by prior vows."

Lamberton pressed a forefinger to his lips, as he always did when in deep thought. He watched the oaks and birches swaying in the breeze near the stream, remaining in this pensive stance for so long that the men began to wonder if he had fallen into a mystical rapture. Finally, he announced, "There is an ancient law of our land, one that the Romish monks have long sought to ban from our memories. A man and woman cannot be made one unless their oaths are uttered under an oak tree of at least a hundred rings."

James brightened. "A fine law that is."

The bishop scowled at the interruption. Regaining silence, he continued with his brief sermon, "If the tree blossoms the next spring, the hearts of the betrothed are confirmed true." He took Belle by the hand. "My lady, did you by chance marry Tabhann Comyn under an oak tree?"

"No, but—"

"Well then, in my bishopric, you remain a free woman. Though I would counsel you to think twice before yoking yourself to this untamed colt. Plenty of better choices abound. Randolph there, and even Frasier, wrinkled as he is."

The men elbowed James aside to offer their proposals to Belle.

Blushing at the attention, she pulled James closer. "Your concern is well taken, Bishop. But I'm told that God gives more to those who need it." She smiled lovingly at James and added, "With all his faults, and they be many, this is the man with whom I've prayed to share my life."

Robert brought Elizabeth into his embrace. "Come to think of it, my love, we'd best renew our vows under the oak, too."

Amid the cheers, the bishop led the wedding procession into the grove near the stream. Choosing what he deemed to be the oldest of the oaks, he positioned the two couples under its groaning branches and intertwined their arms in the ancient symbol of infinity. "Do you, Isabelle MacDuff, promise to be a loving and loyal wife, for as long as you and your husband both shall live?"

"I do."

"And do you, James of Douglas, son of Wil the Hardi, promise to protect and honor this woman as your wedded wife, until death—"

Before the bishop could finish the vows, old Scrymgeour lunged forward.

James smiled at the half-deaf standard bearer's premature attempt to offer his congratulations. He gently braced the aged veteran by the shoulders to escort him back to the others so that he could finally, after all of these years, say the words that he had longed to speak.

Scrymgeour descended slowly to his knees, and fell forward—with an arrow in his back.

The night sky whistled with missiles.

The Scots stood motionless, unable to comprehend what was happening.

James heard another volley unleashed from somewhere above them. He lunged at Belle and wrapped her in his arms, taking the brunt of a glancing arrow. He shouted at Robert, "Get down!"

Several men fell around him, groaning and impaled.

"The Bruce!" cried English voices in the darkness. "Take the Bruce!"

The ambushed Scots reached for the daggers at their belts, forgetting that they had failed to bring their weapons.

An English soldier sprang from trees and ran for Robert, who was bent over the lifeless Scrymgeour, trying to extract the arrow.

James tripped the attacker, stole his sword, and gutted him. He led Belle in a blind retreat toward the stream. Halfway to the banks, he looked back and realized that he had lost Robert. "To Douglas!" he screamed, hoping that Robert would hear him above the din of the desperate fighting. "Scots to Douglas!"

Robert's voice cried out through the black night. "Jamie!"

"Rob, leave them!"

"My standard!"

The screams and moans of Scots falling victim to the English archers on the wooded ridges drowned out James's shouts to muster a defensive line. The long shadow of a man moved a few paces ahead, and James placed Belle behind him. Raising his blade, he braced to confront the attacker.

Robert, dazed, came staggering toward them in the moon's hazy light. "Pembroke deceived me!"

James shoved Robert off with Belle toward the water. Then, he stalked back into the darkness. The fires in the camp had been doused, and the night rang loud with the sounds of desperate combats. He heard hooves coming fast on him. Crouching behind a tree, he pounced on the rider and knocked him from the saddle.

"Bruce!" the unhorsed knight shouted. "Come fight like a man!"

Recognizing that voice, James lunged and drove Clifford against a tree. "When have you ever fought like a man?"

"Jamie!" a woman shouted from somewhere nearby.

He froze—that was Belle's voice coming back toward him. He prayed for just a few more seconds as he pressed his forearm against Clifford's windpipe.

"Jamie!" Belle cried again, this time with raw desperation.

The English soldiers were closing in around him. Denied hearing Clifford rasp his last breath, James kicked the officer coughing to his knees. He corralled his neighing horse, mounted, and rode toward the high rocks where the Bruce brothers were fighting a rear-guard action while the women swam for the far bank. He galloped into the advancing English and cleaved the lead riders from their mounts. The ambushers called a retreat to regroup, yelling warnings that the Scots had mustered reinforcements. Afforded a moment's reprieve from the fighting, he dismounted with a leap and lifted Belle to the saddle that he had just vacated. "Away! At once!"

Robert climbed onto another horse and dragged Elizabeth up with him.

"I won't go without you!" Belle cried at James.

James slapped the flanks of both horses and sent them galloping into the thickets. "Head west! I'll find you!"

SEVENTEEN

The descent of a forked shadow over Belle's hooded eyes startled her from a disturbed slumber. Lifting to her elbows, she peered up into the dim light of early morning and saw two fangs of a snake poised to strike at her nose. She shrieked and slapped at the slithering creature.

Her hand hit something hard.

The menacing reptile was in fact an exquisite brass belt buckle sculpted into the head of a serpent, worn at the waist by a spectral hermit who looked as old as the stone walls that surrounded her. The encrusted tendrils of the cleric's long white beard scraped against her cheeks as he leaned down to examine her more closely. Perturbed by what he observed, he tapped his gnarled staff near her ear and then grumbled an order in Gaelic to a dwarfish, pigeon-breasted monk who stood at his side.

Disoriented, Belle rubbed the sleep from her lids. Wondering if might still be dreaming, she ran her hand across a crude baptismal cauldron blackened by centuries of tallow smoke. Finding it all too real, she crawled to a cruciform slit to glance outside. In the near vale, painted in a hundred shades of funereal purple, lay the most desolate moorlands in all Scotland.

That bleak horizon revived her memory.

During their desperate retreat from Methven, Robert and James had left her and the Bruce women here at Glen Dochart Abbey, a Culdee monastery founded near the cave where St. Fillan had secluded himself for twenty years. Hidden in a rock-strewn valley near Loch Tay and bordered by the snow-capped peaks of Ben More and Ben Lui, the shrine was nothing like the impressive descriptions that she had heard of it as a child. All that remained of the once-thriving monastic community was this crumbling chapel and some wattle huts, and even by primitive Highland standards, the place resembled more a cave than an abbey. The Cistercian missionaries who had crossed the Channel to bring Scotia under Rome's dominion had not bothered to raze the kirk, confident that the few remaining Culdee hermits could not survive another harsh winter here without their stores of salted meat and kegs of ale.

With her head throbbing from the cloying incense, she looked over her shoulder and, still on her knees, found the two mismatched recluses staring at her as if never having laid eyes on a woman before. "Who are you?"

The shorter monk made the introductions. "This is the venerable Dewar of Inchanffray. And I am his novice."

"How long have I been asleep?"

The Dewar tapped his staff again in his mysterious code, apparently demanding a translation from his stumpish companion, who had a pug nose and a balding head crisscrossed with a few strands of straw hair. The novice babbled something in Gaelic to his superior. Then, after they finished what sounded like an argument, the novice turned back to her and answered her lingering question. "Since yesterday."

"Where are the others?"

The dwarfish novice came closer, revealing as he opened his rathole mouth that he had lost all his teeth except four molars. "Your king has departed with Lord Douglas."

"James Douglas is not a lord," she corrected him.

The novice relayed her protest, and reported his superior's animated reply. "My abbot says the man who calls himself Douglas is destined to become a lord, and that the Almighty deems the past and future to be of one unrent weave in time." He paused before imparting the rest of the translation, "He also said you should be in a nunnery practicing the art of silence."

Belle shot to her feet. "You may tell this two-legged relic that not only does he stink—" She was stopped short by the dwarf's impudent grin.

Accosted by the Dewar's quizzical glare, the younger monk bowed to cover his muttered aside to her, "I contrived that last part. My abbot comprehends not a word of the Scot English. It is my only amusement here."

Baffled by the prank, Belle needed no translation to see that the old Dewar disapproved of a female lodging in his sanctuary. When the crusty hermit persisted in glowering at her as if she were Satan's handmaiden, she resolved to remind him that Pict priestesses had ruled this land long before St. Fillan was even a twinkle in his mother's eye. But before she could do so, the abbot's diminutive minion captured her hand and nearly dragged her through a narrow tunnel that opened to an adjacent croft hut that had a pot of oat gruel simmering over a peat fire.

The wee monk shut the door. Then, he filled the ladle with the steaming curdle and offered it to her.

She sniffed its contents. "What's in this?"

"Rabbit marrow. And stock that's better left to the mysteries of Our Lord."

Despite its unappealing ingredients, she gratefully accepted the offering, having not eaten in two days. The gruel had a pungent nip that tasted of soured goat's milk flavored with turnips. In her state of hunger, spiced almond soup could not have been more satisfying.

While she lapped up the gruel, the little monk squinted through the greeting slot to insure that the Dewar was not lurking just beyond the door. "The other lassies are asleep in the Abbot's quarters. Your lord Douglas left before dawn to search for survivors."

Belle huffed, tired of men assuming that she submitted to be ruled by other men of inferior station. "How many times must I tell you? Jamie Douglas is *not* a lord! And he certainly is not *my* lord."

The monk shrugged, granting her protest little credence.

"I am a countess, I would have you know! And thanks to the damnable English, I am not even married to him ... yet." Her voice trailed off in despair, as if not quite believing that fate would ever allow it to happen. With an impotent wave, she gave up the effort to educate the rube. "Do you have a name?"

Amused by her outburst, the monk climbed atop the table and sat cross-legged in front of her while she ate. "Ned Sween. The others here call me Sweenie. Sweenie the Wee-kneed. You may call me Sweenie, Or Wee-kneed."

Distracted by the odd way that his head bobbed on his slender neck, she wondered if the tic was caused by the disproportionate weight of his skull.

The monk mistook her stare for skepticism about his self-styled pedigree. "Christ wished a nickname. Why shouldn't I have one?"

"Christ did *not* wish a nickname!"

The monk raised a finger in the air to repulse her objection. "Scripture says He walked around pestering the disciples to reveal what other people were calling him."

She made the sign of the Cross to blunt the anger of the saints. "The old man permits you to blaspheme like that?"

The monk's pebble-shaped eyes sparked with mischief. "So long as it's not in the Gael tongue."

Now even more dumbfounded, Belle looked around at the spare cell overgrown with lichens and stank of mildew. The only concession this queer monk had made to the biblical command of cleanliness was a pole broom being used by wolf spiders for their webs. The bed, a crude construction of shaved poles and heather straw, resembled more a lark's nest than a clerical abode. Two indentations had been worn into the floor stones from centuries of previous inhabitants kneeling in prayer, and above the cot hung not the traditional Roman crucifix but the cross of St. Bride with its four flanges at right angles in a rotary pattern. She had seen such pagan crosses when traveling the north as a young girl, and remembered being struck by how their traverses resembled fiery tails of the sun. "Does the Dewar know you follow the old ways?"

"He has never thought to inquire."

"Why did you come to live here if you don't follow Christian rules?"

The tonsured dwarf stole her bowl with his stubby, claw-like fingers and waddled over to the pot to ladle another helping of gruel for her. "I was left as a lad on the moors to die. The Dewar found me on one of his sojourns into the wilds to imitate the forty days of Christ's trials."

"Your clan abandoned you?"

Sweenie tested the simmering gruel and flavored it with another dash of thyme. "An English demon named Clifford hung my mother from the highest tree in Ayrshire. In honor of my deformity, he decided I merited a slower death." He curled his lower lip to reveal a scar.

"My Lord."

"He nailed a rag to my mouth scribed with a warning that the same ill use would be *gien* to any who resisted the invaders."

"That man Clifford is Hell's doorman!"

Sweenie shrugged off the memories of his ordeal. "God's ways are inscrutable. The Dewar required a scribe to correspond with foreigners. I had a talent for words, so he took me in and sent me to Iona to learn the Anglian tongue."

She took another sip and coughed painfully from the gruel's burn in her chest. The chill she contracted during the windy ride from Methven had now settled deep into her lungs.

Seeing her wheeze in discomfort, the monk placed his hand over her throat and closed his eyes. After nearly a minute of mumbling incantations, he scampered from the cell and returned with a smooth black stone, about the size of three fists. "Fillan's healing rock. Daren't tell the Dewar that I used it on you. He's of the opinion that lasses steal its power."

She caressed the strange lozenges and spirals that had been engraved into the stone. She felt a strange tingling, and her breath began to deepen and ease. A pressure grew between her eyes, and an inward vision suddenly flashed across her mind's eye: Jamie was on his knees, covered with blood and crawling toward her. She struggled to come to him, but he kept moving away.

She shrieked and dropped it—this was no Christian relic, but an ancient keek-stane, a scrying talisman used by the ancients for divination. She rushed from the cell. Sweenie took a flying leap from the table and waddled after her. Bursting into the Dewar's quarters, where Elizabeth and the other women were asleep on mats, she shook the queen awake. "Something awful has happened!"

Elizabeth arose with a start. "Are you ill?"

Through the window, Belle heard desperate shouts ring out from the valley.

Clutching her cloak around her, she ran out the ice-draped door of the abbey and met Robert and Edward Bruce dragging James up the frozen slope. The king and his brother carried James unconscious into the kirk. They ripped open his shirt to reveal a ragged tear on James's shoulder.

Hearing Belle's cries, James forced open his eyes. "A flesh wound is all."

Robert heaved from the run. "Lorne and the MacDougalls have taken up with the Comyns. Nigel is trying to hold them off near the river."

Belle tore a swath from her sleeve and wrapped it around the gash, which looked more serious than James had let on. "Where is the rest of our army?"

Robert turned aside, unwilling to let her see the shame in his eyes. "Fraser and Randolph have been taken prisoner. There has been no word from the Bishop. I've no more than thirty men left. Lorne will be on us within the hour. Pembroke and Clifford patrol the south. If we fail to make the Isles before they gain our flank …" He could not finish the report.

Sweenie's minikin face darkened on hearing Clifford's name. He told the king and his men, "There's a ford two miles south along Glen Falloch. It offers the quickest way to reach Loch Lomond."

Robert only then noticed the monk lurking in the shadows. "South? That leads me into English hands!"

"Aye," the wee monk said. "And Clifford knows it."

James, dazed and weak from the loss of blood, lifted his head. "Rob, he's right. They'll expect us to cross north of the loch. We should follow the eastern banks and ferry over farther down the water."

Robert stared at the monk, trying to fathom how such a freak of nature could possibly be trusted for directions. "Who is this blathering gargoyle?"

The monk bowed. "Ned Sween is my name, Sire. You can call me Sweenie. Or Wee-kneed. Or Sweenie the—"

"Just call him Sweenie!" Belle shouted at Robert, exasperated by the monk's penchant for babbling on incessantly when there was no time to spare. "He has good reason to see you escape from Clifford's net, my lord. He was once abused cruelly by the man."

Drawn by the shouting, the Dewar arrived and thumped his staff to demand an explanation of the commotion. When Sweenie, reluctantly, revealed his desire to go fight the English, the Dewar's shaggy white brows drooped in sadness. But finally, the old hermit placed a hand on his companion's head in a half-hearted blessing, and Sweenie told Robert, "I'll go with you."

Robert stood speechless, questioning if God Himself had decided to mock his fledgling kingship by restocking his tattered army with grotesques and mutants. Left with no good alternative, he nodded a bitter assent. Resigned to losing his most valued acolyte, the Dewar prepared to retire to his cell and resume his prayers. Before departing, the old hermit fixed his hard grey eyes on Belle and uttered something in Gaelic that sounded like a warning.

Shuddering, but not knowing why, Belle asked Sweenie, "What did he just say to me?"

Sweenie was driven to the revelation by her demanding glare. "He says you must never fail in your faith, for it will be tried."

Belle turned and confronted the Dewar, waiting for an explanation of the strange prophecy, but the hermit merely pulled his cowl over his head and walked off into the tunnel.

While Belle was still trying to make sense of the unsettling exchange, Sweenie perched himself on a stool and drew a map of the Dalry vale on the stones of the wall with a charcoal shard. He traced its route with his finger for the king and his men. "The path across Ben Oss to Falloch is too steep for horses. We'll have to go around it this way." He waited until they nodded their understanding of his plan, and then doused the drawing with skillet grease to prevent the English from finding it.

"Send the women east," Edward told Robert. "They'll only slow us."

James lifted to his elbows to plead against Edward's advice. "They must stay with us! Rob, without them, you'd not have the crown!"

Robert seemed befogged, slowed in his thinking. He glanced at his sisters Mary and Christian, who huddled together in fear with his daughter, Marjorie. After nearly a minute of agonized debate, he pulled Elizabeth into his arms. "Nigel will take you and the lasses to Kildrummy. Atholl is too ill to run with us. He'll go with you. The castle is strong."

James winced, still trying to stand. "No! I'll take them!"

Robert burned him with a hurt look accusing betrayal. "I can't make it to the Isles without you."

James finally managed to climb to his feet. Staggering from faintness, he drew Robert aside and whispered with every ounce of strength he could muster, "I can't leave Belle again."

"You swore you'd never leave *me.*"

James blinked to stay conscious, his blurring gaze resiling from Belle back to Robert. He knew Robert would not survive if left on his own in the wilds. Coddled during his years in London, Robert had never suffered the deprivations of the barren moors. Torn by love and allegiance, James reached for Belle and searched her eyes, silently asking a release from the promise he had made to her on the night at Methven, that he would never again let Tabhann or anyone else separate her from him.

Belle tried to be strong, but the beginnings of a demand dissolved into a plaintive cry. "Jamie, please ... take me with you."

James cupped her face in his hands. "He is our king. You did not risk your life to place the crown on his head only to see him fail, did you?"

Her voice cracked. "I beg of you."

Shouts came from the Dalry valley.

"At once!" Edward warned. "Or we are all lost!"

James kissed Belle, his bloodied cheeks wet with her tears. "I *will* come for you. I promise."

"Our vows! I would leave a husband, at least!"

James looked to Robert, who was pacing anxiously at the door, his eyes fixed on the horizon. "Will you finish our betrothal in the Bishop's stead?"

Robert, preoccupied with his troubles, did not hear the request. Before James could ask again, Edward hurried his brother out of the abbey and toward the horses.

Denied, James braced Belle at her shoulders, locking onto her frightened eyes. "We are married in our hearts. When I get him to safety, I'll find you. We'll take the vows then."

Before she could answer him, Edward ran back into the chapel and pulled her from James's grasp. She escaped the Bruce brother's clench long enough to retreat to her knapsack and retrieve a small, leather-bound volume. Coughing back the emotion, she pressed the book to James's heart. "I'd planned to give it to you on the anniversary of the day you won the ax." Fearing they'd both break down completely, she steeled her emotions and ordered him in the firmest voice she could manage: "I wish the book returned, James Douglas."

He couldn't let go of her. "Never forget I love you."

Edward dragged her away and drove her from the kirk. Outside, he lifted her onto one of the horses. He sent her galloping off only moments before his brother Nigel came running up the valley with the MacDougalls in hot pursuit. Afforded no time to trade even a word of farewell with his fleeing brothers, Nigel leapt on the last horse and lashed to catch the women rushing north.

Edward and the men remaining behind prepared to fight a rear-guard action while Robert led James, staggering, from the chapel. With the shouts of a fight ringing out behind them, they hurried into a tunnel that the Culdees had built long ago to assure access to the miraculous waters of St. Fillan's pool.

Eighteen

riven by the baying of the MacDougall bloodhounds, Sweenie led Robert's band of twenty half-starved men in stitched buckskins and scraggly beards down a narrow shepherd's path that ran along the treacherous face of Ben Oss. The vicious dogs, having picked up their scent, were getting closer, and the waters of Loch Lomond, silver and rippling under a full moon below them, offered their only hope for escaping the turncoat Comyn allies who were on the chase to deliver them up to Longshanks.

Exhausted, Robert knifed to his knees. "Go on! Leave me!"

James dragged Robert to his feet and prodded him to keep running. Despite his shoulder wound, he had held up better than Robert during their three-day marathon, having learned years ago how to survive in the wilderness after Clifford had forced his family into destitution. "If you stop, your legs will cramp."

Robert groaned and staggered with each forced step. "Damn MacDougall! The Comyns will pay for this!"

"Aye, see, you're feeling better already."

"And damn *you*, Douglas! For talking me into this hell on earth!"

James increased their pace in punishment for that indictment. "You're too late. We're both already damned. Even the pope moves faster than you do!"

The other men took turns assisting the king until they came to a lush glen shaded by a thick grove bordering Loch Lomond.

Sweenie waddled off ahead to make certain the MacDougalls were not hiding in wait. Minutes later, the little monk returned, looking shaken. "Not a soul on this end, but ..."

"Out with it!" James demanded.

"I can see their fires. They're patrolling the west banks."

James kicked at a log in hot anger. The MacDougalls had split up and sent a second party north of the peak to the far side of the loch, expecting their small band to cross the water at its narrowest point.

Robert glared at Sweenie. "This misshaped brounie has led us into a trap!"

"Leave off him," James said. "He had one plan more than you did."

Edward Bruce peered off into the darkness, trying to locate the torches of the MacDougall hunting parties. "Lorne will negotiate. We'll offer him lands for refuge."

Robert sank to the ground, defeated. "Longshanks has Lorne caught in his talons. The game is up."

James jabbed a stick at Robert's ribs. "We'll cross farther south."

Robert was too tired to parry the goading thrusts. "A man with a full belly couldn't swim that length."

James studied the loch's mist-shrouded depths. "There's still three hours until daylight. Find where the loch is widest and meet me there at dawn."

"Widest?" Robert protested. "What in Hell's name are you intending?"

James disappeared into the darkness.

A thickening fog descended over the loch, blotting the morning sun and blanketing the environs in an eerie quiet. Robert and his exhausted entourage had spent the night crouched behind boulders, shoving and elbowing one another to stay awake. James had been gone all night, and Robert estimated by the rising loudness of the baying that MacDougall hounds would be on them within three hours.

"Douglas tricked us," Edward Bruce snarled. "He knew he stood a better chance if he—"

The water along the banks splashed. The Bruce men drew daggers, bracing to fight for their lives.

Edward was about to lunge at the approaching shadow when a lone man split the fog and pulled up an abandoned fishing bark.

James captured Edward's hand and deflected the thrust aimed at his chest. Legs buckling from fatigue, he ordered the Bruce men, "Three at a time. Sweenie's the lightest, so he'll row."

Incredulous, Edward stepped into the half-rotten boat to test it. "We'd have a better chance of walking across the water."

James offered Robert a handful of shriveled brae berries. "Go on with your depraved brother. I no longer can endure the company of two Bruces in the same shire. Your poor mother must have gained her sainthood for putting up with your incessant whining."

Famished, Robert savored the scent of the berries, but he gave them to Sweenie. "You'll need these more than me. I'll cross last." He turned to his brother, who was still shaking the boat, unwilling to accept that they were going to attempt to use it. "Eddie, you go first. One of us must survive."

James shoved Edward into the leaky currach, along with another man. "Since I discovered this fine galley, I claim the honor of guarding the king. And when the bards tell of this day, I'll make certain they know it was Edward Bruce who hightailed it first. Now, off with you! Don't worry if you can't swim. The hot air from Bruce's bluster will keep you afloat."

As Edward slouched off cursing, James led those staying behind to the protection of the woods above the loch. Calculating that each crossing would take at least a half-hour, he chose not to confide to Robert that it was well nigh impossible for Sweenie to make ten return trips before dropping from exhaustion, let alone accomplish the feat before the dogs found them. He gathered up a bed of leaves and, settling down to catch a moment's rest, found Robert watching him with an unnerving smile. "You make me more than a little skittish looking at me that way? Has it been that long since you've been cozy with Liz?"

Robert kicked at him. "I would have wagered what little remains of my kingdom that you weren't coming back."

"Damned if I didn't consider it. But then I'd have missed watching you be drawn and quartered." James rolled to his side and felt a hard object against his ribs. He reached into his vest and pulled out a small book.

"Where did you get that?"

"Belle gave it to me at Glen Dochart."

Robert crawled nearer to inspect the book. "At least they'll say you died a literary man. What is it?"

James opened the clasp on the book and held the first page toward the dawn light breaking through the trees. "The *Chanson of Fierabras.*"

"One of my favorites. Your lassie has fine taste, except in men."

James carefully dried the pages in the crisp morning air. "You've read this? Aye, you would have, given your fine English schooling and all."

Robert rested the back of his head on his hands and gazed at the thin band of orange rising over the loch. "My mother would recite *Fierabras* to me when I pestered her for tales about the Crusades. It is the story of Charlemagne and his knights, Roland and Oliver. An adventurous pair, those two were. And bumbling. They stumbled into a hundred battles with the Moors."

"If they were so loutish, how'd they always manage to escape?"

"Mostly by jesting their way through trouble," Robert said. "The infidels thought they were crazed."

James held up the first page and read Belle's inscription:

> *To my beloved Oliver,*
> *May you and your Roland find the warmth of merry*
> *fellowship on your Quest.*
> *Your constant Floripas.*

"Who is Floripas?"

Robert tried to snatch the book from him. "Are you reading ahead? She was the ravishing sister of Fierabras."

"And Fierabras? He was the son of the Moorish king?"

"Aye, and dark-skinned." Robert winked to drive home the barbed comparison. "He was as ugly as Floripas was fair. Fierabras led a fleet to Rome to steal the true Cross. Oliver fights a duel with him to regain the relic, but ..." He delayed for effect. "Something dire transpires."

James thumbed through the book. "What happens to Floripas?"

Robert suddenly understood why Belle had chosen this book as a gift to James. "Floripas leaves her home in Syria to save her brother in France. She falls in love with the enemy of her people."

"She abandoned her family?"

"And her God," Robert said. "Floripas converts to Christianity. When she convinces her brother to spare Oliver from execution, Roland offers her a reward. She asks him to require her Christian knight to marry her." His voice trailed off as he became lost in his thoughts about Elizabeth.

"Are you going to tell me what happens, or not?"

Robert marked a page with a pine needle. "Savor it in small bites, Jamie. We'll have many a night for it, I fear. Here's a taste to wet your whistle."

James read aloud the passage that Robert had pointed out:

"'Sir' said Floripas. 'This man gives me.'
'By my head,' said Roland, 'so shall it be.
Come forward, sir, and this lady take ye.'
'Sir,' replied the knight. 'May God punish me if any but
Charlemagne give her to me.'
When Floripas heard, to rage was she stung.
'By Mohamet,' she swore. 'You shall all be hung!'
'Sir,' said Roland to his fellow knight, 'Do what we desire.'
Sir,' answered the knight, 'just as you require.'"

They both laughed so loudly at the inept attempt by Floripas's lover to avoid the chains of marriage that the other men erupted from their slumber with daggers drawn. They discovered the twosome wrestling over the book in a contest to read the next verse. Robert nearly had it in his grasp when a horn sounded through the fog to signal that Sweenie had returned.

James waved another two men down the embankment toward the currach. Finding them delaying to hear more of the chanson, he threw a rock to chase them. "We'll tell you how it ends in the unlikely event you don't drown." He tossed the book at Robert and told him to read more. "Start from the beginning. And leave off with that insufferable London accent of yours."

Sweenie slumped over the oars as he split the mists and floated to the banks. Miraculously, after just three hours, the little monk had ferried all the men except James and Robert to safety.

James pulled the splintering currach to the shore and whispered, "Wee-kneed, you've earned your perch in Heaven this day."

Robert stepped in, but the bark threatened to swamp, so James swam along-side them to lighten its weight. Keeping silent, Robert and Sweenie rowed into the protection of the fog just as the MacDougalls and their bloodhounds reached the shore.

The icy waters soon drove all feeling from James's limbs. Robert grabbed his arm and held him tightly, requiring Sweenie to double his efforts on the oars. After several minutes, James felt Robert's hand throb and begin to cramp. James tried to hold on, but too fatigued to stay awake, he slipped from Robert's grasp and slid off into the loch.

I wish the book returned, James Douglas.

Belle's voice jolted him back to consciousness, and he felt himself dropping to the bottom. Swallowing water, he fought to the surface and swam through the fog to find the side of the currach. To stay awake, he counted aloud the number of times the oars split the water.

Four hundred and eighty-four strokes later, the boat lurched against land. Robert leapt into the waist-deep water and pulled James to his feet. They heard a distant voice shouting through the fog.

"I'll search over there."

James dropped to his knees on the shore, biting off a curse. The MacDougalls had posted sentries on both sides of the loch. Edward and the others had likely been captured, but crossing back would only land them in the hands of the other search party. They would have to fight their way out, or die trying. He drew his dagger and signaled for Robert to follow him.

The searching voice called out again. "Bruce!"

James coiled, preparing to charge at the man, but Sweenie held him back.

The little monk motioned for Robert and him to stay crouched. Then, he pulled his soaked hood over his head and walked into the mists chanting, "Our Father, who art in heaven, give us up his name!"

"Who goes there?" shouted the shrouded voice.

The fog prevented James from seeing what was happening. He leapt to his feet, determined to go to the monk's aid, until Robert restrained him.

Sweenie was counting the steps he had walked into the blinding soup when the discarnate voice called out again.

"How many fingers on Fillan's hand?"

The shouting man, Sweenie suspected, was asking for a password, and it was probably a trick question. The saint's shriveled arm was kept pickled in brine at Whithorn Priory, but he had never cared enough to go see the relic. Had souvenir seekers hacked off some of the fingers? Maybe Fillan had been born with a malformed arm. Not likely, considering the Roman monks would have banished him as a child of Satan. He stalled for more time. "Left or right?"

"Are you clan Donald or Dougall?"

Sweenie risked a step nearer. "My mother never told me."

"Enough of your cunning tongue! Show your face!"

Sweenie drew up his courage and pushed deeper into the fog, determined to latch onto the MacDougall knave and gnaw him to death with his gums, if necessary. Ten steps into the soup, he bumped his forehead against a knee. He looked up. Above him loomed the tallest man he had ever encountered. He nearly swallowed his tongue.

But instead of attacking, the bearded giant backed away. Eyes bugging, he pulled a coin from his pocket and bounced it off Sweenie's chest. "An offering. Forgive the intrusion. No mischief, please."

Sweenie concealed a smirking grin at his good fortune. This hairy behemoth wrapped in folds of tartan wool was apparently under the delusion that he had just stumbled upon a gnome, one of the Little People who haunted these moors. Unarmed as he was, the monk decided to use the only weapon at his disposal, his cleverness. He puckered his nose into an elfish scowl and seized on the foolish man's superstition. "A six-pence? That pittance for the trouble you've caused me? Your name, mortal!"

"Angus Og MacDonald."

"Your business in my glade?"

"I'm searching for the king of Scotland."

Sweenie scoffed. "You expect me to fall for such nonsense? What monarch in his right mind would be lurking about here in such foul weather?"

"Robert Bruce is his name. I was told he seeks refuge in these parts."

Sweenie made a waddling circuit around the giant's ankles. "I thought Comyn the Red was the leader of you miserable wretches? Who is this Bruce you speak of?"

"Are you as daft as you are wee?" The giant Scot immediately regretted his outburst. "The Red is now under sod. Bruce is our monarch now, but he's hard pressed by his enemies."

Sweenie climbed atop a mossy boulder and sat cross-legged, pressing his tiny fist against his chin in a pose of deep thought. "I might be able to conjure up this king of yours with a little magic. But a six-pence won't even pay for the first incantation."

The distant howling of the hounds from across the loch sped the giant Scotsman to the transaction. He reached into his waist-pouch and relinquished ten more coins.

Dropping the offering into his pouch, Sweenie broke off a twig and tested its flex by circling it above his head as a wand. "Fire and wind, earth and water—eh, I almost forgot. I need a description to inspire the vision. What does this Bruce fellow look like?"

"A man of good height."

"And countenance? Fair or repugnant?"

"Average for a Lowlander. Nothing remarkable."

"How is he with the ladies? Well met?"

The looming scout squinted quizzically. "Is that necessary?"

"Would I have asked it if not?"

MacDonald raised his hands in contrition, fearing he had angered the sprite. "Bruce gains his share of attention, but I suspect it is due more to his wealth than comeliness."

A rustling near the loch was followed by a loud thump.

"Just some of my friends," Sweenie assured the man. "Pay them no heed, or they'll find us and demand more compensation." He began dancing a jig atop the boulder. "Bring me Bruce! Bring me Bruce!"

A hail of rocks rained down on them both.

The frightened MacDonald man looked to the heavens in confusion.

Sweenie attacked his own head with his fists. "I remember now! The one asking the miracle has to perform the dance."

The MacDonald man was about to protest that condition when Sweenie aimed his wand at him in a warning. The Islesman reluctantly began shuffling in an awkward imitation of the monk's gyrations while looking around to make certain no one was observing his embarrassing display.

"You call that a jig?" Sweenie cried. "I've seen slugs move with more abandon. The elements won't congeal unless you stir the wind faster."

Doubling his effort, MacDonald churned a jigging frenzy—until two men appeared through the mists. He glanced at Sweenie in amazement at the efficacy of the spell. Approaching the conjured men cautiously to test their reality, he yanked on the taller newcomer's scruffy beard. He gritted his teeth and cursed in a voice lowered to avoid alerting any scouts around. "Damn you, elf! This isn't the Bruce. You've summoned some half-wit beggar."

"Average countenance?" Robert growled at MacDonald. "The ladies seek me only because of my wealth?"

The giant clansman's eyes bulged. "By the Rood."

Despite the danger of the moment, James couldn't help but rollick with laughter. He slapped the stunned Islesman's broad back in a hearty greeting and whispered, "Well summed, MacDonald. Though I felt you gave him too much benefit of the doubt regarding the lasses."

The MacDonald clansman embraced Robert with a bear hug. "We feared the dogs had gotten you." He brought Sweenie to his side. "I beg you, my lord, grant a benefice to this leprechaun. I'd have never have found you without his wondrous powers."

"Aye, we mustn't forget the spirits." Robert nodded James to the task. "Vassal, give our wee ally here from the nethers his just reward."

James grasped Sweenie by his cord at his waist, flipped him upside down, and scraped his knuckles across the bald oval on the monk's scalp.

MacDonald was horrified by the abuse. "Douglas, are you mad? He'll curse us to our last days!"

Released, Sweenie spun head over heels and landed on his feet like a cat.

"Sweenie, meet the Chieftain of the Isles," James whispered. "No galley sails from here to the Orkneys without the mandate of this oversized bag of hazelnuts. But pray he's never attacked by a navy of faeries."

Red-faced, MacDonald didn't know whether to thank the scheming monk or heave him into the loch. He pointed a threatening finger at all three men and warned, "If a word of this gets out, you'll all swim to—"

The louder barking of the hounds drove them behind the boulder.

MacDonald pushed Robert toward the wooded ridge. "The Earl of Lennox escaped Methven and made his way to my castle in Dunaverty. We found your brother this morning. We'd best not tarry."

Holding back, James turned to assess Sweenie's condition. "You got one more jaunt left in you, Wee-kneed?"

Sweenie flexed his puny biceps. "Aye, my lord."

Robert saw to his regret that James was determined to backtrack and find Belle. "I owe you my life. ... Go on, then."

Clasping Robert's hand in farewell, James instructed MacDonald, "Angus, take good care of our king. I'd not serve a day under his boiled-brain brother." He thumped Robert on the chest. "I'll find you in the Isles."

"Clifford will be patrolling the south," McDonald warned him. "Go by way of Strathyre."

Halfway down the slope, James turned back and called out, "Bruce!"

Robert spun in his tracks, looking hopeful. "You've changed your mind. I knew you couldn't stay long from me."

James motioned with a cupped hand. "Let's have it."

With a guilty shrug, Robert reached under his shirt and tossed over the copy of the *Chanson of Fierabras* that he had purloined while James was slumbering on the far banks. Before James could burn his ears with a flurry of curses, Robert ran off for the ridge to catch up with MacDonald.

Reunited with his precious gift from Belle, James hurried back to the loch and found Sweenie catching a wink in the currach. He shook the monk awake and pushed the boat off into the waters.

Halfway across the water, James broke their weary silence to correct one of the dwarf's more irritating habits. "How many times must I tell you? I am *not* a lord. Leave off such fancy titles for those like your new king who traipsed about the London courts with curled toes."

"But your lady insisted that I address you as such."

"Did she now?"

Sweenie grunted and puffed as he rowed. "Aye, she told me that life had given you so little in compensation of features or wit that we should allow you this one false conceit, at least."

Ears reddening, James stole the oars from the lippy monk and sped their pace to find his Floripas.

ΠΙΠΕΤΕΕΠ

he first rays of the March sun broke over the Don River as Tabhann
Comyn led his mounted mosstroopers into the golden moors of Buchan.
During the six months since Belle had escaped from Dalswinton, he
and his cousin Cam had scoured the North, searching for her and planning
their vengeance against James Douglas and the Bruces. At last, they had turned
up a promising piece of surveillance: MacDougall's spies had reported seeing
several stragglers, including women, running for Kildrummy castle. If his wife
was among them, he was determined to see that she received a proper welcome
home.

Reaching the crest of the Grampian Mountains, he gained his first glimpse
of Kildrummy, the northern keep that had been held by their clan before the
Bruces stole it. Black clouds roiled above its quadrant towers. The castle was
under siege, and had been for at least a week, by the look of the trebuchet
damage to the walls. Scanning the heralds flapping over a white pavilion, he
pointed to the Plantagenet dragon. He was too shocked to utter the possibility.

"Longshanks is too ill to ride this far north," Cam assured him. "It must be
the prince."

Tabhann was relieved that Longshanks was not up here in Mar rutting
around, but Edward Caernervon's unexpected arrival presented him with a
different, and troubling, dilemma. For all his cruelty, Longshanks could be
counted on to act rationally, in accord with England's interests. The Comyns
and the MacDuffs were still in the English king's peace, and so long as Robert
Bruce was at large, he felt confident that Longshanks would find it advanta-
geous to embrace him as a victim of the usurper. The Plantagenet's misspent
arrow of a son, however, was flighty, prone to wild swings of emotion, and at
times reclusive. He might prove to be an unreliable ally.

As Tabhann led Cam and their men into the English camp, which had been
set a mere two hundred yards from Kildrummy's curtain walls, he suffered

the glares of the conscripted Yorkshiremen and Northumbrians, who made little distinction between traitorous and loyal Scots. Spying Nigel Bruce at the crenellations directing the tower's defense, he lashed his horse through the English pike men and nearly trampled several of them in his haste to confront his old clan enemy. "Damn you, Bruce!" he snarled up at the walls. "I'll have my wife! And your head on a pike!"

"She found your bed too small!" Nigel shouted down at him. "At least, I think that's what she said she found too small!"

That retort drew raucous howls from the English archers, who lowered their bows in admiration for young Bruce's witty bravado.

Enraged, Tabhann lashed his horse along the perimeter of the moat in search of some means to attack. Denied a target for his wrath, he retreated through the jeering conscripts and rushed up to Caernervon's pavilion.

From their position in the vale below the castle, Robert Clifford and Aymer de Valence, the newly appointed commander of the English army in the North, had been observing Tabhann's raging performance with amusement. "A magnificent sortie," Clifford remarked dryly. "Those walls suffered dearly."

Tabhann leapt off his saddle and came strutting up huffing indignation. "That is *my* castle you are destroying!"

Clifford pushed the complaining Scot aside. "You expect us to stand back after the fighting while you sweep in to collect the spoils?"

"The Bruces stole it from my uncle!"

Valence half-listened to Tabhann's rant while he signaled for the trebuchet to be reloaded. "I don't give a damn, Scotsman, if your mum suckled you in that tower while the angels sang lullabies. Engage those ramparts again without my permission, and you'll walk to Lanercost in chains."

A helmeted knight arrayed in flashy French silks galloped into the camp. He dismounted and strode into the prince's pavilion without even being questioned about his purpose.

Tabhann looked to Valence for an explanation of *that* privilege, but the earl merely shrugged. Furious that a foreigner was permitted a prior audience, Tabhann marched toward the pavilion.

"I wouldn't do that if I were you," Clifford warned.

Ignoring the advice, Tabhann forced his way inside. He found Caernervon under the sheets, naked and in the arms of Piers Gaveston. Sputtering for words, he was hard-pressed to know which was more shocking: that the prince was intertwined in a perverse embrace, or that his Gascon dandy had so brazenly violated Longshanks's order of exile.

Caernervon grinned and stroked Gaveston's oiled locks for Tabhann's benefit. "It seems, Piers, that the beasts have broken out of the stables again."

Tabhann retreated a step. "I would speak with you, my lord, concerning my wife."

Gaveston kissed the prince and then watched for a reaction from Tabhann. "Has the Scottie lost his bride?"

Caernervon nuzzled and conversed intimately with his favourite, as if Tabhann were not present. "It seems she prefers the company of that Douglas cad. You remember him, Piers. He was the thick-tongued bumpkin who danced like a bear."

"The one with the firm derrière?"

Caernervon, stung with jealousy, wriggled away from Gaveston's arms.

The Gascon knight reassured the insecure prince with a pointed glance aimed at his buttocks. "Not as fine as yours, Poppy."

Mollified, Caernervon rested his head on Gaveston's chest. "I too have suffered the pangs of lost love. We must do all we can to see the Scottie reunited with his lady."

Gaveston leapt from the bed and donned the prince's breastplate, leaving exposed his lower extremities where a codpiece would be attached. He scampered around mimicking a joust with his lance. "Your wish is my command, my lord! Where is the poor damsel held? In London Tower? On some brigand ship?"

Caernervon rollicked across the sheets, toasting the performance.

"My wife!" Tabhann shouted, incensed by the mockery at his expense.

Wiping tears of mirth, Caernervon finally regained breath enough to report, "She is indeed inside those walls."

Tabhann took an impatient step toward the bed. "Then it is true—" He stopped when Caernervon laid back the covers, as if to make room for three.

Primping his curls, Caernervon studied his own reflection in the goblet's jeweled neck. "There is even more good news. This Douglas traitor who cuckolded you now seems to have turned his affections toward Robert Bruce." The prince shot a wicked glance at Gaveston, as if savoring the possibility of a physical bond between the two Scot rebels. "Bruce and Douglas have abandoned those conniving cunts they dragged west with them. Now they share a bed sack on the moors! How scandalous!" He winked with devilish intent at Gaveston, who was prancing around in glee at the irony. "It would be such a shame if such depravity became widely known. That might destroy their reputations."

"Who defends the tower with Nigel Bruce?" Tabhann asked.

Tired of toying with the humorless Scot, Caernervon suspended Gaveston's taunting with an upturned hand. Adopting the practiced façade of the serious monarch that he would soon become, the prince reported, "He is being suckled by that fat sow, Atholl. I intend to roast their loins for ham hocks. They have a small garrison, but Bruce's brother is putting up a stiff resistance.

I fear it will be a month, perhaps more, before you are back in your lady's arms." He winked at Piers, betraying that neither was in a rush to end their secret tryst in this wilderness. "These primitive siege guns commissioned by my father are not worth the kindling."

"A *month?* That is time enough for Bruce to restock his rebel army in the Isles and send a relief force!"

Caernervon waved off the warning. "Do you know what they are calling Robert Bruce in London? King Hob. He hobbles over here and he hobbles over there. That smelly MacDougall oaf reports that the turncoat now resembles a recluse with a beard falling to his belt and his ribs poking out of rags ripped to shreds by hounds. Even by your primitive standards of hygiene, Comyn, that must be something frightful to behold. You needn't worry about King Hob. He can't even scare up a rabbit to roast."

"Even if Bruce remains in hiding, Douglas will come for her."

Caernervon drained his wine goblet. "What can one man do to us?"

Tabhann paced and stewed, desperate to get his hands on Belle before Douglas discovered where she was hiding. He scoured his memory of Kildrummy's layout. One oddity of its architecture, he remembered, had always drawn complaints from the vassal assigned by his uncle Red to hold it years ago. A small chamber situated between the kitchen and the dining hall had been converted into a corn bin. The room had once been used as a waiting station to pass heated victuals, but the aperture had been boarded up rather than refilled with stone and mortar. He asked the English prince, "Is the castle provisioned?"

With affected dejection, Caernervon sank into his pillow and bemoaned his plight. "Alas, it seems so. My spies confirm the granary is full."

Tabhann rushed from the pavilion.

Belle had dreamed for weeks of a night in a warm bed, but now that she had gained the protection of Kildrummy, she could not sleep. She climbed from her straw mattress and knelt next to Elizabeth, who lay shivering under quilts near the altar. Nigel had lodged them here in the chapel for safety, trusting that the English would not aim their slings at holy ground. She placed her palm on the queen's splotched forehead. The fevered chills had not eased.

Elizabeth opened her swollen eyes. "Marjorie?"

"The child is asleep in the kitchen with Mary and Christian," Belle assured her. "There is more heat from the ovens."

She marveled at how well the queen had stood up under the rigors of their ordeal. Growing up in Fife, she had become inured to the brutal northern winters, but Elizabeth had never spent a day outside the London court or her father's castle in Ireland. She recalled the first time she had laid eyes upon Richard de Burgh's daughter, in Berwick city. She had formed an immediate dislike for Robert's new wife, for there had been condescension in Elizabeth's manner, a legacy of her Irish heritage, no doubt. Ulstermen and their women, after all, would stand in rags on Judgment Day and declare all other races inferior. And yet, she conceded, God must have chosen Elizabeth for the role, knowing that Robert would require a queen with a deep reservoir of stubbornness and tenacity.

As if sensing her thoughts, Elizabeth looked up at her with a contrite smile and whispered, "I have never properly thanked you."

Belle turned aside. As an only daughter, she had never enjoyed a close bond with another woman so near her age. Finding it difficult to share her deepest feelings, she deflected Elizabeth's attempt at intimacy by pretending to tend to the hearth.

Elizabeth persisted in trying to draw her out. "There is something I have never told you. The first time I encountered James, I found him infuriating."

Belle could not stifle a rueful chuckle. "Perhaps you and I are more alike than we thought."

"How did you meet him?"

She stirred the fire. "I stumbled into him."

"No, in truth."

"I bounced off his chest like a tossed chestnut. A force seemed to have pushed me into him. I turned to see what I had danged. He looked at me with those daunton black eyes …"

"And?"

"He kissed me."

Elizabeth struggled to her elbow. "Without even knowing your name?"

"Aye, I should have slapped him, but …"

"What *did* you do?"

"He bolted from me before I could do anything." Several seconds passed before Belle found the resolve to ask Elizabeth the question that had haunted her these many months. "Have you ever wondered if the patterns of our lives might be foretold in a lone encounter?"

"What do you mean?"

"Ever since that day, Jamie has been running from me, or I from him."

Elizabeth shook her head in disapproval. "One would think *you* were the Irish of the two of us, spouting such mystical nonsense."

"You don't believe that you and the king were destined to be together?"

Elizabeth lowered her gaze as she thought a moment. "Ours is a different bond. Marjorie's mother was Robert's true love. He and I share a respect, a deep affection even. But I know there is a part of him I will never have."

"You wedded him knowing this?"

"Robert proposed, and I accepted. I did not ask his reasons. I sensed in him some great purpose, and I felt duty bound to my father's approval. Do you judge me harshly for that?"

"Me? A married lady who violates her vows is in no position to judge? But surely love can grow. The seed lies dormant until the spring and—" Belle looked down and saw that Elizabeth had fallen asleep. She tucked the blankets around the queen's neck and quietly prepared to leave the chapel to check upon Nigel. At the threshold, she heard faintly ...

"He always returns."

She turned back, questioning if her imagination had spoken those words.

The queen opened her eyes slightly. "James runs from you. But has he not always returned?"

Her heart surged. "Aye, he has."

"Then perhaps *there* is your pattern," the queen said, her voice trailing off as she slipped back into sleep.

Smiling with a swell of hope, Belle closed the door and made her way through the darkness across the rock-strewn bailey. The English had suspended the bombardment for the night, and the weary Scot defenders on the walls were stealing a few minutes of slumber. The tapers cast flickering shadows across her approach to the great hall. Near the granary, she saw a cloaked figure. She haled the man, who seemed to be in a hurry. "Sir, can you tell me where I might find Lord Bruce?"

The man drew his hood over his head and refused to answer her.

She shivered from a foreboding. "Have we met?" When the man kept his face covered, she backed away in alarm and screamed, "Nigel!"

On the allures, the soldiers leapt to their feet and gripped their weapons.

Nigel came running from the tower and found her shaking, in a panic. Bracing her shoulders, he asked, "What is wrong?"

She needed several breaths to find her voice. "That man."

The cloaked phantom lowered his hood. The defenders on the walls sheathed their swords and muttered curses for having their rest needlessly disturbed.

Nigel calmed her. "It is only Callahan the blacksmith."

The blacksmith bowed stiffly to her, but kept his eyes cast down.

Belle was sick with embarrassment. "Forgive me. I am so tired. My mind must be playing tricks. I thought he was an intruder."

Nigel dismissed the blacksmith to his intended destination, and then escorted Belle back to the chapel. "You must get some rest."

"Is there no word from the king?" she asked.

Nigel smiled to reassure her. "We have enough grain to hold out for two months. Caernervon does not have that kind of patience. You needn't worry."

Relieved, she sank into his arms. Since their escape from Glen Dochart, she had formed an abiding affection for the youngest Bruce brother. Unlike the rash Edward and the ambitious Robert, Nigel was selfless and sensitive. More slender in build and fair in features than his siblings, he reminded her of Galahad, the chaste knight of Arthur's Round Table. He emulated his oldest brother with such devotion that the others called him "Little Rob." He would do anything to further Robert's cause, of that she had seen evidence enough, and there was no one, other than James, in whose protection she felt more secure. She kissed his cheek to send him back to his duties.

When Nigel had departed, she glanced back toward the granary and saw the blacksmith lingering near its door. Had the poor man been trembling? She offered up a prayer for him, thinking how tragic it must be for one trained in the use of his hands to suffer from the palsy.

S ometime later that night, Belle awoke to the acrid sting of peppery smoke. She leapt up from the floor and pulled the dazed Elizabeth through the door. Marjorie, blackened with soot, crawled from the kitchen just before a crackling beam landed behind her. The castle was an inferno.

Outside, Nigel was mustering his men to defend the burning gate. He warned her back. "The granary has been fired! You must get away at once!"

She rushed to the well for buckets. "We can't leave you!"

Nigel intercepted her and pressed a loop of rope into her hands. "I'll lead an attack from the south gate to divert the English." He gathered the other women together and hurried them toward the wall. "Go north to Tain! Seek sanctuary with St. Duthac's monks!"

She heard the shouts of the English massing for an assault. Powerless to help him, she kissed his forehead. "You are every breath the knight your brother is. God be with you."

Her blessing drew his tears. "And with you, my lady."

He warned her away, and she hurried Elizabeth, Marjorie, and the king's sisters to the north ramparts. Climbing to the allures, she looped the rope around a crenellation and ordered Elizabeth to go down first. The drop was more than twenty feet, and when Elizabeth hesitated, she had to push the queen to the rope. "You can do it!"

Elizabeth closed her eyes and slid down the rope, crying out from the burn. Little Marjorie, who had inherited the agility of her father, easily rappelled down. Belle hurried Mary and Christian to the task while she watched Nigel prepare to meet the onslaught of the rams hammering the main gate.

Seeing them safely on the ground, she prepared to leap across the wall when a horrid thought came to mind: How would James find her? She picked up a shard of charcoal and debated the risk.

Elizabeth shouted at her from below. "I see their torches! Hurry!"

Belle scribbled on the wall: *Sanctuary*.

As a child, she had always wanted to travel to Tain and see the Culdee shrine that marked the birthplace of St. Duthac. A lover of all God's lesser creatures, Duthac had saved a herd of runaway cattle from slaughter by coaxing them into the stone fence that surrounded his hut, insisting that the Old Testament required all beasts in the shade of a holy temple be spared for forty days. Word of this Scottish St. Francis of Assisi had spread so quickly that his humble abode soon became crowded with human fugitives from justice. Two hundred years later, King Malcolm III granted legal standing to Duthac's tradition, and ever since, Scot monarchs had made the pilgrimage here to affirm the sanctity of the sanctuary law.

Yet never had she dreamed she might one day require its protection.

Faint with hunger, she peered above the hull of their creaky bark. She hadn't expected a grand church, but St. Duthac's chapel, off high in the misty distance, was little more than a stone hut perched on a knoll above the turbulent waters of Dornoch Firth. A muddy path, overgrown with brambles, spiraled up to its entrance nearly a half-league away. She had lost count of the days since they had made their way by foot to Inverness, where she and the Bruce women had found transport around the tip of Tarbot Ness to Tain. Now, as their bark floated toward the beach, she braced for the perilous run they would have to navigate across the open dunes and through the wooded bluffs. Even if they managed to reach the chapel, the English chasing them might surround the kirk and try to starve them out.

The old fisherman who had risked his life to ferry them across the firth assisted her and the other women from the currach. He waded with them through the freezing waters until they reached the banks. "This is the Earl of Ross's country," he warned. "The Comyns pay him handsomely for his dirty allegiance. His mossers are always out and about. You'd best be scarce."

"We've nothing to offer you in payment."

The fisherman shrugged off her expression of regret. "Remember me to our king, m'lady. When he comes here pray, I'd be honored to row him."

She kissed his hand. "The name MacKleish shall one day grace a herald."

The old man's eyes watered as he climbed back into his currach and pushed off into the mists.

Left to their own wiles, Belle led the Bruce women on a forced run through the dunes and up the winding stairs carved into the limestone juts. They waited there until darkness to avoid being seen by the Ross constables and brigands who lurked in the woods. The debtors, heretics, and other criminals who came here by the hundreds each month were required to carry money or valuables for the donations. Those who could not afford bodyguards or pay for documents of safe passage were easy prey. Unescorted women in particular were always in danger.

When the light finally faded, they made their way with difficulty up the sea cliffs. After an hour of slinking from tree to tree, she caught sight of the girth crosses that marked the sanctuary's boundaries. A large iron ring hung from the door of the ancient kirk. Was it abandoned? Nigel had not told her what act was required to complete the immunity. Would her grasping of the ring be enough? Could they all keep their hands on the handle at once?

Ordering the other women to remain crouched behind a stone fence, she crawled to avoid being seen and took aim for the portal, which stood twenty paces away. Offering up a prayer, she rushed for the ring and pounded it against the worn plate below the grill slot. A sleepy Culdee monk with gaunt eyes and no teeth cracked open the door. He closed it just as abruptly, nearly crushing her fingers. Fighting faintness, she knocked again. "We seek sanctuary!"

The monk poked his head out. "Sanctuary from whom?"

She signaled for her companions to hurry to the kirk, and when they staggered up, she brought Elizabeth into her embrace and told the monk, "This is your queen. The English seek to capture us. You are our last hope."

The monk looked beyond her shoulders and searched the dunes. He shook his head and tried to close the door. "I have trouble enough with the abbeys."

Belle thrust her foot onto the threshold. The monk, she realized, had mistaken her whispering for irresolution. If they were going to be turned away, she decided her muted voice would be of little use now. She forced the door wider with her knee and shouted, "I was told that the Culdees were the true descendants of Christ! I now see that I was misinformed!"

The monk recoiled from her sudden fury. "Who told you such thing?"

"A brethren of yours. Ned Sween of Glen Dochart."

The monk broke a gummy grin. "You know the Wee-kneed?" He scanned the grounds behind her. "Is that half-devil with you?"

She was taken aback by the swift alteration of his temperament. "He is in the West risking his life to save your king. But I shall advise him of the base hospitality you showed us." She huffed off, taking the women with her.

"Wait!"

She turned, praying he would reconsider. The monk debated the risk, then finally, with a roll of the eyes toward the heavens, waved her and the other women into the kirk. She was first to step into the enclosed darkness. The sanctuary's floor of pounded dirt didn't even have a chair or table: it made Sweenie's hovel at Glen Dochart look like a palace. She looked around and wondered how many thousands of criminals and desperate refugees had trod in there.

The monk locked the latch behind them. Settling on the straw mat in the corner to resume his holy contemplation, he said flatly, "What I have is yours."

The Bruce women dropped to their knees and rolled to their sides in exhaustion. After covering them with robes, Belle slid against the dusky wall and slipped into a deep sleep.

hours later—just how many she did not know—she heard the ballad that James had always sung to her:

> "On quiet glen
> where old ghosts meet
> I see her walking now
> Away from me so hurriedly
> My reason must allow …"

She staggered to her feet and rushed to the window. Was that him walking up the causeway? What was he carrying? She threw open the sanctuary's door and ran to him until her legs nearly failed. He held a swaddled infant in his arms. She reached for him and looked down at the child. It was a baby boy with dark skin and—

A pounding at the door wrenched her from a vivid dream.

Disoriented, she climbed to her knees. The other women were still asleep, but the Culdee monk was not in the sanctuary. The torches had gone out, and it was night.

The door pounded again.

James's distant voice still lingered in her ear.

Her heart leapt. He had found her at last! She crawled to the entry, whispering a prayer of gratitude to St. Duthac for sending her the prophetic dream to announce that James had come to take her home. She pushed back her hair and wiped the grime from her face, then she drew back the bolt and threw open the door, desperate to fall into his safe embrace.

TWENTY

espite having searched the mainland for all of a fortnight, James had found no trace of Belle and the Bruce women. Now, chased west through Argyll and Kintyre to this desolate isle of Arran, he was growing more desperate by the hour. The English galleys had anchored at Brodrick Castle, less than a mile away, and Clifford was sweeping the headlands with two pincer columns of foot soldiers to flush him out. Famished to the edge of losing consciousness, he had no choice but to abandon the cover of the forested cliffs and attempt a dangerous run for the beach.

His only hope was to find an abandoned bark and try for Ireland.

One last time, he shouted Robert's name. Cupping his ear against the crashing waves, he prayed for an answer to the call that he had aimed at every cranny and grove between here and Kildrummy. He thought he heard the weak blare of the royal ram's horn in response, but when it was not followed up with a second blast, he dismissed it as just another hunger hallucination.

Burning with a fever, he arose unsteadily and staggered toward the shoreline while holding the aching shoulder that had become infected with an aching mass of pus. He knelt behind a dune, breathing hard to gather strength for the effort. In recent days, an enemy more insidious than Clifford had begun dogging him—his own traitorous mind. Everywhere he went, he caught fleeting glimpses of Belle and Robert, only to be cruelly disappointed.

That damnable horn of his imagination sounded in his ear again. Half-crazed, he banged his head against the ground to chase the torment. He crawled over another dune to find shelter from the howling wind and—

Robert's death mask, shining ghoulishly in the moonlight, stared up at him.

This time, the demonic vision did not recede. He tried to plunge his dagger into the demon's heart, but a tremoring hand restrained his wrist.

"Roland would have come sooner."

No wispy spectre of his mind had spoken *those* words. Robert, in the flesh, lay half-buried before him under a crest in seaweed and sand.

Still not quite believing his eyes, he resurrected Robert from the detritus and brought his wasted frame into his arms. "Roland didn't have half of England on his heels." Seeing Robert's lids swollen nearly shut and his hands shaking terribly, he pulled out the last slither of his salted rabbit meat and brought it to Robert's lips.

Robert shoved the morsel aside. "What has happened?"

James finally gave him the bad news. "Kildrummy is burned."

Robert slumped, aggrieved by the loss of his invaluable northern castle. Yet he took refuge in hope. "Nigel must have escaped and fled north."

James chose to let him think that for now. Given Robert's fragile mental state, he thought it best not to reveal that he had discovered discarded wine casks from Brittany and tins of spiced meats outside Kildrummy. The campsite had served as headquarters for someone with more refined tastes than those cultivated by the Comyns. He felt confident that if Belle *had* been at Kildrummy, she would have left him some indication of her destination. He had searched the burned castle for evidence of her presence, but the walls had been charred and the rooms ransacked of any documents. Seeing Robert's eyes fluttering, he gently slapped his cheeks to revive him. "Edward abandoned you here?"

Robert licked his cracked lips, searching for moisture. "Percy and Clifford attacked us at Dunaverty. Angus set sail to save his galleys and divert the English to Ireland. Eddie has gone west to God knows—"

Voices shouted out on the bluffs. Overhead, hooves pounded the ridges.

James motioned for him to remain silent. "We can't stay here."

"My legs … I can't move them. What's happening to me?"

James waited for the English search party on the bluffs to pass by. Then, he lifted Robert to his shoulder and gagged his mouth with a slither of bark to stifle his delirium screams. The drizzle was threatening to turn into a hard, chilling rain, and he feared if he did not find shelter soon, Robert would not last through the night. Despite the danger, he dragged him down the beach, praying that Clifford would suspend his search until the storm passed.

A cry echoing through the cave raised Robert from an unsettled sleep. He rolled over and, wincing, levered to his elbows. "How long have I been out?"

Hovering over a pitiful fire, James bit down on his sleeve and held a scalded knife to his festering shoulder to cauterize the inflamed gash that now threatened the use of his arm.

"Jamie … how long?"

In pain, James muttered through gritted teeth, "Three days."

Robert stared at his own shaking hands, white as those of a corpse. "Am I dying?" Receiving no answer, he crawled toward James, his fingernails raking at the dirt. "Promise me you'll not let me die an excommunicate."

A raven flew into the cave and alighted on a boulder near the entrance. James recoiled into the shadows. Morgainne was stalking her two souls again. He hurled a stone at the death harbinger, remembering that she had followed him all the way from Kildrummy. When the blood-lusting bitch did not move, he lurched toward the entrance to chase her away. The wily goddess merely laughed at him. His stomach burned from hunger. By God, if they were going to die, they'd have a last meal, at least. Nothing would give him more pleasure than to roast that taunting harpy and gnaw on her bones. He reached behind his haunches and gathered up another sharp rock. The raven remained on her perch, daring him. He lifted to his knees and fired, but the raven dodged the rock and danced away with a taunting screech.

He sank in defeat, but then remembered that Robert was watching his every move. "You'll not meet your Judgment Day on my watch," he promised. "We still have that journey to make."

The reminder of their boyhood pact galvanized Robert. "Aye, the Holy Land. Once we've mended, I say we take one of MacDonald's galleys and dry our feet in the sands of the Lord."

James sat back against the dank cave wall to steady against the dizziness. "You think the Moors ever laid eyes on a Lochaber ax?"

Robert closed his eyes. "The first time would be their last."

"That it would."

Wearied from just that brief exchange of false bravado, James became silent, laid low by the realization that in truth they had forfeited the chance of ever fulfilling their dream of taking the Cross. If they could not defeat the English and protect their own womenfolk, how would they throw back the infidels? They were likely being derided as incompetents in courts all over Christendom. The King of Jerusalem would never welcome into his service two excommunicated traitors turned beggars. Robert had always been the melancholic one, but now he felt himself falling into the black abyss of hopelessness.

Robert resorted to the one subject that never failed to bring a smile to his friend's face. "That lass of yours loves you more than life itself. If I were a wagering man—"

James snorted cynically. "If you're anything, you're a wagering man. Why else would you have listened to my nonsense about seizing the crown?"

"You're the one who made the more foolish bet, putting all you had on me." Robert reached into his jerkin and tossed an English pence at him. "Here's another wager. I'll give you odds that Belle and Liz are quilting a sham near some raging hearth right now. Nigel wouldn't let me down. Norway is where they are, I'm certain of it. With my sister in Haakon's court."

James ran his finger across Longshanks's inscription on the coin. Suddenly, he was swept by a wave of despair. "I'll never hold her again." He turned aside and rolled onto to his stomach, trying to chase the shooting hunger pangs.

"Don't go down on me, Jamie. I can't see it through if you give up."

James blinked hard, trying to focus his tunneling vision. He groped his way to the fire and tried to stoke the embers, but what little driftwood he had managed to find was too green to take a flame. The oystercatchers had grubbed the bluffs clean of all the pignuts and tubers, and he didn't have the strength to wade into the water and spear a fish. As the night's cold descended on the cave, he felt an encircling darkness in his soul. He gave up on the fire and muttered in anguish, "I can't see a light ahead."

Robert crawled closer to the pitiful pile of kindling and blew weakly on the ashes. "It'll be dawn in a few hours."

"No, I mean … I can't see how we can defeat the English. Wallace had ten thousand men with him. Five hundred came to our call. Half of those we lost at Methven. Longshanks holds every castle north of Carlisle. Your brothers are scattered. Angus has been forced to take to the sea."

When Robert could not summons a rebuttal to that grim assessment, James lowered the back of his head to the ground. Fearing he would never wake up if he fell asleep, he stared at the ceiling to fix his eyes against the vertigo. Above him, a large black spider dangled on a thread. The wiggling creature had fallen from its corner and was retracting its legs in a frenzied effort to regain its web.

The spider threw itself against the limestone but failed to secure a hold.

Summoning what little strength he had left, James climbed to his knees for a closer view. Again and again, the spider launched an improbable quest to regain its home, only to fall short. "Rob, look at this."

Half blind, Robert leaned on his elbows and watched the blurry image of a spider twirl toward him. On the spider's back was a red and yellow streak, the colors of his clan's heraldry. Nearly exhausted, the spider climbed its thread in preparation for one last attempt.

"He's going for the rebound."

Robert squatted under the spider and reached to assist it. "That thread won't hold."

He held back Robert's hand. "No, he can do it. Come on, laddie!"

The spider continued its perilous ascent up the thread, stopping to rest every inch or so. When it could climb no higher, it paused as if to summon courage—and dropped to its death or freedom. The thread stretched and rebounded. The spider catapulted toward the web and clung fast.

They cheered as the spider crawled to the center of its web in triumph.

"A sign, Rob! See how he preens on his regained throne. A king speaks to a king! He is telling you never to give up!"

"You believe it so?"

A light flashed near the mouth of the cave.

James pulled Robert behind him. Clutching a rock, he cursed under his breath, fearing that their shouts had drawn Clifford's scouts. As the torches approached, he came to his knees, preparing to fight to the death.

The outlines of a woman in black robes appeared within the blinding aura of the torches. Her sleeves resembled wings, and her hood fell to a point like a predator's beak.

James backed away. Not Clifford, but the raven goddess Morgainne, had come back for them. He remembered that she always melded into her mortal shape when arriving to announce a death. He scooped a handful of rocks and threw one of them at her. "You'll not take him!"

"Who gives me orders in my own land?"

He flashed another stone to scare off the carrion bitch. "Take me, damn you, if you must have a soul to slake your blood thirst!"

The death goddess retracted her hood, revealing strands of wild red hair and pale skin. Several men with torches came up from the shadows and stood aside her. The shortest of them rubbed his arm and threw the rock back at James, grazing his ear.

"That'll require a severe penance!" Sweenie cried, rubbing his scalp.

Edward Bruce rushed up to embrace his brother. "We've been searching under every rock from here to Mull for you. MacDonald has his galley waiting in the bay. The English patrols are on the eastern side of the isle. We must hurry. They'll sail around the cove within the hour."

Edward helped Sweenie and the other men carry Robert from the cave.

James held back, seeking his equilibrium from the discovery that the woman was not Morgainne. Still struggling to squint his eyes into focus, he asked her, "Who are you?"

She offered a hand to assist him to his feet. "Christiana of the Isles."

"The daughter of Gamoran, the chieftain?"

She nodded. "My father is dead. I now lead my people."

"How did you find us this far south?"

Christiana rolled her eyes into her upper lids, as if overtaken by an inner vision. She looked up at the spider hanging above her head and stroked its spine. The spider arched its back as if to acknowledge her greeting. She whispered something to it in what seemed to be some form of oracular communication. Then, she looked down at James and warned him, "A lady suffers for you."

James's weakening knees knifed him to the ground. "Belle?"

Christiana translated the rest of the prophecy from the spider. "She dangles. Bait to catch a king."

He crawled closer. "Speak plainly, woman! Do you know where she is?"

Christiana's voice turned husky. "Many years from now, a great nation is promised on the far side of the world. But this shall come to pass only if you and your king gain victory here." She placed her ear near the spider to better hear its message. "Look to the blood crosses. They bear the salvation of the Light in your hour of travail." After a long silence, she finished with another warning, "This war cannot be won by you alone."

"Blood crosses? What in God's name does *that* mean?"

She turned and walked away.

"Damn you! Answer me!"

At the mouth of the cave, Christiana looked over her shoulder at him with a heavy-lidded glare of contempt. "For you to prevail in this war, the women of your land must prove stronger than the men of your enemy."

"Of *my* land? Do you forget that you are a Scot, as well?"

"I am an Isleswoman. Whether I shall one day be a Scot depends on you and your king. From what I've seen so far of your skills in governance, I doubt there's much chance of it."

"Babbling hag! What do you know of our war!"

Christiana whipped her cloak across her face, leaving only her flaming eyes bared. "I know this much. Only the female spider bears the colours of royalty. The truth of my vision has already been confirmed."

James was utterly baffled by all of these shrouded declarations. "And, pray tell, how?"

"Had that spinning lass and I not come to your aid this night, you and your fair-weather king would have been dead by morning."

TWENTY-ONE

Blindfolded, Belle was dragged from a mule and shoved down a cobblestone path. The past week had been a whirlwind of confusion and terror, ever since that desperate night when the man pounding on the door of St. Duthac's kirk turned out to be not James, but the Earl of Ross, a Comyn ally who had found and deciphered the scribbled message she had left at Kildrummy. Taken from the Tain sanctuary with the other women, she had been kept uninformed about her whereabouts. Now, as her eyes were uncovered, she adjusted to the harsh sunlight and saw a Latin inscription on the keystone of an archway.

Her heart sank.

She was standing at the gate to Lanercost Abbey, the English army's headquarters just south of the Borders. The guards drove her into the abbot's quarters. Inside, the windows were draped with black bunting and an odor of camphor filled the stifling air. Prodded another step forward, she saw a group hovering around a canopy made of gauze-thin linen. As a candle's flame flickered, their faces became clearer: Caernervon stood aside a bed, flanked by the Earl of Ross and the Dominican Lagny. Elizabeth Bruce, her stepdaughter Marjorie, and the Bruce sisters knelt at the foot. They turned toward her with fright in their swollen eyes.

Caernervon retracted the sheer canopy. "Father, I have captured the bitches."

A desiccated hand reached through the gauzy folds and beckoned Elizabeth Bruce closer. "Dearest Liz, praise God you are saved from that felonious husband of yours. … Where is he hiding?"

Elizabeth's breathing shallowed. "I do not know."

"Light!" the king shouted. "I am not in the grave yet!"

The royal physician rushed up to massage the old monarch's chafed temples, muttering a warning about the sun aggravating the headaches.

Longshanks, shriveled to half his normal weight, repulsed another invasion on his person and tore the canopy from its supports. He dragged up against the headboard and captured Elizabeth's hand. "Am I too frightful to look upon?" When she tried to retreat, he forced her ear to within inches of his labored breath. "Vile rumors are being spread about you, Liz. They are saying you counseled Bruce to turn against me."

Elizabeth's words quavered. "Your Highness—"

"Of course, I protested that slander. My favorite daughter of the loyal Carrick would never betray my trust." Finding her too distraught to form a response, he caressed her tangled russet hair, each stroke firmer in its threat. "My little songbird. You were always so facile with the quips. Perhaps you need some time in a nest to regain your voice." He shoved her away. "Take her to York dungeon!"

Little Marjorie screamed as Elizabeth slid to her knees, her mouth gaped in a silent shriek.

Belle rushed up to prevent Elizabeth from collapsing. She pleaded leniency for her queen. "Robert Bruce cares nothing for this woman. He abandoned her in his haste to escape from Methven. You will only be doing his bidding if you allow her to languish and suffer."

Stunned by Belle's intercession, Elizabeth was about to contradict that falsehood when Belle glared a warning at her to remain silent.

The Earl of Ross, seeing that the king could not place Belle's face, came to his aid. "The Earl of Buchan's absconding wife, Sire."

Belle caught a shadow of movement in the corner. Isabella of France, standing off in the dark to avoid the king's detection, came into the dim light. The French princess shook her head in a covert plea for Belle not to draw more attention. But Belle ignored the warning and stepped in front of the prostrate Elizabeth to deflect the king's ire. "I now belong to James Douglas."

Longshanks covered his scabrous shoulders with a velvet robe stained in blood and phlegm. Wincing from the painful effort, he stood and, tottering before finding his balance, shuffled a few steps toward her. "So, it was *you* who placed the crown upon the traitor?"

"Upon the rightful king of Scotland."

Longshanks enjoyed the bemused reaction of his son—and spun back on Belle, slapping her to the floor. "Perhaps you've not been informed of what we do to traitors."

Disoriented for a breath, Belle looked up from her knees. Through stinging tears, she saw the king nod to the Earl of Ross. A side door opened, and attendants carried in a board draped with a sheet.

Longshanks ripped off the covering.

The severed heads of Nigel Bruce, the Earl of Atholl, and Christian's husband, Christopher Seton, sat impaled on spikes, their faces frozen in their last agonized repose.

Belle stifled a gasp. The mouth of a fourth head—which looked disturbingly familiar—had been grotesquely stretched open. She nearly vomited, sickened by the smell of putrid flesh lathered with preserving tallow.

Longshanks seemed to draw strength from the macabre display. "Atholl protested that his rank did not merit a common hanging, so I had him strung up twice as high as the others." He laughed so hard that a hacking spasm nearly choked him. Regaining his breath, he grasped the bloody scalp of the unidentified head and held it in front of the women. "Do you not recognize him?"

Sobbing, the women shrank from the bloody stump.

"Kildrummy's blacksmith. He sold you out for gold. I always pay my debts. I had his throat filled with his reward."

Belle turned from the dangling sinews, struggling to maintain her wits. If Longshanks inflicted such horror on these men, what diabolical tortures would he devise for James and Robert? She saw a scalpel on the bed stand, three paces away. Calculating each movement required to capture the blade and plunge it into the king's chest, she looked across the room. As if sensing her plan, Princess Isabella edged in front of the guards, watching the aim of her eyes.

Longshanks limped and lurched around Belle. "I suggest you speak, woman, while I am still in the mood to listen. … Where are Bruce and Douglas?"

She tensed to lunge for the scalpel, and—

Longshanks erupted in another coughing spell. He staggered into the table, sending the surgical instruments flying across the floor.

Denied, she glanced helplessly at Isabella, who closed her eyes in defeat.

Steadying against a bedpost, Longshanks nodded to the door watchman.

The Comyn cousins were escorted into the room.

Tabhann had to be restrained from rushing at Belle. "Faithless cur!"

"Now, then, is that forgiveness?" Longshanks chided between hacking coughs. "She is of the weaker sex, a victim of temptation. We must allow her to redeem her soul." The king looked to the Dominican Lagny for confirmation. "Is this not the Christian way, Abbot?"

The inquisitor inspected Belle with a long-snouted sneer. "This harlot takes orders from the Devil's henchman, the Bishop of St. Andrews. Scotland must be cleansed anew of heresy and brought again under Rome's authority. Cut off the head of the dragon, and the body will die."

Longshanks placed an unsteady hand on the inquisitor's bony shoulder for balance. "Fear not, friar. That Fife warlock now conducts his black Masses in

Winchester dungeon for a congregation of rats." The king glared at Belle as if plumbing her resolve. "Being a godly ruler, I am inclined to give this fallen woman another chance for redemption." He grasped her arm and led her to a large wooden chest that sat below the windowsill. "Place your hand on this stone and renounce the coronation of Bruce. Confess that you were coerced and agree to return to your husband. Do this, and I will be merciful."

Belle stared at the ugly lump of limestone that had been transported from London for viewing in York cathedral. The block still held the scars that the English king had inflicted on it during the signing of the Ragman Rolls. What harm would be caused by speaking the oath over it? After all, this was not the true Stone of Destiny, even if Longshanks believed otherwise. She could plead ignorance of the import of Robert's coronation and claim that she had acted out of passion. Yet if she complied with the demand, Tabhann would contend that Robert had been crowned illegally, and the few clans that still remained loyal to the rebellion would turn their allegiance. If that happened, the sacrifices that she and James had accepted to bring Robert to the throne would be in vain.

Elizabeth, shaking uncontrollably, looked up from her knees at her, trying to divine what she intended to do.

One of them would suffer the king's wrath, Belle knew. Elizabeth's womb held Scotland's only hope; the queen had only a few childbearing years left, and if she were left to die in England or, God forbid, be executed, Robert's dream of uniting the clans under a new line of succession would fail, dooming their country to English dominion forever. She prayed to St. Bride for courage; then, taking a step forward before she could lose resolve, she challenged Longshanks, "Bring me the true Stone, and I will name the true king."

The king's patchy brows narrowed. "This *is* your Stone."

She pressed his hand to the rock. "Why then does it not scream?"

Longshanks repulsed her grasp and shoved her to the floor. "Throw her in a Welsh nunnery! She can listen to her own screams!"

The soldiers were about to drag Belle away when Caernervon delayed them. "Father, Robert Bruce is too cowardly to care what happens to his women. But his fellow conspirator has always labored under a foolish code of chivalry."

"Speak plainly, damn you!"

The prince shot an evil glance at Belle. "By all accounts, James Douglas alone has kept Bruce alive."

The king glowered at his son. "I need no lessons in surveillance from you."

Undeterred by the dismissal of his competence, Caernervon persisted in spinning out his proposed scheme. "Bruce will let his wife rot first before he shows his face to us."

"What are you suggesting?"

Caernervon removed the gold chain from around his neck and swung it in front of Belle. "Douglas is a different cut of cloth. If his wench here will not lead us to the rebel, why not let *her* lead the rebel to *us*?"

Princess Isabella, alarmed, stepped forth from the shadows. "Sire, these ladies have no choice but to follow the orders of their lords."

Longshanks patted his daughter-in-law's hand with mock compassion. "Then I would have you, my young French swallow, follow *my* order by holding your insufferable tongue!" He released her hand with a rough snap of his wrist.

Shaken, Isabella retreated with her head bowed.

Longshanks pulled Elizabeth from her knees and into his vulturous embrace. "A propitious change of fortune, darling. I have decided that you, not your treasonous accomplice here, will be housed with the nuns of St. Catherine. Holderness should be far enough from the Borders, don't you think?"

Elizabeth looked rattled, uncertain if she should be grateful or distraught. "My stepdaughter and attendants. I beg you show them equal mercy."

"Your treacherous husband's brood will be held in secure confines." The king turned on Belle, forcing her to wait to hear her fate. He slithered his fleshless arm across Caernervon's shoulder to acknowledge a nascent maturity developing in his son. "You speak true about this one, Eddie. She deserves special treatment. Was it not in Berwick where we dealt old man Douglas his defeat?"

"I was there with you," Caernervon reminded him with an unctuous grin.

"That city must hold fond memories for the son. Perhaps we should give young Douglas a reason to visit it again." The king then posed to Tabhann a question that was more of a threat, "You don't mind if I borrow your wife?"

Tabhann glared revenge at Belle. "Do with her what you will."

"How generous of you." With a smirk, the king circled Belle while thinking. Then, he turned to his officers and ordered, "Lodge our crown-toting traitoress here in an open cage from Berwick tower. Raise it high enough so her countrymen can see the reason for the chastisement they are about to suffer."

Belle stood numbed, unable to comprehend the sentence.

Horrified, Elizabeth reached for her, but the guards pulled them apart.

Longshanks lapsed into another fit of coughing. When he recovered his breath enough to speak, he taunted Belle, "Berwick offers a splendid view of the Tweed valley. You'll be first to see Douglas coming for you."

Suddenly she remembered what Idonea Comyn had told her on the day they had first met: *To survive, you must make the whoresons believe you possess the power to conjure the spirits.* Consumed with a fury, she escaped the guards and stole a candle from its holder. Before she could be wrestled back, she dripped wax on the king's chest, evoking an old Highland sorcerer's ritual used to predict who next would die among all persons present in a room.

The Earl of Ross retreated a step, having seen crazed Scot widows perform this pagan soothsaying incantation for troops on nights before battle. A dozen hands clutched at Belle, pummeling her to the floor.

Wrestled away from the king, she shouted, "Burgh upon the sand!"

His chest hairs singed, Longshanks lurched back in confusion.

The guards threw Belle to the floor again. She clawed to her knees and screamed the rest of her death fey at the monarch, "I will outlive you! I will see Scotland freed of your tyranny! You will take your last breath in the burgh upon the sand! At that hour, God shall reveal on whose side He fights!"

Longshanks staggered until he found his balance. He looked to his councilors for an explanation of the incoherent curse, but none dared offer one.

Finally, the inquisitor Lagny broke the disconcerting silence. "The burgh upon on the sand, Highness, can be none other than Jerusalem. The witch has just predicted that you will one day again take up the Cross in the Holy Land. Let us rejoice that you will live many more years."

Reassured by that exegesis, Longshanks laughed and raised his goblet in a toast to the women being dragged from his presence. "I vow that I will bring these heathen Scots to justice before I kneel at the Tomb of Our Lord."

The warden of Winchester dungeon rattled the bars of the cell. "Up with you, Scot. Priests to hear your confession."

Bishop Lamberton tried to stand and come forward, but the manacles on his legs restrained his movement. Through the haze, he saw the grille swing open and two hooded Augustinians enter the cell.

The tallest monk handed a document to the warden who was lingering at the entry. "The confession is to be private, by order of Canterbury."

The warden slinked off in a huff, denied the chance to collect surveillance and hawk it for a few pence.

Lamberton rattled his chains to chase them. "I'll give my confession to the Devil before spilling to Longshanks's spies!"

The taller monk lowered his hood slightly.

Lamberton blinked hard, not trusting his sight in the dim light.

Peter d'Aumont, the Templar he had argued with in Paris, raised a finger to his lips and nodded toward the door where Jeanne de Rouen, the female student of Giles d'Argentin, stood watch. They stared at the bishop, stunned by his wasted condition.

D'Aumont clasped the bishop's feeble hand and, kneeling aside him, whispered, "Philip has ordered the arrest of every Templar in France. The Jerusalem and Paris Masters have been imprisoned in Chinon."

"Clement does not defend you?"

"The pope is in cohorts with the French king. He affirmed the arrest order *ex cathedra* in Avignon. The commandery treasuries are being confiscated, and many of my brothers now endure unspeakable tortures."

Lamberton was surprised only because it had taken Philip this long to make his move on the Temple with the aid of nefarious influences in the Curia. "The Dominicans have finally played their hand."

D'Aumont checked the grille as he hung a purple stole around his neck to act out the confessional sacrament. While setting out the oils of the sacrament from his pouch, he revealed under his breath, "A few of us escaped."

Lamberton bowed to bring his ear closer to the report. "How many?"

"Fifty from France," d'Aumont whispered. "Another thirty from Tomar in Portugal. We pray as many from Spain."

"Has the edict been issued in London?"

Jeanne hissed a warning as the warden walked past the cell.

D'Aumont signed Lamberton's forehead with the Cross. Assured that the grille was clear again, he continued his report. "The inquisitor Lagny has infiltrated the Plantagenet court. He presses for our arrests. London Temple has been placed under guard with royal troops."

"Longshanks may test you, but he won't enforce the warrants. He despises Philip too much to do the French bidding. He also owes the Temple for past support." Lamberton glanced at the grille. "But the Prince of Wales comes from a different kettle of fish. If the old man dies, you will be in grave danger."

D'Aumont eyes hooded with shame. "I was too blinded by pride to heed your warning in Paris. I ask your forgiveness … and beg your help."

The bishop displayed his chains. "What assistance could I offer you?"

"Those brothers who escaped Phillip's snares have set sail from La Rochelle. The French royal galleys are in hot pursuit. I must find refuge for them soon, or they will be captured. We have come to seek your blessing."

"Blessing?"

"To hide in Scotland."

"There is no more Scotland. The English have the run of our castles. And I have heard nothing from Robert Bruce in over a year."

Jeanne abandoned her watch and hurried to the bishop's side. "Perhaps we can serve as your eyes and ears. Our spies in London tell us that your king was last seen with the chieftain MacDonald near Arran." She glanced at d'Aumont, uncertain if she should convey the next piece of news. "Your queen and the Countess of Buchan have been taken prisoner. Longshanks has ordered the countess displayed for ridicule in a cage above Berwick tower."

Shaken by that news, Lamberton whispered a prayer that the MacDuff lass would find the strength to survive her ordeal. He knew James and Robert had to be in dire straits if they had abandoned the women on their retreat to the Isles.

The warden's footsteps echoed down the stairwell again.

D'Aumont and Jeanne waited for the bishop's answer.

Lamberton feared that if he conspired with these Templar emissaries to protect what remained of their Order, Philip would abstain from offering assistance from France, and the papal edict of excommunication that so tormented Robert would remain in force. He shook his head to indicate the futility of their hope. "The Bruce will never grant your request."

D'Aumont grasped the bishop's hands to convey the depths of their desperation. "We ask only for time to plead our case. If your king is a fair man, he will see that we have been wronged by the pope, just as he has been wronged."

Lamberton studied the monk, marking the fervency in his sleep-denied eyes. He had long suspected these Templars of possessing evidence that the papacy wanted quashed, just as Rome had suppressed the Culdee testimonies of Christ's presence in Britain. They were haughty in their ways, for certain, but if his dream of a nation honoring freedom of conscience was ever to take flight, then these monks deserved Scotland's protection. Though not convinced about the wisdom of such a dangerous course, he finally nodded his assent to their sanctuary request, taking on the responsibility of trying to convince Robert Bruce of its justification if he ever gained his release.

Eyes welling up in gratitude, D'Aumont pressed a kiss to the finger where the bishop's ecclesial ring would have resided.

Lamberton brought him back upright. "Avoid the Temple's preceptory at Ballentradoch. Clifford will expect you to try for Sinclair's lair. Kintyre is good country for laying low. There are hundreds of inlets and hidden harbors there." He pinched the *cross pattée* on the Templar's mantle. "And you should rid yourselves of these red crosses for a time."

"God be with you."

The two French imposters draped their heads with their cowls and slipped out through the grille. Making fast for the stairwell, Jeanne turned back on the first step. "Your scribe in Paris ... did he ever learn to use the sword?"

Smothering a smile, Lamberton shook his head, affecting regret and disappointment in his adopted son. "The lad had no skills for the military life. Should you ever encounter him again, it would profit you to coax him into a rematch."

Part Two
The Ax Descends

1307–1314 A.D.

James of Douglas, always bent on plots.
— Vita Edwardi Secundi

TWENTY-TWO

Robert carried two flagons of steaming ale to the rocky shore below Castle Tioram and offered one to James. "You needn't keep a lookout."

Waving off the drink, James continued pacing the dunes surrounding Christiana Gamoran's secluded islet. As he had done every morning for the past three months, he searched the watery horizon for the masts of Angus Og MacDonald's galleys. Each passing day he spent trapped here made him more despondent. Buffeted by storms, Clifford had given up the chase across the Firth of Lorn and had thrown up a cordon of patrols around this narrow channel into Loch Moidart. As a result, the haggard survivors of Robert's army, unable to forage sufficient provisions for the winter, had been forced to disperse across the Isles to survive on their own until spring, when the Bruce brothers would scour Ireland for more volunteers.

"Chris's scouts assure me that the English are anchored at Tobermory."

Plied again with the offer of drink, James refused it and turned his back on Robert in disgust. "I'm not worried about the English."

"What so vexes you, then?"

"You've read the *Iliad*?"

"One of my favorites."

"Then you know the misfortune a woman can cause a fighting man."

Robert followed James's gaze of accusation toward Tioram's tower, where Christiana, still in her night robes, stood watching them in the window. Finally taking the import of this line of questioning, Robert set his jaw and reminded him, "We wouldn't be alive without her."

"Do you forget you still have a wife?"

Robert slung the second ale cup at him. "I'll not be lectured on the sanctity of marriage! Not by one who asked me to break them for that MacDuff lass!"

James kicked the empty flagon back at him. "Aye, you're already damned to Hell by the pope. Why not make the best of it?"

Robert leapt from the bluff and flattened James in the wet sand. They scuffled and traded punches as the waves crashed over them. Pressing his forearm against James's chest, he demanded, "What would you have me do, damn you?"

James heaved him aside and came back to his feet with fists clenched. "I'd have you remember how many men are dying while you sit here idling away in that soothsayer's arms!"

"I have no army!"

"You have me! But not much longer!"

Robert kicked sand at him. "Go then! What good have you been to me anyway? It is a king you address! Do you forget that?"

"Aye, a king who rules from the bed of a mistress while his realm is being ransacked!"

Robert was fast on his heels. "Abandon me, then! That's what you've been planning all along! You accuse *me* of being blinded by a woman? Look at you! That MacDuff lass is all you talk about! Chris has maids. Take one to your bed."

James turned away to hide the hurt in his eyes. Ten lasses in his bed wouldn't make him forget Belle—nor the fact that Robert had made him break his promise never again to abandon her. Whirling back to face him, he hit him in his most vulnerable spot, his insecurity. "Do you know why only five hundred men joined us at Methven?"

Robert glanced aside, as if not believing the defense he was about to offer. "The summons was too hasty."

"Nay, it was because few trusted you to stay the course."

Robert reacted as if cut to the quick. "Stay the course? I *have* stayed the course! And the course you led me upon has brought me to this! A prisoner in my own kingdom!" He drew a deep breath to calm himself, allowing the heat between them to cool. "We must bide our time until we get more recruits. Clifford patrols every foot of Carrick and Galloway."

"And by spring, there will be nothing left to recover. Longshanks will hold every castle from Stirling to Inverness." After a pensive breath, James revealed his intent. "I leave on the morrow, with or without you."

"We haven't eighty men within the day's call."

"I'll make do with ten."

Robert caught his arm. "The dampness here has sogged your head."

James waited for him to remove the hand. "There's another way to fight the English. Clifford may own the day, but I will own the night."

He climbed to the bluffs and unexpectedly came face to face with Christiana, who had walked down from the castle after observing their fight. Looking distraught, she held a folded parchment in the fold of her sleeve.

Robert, still on the beach below, waited for her to reveal what was on her mind. "Well, out with it, woman!"

Clutching the letter with its seal broken, Christiana could not look at him. "Your brother Edward says he has a hundred men with arms on Arran. Thomas and Alexander wait in Ulster with two hundred more."

Robert reacted as if convinced that she had misread a coded message his brothers had sent. "That cannot be all they've managed to muster."

Christiana glanced sharply at James; then, she flung the letter at Robert. "Edward says you must come now, or never."

Robert shook his head in disbelief as he read the few hastily scribbled lines on the message. "How does he expect me to transport them across the sea?"

Christiana turned aside to hide her tears. Driven to the task by James's forceful glare, she finally admitted to Robert what she had promised James privately several days ago. "I've ordered ten of my galleys up from Doirlinn."

Her willingness to risk her navy for his cause stunned Robert. He climbed to the bluff and reached for her hands, whispering softly, "Chris, how can I ever repay you?"

She repulsed his attempted embrace. "The ships come with one condition."

"Name it."

"Never return to me."

Before Robert could argue against her decision to deny him her bed, she hurried away. Several steps up the path, she turned back to confront James. "And I *have* read Homer."

James realized that she had overheard their shouted argument while she had been walking down from the tower through the mists.

"It was *not* a woman who set those Greeks upon that journey," she reminded him. "It was a man's lust for war and revenge for a wife stolen by another man." She whipped her cloak across her shoulders and did not look back as she walked away.

A week later, as their small invasion fleet sat at the ready in Whiting Bay, James paced the swaying deck of the lead galley. Below him, the white-capped waves sheltered by the grey cliffs of Holy Isle lapped at the hull with deceptive calm. Fearing the sea would turn violent with the approach of night, he looked up again in exasperation at the crag where Robert had stood fixed for two hours, peering across the Firth of Clyde toward his birthplace at Turnberry. To the south, off the Irish coast on Rathlin Isle, a second small force led by Thomas and Alexander Bruce had been sent orders to sail at dusk, which was now only minutes away.

From his lofty vantage overlooking the bay, Robert called down to him on the ship again. "You are certain the watchmen saw the signal?"

Green from the churn, James braced against the riggings to avoid retching. Behind him, their three hundred volunteers huddled on the row benches for warmth and muttered complaints that they had wasted enough time waiting to launch for the mainland. Most were fast losing faith in this new king. Yet with the other claimants to the throne now dead or firmly under the Plantagenet thumb, their only alternative to Robert's irresolute rule was English oppression. Lust for revenge, not loyalty to Bruce leadership, had driven most of these refugees to this desperate hour.

Robert peered across the sea again. "I can't see beyond that far bow!"

"Three fires!" James shouted at him. "With the middle extinguished if all is clear! Cuthbert can be trusted! We'll find the English bedded down when we land!" When that assurance did not move Robert from his rooted stance, James leapt across the gunwale and clambered up the rocks to speed him to the task. "If we don't go now, your brothers will be left stranded."

While Robert studied the ten bobbing coffins that Christiana had supplied him, a seal lounging on the rocks began barking at him, as if to mock his indecision. The king shook his head in dismay, rudely reminded that even the lowliest of his subjects afforded him no respect.

Although he would not admit it, James conceded that Robert had good reason to doubt the likelihood of their success. The condition of Christiana's ships did little to inspire confidence. Unlike the English galleys with their fortified forecastles and keels of bolted timbers, these steep-pitched Highland barks had been clapped together with rusted clinch nails and moss caulking, and their rectangular sails of dun-colored wool were so thread-worn that they appeared on the brink of ripping from their frayed hemp cordage. In truth, the hulls were no better than those of the dugouts that had carried their Norman ancestors to these isles centuries ago. Despite these misgivings, he put up a false bravado and assured Robert, "The Danes reached Ireland in hollowed logs with less ballast than these offer. We'll easily manage the fifteen miles to Ayrshire."

With a heavy sigh of resignation, Robert climbed down from his perch and walked to the shore. Relieved that a decision had finally been made, the men raised their oars before he could change his mind. Assisted to the lead galley, Robert glared at the bowsprit crowned with the head of a red dragon. Touching it for good fortune, he ordered Sweenie, "Bless this sailing, monk."

Sweenie climbed atop James's shoulders. Lowering his head, he prayed loud enough for all the men to hear: "Lord, you parted the waters for Moses. But we're not asking for a miracle like that on this night. We're Scotsmen here. We'll make our own fate. Just ease the gales a bit and we'll take it from there."

Appalled by the blasphemous benediction, Robert stood glaring at the shrugging monk, until James chided him, "You're damned for eternity anyway. So stop your bellyaching about not getting a High Mass."

Robert shook his head as he coldly regarded his scruffy band of ill-clad men and questioned how he had been brought so low. But, at long last, he gave a half-hearted signal for the helmsmen to push off, and one by one, the galleys, each limited to a solitary covered lantern to avoid detection, formed a line and bit the water with supple quickness.

Soon the sun fell to the horizon, requiring the armada to keep the moon's shimmering beam in its sights, remaining just north of its light to avoid detection. The oars slapped the water in a rhythmic beat.

Robert caught James staring mesmerized at the roiling storm clouds passing to the west. He remarked dryly, "I trust the heavenly signs are well met?"

James pointed to Columba's pulsing star, which had just appeared in the clearing sky. "I was thinking how fortunate I am. The exiled saint never saw his homeland again. Whatever happens, at least I'll see mine this night."

An hour into the crossing, the Scot pilots could no longer tack by the fires on Arran Isle behind them. The outbound currents had strengthened, insuring that there would be no turning back before the tide reversed in the morning, and the men had abandoned their nervous prattle and now rowed in tense silence. Robert stood uneasily at the bow, shrouded with the stricken look of a condemned man going to his execution.

To raise their spirits, James signaled Sweenie to a task that they had previously conspired. The monk climbed the mast and shouted against the wind:

> "Scots, who have with Wallace bled!
> Scots, who now with Bruce are led!
> Welcome to your gory bed!
> Or to victory!"

James slapped Robert's back. "Now you'll get your blessing."

As he sang, Sweenie clung fast to the rigging with his blunt legs flapping like pennons. The men in the rear galleys, taking heart from the little monk's fearlessness, unleashed a roar of admiration above the crash of waves.

Try as he might, Robert could not suppress a grudging smile at the feat.

James climbed the mast behind Sweenie and chimed in with another verse:

> "Now's the day, and now's the hour;
> See the front of battle lower;
> See approach proud Edward's power
> Chains and slavery!"

The Scots rowed faster to the cadence of the ballad that had been sung by Wallace's soldiers at Stirling Bridge. Even Edward Bruce, who despised all such acts of frivolity, joined in the chorus:

"What, for Scotland's king and law,
Freedom's sword will strongly draw,
Freeman stand, or freeman fall,
Let him on with me!"

When they had finished their song, James slid back down the mast. Finding not a dry eye on the decks, he gripped Robert's arm to firm his resolve. "Do you know how many are with us this night?"

Robert gave him a dubious glance, as if suspecting he had fallen into one of his infamous dreaming spells. "Three hundred, unless you count the fish. And I wouldn't put that past you."

James looked across the galleys to burn each face into his memory. "I'll wager you ten thousand old men will one day tell their grandsons how they sailed with Bruce and Douglas on this wee sneak back into Scotland."

Two hours before dawn, the galleys floated in creaking silence toward the mist-shrouded Ayrshire coast. The English had destroyed the old Turnberry lighthouse, forcing the Scots to rely on the instincts of Christiana's pilots to navigate the dangerous reefs. Despite the roughening of the sea, they maintained good formation, and when they came in danger of grounding, James signaled for the rowing to stop.

He dived into the chilly waters and swam ashore. Finding the dunes unguarded, he whistled the others down the hulls to join him. The shivering men waded in and mustered under the overhanging bluffs. They had gone over the plan a hundred times. Their scout on the mainland, Cuthbert, was not to light the signal fire until Clifford had depleted the garrison for one of his many forays into the countryside. Then, they would follow Cuthbert into the city by the cow gate and attack the sentries in their sleep.

Minutes passed, and then an hour, but Cuthbert did not arrive.

James prepared to reconnoiter Turnberry's walls when the bluffs suddenly came alive with torches and voices. He held the others in their crouches while he slithered up alone to the headlands for a better look. He was about to tear into Cuthbert for his tardiness when the English cavalry came galloping over the brunt, followed by foot soldiers thrashing at the gorse brush with pikes.

He crawled closer to the castle and saw English scullions tending a large bonfire. He slammed a fist into the sand. Their watchmen on Arran had mistaken a burning refuse pit for the signal. The garrison would still be at full force, and Clifford now had his troopers patrolling the coast for landing parties.

He waited until the last of the horsemen had passed overhead. Then, he slid back down the dunes and reported to Robert: "A fire …"

"And?"

"Not ours."

Robert stared at him in disbelief. Shuddering with a look of panic, he ordered his brother Edward to recall the galleys. The exhausted men moaned and cursed as they began crawling back toward the water.

James held back. "I won't go."

"Percy and Clifford must know we are here," Robert reminded him. "We'll be butchered if we stay."

"And if we go back to Arran, we'll never keep enough men with us for another invasion. I say we split up and regroup in Galloway."

Robert studied his men behind him, reminded that they had risked everything to reach this shore. Seeing the desperation in their eyes, he finally agreed to stay. "We'll scatter in threes and meet up in Glen Trool within the fortnight."

"I'll go with you," Edward said.

Robert shook his head at Edward's smothering insistence to always be at his side. "We can't be captured together. Jamie goes with me. And the monk."

Denied again, Edward sneered at James as he dispersed the other men across the dunes to make the run inland.

Sweenie sent them off with a whispered verse from the ballad that he had sung on the galley. "Welcome to your gory bed, lads. Or to victory."

On their third night of running from Clifford's patrols, James, Robert, and Sweenie finally reached the forest around Glen Trool. To avoid leaving tracks, they followed the puddled banks of Loch Moart and eventually came upon a thatched hut that churned smoke from a stone chimney nested with hundreds of jackdaws and puffins. Overgrown with sphagnum and wadded with twigs, the cabin resembled a giant sett formed by badgers. It would have passed for any hunter's winter outpost except for one remarkable oddity: a maturing hawthorn tree split the roof, evidence that whoever called this place home had long ago given up the pretense of maintaining the border between nature and civilization.

When darkness fell, James ordered Robert to remain behind with Sweenie while he stalked the cabin, hoping to find something to eat. He ran in stealth toward its window and, arriving, looked through the vined aperture. A pot of stew sat boiling over a fire, giving off an aroma that nearly buckled his knees. He drew his dagger and cautiously opened the door to the hut.

Tending the hearth was a shrunken crone with thinned white hair drawn severely over the tops of her ulcerated ears and a cob-nosed face that was all creases and moles and hanging skin. Seeing him, the woman did not frighten, but merely arose from her stool and, as if having performed this sacrifice many times, poured a ladle of root soup into a wooden bowl and set it on the table.

James stared at the first food he had seen since the invasion. He couldn't remember ever having smelled anything with such a heavenly tang, but he declined the offering. "Two men are with me. I can't eat without them. I see by your circumstances that you haven't enough for three."

The old woman ladled two more helpings and set them on the table.

Moved by her generosity, James stuck his head out the door and signaled Robert and Sweenie up from their hiding. They entered warily and stared wide-eyed at the gruel. When the crone nodded them toward the table, Robert and the monk bowed to her and attacked the helpings like wild animals. James paused long enough from his ravenous eating to thank the crone. Yet she persisted in not speaking, and when they were finished eating, she merely removed the licked bowls from the table for washing. After lapping his bowl clean, he tried again to draw her out. "Your name, my lady, so that we might one day repay this kindness?"

At last, she proved that her tongue worked. "There's nothing ye could do for me, unless ye can raise the dead. I give sustenance to all who come to my door in the hope that some charity might be visited upon our king. None's heard from him for months. I pray he's still alive."

Her earnest prayer heartened James. If the common folk like this woman still supported Robert, he held out hope that they might yet redeem themselves in the eyes of the oppressed and save the kingdom from English domination. "Your prayers have reached God this night," he told her. "You have just served your liege."

The crone rushed at him and thumped his head with her ladle. "This is how ye repay me? Festooning me with jests? Get out of me abode!"

Robert stood from the table and tried to calm her. "Good woman—"

The crone turned on him, aiming her kitchen weapon in threat. "When King Robert returns, and I swear by Fillan's hand he will, he'll bring a host so great that Edward feckin' Longshanks, God damn his malformed soul, will run south like a Irish hare in heat!"

Robert gently grasped her shaking hands. "My man here speaks true, good mistress. You have indeed just fed that host ... I am the Bruce."

Squinting to take in his features, the old woman spat a wad of saliva into the fire to deny that claim. "I saw young Bruce once in a Glasgow tavern. Served him and his grandfather with tankards, I did. You wouldn't suffice for his bootlick." But when Robert reached into his cloak and pulled out the gold brooch with his clan herald, she stared at the talisman and slowly raised her gaze to his scruffy face again. Eyes bulging, she staggered to her knees. "Forgive me, m'lord."

Robert raised the woman back to her feet. "I am the one who requires forgiveness. I have left too many of my subjects in such straits. My wife could use a good matron like you."

The crone blanched. "Ye've not heard? … No, how would ye?"

"Heard what?"

The crone's eyes darted as tried to evade the answer. Finally, she swallowed hard and revealed, "Your queen has been captured. Those traitorous Comyns handed her over to the English six months ago."

"God help me! My daughter and sisters?"

The crone nodded, her hands shaking from witnessing the king's outrage. "Scattered off to English prisons."

James leapt up from his stool. "Another lass was with them."

The woman ran her fingers through his thick hair, trying to place his face. "Are you the son of the Hardi? The one they call the right hand of the king?"

"Aye."

She hesitated, until his fearsome glare demanded that she say what more she knew. "Some of the English soldiers were puffering in the village. The Countess of Buchan is being paraded about in a cage to be abused by all who pass."

James overturned the table in a rage. "Where?"

The woman backed away, frightened by his outburst. "I daren't know."

Robert was certain that the woman had just heard a wild, unfounded tale. "Longshanks would never deal with a lady in such base manner."

James glared darkly at him. "Aye, you'd know well enough!"

Robert's face drained at the insult. "I'll not suffer that from—"

The door squealed open.

James turned to find three men, armed with axes, at the threshold. Cursing his failure to keep watch for Clifford's men, he grabbed a chair and prepared to fight them off. He motioned Robert and Sweenie behind him, and then waited for the attackers to make the first move.

The old woman shouted something in Gaelic.

The intruders lowered their weapons and descended to their knees.

The crone brought Robert to them. "These are me sons. Now you have a start on resurrecting that army ye lost to those whoresons at Methven."

Robert was stunned by her selfless offer. "Who will see to your safety?"

She glared a warning at her sons not to speak. "Me husband will be back from hunting soon. He'll watch over me." She raised her lads to their feet and pushed them to the door. "Now, off with ye. The English demons are on the far side of Loch Trool, thicker than spring gorse and begging for a bloodletting."

Ten hours into their run for Glen Trool, Robert begged a moment's
rest. Gaining his breath, he asked the sons of the crone, "You lads
have names?"

The tallest answered. "I'm Murdoch. This is McKie and McClurg."

"From three different clans?" James asked.

"We're half-brothers," Murdoch explained. "My father was killed on Roslin
Glen. McKie's old man fell at Stirling Bridge."

Until that moment, James had given no thought to their markedly different
features. Murdoch was dark, lithe, and angular, and carried himself with the
quiet somberness of a friar sworn to silence. McKie, the second oldest, was raw-
boned and ruddy and kept his head perpetually down as if determined to ram it
against a wall. The youngest, McClurg, was blond and moon-faced with peach
fuzz for a beard, and he was the only one of the three who had even threatened
to crack a smile. In fact, the only characteristic all three shared was a remarkable
ability to travel on a half-run for hours without becoming winded.

Robert asked McClurg, "Your father is away hunting?"

"He died on Falkirk field."

James shared an astonished glance with Robert, realizing that the mother of
the boys had lied about having a husband who would protect her. He admired
their pedigree, spawned as they were from a clan of hardy fighters. "You lads will
be in my service from here on. Any of you feel like going on a little excursion
into Northumbria to visit to the English scum who murdered our fathers?"

The brothers nodded eagerly at the prospect for revenge.

That was the first Robert had heard of the dangerous plan. He warned
James, "There's fighting enough here in Galloway still."

Since leaving the crone's cabin, James had pointedly refused to speak to
him, making it clear whom he blamed for Belle's capture. Only now, without
the courtesy of a direct glance, did he reveal his intent to plunge into the
Borders and the northern English shires to harass the garrisons there. "I'll stay
with you until we deal with this English army on our heels. Then I'm going
south to find her."

TWENTY-THREE

James placed his ear to the shepherd's path that led into the Glen Trool wilderness, but the ground remained quiet. After three days of scouting this meandering loch that fed the Black Water of Dee, he had found no sign of the English army that the Galloway crone had reported was here. He was starting to suspect that the old woman had simply imagined it all.

He prayed that she had also been mistaken about Belle's capture, but somehow he had to find out for certain. In the old days, to locate the whereabouts of an enemy or lost comrade, his father had often employed an ancient Pictish trick called 'riding the wind.' The hags who taught the magic warned that separating one's spirit from the flesh to travel to far places was a tactic full of peril, for one could easily become lost forever in the netherworlds.

Despite the dangers, he decided to risk it. He sprawled out on his back with eyes closed, imagining a map of England against his lids. The sun's rays warmed his face and brought a tingling numbness to his legs, and soon he slipped into that liminal space between sleep and wakefulness. He felt his spirit rising to his head and leaving his body.

Moments later, a shadow came over him.

Had he been transported to Belle so quickly? He resisted the urge to open his eyes and instead allowed the vision to congeal. A soft hand caressed his face. He sank into her touch, amazed at how real this conjuring seemed. She slid her fingers past his throat, untied his shirt, and searched for the heart stone she had given him. Clever lass. He captured her face to bring her lips to his.

Her scream scattered the corbies in the trees.

He leapt to his feet, shielding his eyes from the blinding sun. The silhouette of a girl stood before him. He was disoriented, uncertain if they were still in Glen Trool. Had his wind riding reversed the spell by bringing Belle's spirit to him? This apparition before him had her height and long black hair. She stared at his face for several seconds, as if she didn't recognize him.

"I thought you were dead," she said.

Overjoyed, he reached for her. "I searched for you at Kildrummy—"

A scrawny girl in rags pushed him away. "Don't hurt me!"

He rubbed his eyes. What was this curse that every woman he now encountered looked like Belle? Was Morgainne playing games again with her glamourie? Recovering from his disappointment, he reached into his pouch and offered the half-starved lass a piece of jerky. "Are you from these parts?"

She stopped her chomping long enough to mumble, "Muldonoch." She kept looking beyond his shoulders. "Where are the others?"

"What others?"

Her eyes darted from side to side. "I heard the king was in these woods."

"Who told you that?"

She wouldn't look at him directly. "Is there more food?"

He noticed a rip on her blouse edged with bloodstains. He tried to examine a whip mark on the top of her back, but she fought him off. He steadied her with a grip on her arm, then pulled down her collar and found her shoulders marred with flogging scars, recently inflicted. "Who did this to you?"

She tried to yank her arm free of his grasp, refusing to answer him.

He threw her over his shoulder. "You'll damn well get your wish to see the king!"

James walked into the camp and dropped the kicking lass in front of Robert. "One of your subjects wishes an audience."

"I sent you for venison. She looks too scrawny for roasting."

James prodded the crawling girl forward on her knees. "We're the hunted ones. And she's the flush hound."

Robert clamped the lass's chin. "Who sent you into these wilds?"

The fierce glares from the men around her finally drove the frightened girl to an answer. "An Englishman named Clifford. He holds my family and said he'd kill them if I came back without learning your numbers."

James roughly hoisted her to her feet. "Clifford is in Glen Trool? Lie to us, scamp, and you'll wish you were back in his hands."

"You think I don't know who thrashed me? Another lord rides with him! They call him the Flower of Northumberland!"

He glanced at Robert with kindled anticipation on hearing the sobriquet of Pembroke, the treacherous earl who had deceived them at Methven. He tightened his grip on the girl's shoulders. "How many are with him?"

"Three thousand, maybe more. They're coming up the loch like locusts and bragging they ain't leaving until they have King Hob's head on a pike."

Edward Bruce drew his dagger and grabbed the girl's hair to bend her throat for cutting. "Traitorous hizzie! You've led him to us!"

"Lay off her," Robert ordered.

Edward threw the girl aside, incredulous at his brother's refusal to punish the treason. "We've waited for three months. All the English have done is gotten stronger. I say we attack them now!"

As the lass staggered coughing and gagging to her knees, Robert searched the dark depths of the wilderness below for more evidence to confirm her unlikely claim that an English army was here in the west, hunting them. If she spoke true, they would soon be surrounded and outnumbered. Although a few more recruits had trickled in to him from Carrick and Annandale, his younger brothers with their three hundred volunteers had not yet arrived from Ireland. "We can't move against Pembroke without Tom and Alex."

James saw that the girl became even more jittered at the mention of the Bruce kinsmen. He clamped on her arm to draw out what information she might be withholding. "What do you know about them?"

Her face turned white. "They landed in Galloway, but …"

"Out with it!" Robert shouted.

"The English captured them! They butchered your brothers and scattered their limbs for the crows to feed on!"

While Robert stood frozen, unable to believe what he had heard, Edward raced for his armor, frothing and swearing like a madman. Several of the men followed him to the weapons while others waited for the order to march on the English and take revenge.

James drew Robert aside. "If we splinter now, we're lost."

Robert dropped his hands to his knees. "What would you have me do?"

"We don't have the numbers to fight them in the open."

Edward, blind with rage, had to be restrained from rushing at James. "They weren't *your* brothers!"

"Question my loyalty again, and I'll do Clifford's work on you!" James shoved Edward aside and climbed a boulder to be heard by all. "Have you forgotten Falkirk? The English bring warhorses and outnumber us six to one! I say we fight them at our time and in the manner of our choosing! Make the forest our field of battle and burn every path before them! Let them share the hunger we now suffer!"

Horrified, Edward looked to Robert, expecting him to countermand such a craven strategy. "Rob, Douglas would make us the laughing stock of every court. Do you want to be remembered as the king who turned Scotland into a land of cutthroats? If we're to die, let us die with honor here."

"Did Tom and Alex die with honor?" James asked Robert. "I say we send honor to Hell with the bloody English bastards!"

Still choked with grief, Robert waved up the little monk who now served as his chaplain. "I'd have the Almighty's counsel on this."

Sweenie pondered the dilemma. Then, he waddled up the boulder and climbed atop James's shoulders to be heard by the ranks. "St. Peter carried a sword to defend our Lord. Did he not slice off the ear of a Roman soldier?"

McClurg nodded. "Aye, but Christ told him to lay down the blade in the garden of sorrows."

"That He did, wise Master McClurg!" Sweenie cried. "Yet is not Our Lord all knowing? Christ knew that St. Peter was carrying the blade long before He ordered it sheathed. So, I ask you, why would Christ allow the apostle to bring the weapon in the first place if He did not believe there be a time and a place for its use?"

The men traded amazed looks; they were never disappointed in Sweenie's ability to read signs and justifications for their cause in Holy Writ.

Sweenie kicked at James's ribs, spurring him to keep moving along the high rock. "I once asked the Dewar about this very conundrum." He delayed the revelation to heighten their expectation and draw the men even closer.

"Damn it, Sweenie!" McKie shouted at the monk, who was winking as if armed with a secret. "Are we going to have to beat it out of you?"

Sweenie grinned slyly. "Aye, lads, the Dewar did indeed tell me of a more satisfying explanation. One revealed in a long-lost gospel brought to our fair land by St. Joseph of Arimathea. St. Peter, it seems, was not a simple fisherman."

"What was he, then?" Edward asked.

"A freedom fighter."

"Like us!" McClurg observed.

Sweenie pounded his tiny palm against the top of James's head to emphasize the point of his sermon. "Aye, like us, lads! The good saint of the sword and his mates were called Zealots. Why? Because they fought like madmen to rid their people of a conqueror's yoke. And like us, they hadn't the numbers or weapons to overcome the Romans in open battle. So, what'd they do, you ask? They relied upon raids and the fomenting of trouble in the night." He paused to allow the import of this to sink in. "Now I'm asking myself why should we fight our war on the Devil's terms? God intended no man to be a slave to another. Give to Caesar what is Caesar's, saith the Lord. I say we give to Longshanks what he's given us. Hunger and fire and terror!"

Robert regarded Sweenie skeptically, but finally he begrudged the monk a nod of approval. His new Culdee chaplain might not be the most orthodox of churchmen, but he knew how to spiritually prepare men for war.

James heaved Sweenie off his shoulders and landed him with a knuckle-scrape on his tonsured dome in congratulations. "Well-preached for an excommunicated homunculus."

Motioning James and Sweenie down, Robert climbed atop the vacated boulder to address his men. "Let this be our testament! Tell our people that we will harry the English on foot and draw them to the darkest corners of our terrain! Turn the forests and moors and mountains into our allies! Our war will know no season! Let the English come north and find fields burned and laid waste! Soon enough their empty guts will have them longing for home!"

James saw the traitorous girl listening spellbound to the speech. He looked up to Robert and asked, "What about the lass?"

Robert glared down at the girl. "Are you a true Scot?"

She cowered on her knees, expecting her throat to be cut. "Aye, my lord."

"And you're willing to prove it?"

"For your forgiveness, anything."

Robert forced her to suffer another moment's penance, then ordered her: "Return to Clifford and tell him that King Hob sits at the mouth of Loch Trool licking his wounds."

"What if he asks of your strength?" she asked.

Finding her counting the men with her fingers, James curled her hand into a fist to save her the trouble. "Tell our old friend Clifford the truth. Our king is accompanied by five hundred miserable skeletons who never cease scrapping."

The next morning, James led ten men on a run across the western traverse of the steep Trool. On the opposite banks of the loch, Edward Bruce and his detachment of two hundred Scots hid behind the trees high on the ridges while Robert and the rest of the army remained in the camp to stoke the fires that would hopefully seduce the English into the glen.

James conceded that this plan to split their small troop was fraught with risk, but he could see no other choice. If the English were allowed to pass through the forest uncontested, Pembroke and Clifford would reach the sea and burn the coastal cities between Straener to Turnberry.

He felt behind his back for his ax, making sure it was still there. All now depended on his suspicion that the stubborn English whoresons had not learned the lesson of Stirling Bridge. He would apply Wallace's famous feint again, allowing them to chance upon him in the glen. Once discovered, he would retreat on foot and draw the English cavalry deeper into the wilderness on a chase. When Clifford's knights became separated from the protection of their infantry, he and his Scot raiders hidden on the hills above would introduce the English to Hell's new location.

After positioning his men in their lairs at the bottom of the glen, he sent the three sons of the Galloway crone ahead to scout. The elusive lads had earned the nickname "the Trinity" because they seemed everywhere at once; Murdoch, the fastest and quietest runner of the three, had been dubbed the Unholy Ghost.

Minutes later, the Trinity brothers returned from their reconnaissance and hightailed it around a bend where the loch angled sharply. They found their comrades hidden behind the brush on the mountain's side of the path.

"Three hundred yards," Murdoch whispered to James. "Clifford leads the column in full armour."

James grinned. Just as he had hoped, Pembroke and Clifford had divided their forces and were now marching down both sides of the loch. Now, he needed one more break to fall his way. Pembroke was too clever to bring his knights into such a narrow confine without infantry at his front, but Clifford did not have the patience to be slowed by a large number of foot soldiers. With a series of prearranged hand signals, he set the rest of his men in the brush on the steepest side of the path. Satisfied with their concealment, James abandoned his hiding and walked casually down the path toward the sounds of clanging breastplates and pikes.

Clifford, riding at the head of the knights, kept his attention locked on the high ridges overhead. Behind him, two hundred infantrymen marched warily, two abreast. The English officer rode several more paces down the path before discovering a bearded man in buckskins standing with his fists set on his waist. He cantered closer—and lurched forward from sudden recognition.

James retreated in a slow run back up the glen.

Clifford dug in his spurs and charged. "A hundred pounds to the man who takes Douglas alive!"

The single line of mounted English knights imploded in a greed-fueled rush to fight for advantage on the narrow path. Pinned by the loch on one side and the wooded rise on the other, several drove their mounts into the water in search of a shortcut.

Luring them closer, James ran along the banks while looking over his shoulder. Clifford was gaining on him. He counted off the seconds to estimate how many more English had passed the position of his hidden men. When Clifford came within a lance's throw of him, he darted off into the thicket.

"Don't let him escape!" Clifford shouted. "Leave the horses!"

Screams rang out from the rear of the English column.

Clifford spun in his saddle.

The Trinity lads were ambushing his stragglers and slicing the throats of those who could not move forward. Thwarted from going to their rescue by the mash of his own column, the officer had no choice but to drive deeper into the glen. A rumbling shook the ridge above him—felled trees and boulders came crashing down the slope. He and his English knights leapt from their horses and dived into the loch to avoid the avalanche.

From behind the trees, James jumped out and flogged the abandoned horses up the path toward their Scot camp while the Trinity lads hacked away at the rear echelon of the trapped foot levies. Satisfied at last that enough carnage had been inflicted, he blew his horn to signal the retreat. After his men disappeared up the ridge, he captured a horse and rode headlong toward Clifford, who was thrashing the water in a frantic effort to discard his slogged armour.

On the far side of the loch, Pembroke and his two thousand infantry could only stand by and watch as Clifford's mangled force retreated in a panic. Suddenly, sounds of thunder shook the wooded scarp above Pembroke.

"Get out!" Clifford shouted at him from across the loch.

The English earl looked up and saw boulders hurling down the ridge. Edward Bruce and his men rushed from their hiding behind the high trees and came charging down the embankment at Pembroke's troops.

On the near side of the loch, James drove his stolen horse into the water and fought off the English infantry who came swimming into his path. He reared the animal in an effort to stomp on Clifford. "Where is she?"

Clifford stole a sword from one of his drowning knights and slashed at the attacking horse's forelegs. James leapt from the saddle to finish his old rival, but the survivors of the decimated English infantry turned from their retreat and closed in on him, itching to claim their bounty.

"Come on!" Clifford taunted him. "I'll take you to her!"

James pulled his ax from behind his back. He heaved the death stroke—but his collar was captured from the rear, causing his swipe to miss Clifford's jaw.

The Unholy Ghost was dragging James to the safety of the woods.

A month after their ambush of the English army at Glen Trool, James stood with Robert atop Loudon Hill and surveyed the pog that had been used as a fort by the ancient Dalradian kings many centuries ago. Around them lay hundreds of dead English conscripts, cut down during their second improbable victory over Clifford and Pembroke.

Amid the stench of second-day blood, spring rhododendrons had exploded in purple all over the Galloway valley, auguring a new season in Robert's fortunes. In the eleven months since their invasion from Arran, his destitute band of refugees had driven the English back across the border to Carlisle. The Culdee monks in the North were now spreading news of the miracle and reminding the clans of Merlin's ancient prophesy: Upon the death of Le Roy Coveytous, a new king of the Celts would unite Wales and Scotland and win a peace that would last until the end of the world. As a result, nearly two thousand more volunteers had poured south to join the insurrection.

Despite these remarkable successes, Robert remained sullen and down in the mouth. Stirling, Berwick, Edinburgh, and Inverness were still in English hands, and Clifford continued to prosecute his reign of terror in the Borders. Their small invasion force had merely turned back the vanguard of the English onslaught. "We've gained success too soon," he warned James. "We should have waited until Longshanks was dead. Now he'll come at us again with every-thing, and soon."

James never failed to be amazed by his insistence on seeing good fortune as a dire portent. "Then let's go at him first."

"Still you clutch to that fantasy of invading England?"

"It would gain us time to bring in a harvest. Lanark and Annandale are burned out. Why not let the burghers of Carlisle and York suffer the privations for a season?"

Robert gazed south toward the Solway Firth coast, where St. Ninian had first stepped foot on Scotland to live as a hermit in a seaside cave. "I can't win this war with the Comyns biting at my rear from Mar and Fife. So long as they persist in their claim for the throne, half the country will refuse to join me. I must bring the Comyns to heel before I challenge Longshanks."

"You mean to abandon all we've gained down here?"

"I cannot fathom going north without you, but you've given me more than any friend could ask. Take as many men as you need and go save your lady. Her return would do more for the morale of our people than a dozen victories. Perhaps if you cause enough mischief in the Borders, Longshanks will be less inclined to send reinforcements to the Comyns."

James brightened at the prospect of finally attempting Belle's long-delayed rescue. "Give me Sweenie and the Trinity lads. I'll recruit the rest in Lanarkshire. But you must promise me one thing."

"Name it."

"You'll not let Tabhann Comyn meet his end until I return to join you. He's mine for the gutting."

Robert grasped James's hand to seal the vow. "Be careful, Jamie. Clifford will have his spies out."

"And soon enough, I'll have mine."

James hurried down the crag, eager to return to Douglasdale and see what remained of his home. Stopping, he clambered back up the hill and held out his palm at Robert in a demand.

With a guilty shrug that was becoming all too familiar, Robert reached under his hauberk and tossed over the purloined *Chanson of Fierabras*.

TWENTY-FOUR

Summoned back to Carlisle to answer charges of incompetence for their defeat in the Galloway campaign, Clifford and Pembroke stood with what remained of their army on the tourney field below the castle and watched as a crane lowered a set of armour onto a white Arabian whose livery had been rigged with four wooden flanges. Loaded with its burden, the steed was led by a squire toward the waiting troops. Walking behind it came a procession that included Caernervon, Gloucester, the Dominican Lagny, and a host of physicians and court minions. Every few paces, the saddled armour wavered and threatened to fall, requiring attendants to rush forward and set it aright. When this faltering entourage at last reached the field, Gloucester removed the helmet from the stooped torso that sat astride the horse.

A gasp swept across the waiting ranks.

Longshanks, completely bald and so pale that he appeared embalmed, accepted a vial from the royal surgeon. He struggled to bring its greenish liquid to his lips and managed to swallow a third of the contents before spilling the rest down his chest. He spat out the medicinal, convulsing with painful coughs, and gagged, "What is this wretched poison?"

"Amber and jacinth, liege," his physician said. "Marinated in silver."

Unsteady on the skittish mount, Longshanks bent over and lifted his bony buttocks, fouling the air with a loud fart. "If I have to drink all the silver in my treasury, I may as well shit out what remains of it!" He glared at Clifford and Pembroke. "That is what my officers do!"

The king thrashed and cursed, struggling but unable to raise his forehead from the pommel. At Gloucester's command, the royal retainers attached cords to the back of the king's breastplate and levered him aloft like a tent pole. When upright again, Longshanks became transfixed on the barren Cumberland horizon spread out before him to the north. He slapped at his thigh in a frenetic attempt to find his absent sword. "Hold the cavalry! Gloucester! Where are my archers?"

Alarmed by the king's worsening dementia, Gloucester signaled for the standard bearers to raise their heralds, hoping the sight would revive the old man's memory. "My lord, these are our troops. You called them back for an inquest."

"Bring the Scot traitor to me! Where is Bruce?"

Clifford saw Pembroke glaring at him from across the ranks, refusing to make the first move. Being inferior to the earl in rank, he knew that delay would only bring more ire down upon him, so he reluctantly stepped forward. "Sire, we don't have the Bruce."

"Where is he?"

"We do not know, Your Grace."

That admission jolted the king to a chilling lucidity. "He always seems to know where *you* are!"

Clifford bowed, hoping to deflect the king's glare of recrimination. "Bruce and Douglas now fight like common bandits. They crawl upon us at night and burn all that stands in their wake, even their own castles and fields."

Restricted by his armour, Longshanks turned to and fro in a frantic effort to locate Gloucester, who was standing only a few paces away. The king kicked at his horse to make the angling maneuver for him, and finally he found the target of his wrath. "Gloucester! Cursed traitor! This is your knavery! You protect your kinsman!"

Gloucester seethed, burned by the haughty smirks of Caernervon and the other court lackeys. "More than once I have placed my life in harm's way for the sake of the Realm. And still Your Highness questions my loyalty?"

Caernervon seized the opportunity to stir his father's bile against the baron who had supported Gaveston's banishment from England. "Is it not odd, father, that Lord Gloucester has not once requested permission to take the field against his cousin? As I recall, he also advised leniency for that Scot woman at Berwick."

Longshanks growled and drooled as he punished the flanks of his faithful mount with his mailed fist. The aged warhorse, which had survived campaigns from Wales to France, fell into a hesitant trot. The attendants tried to halt the confused animal, but the king, convinced that he was being rushed upon in battle, drove them back with blows to their heads.

Gloucester captured the king's reins. "Sire, where are you going?"

"If these fools cannot defeat Bruce, I will do it myself!" Longshanks cudgeled the earl from his path and rode roughshod through the flustered soldiers, who did not know whether to fall out or risk being trampled.

As the king trotted past them, the men cast their gazes down, saddened by the pitiful deterioration of their once-feared warlord. He had launched his impromptu invasion not on the main route that skirted east of the Solway Firth toward Dumfries, but down a sheep trail that snaked through the rolling gorse fields and led to the Irish Sea. Of those present, only Caernervon was of sufficient stature to countermand his father's confusion, but he chose to let the spectacle proceed for his own amusement.

After several minutes of this idle riding across the moorland, Longshanks halted and slumped over his saddle. He tried to speak, but his quivering lips could only dribble saliva.

Gloucester hurried to him. "Sire, you must rest."

"Camp," Longshanks managed to mutter.

Gloucester could not be certain if he had heard the king correctly. These marshlands around him were so slogged from the recent rains that the horses were in danger of sinking to their forelegs. There was not a dry patch to set grappling irons for the tents. Fatigued, the troops crumpled to their haunches in the muck, some even falling asleep. The baron looked to Caernervon for assistance in the matter, but when the prince refused to dissuade his father from the decision to set camp, Gloucester could only shrug with disgust and motion the wagon masters to unload the provisions and luggage.

While the royal shelter was being raised, Longshanks sat in the saddle gazing at the dunes with a bewildered look. The recession of the afternoon's tides had revealed a broad beach crowned by scruffy bluffs and pimpled with a few abandoned huts. "What is the name of this place?"

"Burgh On The Sand, Sire," Gloucester said.

Longshanks stared at the village as if it should hold a place in his failing memory. Suddenly, his eyes bulged and he stiffened in terror. *Burgh upon the sand.* Hadn't that Scot witch prophesied he would die at such a place? He tried to rein to a retreat, but his legs cramped with spasms and his feet slid through his stirrups. "No! No! Jerusalem! It must be Jerusalem!"

Spooked by his shout, the horse shot off into a wild run.

The soldiers finally corralled the charger and released the jangled monarch from his saddle's restraints. Six attendants were required to carry him to a litter that had been raised off the wet ground by poles. Gloucester and the physicians surrounded him and tried to make sense of his incoherent screams.

The Dominican Lagny ordered all but Caernervon from the king's presence. "I must take his confession and perform the last rites."

Informed that his death was imminent, Longshanks lapsed into a spell of shaking so violent that his joints locked in an agonizing rigor. "My son!"

The friar daubed penance oil on the king's forehead and leaned to his ear, whispering, "Your Highness, we must insure your soul's salvation."

"Eternal peace!" Longshanks cried. "The sacrament!"

Out of earshot of Gloucester, the inquisitor glanced with anticipation at Caernervon as he placed a quill in the king's unsteady hand and whispered, "The Holy Father has issued an edict calling for the trial of all Templars. The last rites cannot be given until you sign the warrant for the arrest of those who hide in England."

Longshanks slapped away the quill. "Scheming Frenchman! You'll not steal my kingdom for Philip!"

The inquisitor held back the unction oil in an act of extortion. "Those who aid the Temple are condemned to Hell's fires."

Longshanks thrashed the monk aside and motioned his son closer. "Promise me, damn you! Promise me you'll not squander all I've gained!"

Caernervon grinned at him in a taunt. "I can't hear you, Father."

"I'll plague you from the grave if you fail me on this! Boil my bones! Take them with the army to Scotland. I want to be there when Bruce and Douglas are captured." Swarms of flies attacked the king's striated face under the broiling midday sun, but he could not raise his arm to chase them. He begged his son, "Give me shade."

Caernervon waved his hand back and forth across his father's eyes, merely increasing the heat's torture. "Are you burning, Father? Where you now go, it will be a thousand times hotter."

Longshanks bolted up and captured the prince's throat. "That Scot woman tricked me! Give her no—" He arched in convulsions and fell back.

Caernervon fought to escape the sharp-nailed fingers twisting his collar. Even in death, his father was proving stronger than him.

At last, the prince peeled the rigored hand from his neck and staggered to his feet. He calmed his nerves and composed his disheveled hair while standing over the corpse and, for propriety's sake, acting as if he were whispering a prayer over it. Then, he turned and strode toward the waiting royal entourage with the postured authority that he had practiced for so many years. Arriving in their fretful midst, he nodded with a firm chin and offered his hand to the councilors and barons for the requisite bows of homage.

Gloucester rushed to the king's litter, unable to believe that the old man was truly dead. He lifted Longshanks's limp head, feeling its neck for a pulse. Finding no sign of life, he pressed the king's eyelids closed.

Caernervon came hovering over the earl with a vengeful sneer. "Send word for Lord Gaveston to return from France at once."

Gloucester looked up in protest. "The king had the Gascon banished."

"I am your king now!" Caernervon shouted. Just as abruptly, he turned ominously cold, imitating what he had witnessed his father do on many occasions with great effect. "Lord Gaveston will be joining my court and taking a wife. I should think your daughter might offer a suitable match."

Gloucester signed his breast and muttered, "I pray for England."

The Dominican bent to a knee before Caernervon and pawed for his hand to kiss the ring of King Edward II. "Sire, shall I attend to the funeral?"

Caernervon paused to enjoy the first time he had heard himself addressed in the royal manner. Preening in the moment, he repulsed the monk's fawning hand and walked away. "Throw his bones in the nearest hole, for all I care."

Awakened by the dawn cries of the Berwick fishermen on the Tweed, Belle crawled onto her scabbed knees to offer up her morning prayer to St. Bride. The days were growing longer now, which was both a blessing and a curse. There would be more warmth from the sun, but also more stares and taunts from the curiosity seekers who came from as far away as London and Salisbury to gaze at her like a festival freak. She pulled herself up by the prongs of the cage, which hung from a high beam and overlooked the river's bend to the west. Her only refuge from the harsh sea wind was an open-sided privy, built in a corner and diabolically designed with a headboard so low that she could not remain inside it long without great discomfort.

She saw the washerwomen and scullions coming down the path from the town to use the pounding stones on the banks. Having vowed never to let them find her in despair, she gathered strength and prepared for the same ritual that she had performed every morning during the eight months of her imprisonment. She coughed to loosen the phlegm from the cold in her lungs and, looking toward Scotland, imagined James galloping across the Lothian meadows to come for her. With the sea gulls cawing in accompaniment, she sang the ballad she had learned as a child:

"Oh the summer time is coming
And the trees are sweetly blooming
And wild mountain thyme
Grows around the purple heather.
Will you go, lassie, go?"

The scrub hags tried to silence her with a volley of rocks, but their attacks only inspired her to sing louder:

"And we'll all go together
To pull wild mountain thyme
All around the purple heather.
Will you go, lassie, go?"

She sank to her knees, faint from even that slight exertion. This time, however, her tormentors did not dissipate as they usually did after her defiant serenades. Instead, the cage rattled and lurched from the impact of another round of missiles. She curled up in the corner, turning her back against the assault. She risked peering over her forearm and saw a black spider on a thread descending toward her nose. She tried to warn it away. "You best go back where you came from, if you know what's good for you." When the spider refused to heed her advice, she smiled. "Aye, you must be a cussed Scot like me. Crossed the river, did you? No English spinner would be caught in here."

Remembering that Idonea Comyn once told her that all of God's creatures carried messages from the spirits, she reached up and ran her finger across the ridged back of the spider. "What are you trying to tell me?"

At that moment, a ray of sun broke through the clouds and illumined three tiny dots of robin-blue on its spine.

The specks, she saw, formed an image that resembled the Douglas herald. She brightened with hope. "Is Jamie alive?"

The spider arched and retracted its legs, as if in confirmation—but a stone whistled through the prongs and sent the spider tumbling. She lunged to save her newfound friend, too late.

"Witch!" screamed a voice from the mob below. "You killed him!"

She crawled to the far side of the cage to find the source of that condemnation. Across the bridge, a procession of English knights led a gurney laden with a coffin wrapped in gold cloth and emblazoned with the heraldry of a red shield and three rearing lions. The lone rider following the cart wore a crown. She squinted, trying to identify him—and her heart leapt with hope. She followed the progress of the procession as it reached the bridge and threaded along the river toward a flotilla of ships anchored in the harbor. Peasants walked behind the casket, sobbing and clamoring to touch it. When the gurney passed under the cage, Caernervon halted his caparisoned horse and looked up at her. She pulled to her feet to demonstrate that her prophecy that day in Lanercost—that she would survive Longshanks—had come to pass.

Caernervon announced to the gathering crowd: "I am compelled by tradition to show mercy to all who look upon my father's body before its burial." He gazed back up at Belle. "Renounce the rebels Bruce and Douglas, woman, and this day I shall set you free."

The mob hushed to hear her answer.

She gripped the bars, fearful that her weakened legs would betray her. At that moment, she saw the spider climbing back to the cage on a thread that dangled from the bottom plank. Tears filled her eyes. Her companion had not been crushed in the fall, after all. A strange lightness suddenly came over her, and she then understood the spider's message: *She was not alone.* Drawing a painful breath, she sang the final stanza of her ballad:

"I will range through the wilds
And the deep land so dreary
and return with the spoils
to the bower o' my dearie
Will ye go lassie go?"

Exhausted, she rested her head against the rails and reached through the prongs to assist the struggling spider to her side.

Caernervon's upper lip quivered as he stared up at her. Could this pig-headed woman not see that he was now king? Within the week, he would marry Isabella in Westminster with the full array of the kingdom's nobility in attendance. He could not let this Highland shrew defy him in front of his new subjects, or it would be the talk of London. He pointed his finger at her in threat and prepared to—

Belle turned away to ignore him.

Humiliated in his public act as monarch, Caernervon could not summon words sufficient to bring the Scotswoman to heel. He sat impotent in the saddle, burned by the judging stares of his subjects. Finally, he cursed to his officers, "God damn that woman! Let her rot up there, then." He spat at her, but the wind drove his spittle back into his face. As the crowds rippled with derisive laughter, the new king angrily wiped his eyes and lashed his horse toward the ships that would carry the remains of his father to Westminster.

The transplanted English inhabitants of Berwick, embittered by what fate had brought them to succeed Longshanks on the throne, gathered up more rocks and renewed their assault on the cage.

Belle hovered over the spider to protect it. When the procession had passed, she risked rising to her feet again, and saw a Latin epigraph inscribed on the rear of the coffin being transported by the gurney:

Edward Primus
Scottorum Malleus
Pactum Serva

She sent the long-legged English devil to his tomb with a scream, "Aye, you were the Hammer! But the Anvil has outlasted you!"

The mourning throngs rushed back at the cage and launched a second volley of stones at her. Amid the debris raining down on the cage floor, she found a small package tied with string. She shielded her discovery from the onslaught and carefully unwrapped it.

A loaf of bread!

She dug her teeth into it and bit upon something hard.

A tiny cross of St. Bride and a rolled slither of parchment fell out. Baffled, she unfolded the ribbon of lambskin and found a message scribbled on it:

An ancient oak at Methven blooms this spring. Keep faith.

Dodging more rocks, she searched the mob for her benefactor, but she saw only angry faces staring up at her. Beyond them, a hundred yards to the south, a hooded woman hurried away along the river's edge.

She studied the note again. The script was embossed with Latin flourishes, evidence that it had been written by a learned cleric. The "T" had been formed using the Saltire of St. Andrew. Below the words in a different ink had been sketched a pair of spurs. She brought the parchment to her nose. *That* rare lavender perfume she would never forget. She had encountered it once before, on the dance floor of Berwick's great hall.

TWENTY-FIVE

In the kitchen of the old Douglas tower, Eleanor Douglas removed a pot from the hearth to silence its boiling so that she could follow the footsteps creaking the ceiling boards above her. On the ramparts, Robert Clifford was inspecting the walls, and with him walked John Webton, an inexperienced Sussex knight appointed castellan, and Thomas Randolph, the former Bruce ally who had been forced to join the English after his capture at Methven.

She could no longer make out faces from afar, but her hearing was still sharp, and she had put that faculty to good use in gathering surveillance. Longshanks's death had proved a mixed blessing for the few villagers who remained in Douglasdale; Caernervon's abandonment of his father's invasion with a new army had allowed them to gather the first full harvest in ten years, but it had also freed Clifford to come north to collect on back rents. She placed her ear near the air vent to overhear Clifford giving orders.

"Take ten men out tomorrow and cut some timbers," the officer told his subordinate, Webton. "I intend to reinforce these foundations."

"My scouts tell me that Bruce and his mossers still lurk in Carrick."

"You needn't worry about Bruce," Clifford assured Webton. "He fled north after that dolt Pembroke was replaced by Richmond in command of the army."

"The king intends to renew the campaign?"

Clifford snorted. "Edward campaigns only to Piers Gaveston's ass. But Bruce will be brought to heel soon enough. The lords will see to that. Until then, we will fortify this keep to use as a bolt hole for scouting raids."

Randolph reminded the two Englishmen, "You've forgotten about James Douglas. You will come to regret the day you hung his woman in that cage."

In the kitchen below, Eleanor, learning of Belle's plight for the first time, stifled a cry of anguish just as Thomas Dickson, her late husband's elderly servant, entered the kitchen to gather plates for breakfast. Wiping tears, she motioned him over to attempt to listen with her, despite his hardness of hearing.

Clifford's laughed off Randolph's warning. "Douglas never leaves Bruce's side. His whore has been languishing in Berwick for over a year. If he intended to launch a raid to save her, he would have attempted it by now."

Eleanor slumped against the wall. Although Robert Bruce had returned to Scotland eleven months ago, her stepson had not come back to Douglasdale, and she had become resigned to the permanency of the occupation. She had not seen her youngest son, Archie, since sending him off nine years ago to be cared for by kinsmen in the North. She looked out through the window toward the valley. How many times had she stood here in despair, thinking about jumping to her death? Below the village, several soldiers from Clifford's garrison were entering St. Bride's kirk to attend Mass. Farther north, across the Leith water, a woman, hooded and cloaked against the harsh wind, drove a herd of scrawny cattle toward a communal pen. Clifford must have seen the cattle, too, because she now heard him comment that a beefsteak would make a fine Sunday repast.

Webton protested that plan. "These people here depend upon the milk."

"I am beginning to question if you have the resolve to serve me."

"I'll fight any man of arms," Webton told Clifford. "But to commit thievery on starving womenfolk and children—"

"Send two men to take that herd at once. I want a flank cut delivered to the kitchen within the hour. And if the wench is comely, bring her along as well. There's nothing more satisfying than a Highland cow, eh Randolph?"

Eleanor whispered a curse on the English officer, as if another malediction added to the previous thousand might tip the balance of God's favor.

I n the great hall, Clifford watched with amusement as the lame Dickson floundered out of the kitchen dragging his bad leg while balancing goblets of wine on a tray. Laughing at his pathetic effort to hurry, Clifford stuck out his boot and sent the feeble servant sprawling across the floor amid spilt wine and shattered glass. "There's a Douglas for you! At home on all fours."

Helpless to halt the abuse, Randolph assisted Dickson to his feet while Cull and Chullan, mangy and half-starved, snarled at Clifford from their tethers. The miserable dogs were approaching the age when most mastiffs broke down and died, and Randolph marveled at how they hung on despite their sporadic feedings, as if fueled by a sheer hatred for Clifford and nothing else.

Clifford taunted the wet noses of the hounds with his cutting knife. "Ale, Scottie!" he demanded of Dickson while hissing at the dogs. "No more of that insufferable French piss water!"

Dickson gathered up the goblet shards. "Aye, my lord. Clumsy, I am."

Eleanor rushed in to see what had caused the commotion.

"Well, woman?" Clifford barked. "I'll not wait all day!"

She pursed her lips in anger, but then quickly retreated into an affectation of submission. "Cooking, my lord. Cooking."

"Make certain the beefsteak cut is generous."

She turned back in confusion. "I've been delivered no meat."

Clifford marred the table with his knife. "You will be, soon enough. And I'd best not find a sliver of the flank missing."

Eleanor returned to the kitchen grumbling curses. The door slammed—and a hand reached from behind to cover her mouth. She struggled to escape, until an old woman in a hood and herder rags pressed a kiss to her cheek. The widow made out the blurred features of three men at the rear entry, with blood dripping from their daggers. She recoiled with fright, and turned back to the strange hag who had invaded her kitchen with the men.

The female intruder shed her outer garments.

Eleanor gasped, her eyes flooding with tears. She reached out for an embrace to confirm that it was really her stepson in the flesh.

James looked over her shoulder and nodded for the Trinity brothers to drag in the side of beef they had just carved from the butchered heifer. He glanced through the window to insure that the English guards had been dispatched and their places taken by two of his raiders. Then, he hung the beef on a ceiling hook and motioned for his stepmother to carve off a cut for Clifford's steak.

Eleanor suddenly realized that James had been the cloaked woman herding the cattle across the vale. His men had stolen upon the castle with the migrating cows, a ruse her husband had often used. She made a move to ask what was happening, but at that moment Dickson limped into the kitchen with his head lowered. The old servant looked up and stiffened as if seeing a ghost.

Before James could muffle his reaction, Dickson dropped the tray in shock.

In the great hall, the loud report from the kitchen drove Clifford to his feet. The officer rushed to the window and gazed down at the bailey. The cow's carcass was draining from a butcher's hoist, and his guards stood at their posts. Still suspicious, Clifford drew his blade and motioned for Webton and Randolph to watch for intruders at the front door. He burst into the kitchen.

Carving on the hanging side of beef, Eleanor turned with a glare of disgust at the intrusion. "Did you expect the steak to jump to the spit on its own?"

Clifford clamped a hand to her throat. "You do rattle on, don't you? That useless stepson of yours suffers from the same malady. Did I ever tell you how I laid him on his bony rump at Berwick?" He shoved her toward the hacking block. "If I'm not fed soon, I may fall into a foul mood." He kicked Dickson as he marched back into the hall.

When the kitchen door slammed shut, James leapt down from his perch on the rafters and drove his fist into the beef slab to vent his anger. He stared at the steak that Eleanor had just cut. Then, struck by a thought, he whispered, "This meat won't do for such a fine English gentleman." He pulled the ax from behind his back and told Dickson, "Tom, keep our guests drinking."

Eleanor and Dickson carried three sizzling steaks into the hall. After serving Webton and Randolph, the widow delivered the largest cut to Clifford. "Rare, my lord. Just as you like it."

Clifford impaled his knife into the steaming strip and took a bite. After several chews, he pointed the blade at Eleanor. "Not bad for a cow raised on Scot shit." He stuffed his mouth with another morsel and studied her with a look of suspicion. "What is this flavoring?"

"Rosemary. Mixed with thyme and cinnamon."

Clifford savored the beefsteak's juices. "By God, this is succulent." He turned to Randolph and Webton. "Does yours have an unusual bite to it?"

Randolph shrugged as he kept his eyes on his plate, his appetite ruined by the loss of the cow for some poor fellow countryman.

In the corner, the mastiffs whined, tortured by the aroma.

Clifford teased the hounds with another slither before stuffing it into his mouth. "What would you know about delicacies, Randolph? I'm telling you, this has a hint of the Continent, maybe Sussex even. My sensibilities are so keen that I can identify the shire where the heifer has grazed." His nostrils flared. "I'll wager a week's pay that this cow was stolen from Yorkshire."

Eleanor asked him, "Will there be anything else, my lord?"

Clifford searched his plate. "Did I not order artichokes with this?"

"Artichokes? You said nothing about—"

Clifford slung the grease in his plate at her. "I'd best be tasting marinated artichokes before I finish!"

Splattered, Eleanor bowed and hurried back to the kitchen with Dickson.

James had been watching the encounter from the cracked door. He wiped the grease from his stepmother's face with a rag and hurried her toward the back entry. "The Trinity lads will take you north."

Eleanor held back. "Your father built this tower, Jamie. Don't let them defile his memory."

Her plea took him by surprise. "I haven't the men to hold it."

She glared at him fiercely. "I don't mean for you to hold it."

Suddenly taking her meaning, James was stunned.

At the rear door, McClurg reappeared. "The English are coming back from the kirk."

James saw that his stepmother was resolved not to leave until he agreed to her request. With a heavy sigh, he ordered McClurg, "Get her to safety. Then draw Clifford out from the tower."

Clifford belched, leaned back, and loosened his belt. "That old hizzie may be blinder than a cross-eyed bat, but she can still work a stove."

Disgusted by the officer's boorishness, Randolph cracked, "I'm surprised you managed to get it down without your artichokes."

Clifford angrily spat out a cud of gristle, reminded of his absent side order. "Damn that dotaged bitch! Where is she with those artichokes?" He clanged a flagon with his knife. "Woman! Get out here!"

Receiving no answer, the officer erupted to his feet and charged into the kitchen. His eyes bulged with a ghastly discovery.

Two of his guards hung from hooks—with the flesh hacked from their ribs. The pot was still boiling over the hearth. Human bones and sinews lay on the butcher's block, and a message had been written in blood on the table:

Bon Appetit, this is only the first course.
James of Douglas

Clifford staggered out into the bailey and vomited. Taking the bait, he rushed to his horse and led his garrison out the gate, hell-bent on gaining the blue Douglas banner that fluttered near the kirk.

Hiding on the ramparts, James hoped the Trinity lads would run Clifford in circles for a few hours. When all was clear, he quietly descended the stairway into the great hall and found his father's herald still hung over the hearth, slashed and pierced with arrows. He ran his hand across the trestle table where the Guardians had held their meetings when he was a boy. A wisp of cold wind creaked open the door, and he was now staring at Wallace's ghost in the shadows.

With honor comes duty, lad.

He walked to a window and stared down at the spot where Clifford had shackled his father on the day he was dragged to London Tower.

A bloodied face looked up at him.

Remember, you are a Douglas. You bend to none but God and your conscience.

His nostrils stung from the putrid smell of camphor lingering from the pomander that Clifford wore on his belt. He had never been able to rid his head of that noxious odor in the Berwick breeze that swung Gibbie to his death.

His stepmother was right. Too many dark memories lingered here now.

He hammered at the table with his ax, until nothing was left but a pile of kindling, and then he removed his clan's herald from the wall. He threw it onto the stack of broken wood and was about to fire the wood when a whimpering came from the darkness. He stalked the pining sound into an antechamber. Gripping his ax, he threw open the door.

Cull and Chullan, too weak to bark, stared up at him with pained eyes. Pocked with scab wounds from Clifford's beatings, the mastiffs struggled from their haunches to greet their old master.

He knelt to cut the hounds loose and brought them into his embrace. He looked around and remembered this room had been the old study, where his father had planned the muster of the army at Berwick. In the corner, on the writing stand, he spied a black lock box. He had never seen that here before. He pried it open with his dagger and found military orders, coins—and a letter perfumed with a nutmeg fragrance. He opened the letter and read:

> *Dearest John,*
>
> *I have not slept a night since your proposal. My father does not look with favor upon our arrangement. He holds you wanting in the qualities essential for a soldier and believes you best suited for the clergy in temperament and resources. I protested this harsh indictment, but he has relented only in degree by agreeing to a probationary period, with a condition that I fear will prove too costly for the reward. I have just learned that, as a test of your fortitude, he has arranged for you to serve under Robert Clifford, a man whose reputation here is less than honorable. The assignment is to hold a certain keep in the Scot borders for one year. If you succeed in that task, my father has promised to grant his permission for our marriage. My confidantes in the court warn that this is tantamount to a denial at best and a death sentence at worst. The tower was captured from a Scotsman named Douglas who, by all accounts, is a savage bent on bloody revenge. I beg you not to accept this challenge, for I would sooner have you alive in another's arms than dead because of me.*
>
> *Yours in love, Rosylann*

James stared at the letter, astonished that his Galloway raids had spawned such a reputation for him all the way to—

The zing of a blade startled him.

He turned to find an English knight standing at the door. He cursed his failure to check the courtyard again. When the intruder did not make a move to attack, he warned him, "You are in my home."

The Englishman only then identified the Scotsman he now confronted. He tried to maintain a defiant stance, but his trembling hand betrayed his fear. "It may be your home, but it has been put in my charge." He saw the letter in James's hand. "Is it your practice to plunder private correspondence?"

James reread the name "Webton" on the address. "I do when the recipient serves a king who seeks to destroy my country."

Webton glanced toward the window, but saw no sign of Clifford returning. Ashen-faced, he admitted, "I have no hope of taking you, but I must try."

James kept the man in the corner of his eye while he studied the signature on the letter. "Tell me of your lass."

Webton blinked with affront. "What is that to you?"

"She claims to know me. Enough, at least, to slander me."

Webton was denied in his attempt to retrieve the letter. "She is the Earl of Sussex's daughter. That is more than you are entitled to know."

James paced the room, watching for a threatening lunge. "How long?"

"Until what?"

"Your year is attained."

Humiliated, Webton cast his eyes down. "On the morrow."

James dragged up a chair, causing the skittish officer to flinch from the screech of its legs. He sat at the writing table. Gripping his ax with his left hand, he dipped a quill into the inkstand while keeping Webton in his periphery. When he had finished writing on the back of the letter, he refolded it and kicked another chair toward his opponent.

Bewildered, Webton asked him, "Am I your prisoner?"

"Sit with me awhile."

Webton warily took the chair across the table.

They sat together in tense silence while James watched the window for Clifford's return. As the minutes passed, every happy moment that he had spent in this tower came back to him. The first time he had laid eyes on Belle in the vale below, she had lifted him to his feet and had spurred him on during the race. Would he have won this ax if not for her help? Would she be suffering in that cage now if he had not stalked her along that burn out there? A man caught in this cracked world, it seemed, was nothing but a stone tumbling down a glen, striking others in its path until all were cast into the abyss. Once lost, a stone never returns to the top of the mountain.

Were the best times of his life now behind him?

At midnight, the bells of St. Bride's kirk rang out from the village in the vale. James stood and, without offering a word of his intention, walked into the great hall. He retrieved a torch from the wall sconce and threw it on the pile of smashed furniture. The panels quickly erupted in flames. When the fire was sufficiently seeded, he retreated down the staircase, too overcome to look back.

Webton followed him out to the bailey, uncertain what was happening.

James mounted the Englishman's horse. "In return for your life, will you grant me a small favor?"

Webton hesitated, suspicious. "I'll not betray my oath to my king."

James handed him his lady's letter. "See to it that this is sent to London." Followed by the two mastiffs, he rode off before the Englishman could protest the unseemly arrangement.

Left alone inside the castle, Webton opened the letter and read what James had written on its reverse side:

> To the Earl of Sussex,
>
> On this day, Sir John Webton subdued me in a contest of arms and held me prisoner in the defense of Castle Douglas. In compliance with his command, I have rendered this account of the incident. I beseeched him not to fire the tower, but he chose to destroy it rather than leave it to the capture of my men, as would I have done had the circumstances been reversed. My only solace in this unhappy affair is the knowledge that England sends incompetent men such as Robert Clifford to command their armies instead of stalwart officers such as Lord Webton.
>
> > James of Douglas

A hundred miles east of Douglasdale, the citizens of Berwick crowded along the banks of the Tweed to witness the unthinkable scene. In the river's swirling currents, their new king swam naked and cavorted with Piers Gaveston, who only a week earlier had rushed across the Channel from Brittany. For the two men to indulge their passion for swimming in private was scandalous enough; skill in floating, after all, was a vice inspired by the Devil. But to engage in such behavior under the very public gaze of the Dominican inquisitor Lagny could only be explained as the wanton fruit of sinful pride.

On the Northumbrian side of the river, the most powerful earl in England, Thomas Lancaster, sat mounted in ceremonial garb, accompanied by a hundred knights. He had been forced to wait for more than an hour, a snub that even the lowliest peasant understood. The last of the high lords to recognize Caernervon's succession had finally come north to give homage, a condition for reclaiming his forfeited lands of Lincoln, Salisbury, and Leicester. Yet Lancaster refused to be brought completely prostrate. As the leader of those barons who had schemed to weaken the monarchy, he drew the line at bending knee on ground stolen by the Plantagenets with illegal royal levies. For this reason, the earl would not cross into once-Scottish Berwick, and instead had insisted that Caernervon travel the paltry distance of the river's breadth to meet him.

In the river, Gaveston, who had convinced the king to make Lancaster wait in penance for his initial recalcitrance, splashed playfully and pulled his royal lover's feet underwater to steal a kiss.

Edward surfaced in a panic. "Have you taken leave of your wits?" He looked toward the horizon to see if Lancaster had witnessed the indiscretion. "I should never have allowed you to talk me into this."

Gaveston whipped his long black hair behind his head and waved contemptuously at the haughty baron he so despised. "Black Dog of Arden!" he screamed at the morose-tempered Lancaster. "Your king commands you to bark!"

Edward saw Lancaster staring down his long nose at them, pecking and bobbing like a snorting basilisk. "Look at him! He gives me the Evil Eye!"

Gaveston loved to mimic the earl's quirky mannerism; this enraged reaction was precisely what he had hoped to elicit with his taunts. He shouted even louder so that all of Lancaster's courtiers could hear. "I'm looking forward to our next tournament! How many months has it been since I wiped Nottingham field with your hairy ass?"

"Don't stir his bile!" Edward begged. "I must deal with him on the treasury."

Gaveston flipped onto his back in imitation of Lancaster's fall during their last jousting match. "What can he do to you?"

"He conspires with Gloucester and Warwick to force the ordinances on me!"

"What ordinances?"

Caernervon swam farther down river, hoping to escape Lancaster's spiteful gaze. "The barons are scheming to take control of my purse."

"Cretins!" Gaveston shouted. "Blood-sucking beasts!"

"Piers ... do you truly believe I am king?"

Gaveston swam closer to embrace him. "Not that again."

"The rumors persist that I am not my father's son."

"Lancaster pays his men to spread those lies."

"They all find me repugnant. The commoners won't even touch me for the scrofula cure. I am told the monks at Canterbury have discovered precious oil in the crypts there. The Virgin appeared to Becket and offered it to him to be used for miracles. I have petitioned the Holy Father to allow me to be consecrated again with the oil. Perhaps then the people will accept me."

"That papist puppet in Avignon will demand a pretty compensation for that crock of magic piss," Gaveston predicted. "Clement favors France in the present diplomacy."

Beset by a host of worries, Caernervon climbed to the bank and retrieved his robe. Drying himself, he looked toward the tower in the distance where Belle's cage swayed in the wind. "That witch is the cause of my misfortune! She cursed my father! Now she has blackened me! I should send her to the stake!"

Gaveston climbed out of the river and waved off that idea. "Death would only strengthen her powers."

Caernervon pulled at his own hair, powerless to enhance his standing with both the commoners and the lords, "To the Devil's dungeon with them all!"

Gaveston rested against a tree and watched a line of wood mites march from a rotten root toward the river. When Caernervon came closer to see what had caught his attention, the Gascon drew a circle that intersected the path of the mites. To Caernervon's astonishment, the insects inside the circle refused to cross the imaginary border. Gaveston enjoyed the king's reaction to the magic and, with an evil smile, directed his lover's gaze toward Berwick tower. "If that Scotswoman truly is a witch, perhaps you should learn from her and adopt the methods she used to bring down your father."

"You mean ... " Caernervon turned a glance of alarm toward the inquisitor conferring with Lancaster beyond the river. "Conspire with demons?"

Gaveston gathered two flat stones and a burnt twig at the river's edge. On one stone, he sketched a caricature of Lancaster, and on the other he drew the image of an ax. Mumbling an incantation, he smashed the stones together and looked toward Lancaster. "He'll meet the edge of a blade soon enough."

Caernervon was stunned. "You've learned to cast the glamour?"

"My mother taught me the art when I was a lad." Gaveston became uncharacteristically solemn, darkened by the memory. "She was an Albigensee. The Dominicans"—he shot a sneer at the observant inquisitor—"forced me to stand at the pyre and watch her burn."

"What other sorcery do you know?"

Gaveston led the king away from the banks and to a wooded spot near a bend in the river. There they knelt together on a smooth boulder above a still pool. The Gascon stared at the water for nearly a minute. Suddenly, he pointed at the king's reflection. "Keep your eyes on your spirit!"

Caernervon meditated on his image floating in the water. After several moments of his intense concentration, his face faded from sight. He erupted to his feet, blinking, astonished by the magic. "I've disappeared!"

Gaveston chose not to reveal to the gullible king that one's eyes lose their focus after staring on an object too long. "The angels have erased your past. You are free to create your future. Scry the mirror of the world for what you wish."

Caernervon whispered aloud his heart's desires. "Lancaster ascends the scaffold. Warwick and Gloucester follow him. I see us together always in London court. But how can that be?"

"What prevents it?"

"That damnable French she-cur that my father forced on me as queen. She will accuse me of avoiding her bed to provoke Parliament to humiliate me."

Gaveston stared at the currents for so long that Caernervon feared he had fallen into a trance. Suddenly, the Gascon grasped his lover's head to aim his gaze. "Do you not see it?"

Caernervon frantically searched the water. "See what?"

"Isabella is on a ship to France. Look! She holds a document and is crying."

"A divorce! I am to have a divorce! But how?"

Gaveston cocked his ear to better hear the spirits speak to him. "You must petition the Holy Father."

"But Clement is under Philip's thrall. What could I possibly offer the Church for release from my vows?"

Closing his eyes, Gaveston reached a hand into the swirling water and pulled out a reddish stone shaped like a splayed cross. "It must be a sign."

Caernervon caressed the stone as if it were a precious relic. "The Templars."

"That's it! They are telling you to arrest the scheming monks!"

"But the Temple has always supported our cause."

Gaveston stroked the king's chest. "Philip has confiscated their commanderies in France. If the French king is also allowed to gain the monies in the London Temple, he will strengthen his armies, and you will suffer an odious defeat. Do you not see the divine answer? This solves all of your problems. The Holy Father will look kindly upon your petition for divorce. The Temple's funds will free you from domination by the barons. And we shall forever be together, without the shadowing presence of that Frenchwoman."

Caressing the stone, Caernervon suddenly made up his mind. "Yes, send the order to London."

Gaveston rewarded him with a kiss. But then, the Gascon turned away, his eyes hooded in sadness.

Overjoyed at the prospects of finally being rid of Isabella, Caernervon could not understand why Gaveston had suddenly become downcast. "Tell me, Poppie. What is wrong?"

Gaveston choked back tears. "Lancaster and the other lords despise me so. I can no longer bear their shaming. Mayhaps they *are* right. I am not worthy to be with you."

"I am king! And I say who is worthy and who is not!"

Gaveston stifled sobs. "If only I were equal to them in rank. I wish they could not treat me so basely."

The king grasped him by the shoulders. "I was waiting to tell you this eve when we supped. I have decided to name you Earl of Cornwall!"

Ecstatic, Gaveston embraced the king. As they hugged, the Gascon looked across the river and, making certain that Edward did not see his gesture, nodded furtively to the inquisitor Lagny on the far bank.

TWENTY-SIX

The surly stares of former comrades accosted Thomas Randolph as he galloped into the northern Bruce encampment below Inverurie. After being captured during the Methven ambush two years ago, he had been forced by the English to choose between execution and swearing allegiance to the Plantagenet. Yet none of these Scots now surrounding him were moved by his plight, for most still mourned kinsmen who had accepted death rather than break fealty to the cause of independence. Despite this hostile greeting, he held his head high and insisted, "I must speak with the king."

Edward Bruce dragged his nephew from the horse. "Say your piece to me."

"I gave an oath. I must present myself to your brother."

"An oath to whom?"

"Jamie Douglas. He captured me in Lanarkshire. As a condition for my release, he ordered me to come north and accept the king's judgment."

The men gathered around Randolph, heartened to hear that James was not only alive but thriving well enough to take prisoners.

Neil Campbell asked him, "How goes it for Douglas?"

"By the looks of it, better than it goes for you," Randolph said. "He harries Lanark at will. He even burned down his own home rather than let Clifford to use it for raids."

Campbell was shocked. "He left Castle Douglas in ruins?"

"Aye, and that's the least of his mischief. He fed Clifford the flesh of his own guards. Cooked it up himself in his own stepmother's kitchen."

The men whistled at the first good news heard from the South in months.

Lennox shouted over them, "I hope he sent a tasty sampling from the Douglas Larder to Caernervon! By God, our Jamie's making a name for himself!"

"A name cursed on every crossroads from Yorkshire to Bristol," Randolph added. "The English are now calling him the Black Douglas."

Boyd slammed a fist into his palm in delight. "Did you hear that, lads? The Black Douglas! We could use some of Jamie's black art up here, eh!"

In the midst of this celebration that seemed fueled by desperation, Randolph saw that Edward Bruce, alone of all the men, was not buoyed by the report of Douglas's success. The hotheaded Edward had never hid his suspicion that Douglas was scheming to carve out his own kingdom in the South.

Pulled away from the others, Randolph listened with growing alarm as Edward described the calamity that had just befallen this army. At the height of their assault on the Comyn stronghold of Invurerie, Robert had been struck down by a mysterious illness that locked his limbs in a catatonic trembling. The sight of him being carried frothing and unconscious from the field had so unnerved the volunteers that Edward had been forced to lift the two-week siege. The Comyns, whose defenses were only hours from collapse, had been gifted with a miraculous reprieve.

Yet what Randolph heard next stunned him even more. Many of the men, Edward admitted, blamed this reversal on divine retribution for Robert's failure to honor his promise to hold off on the Comyns until Douglas could come north and join the attack. All Scots knew that Douglas had a score to settle with Tabhann. The Bruces had been freed to cut a swath of vengeance through the western Highlands only because Douglas had kept Clifford pinned down in the Borders. During these past months, Robert had marched his army over the snow-capped peaks of the Great Glen and had captured John of Lorne, the MacDougall chieftain who had handed over their brothers for execution, and the Earl of Ross, the traitor who had sold out the women at Tain to the English. The last obstacle to Robert's consolidation of Fife and Buchan now stood behind those walls in the distance. If the Bruces could take Inverurie, they would at last be free to march south and confront the English.

Randolph challenged Edward to explain his actions. "You convinced the king to attack? Without first sending word to the Borders?"

Edward glanced worriedly at Robert, who lay writhing near a fire, blind and paralyzed and with pus-weeping blotches inflaming his skin. "I feared delay would allow the Comyns to escape. Those whoresons sent David Brechin into our camp this morning to offer terms for our surrender. I agreed to the meeting only in the hope that it would quash the rumors of my brother's death."

"And?"

"Rob could not form a coherent word."

"Then the Comyns will attack on the morrow, for certain."

Edward shrugged like a man resigned to the gallows. "We will fight to the death rather than relinquish the crown."

Randolph shook his head, dismayed at discovering that he had ridden hundreds of miles north to escape execution, only to be penned in with a disgruntled army whose demise appeared imminent.

"Jamie!" came a cry from the far side of the encampment.

The men turned toward Robert, who lay shivering under a cloak near a fire. "Bring Jamie to me!"

They were stunned to hear the first words from his mouth in three days.

Relieved to see his brother conscious, Edward prodded Randolph forward, determined to disabuse Robert of the mistaken identity and have him mete out severe punishment for their nephew's treason.

Soaked in fever sweat, Robert looked up at Randolph with tears of delirious joy. "I knew you'd come!" He crawled closer and reached out. "Forgive me, Jamie! I had to attack! There was no time to lose!"

Randolph was shocked by the king's ghastly appearance. "My lord ..."

Robert clawed for Randolph's hand. "God has answered my prayers. Tell me of the Marches, Jamie! No, you must sleep first! On the morrow we renew the siege."

Edward had never noticed the striking resemblance between Randolph and Douglas. Indeed, they were the same height, and could even pass for brothers. Signaling to the other men for silence, he whisked Randolph away before Robert could come to his senses. "Rob, get your rest," he told his brother as he hurried off. "Douglas and I will make plans for the assault."

Levering to his elbows, Robert searched the camp to count how many were still with him. "Jamie, you'll lead the left flank! We'll give them Loudon Hill again! To see the look on Comyn's face when he finds you at my side!" He fell back to a fitful sleep as his voice trailed off.

Edward summoned a monk warming his hands over a fire and told him to bring his needle and thread. He led the two men to the edge of the camp, out of earshot of the others. Sizing up his prisoner's face, he smeared a dollop of boot black on his palms and whispered to Randolph, "Do as I say, and you may yet save your neck from the block."

Inside the defended city of Inverurie, David Brechin returned from his parlay with the Bruces and found the Comyn cousins pacing the allures while studying the distant fires of the royal encampment. "Bruce has one foot in the grave," Brechin assured them. "A fever has curdled his mind to mush. I give him no more than a day."

Tabhann tempered his elation. He had seen Robert falter on the field with his own eyes, but his old nemesis had overcome so many legendary hardships and near deaths that he found it difficult to believe that fate could turn so capriciously. "You are certain of this?"

"I could smell the death rot on his breath."

Cam was hot to attack. "We should strike before Douglas arrives."

"Edward Bruce leads in the king's stead," Tabhann reminded them.

Cam grinned. "And he'll come bulling right into our slaughter pen."

At dawn's first light, Tabhann and Cam led their three thousand men from Inverurie and into the open pastures below Meldrum. Certain of victory, they took their time forming up ranks and parading across the lines, promising booty and titles when the throne was filled with a Comyn. Their troops fell silent on seeing the Bruce ranks emerge from the far grove.

Tabhann rode into the gap between the two armies to confront Edward Bruce. "Give up the crown, Bruce, and your men will be spared!"

"The crown lies where it belongs."

Tabhann laughed. "You didn't bury it with your brother's corpse, I hope. Are we going to have to dig him up?"

A helmeted knight wearing a gold band and brandishing the royal herald rode forth from behind the Bruce line. He called out through the air slits of his faceplate to Tabhann, "Come take it!"

Tabhann cantered closer, determined to expose the trickery. "If that's the Bruce, then I am the queen of England!"

The approaching knight halted and removed his helmet. "I am certain Caernervon will gladly make room for you in his bed."

Robert sat in the saddle.

Tabhann stared gape-jawed at his old nemesis; then, he turned a punishing scowl on Brechin for the erroneous report about Robert's health. Still, he was confident. Edward had managed to hoist his brother onto a horse, but clearly Robert, swaying and groggy, could do no more than watch his ragged army be annihilated. He decided to call their bluff on this desperate ploy to make the royal troops believe that their king was in fighting condition. "Why should we force Scots to kill Scots, Bruce? Let us settle this between us in single combat!"

Robert fought against his debilitating vertigo to remain upright. "As Brechin no doubt advised you, I am recovering from the ague. I shall offer you my second, as the code allows."

Another knight on a black stallion split the tree line. In full armor, this second, unidentified rider carried on his lance a pennon featuring a blue field and three silver stars. A gasp of disbelief cascaded across the Comyn ranks—*that* was the Douglas herald.

Tabhann looked back at Cam and Brechin, demanding an explanation for the apparition.

"They are so desperate," Cam scoffed, "they resort to blatant fakery!"

From a hundred yards away, Tabhann saw the knight briefly remove his helmet to adjust his flowing hair. A familiar dark face glared back at him in the faint light before the helmet was returned to its head. His mannerisms were those of Douglas, for certain: The askew way he sat in the saddle, the high grip on the reins, the haughty arch of the head. But how could Douglas have made it this far north so quickly? When the knight cantered across the lines and motioned for a challenger, Tabhann ordered up his most accomplished mercenary, Robert Bingham, a brutish malcontent from Northumbria. "Kill that man," Tabhann told the English cutthroat, "and this land you now ride on is yours."

Both armies backed off to allow a clear field for the single combat.

Without the usual ceremony and mutual signal of attack, Bingham lashed his steed toward his opponent, who sat waiting without a flicker of motion. Nearing the collision, the Bruce champion spun his horse in a deft maneuver to avoid being impaled. He whipped an ax from behind his back and hammered Bingham with a stroke to the crease between his shoulders and neck. The Northumbrian mercenary hurled to the ground and thudded in a cloud of dust.

Blood oozed from the vents of Bingham's writhing helmet.

Tabhann reined back—he had witnessed *that* death stroke before.

The ax-wielding champion came riding up aside Robert, and together they led their ranks forward. A hundred paces from their lines giving battle, Tabhann and Cam turned tail and galloped south.

Abandoned, the Comyn troops broke into a disorganized retreat.

Five hours later, the victorious royal army escorted Robert through the deserted streets of Inverurie. Reaching the tower, the king slumped over his saddle in exhaustion. Edward Bruce and his officers untied the tethers that had been used to strap Robert upright to the hidden flange and lifted him from the restraints. They carried the king into the hall and placed him on a blanket that had been set out near a warming fire.

"Jamie!" Robert muttered, half-conscious. "Bring Jamie to me!"

The men were uncertain how to respond. Reluctantly, Edward motioned his brother's champion that day to the bed. The knight who wore the Douglas insignia on his breastplate removed his helmet.

Randolph, not James, knelt at Robert's side.

This time, Robert was not fooled. He burned his nephew with a wrathful glare. "Traitor! You fought with Comyn this day?"

"No, my lord," Randolph said. "With you."

Robert searched the faces around him, fearing that the illness was still twisting his mind.

Edward finally admitted, "Douglas remains in the South. He sent Randolph north to you as a prisoner. Our kinsman agreed to disguise himself as Douglas during the battle."

Robert took a closer look at Randolph, and sank in sharp disappointment. The victory established his dominion over the northern shires, but his betrayal of James had taken a heavy a toll on him in guilt. He had miraculously recovered his strength only because he thought all had been made right between them. Now he dreaded even more the hour he would have to explain his shameful action to his wronged friend. He stared at Randolph for several tense moments. Perhaps, he prayed, forgiveness would beget forgiveness. "I have wronged Jamie, as you have wronged me. Join me, nephew, and all is forgotten."

The men cheered the offer of leniency.

Yet Randolph remained unrepentant. "I performed this service to repay Douglas's kindness. I made a grave error in judgment by submitting to the English. For that, I will live forever with the shame. But I shall not do penance for one malfeasance by committing another."

Edward spun Randolph by the shoulders to confront him. "Have you lost your senses? The king has just offered you your life."

Randolph rebuffed the crass bargain with a contemptuous jaw. "The English are duplicitous, but you Bruces have refined the vice to a fine art. You refuse to fight honorably, and you speak oaths too easily. Douglas and his lady put the crown on your head, my lord. You chose personal glory over the duty of *a man* friendship."

Robert struggled to his feet. "I should have you strung up!"

"Aye, if by the continuance of terror you would enforce your rule."

Robert stumbled, wincing from the ache in his ribs. The men rushed to brace him, but he pushed them aside. He commanded a rope and with trembling hands noosed Randolph's neck. "You accuse me of waging this war by base means. Do you know who fathered that strategy?"

Randolph, glancing at the beam above him, shook his head.

"Our mutual friend for whom you have such high esteem." Robert waited for his nephew to break. Finding him still defiant, he nodded in a grudging admiration for his principles and removed the noose from around his neck. "You resemble Jamie in more than just features. You'll stay with me, Thomas. Fight or not, that is your choice. But I'll not give you the satisfaction of taking leave of this cracked world before I do."

TWENTY-SEVEN

ames crawled out from his leafy lair in the outskirts of Ettrick Forest and listened for the rustling of Clifford's patrols. Finding the wilderness trail near Jedburgh deserted, he signaled for his three hundred raiders to join him in the clearing. Pale from weeks of no sun, the men emerged from the cover of the foliage and sprawled along a high ridge south of the Tweed River, taking advantage of the rare opportunity to bask under the warm spring rays.

As they lounged, James walked among his small band, checking on the condition of their feet and weapons. He had driven them hard during these three years since the Douglas Larder raid, but their punishing sorties against the occupied Borders burghs had prevented the English from sending reinforcements against Robert's army in the Highlands. Clifford was always predictable in his retaliation, burning the same Scot castles and abbeys and ordering his officers into this wilderness on a fruitless search for prisoners. Inevitably, Clifford would become overconfident, convincing himself that the Scot raiders had finally fled north, and then he and his Lanark men would then strike again at the occupation garrisons, poisoning their wells and ambushing their supply trains.

Despite these successes, he was growing frustrated with the gadfly role that Robert had assigned him. Berwick remained out of his reach, and he feared Belle would not survive much longer in that miserable cage designed for her humiliation. He had scoured his brain for some way to rescue her, but in the end, he knew an attack on the impregnable port city with such a small force would be suicidal.

While the others caught up on their sleep, he unrolled his tattered pack and took refuge again in the hope that had always kept him from despair: He and Belle with a dozen children in some manor house above a salmon stream. As he daydreamed, he gazed down at this lush valley lined with oaks, and blinked hard. Before him lay the very landscape that had always appeared in his reveries, accurate to the covering groves that would protect against the harsh winter winds. This rock-strewn clearing guarded the ancient Roman way that offered the only route into England for twenty leagues in either direction. The horse path snaked around the hill and descended into a cranny with steep shoulders. No one could cross the border here without passing through this natural gateway; it would make a perfect spot to situate his headquarters and build a home for Belle. Inspired, he rousted Sweenie from his slumber.

"That was an hour?" the monk grumbled.

"What is the name of this place?"

Rubbing his bleary eyes, Sweenie pulled out the sheepskin map that he kept hidden in his sacerdotal. He ran his stumpy forefinger down the angling line demarking the border and stopped at an insignificant "X" that represented a desolate shepherd's pass. "Lintalee."

"Lintalee? What does that name mean?"

"It's Gaelic for the only place in God's kingdom in which I've managed five minutes of sleep since I had the misfortune of encountering you."

"Bless this hill," James told him. "Or do whatever you churchmen need to do to make it mine."

"Make it *yours*?" Sweenie leapt to his feet and stamped his short staff in protest. "What makes you think the Almighty fashioned this landscape for *you*?"

"I was just visited with a holy vision." He captured the little monk by the scruff of his neck and led him down the valley toward the creek. "I'm thinking of building a chapel here, maybe even an abbey." He winked in conspiracy. "Of course, its abbot will enjoy a rich endowment."

Sweenie escaped his hold and harrumphed at the bribe. "You think I'm fool enough to squander away my days of old age under your—"

A thunder of hooves came rumbling up from the south.

James whistled the other men back to the woods. Too far away to rejoin them without being seen, he led Sweenie on a run toward the ravine. He gave his dagger to the monk and swept his hand across his own throat to instruct him on the swiftest technique for the kill.

The approaching patrol galloped into the sunken path with none of the cautious manner typical of Clifford's troopers.

James pounced into the crease of the first two riders. He dragged them from their saddles while Sweenie leeched on the third rider's back and rode him like a snorting bull. James stunned a fourth intruder with a knee blow, then jumped astride a fifth rider and pinned him. In the midst of the scuffle, he felt a strange softness on the man's chest.

"Hold off!" one of the unhorsed riders shouted.

The rest of the Scot raiders jumped down from their hiding in the trees and appeared above the ravine with their notched bows aimed at the trespassers.

The leader of the mounted patrol stepped forward with his hands raised. "We have no quarrel with brigands. Allow us passage, and you will be well compensated."

James collared the man. "Brigands? I'll sever that slandering tongue!"

McClurg restrained him from gutting their captive. "At least find out where his lucre is stashed before you render him speechless."

"Finian's teeth!" Sweenie shouted.

The Scots turned to find the monk still wrestling with his victim, biting and cursing like a landlocked Islesman. Outsized, Sweenie finally ripped away the man's cloak and exposed a mantle sewn with a splayed red cross.

James removed the helmet from one of the riders he had just unhorsed. Standing before him was Jeanne de Rouen, the lass who had bested him in swordplay in Paris. He stripped off her riding cloak and discovered that she wore a black mantle stitched with a red, eight-pointed cross.

Driven to the task by dagger points, her companions removed their own cloaks, revealing splayed red crosses on their mantles.

"Murderous bastards!" Sim Ledhouse snarled at the crusader monks. "I lost two kinsmen at Falkirk to these conniving Templars. Caernervon sent them slithering up here to do his assassin work. I say we slice them from ear to ear and send their heads back to London."

James recognized their leader as Peter d'Aumont, the haughty Auvergne monk who had shouted threats at him in Paris. He twisted the knave's collar to demand an explanation for this trespassing so far from France. "What skullduggery brings the French Temple to Scotland?"

"Philip has imprisoned our brothers on false charges of crimes against the Church. Those still alive are now at the mercy of torturers."

Ledhouse got into d'Aumont's face. "This one's a coward as well as a traitor! He leaves his men behind while he flees to save his own hide."

"To fight on!" d'Aumont insisted. "I led what few I could muster into the Orient Forest near Troyes. We made our way by night to La Rochelle and sailed across the Channel."

"Longshanks favored the Temple," James reminded the French monk. "And Caernervon was knighted in your sanctuary."

"Piers Gaveston is in league with the Dominicans," Jeanne de Rouen said. "The friars have turned Caernervon against us. Your Bishop of St. Andrews languishes in Winchester dungeon. He told us to head west to Kintyre and the Isles."

"Lies!" Ledhouse shouted. "Lamberton would never aid these popish swine!"

Sweenie circled the Templars while debating their claim. "Even if what they say is true, the Bruce will not sanction this. If he is discovered harboring heretics, the Church will never release him from excommunication."

"And if we let them live," Ledhouse warned, "they'll lead Clifford to us."

James twirled his dagger under d'Aumont's nose. Nothing would give him more pleasure than to gut the arrogant Frenchman. He was about to dispatch him when a raven's shriek shook the treetops—Christiana Gamoran's enigmatic warning in the Arran cave came to his memory.

Look to the blood crosses.

He stared at the Templar mantles. Could *these* red insignias be the blood crosses that the clairvoyant Isleswoman had promised would one day show him the way to victory? He shook off that notion as ludicrous. How could these outlawed monks, notorious for being loyal only to what benefited their order, possibly help Scotland? His father had told stories of their treachery in the Holy Land. The Temple Master there had accepted bribes from the Saracens to raise the siege of Damascus and leave other Christians to die.

No, he would not fall for their trickery. If Lamberton had sent them into the Borders with his blessing, he would have supplied them with a sign to confirm his patronage. On his signal, his men threw ropes over the limbs to string up the Templars.

Jeanne stepped forward to be the first to die.

James admired how his former tourney-field opponent had flowered into a ravishing woman, no longer able to hide her curves under her mantle. "I thought only men were allowed to join the Temple."

D'Aumont answered for her. "She is a Cistercienne. Attached to our commandery to assist in the education of the brothers."

James scoffed at that claim. "She educated you, all right. With the business end of a steel blade, just as she did me once."

Jeanne blanched in sudden recognition, only then making the connection between her former opponent in Paris and the legendary Scot raider she had heard tales about. "*You* are the Black Douglas?"

"You seem surprised."

"I never expected to find you in the company of soldiers."

"And why would that be?"

"Your bishop said you had turned out more suited for the monastery."

Regaled by laughter, James begrudged a sheepish smile. "Did he now?"

Their raucous reaction to her observation confused Jeanne. "When I asked if you had continued with your martial study, the bishop said you had proven not cut out for the warring life. He also suggested that it would be to my advantage to challenge you again."

James chortled, nodding at what he knew was a confirmation of their claim; *that* clever quip carried the bishop's imprimatur, for certain. Eager for a rematch, he cut the bindings on Jeanne's wrists and threw a sword to her.

Jeanne reddened, informed that she had been the brunt of a jest at the bishop's behest. She returned the blade. "I was also told that the offer of shelter was an ancient tradition in your land. If you cannot see it in your heart to give us refuge, I will not fight you for it to provide amusement." She stepped in front of d'Aumont and brought James's dagger to her slender throat, daring him to follow through with his threat.

James maintained his threatening glower, but she did not waver. Then, another warning from the past rang in his ear: *The women of your land must prove stronger than the men of your enemy.* This French lass possessed more courage than any of these monks who rode with her. He severed the bindings on the wrists of her fellow Templars, then cut a swath from his own surcoat and gave her the shred of cloth embroidered with his clan's crest. "Show this to any who threaten you with harm."

His raiders shook their heads in disgust, forced to stand down. The Templars, stunned by the reprieve, mounted quickly and headed north.

Galloping with them, Jeanne halted several lengths away. She split off from her comrades and doubled back to James. After a hesitation, she whispered, "The lady held in Berwick ... I have heard it said that she is your woman."

"Aye."

She cantered a few steps off to lead him farther away from his men. "Our spies in London tell us that Edward plans to visit Roxburgh on the fortnight. The queen and his favourite will accompany him. He has ordered the towers festooned to his meet his taste in fashion."

"Thank you for the surveillance about Caernervon's weakness for fine furnishings," James said sarcastically, giving little care to the fact that prissy monarch would be visiting yet another of the strongly defended Borders castles.

Jeanne looked fiercely into his eyes to drive home the import of her report. "Half of Roxburgh's garrison is to be redeployed in neighboring towns to make room for Edward's bloated entourage. It is also rumored ..." She hesitated again, as if debating whether she should finish.

James was suddenly more interested. "Go on."

"The king intends to bring your countess in her cage to Roxburgh. To further humiliate you and the Bruce."

James nodded to her in gratitude, realizing that he had been too hasty in dismissing the information. When she reined up to leave, he made a strike for her sword, but she deftly parried his thrust. He grinned, remembering that quick maneuver. "I'm not certain I could have taken you."

"I've had little time for practice."

"You still owe me a rematch."

"I pray we both live long to see that wish granted."

He had expected to be answered by the same old brashness that he had witnessed from her on the tourney field in Paris, but he found only despair in her face. He squeezed her hand to instill her with hope. "When you reach Kintyre, ask for Christiana of the Isles. She is not particularly fond of me, but she has a compassionate heart. She'll not turn you away."

"Do you know what they're saying about you in London?"

"Whatever it is," he said with a smirk, "I suspect it's not fit for a lady's ears."

"Mothers sing lullabies warning their children that the Black Douglas will come take them if they misbehave. You have all of England in a fret. Wagering parlors on Market Street are even taking coin on when you will raid York."

"What odds are they offering?"

"Two to one, within the year."

"Maybe you should have laid some of your Templar gold on the table."

"If I placed a bet, it would be on Roxburgh, not York."

James grinned at her confidence that he could carry off the seemingly impossible task of rescuing Belle. He sent her on her way with a slap to her horse's flanks. After lingering on her as she rode off, he turned to find his men confronting him with frowns. "You lads have a grievance with me?"

Ledhouse stepped forward. "Some of us think you've gone soft. Every time a lass shows up, we seem to get the worst of it."

James locked onto the blacksmith in a match of glares. "Speak what's on your mind."

Ledhouse spat a phlegm wad at James's feet. "We could be setting Northumbria and Yorkshire aflame, but instead you keep us holed up in this forest for months while you scheme to save Buchan's wife. Now you let these Templars ride off with their French whore to report our position to Clifford."

The Trinity brothers drew their swords and came standing aside James, prepared to defend him.

James shoved the mutinous blacksmith back from breathing down his neck. "You and me, Ledhouse. Leave the others out of it."

Ledhouse ran his fingers down the buttons of James's jerkin in an old Highland challenge. "I don't give a damn if you are the king's drinking mate." He swung his Lochaber ax and narrowly missed James's shoulder. "When I'm finished with you, I'm going after those feckin' monks who killed my brother."

On the ridge, Jeanne and the Templars had turned on hearing the shouts. They delayed their departure to watch the fight between the two Scots.

TWENTY-EIGHT

Forced to keep moving to avoid freezing, Belle crawled to the far corner of the cage and turned her back against the night's shifting wind. As she had done each night for the past four years, she pulled herself to standing and offered a prayer of gratitude to St. Bride for allowing her to survive another day. This time, however, she knifed back to her knees, too weak to sing the defiant ballad that she always offered up to bless the setting sun.

The English townsfolk attributed her survival in such harsh conditions to witchery. But in truth, Caernervon had become so determined to keep her alive as a hostage that he had secretly ordered two concessions made to her confinement: She had been given an extra woolen blanket, and once a week, veiled nuns were allowed to enter the cage to bathe her. The townspeople had become so accustomed to her hovering presence that now they mostly ignored her.

This eve, the guard arrived tardy as usual with her gruel. "Special treat, wench. A bit of Bruce's flesh in it." He slung the slop at her feet.

She sniffed the wretched pulp and fired it back at him. "You English don't know lion flank from hen meat. It tastes like Caernervon's breast. Perfumed and tenderized from too much handling."

The guard rattled the prongs of her cage with his pike. "You may be wasted to the bone, but you still wag a fat tongue. I'm guessing by your sass you ain't heard what happened to your Scot rooster."

She crawled closer. "You have news of James Douglas?"

The guard grinned at her desperation. "He's dead as that rat in your stew."

"I don't believe you!"

The guard was amused by her plunge into despair. Only when she turned away, unwilling to be the object of his torment, did he finish his report. "One of our spies saw your fancy get into a scrap. He was gutted like a perch by another Scottie named Ledhouse. There's a fine end for him. Won't be long before your King Hob gets the same treatment."

Ledhouse.

She raked her memory. Hadn't she heard the English fishermen curse that name? The report rang horribly true. She looked west for some sign from the heavens to negate Jamie's death, but her eyes had so weakened that she could no longer make out even the ships coming up the Tweed. Of all the maladies she suffered, this was the cruelest. The first three years had been tolerable only because she could watch the horizon for Jamie. But now, all that appeared to her distant field of vision was a blur of greens and browns. She looked up at the ceiling for solace from her only friend.

The spider's web was empty.

She frantically searched the cage. The spider had miraculously survived three winters with her, appearing again each spring to spin another home in the corner of the cage. She had always sensed that its return held a mystical connection with Jamie. Below her, the market din in the city had quieted with the onset of night, and she could hear the townspeople reveling in a celebration near the sparks of a bonfire in the square. She cocked her ear toward a woman's voice that sang out from one of the corbelled houses on the bluffs:

> "Hush ye, hush ye,
> little child ye,
> do not fret ye,
> no more can
> the Black Douglas
> come and get ye."

Hope for Jamie's arrival was all that had sustained her. Now, even that had been wrenched away. She curled her legs into her chest, too distraught to maintain the façade of courage. On the tower above her, she heard the guards placing bets on what hour they would find her dead.

Seated at the far end of the royal table in Roxburgh's great hall, Queen Isabella made a silent wager on how long it would take for her temperamental husband to erupt with his usual explosion of childish rage. She guessed it would be within the minute, given how Tabhann Comyn was now edging up next to the king, nudging him like a wet-nosed hound and demanding an answer to the same question that he had been blathering the entire night.

"You are certain Douglas was killed?"

Caernervon ignored the annoying Scot and applauded the next course of his birthday feast being carried in. "Cockentrice!" He squeezed Gaveston's hand with excitement. "What a marvelous surprise, Piers!"

Isabella turned aside to hide the flush in her cheeks. She dared not reveal her grief at the news of James's death, not even to Gloucester. Although there was no reason to doubt the Templar informant's account, Caernervon had ordered him racked to confirm his veracity. Under torture, the monk had insisted that he saw the Black Douglas fall under the ax of another man in his troop.

She fought back a tear for James as she looked down the table. Tabhann, forced to endure yet another of Caernervon's drunken theatrical fetes, was tapping his fingers with simmering impatience. After his Inverurie defeat two years ago, the Comyn chieftain had taken asylum here with the English court to press for renewal of the Scotland campaign while his cousin Cam remained in the North, trying to rally their scattered allies. The Bruces were burning every Comyn castle and barn in Fife, and Tabhann warbled on incessantly that if he did not return soon with English reinforcements, there would be nothing left of his domains to salvage. But her husband, she knew, would not move without Gaveston, and the royal favourite, recently installed as the Earl of Cornwall, saw no reason now to endure the hardships of the Scot frontier.

She scooted her chair to gain a better vantage of Thomas Lancaster and the other barons who had been commanded to attend this feast, ostensibly to honor the king's birthday, but in truth to put their loyalty to the test. On this night, she sensed a heightened tension in the hall. Clifford seemed edgier than usual as he patrolled the outer walkway surrounding the tower. The sentinels had been doubled, a precaution against the danger created by the removal of half the garrison to Jedburgh to make room for the festivities. She noticed that with each pass, Clifford peered through the window at Lancaster, who in turn met the officer's eyes coldly.

This time on the officer's circuit, the scullion serving the king also returned Clifford's furtive glance. Clifford nodded to the server and then swiveled his gaze toward Lancaster, who seemed to answer him with a half smile.

Throughout these enigmatic exchanges, Tabhann, oblivious, continued to prattle on. "My lord, your own officer told me he harbors doubts about—"

Caernervon threw a ladle of gravy at the Comyn chieftain to shut him up. "If I am required to suffer your presence, Scotsman, do me the privilege of leaving off with the incessant nagging! I am finally rid of this Douglas miscreant! And I intend to celebrate!"

After calming Caernervon with a peck on the cheek, Gaveston aimed his carving knife at Tabhann. "Persist in perturbing the king, Comyn, and we will feed *your* boiled tongue to your wife." The Gascon made a motion with his head toward the ramparts. "Shouldn't you be out there comforting her? I can arrange for you to spend the night in her lodgings."

Tabhann was too stupefied to wipe the gravy from his shirt.

With the pesky Scot finally silenced, Isabella turned her attention back to the kitchen entry and the scullion who had just dished the king's victuals. The man careened clumsily, nearly dropping the empty tray while displaying all the grace and refinement of a chimneysweep. For surveillance purposes, she had made it her practice to know every member of the royal staff, and she found it odd that an inexperienced newcomer would be added to the kitchen retinue for such an important occasion. She locked onto the ham-handed cretin and saw him shoot another nervous glance at Clifford who, standing outside, looked through the passageway window as Gaveston was dished a slice from the roasted pig.

"I've not tasted such divinity since Paris!" Gaveston purred, nuzzling Edward's cheek. "Did you change your cookery staff as I asked, Poppie?"

The king nodded while he stuffed his mouth with creamed dates.

Isabella saw Lancaster wave the wine steward aside for a better view of the chattering Gascon. The choleric earl, ascetic in personal tastes, rarely touched spirits or wine, but on this night he was indulging freely. How strange, she thought. The baron had made no secret of his hatred for the king's favourite. And yet now Lancaster was calm and good-humored, as if a burden had been lifted from his shoulders. He even seemed to be enjoying the wisecracks that Gaveston hurled at every hapless person who came within his sight.

The new scullion returned again from the kitchen, this time with a platter of basted deer steak. When it was presented to the royal table, Caernervon ignored the offering and instead stuck his nose into Gaveston's serving. "You've convinced me, Piers. I must have some of your spiced piglet." The king dug his knife into Gaveston's plate and extracted a steaming slither of pork.

The waiting scullion turned toward Lancaster with a look of alarm.

The earl lost his expectant smile as Caernervon brought the loaded knife to his drooling mouth. Lancaster signaled the servant with a sharp thrust of his chin—and the scullion dropped his tray into the king's lap.

J ames crouched at the foot of Roxburgh's walls and counted the lit tapers on the crenellations above him. He had gained a stealthy approach with his time-tested tactic of walking in the middle of a herd of cattle. The castle appeared less heavily garrisoned than usual, just as the French lass with the Templars had predicted. He nodded for McClurg to pass the word to the other men.

They would make the attempt.

His plan to rescue Belle depended upon the success of two tasks. The first had already been accomplished. Months earlier, he had contrived a ruse to be acted out whenever they encountered the English on raids: Ledhouse would incite a fight and feign killing him. He and his raiders had even choreographed the blows to make their struggle appear more realistic. During their ambush of the Templars, he had sensed that one of the monks was disloyal to d'Aumont.

The traitorous Templar, taking the bait, had reported his contrived death to Caernervon in the hope of being given sanctuary.

The second task, now at hand, was even more daunting. These high curtain walls were designed to prevent easy scaling, and the English believed that he and his Scot raiders carried no siege equipment. But Sim Ledhouse had put his mind to an invention that might turn the tide of the war, if it performed as promised. The clever blacksmith had calculated that by connecting two lengthy hemp ropes with a series of folding planks, they could roll up the flexible ladders, carry them on their backs on the quick, and unroll them when they were positioned under these walls.

Two shrill whistles came from the far side of the keep. That was Ledhouse's signal. He was in position at the postern gate, ready to create the diversion.

James nodded for the sons of the Galloway crone to load their crossbows with the grappling hooks, which had been attached to the top ends of the rope ladder. The timing of their launches would have to be precise. He and the lads whispered to three together—and fired at the rampart nearest to Belle's cage.

The hooks snaked the ropes into the black sky ... the iron claws held. The ladder planks cascaded into place, just as Ledhouse had designed.

James went up first, promising to signal when he reached the top.

Scalded with hot juices from the tray dropped into his lap, Caernervon howled and shot up from the table to his feet. He ripped down his wet leggings with no consideration for modesty. "Idiot! I'll have your head sewn on that sow's neck! My God, I am boiled! Piers, help me!"

Alerted by the shouting, Clifford rushed from the allures outside the tower and came running into the hall. He found the chamber in chaos and the king rolling on his back with his breeches halfway to his thighs. Despite Caernervon's ravings, Clifford did not hurry to the king's side, but kept his gaze fixed upon Gaveston, who sat limp, negligent to his lover's plight.

Gaveston looked down in horror at his sleeves and found them soaked from sweat chills. Trembling, he tried to rise from the chair and fell to his knees, clutching his stomach. His green face contorted from confusion to agony.

"Piers!" The king writhed on the floor like a hooked worm. "Help me!"

Clifford glanced through the window toward the tower defenses. His guards were no longer at their stations. He turned and scanned the tables.

The queen had disappeared.

The officer ran out through the door, leaving the king and his favourite writhing on the floor. The servants and other guests, fearful of being blamed for the poisoning, had scurried off.

"I am dying!" Gaveston screamed. "Poppie, I am dying!"

Caernervon tried to assist the retching Gaveston to a chair. He called for his physician, but no one answered him. Abandoned, he dragged his favourite out of the hall and down a dark corridor, crying for his guards.

Hands reached from the shadows and stifled the king's screams.

The top edge of the rampart crumbled, forcing James to hang on by one arm. Regaining his grip, he pulled himself over the wall.

Two English guards stood across the allure, not twenty paces away.

His breath quickened as he surveyed the battlements.

There was the cage. And Belle, covered by a hooded robe, sat huddled in the corner with her back to him.

He could have used the Trinity lads at his side now, but he feared another crossbow shot to bring them up would give his presence away. He slid alone along the shadows between walls and the tapers. As the guards strode closer, he drew his dagger and slit the throat of the man on the left. The second guard turned to speak to his fellow sentry—an uppercut to his jaw sent him tumbling over the ramparts.

That would be signal enough for the lads.

Rubbing his knuckles, he stalked his way toward the cage, hiding behind each buttress along the tower wall. How long he had dreamt of this moment. What would he say to her? How would he explain his failure to come for her at Kildrummy? Would she even recognize him now?

He stole along the wall from corbel to corbel and came to the hoist beam that dangled the cage over the moat. He dared not call out for fear that her reaction would alert the guards. The beam's edge was no wider than his foot, forcing him to inch his way slowly toward the roof.

Atop the cage, he reached down to test the latch. The door was unlocked. Strange, he thought. Grasping the edge of the cage's roof, he flipped head over heels, kicked in the grille, and landed on the cage floor.

Belle sat slumped over in sleep.

He quietly crawled across the cage. Closing his eyes, he grasped her shoulders and turned her, pressing a kiss to her lips to prevent her from screaming.

She returned the passionate kiss and pulled him closer.

How desperately he had missed that embrace! She edged him into the shadows and lay next to him. She felt so vibrant and strong. Thank God for that. He opened his eyes to see the face that had remained etched in his mind for five long years.

A firm hand replaced her lips on his. "Get away! At once!"

Had her voice become so altered? Confused, he pulled back her hood. In the dim light from the torches, he saw, for the first time, the face that had spoken those words of warning.

Isabella of France pressed her hand against his chest to ease the shock to his heart. "Clifford suspects you are here."

He reeled against the bars. "But where is …" His question died with a gasp.

Isabella took his face into her hands to bring him back to the moment's urgency. "Your lady remains in Berwick. Clifford placed an imposter here in her stead. I bribed the woman to take her place and warn you."

Despairing, James could not force himself to move.

"Do not fail your countess now. Live, and come for her another day."

Shouts rang out near the north walls—Ledhouse and his men were in a hot fight. Outnumbered, they wouldn't hold out for long.

Isabella pulled him, listless with a heavy heart, to his feet. She climbed out the door of the cage and clambered onto its roof, beckoning him to follow. When they were both atop the cage, she led him across the beam that extended several feet from the tower's wall. They reached the allures just moments before the English soldiers poured down the gangway. She dragged him into the shadows and swept him into a side alcove. When the pounding of boots receded, she inched her eyes beyond the corner of the buttress and saw that the way was clear again. She kissed his hand and sent him running for the wall to escape.

Covered by the flickering darkness, James slid to his stomach and dived under the protection of a crenellation. He reached up and groped the edge of the walls until he found the grappling hook that the Trinity lads had shot up again. He wrapped his leg over the merlons, grasped the rope in preparation to rappel down, and—

He fell from a blow to the back of his head.

Tabhann raised his sword, hot for the kill. "Aye, I never believed you were gutted. I was born for that deed, not Sim Ledhouse."

James rolled aside, narrowly avoiding the blade's thrust.

Tabhann chased him to the rampart's edge and pressed the sword to his throat. James arched over the side with his head dangling. Tabhann raised his weapon for the finishing blow—

A grappling hook shot over the wall and jerked the blade from his grasp.

Hiding in the shadows, Isabella slid an abandoned pike across the stones.

James pounced on the weapon. Behind him, the shouts came closer—the English guards were rushing up the ramp. He prodded Tabhann toward the beam that extended the cage over the wall.

Tabhann tried to delay until Clifford's men arrived, but the punishing thrusts drove him backwards.

"Climb it," James ordered.

Given no choice, Tabhann crawled onto the beam and backed away from the rampart. When he was atop the cage and beyond James's reach, he grinned. "Fool! You can't reach me now! You've condemned yourself!" He pointed out James to the onrushing English soldiers. "Douglas! Over here!"

James slithered back into the shadows with Isabella. Hidden from view, he shouted in his best Yorkshire accent, "Douglas escapes! On the cage!"

Tabhann lost his preening grin. Unable to kneel and hide without risking a fall, he tried to stave off a volley. "Don't fire"

Hearing the Scot voice in the darkness, the guards unleashed their arrows.

Tabhann looked down at blood oozing over the gravy stain on his shirt—his chest was riddled with fletches. He tried to shout a curse at James, but his words faded as he fell to his death.

The door to the queen's chamber flew open, moments after Isabella slid into bed and wrapped herself in the covers.

Armed with a torch, Clifford marched in with a contingent of soldiers.

Thankful that she'd had time to put on her gown, Isabella pulled the sheets to her neck and acted dazed, as if she had been asleep. She had seized on the chaos of Gaveston's attempted poisoning—she suspected Lancaster, but the culprit could have been any of a dozen men in court—to rush from the hall and exchange places with Belle's impostor while Clifford was distracted. She hoped the officer wouldn't notice that her hair had not been brushed out, or that the candle next to the bed was still smoking from having been snuffed only seconds before he entered. Shielding her eyes from the harsh light, she shouted at him, "How dare you, sir!"

"Orders, my lady."

"Orders to invade the privacy of my *boudoir*? Issued by whom?"

Ignoring her demand, Clifford searched behind the curtains and furniture.

She was infuriated by his refusal to answer her with anything but a smug smile, a gesture that she knew was aimed at the irony of her sham protest. Because of the king's neglect of her, many whispered behind her back that she had come to regard nights alone a privilege.

"I will lodge a protest of this with my father!"

"You must be a sound sleeper," Clifford observed in a veiled challenge. "To remain undisturbed by the shouting outside."

"If you intend to persist in this debasement, then dismiss these men!"

She held her breath while the officer debated her demand. She might be a despised Frenchwoman among the English courtiers, but she knew Clifford needed no reminding that she could still cause him problems should her flighty husband decide to appease her at the officer's expense. As she hoped, given the man's reputation for caution on the military field, Clifford chose the better course of discretion and ordered his soldiers out.

Alone with her now, Clifford kept searching the chamber, rifling through the intimates in her wardrobe. "The Black Douglas lurks in this tower."

She cackled to dismiss that suggestion as absurd. "That coward would never show his face in Roxburgh!"

"You left the feast at a very convenient time."

Her heart raced. Did he suspect her? "Where is my husband?"

"For his safety, he is being escorted back to Berwick."

"And he leaves me in this sty? Without a word of his departure?"

Clifford saw the covers ripple near her on the bed. He raised his blade, ready to impale the intruder—and tore away the sheets.

Gloucester, half naked, lay next to the queen.

The earl erupted from his hiding in the bed and drove Clifford with a pointed finger toward the door. "You pox-cheeked trough maggot! Do you forget your fucking station? Speak a word of this to anyone, even to those cunted hedgehogs you whore on, and by God I will see you remanded on the next ship to Brittany for violating the privacy and honor of the Queen!"

Speechless, Clifford bowed in contrition and hurried from the chamber.

When the door slammed shut, Gloucester tapped the footboards.

James crawled out from under the bed frame.

Isabella hurried the two men toward a side door.

James delayed to thank her, but she sped him off with a whispered assurance, "Your lady has all your stubbornness and more. She survived to see Longshanks admitted through the gates of Hell. She will not allow my titmouse of a husband to outlast her, either. Now go, and God be with you."

TWENTY-NINE

Three sharp whistles—the signal of Robert's courier—flushed a bevy of swallows from the treetops of Ettrick Forest. James leapt from the dense brush and flagged down the approaching riders, hoping to learn why the English had not retaliated for his Roxburgh raid. In the four months since his failed attempt to rescue Belle, the Borders had been so quiet that he feared Caernervon had already launched his invasion of Scotland by sea.

Twenty horsemen arrived, led by a dark-faced man who reined to a halt and sniggered, "St. Fillan must have cast a spell on Clifford's nose! I could smell your sorry Lanark asses all the way from Peebles."

James stepped back and cursed under his breath. *Thomas foccin' Randolph.*

His raiders, aware of the simmering rivalry between the two men, grinned at the promise of entertainment that this encounter held. Instead of dispatching the traitor to the block, Robert was now grooming his turncoat nephew into one his most trusted lieutenants. Even more galling to James were the rumors that Robert had mistaken Randolph for him at Inverurie.

Dismounting with a flare, Randolph reached into his saddlebag and tossed a charred brick at their boots. "A souvenir from Edinburgh Castle."

James examined the kiln marks on the brick while his men hooted down Randolph's claim that he had retaken the well-defended crag fortress from the English.

"No mortal could scale those walls," McClurg insisted.

Randolph greeted his old comrades with handshakes and backslaps. "There you're wrong, you stinking Unholy Ghost!"

James kept a skeptical distance. "Edinburgh is truly ours?"

"Aye, Jamie! You should have been there!"

As the Lanark men crowded around Randolph, mesmerized by the vision of the Scottish Lion once again flying above those hallowed heights, James threaded their ranks to protest, "I *would* have been if you had told me—"

"We sat under that rock for two months," Randolph bragged. "One fine summer morn, I told the lads, 'I don't have the patience of Jamie Douglas, just waiting for starvation to take its course.'"

James reddened. "The Hell you say! When did I ever—"

Sweenie threw an elbow at James's ribs. "Will you let the man finish?"

As James was shoved to the rear, Randolph rubbed the dust from his mouth and continued his report. "Now, where was I?"

"Below Edinburgh's walls!" Ledhouse reminded him.

"Aye, lads." Randolph turned to each man with exaggerated intensity, regaling his rapt audience in the round. "There I was, staring up at that rock thrice the height of St. Andrew's spire, and I said to myself, 'If Jamie Douglas can scale Roxburgh, then by Christ I owe it to him to have a run at these ramparts, even if they make Constantinople's towers look like Aberdeen cattle pens. The English had raised the walls ten—no, twenty lengths higher. Mind you, the fact that you lads failed to hold Roxburgh tower longer than it takes a Northumbrian to enjoy a good shit gave me pause, but not for long."

Sweenie kept hammering at the kneecaps of those around him to keep from being crushed in the listening scrum. "How many English defended it?"

Randolph swept his hand across an imaginary parapet. "A thousand if there was one, my tonsured heretic sprite."

"Two hundred half-starved conscripts," James insisted from the rear.

"So up we go, one at a time. Thirty against two thousand. The night was so pitched you couldn't see your hand at your nose. A good thing that was, lads! No looking down into the depths of Hell that awaited us if we fell. I'm leading the way, of course. When I gain the crest, I reach for the ledge. And a rock breaks off and lands with a crash that would wake the dead."

"Guards?" Sweenie cried, flinching from the vision.

Randolph stood shadowing over the monk. "Aye, you boot-stomped plug of devil dust! English men-at-arms as thick as these oaks! And just as stout! One calls out, 'You're a dead man, Scottie!'"

Sweenie slammed his knuckle of a fist against his tiny palm. "Damn the ill fortune!"

Randolph lowered his voice to draw them all closer. "Lads, I'd be lying to you if I said I wasn't calculating the very words I'd soon be saying to my Maker. But St. Fillan be my witness, a miracle was granted me that very instant, for the guard just laughed and moved on. The brainless scouser was only trying to scare his mate with a false alarm."

"The Almighty be praised," Sweenie declared, releasing a held breath. "Truly, a sign of the righteousness of our cause."

Randolph parried and punched at James to imitate his fight with the sentry. James fought to escape the clench, but his struggling only served Randolph's purpose in reenacting the scene as he described it, blow by blow.

"When the last man was up and over, the alarums rang out," Randolph said. "And the garrison came on us like the locusts on Pharaoh. But when, I ask you, lads, could three thousand Yorkshiremen could hold thirty Scots?"

Untangling from Randolph's hold, James was determined to put a stop to the yarn before the number of Edinburgh's defenders grew to be half the population of England. "You failed to explain how you got to the top of that tower."

"Did I now?" Randolph reached into his saddlebag again and emptied the remainder of its contents at James's boots.

A rope ladder, threaded with wooden planks, unfolded across the ground.

Randolph smothered a chuckle. "We plundered this marvel from an English patrol near Falkirk. "Someone carelessly abandoned it at Berwick."

Ledhouse's eyes rounded. "That's *my* ladder!"

Randolph slapped Ledhouse's back in mock commiseration. "I'm sure the bards will mention that when they sing of my conquest."

James nodded with a grin, good-naturedly accepting the brunt of the jest. "You came all this way to regale us with your exploits, did you?"

From the shadows, Randolph brought forward a horse that carried a blindfolded man whose hands were bound.

"A prisoner?" James protested. "What do you expect *me* to do with him?"

Randolph dragged the captive from the saddle. "He came to us demanding to speak to the Black Douglas. Apparently he couldn't find you on his own."

Suspecting another prank, James waved off that claim and prepared to return to his seat at the fire. "I've had my fill of your amusements for one night."

"I carry a message from the King of England," the prisoner said.

James spun on his heels at hearing that familiar voice.

The Lanark raiders tightened a circle around the imperious Englishman. But despite their glares of intimidation, the blindfolded captive remained adamant in his demand. "What I have to say is for the ear of Douglas only."

James circled him. "I have nothing to hide from these men."

"I must first confirm that you are Douglas."

Ledhouse pressed a dagger to the prisoner's throat. "No Englishman sees the Douglas in Ettrick and lives to tell of it."

When the messenger refused to retract his condition, James yanked off his blindfold. Before him stood John Webton, the knight whose life he had spared in the attack on Castle Douglas. "Your letter-writing lady is well, I trust."

Webton displayed a betrothal band on his finger. "She sends her regards."

"I hope you didn't come all this way expecting a wedding gift."

Webton lowered his voice to soften the impact of what he next related, "You are to come to Melrose Abbey on morrow eve. Alone and unarmed."

"By whose demand?"

"On that I have been sworn to secrecy." Webton was reluctant to finish his report. "I was also commanded to tell you … if you wish to see the Countess of Buchan again, you will be there."

Ledhouse drove the Englishman against a tree. "Let's string him up!"

Impressed by Webton's courage, James held his men at bay while he tried to divine the purpose of such a strange message. After mulling the risk, he cut the bindings on Webton's wrists and led him back to his horse.

Webton mounted. "What answer shall I convey?"

James slapped the flanks of the horse and sent his former deskmate galloping off without a reply.

"I'll follow him," McClurg said.

"No," James ordered.

Randolph glared at him with a slack jaw. "You're not thinking of going?"

James turned over in his mind all of the reasons the English might have for seeking such a meeting. He had recaptured many of the castles in the south, but Clifford still held Stirling, Bothwell, Jedburgh, Dunbar, and Berwick. If one of the garrison commanders sought the parlay on his own initiative, Caernervon's army would not yet have launched its invasion. Could this be a ruse to capture him? Or confirm that he was still in the Borders? No, Clifford would never expect him to walk alone into such a trap. Something else had to be afoot. Perhaps Lancaster was signaling a desire to join Robert in the war against Caernervon.

"Jamie?" Randolph said, reminding him that they were all waiting.

James wrapped his arm around Randolph's shoulder and led his rival below a limb where their battle gear was hung. "Tom, I suspect your life has been a long series of disappointments since that day you traipsed into Inverurie playing me. I'm going to give you an opportunity to experience the thrill again."

Randolph turned to the other Lanark raiders for an explanation. "I've heard about these daft spells of his."

James sized up Randolph's height and measured him with his own black hauberk imprinted with the robin-blue Douglas crest. Marveling at how well it fit Randolph, he now understood how Robert could have made the mistake of identity at Inverurie. "With your scrawny frame, you may buckle under its weight, but hopefully you'll find a way to manage."

"You going to let us in this cockeyed plan?" Ledhouse asked.

James rifled through one of the bedrolls. Finding a monk's cowl, he slipped it over his shoulders for a disguise. "Tomorrow night, the Black Douglas attacks

Jedburgh. Too bad I won't be there to enjoy it." He playfully thumped Randolph's chest with his fist. "Try not to ruin my reputation."

The next night, James stalked the roofless hull of Melrose Abbey, a Cistercian monastery abandoned after repeated English raids. He slipped alone into the ashlar ruins and searched the dark nave, moving with stealth from pillar to pillar. By now, if the English had taken the bait, Randolph and the lads would be drawing Clifford toward Jedburgh with their diversionary raid. Whoever was meeting him here would expect him to approach from Ettrick in the west, so he had come in from the direction of the coast, but he had seen no tracks or fresh horse chips around the grounds.

Pipistrelle bats squealed from their perches on the vaulting and dived at him. He spun around with his hand on the dagger under his cloak. From the shadows at the high altar, the silhouette of a draped figure appeared. He halted and waited for an indication of the man's intent.

A black-robed figure walked into the diffused light. "I bring a proposal."

He couldn't see the face receded in the hood. "From whom?"

The messenger hesitated. "The King of England."

Why did that voice sound familiar? He turned and scanned the colonnades to insure again that no one was lurking behind him. Taking a step closer, he saw from the messenger's garb that he was a monk. "Churchmen now conduct England's diplomacy?"

"Your lady will be delivered."

He closed in on the monk. "Edward Caernervon is not so generous."

The monk retreated a step to avoid being identified. "Keep your distance. … Someone dear to the king is in danger. You will give him refuge."

He narrowed his blinking gaze, astonished by the extraordinary demand and its peremptory tone. "And if I refuse?"

"The Countess of Buchan will not survive another winter."

He drove the insolent monk against the altar and ripped off the knave's hood, exposing his face.

Staring up at him was the Dominican Lagny, the inquisitor he had first encountered as a young man in Paris. The monk signaled with a weak turn of his head at the shadows behind the altar. From the protection of a column walked a skeleton of a man wheezing with labored breaths. The Dominican brought the half-dead wretch forward. "The king wishes him protected."

Several seconds passed before James recognized the invalid. Hollow-eyed and pale as a ghost, Piers Gaveston no longer resembled the blustering scoundrel who had sat laughing at him during the signing of the Ragman Rolls, when his fellow countrymen had been forced to submit in humiliation to Longshanks.

His mind raced with the implications of this astonishing offer. Although installed as the Earl of Cornwall, the Gascon had to be in grave danger with the other earls if Caernervon was resorting to such risky measures. If Lancaster were to discover that Caernervon was negotiating to place the safety of his favourite over the interests of the realm, the foundations of the Plantagenet house would certainly crumble. Still, he sensed that this monk's plea for sanctuary rang true. His own spies had reported rumors from Yorkshire that Caernervon could not sleep and was refusing food for fear of ingesting more poison intended for Gaveston. He had initially dismissed such reports as scurrilous gossip planted by enemies of the Plantagenet intent on removing Gaveston from his position of influence in the court. But now, seeing the Gascon so deteriorated …

"Robert Bruce takes the credit for your victories," the Dominican said. "His queen enjoys the warmth of a nunnery while your lady languishes in torment. You can still save her."

He cocked his ear toward the dark recesses. Caernervon might be desperate, but would that coward really send this cleric skulking across the border without an armed escort? He glared at Gaveston and tried to find some quality in the cretin justifying such loyalty. "Caernervon risks his crown for *him*?"

The monk did not break his cold, emotionless gaze. "The king has instructed me to ask *you* a question."

"And what would that be?"

"Have you ever known a love for which you would abandon all?"

He came nose to nose with the supercilious inquisitor. "Aye, I have known two. And both have suffered at Caernervon's pasty hand."

The Dominican flinched as if expecting a blow. "The king asks only that you take Gaveston into your custody until he can consolidate his forces against Lancaster. The Bruce need not know of the arrangement."

James held back his cocked fist. "The countess will be released?"

The inquisitor nodded. "She will be taken to a nunnery and nursed to health. Within the year, on Lord Gaveston's safe return, she will be delivered to you."

He weighed the desperate offer. Holing up Gaveston in one of his Ettrick hideaways would not be difficult, but if the Gascon were forced to remain at Caernervon's side, the English lords would be too preoccupied with scheming their king's demise to unite and mount an invasion. Such a delay, even for just a few months, would give Robert precious time to strengthen his army and drive the English garrisons from Stirling and Berwick. If he accepted this arrangement to save Belle, he might well be dooming Robert's kingship.

Rob or Belle, again.

A jolt shook Belle from her stupor.

She lifted her head, cursing at her mind's tricks. She could no longer make it through the nights without being attacked by hallucinations of falling into the river and drowning. Half blind, she levered to her elbows and crawled in the darkness to the bars, navigating by the flickering of the distant flames on the rampart tapers.

Yet this time it was no nightmare—the cage was being cranked down.

The blurred outline of a towering form came rising toward the gate. For a fleeting moment, she thought she saw Jamie's face. Her heart leapt. Had he come to take her home? She folded her hands to St. Bride in gratitude. Yet she dared not utter his name for fear that any act of desperation to rush to him might cause the English to reconsider.

She had not touched the ground in years. How she had dreamt of whisking her toes again through the wet grass. Then, she remembered her weakened condition. She could not let Jamie see her in such a frightful state. She poured what little water remained in her drinking cup down her face to cleanse the sea salt from her rough cheeks. She ran a hand across her forehead, knowing that she must be hideous with her skin so windswept and cracked. Would he still love her looking like this?

A new angle on the world came into her vaporous view—and the cage halted, several feet yet from the ground.

Caernervon, in armour, rode up on a charger and sat staring at her.

The king's altered appearance stunned her. He had lost several stones in weight, and his drawn eyes were bloodshot and full of bitterness. She tried to make out what moved beyond his shoulders. A long column of soldiers, including Gloucester and Clifford, sat arrayed in mounted formation with banners flying. She searched their blurred faces in vain to find the man she loved.

"No song for me this morning?" Caernervon asked her. "I was looking forward to a performance. What has it been since you last serenaded me? Five years?"

She squinted again at the mounted men behind him. Where was Jamie? And why had Caernervon traveled here to Berwick with such a large entourage? Of course! Jamie had refused to cross into enemy land. The English were preparing to escort her to the border for an exchange of prisoners. She pulled up from her knees, determined to walk out just as she had walked in. The river was lined with townspeople who had come to see her depart.

Caernervon extended his hand to her through the prongs.

As his reach came closer to her blinking eyes, she realized that he was offering her the key to the cage latch. She smiled through tears. It was just like Jamie to demand that she be allowed to open the door herself. He would suffer no Englishman to boast of that deed. She reached for her freedom—

The king pulled back the key, inches from her grasp. "They beheaded him."

She collapsed to her knees. *Please God, no!*

"On Blacklow Hill. Lancaster and Warwick dragged him from his bed in dead of night. Thousands packed picnic lunches and blew horns as he was led to the block. I am told it was like a festival."

She fell back, sinking in grief, and drew her wasted legs to her elbows. She heard soft weeping, and looked up. Tears were streaming down the king's cheeks. Why was *he* crying?

They executed his favourite—not Jamie!

She pulled back onto her knees in numbing relief. She was not leaving England, after all, but she didn't care. Jamie was still alive.

"You will see Douglas soon enough," Caernervon promised her. "I will not return from Scotland until I have him at the end of a rope. Here, under your gaze, he will meet the same end that Piers suffered. I should think you would want to live long enough to witness that."

In her periphery, a sudden movement high on the tower caught her attention. She shielded her failing eyes from the harsh sunlight and forced as much distance as she could into her sight. A hand quickly pulled the covering over the window. The royal chamber, she remembered, was in that section of the tower. Had Isabella been watching her speak to her husband? Why, she wondered, had the English queen remained here in Berwick instead of returning to more hospitable accommodations in London or York? She shuddered with a horrid thought: Had Isabella conspired with Lancaster to murder Gaveston? She drew strength from knowing that the plucky Frenchwoman had learned to survive among these English, who despised her also. Turning back to Caernervon, she locked onto his vengeful eyes and asked him, "Does it not seem strange?"

Alerted by her distraction, Caernervon glared at the now-abandoned window in the tower. "Strange, you say?"

"That God places inferior men on thrones."

Caernervon seemed to take refuge in an inward glare of hatred for the world. "Do you still love James Douglas? After what he has done to you?"

"More each passing day."

"*That* is what strikes me as truly strange. Considering that he could have had you removed from this misery."

She steeled her reaction. But inside, she was shaking with confusion.

Caernervon motioned his entourage off, out of hearing range. Clifford delayed his departure, concerned that the Scotswoman might strike out at the king with her nails if he came too close to the cage, but Caernervon demanded that the officer peel off toward the bridge with the others.

Alone with Belle, Caernervon whispered through the prongs, "Last month, I offered Douglas your release. He refused to respond to my merciful proposal for an exchange."

"Liar!"

"Nay, in truth, he told my envoy he considered you dead. Robert Bruce is all he cares about now. But fear not, my lady. I intend to defend your honor. The man who jilted you will soon suffer the agony that I now endure when Bruce climbs to the block."

She saw him waiting for her to crack with emotion, but she turned away, refusing to give him the satisfaction.

He slammed his fist against the cage. Punishing his mount with the reins, he wheeled and galloped north toward the bridge.

Clifford circled back and came up, alone, to the lowered cage. Glancing over his shoulder as the royal column crossed the Tweed into Scotland, the officer curled a treacherous smile at her. "I must commend you, my lady. Your stubbornness to stay alive has served us admirably."

"I have never served *you*! And never will!"

"You must not sell yourself so short in your influence. You have proven more valuable to England than a dozen divisions, for you have accomplished what none of my countrymen could manage. You have turned our king into a warrior."

She squinted at Caernervon riding over the distant hills. Had she unwittingly doomed Robert and James to annihilation, as the officer claimed? Sensing her doubt, Clifford grinned at her and bowed his head with mock courtesy. As he rode off to rejoin the invasion force, the guards on the ramparts hoisted her cage back into the drizzling sky.

thirty

Tethered together by ropes at their waists, three hundred volunteers from the western Isles waited anxiously in their hollow-square formation, uncertain if the attack would come from the Torwood at their front or across Giles Hill behind them. In the hazy distance to the north, a besieged English garrison stood atop the ramparts of Stirling Castle, shouting taunts and placing wagers on whether the Scot infantry would run.

A low rumbling from the south sent rabbits scurrying up the old Roman road that led to the small milling village of Bannock. Moments later, a frothing herd of long-horned Angus broke through the Torwood pines and stampeded toward the raw Scot recruits.

The officers in the center of the schiltron shouted orders for pikes to be lowered in a practiced maneuver that resembled a giant hedgehog bristling to repulse a predator. When the thundering cattle closed within a stone's throw of the front ranks, the volunteers abandoned their sharpened poles and broke for the cover of the burn. Those veterans stationed behind them struggled to hold the line, but they too were finally dragged off in the panicked scramble.

Punished by the hoots of the Stirling defenders, Robert Keith the Marishal led his small contingent of Scot cavalry down the ridge and rustled the cattle back to their pens.

Watching from Coxet Hill, Robert Bruce bit off a flurry of curses at the shameful result of the drill that he had devised to harden his green troops. He lashed his palfrey into the midst of the hangdog volunteers and flayed them with a stinging critique. "God's blood! Shall I send sheep upon you next? If you won't stand up to thirty heifers, how do you expect to face down English knights?"

"We've had our fill of this foolishness!"

He turned in the saddle to find the source of that challenge in the fractured ranks. "Show your face!"

A thick-bearded Islesman armed with a spiked targe stepped forward. "I'll fight the damned Angles! But I'll not stand idle for bovine to gore me!"

Edward Bruce, determined to be his brother's enforcer of discipline, rode up and circled the mutineer. "You'll do as ordered, or you'll hang!"

The obstinate Islesman looked for support from his comrades, who had been sent by Angus Og MacDonald from the hinterlands of Kintyre, Skye, and Gamoran. These sailors were more accustomed to the hit-and-run of galley raids than the tedious repetition of ground maneuvers, but none showed the stomach to stand up to the Bruces. The Islesman was thus forced to be satisfied with hissing at Edward's horse and growling, "If I'm still welshing livestock a week hence, I'm shanking it back to Jura."

From the corner of his eye, Robert saw his brother waiting for him to punish the insubordination. Yet he waved off the confrontation as futile. No Scotsman could be forced to fight if his heart was not in the cause. He had tried to forge this motley collection of feuding clansmen and firth ruffians into an army, warning them that they would suffer the same fate as Wallace if they did not abandon their petty animosities, but his exhortations had met with little success. Randolph's northern men from Moray and Inverness would not even share a camp with Edward's levies from the eastern provinces. With a heavy sigh, he ordered Keith, "Bring up the Annandale lads. God willing, they'll shame the others to—"

"Douglas comes!" shouted a hundred voices.

Interrupted by the roar of excitement, Robert broke a rare grin. Blessed with the arrival of the one man who could raise his spirits, he nodded permission for his volunteers to run down the slope and greet the rider galloping up on the famous sleek black Yorkshire horse captured at Roxburgh. He cantered through the cheering throngs and reached for the hand that he had waited for months to clasp. "We feared you'd found the end of Clifford's rope."

James heaved to catch his breath from his forced ride through the Torwood. "That's one worry you needn't lose sleep over. There's nary a tree left in the Borders to hang a good Bruce man these days."

Despite the jest, Robert sensed an uncharacteristic gravity in his old friend's manner. "What news from the South?"

James held back his report for discretion's sake, but that only caused the men on foot to press closer and balk the horses. He had agonized for weeks over whether to reveal his clandestine meeting with the Dominican at Melrose Abbey, until the offer for Belle's release was rendered moot when the Earls of Warwick and Lancaster captured Gaveston and executed him on Blacklow Hill. He had deemed it best to say nothing of the matter, lest Robert forever regard him with suspicion. Jostled by the soldiers eager to hear, he found Randolph holding back on the periphery. He shouted at his friendly rival, "Tom, is this what now passes for discipline in the King's army?"

Shamed at being called out, Randolph rode through the scrum and tried to flog the men back to their stations with the tails of his reins. "Did you not hear Douglas? This is not a fete!"

Robert shook his head at the fractious scene. He knew any attempt to keep the reconnaissance secret would only make matters worse, for the news would just spread through the camp anyway, skewed and inflated by rumor. With a wan look of trepidation, he nodded for James to give the report.

As the men fell silent, James revealed, "Caernervon has reached Falkirk. The first elements of the English army will be here before sundown."

Robert's face flushed. His scouts had last placed the invasion force in York, leading him to believe that he had another week to prepare. Worse, the disappointment in James's eyes confirmed what he already knew: This wapinshaw army of sixty-days farmers and fishermen was in no condition to fight veteran English knights. He braced against the pommel to steady and asked the question on all their minds: "How many?"

"The English train stretches to Coldstream ford," James said. "Thirty thousand foot and two batailles of archers. Three thousand knights lead them." Hearing the men around him murmur that the invaders were bringing thrice their own number, he added to their consternation. "Clifford and Gloucester are in the van, with Cam Comyn and his turncoats."

Randolph tried to put up a brave front for his uncle. "If that is all they—"

"D'Argentin has joined them," James added, leaving even Randolph speechless.

Those names came hurling at Robert like body blows, none more stinging than the last. "Caernervon has opened his coffers for the best knight in France?"

"Aye, and …" James hesitated, his voice trailing off.

"Out with it!" Robert demanded.

James angled his horse to shield this next bit of news from the crowding men. "Elizabeth's father is at Caernervon's side … with the Bohuns."

Robert sat staring at him blankly, as if not quite believing what he just heard.

James did not need to spell out what all of this meant: Caernervon and the English lords had ceased their bickering and were now united in their determination to subjugate Scotland. Robert's father-in-law, the Earl of Ulster, was bent on wresting Elizabeth back from a treasonous marriage, and Gloucester had likely been given the choice of taking up arms or suffering the same fate as those lords who had been executed after their unsuccessful coup attempt for the throne. D'Argentin, unemployed since the English treaty with the French, had no doubt been seduced into the English service by the Dominicans with a promise that the campaign would be a holy crusade. Yet what galled Robert most, he suspected, was the arrival of the Earl of Hereford, Humphrey de Bohun, and his freshly knighted nephew, Henry. The pompous elder Bohun had once been engaged to Elizabeth, and when she broke off that arrangement, the cad had besmirched her honor by claiming that she had become embroiled in a scandalous dalliance.

Edward Bruce edged his pony closer to roust Robert from his vexed thoughts. "We have no heavy horse."

Robert whirled on his brother in hot anger. "What in the Devil's womb would I do without you always revealing the obvious to me?"

"To Hell with you, then!"

His fiery temper flinted, Robert quarreled at full voice with Edward, giving no regard to the effect it would have on the already disheartened men who milled around him. "Had you not agreed to that fool-headed pact with Mowbray to lift the siege on Stirling, Caernervon would never have gained the support of the English barons!"

"Bridle yourselves," James warned the two brothers, glancing at the ranks to remind them both about the fragile morale of the volunteers.

Robert required a moment to recoup his steely composure. Finally, he turned a cold shoulder on Edward and whispered to James, "This army has one battle in it. If we fight here and fail, we are done."

Like his father, James had been born with the gift of sensing the critical points of a battlefield. He felt certain that Caernervon's first objective would be not to form up for battle, but to relieve the besieged garrison at Stirling Castle, which stood a league to the north and offered an ideal springboard for an invasion of Fife and the Highlands. More to the point, the pampered Caernervon despised sleeping in tents. That June had been the hottest in memory, and the stifling humidity and stagnant water had spawned a plague of midges that attacked exposed flesh at night. He was confident that the impatient English king would first try to force an entry into Stirling and gain its dry comforts without delay.

He remembered once, as a boy, having crossed this soggy terrain around the croft huts of Bannock village. The forest of New Park merged with the meandering stream here to form a natural funnel that had a deceptive, changeling nature. The overgrown shocks of cotton grass appeared to offer firm footing, but below their thin layer of peat trickled hundreds of rivulets that became gorged with rain. The only stretch suitable for heavy cavalry was a ridge called the Dryfield, a sloping terrace adjacent to the Carse where the marshland rose gently east of the Roman road. He looked to the west and saw that the horizon had turned the color of aged pewter. The air was unnaturally still. If the skies opened up during the night, the Carse would become a quagmire. He turned back to Robert and counseled, "I say we force them to fight us here."

That suggestion nearly catapulted Edward Bruce from his saddle. "You're the one always telling us to fall back, Douglas!"

James kept his insistent gaze fixed on Robert. "They've got us in fists. But we've got them in wits."

Robert gave up a jittered half-laugh at hearing the words he had quipped years ago when the Comyns surrounded them as lads.

Before Robert could think up a hundred reasons why defending the road to Stirling could not succeed, James rode up to a swell along the ground and shouted at the troops, "I stand with our king on this field! Will you stand with us for Scotland's freedom?"

The cattle-hating Islesman spat at the hooves of James's horse, making clear that he had heard his fill of Southerners boasting about the exploits of this Black Douglas of Lanarkshire. "I don't see you doing any standing. Freedom is a word that rolls slippery from the lips of a man on a horse. You can hightail it when the fighting gets hot. Wallace couldn't stop the Angles. What makes you think you can?"

James rose in his stirrups to be heard by all. "What gave you galley rats the notion that I intend to just *stop* the English? Haven't we always been satisfied to just stop them? And haven't they always come back like vermin? Hell, I'm going to drive them to London and wipe my boots on their asses in the Tower where they murdered my father!" He glared down at the disgruntled seaman from Bute and added, "Any man who doesn't want a part of that can go home and empty his salmon lines to feed his new English overlords!"

The Lanark men stomped in approval and threw taunting elbows at the mouthy Isleman, who finally begrudged a nod of admiration. At last, he and his fellow Northerners had found a man who, unlike these English-bred Bruces, talked their language.

With a sly smile, James leaned to Robert and whispered Sweenie's favorite benediction, "Welcome to your gory bed, or to victory."

Robert gave the impression of a coiled spring as he turned to and fro in his saddle, playing out the potential battle in his mind and weighing the conse-quences of a retreat.

James was aware that Robert had never been able to shake the memory of those Welsh archers decimating Wallace's schiltrons at Falkirk. He could almost hear the doubts rattling in his head. None of them had ever commanded a full-pitched battle. Loudon Hill had been no more than a skirmish against the incompetent Pembroke, and most of these lads had never been locked in anything fiercer than a wrestling match. They whooped and bellowed for a fight now, but what would they do when they faced Flanders warhorses? There were three months of campaigning left until the harvest season. Robert might try to stare down Caernervon long enough to convince the English to turn back. He might also order Keith and his light cavalry to protect the escape route to the West, and if hard-pressed, run for the Isles during the night.

Robert turned on him with a questioning glare, as if sensing the invasion of his thoughts. Met with an arched brow to goad his decision, he took a deep breath of resignation and ordered his brother, "Bury the spikes."

Edward lurched forward in the saddle. "You can't mean to hold this ground!"

"It will do no harm to listen to what Jamie proposes."

After failing to convince his brother to change his mind, Edward angrily waved his sappers into the grassland between Coxet Hill and the Torwood. The diggers began excavating hundreds of potholes and filling them with four-pointed wooden caltrop jacks designed to pierce the hooves of the sturdiest horses. Others followed behind them, camouflaging the spikes by covering the holes with the thin first layers of the uprooted sod.

While the Torwood entry was being mined, James led Robert and the other officers on a gallop toward St. Ninian's kirk, an ancient Culdee chapel that sat on the road to Stirling. Arriving, James dismounted and walked through the surrounding graveyard that was filled with leaning stone crosses, many marking the remains of Wallace's veterans killed at Stirling Bridge. He entered the kirk and upended a pew. Finding a nub of charcoal, he drew a map on the back of the sitting boards.

His blood still up, Edward Bruce was on James's heels. "That was a bonnie speech, Douglas! Now tell us on how you intend to prevent three thousand English knights from sconing our infantry."

"Clifford will bring his heavy horse up the Falkirk road," James predicted. "We'll keep them from forming lines longer than ours by funneling them between New Park and the burn."

The other officers traded skeptical glances, unable to fathom how their poorly armed and outnumbered troops could stop Caernervon's advance, even on such a circumscribed field.

Randolph shook his head. "To reach New Park, our left flank would have to be stretched to the breaking. We don't have enough men to form two ranks."

"We won't strengthen the left," James said. "We'll weaken it."

Aghast, Edward came nose to nose with him. "This is war, not chicken thievery. Leave the tactics to those of us who have been trained in them."

James shoved Edward aside and traced a serpentine line across his map to represent the flow of the Bannock stream through the low valley that led up to the castle. "Caernervon will see the weakness on our left. He'll try to cross the burn to the east and circle our rear."

Edward elbowed back to the fore. "Here's a bit of military wisdom that has apparently escaped you, Douglas. We don't *want* the English in our rear."

"No, but we want Caernervon to try for it." James pointed Robert to the spot on the map where the stream turned back and formed a bulge of marshland with a narrowing neck. "When he does, he'll meet his watery grave right here."

Robert studied the etched map. "Your plan assumes that Caernervon does not mass his infantry on the Dryfield and turn to fight us."

"He won't lead with his foot levies," James promised. "He'll expect us to run at the first sight of his armoured horse, just as we always have. Half his army is still a day's march from Falkirk. He doesn't have the patience to wait. If we fall back to New Park tonight, he'll think we've decided to retreat. When he sends in his knights to gain the castle without foot support, we'll slice the head of the snake before the tail knows what hit it."

As they waited for Robert's decision, the only sound to be heard in the kirk was the clatter of a trapped curlew in the rafters. James knew his proposed strategy was fraught with risk, for Robert's caveat had exposed the weakest link in the chain of events that would have to happen to cause it to succeed.

Edward broke the tense silence. "Rob, this is madness. If they wheel west and draw up for battle, we'll be crushed."

"Aye, I *am* a madman," James said. "I'm about to fight the largest army ever mustered on this Isle with men who hate each other more than the English. And if that's not the Devil's work enough, I have to put up with a bawheid with haggis for brains like you leading one of our divisions."

Randolph had to restrain Edward from charging at James.

While his officers bickered over the best course of action, Robert walked to the cruciform window and gazed at the rising mists below the Bannock burn.

James prayed that, for once, Robert would be unconventional in his strategy. Longshanks would never have fallen for such a trap, but Caernervon was a notorious creature of habit, devoid of creative thinking, impatient of subordinates, ever suspicious of those who displayed brilliance and dimmed his own haphazard light. Gloucester and Clifford would be on guard for such tricks, true. Yet Gloucester suffered from the taint of suspected treason, and Clifford had never been knighted. Caernervon would take his counsel from the Bohuns and the other court schemers who were eager to load their booty wagons.

Robert slapped his thigh, bringing them to attention. "Tom, set your schiltrons below this kirk. Eddie and I will guard the approach up the Falkirk road."

James waited to hear his name in the battle plan, but Robert retired to the altar and knelt for prayer without even looking at him. Coldly rebuffed, James dropped his head in defeat, burned by Edward's infuriating smirk. Robert was preparing a retreat by keeping his Southern men in the rear to lead the escape west while Edward and Randolph fought a rear-guard action. Despondent, James walked toward the door while searching for the words to explain the shameful decision to his troops.

Robert, kneeling at the altar, asked, "Jamie, can your lads hold the center?"

At the door, James turned, uncertain what he meant.

Robert arose from the kneeler. "You will command the third division."

Edward's condescending grin gave way to a dropped jaw. "Douglas has never led more than raiding party! You cannot place our fate in the hands of—"

"Enough!" Robert shouted.

Having silenced his brother, the king walked to the map and aimed his dagger at the spot called the Way, a drover's path between the high ground and the marshes along the Bannock stream. Looking at James pointedly, he ordered, "Leave a gap between your schiltrons and the burn." He drove the cutting edge of his dagger into the ancient pew to demonstrate what he prayed would be the result. "Just wide enough for the head of a snake to slither in."

Clifford rode ahead of the lumbering English army to scout the narrow cart track through the Torwood. He despised this damp, endless forest and its threatening silence broken only by the occasional upshoot of leaves or flap of wings. His entire career had been wasted putting down raids in this wilderness; he had chased Douglas so many years that he could now feel the scoundrel's proximity in the prickliness of his skin. His repeated failures to capture the felon had turned him into an object of derision in London. Had he delivered up Douglas's head, by now he would have been stationed in the king's court, perhaps even elevated to an estate. Instead, he was relegated to these Marches for the rest of his days, denied even the privilege of a knighthood.

A sharp crackling of branches chased black grouse from the treetops. He reined off the path and hid behind the brush. The dull sucking of ironclad hooves against the mud became louder, and he drew his blade, certain that Douglas was shadowing his advance. When the oncoming riders closed within range, he cut across their approach.

Gloucester and Cam Comyn reined up, causing their spooked horses to whinny and rear to their hinds.

"Damn you, Clifford!" Gloucester shouted, finally regaining control of his mount. He looked over to see Clifford's fingers quivering at his side. "What in Hell's name is wrong with you? Are you not well?"

Clifford could not steady his hand sufficiently to sheath his blade. "I was well enough until you came up on me like scofflaws!"

"Bohun requires your presence."

Clifford persisted in staring at his own traitorous fingers.

"Did you hear me? I said Bohun—"

"I am not a goddamned wet nurse!" Clifford spat to curse Henry Bohun, the king's hotfoot brother-in-law, a poseur who had never come near even a tavern brawl, let alone a battle. He had wasted half his time on this invasion attending to that coxcomb's complaints. "He can find his own way, by Christ!"

Gloucester despised Clifford, but he agreed with the officer's indictment of the stupefying manner in which this invasion was being conducted. Bohun was merely the most recent addition to the bloated influx of court dandies being brought north. Also in the slowly advancing retinue rode the king's new favourite, Hugh Despenser, a dolt whose ambitions were exceeded only by his appetite. Although Despenser could not have been more different in appearance and temperament from Gaveston, Caernervon had somehow become convinced that the Gascon's soul had returned to him in Despenser's youthful but dissolute frame. He searched the path up ahead. "Where is Bruce?"

Clifford squeezed his fist, finally regaining control of his hand. "North of this bramble wood, by my surmise. I can smell the piss trail from him wetting his pants with fright."

"His bed-warmer Douglas will be with him," Cam Comyn predicted.

Clifford shielded his eyes from the first morning rays piercing the tall pines. He was determined to avoid battle until the entire army had mustered on the same field. The van marching up from Falkirk would reach the outskirts of Stirling within the hour, but its arrival would present him with a new difficulty. He was coordinating a procession, not an invasion. Caernervon alone traveled with thirty baggage wagons, and Humphrey Bohun was so certain that Stirling Castle would be his new residence that he had commissioned a small navy to transport his furniture up the coast. Clifford had begged permission to divide the army and come at Stirling from three sides. Yet Caernervon, an aficionado of theatrics, insisted that the Scots be forced to witness his thirty thousand men marching together for dramatic effect. This narrow path through the Torwood required bringing the troops north in a single line, three abreast. The second division, escorting the king, would not arrive before nightfall.

Henry Bohun, bouncing in the saddle like a sack of apples, came galloping up with his splashy gaggle of thirty knights. Against orders, he and his band of ale-swilling blowhards had left the king behind and were now hurrying ahead, lusting for blood sport with their silk banners flapping. The portly Bohun lifted the visor of his shiny new bascinet and, unloosing his white whiskers that resembled tusks, advised Clifford, "If you don't increase the pace, we will run out of daylight before we can scare off the Scots."

Clifford felt his hand shaking again. "You and your tourney poltroons will frighten them enough with those fox plumes flying from your scalps. Perhaps you might make more noise to alert them."

"The king wishes Stirling taken before dusk," Bohun insisted.

Clifford bristled at the man's incessant name-dropping regarding his private confidences with the king. "The infantry can cover barely a league at three hours."

"Then we shall ride on."

"The Hell you will! I command this—"

Bohun ignored Clifford's demand to wait for the rest of the army and instead drove deeper north into the Torwood with his thrill-seekers.

An hour later, Henry Bohun outraced his comrades to a clearing at the northern edge of the Torwood. He rode out into a sun-drenched meadow below Stirling Castle in the distance and found the Scots practicing their battle maneuvers on the far side of the burn. He pranced his magnificent steed to give the foot-bound bumpkins a fright.

Clifford, giving chase, galloped out from the tangle of brush and saw to his dismay that the London popinjay was about to ruin his careful plans for a coordinated surprise attack. "Bohun! Back, damn you!"

Bohun ignored the command and strutted closer to the burn. On the far side of the stream, the astonished Scots stared wide-eyed at his caparisoned warhorse. He spied a Scot officer on a palfrey riding across their lines in a harried effort to set them in battle formation. Grinning, he turned over his shoulder and shouted at Clifford, "God's blessing! That's the Bruce!"

Clifford wheeled on hearing that cry. In his bumbling haste, Bohun had caught Robert Bruce on a transport pony without a stint of armor. The Scots around Bruce were in disarray, with a gap between their flank and the burn. He tensed with anticipation. Fortune had finally shined on him. He and his arriving knights would stare Bruce down and freeze the unprepared Scot levies in place until the first column of his English infantry came up. Then he would launch a flanking charge and order his archers to finish them off. At last he would gain his due glory, even before Caernervon even reached the field and—

Bohun slammed his visor and galloped toward the burn.

"No!" Clifford shouted.

James shouted from across the field, "Rob!"

On the near ridge, Robert turned on his palfrey toward the Torwood and saw the first elements of the English cavalry trickling out from the thick brush. A lone English knight had splashed across the burn and was now bearing down on him. He sat exposed on the open ground with no weapon.

James reached behind his back for his Dun Eadainn ax. Too far to intercept the onrushing knight, he galloped up and heaved the weapon toward Robert.

Robert caught the ax and held it on his pommel, restraining his frightened palfrey as the Englishman kicked his charger into its final approach. Bohun lowered in the saddle on the gallop and took aim at Robert's exposed right pectoral. Seconds from impact, Robert reined his palfrey left, rearing it to its hinds, and shifted the ax to his right hand. Bohun swept past without finding his target. Robert drove the ax into the Englishman's helmet—the handle splintered, but the blade impaled the crease of Bohun's visor.

Bohun dropped his lance and slumped against the cantle. His head dipped, his plume fluttering in the wind as his charger pawed for direction. With a sudden heave, he careened to the ground, crashing with a great clang of metal.

Blood seeped from the slits of his bascinet.

A stunned silence fell across the field.

Several of the Scots in the ranks rushed up to pull off Bohun's helmet. They found the Englishman's head crushed between his bloodied side-whiskers.

At the entry to the Torwood, Clifford scrambled to form a battle line with the hundreds of his knights pouring into the clearing. Across the burn, he saw a dark-faced officer point toward the mounted English ranks and then lead a screaming charge down the slope.

Was that Douglas's banner with its field of robin-egg blue?

Clifford reined his horse back a step. The Scots were hurling themselves at him like savages. *Damn that fool Bohun!* He signaled Gloucester and fifty knights forward, but when Cam Comyn held back, he demanded of the Scot, "Are you going to fight, or just watch?"

"I'll fight," Cam said. "On my terms, not Douglas's."

Halfway to the burn, James halted his Lanark men and back-stepped them into a slow retreat.

Clifford laughed at their sudden loss of courage. Stoked for the easy kill, he signaled for his mounted knights to double their pace and charge the fleeing Scots. In an act of sheer luck, Bohun's festoonery had seduced the undisciplined Scot mob into giving battle too soon. He was about to give the order for his archers, now rushing forth from the brush, to finish the Scots off when he saw Gloucester and his knights plunge into the earth. Confounded by their disappearance, he stood in his stirrups to search the terrain for his cavalry.

One by one, his dazed English knights climbed out of the holes that had been hidden with sod. Their mounts, impaled on the caltrop spikes, writhed and whinnied in agony. Gloucester staggered across the piles of mangled horse-flesh in a frantic effort to rally his survivors.

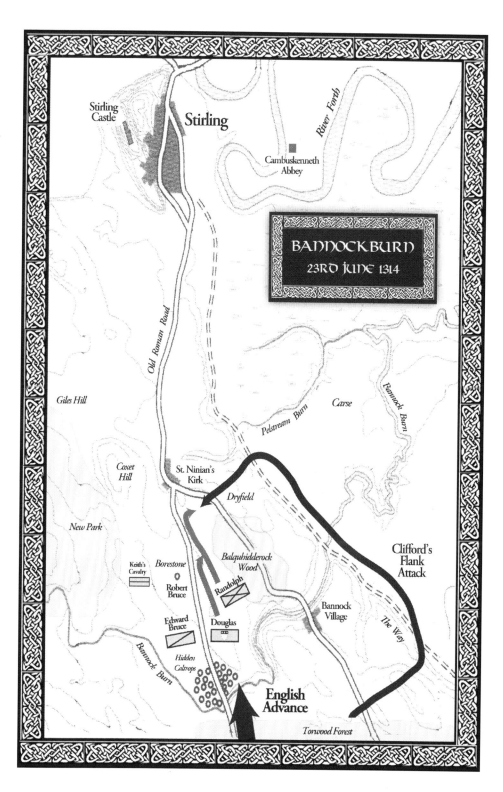

The Scot retreat had been a sham.

Clifford watched, stunned, as Douglas turned and led his Lanark men back into the valley. With bloodcurdling yells, the Scots descended on the confused English knights and hacked at them with their clubs and claymores. Rattled, Clifford rushed his Welsh archers to the front and gave orders to fire. The sergeant of the archers delayed, fearful of hitting their own men, but Clifford nodded grimly for the enfilade to proceed. Commanded to the task, the archers reluctantly drew their bows and unleashed a hail of missiles that darkened the sky.

Shouts of warning shook the field, and James and his men fell in unison, retracting their legs under their shields. The English knights who had survived the pits now suffered the impact of the arrows from their own archers. The vale filled with screams and the pings of iron points. Gloucester dodged the enfilade as he fought his way back to the Torwood.

James and his men sprinted toward the forest to finish off Clifford's unhorsed knights, but they were halted by hundreds of English infantrymen flooding out of the Torwood onto the Roman road. Only a few yards from Clifford, James found himself surrounded by Yorkshire pikemen. Outnumbered, he fought his way out and led his men back across the burn. Edward Bruce's schiltrons broke ranks to provide him cover. The hellish maze of pits and wounded men slowed the English infantry, which finally gave up its chase and retreated to the Torwood. The Northern Scots mobbed their returning comrades and lifted James onto their shoulders.

"You gave them a bonnie taste of Lanark steel, Jamie!" Randolph shouted.

The risky charge had given Robert time to retrieve his armour from Coxet Hill, and now he rode down the lines on his battle charger. "To your squares!"

Sobered by that warning, James ordered the celebration to cease and reformed his men to meet the inevitable English counterattack.

◆n the Torwood, Clifford marched up to Bohun's mangled body and kicked it so hard that some swore they saw it twitch. In the span of mere minutes, the London upstart had managed to destroy what had taken Longshanks two decades to gain: Scot fear of heavy cavalry. For the first time, those clan savages hooting and hollering beyond that burn had witnessed one of their own vanquish an English knight on an open field.

Clifford looked across the rising ground that ran through the Bannock village. This opening skirmish had allowed Bruce time to set his defenses. The Scot right flank, commanded by Edward Bruce, appeared strong and fixed against the dense foliage of New Park, and Douglas was now stationed in the center. But Randolph's division sat farther north, overlooking the road to Stirling. Bruce's nephew would command Northern men, many who were deserters and disaffected conscripts from Comyn's old army. Clifford smiled grimly as he traced the battle line toward Stirling Castle. Bruce had been forced to stretch his reserves so thin that he had left a gap in the crease between the divisions led by Douglas and Randolph.

There was their soft underbelly.

"We should renew the attack before they mass," Gloucester advised.

Clifford mounted. "Wait here for the king to arrive."

Gloucester tried to capture Clifford's reins to delay him for an explanation. "Where in Hell's name are you off to now?"

Clifford brushed the baron aside and disappeared into the Torwood.

After positioning his troops atop the high ground overlooking the Carse, James hurried toward a brae below Coxet Hill, where the royal standard had been planted on a borestone. In the three hours since the morning fight, a disturbing calm had descended on the vales. Roiling clouds were now gathering in the west, making it look more promising that his prayer for rain might yet be answered. If he and his men held off the English until dusk, they could move back off the ridge during the night and find shelter in the New Park. Yet it was that turn of season when the light lingered well after midnight, affording Clifford time yet to launch another frontal assault.

At the borestone, he found Robert pacing the summit, guarded by Keith's light horse of five hundred, the only cavalry in their army. He reported to Robert, "The English still won't make a move."

"Where is my brother? I ordered him up here an hour ago!"

"No doubt parlaying with Caernervon for another truce. Perhaps this time he'll hand over Edinburgh." He knew how to light Robert's fuse; Edward was loyal to be sure, but the hotheaded Bruce brother had become increasingly jealous of Robert's stature. Denied the Scottish throne because of his birth order, Edward was now so obsessed with invading Ireland and declaring himself that isle's monarch that James suspected him of agreeing to suspend the Stirling siege to hasten the decisive battle that would free him to pursue his Irish fantasies.

"Leave off him, Jamie," Robert ordered. "I have enough to worry about without the two of you constantly wrangling."

"If he crowds my division, I'll kick him back to Ireland."

Robert fixed his worried gaze on the old Roman road that disappeared into the Torwood. "Why does Clifford wait?"

Before James could offer a guess, screams came from their rear. He and Robert turned toward the sounds of battle and saw five hundred English knights making fast for Stirling below the brow of the Carse, east of St. Ninian's kirk.

Clifford was attempting to outflank them.

Stationed there to prevent such a ruse, Randolph had failed in his duty. He spurred up Coxet Hill in a sweat and cried, "They stole on us under cover!"

Robert made no attempt to hide his anger at his nephew for failing to protect their left flank by keeping the far bank of the burn scouted. "A rose has fallen from your garland, Thomas!"

Randolph came to a ragged halt, crushed by the king's condemnation.

"We're all to blame," James said. "We had equal vantage."

Robert had no time to soothe Randolph's injured pride. "Jamie, hurry to Tom's aid before the lads break!"

As James rushed his fifteen hundred men toward St. Ninian's kirk, Randolph galloped back to his division and led his Northern men into the low ground in a last-ditch attempt to intercept Clifford's knights. Despite Robert's orders, James held his troops back while he watched Clifford form his cavalry into a broad line for an assault against Randolph's schiltron. Now dismounted, Randolph steeled his men to remain steadfast in their square. The first ranks dropped to their knees and lowered their pikes just seconds before Clifford's knights crashed into them. Randolph's schiltron wavered but held, repulsing the first onslaught.

Robert cantered with rising agitation back and forth across the brow of Coxet Hill. He shouted at the Lanark men, "To him now, Jamie!"

Yet James stood back, monitoring the grinding shifts of momentum between Randolph's schiltron and the English knights. If Randolph could turn back Clifford without his assistance, it would do more for their army's morale than a thousand new recruits. Fixed to his stance inside the hollowed square, Randolph saluted him in gratitude for the show of confidence.

Despite his repeated assaults, Clifford could not break the Scot square, and his knights, growing frustrated, began throwing their maces into the schiltron in wild attempts to pick off Randolph. James and his Lanark men shouted encouragement to their northern comrades as Clifford and the knights regrouped for one last assault. Randolph's men buckled under the impact, but they regrouped and threw off the skittish English chargers yet again.

Exhausted, Clifford and his surviving knights finally retreated down the muddy banks of the Carse and headed back toward the Torwood.

James led his men into the valley to embrace Randolph's lads and offer water skins to slake their thirst. Arm in arm, James and Randolph looked toward St. Ninian's kirk, hoping for some gesture of commendation, but Robert had disappeared behind Coxet Hill.

F our hours later, darkness finally fell over the village of Bannock. In the Torwood to the south, Clifford's camp was chaotic and tense. The fresh English troops marching up the old Roman road from Falkirk had expected to find a comfortable bivouac. Instead, they stumbled into an infernal mash of wounded and exhausted men who lay amid the stinking dead bodies of their comrades killed in the day's disastrous charges. Scuffles broke out as a cold rain began to fall and turn the ground into a muck of manure and urine.

A commotion of horns and heralds drove the slumbering soldiers off the road to make room for a squealing caravan of baggage wagons. Caernervon climbed out of the lead carriage. Accompanied by Amery Valence, D'Argentin, Richard de Burgh, and Hugh Despenser, the king marched toward a litter that had been hoisted on poles.

The soldiers lowered the canvass sheet to display Bohun's bloodied corpse.

Staggered by the grisly sight, Caernervon flung his hands to his head. "How did this happen?"

"He gave battle against orders," Gloucester said.

Caernervon took a slobbering swallow from a wine skin to steel his nerves. "He charged to avenge my honor! And where were you?"

"After the initial assault, I deemed it prudent to wait for the full army."

Caernervon flung aside his new helmet, which was crowned with a sculpture of a coiling leopard. "All you have ever been is prudent! You allowed Bohun to be ambushed by your own kinsman! And you walk away without a scratch?"

"I will not be slandered—"

"You will speak only when ordered!" Kicking at anything within his reach, the king grabbed at Clifford's breastplate and ranted, "Why am I not sleeping this night in Stirling?"

"The Scots have contested the entry."

Caernervon angrily stripped his soaked cloak and threw it to the ground. His servants rushed to shield him with a canopy, causing the runoff to fall on his officers. The king turned on Clifford again and demanded an explanation. "You have not flanked them?"

"The river blocks our approach."

"River? You call that offal trench a *river?*"

Cam Comyn spoke up to warn the king against any attempt to cross the ground that lay between them and Stirling. "Those vales are impassable."

Caernervon slogged a raging circle around his drenched officers. "Am I to understand that all that stands between me and the capture of Bruce and Douglas is *mud?* My treasury spent on the largest army ever assembled this side of the Channel! Months of suffering this miserable hellhole to be denied by *mud?*" He kicked up globs of muck onto Gloucester's breeches.

Gloucester was forced to suffer the smirks of Hugh Despenser, who was clever enough to remain in the shadows when the king was in one of his black moods. The earl tried to reason with Caernervon. "Sire, the heavy armor—"

"You *will* take our horse across that stream!" Caernervon shouted at the earl. "By dawn, we *will* stand between the Scots and Stirling Bridge!"

Gloucester looked to the other lords for support in his protest, but none in the royal council were willing to come to his defense. He knew that his standing with this incompetent monarch could never be repaired; it was England he now hoped to save. "Such a position will expose us needlessly. The river would be to our backs. Should we need to retreat—"

"Do as I command! Or I will have you arrested!"

While the king ranted on, Clifford pulled Cam Comyn aside and whispered, "You're familiar with this ground?" Receiving a nod, Clifford looked across the carse and ordered the turncoat Scot, "Meet me at the picket line in an hour."

Unable to sleep, James lay on his bedroll, rehearsing in his mind the order in which the next morning's battle might unfold. The day's unlikely victory had bonded their men into an army, but he was under no illusion that the morrow would offer up another Bohun to lay waste to Clifford's cautious tactics. Assured that his division had been fed and given its orders, he arose and walked the ridges along the New Park, where hundreds of desultory fires flickered through the swirling shrouds of rain and mist. He was not a praying man, but on this night he felt the need.

He came up the hill to St. Ninian's kirk, and entered the sanctuary. Inside, he found Robert, still in his muddied battle gear, bent over the kneeler under an icon of the kingdom's patron saint. "You should get some rest."

"Do you ever think about Hell, Jamie?"

Alarmed by that tone of flagging resolve, James offered him his cloak for warmth. "I think about what Belle endures. And I know God could not surpass the English in devising torments."

Robert dropped his head in weariness as he draped his shoulders with the cloak. "I'm not as strong as your lass."

"You're strong enough."

Robert lifted himself from the kneeler, wincing, and walked to a crude crucifix above the altar to study the mutilated image of Christ. "The churchmen say if we die denied the grace of God, we will burn for eternity."

James had seen that same tortured look of doubt in Robert's eyes on the night of their Turnberry invasion. He backed against the wall and slid to his haunches. "Do they not also promise that every man is to be given his Day of Judgment? I'll take eternal damnation, provided I can confront the Almighty and ask Him why a good woman is caused to suffer so. If you go to the fires, Rob, you'll go surrounded by the best men God ever fashioned. And Satan will have an army that will make the archangels tremble."

Robert's pugnacious jaw still led, but his shoulders had become rounded from the burdens of the war, and a slight paunch now hung above his belt. On this night, he had a soulful urgency that verged on desperation, a crisis of resolve that surpassed even their darkest days on Arran. They both knew that, if captured, they would face the same fate dealt to Wallace.

"We could still make for the Isles. Cross Stirling Bridge and burn it." Ashamed of his weakening resolve, Robert could not bring himself to look up.

James stood to leave him to his prayers. He had dealt with Robert's low moods too many times to count, but the irony of this night did not escape him. He had shaped the very strategy that Robert was now proposing—the slash and burn, the patience to fight another day. All that had been fine when they were young. But he could no longer endure the thought of running across the Isles again, lurking from cave to cave and surviving on hope alone. "Aye, we could fight from the mountains, come out at night like we have since we were lads. And our sons and grandsons could do the same. And it would never end."

Robert returned the loaned cloak. "Jamie ..."

James saw a hesitant look in his eyes. "Rob, what is wrong?"

Robert turned away, as if thinking better of uttering what he had nearly revealed. "Be careful tomorrow."

James left the kirk troubled. Had there been a hint of clairvoyance in Robert's voice? Or was his own gut warning him of something more ominous? He crossed the crown of the Dryfield in the drizzle, memorizing every swale and copse for the coming battle. When he neared one of the burn's offshoots, an arrow landed near his feet. A spooked sentry, most likely.

He walked guardedly toward the direction of the arrow's firing.

"We can avoid this," a voice called out through the fog.

He risked a few steps closer. As the shrouds of mist slowly cleared, he saw Clifford and Cam standing across the Pelstream. He reached for his dagger, but they were too far for an accurate throw. He tried to coax them closer. "Come over here. I can barely hear you."

Clifford laughed. "After all these years, you think we'd fall for that?"

"Join us, Douglas," Cam said, "and all is forgiven."

He suspected a trap. "Your bribes are nothing to me. Ask Caernervon."

"The Bruces intend to abandon you," Clifford warned. "My scouts say their baggage wagons are loaded for a retreat to the Campsies. They will leave you to fight while they escape to the Isles."

He couldn't help but wonder if that distant look in Robert's eyes had indeed been betrayal. Why had Robert placed the royal standard on Coxet Hill, which sat near the only escape route to the West? In battles past, Robert had always been in the middle of the fray. Determined not to let Clifford and Cam detect his doubt, he picked up a stone and hurled it across the burn, then retraced his steps back into the fog.

Clifford edged closer to the stream. "I have convinced the king that imprisoning your woman no longer serves our purpose!"

Hopeful, he stopped and turned back.

Clifford grinned at the silence, having exposed his old rival's weakness. "Tomorrow, my courier will deliver an order to Berwick ... for her execution."

Cam laughed. "She lost her head once when she crowned Bruce. We'd not see her lose it again, eh Douglas?"

"You can still save her," Clifford offered. "Bruce need not know. When we move for Stirling in the morning, hold back your division until we gain the high ground. It will be over before you engage. I will see to it that the execution order never arrives."

James dived into the burn and swam furiously to overtake the two scoundrels. When he reached the far bank, he pulled his dagger for the kill, but they had disappeared into the mists.

thirty-one

"**B**ring her."

That command, from somewhere in the morning's darkness, startled Belle out of a fevered sleep. Lifted off the cage floor, she went rigid with fear. Had Caernervon finally ordered her to the execution block? Nearly blind from the hunger glaze that had hardened over her eyes, she could make out only flashes and shadows as she was removed from the cage and carried up the tower stairs.

The howling of the sea wind silenced suddenly.

She heard the crackling of a hearth. Tears of bitter irony stung her swollen lids. She had languished in the harsh elements for seven years, freezing during the winters and sweltering during the summers, but now she would meet her end under a dry roof in a chamber heated for comfort. The soldiers laid her on what felt like piles of straw, no doubt strewn to soak up her blood. Even at death's approach, she couldn't help but sink into the luxurious softness of the matting. Deprivation had heightened what she had once taken for granted. This nesting, better suited for mules, felt as heavenly as a feather bed.

Was Caernervon watching her from the balustrade? Aye, he would expect her to break and beg a chance to renounce her allegiance to Robert Bruce. But she would not give him the satisfaction. She lifted to her knees, struggling against the faintness to remain upright. She stretched her neck to offer the executioner a better target and shouted at the English king, "Come strike the blow, eunuch!"

A door slammed.

She shuddered and collapsed—but her head still pounded horribly. She risked opening her eyes and saw the same swirl of blurs that only seconds before she thought would be her last view of this world. Her heart sank. She was still alive. She reach up and felt for the wound on her neck, but found none.

Incompetent swordsman! Why does he not finish me?

A bowl of warm liquid redolent of cinnamon came to her lips. She tried to sip it, but her throat was too swollen to swallow. She coughed and retched with spasms. Her lungs felt as if they were on fire. *They are reviving me only to suffer the blade again.* She shoved away the bowl in a rage.

"You are safe here," a woman whispered, restraining her thrashing arms.

Smooth hands caressed her forehead ... and then a blurred face, framed in blonde hair, came hovering over her.

The English queen?

She reached out, clawing at the softness under her, and found that she was not on execution straw, but a bed. She sobbed, undone by the discovery. "You must take me back. If your husband learns—"

"You needn't worry about him," Isabella of France said. "At least for this night. He has taken an army north to fight your people."

Alarmed, Belle tried to arise. "Jamie must be warned."

Isabella eased her back to the pillow and brought more tea to her lips. "There is nothing you can do for him now."

Belle tried to marshal her fragmented thoughts. More and more, her mind now lapsed into periods of forgetfulness, and each time it happened, she feared that she would not return to sanity. She fought against these involuntary retreats from the world, worried she might not recognize Jamie when he came for her. Having lost track again of the months again, she had to ask, "What year is it?"

"1314. The 24th of June."

"Midsummer day?"

The queen nodded wistfully. "When I lived in Paris, I so looked forward to the festival. I'd stroll the gardens picking roses to offer to my *beau*."

Belle smiled. "I'd swim naked in the sea like Aphrodite."

"You Scots are mad!" Isabella covered her mouth immediately, concerned that she might have given offense.

A burst of frantic chirping came from outside the window.

Belle turned at the sound, realizing that the larks that nested atop her cage had been thrown into perturbation by her disappearance. "Aye, I suppose we *are* mad. But only a Frenchwoman touched in the head by glamourie dust would risk her position with king and Parliament to keep a Scot prisoner alive."

The two women shared a nervous laugh that died with a sad silence.

"I do have one quibble with you," Belle added, wishing to chase the melancholy that had overtaken the moment. "That loaf of bread you tossed me on the day of Longshanks's funeral was week-old and moldy."

"The harder the crust, the easier the throw."

Belle sensed that the queen was examining her wasted condition, trying to fathom how she had managed to stay alive. They were nothing alike in features or temperament, but their lives had taken parallel paths. Both had been thrust into the same foreign land and made prisoner to the same despicable monarch. Her suffering in that cage was nearly unbearable. Yet she would not trade it for Isabella's fate; to be cast off for another woman would be crushing enough, but to be abandoned for another man's bed with no hope of enjoying the intimacy of passion was a cruelty that only the Plantagenets could design.

She remembered the first time they had spoken, on the dance floor of this very tower. She had always wondered why the presumptuous French girl came to her rescue that day. How angry Jamie had been at them both; she could still feel the heat from his wild eyes. The Almighty's ways were passing mysterious. Had Isabella not contrived that reunion with James, she would never have rushed to Scone to place the crown on—

A wail startled her.

A matron stood at the door with a crying infant. "Mum, it is the hour."

Isabella untied her bodice and took the swaddled child to suckle it. She indicated for the matron to leave, but before doing so, the matron retracted the curtains in a protest against the French practice of coddling babes.

Belle was stunned. "Your husband has proven a man, after all?"

When the queen did not answer her, Belle raised her head to examine the infant cocooned in strips of linen and lace. She caressed its downy head and saw from the embroidery of the cloth that it was a boy. These cruel English imprisoned their children with such bonds in the belief that the natural act of crawling was insubordinate. Was it any wonder that their men turned ravenous for war?

As if to confirm that judgment, the infant lunged at Isabella's nipple.

Belle was suddenly swept by a wave of revulsion. This birth meant that the Plantagenet house would survive for another generation. How many more of her countrymen would die under the watch of this child? And then, a revelation came: Had God asked her to endure this diabolical confinement to bring her to this moment of opportunity? She turned an ear. The floorboards were no longer creaking—the guards must have departed with the matron.

A stream of golden light revealed the location of the window.

She had not walked that far in seven years. Could she summon the strength to commit the deed? Deprived of his heir, Caernervon would lose the flagging support of the earls, and the English invasion would be rendered stillborn.

"He is ten months old," Isabella said.

Belle struggled to her elbows, shifting nearer to the edge of the bed while continuing to talk to disarm Isabella. "Have you named him?"

"Edward."

Belle winced at hearing the surname that had been a curse on Scot lips for two generations, and now a third. Malevolent fate. A woman who did not love her husband had been given a child whose destiny marked it for the oppression of thousands. How many times had she replayed that night in Methven, when she and Jamie had talked of raising a family? Her best years had been wasted in that cage, and she feared from the dead feeling in her womb that she could never provide him with those children."

"Would you like to hold him?"

Before Belle could answer, she felt the infant placed in her wasted arms. The boy stopped crying and grinned up at her, as if daring her to do it. The shutters on the window rapped against the stones. Could the guards on the ramparts see her through the open panes? Her hands were shaking. If Caernervon discovered that she had been allowed to hold his heir, the queen would suffer gravely. *Why does she take such wanton risk?* She saw Isabella's drawn face staring down at her with a look of desperate expectation.

She *wants* me to kill it.

Was this why she brought her in from the cage?

Aye, she also abhors the thought of Caernervon's progeny ascending the throne. It all made sense now. If Isabella committed the deed, her husband would have his justification for ridding himself of the marriage that he despised and thus freeing England from its treaty with France. If, on the other hand, an imprisoned Scot woman was the culprit, Isabella would be vilified for weakness and negligence in showing mercy to a fellow lady of noble rank, but the English barons would never permit her to be exiled or executed, not after she had proven capable of bearing children with the unreliable Caernervon. His preference for men was now widely rumored across the Continent. Longshanks had beguiled Phillip into the marriage when his son had still been a callow youth. No monarch would risk bonding a daughter to Caernervon now.

She felt the infant's head pressing against her shriveled bosom. The wind was rising, and the first rays of dawn were forming on the horizon. The matron might return any moment to close the rattling shutters. She covered the babe's head with the corner of the blanket. *Why did I do that?* The infant nuzzled closer to her and fell asleep in her arms. She tried to quell the trembling in her hands. "My eyes are poor. May I take him to the light?"

Isabella assisted her to her feet and helped her walk with unsteady steps toward the bay window. She felt the queen's hands trembling against her elbows as she ran a finger across the child's matted sprouts of hair. A blast of sunlight suddenly hit her face, warning her that she had reached the ledge. This wee monster that ran with the ancestral blood of Longshanks reached for her breast. As she tightened her hold, her long nails brushed the infant's pink neck, and its mucous-rimmed eyes looked up at her in accusation. The queen eased the grasp on her elbow, allowing her the required freedom of movement to lean into the window. One more step and—

Heavy boot steps came thudding down the hall outside.

Isabella quickly took the child back, a moment before the chancellor of the royal household, accompanied by the sneering matron, entered the chamber.

The official took the infant from her. "The prince must be returned to the nursery. And you will be kind enough to join us, madam."

Belle silently cursed the meddling matron for reporting the request that they be left alone. Isabella had already tested the court's forbearance by ordering her to be temporarily removed from the cage. She could not risk a report of her unpopular leniency to a Scot prisoner being sent north to her husband.

"A minute more," Isabella begged the official. "I must help the lady walk a bit to regain the strength in her legs."

The chancellor would not relent. "Your chambermaid can attend to that."

Belle's spirit sank. Her delay had cost them the opportunity.

As the queen reluctantly prepared to leave with the court official, the infant wailed in protest and fought to return to Belle's arms. Isabella looked quizzically at the infant, then at Belle, unnerved by their sudden bonding.

Belle knew this might be her last chance to ask the question that had burned in her heart for years. Risking the suspicion of the chancellor, she turned aside and whispered to Isabella's ear, "Do you love him?"

Isabella acted as if she had forgotten something near the bed. She told the chancellor, "The lady has womanly needs I must attend."

He glared at her, but finally acquiesced to the delay in her departure. He handed the infant to the matron and followed her out.

When the door finally closed, Isabella walked to the window and stared across the Tweed meadows. "He is my child. Of course I love him."

"No, do you love *Jamie*?" She heard Isabella fussing at her gown in an attempt to avoid the subject. Try as she had, she could not shake the doubts that she had harbored since the night of Ragman signing, after she saw how Isabella had looked into James's eyes while dancing with him. He had always refused to talk of his time in Paris, and that, she feared, was telling. She could just make out the lines of Isabella's firm figure. "You are more beautiful than me. Any man would have chosen you."

Isabella stifled a cough of raw emotion. "It is true. I was drawn to your James. He was rough-hewn, but I could see the sculpture that would emerge."

"You shared his bed?"

The queen took Belle's hand to reassure her. "He was always faithful to you. I still remember how he described you. The most bonnie lass in all of Scotland."

Belle, fighting tears, nearly collapsed.

Isabella caught her and, leading her back to the bed, tucked the covers against her neck. "But he neglected to mention how stubborn you were. You must sleep while you can. I fear I will not be allowed to keep you here long." She had nearly reached the door when she turned back and asked, "That day at Lanercost?"

Belle reopened her heavy eyes. "Aye?"

"Longshanks would have sent you to a nunnery. Yet you taunted him into a rage. I have never understood why."

Belle looked up at the dark blurs above the rafters, reliving that horrid moment when her ordeal began. "My people have clawed at one another for centuries. We will never be free until we put aside our bickering and become united."

"How can your suffering change that?"

"My queen would have felt the full brunt of Longshanks's wrath. He was bent on setting an example with one of us. I knew Elizabeth Bruce could not survive a stark confinement."

"But even had that been so, Robert Bruce would still rule Scotland."

"Scotland's future depends as much on Lady Bruce as on my king," Belle explained. "If she fails to give birth to a son, there will be another clan war for the throne. And the Comyns will conspire to barter away our freedom."

A raven flew into the chamber and perched on the ledge.

Isabella tried to chase the intruder with a flap of her sleeve, but the harbinger insisted on sitting in vigil and cawing loudly.

Belle shivered from a chill—she began coughing and hacking.

Isabella looked down in horror at the sheets—they were stained with globs of blackened blood. Fearful that consumption was eating into Belle's lungs, the queen turned for the door. "I must call the physicians."

Belle heaved for breath to call her back. "No, please." Fighting off an encircling darkness, she begged, "Could I have a quill and parchment?"

Isabella nodded to indicate that she understood Belle's reluctance to trust the English doctors. She retrieved the writing instruments from a table and brought them to the bed with a small lap desk. She sat aside Belle and, placing the inked quill in her hand, brought its tip to the parchment laid out across the slant board.

Too blind to form the letters, Belle could only manage a few scratches. After several unsuccessful attempts to write the note, she fell back to the pillow in frustration.

Isabella took the quill from her failing hand. Glancing at the door, she whispered, "Speak the words to me."

Thirty-two

As the clear dawn of Midsummer Day broke over the soggy fields below Stirling Castle, three slashes of the royal standard atop Coxet Hill launched the Scot advance.

Led by James on horse, the Lanark men, with their pikes shouldered and their bowl-shaped helmets glistening in the low sun, emerged from their tree-covered encampment in the New Park. During the night, many had sewn white St. Andrew's crosses onto their bright yellow tunics and cowhide jerkins to distinguish comrade from foe. They marched in determined silence toward their assigned battle position just south of St. Ninian's kirk, where they would stand as the last barrier between the English army and Stirling Bridge. The passing of the rain clouds had tinctured the eastern horizon with a crimson haze; veterans of the Wallace campaigns whispered of having witnessed the same omen of drenching blood before the calamity at Falkirk.

James rode ahead to scout the dense copse that obstructed his vantage of the English encampment. He knew from memory that this carse descended gradually toward bogs veined with hundreds of sluggish rivulets. He had ordered the banners kept furled and the battle horns lowered, for if the English spied their approach too soon, Clifford might rush his knights to the Dryfield and destroy any chance they had of slowing the heavy destriers in the wetlands.

Moving swiftly, he and his men cleared the brush harls of Balquihidderoch Wood and came to a halt at the crest of a ridge. Below them, on the near side of the burn, hundreds of caparisoned chargers were forming up under heralds from Gascony, Holland, Brittany, Poitou, Aquitane, Bayonne, and Germany. Behind these knights in the service of England streamed an unbroken column of infantry reinforcements from the south.

On his flanks, the divisions commanded by Randolph and Edward Bruce stopped and descended to their knees. The Dewar of the Culdees, his white beard flowing in the wind, walked out of St. Ninian's kirk and, with the aid of

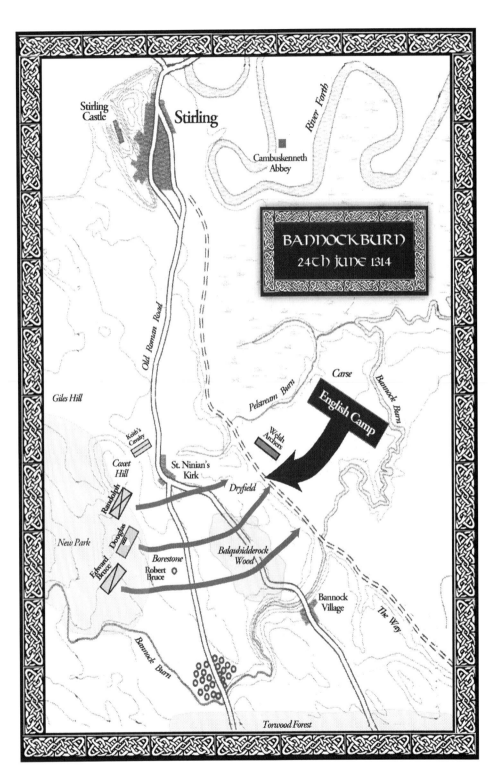

his staff, limped across the bowed ranks. The patriarch of the old Celtic Church had rushed here from Glen Dochart during the night to bless Robert's army with Caledonia's most hallowed relics. Following him came a procession of friars from the northern abbeys, including the sallow-faced Abbot of Arbroath, who held aloft the venerated Breacbannoch, the silver reliquary that held the bones of St. Columba.

Sweenie had not seen his spiritual father since the day he had left the Culdee hermitage in the Highlands to lead Robert's survivors across Loch Lomond. The squat little monk ran to a tearful reunion with the old abbot. The Dewar gifted his former acolyte with a long pole crowned by a wooden box that contained St. Fillan's shriveled arm. All Scots knew the story: When Fillan had prayed for light by which to read Scripture in his cave, his arm had miraculously glowed with the effluence of the Holy Spirit.

From the ranks, a shout rang out: "How many fingers on Fillan's hand?"

Sweenie turned with a grin toward that familiar call.

Angus Og MacDonald had arrived with the Culdees to take his assigned position on the right flank, an honor granted to his clan in perpetuity for rescuing the king and his ragged band on their run from the ambush at Methven.

Spurred by the Isles chieftain's mischievous nod, Sweenie opened the reliquary to solve the riddle of the giant Islesman's favorite password. The saint's desiccated hand—with all five fingers still intact—had curled into a fist. Inspired by the portent, Sweenie ran in front of the ranks and shouted, "The blessed Fillan clenches to hammer the Anglish swine!"

The men nearly trampled the little monk to witness the miracle.

The Dewar thrust his gnarled staff to the sky and shook the heavens with a cry. "The saints fight with ye to drive the papish devils back to Rome!"

James's throat seized with emotion. How he wished Lamberton were here to witness this battle that would be fought not by men alone, but alongside the gods of ancient Alba. The bishop had once told him the story of how Caesar's legions had butchered the Druids on the Isle of Anglesey. Centuries later, the papal missionaries had treated these descendants of the old religion no better. Now, the Dewar and his long-suffering Culdees had come to inflict their own spiritual revenge on the pope's English pawns.

Word of Fillan's clenched fist spread down the battle line, and the Scots began weeping and shouting names of murdered kinsmen. A quarter-mile to the south, Edward Bruce lashed his black pony across his ranks while reciting the English atrocities inflicted on his dead brothers. On the left, Randolph remained calm and cheerful, thumping the helmets of his men for good fortune. Behind the king's nephew, atop Coxet Hill, Keith the Marishal and his paltry cavalry of five hundred waited, their scrawny hobbins champing and pawing at the tumult.

Cull and Chullan, drawn by the cheering, came running from the New Park camp. Sensing the onset of battle, the old mastiffs had gnawed through their tethers to join their master.

"Back, you hounds!" James shouted, to no avail.

He shook his head in wonder at how the two grizzled dogs had survived for eighteen years under such affliction and deprivation. They came from hardy stock, bred from a father that had lived past the usual age of twelve; they seemed determined to hang on until vengeance was gained against England.

Sim Ledhouse laughed at how the frothing mastiffs would not retreat. He bared his teeth at them and smacked their noses, admiring their stubbornness. "Aye, Douglas, you're not the only one who has a score to settle."

Suddenly, amid this tumult of preparation, the field fell silent.

Robert, wearing the circlet of gold forged for his battle crown, galloped down from his signal station and dismounted in front of the Lanark division. With a set jaw, he drew his blade and strode toward James. "Douglas! On your knees!"

Surrounded by glares of suspicion, James descended as ordered. Had Robert learned of the secret meeting in Melrose Abbey? He lowered his head, fearing that rough justice was about to be meted out for treason. Robert came up with sword twitching and took aim at his neck. James braced for the blow—but the blade merely tapped his shoulders. He opened his eyes in confusion.

"James of Douglas," Robert shouted. "For brave service to Scotland and thy king, I knight thee banneret!"

The divisions on his flanks turned to witness the honor that could only be given in battle. Shouts of "Douglas! Douglas!" cascaded down their lines.

Edward Bruce muttered curses and refused to acknowledge the honor, but Randolph circled his horse to salute his friendly rival.

Sweenie rubbed away a tear. "He's going to be insufferable now. Come on, Douglas. Up with you. No time to rest on your laurels."

That jest drew laughter from the men. James had tried for years to break the monk's habit of referring to him as a lord. Now that he was due the deference, Sweenie, ever the true Scot, refused on principle to grant him the lofty title.

Robert mounted again and cantered before his infantry, who rested against their pikes, bracing for the inevitable speech recounting their travails and injustices over the decades, a litany they had heard a thousand times from their fathers and grandfathers. All had been issued the usual pardons and abeyances of debts, but such enticements meant little to men facing death. He stared at their expectant faces, trying to find the words sufficient to express his gratitude for their trust. Finally, he shouted, "My hope is constant in each of you! I leave airy speeches to the English! Few from their lips have ever been worthy of trust! I am told their king brings a chronicler paid gold to record his victory! I would send that wordsmith to his scrivener's bench to recount a tale of how we Scots won back a nation this day!"

Not one cheer met his call to arms.

James feared that Robert had lost them before the first blow was struck.

The mutinous Islesman who had threatened to desert during the cattle drill stepped forward. Making known his intent without words, he spat a black wad of oatcake onto the heather and thrust the butt end of his spear into his belt mount.

Seven thousand Scots followed his example and fixed their weapons.

Unaccustomed to rising so early, Caernervon yawned and rubbed the sleep from the dark circles under his eyes. His head pounded from a hangover. He had tossed and turned all night, kept awake by the infernal din in the camp. Leaving Hugh Despenser still asleep inside, he arose and staggered through the flaps of the pavilion in his nightshirt to search for the nearest wine casket.

For the first time, he confronted the logistical chaos spawned by his order to wheel the army east of the Scot encampment. Thousands of hooves and boots had churned the muddy ground around him into a morass of manure and piss, requiring the engineers to dismantle every shack in the nearby village to lay planks for footing. Weighed down by their soaked gambesons, his conscripts, forced to choose between sleeping in the muck and standing all night in their battle gear, stared up at him with the deadened eyes of cadavers. The victual wagons remained halted on the far side of the river to allow the baggage trains carrying the livery of his knights to cross first. The few sacks of oats ferried across to feed the infantry had become drenched, and those who had risked eating the rancid meal were now doubled over with the scours. The entire army stank from rot and the runs.

He slogged through the camp until he found his officers.

Slumped with fatigue, Clifford, Gloucester, Cam Comyn, and D'Argentin sat at the ready on their loam-spackled steeds.

"In God's name! Why have you not taken Stirling?"

"Our rear echelons have not yet come up," Gloucester told the king.

"And pray tell, why not?"

"Only one ford is passable."

Caernervon slung the remnants of his wine at the earl, spooking the horses and setting off a chain reaction of curses and jostling through the crowded ranks. "You don't need the entire army! The castle is right over *there*!"

Clifford managed to calm his skittish mount. "Bruce waits on the high ground."

"He *waits!* And he will continue to *wait!*" Caernervon turned to Cam Comyn for his opinion. "What say you on this, Scot?"

Cam shrugged, confident. "Bruce is no Wallace. When he sees our knights on the move, he'll run for the Isles."

Gloucester had become alarmed by the king's recent transformation. As a young man, Caernervon had shown no interest in military affairs, leaving tactical decisions to his father's officers. But on this campaign, he had fallen under the grandiose delusion that his father's genius had spontaneously blossomed in him. The unexpected—and in some quarters, unexplained—birth of a son seemed to have filled him with a sense of invincibility. "The men and horses are fatigued, Sire. If we rest a day and gather strength, the ground will firm."

"Look!" Caernervon pointed to Dryfield, where the Scots had descended to their knees. "Did I not tell you? They beg for mercy!"

"Mercy from God," Gloucester said. "Not you, my lord."

"If you are too craven to fight, I will order Clifford to lead the advance!"

His honor besmirched, Gloucester unbuckled his breastplate and threw it to the ground. Caernervon smiled with the presumption that the troublesome earl had just relinquished his command, but Gloucester slammed down his visor and spurred to the fore of the waiting knights. The monarch was about to wave off the baron's bluffing theatrics when he heard a distant roar. He turned to his French mercenary and inquired, "What is that commotion at their center?"

D'Argentin nodded with pride. "Douglas has been knighted."

The king laughed. "Then both he *and* Bruce will retreat in grand style."

"I have never met Robert Bruce. But I assure you, Sire, Douglas will not run."

"What makes you so certain?"

D'Argentin tightened the bindings on his breastplate. "I trained him."

As the French knight rode off to join Gloucester, Caernervon saw Despenser sauntering out of the tent to take a piss. "Hah! Instructed by a Parisian, Hugh! All the more reason we have nothing to fear from that rabble. Where is my cook? I cannot ride without breaking my fast." From the corner of his eye, he saw James Douglas on the far ridge being mobbed with congratulations. With a scheming gleam, he retrieved a sword and approached Clifford. "You and this Douglas have been like Cain and Abel, no?"

Clifford kept his steely gaze fixed on the Scot army in the distance. "I am no brother to that man, my lord."

"Still, Douglas should not enjoy all the glory this day." The king flippantly buffeted the officer on each shoulder. "Sir Robert Clifford." He tossed the sword to the mud and renewed his search for a repast.

Clifford smoldered at the bitter irony. The knighthood unjustly denied him all of these years had been granted as an afterthought, not in recognition for his accomplishments, but as a meaningless parry to Douglas. Empty accolades from this frivolous monarch meant nothing to him. He should have received the honor from Longshanks years ago. Now, too old to prosper under the rank, he lived only to gain revenge against that Scotsman who had ruined his career.

He pulled out the order for Belle's execution and took grim solace in its contents, having convinced the king to sign it as a precaution should one of the rebellious barons back in Yorkshire attempt to abduct her. He handed the order to Cam Comyn. "On my signal, deliver it to Berwick."

J ames watched as Clifford, d'Argentin, and Gloucester led their knights out from the English camp in single file and fell into a faster pace along the bridle path that ran parallel to the old Roman road. He held his breath in rising hope: Just as he had predicted, Clifford appeared intent on making for Stirling Castle rather than forming up battle lines. He had read his old enemies perfectly: Caernervon had positioned his infantry to the far side of his cavalry, where they could offer no protection.

The whoresons had taken the bait.

Three blasts from the horn sounded by Robert's herald sent Randolph and Edward Bruce hurling down the escarpment.

Clifford and his knights wheeled left in a stunning maneuver.

James lurched forward in his saddle. *Damn him! It's a feint!*

He tried to stall the other schiltrons, but he was too late. Clifford had only mimicked the attempt for Stirling to draw them out. The English knights lowered their lances and drove their chargers toward the Carse.

Both armies were locked in a desperate race for the Dryfield.

The Lanarkshire men waited for his order to join in the charge, but James sat motionless in the saddle. He spotted the Comyn banner at the royal pavilion. Why was Clifford keeping Cam in the rear?

Comyn is the courier to Berwick.

"Jamie?" Ledhouse shouted. "On them, or the lads will be turned!"

James heard his name called out by a hundred pleading voices, but one rose above the others. He looked to his right, where a dead oak had been splintered and blackened by lightning. A solitary bloom sprouted on one of its pocked branches.

"Jamie! I love you! Give the order, Jamie!"

Belle's voice seemed to inhabit the hollowed tree trunk.

Perplexed, he rode closer to the log to examine it.

A raven crawled from the detritus and pecked at the bloom until the last vestige of life in the oak was destroyed. The raven shape-shifted into the goddess Morgainne, who confronted him with a fearsome glare. "You plot to deny me?"

"Away!" James screamed at the death hag. "Not this day!"

"Aye, this day it is. I *will* have a soul dear to thee."

"Not her!"

Morgainne shot him a wicked smile, and before he could accost her again, she melded back into the raven's form and flew off.

All around him, the men were staring, as if questioning his sanity.

Randolph and Edward Bruce's divisions careened into Clifford's knights across the Carse, their long-necked axes and claymores clashing against the English armor with a rat-a-tat-tat that was overtaken by screams and groans. The sky exploded with splinters as the Scots rushed to the underbellies of the English horses and hacked at their fetlocks. The field erupted into a bedlam of flailing limbs, agonized neighing, dying curses, bleeding horseflesh, thumping cudgels, and hurdling maces.

On the summit, Robert watched James from afar, vexed by his delay.

I n his tent, Caernervon's attendants attired him in the black hammered armor that his father had worn in the French and Welsh campaigns. He had ordered the breastplate tailored to his specifications for this long-awaited day. Within the hour, he would ride into Stirling and finally silence the insults that he had suffered since childhood. He was about to prove beyond all doubt that he was indeed the son of Edward the First, conqueror of Wales. He would accomplish what even his even father had failed to attain: The complete subjugation of Scotland.

Of course, he would have to chase Bruce into the Highlands to finish him off, but the fickle clans would deliver up that ungrateful brood with Douglas rather than suffer the consequences, just as they had done with Wallace. For years he had dreamt of marching the two cutthroats back to England in a triumphant procession reminiscent of Caesar's return to Rome with the Gaulish savages. He had promised to hold Douglas's execution under that Scotswoman's cage. But he would save Robert Bruce for a public quartering at London Tower.

He peered through his tent flaps and saw Cam Comyn waiting on a horse. "How goes Clifford's progress?"

Cam could barely sputter the reply. "Slow, my lord."

"Whatever do you mean?"

"The Bruce ... " Cam had trouble finishing the report. "... has attacked."

Caernervon rushed out of the pavilion. Instead of retreating, the Scots were charging down the sloping ground toward his encampment. Stunned, he commandeered his mount and, after several awkward stabs at the stirrups, leveraged to the saddle. As he spurred toward the lines, his frown of confusion became a broad grin. "Bruce, you fool! This is even better than I could have imagined! I will destroy you before the hour is up!" He saw the Lanarkshire division still holding its first position. "Does Douglas not engage?"

Cam followed the king on the precipitous ride toward the front. "He is learning a rough lesson from Clifford!"

"Indeed?" cried the king, laughing. "What lesson would that be?"

On their rush to victory, Cam reached under his gambeson and felt for Belle's execution order. "Never go to battle pining for a wench!"

R obert galloped down from Coxet Hill and hurled an ax into the sky. James deflected the falling weapon with his forearm. He looked at the trampled grass and could barely believe his eyes. During the night, Robert had recovered the splintered remnants of the Dun Eadainn relic and had cobbled its handle with twine and nails. The ax still bore the markings where Belle had retraced his name to preserve the memory of his boyhood victory.

Rob or Belle, again.

How many times had he been forced to make that choice?

He took a deep breath and brought Belle's face to his memory. One soul was what Morgainne demanded this day. By God, he would give it to her! If he could never see Belle again, he would make certain *she* would not be the one to die.

Nodding sternly to Robert, he led his division into the Dryfield.

On the run, he found Randolph and Edward Bruce being thrown back into their outnumbered hedgehog formations. Clifford's knights were trying to break their schiltrons by hurling maces at them. Gloucester, unidentifiable without his heraldic armor, was swallowed up in the scramble of English knights and pike-thrusting Scots. The earl's helmet was ripped from his head. He fought bravely, but there was a wearied resignation in his eyes. As the Scots dragged him from his horse, he left his chest exposed, as if wishing to die.

James shouted, "Spare that man!"

The din of the battle drowned out his plea.

He fought a path toward Gloucester, but the baron fell to the bottom of the bloody scrum.

J ames stood in the center of his mangled schiltron, barking orders and whipsawing maces while Cull and Chullan attacked any Englishman who had the misfortune of breaking through. Hours had passed since the first clash of arms that morning, but the sun now seemed locked at its apex, turning the battle into a desperate struggle of endurance. Stout legs and hearts would win this day, he knew, not more tactics.

Clifford's banner suddenly appeared above a pack of English knights trying to hack a path through the Yorkshire conscripts pressed upon its rear. Ledhouse was about to reach for Clifford and hammer him from his horse, but James pushed his officer aside and lunged to strike the deathblow.

Cull sprang over his master's head and dug his fangs into Clifford's biceps. Wrangled from his saddle, Clifford pummeled the mastiff with his spiked arm-guards. The old hound, gushing blood from its nose, dropped lifeless. Clifford heaved James to the muck and shouted for more English reinforcements to pour through the breach and drive back the schiltrons.

James sank deeper into the loam, trampled by the rush of boots.

Clifford dug a heel into James's neck and shouted, "Bring up the longbows!"

A thousand Welsh archers blazoned with the crosses of St. George formed a wedged herce across from the Lanark division. With practiced precision, they impaled their staves into the ground for quick loading and leveraged their tall yew bows by malleting them into holes. The masters threw tufts of grass to judge the wind and then barked orders for their bowmen to error on the side of overshooting to increase the odds of hitting deserters.

The Scot ranks groaned with despair, bracing to suffer deadly volleys from the same sharp-eyed mercenaries who had brought down Wallace at Falkirk.

With a slight incline of their heads, the Welsh archers leaned into their bows and filled the sky with a shrill whistling. Seconds later, both Scots and English knights fell impaled. The schiltrons lurched back and crumbled, and some of the men threw down their pikes and ran.

Half buried in the mud, James slipped from consciousness.

Leaving him for dead, Clifford rushed ahead to lead the charge that would win the day.

My time. Not yours.

Morgainne's command in his ear revived James. He resurrected from the mire with his face streaked in loam. Coughing and gasping, he turned and found Robert galloping across the Dryfield, leading Keith's cavalry in a frantic effort to rally the survivors back to the New Park.

Clifford drove his panting levies up the Dryfield slope.

Just as the last of the Scot squares were about to break, an unnatural stillness overtook the field. Both armies lowered their weapons and gazed toward Giles Hill, behind the Scot lines, where a hundred mounted knights now appeared on the horizon. Framed by the crimson sun, the riders unrolled the packs from their saddles and donned white mantles blazoned with red crosses. One of the knights raised a banner with a black square adjacent to a white square.

Clifford spotted the Beausant insignia. Breaking a triumphant grin, he shouted Longshanks's famous quip from the Berwick tourney years ago. "The Templars always pick the winning side!"

Those Scots who were still holding the lines now backed away, stricken by the unexpected arrival of the crusader monks.

James's heart sank. Here was Falkirk all over again.

Clifford signaled for his archers to move forward. "Finish them!"

The Templars lashed to the charge, taking aim at the Scot schiltrons.

Trapped, James quickly revamped his depleted squares and ordered his survivors to face both directions. He had no choice but to sacrifice a few to save many. "Those in front! At my command, fall on those behind you!"

His men in the front row turned ashen glares on him, stunned that he was ordering the veterans to take the brunt of the arrows.

Now even more confident of victory, the Welsh archers methodically notched their bows and waited for the Templars to drive the Scots from the squares and expose the enemy to their murderous fire. A few lengths from the schiltrons, the Templars veered to their left and charged instead at the Welsh.

The archers, panicking, wavered and broke without firing their bodkins.

Undone by the Templar perfidy, Clifford clambered across the wounded in a desperate effort to marshal his retreating archers. "No! Damn you! Hold!"

James thrilled at his sudden turn of fortune. The Templars had merely dissembled an attack on his Scots in a ruse to escape the range of the Welsh arrows. The crusader monks drove into the phalanx of archers shouting the names of their brethren who had been murdered by the Roman Church and its allies, the French and English monarchs.

Peter d'Aumont and Jeanne de Rouen threw off their helmets, gasping for breath in the stifling air. Riding hard, they took aim at Caernervon's encampment, where a cadre of Dominican friars had congregated in preparation to take over the Scot abbeys. As Jeanne raced past the crumbling Scot schiltrons, she glanced fiercely at James to spur him to the promise of the moment.

James rallied his survivors back down the scarp. The English infantry, no longer certain who they were fighting, broke for the protection of their camp and swept up Clifford and his knights in the retreat.

"On them!" James screamed. "They fail!"

Clifford stumbled in the quagmire. On his knees, he looked up to see James swinging his ax. The officer rolled and kicked James's feet from under him, then crawled toward the burn.

James dropped to his knees, too exhausted to give chase.

Chullan, circling his dead twin in grief, pinned its ears back on hearing Clifford's shout. As if inspirited with a miracle of returned youth, the old mastiff darted through the whirlpool of legs and dived into the burn. Slowed by his armour, Clifford tried to escape. Chullan paddled furiously across the burn and pounced for the officer's jugular. Clifford thrashed to parry the attack, but the mastiff latched onto his neck and dragged him under the water.

Moments later, Clifford's head—torn from its neck—bobbed to the surface.

Caernervon watched in disbelief as his army stampeded back toward him. The Scots were driving his infantry into the burn; those levies who could not swim sank under the weight of their padded doublets.

D'Argentin high-stepped his charger over the crawling mass of panic to reach the royal pavilion. "Sire, I must remove you to safety at once!"

Caernervon threw off his helmet and tore at his hair. "Rally them!"

"You must flee! Else England will pay a ransom it can ill afford!"

Finding Caernervon too disoriented to move, d'Argentin dragged him to a horse, leaving behind the royal shield and armory. Accompanied by Cam Comyn and an escort of twenty knights, the Frenchman led the king across a ford in the burn and circled the battle in a race to reach Stirling Castle.

Minutes later, the royal entourage reined up under Stirling's battlements.

Caernervon, his eyes wild with panic, looked up at the walls and shouted a demand for sanctuary. "Open these gates!"

Philip Mowbray, the English commander of the besieged castle, had been watching the battle from the ramparts. His scowl betrayed his disdain for this king who now begged protection under the very law he had violated in abducting the Scotswomen in Tain. "I gave my word to the Bruce. If you do not relieve this castle by dusk, I must relinquish it."

"To Hell with your word! I am your liege, damn you!"

Mowbray remained adamant in his refusal to violate his oath to the Scots.

While the king raved on with hysterical threats, d'Argentin spied Keith's cavalry massing near St. Ninian's kirk. Seeing that they were about to be trapped, the French knight ordered Cam, "Take him to Linlithglow without delay."

"Where are *you* going?" Caernervon demanded.

"Back to the battle."

"I paid for your protection!"

D'Argentin's eyes hooded with revulsion for the sobbing king. "There has been dishonor enough this day. I do not intend to add to that roll."

Caernervon reached into his belt pouch, pulled out a gold groat, and threw the coin at the knight. "Inconstant Frank! Take your Judas pay with you!"

D'Argentin stared at the king's profile on the coin, as if searching an explanation for how he had been seduced into the service of such a feckless monarch. "All my life I have fought for gold. This day, I will fight for something else, as do Gloucester and those Scots." He flung the coin off the wall and rode off to join the overwhelmed English troops.

Robert spurred his frothing destrier down the Carse to exhort his men to leave off taking booty and finish the victory. He found James below the scarp, tending to the wounded. "Jamie, are you injured?"

Surrounded by slashed and writhing bodies, James struggled to his feet to show that he was unscathed. "The field is ours!"

"Aye, but not the prize." Robert pointed toward a band of horsemen circling around Stirling crag. "Caernervon escapes!"

Belle's execution order.

In the heat of battle, he had forgotten about Cam Comyn.

He captured the nearest horse and galloped west along the burn, accompanied by a contingent of Templars. His only chance to stop Caernervon and Comyn now would be to head them off before they reached the bridge that led to the only passable road west. He cut through the bramble of New Park and came upon the royal entourage hurrying toward the river. The far bank was thick with English pike men—and Caernervon had already gained the bridge.

Seeing Cam still waiting to cross, James lashed to the chase. "Comyn!"

Caernervon sped on, but Cam stopped to taunt James with a finger in the air. James heaved his ax at the turncoat Scot, and Cam laughed as the weapon bounced short off the bridge. He waved the execution order and shouted, "Any last words for your Fife whore?"

James leapt from his staggered horse and charged the bridge, but a hail of arrows stopped his advance. When he lifted his eyes from under his arm, Cam was halfway across. He shouted at Cam, "I'll see you in Hell!"

"Save me a place when you—"

Cam stared down at his chest. He ripped open his gambeson to find an arrow point emerging from his sternum. He held a perplexed look, as if questioning how a missile had reached him from that distance. With blood dribbling from his mouth, he tried to hand the order to a sergeant at the bridge gate. A second arrow whistled through the air and sent his horse plummeting over the abutment. He was caught in the stirrups and dragged under the river's currents.

The order slipped from his grasp and floated away.

At the river's edge, James searched for the source of the arrows.

An English knight armed with a spent crossbow rode out from behind a tree on the far side of the river. James Webton, the officer whose honor he had spared seven years ago at Castle Douglas, nodded to confirm that his debt was paid, and then galloped off rejoin his king in the retreat.

For two weeks, James and the Templars had stalked Caernervon in a circuitous chase west and south of Stirling. Yet despite fighting a series of hard-pitched skirmishes, they had failed to break through the royal guards, and now Caernervon was approaching the port city of Dunbar, where a galley waited to take him down the coast to Berwick.

Randolph, hurrying south from the battlefield, intercepted James and his fellow pursuers riding north along the Tweed River in a desperate attempt to intercept Caernervon's fleet before it reached the sea. "Hold off, Jamie! The king wishes you back to Stirling! I am to take command here!"

James reined up reluctantly, suspecting Randolph of instigating the recall so that he could gain all the glory. "Another night and I will have him."

"His orders were for you to come at once."

James cursed his failure to capture Caernervon. "How many men did we lose in the battle?"

"Less than three hundred. Fillan's miracle, for certain."

"And the English?"

"Four thousand, maybe more," Randolph said. "Half of those sank in the pols or drowned in the burn. Caernervon abandoned his baggage train with two hundred thousand pounds of gold and silver."

"That's more than our entire treasury."

"Aye, and weapons enough to arm us ten times over." Randolph led him several lengths from the others to finish his report. "The king has fallen into one of his black moods. He refuses to break his vigil over Gloucester's body."

"Your uncle has never been able to abide good fortune. He'll not be content until he reaches the fires of Hell to confirm the low opinion he holds of his own soul. Did he say why he required me so urgently?"

Randolph's eyes flashed a mischievous twinkle. "A prisoner exchange has been arranged. The English have agreed to hand over our queen for Hereford and Thweng."

"You came all this way to tell me that? Why in heaven's name must I—"

Randolph's smirk spread into a wide grin, leaving James speechless. "I also recall him mentioning something about another lady being part of the agreement. What was her name? Oh, aye. I think he called her the Lass of Scone."

James repeated those last words silently. Then, he lashed his horse into a gallop, cursing, "Damn you, Randolph! Why didn't you say so right off?"

As his old rival rushed north in a heat, Randolph winked at Jeanne. "Douglas would never make a Templar, eh? No vows of chastity for him."

His cruel withholding of the news did not amuse Jeanne. She sidled her horse next to him and offered her opinion on the matter. "One thing is certain. No lady would ever wait seven years for *you.*"

For once, the wisecracking Randolph was cast mute as a stone. Before he could protest that charge as undeserved, the French Cistercienne spurred off to catch up with James.

James and Jeanne crossed the battlefield below Stirling and made haste for Cambuskenneth Abbey, an Augustinian monastery ensconced in a loop of the River Forth. On the lowlands between the Pelstream and the Bannock burn, the sun had combined with the macabre effects of rigor mortis to disgorge hundreds of submerged corpses and horse carcasses. Many of the dead soldiers had been pushed upright from shallow graves, some to their waists, others to their necks, all serving as carrion for the crows.

James rushed ahead along the Forth's banks and found the abbey grounds piled with English shields and abandoned armour.

Robert, haggard and bleary-eyed, walked out from Cambuskenneth's doors. His physical deterioration was alarming; his skin had broken out in red splotches and he clawed nervously at an open sore on his forearm.

Despite these misgivings, James leapt from the saddle before his horse had even halted and grasped Robert by the forearms. "Is it true?"

Robert led him out of earshot of the men-at-arms mingling along the riverbank. Agitated, he brushed his wild black hair in an attempt to affect nonchalance, but he could not hide the fact that he was as flustered as a schoolboy. "We must prepare ourselves. They have no doubt altered greatly in appearance."

"Where are they?"

Nodding with a turn of his head toward the Abbot's quarters, Robert held James back from running to its entrance. "We must give the English no cause to think us too eager to negotiate."

James closed his eyes, trying to calm his nerves. His heart was beating so fiercely that he found it difficult to breathe. At the well, he drew water to wash the grime from his face and saw his reflection in the bucket. He had been in his mid-twenties when Belle had last seen him. Deep lines now creased his face, and he slumped slightly from the aches in his back and knees. He conjured up for the thousandth time the image of her dark, penetrating eyes and soft lips. The memory of her radiance that day in Glen Dochart was the only thing that had kept him from despair.

I wish the book returned, James Douglas.

Reminded of Belle's last words to him, he felt for the small volume under his shirt. He sighed with relief. The *Chanson of Fierabras* had survived the battle.

He pulled the book out and dried its pages in the breeze. This day, he would fulfill that promise. Through all the years, he and Robert had read the tale over and again in the saddle and during long nights. He had heard every word of it in Belle's voice, and had saved the last chapter to read with her. All of that was now past. The Comyns were dead and the English repulsed. He had already picked out their wedding oak, near the chapel on Stirling Crag. They would finish their vows before this day was done. Nothing would keep them apart again.

Edward Bruce, escorted by Keith's cavalry and the Templars, came trodding on horse across the bridge. Envious of the accolades that James was receiving for the successful battle strategy, Edward refused his rival even a nod of acknowledgment as he prodded up ten English prisoners tied to a cart that carried three large wine casks. Then, remembering his place, Edward stopped and waited for his brother to take the lead.

Robert paused at the top step of the abbey to fix his grandfather's gold brooch on his cloak. In a gesture of celebration, he firmed his hold on James's forearm to share the moment they had both so fervently awaited. Then, with a deep breath, he nodded for Edward to open the doors.

Their boots echoed off the flagstones as they strode down the nave's central aisle. Robert stopped several paces from the altar, indignant at not finding the English emissaries waiting for him. He had won the battle, not Caernervon. He would not cool his heels for a defeated opponent. He turned to leave.

The Abbot of Lagny, surrounded by a guard of English knights, walked forth from the sacristy. The inquisitor appeared so disgusted with his assigned diplomatic task that he refused the Scots a direct look.

Robert ordered forward the Earl of Hereford and Sir Marmaluke Thweng, the two ranking prisoners. He also called up a plump Carmelite friar named Baston, the English scribe who had been found wandering aimlessly along the burn after the battle.

Lagny glared disgust at the captured chronicler. "This coward is not part of the arrangement."

"He is now," Robert said dryly. "The friar intends to give a different account of the battle than the one commissioned by your king."

For the first time, the Dominican saw the Templars in the Scot entourage. The inquisitor made a menacing move toward the monks who had ruined his plans for dominance over the rebellious Church of Scotland. "Traitorous heretics! I watched your sodomite De Molay burn on the pyre!"

Jeanne came face to face with the man who had helped conspire the arrests and executions of her spiritual brethren in France. "*Oui*, and as he suffered in the flames, our grand master called the pope and the French king to God's tribunal within the year to stand for their crimes. Clement has already answered his summons in Hell. Phillip will follow soon enough. As will you."

When the Dominican raised his hand in threat, James drew his blade and brought it to the monk's throat. "Your reign of terror holds no office here."

"I have authority to call off this exchange," the Dominican warned.

James nodded for Keith's men to bring up the English privy seal and royal shield, priceless accoutrements that Caernervon had abandoned in his haste to leave the field. "The shield appears unused," he said pointedly. "I wonder how your king will react when told that they hang it on display in Dunfermline because of your impertinence."

The Dominican suddenly lost his bluster.

Robert signaled up the large wine casks that held the bodies of Gloucester, d'Argentin, and Clifford, all pickled in brine. "My cousin and the Frenchman are to be buried with honors. You can throw Clifford's bones into the Thames for all I care."

"Lord Gloucester's family has asked his armour be returned," Lagny said.

"He wore none. He preferred an honorable death to serving a dishonorable monarch." James allowed Hereford and Thweng to pass into the hands of the English. "We have complied with our terms. Now, you will fulfill yours."

Shaken by the report of Gloucester's martyrdom, the Dominican reluctantly signaled for his guards to enter the sacristy. They brought out Elizabeth Bruce, Mary Campbell, Christian Seton, and Robert's daughter, Marjorie.

Gaunt and pale, Elizabeth rushed to Robert's arms. But Marjorie, eyes crazed with fear, held back.

Robert reached for his daughter, now eighteen, and tried to coax her to him, "Come, child. It is over."

Marjorie screamed and slapped away his hands.

Elizabeth brought the shaking girl to her side and shielded her eyes from the stares of strangers. She whispered to Robert, "She's not in her right mind."

From the shadows of the choir stall, an old man shuffled into the dim light. He limped toward James with bated steps, as if his ankles were shackled. "By God's grace," he muttered as he reached for James. "By God's grace."

Lagny turned with a huff to leave, revolted at being forced to give up the one man he deemed most responsible for this unthinkable calamity.

Fighting tears, James rushed to embrace Bishop Lamberton. He looked over the old cleric's shoulder and counted the faces of the women who had been delivered. Grinning, he pulled away and searched the recesses behind the choir and altar. He knew Belle's tricks. She was hiding to surprise him. After all this time, she still played with him as if they were youngsters. He would find her out and lift her to the rafters. He shoved open the sacristy door and waited for her to spring upon him.

The anteroom was empty.

Suddenly cold with dread, James rushed back into the nave and captured the inquisitor's arm in a demand. "The Countess of Buchan?"

Savoring a smile, the Dominican brushed off his imploring grasp.

Lamberton braced James at the shoulders, and shook his head.

"But Randolph told me … Is she not well enough to endure the journey?" James turned to Robert. "I'll leave at once for Berwick to bring her back."

The frail bishop firmed his grip. "Jamie … she is dead."

A raven's shriek shuddered the nave.

James staggered and nearly fell, until Lamberton caught him.

When the Dominican lingered to enjoy James's grief-stricken prostration, Robert charged at him in a fury. "Out! Out of my sight!"

The inquisitor quickly herded his ransomed lords from the abbey before the exchange could be renegotiated.

Robert turned back to find James on his knees. He tried to bring his friend to standing, but James repulsed the effort. Robert stood over him in anguished silence, at a loss what to say. When James refused even to look up at him, Robert could only nod for the others to depart with him. As the Scots walked from the abbey in silence, they pressed a hand to James's shoulder to acknowledge his loss.

Jeanne lingered behind in the shadows of the narthex, determined to make certain that he did no harm to himself.

PART THREE
The Heart Returns

1315–1330 A.D.

If a stone falls down the glen, it's in the cairn it will rest.

— ancient Scottish proverb

thirty-three

As Jeanne de Rouen led the king's daughter, Marjorie, on horse into the Lintalee defile, she reached for her dagger, a reflex from that day six years ago when she and the Templars had been ambushed by James and his raiders in this shadowy archway of hanging firs. The path was still littered with carts and helmets abandoned by the English army on its retreat from Stirling. Overhead, magpies chirred frantically above the broom thickets. Were they warning her away?

Just then, the new Douglas manor came into her view, rising beyond the leafy tunnel and shimmering under the golden summer sun on a half-moon curve of high ground. Two rows of concentric walls surrounded the round tower of whitewashed logs; its steep roof rose to a point, giving the place more the appearance of a small Loire château than a Highland keep. This new fortified headquarters was perfectly situated to serve as a bolthole for raids into Northumbria. Below the manor, Sweenie and the men lazed along the stream trading stories and arm-wrestling while James, stripped to the waist and alone in the vale, attacked a tall pine with a notch ax.

Apprehensive, the French Cistercienne slowed their approach. Two years had passed since she had last seen him. The Almighty, it seemed, never gave without taking, for although the English had been bloodied at Bannockburn and the queen restored to Robert, the victory had come at a heavy price. News of the battle's outcome had not yet reached Berwick when the Countess of Buchan was found dead. To calm the Yorkshire populace until he could sail to London, Caernervon had sent couriers ahead to spread word across northern England that both Robert and James had been killed. Many Scots believed that Belle had given up her spirit in despair after hearing the scurrilous report.

Despite his crushing defeat, Caernervon continued to press his illegal claim on the Scottish throne. As a result, James had been required to renew his war of attrition here in the Borders, and there were rumors that he had fallen into such a debilitating despond that he now broke his seclusion only to vent his rage by pillaging the English marches.

The men finally spotted the two women and rushed up from the clearing to pepper them with questions about news from the North. Sweenie applauded their arrival. "Now we can hold the housewarming."

From afar, Jeanne kept watching James, who remained in the vale, refusing to acknowledge her. She made a move to ride over to him, but Sweenie captured her bridle to insist that she not grovel. She thought he looked gaunt. Had he not been eating? Why would he not come to her? When the tree he was attacking finally fell, he seemed to take satisfaction that another of God's creations shared his pain. He threw the ax over his shoulder and walked toward the lodge without offering her even a nod in welcome.

While the men helped Marjorie from her pony, Jeanne dismounted and took off her gloves. Brushing back her hair, she whispered to Sweenie, "Do I need to go in there armed?"

The little monk, seeing her determined to speed the confrontation, reluctantly escorted her to the gate of the manor. He offered some counsel before allowing her to enter alone. "Pay him no mind. He's not been his old self."

Inside the hall, she found James slumped on a stool, aimlessly stirring the logs in the hearth. When he refused to turn and greet her, she risked a step closer. "The king has appointed you Warden of the Marches."

He erupted to his feet and kicked the stool against the wall. "I suppose he thought that one up in the queen's embrace!"

She was disappointed to find that his brooding anger had not dissipated with the passage of months. Randolph had been sent south several times to negotiate a reconciliation with Robert, but the king's nephew had only inflamed James's bitterness with reports of how Elizabeth had turned Dunfermline into a jovial home. She suspected that Robert had dispatched her here, too, for a purpose other than delivering orders and escorting his daughter on a diversion in the countryside. But now she saw from this cold welcome that she was the last person suited for such a diplomatic task. During those black days after the battle, she had remained at James's side, secretly falling in love with him. Yet the more she attempted to break through his pain, the deeper he seemed to resent her for not being Belle. He had fled Stirling without even offering a goodbye to her. She had hoped to find his heart healed, but she saw that her arrival had merely reopened the wound. With regret, she retreated to the door. "I'll not impose upon you further."

"Why did you bring Marjorie here?"

She turned back, grateful, at least, for those few words. "The physicians have given up on her. The king hoped you might raise her spirits."

James angled toward the window and watched the men entertain Marjorie with a game of cards outside. He had always held a warm place in his heart for the star-crossed lass. Although she was now twenty years old, her maturation had been stunted by the years spent in English confinement. A child still in both temperament and intelligence, she had become withdrawn, frightened by the most harmless of noises, and was a constant irritant to Robert, who cared about her well-being only because she was now seven months with child. All Scotland watched the progress of her pregnancy with great concern, for Elizabeth had not produced a male heir and Robert now suffered more frequently from his mysterious illness. The commoners constantly pestered the poor lass to touch her womb, and the nobles whispered fears about the mental condition of the infant she would bring to term. It was an unbearable burden for the painfully shy girl, who found it difficult enough to make it through each day without breaking down.

Earlier that year, fearing another struggle for the crown should Marjorie's infant not come to term, Bishop Lamberton had reconvened the Parliament to establish a line of succession. Edward Bruce had been chosen first for the throne, but he was so reckless that few expected him to outlive his older brother. At long last giving up hope of siring a male, Robert had betrothed Marjorie to the son of one of his oldest allies, Walter Stewart, the High Steward of Scotland. Young Stewart had performed his marital duties with admirable swiftness. Everyone—except the Comyn expatriates—prayed for a boy.

Jeanne scanned the mud-spackled walls and considered how she might make the place more hospitable. A good soap rubbing would chase the harsh aroma of cut wood, and she would replace the floor straw with sprinkled lavender and sweet fennel. The rafters begged for tapestries, the creaking floorboards for the warmth of rugs. She had seen an elmwood armoire in Stirling that would fit perfectly in the alcove. "Did Castle Douglas look like this?"

He shook his head. "That is a memory I wish forever banished."

She spied two swords propped in the corner. Perhaps there was another way to rouse him from his self-pity. "Did I not once promise you a rematch?"

He waved her off, in no mood for such nonsense—until she retrieved one of the swords and prodded him in the ribs. He tried to steal the weapon from her, but she demonstrated the same quickness he remembered when they fought under the shadows of Notre Dame. He took the other blade and squared off with her. "What do I get if I win?"

"From the smell of things around here, you could use some laundering."

He kicked aside the soiled clothing—and lunged at her with a quick wrist snap, severing a couple buttons on her blouse.

She looked down at her partially exposed chest. "That is base chivalry!"

"What would a French hussy know of chivalry?"

When she dropped her chin with hurt, he lowered his sword and came closer to beg her forgiveness. She spun and drove the weapon from his grasp. Disarmed, he backed away and felt for the blade on the floor with his boot. If he bent to reclaim it, she would have the advantage.

"What are you waiting for?" she taunted. "At your advanced age, if you tarry much longer, you'll not be able to reach the floor."

"And you? Your reward in the unlikely event you prevail?"

"I've not been on a picnic since Paris. Cheese, wine, and pastries."

He toed his blade closer. "Where would I get pastries around here?"

She poked him in the gut. "Are there not bakeries in York? Or is that city beyond your reach?" When he made a move for his weapon, she kicked it across the floor and backed him into a corner. He raised his hands in concession. With a smirk of conquest, she lowered her blade. "And don't think you can slip that cheap Lanark cider—" The sword was knocked from her grasp.

He grasped her wrists and pinned her against the wall. The more she struggled, the tighter he restrained her. Pressed under his weight, she was about to bite his arm when she found his gaze transfixed on her heaving chest revealed by the ripped blouse. She tried to cover her breasts, but he kept her arms splayed to enjoy the delightful view.

He whispered hotly to her ear, "A surrender must be accompanied by word of mouth." His rising breath traveled down her neck. "A lass too clever by half once taught me that."

"I surrender."

She moaned as he kissed her hard, giving vent to all the rage that had festered inside him. He tore the shredded blouse from her shoulders. She closed her eyes and became lost in the rising passion, but then cold tears streaked down her breasts, startling her. She looked down and saw that he had dropped sobbing to his knees, the grief pouring out in waves. She removed what remained of her blouse and, raising him, pressed another kiss to his lips to draw out his pain. She whispered heavily, "I don't want you to stop loving her."

"I cannot give what you deserve," he said, still heaving.

Taking his hand, she led him into the bedchamber. "I will never ask for your heart." She closed the door behind them, praying for the strength to honor that vow.

Robert Neville, known in every tavern and whorehouse from Dover to York as the Peacock of the North, disembarked from an English galley at Berwick port. Accompanied by his two younger brothers, the knight strutted up the tower steps with his flaxen curls bouncing to the lead of his famous blue helmet plume. On the ramparts, he looked down and laughed at the Scots who were scurrying to mount an assault from their siege trenches below the fastness. The pomp of his arrival had apparently deluded the attackers into believing that Caernervon himself had arrived to take command of the only city north of the border that still remained in English hands.

The Nevilles entered the main hall of the tower and found a wretched tableau of crumbled walls, hacked furniture, and torn tapestries. John of Richmond, the commander of the beleaguered English garrison, sat slumped at a table with his officers, who refused to stand and offer the traditional greeting demanded in a nobleman's presence. The Peacock inquired of them in a tone of mock confusion, "Might you direct me to the quarters of the gentleman in charge of this enterprise? I seem to have taken a wrong turn into the coal bin."

Richmond sneered at this latest addition to the long list of fools who had been banished to his corner of Hell. During the two years of the siege, the king had used Berwick as a refuse pit for exiling malcontents, paroled criminals, and barons in disrepute. The officer kicked a rickety chair toward the eldest Neville and growled, "Dine on dog meat for eight months and we'll see how rosy your cheeks turn. When will I be reinforced?"

Robert Neville gingerly navigated across the debris, careful to avoid scratching his spit-polished boots. "Not soon. Edward has levied more taxes to pay for the losses at Stirling. The earls are marshalling their forces in the South. There is civil war afoot."

"You must have offended someone of high stature to merit this assignment," Richmond said. "We usually get the Tower rejects."

The Peacock rocked the dusty wine kegs in a search for anything suitable to imbibe, choosing not to reveal the true offense that had given rise to this present punishment: He had killed one of the king's sycophants, Sir Richard Marmeduke, in a squabble over who was the more ranking lord at the royal dinner table. Instead, he lied: "Caernervon's newest bed doll, Hugh Despenser, could not abide my good looks so near the royal pillow."

Offended, the officers reached for weapons, but Richmond held them at bay and warned Neville, "Mind your tongue here."

"I don't intend to be here long enough to mind it."

"You have some ingenious plan to get us out, do you?"

The Peacock lingered at the arrow slit, inspecting the defensive cordon that the Scots had thrown up around the city. The besieged tower could only be provisioned by sea, a dangerous enterprise that required running the gauntlet of archers on the beaches at night. "I never thought I'd see Englishmen cornered by Highland rats." He searched the Scot pennons beyond the Tweed. "Where does Robert Bruce make his headquarters?"

Richmond snorted at Neville's ignorance of this war. "Bruce is not here."

Neville turned in astonishment. "Who commands the savages?"

"The Black Douglas."

Neville loosed a sibilant puff of hilarity. "The *Black* Douglas? Why not the Lavender Douglas? Who is this brigand with such a ridiculous name?"

Richmond had endured that same question from dozens of hotspurs who had dashed north to try their hand against the infamous rebel leader. "The man has never been defeated."

Neville peered beyond the walls. "Point this black phantom out to me."

Richmond hesitated before admitting, "He's not in their camp."

"Does he command from a galley?"

"His new manor is thirty leagues west of here."

Neville held a contemptuous glare of disbelief. "Manor? Have you built a cathedral to him as well? Mayhaps I should make a pilgrimage and light a votive candle in his honor. It seems the brigand has performed the miracle of besieging the king's forces without even being present. St. George himself could not have accomplished such a feat."

"You have never met him on the field."

The Peacock flipped an upturned hand toward his brothers, beckoning a bottle of wine from their own transported stock. After enjoying a long draught, he licked his lips and declared, "I am going to do you a favor, Richmond. Not that you merit it, but you and this rabble of yours are in dire need of an exorcism. Where is this Black Devil's manor, as you call it?"

Richmond brightened at prospects of getting the braggart out of his hair. "At a place called Lintalee, south of Jedburgh. I'll even mount a counterattack to give you cover."

The Peacock took another long drink and, belching, tossed the empty bottle through the window. "I managed to get into this piss hole without your aid. I shan't require it to get out."

James led Jeanne and Marjorie on horse into the low vales of Lanark and spurred into a playful dash. After entertaining them for a week, he had agreed to accompany the women back to the Stewart castle at Renfrew. He wouldn't admit it, but he was enjoying this respite from the campaigns.

Jeanne caught up and prodded him to open up. "You needn't have come all the way with us," she said, clearly not meaning it. For the first time since Bannockburn, she felt a lightness of heart in him. Marjorie's spirit had also lifted; the lass's cheeks were flushed and, though she still rarely spoke, an occasional smile now crossed her face. Robert had been prescient in sending his daughter to James for a visit, and James had benefited from her company. Despite his initial brusqueness, he had warmed up and had even regained some of his old bounce. She asked him with a flirting glance, "You are certain Murdoch can handle the Borders without you?"

"The English haven't rustled from their fouled nest in Berwick in months. Besides, there's something I want to show you."

They turned off the road toward Glasgow and entered a blue vale split by a meandering stream and guarded by an abandoned tower.

An inhuman shriek cut the air.

James drew his sword, signaling for the women to remain behind as he rode ahead. In a lek clearing near the river, he found a covey of black grouse strutting and booming in a spring mating ritual. The males puffed their chest sacs and fanned their white tail feathers to chase their rivals and to attract the females, who danced away in feigned outrage. He stole a sheepish glance at Jeanne and wondered if she too saw in this encounter a mockery of their lovemaking, which had been anything but genteel.

She shooed the aggressive grouse bull with a loud clap.

"What is this pile of rock?" Marjorie asked him.

He sat staring at the ruins. "My childhood home."

Marjorie reddened. "I'm sorry. I did not mean ... How long has it been since you last saw it?"

"Fifteen years." He rode past the crag that he had climbed as a boy to win the Dun Eadainn ax and led them west toward the Douglas Water, until they came to the boulder where he and Belle had held their childhood trysts. After staring at the spot for several moments in silence, he asked Jeanne, "Would you allow me a moment with Marjorie?"

Thrown by the odd request, Jeanne interrogated him with a look of suspicion. But finally she rode up the hill toward the ruins to prepare the picnic that they had brought.

Alone with the king's daughter, James bridled her pony closer to the river and assisted the pregnant lass from the saddle. He walked with her to the boulder and stood there in silence, aimlessly throwing stones into the currents. The water was low, even for summer. He never could have hidden from Belle under its surface on a day like this. He stole a quick glance at Marjorie and saw that she had closed her eyes to bask in the sun's warmth. Her belly had grown in the two weeks that she had been with him, and he was now more hopeful that she would survive the coming ordeal. She had eaten heartily, even fishing and hunting with the men in the bracing outdoor air.

The pangs of childbirth could be no worse than the English prison she survived, he told himself. Still, Marjorie was so slender, a mere sparrow of a girl with spindly legs and the melancholic Bruce temperament. And what if there were complications? This might be his last chance to find out about those last days in the Highlands when Belle and the Bruce women had been on the run. Had Belle blamed him for abandoning her? Why had Longshanks imprisoned her in the cage and not Elizabeth? In his darkest moments, he even questioned if Robert had secretly bribed Longshanks to show leniency to Elizabeth, to the detriment of Belle. After a deep breath, he risked, "Marjie, there's something I have long meant to ask you." When she turned away, as if divining what was on his mind, he apologized. "I'm sorry. I shouldn't have, but—"

"Do you love her?"

He hesitated. "I'll always love Belle."

"No! I mean, do you love Jeanne?"

James scooped another handful of pebbles and skipped them across the stream to avoid answering her. Each throw carried more anger.

"She loves you. Can you not see that?"

He flung the last rock so hard that several low-flying razorbills dived in retaliation. "There are things you don't understand."

Marjorie lurched to her feet, nearly losing her balance. "You have no right to say that! Seven years I spent in that English hole! There are things *you* don't understand! You *and* my father!" When he gently lowered her back to sitting, she began weeping. "Belle had a choice. I did not."

"Choice? What do you mean?"

Marjorie reacted as if wishing to retract that last utterance, but his fierce glare demanded an explanation. Finally, she revealed, "The English king was going to make an example of me and Liz. ... But Belle took our place."

James captured her arms to speed the revelation. "Why?"

"I don't know why! Why does anything happen? Why didn't I die instead of her? No one loves me! There's not a night I don't pray to wake up dead!"

"Don't say that! You carry Scotland's hope."

She struggled to escape his grip. "I don't want to carry anything! I hate this miserable world!"

"You must remember your father—"

"My father cares nothing for me! He uses me only for his designs! All of you use us! You used Belle! And now you use Jeanne!"

She shoved him away and ran up the hill. Before he could catch her, she pulled herself atop the mare and galloped north, spooking off his horse.

Jeanne had shared only a few words with James during their frantic gallop north to find Marjorie. Her banishment at the river could only mean one thing: He had asked the lass about Belle. She wasn't certain what incensed her more—that James had recklessly brought up the subject despite Marjorie's fragile state, or that she had deluded herself into believing that, by sleeping with him, she could help him forget the dead countess. At this moment, she had more pressing concerns than bruised feelings; the king would hold her dearly responsible for allowing his daughter to run off.

Chilled by a gale brewing in the east, James drew his cloak tighter around his neck as he scanned the moors along Knock Hill on the road between Paisley and Renfrew. Finding no sight of Marjorie, he stole a glance at Jeanne, trying to divine the reason for her enforced silence. "The day has turned cold enough without you frosting it."

Jeanne reined to a sharp halt. "I was warm enough in your bed!"

"I didn't ask you to come to me! I was doing well enough without you!"

"You are a pig-headed man!"

"And you are a conniving French changeling of a—" A loud cawing cut him short. He saw a bevy of sparrow hawks circling just beyond the hill.

Jeanne watched as the birds hovered and tightened their formation. She had seen that same chilling pattern of flight on battlefields. Before she could ask what was wrong, James galloped across Knock Hill. He found Marjorie's horse, with its saddle slipped, watering at the river. Several feet away, Marjorie lay bloodied and unconscious. He leapt down and hurried to the girl, feeling for a pulse. Jeanne came riding up and, dismounting, knelt at his side. She took one look at Marjorie and turned aside, shaking her head.

James pressed his ear to Marjorie's breast and slapped her bloodless face, trying to revive her. "She's not dead!"

Jeanne restrained his hand. "It's the child."

"How long ... can it live?"

Jeanne made the sign of the Cross to speed mother and infant to Heaven. "There is nothing we can do." She tried to stop him from tearing at Marjorie's chemise to expose her stomach. "What in God's name are you doing?"

He pulled a dagger. "Damn it, woman! Tell me where to cut!"

Driven by his crazed eyes, Jeanne traced the path where the incision should be made. He sliced open Marjorie's womb and retracted the cavity walls. She removed the fetus and exposed the umbilical cord for him to sever. She wrapped the infant in the shreds of the chemise.

"Is it alive?" he asked.

Jeanne cradled the child and felt a tremor. She nodded, overcome with hope and grief. It was a boy—a future king.

He kissed Marjorie's cold cheek. For the first time in the lass's short but discontented life, she held a look of blessed repose. Her existence had been filled with more horror and suffering than most men could have endured. Yet Fate had chosen to withhold its cruelest indignity until the end. She had been taken from this cold-hearted world without even the comfort of knowing that she had delivered Scotland's salvation.

J eanne had insisted on staying with the Stewarts at Renfrew to help care for the premature infant, so James made the journey back to Lintalee alone. Robert had yet to be informed of the birth of his heir, named David after Robert's maternal grandfather; he was still in the west near Loch Ryan, preparing to lead an army across the sea to Ireland to go to the aid of his brother. Edward had captured Carrickfergus and, with characteristic bluster, had declared himself High Monarch of Ireland. His power grab had miraculously united the squabbling Irish earls, spurring them to side with an English monarch they'd never seen rather than submit to a Scottish invader on their doorsteps. Hard-pressed, Edward had sent a desperate plea to Robert for aid.

He muttered another curse at that nonsense. Before leaving for Ulster, Robert had issued an order appointing him as Lieutenant of the Realm during his absence. He had always counseled Robert against such dangerous diversions, but the king suffered a blind spot when it came to Ireland. His Celtic mother had weaned him on stories about Culchullan and the Stone of Destiny, and Robert had come to see himself as a resurrected Arthur who would reunite Ireland, Scotland, and Wales, as Merlin had prophesied.

Now, as he approached the Lintalee defile, the acrid sting of black smoke attacked his nostrils. He rushed through the pass and saw a billowing cloud churning over the ridge. His manor was charred and ransacked. Galloping up, he leapt off his saddle and ran through the smoldering doors. Seven Scot corpses lay burnt on the smoking floor. Murdoch's mutilated body hung from the rafters with a placard tied to its neck:

> *Salutations to the Blackened Douglas,*
> *Your abode now matches your name. Should you wish to*
> *thank me in person for the alteration, I am accepting visitors at*
> *Berwick on the Tweed.*
> > *Yours truly, Sir Robert Neville*

L ashing his frothing horse into Berwick, James rode behind the siege moat surrounding the city and called his Scot fighters to him.

Sim Ledhouse, who had been placed in command of the encirclement operation, tried to draw him back to safety behind the lines. "Can you not find another fight of your own, Jamie?"

In a wrathful state, James high-stepped his steed below the walls, giving no care to the range of the English arrows. "Who is Robert Neville?"

"The Peacock?" Ledhouse asked. "How did you know he was here?"

"Damn you! Answer me!"

"A knight from Durham with a mouth that exceeds his stature. What's gotten your hackles up?"

"McClurg and McKie?"

"On the lines near the beachhead."

James raced down the moat trench toward the coast, nearly trampling several of his own men in his path. He found the two Trinity brothers stationed behind the barricades. "Up with you, lads!"

Baffled by his cryptic summons, the brothers from Galloway mounted their ponies and followed him in a sortie around the walls.

James shouted at the defenders on the ramparts, "Bring me Neville!"

"He dines this hour!" a sergeant said. "Call back tomorrow!"

Not recognizing him without his banner, the garrison shouted catcalls at him, convinced that he was a raw recruit too eager for his first fight.

After studying the window in that section of the tower where he remembered the officers used to take their meals, James returned to the trenches and circled the trebuchet that Ledhouse had constructed, the only stone thrower possessed by the Scots. He had never been an advocate of siege guns, deeming them too unwieldy for his slash-and-run tactics, but on this occasion the contraption might serve his purpose. "Sim, can you aim this thing with any accuracy?"

Ledhouse grinned. "I can hit the lip marks on Caernervon's ass."

James nodded him to the task. "Third window."

Ledhouse ordered beams wedged under the running ramps to increase the trebuchet's leverage. When the gun was angled to his satisfaction, James slashed the restraining rope. The stone crashed through the tower's aperture and drew a stream of invectives inside.

Moments later, Neville appeared on the ramparts with a brown soup stain marring his robin-blue satin blouse. "A plague upon the knave who—"

"At the river!" James shouted. "Within the hour!"

Richmond arrived on the walls a step behind Neville. Recognizing the hero of Bannockburn, the English commander crouched behind a merlon thrust, leaving Neville exposed.

Neville laughed at the officers cowering around him. "Who is that piss ant down there?"

"The Scotsman you're hunting."

"*That* black root stump has been terrorizing you?"

"You can easily take him," Richmond assured Neville, turning to silently warn his officers against countermanding the prediction.

Grinning at the chance to add to his reputation, Neville shouted down at his challenger, "Thirty men each."

"Three! And bring along those bastards your mother calls your brothers!"

Liking those odds even more, Neville dug a slither of meat from his teeth and spat it. "Between the river and the west tower. I hear that's where they threw your whore. You can join her after I carve you up."

James and the Trinity brothers rode into the open field and waited.

A half hour later, Neville, attired in a fancied breastplate of hammered silver, emerged from the gate on a sleek Flanders charger jingling with bells. Accompanied by his two brothers, the Peacock paraded back and forth under the walls as if entering a tournament. The soldiers in both camps lowered their weapons in a temporary truce to watch the encounter.

After enduring Neville's flashy antics for several minutes, McKie turned to James. "Are you going to tell us what this is about?"

James delayed answering him until the Peacock reared his courser again, trying to taunt a charge. Then, he looked directly at the two Galloway lads who had shared his every hardship since the Turnberry invasion. "These Englishmen before us murdered your brother at Lintalee."

The Trinity brothers, turning ashen with anger, drew their swords.

As they watched the Peacock strut and bark insults, James whispered, "The order I am about to give you, lads, I would not obey it if I were in your stead." His only indication that the brothers were listening was the whitening of their knuckles as they gripped their weapons. "The first-born Neville is a menace. I will deal with him. But his kinsmen must be taken alive."

McKie and McClurg said nothing, but kept their gazes fixed on the prancing Nevilles. Despite their lust for revenge, James knew they understood the realm's need of such high-ranking prisoners for ransoming comrades who still languished in Caernervon's dungeons. Still, he felt the same knot in his gut he had suffered on the day Clifford had dragged his father to the Tower. A Scot denied blood justice was never again a whole man. He offered them the only words of consolation he could summon. "Murdoch was like a son to me. There's none in this world I'd rather have at my side than the two of you. When I charge the Peacock, circle behind his brothers and cut off their escape."

The Peacock, unable to hear what James had whispered, threw up his hands in exasperation. "I dine at six, blackbird! Dally much longer and I'll hang another ten of you!"

James inched his horse forward. "You and me."

The Peacock gave up a confused half-laugh. "First you said three. Now one? I'm beginning to think you don't want to fight at all."

James reached into his saddlebag and removed the placard that Neville had hung from Murdoch's neck. He threw it at the hooves of the Englishman's horse and, in a ploy to shame him into the single duel, shouted his reply loud enough for the English defenders on the walls to hear. "The invitation was for me alone! If this tourney shill you have sent out is not up to it, I will allow you to send another more seasoned knight in his stead!"

The Peacock glanced up at Richmond. The officer, watching from the tower, eagerly nodded him to action. After debating the proposed change, Neville forced another laugh and taunted James, "Are you going to sit there and prattle on until darkness gives you an excuse to retire?"

James tossed his sword to McKie. He pulled the Dun Eadainn ax from behind his back and rested it on his pommel. The Peacock lost his preening grin. On the ramparts, Richmond and his soldiers murmured with anticipation. They had seen the effectiveness of *that* weapon at Bannockburn.

The Peacock retreated a step and whispered to his brothers.

James spurred to the charge.

The Peacock came at him—with his brothers joining in the assault. James had expected the treachery. He glanced over his shoulder and shook his head at McKie and McClurg to enforce his order not to come to his aid. Nearing the collision, he veered left of the onrushing brothers and caused the Peacock sweep past him, too late in altering his aim. He hammered the youngest Neville from his horse.

Stunned by the maneuver, the second Neville brother retreated for the gate, but the Trinity lads had circled around to block his retreat.

The Peacock reined his horse back into a tight turn.

"You've lost your escort!" James shouted at him.

The Peacock came on again with a fury. James calmed his steed, waiting without a jerk of movement. When the Peacock was within three lengths, he hurled his ax at the forelegs of the charger. The ponderous animal crumpled, whipping its rider over its neck. Thrown to the grass, the Peacock dragged himself up from the tangled stirrups to avoid being crushed.

James dismounted and stood over him. "Your feathers are ruffled."

The Peacock tried to crawl to his feet. James doubled him over again with a kick to the groin. The Englishman lunged at him with his dagger drawn.

James was caught unarmed—his ax lay several paces from his reach.

The Peacock laughed at his turn of good fortune. "Did you know my father served with Clifford?"

James eyed the ax. "I'm told swine run in pairs."

The Peacock angled between James and the weapon. "He was there when they dragged your old man to the Tower."

James ripped off his padded shirt and wrapped it around his forearm.

The Peacock stalked him. "When that Scot felon that spawned you fell from exhaustion, they tied him to a mule's tail."

"The man you hanged was the brother of those lads behind you."

The Peacock swung his dagger at James's face, narrowly missing his mark. "Remind me to say a Mass for his pagan soul."

James parried his wild thrusts. "Take a last look at *your* brothers. I'm going to ransom them for so much coin, your family will be rendered penurious."

Neville bared his teeth in a snarling grin. "I'm told that caged bitch of yours also had a wagging tongue."

James lowered his arm to offer an inviting target. "I'm going to make certain your name is never uttered without mine."

The Englishman swung at his ribs and missed.

James lunged at his neck. "Speak my name!"

Trapped in the chokehold, Neville crumpled to his knees. "Black!"

"My name!"

The blood drained from Neville's distended face. "Douglas!"

"I am a lord!"

Heaving for breath, Neville croaked, "Sir ..."

James twisted the knave's neck to the limit.

"James!"

"Now the bonnie finish!"

"Douglas!"

James threw him to the ground and retrieved the ax.

Neville crawled away clutching his throat. He looked up from his hands and knees to shout a curse—and heard a swish of air.

"When you arrive in Hell, commend *that* name to Longshanks!"

The Peacock's plumed helmet rolled down the river's embankment—with his head still inside.

THIRTY-FOUR

James forded the River Isla near Perth and found the royal cavalry guarding the approach to the ruins of an old Roman camp. Exhausted and battered from their recent rough crossing of the Irish Sea, Keith the Marishal and his dejected troopers sat around the abbey grounds with their heads hung low. James made an attempt at joviality to stir them from their morose slumber. "Did I make a wrong turn into Northumbria? If not for your rabbit-spooking face, Keith, I could have sworn I'd interrupted an English burial party!"

Keith, gaunt and pale, was in no mood for banter. "Why don't you go back to the Borders, Douglas. We've no need of you here."

"Where is he?"

Keith winced to his feet and stood with arms akimbo in front of the abbot's quarters. "The king has given orders. No one sees him."

"Bishop Lamberton?"

"Gone to St. Andrews to take care of his own damn business."

Alarmed at their low morale, James now understood why Lamberton had so hastily summoned him north. Robert, although coldly unmoved by the death of his daughter Marjorie in childbirth two years ago, had become so distraught over his disastrous Irish campaign that he had sequestered himself for weeks in this isolated Cistercian monastery at Couper Angus. This most recent of the king's increasingly frequent spirals into the black abyss of melancholy had come at an inopportune time. After five years of siege, James and his Lanark raiders had finally captured Berwick, but an English relief army was reportedly being raised in York that would dwarf the host brought to Bannockburn. He had left young Walter Stewart in charge of his siege troops with orders to avoid giving battle until he returned.

He dismounted and made a move to go around Keith. Pushed back, he drove the cavalry officer against the wall with a steely glare of warning to unhand his arm. Keith decided not to test the threat, and stepped aside.

James lit a candle from the entry's votive grille and walked through the sanctuary, which had been darkened with black bunting. Plates of rancid food littered the chapel, and it stank from rot and burning incense. As he neared the altar, he stepped on what appeared to be a corpse wrapped in a blanket. Lesions pocked its chest, whose hair had turned white with an oily sheen. Groaning, Robert looked up at him with eyebrows thinned and cheeks riddled with sores that seeped pus in his patchy beard. He crawled off into the shadows to hide. "Don't touch me!"

James tore off the window coverings. "What has happened to you?"

Robert shielded his swollen eyes. "Malachy's Curse. I'll never be rid of it."

He was exasperated to find that Robert was still bedeviled by his deceased grandfather's tale of the traveling hermit who had cast vengeful incantations. "Where is that whoreson brother of yours?"

"Those Irish savages ... cut off Eddie's head. They sent it to London."

He wasted no breath in mourning the greedy Edward, who had earned his fate with his unseemly lust for a crown. As he pulled Robert to his haunches, his hand brushed against carved ridges on the altar lintel. He brought the candle closer. "What in God's name is *this* doing here?"

Robert pressed his splotched forehead against the Stone of Destiny's cool surface. "I ordered the bishop to send it. If I sleep near it, a healing miracle may be granted me."

He found a water basin and dipped a cloth to wash Robert's face. "These sores are getting worse."

"Did you come all the way up here just to mother me?"

He increased the rigor of his rubbing to punish him for the self-pity. "*You* have conjured a miracle, for certain. Thanks to your Irish adventuring, Caernervon and Lancaster have set aside their bickering to join forces. If they retake Berwick while I am here tending to your fragile wits, we'll lose the Marches."

Robert dismissed that possibility. "Caernervon would not have brought his queen consort and son to York if he planned to invade so soon."

Galvanized by that news, James stood from his knee so swiftly that he overturned the basin. "Isabella is in the North?"

"Aye, Liz received a letter from her father last week. De Burgh mentioned hearing in court that she intends to spend the summer in Boroughbridge."

"Heard from whom?"

"The English queen herself, of course."

He lifted Robert to his feet with a surge of excitement. "Boroughbridge is only two leagues from York!"

Robert staggered before finding his balance, having not stood for days. "Who could blame her? London in the summer is a piss pot of humidity—"

"Damn it, Rob! Don't you see what the French lass has done?"

Scratching at his own scalp, Robert stared blankly at him. "What in Finian's name are you bleating about?"

James paced the flagstones in a tightening circle. "Isabella had to know that Liz's father would gossip every detail of their conversation. I tell you there is more method than idle chatter in this."

"De Burgh has a loose tongue, but—"

"Isabella would never willingly travel to Yorkshire with Caernervon and Despenser, unless …"

Robert leaned in, waiting to hear the rest of the thought. "Unless what?"

"Unless she had a damn good reason." James looked down at his muddied boots and became distracted by an army of ants scurrying along the walls toward a dollop of spilled honey. Intrigued, he traced their trail outside the nave.

Baffled by his interest in the ants, Robert followed him through the abbey's door. Outside, the two men tracked the ants to a newly constructed mound of dirt near the gardens. Keith came to attention, surprised to find the king breaking his seclusion. The marishal and his troopers watched in confusion as Robert and James hovered on their hands and knees over the ant mound.

James scooped up half of the dirt pile and carried it several yards away. When he dropped it to the ground, the exiled ants abandoned their quest for the honey and retreated in panic to their queen, who remained in the original pile. He turned back to Robert with a grin of discovery. "The English queen is coming north for more than just a change of scenery."

Robert suddenly understood what James was proposing, and he shook his head sternly. "It's too dangerous."

"Isabella has schemed this to be captured. If I go after her, Caernervon will have to abandon the Berwick siege and rush south to save her."

Robert drew him away from the others. "The Borders must be defended. I cannot send you off into the heart of England on some wild sortie for revenge."

"Revenge? This has nothing to do with revenge. And you are the last one to lecture me about wild sorties!"

"The MacDuff lass is gone. You have to chase the spell this memory of her has cast over you."

He seethed at Robert's patronizing tone. "Back from Ireland with your ears boxed because of your own chimera! And now you lecture me? Easy enough for you to advise temperance! You still have your woman!"

"There is nothing I can do to bring the Countess of Buchan back."

"You can send me to Yorkshire to take Caernervon's queen."

Robert had hoped the passing of the years would soften James's grief, but he now saw the flame that James held for Belle still burned white-hot. He had received reports that James had grown so reckless in his raids that some now feared he was intentionally courting death. James had never led him astray, true. Still, he questioned if he could trust his old friend's judgment on such a risky stratagem. "If Edward leaves a garrison at York and comes at you from Berwick, you'll be caught in a vise."

James slammed a fist into his palm to drive home the point. "And if I capture Isabella before Edward returns to York, the English barons will have their cause to remove the knave from the throne for incompetence."

Robert turned aside and stared down at the ants, admiring the loyalty they showed to the greater cause of protecting their queen. The warrior members of their colony had already reunited their displaced army and were fast at work rebuilding their defensive hill. He looked up again and studied James intently. "Do you know the worst kind of counselor a king can have at his side?"

"Pray tell."

"A man who has nothing to lose."

He came within an inch of Robert's pocked face. "I once shared a cave with such a man."

Robert turned aside, stung by the implication that he had gone soft. He looked across the Sidlaw Hills and calculated the distance that James would have to cover to accomplish the improbable feat. No Scot army had ever made it south of the River Tees, and York was another three days of hard riding beyond that vale. Since his ignominious return from Ireland, even the commoners whispered that he had lost his nerve. Perhaps he *had* grown too predictable and cautious since Bannockburn. He could not allow the English to sniff even a whiff of weakness, particularly after his failure in Ireland. With a slap to his thigh, he nodded his agreement. "Take Randolph with you."

Thrilled to see the old gambler returned to form, James punched Robert on the shoulder, a bit too hard. "I don't need another jester. I have Sweenie."

"Take Randolph," Robert insisted, rubbing his bruised arm. "I'll not have you and the Queen of England traipsing across Yorkshire without a chaperone."

◆ sabella strolled along the River Swale, filling her lungs with the crisp Yorkshire air. The unusually cool summer of that year, 1319, had caused the leaves to turn early. She had not enjoyed such a pleasant outing since her days in Paris, when she would listen to the minstrels rowing on the Seine. How long had it been? Eleven years. It seemed like a hundred. She leaned over the water and saw more age lines in her reflection. Accursed isle! This slither of frozen rock and its horrid clime had taken a frightful toll on her fair features. Even those randy cads in court no longer stared at her as they once—

A pebble bounced off her back.

She turned to find her seven-year-old son scooping another handful of stones. "Put those down, Edward! At once!"

The prince stood his ground with a defying smirk. Even at such a young age, the boy was forever testing her, having developed a cunning sense of the balance of power that compromised her position with his father. There had been scurrilous rumors about his paternity, but she had put to rest that gossip by proudly trumpeting how the boy had inherited his aggression from his grandfather. Nor did it hurt her cause that she had given birth to three more children, who were still too young to bring on this journey. So fervent was England's hope that another Longshanks would follow her husband as king that the barons had gladly accepted her firstborn's legitimacy.

The boy sailed the stone over her head. "I killed the Black Douglas!"

Aghast, Isabella stopped her advance. "Where did you hear that name?"

"I'm going to kill the Black Douglas."

"It is not Christian to speak of murder."

The boy pointed an accusing finger at her. "You fancy the Black Douglas."

Isabella glanced with alarm at the Myton Bridge, where her escort, the Archbishop of York, knelt in prayer with his retinue of monks and acolytes. She captured the boy by the hand and marched him down the bank, safely out of earshot of the monks. "Who told you such nonsense?"

"If you don't want to kill him, that means you fancy him."

She released a sigh, relieved that the boy had just made up the accusation from his overheated imagination. "I forbid you to speak that name. The man is your father's enemy. The king would be very upset to hear you talk like this."

"Why hasn't Papa killed him?"

"He has tried, but—"

"Am I French or English?"

She could not fathom how the child managed to form such astonishing questions. "You are both."

"Then where will I be king?"

"It is complicated. Your grandfather Philip has a son in Paris. He will be king of France if—"

"I'm going to kill the Black Douglas! Then I will become king of England *and* France!"

She huffed in exasperation. "Did you not hear me just tell you—"

A commotion near the bridge cut short her admonition.

"My lady!" The archbishop was waving his meaty arms and running toward her. "We must leave at once!"

"But we only just arrived."

The portly cleric arrived at last and bent to catch his breath. "The sheriff's scouting party has captured a Scot spy not ten furlongs from here. We must remove you to safety."

Isabella feigned shock to hide her elation. Had James deciphered her plan? She returned to her picnic spread and tried to ignore the archbishop's fervent entreaties. "A Scot this far south? That is nothing but a foolish rumor!"

"The Black Douglas!" young Edward shouted. "I'm going to gut the Black Douglas like a mackerel and skin him alive!"

The archbishop wiped sweat from his brow. "I assure you, my lady—"

"I wish to speak to the prisoner," she insisted.

The archbishop's pasty mouth fell open, as if he could not decide which was more outlandish: the boy's screams or the queen's demand. "That would not be prudent, my lady."

Horsemen galloped up dragging their captive across the bridge.

Isabella marched toward them, praying that the cleric would back down to her boldness. "I must know what is happening in my husband's absence."

The archbishop waddled after her, discomposed by her insistence on interrogating the prisoner. "That is no proper sight for your ladyship!"

Isabella knelt over the bloodied prisoner. "Your name?"

After suffering several kicks to the ribs, the man mumbled, "McCraig."

"In whose service?" she asked.

Flogged to answer, the prisoner muttered, "Jamie Douglas."

Young Prince Edward bastinadoed the bound Scot prisoner with his stick. "The Black Douglas! The Black Douglas is here!"

The archbishop turned whiter than his frock. "Douglas comes for York?"

The captive turned his pained eyes on the queen again. "And for you."

Exhilarated, Isabella quickly retreated into an affectation of disbelief. She had convinced Caernervon to allow her to bring the prince to York with the excuse that the boy should witness his father's victory over the Scots. Her scheme had succeeded in all but one aspect; she had not counted on one of James's spies getting captured. She tried to glare the prisoner to silence, and then forced a laugh of derision at him. "James Douglas in Yorkshire? That is preposterous!"

"Nevertheless," the archbishop said, "I must insist that your ladyship return to York at once."

Isabella waved off the demand. "The Scots have allowed this man to fall into your hands to stir up fear among the populace. Douglas has never raided this far south. He knows my husband would cut him off. If I am seen driven away by such a wild fantasy, I will appear craven. Now, I have packed a basket of delicacies, and my son and I are going to continue with our outing."

"I cannot allow it!" the cleric cried.

"Who has been placed in command of York's garrison?"

"There is no garrison. The king has taken the royal troops stationed in the city with him to Berwick."

Isabella suppressed a smile of triumph. *Ah, Edward, you fool. You have played right into my hands.* She told the cleric forcefully, "There is your answer, then. The king would certainly have left defenders in York had he considered such a raid even a remote—"

"Maman's sweet on the Black Douglas!" Young Edward tugged at the archbishop's sleeve. "She wants to kiss him! But I'm going to hang him!"

Until that moment, both the archbishop and sheriff had paid little attention to the prince's ranting. Now, turning on Isabella with suspicion, they found her scowling at Edward in rattled anger. Intrigued by the boy's claim, the cleric signaled for the queen's horse to be brought up.

She fought the soldiers from taking him. "My son stays with me!"

"Orders from the king, my lady," the archbishop said coldly. "Should any danger arise, I have been instructed to send the prince to Nottingham."

"Unhand me, or by God I will see you sent to the Tower!"

But the archbishop would not relent, and Isabella, resigned to his insistence, resorted to another tactic. "At least allow me to send correspondence to the king. I shall raise this offense with my father if you deny me that right."

The archbishop granted the innocuous request with a dismissive wave to the sheriff. "One of my acolytes may transcribe the letter for her."

The prince threw rocks at his mother while she was escorted away. Ecstatic with her removal from his oversight, the boy swung his stick as a sword at an imaginary foe. "Is the Black Douglas going to capture us?"

The archbishop patted the prince's head. "Rest assured, my son. We have nothing to fear from that mortal sinner. The Holy Father has excommunicated the Douglas felon and all who follow his evil path. His name is damned thrice daily in all our churches. Look above you. What do you see?"

Edward gazed at the sky. "Clouds."

"Nay, those are St. George's angels forming his angelic ranks for battle."

"Will my father come to save us?"

The cleric smiled with confidence. "We need not burden the king about this heathen Scot. I have sent an order to York for the local burgher militia to muster on this field. If the fiend is foolish enough to attack us, we will send him back to his pagan hole with his tail severed."

"I want to watch," Edward said with a frisson of excitement.

"You are still a bit wet behind the ears," the archbishop cautioned. "But soon your day will come. Has your mother told you of the brave exploits performed by your grandfather?" When the boy shook his head, the cleric glared at Isabella as she was led away. "A lesson must be learned from that malfeasance. Never trust one's education to the French. Edward Longshanks was a fearsome warrior. He captured the criminal Wallace and sent him to Hell, limb by limb. You must strive to be like him in all ways."

"If he *was* so fearsome, why did he not capture the Black Douglas?"

Astonished by such precocious impudence, the archbishop signed his breast to bless the memory of the deceased monarch. "The Lord left that task to us, so that we might more fully bask in His glory."

J ames trotted along the banks of the Ouse River, searching the purple Yorkshire moors to the south for some sign of John McCraig, his spy in England. His old shoulder wound ached, an unerring portent that danger lurked ahead. The morning fog obscured his vantage, and what little of the bleak landscape he could see looked so alien that his tacking instincts had been thrown askew. McCraig had never failed him, but the man was a half a day late for their assigned meeting.

"Give him another hour," Randolph advised.

"We don't have an hour." James nervously stroked his pony's mane as he glanced over his shoulder at his exhausted men. They had become accustomed to living in the saddle without sleep, but he had never driven them so hard. After reaching the outskirts of York in only eight days, they had left behind a swath of burned villages and ransacked abbeys. Although he had gained the jump on Caernervon, he knew that word of the invasion would have made it to Berwick by now. Every minute of delay decreased their chances of making it home before being encircled. He had even heard some of the men grousing behind his back that he was risking their lives to settle an old score, or perhaps revive an old romance. Jangled by the lack of good surveillance, he turned to Sweenie and, cursing the fog, ordered, "Up with you, monk!"

Rousted from his attempt to steal a few winks of sleep, Sweenie, startled and nearly fell from his pony.

"Make your pilgrimage," James ordered. "And be quick about it."

S weenie grumbled as he pulled a white robe from his saddlebag and donned his usual disguise of a Cistercian friar. Staff in hand, he waddled into the mists and broke an occasional branch to avoid becoming lost. He had performed this ritual of espionage hundreds of times; he would go find the local kirk and beg a meal from the priest, all the while gathering information about the defenses of the nearest city.

After half an hour of this blind searching, he came to a wooden bridge that crossed a small river. The sun broke through and burned away enough fog to reveal the clover fields on the far side of the banks. He rubbed his eyes in disbelief: the valley beyond the bridge was filled with hundred of white-robed canons and priests, all armed with pitchforks. Behind them stood a second line of burghers and farmers, disorganized and dispirited as the canons were disciplined. Clad in an archbishop's raiment, the leader of this strange host waved a towering silver crucifix for a battle standard as he strode confidently toward the bridge.

Sweenie ducked into the grass to avoid being seen, but he was too late.

"You there!" the Archbishop of York commanded him. "Back in line!"

Sweenie slowly stood from the weeds, thankful at least that the cleric thought him to be a stray from his own motley militia. He didn't know whether to retreat or obey the command, so he decided to play the fool, his most accomplished role. "Preachers take up arms?"

"A Scot felon lurks not far from here!" the archbishop shouted.

"I've just come from the north! I saw no such knave!"

"Then we'll have to smoke the Black Douglas from his den!"

"I've heard of this Douglas!" Sweenie said. "God's curse he is! You mean to fight him with churchmen and farmers?"

"Of course not!"

Sweenie forced down the lump in his throat, now certain that English reinforcements were on the way. After all, priests only hurried to a battlefield to share the booty and proclaim the Almighty's hand in—

"Our Lord and his angels are with us!" The archbishop waved his crucifix. "The Scots will fall just as the pagan Goliath fell before David!"

Sweenie questioned his own hearing. Could this English Moses and his Yorkshire Israelites truly intend to fight a *battle*? He stole a glance behind him. The fog was lifting, and he might regain the protection of the receding mists if he got the jump. He pointed his finger toward the low sun rising behind the priests and shouted, "A sign! The sun reverses its course!"

When the archbishop and his canonicals turned to witness the miracle, the little monk took off in a dash for the bridge.

Crimson patches of rage flamed across the archbishop's forehead as he slowly realized that he had been duped. He spun to his canons behind him and ordered, "Take that Devil's gremlin!"

Hundreds of his white-robed clerics charged after the Scot monk.

Sweenie pumped his stumpish legs and threw off his robe to gain speed. He reached the swirling mist just in the nick of time and curled into a ball behind a clump of gorse. There he remained hidden until the voices around him receded. Moments later, an arm reached through the fog and captured his chin.

"What in Satan's name?"

James had come looking for him. Sweenie brought a finger to his lips to beg his silence.

"Are you stealing a nap?" James demanded.

Sweenie dropped an ear to the gorse and listened. The pounding of feet across the timbered bridge had receded. God be praised, the canons had given up their search and had crossed back over the river. He leapt up and led James on a run back to the other Scots while whispering the result of his reconnaissance: "Two thousand, maybe more."

James kicked the ground in frustration. "We can't take on that many."

Sweenie halted his retreat to tug at James's sleeve. "You promised that one day you would allow me to lead a charge into battle."

James dropped his hands to his knees, catching his breath. "Stop talking nonsense. We have to run north, and fast."

"Give me thirty men," Sweenie pleaded. "I'll put up a feint, hold them off until you and the others get away."

"That would be suicide."

Sweenie lowered his eyes and assumed a pious pose. "I have lived a bonnie life, and now it's time for me to pay back my king. I ask only one favor." He stole a glance up at James to determine if his act had cast its spell.

"And what would that be?"

"Compose a song lauding my sacrifice and sing it to King Robert in my memory."

James was ashamed for having wrongly judged the selfless monk. There would be detachments from Berwick heading north to cut them off, he knew, and his only chance of saving most of the men would be to leave a small contingent to fight a rear-guard action. If any of the volunteers survived, they would have to find their way back to Scotland on their own.

McKie and McClurg stepped up. "We'll stay with the Wee-Kneed."

Thirty more men also came forward and stood with Sweenie.

James pressed the little monk's head to his breast. "I'll not forget this."

Sweenie snickered under his breath, "Aye, you won't."

Before James could change his mind, Sweenie led his band of volunteers into the thick fog toward the direction of the oncoming legion of clerics. When the escaping Scots finally rode out of sight, the monk stopped his small troop halfway to the river and traced a line through the grass with his staff. "Gather up all the hay and brush you can find and set them afire here."

His volunteers traded skeptical glances, but finally they obeyed him.

Sweenie trusted the smoke from the burning brush would give them more cover. He stripped off his shirt, dug his hand into a crock of pitch, and painted his face with pagan emblems. Satisfied with his artwork, he threw the crock to McKie. "Pretty yourself up, lads. When you hear Heaven shout St. Finian's name, run toward the river and don't stop until you've been baptized in its bloody waters."

As Sweenie crawled alone beyond the smoke to survey the valley, the men stared at the little monk, wondering if he had lost his wits under the strain. Below him, the English archbishop was leading his canons and burghers across the bridge as if on a Good Friday procession. *Come on, sweet cherubs. Your heavenly reward awaits you.* He waited until the last of the English militia had followed the canons to the near side of the river, and then he stood up in the high grass and shouted, "Who's the holiest saint that ever walked this isle?"

The archbishop fixed a banishing eye on the black-streaked demon. When the incubus would not dissolve back into the smoke, the cleric held up his towering crucifix for protection and answered the challenge, "St. Michael!"

Sweenie rejected that suggestion with a back flip. "Nay! Who's the holiest saint ever walked this isle?"

The archbishop was not accustomed to having his theological authority questioned, particularly by an evil sprite in front of his canons. He tried again: "St. George, may he protect us!"

Sweenie leapt into the air again and smacked his feet together. "Nay!"

Now in a tempestuous snit, the archbishop marched toward the blaspheming cretin. "Damn you to Hell! Who then?"

Sweenie ran at the oncoming clerics and screamed, "St. Finian!"

Hearing the signal for the attack, McKie, McClurg and the other Scots shot forward through the smoke and fog. Half naked and painted like savage Picts, they split the burning brush shouting at the top of their lungs. When they reached the clearing, they found only priests arrayed against them.

The two bizarre armies stopped, confused, and stood staring at each other.

Sweenie broke the brittle silence by resuming his sprint toward the archbishop. "St. Finian was a Scot! And it's a Scot saint come to take you to Judgment this day!" He glanced over his shoulder and laughed as his volunteers charged down the hill and cut down the first ranks of canons.

The archbishop suddenly lost faith in the certainty of God's protection. He dropped his crucifix and fought a path back through his frightened charges in a frantic dash back to the bridge. Left without their spiritual leader, his canons abandoned their weapons and followed him in the retreat, careening into the burghers who were just then trying to cross the swale. Those in the rear of the hightailing mob had to jump into the river to avoid being slaughtered. The currents became filled with so many floating monk robes that the river resembled a rushing stream of lily pads.

While James waited for the last of his mounted troop to ford the river, he heard the distant screams of battle through the fog. He was about to offer up a prayer for Sweenie and his martyred volunteers in the rear guard when he spied a white robe floating downstream.

Randolph circled back. "Sweenie and the lads won't hold them off for long."

More robes came bobbing past, and it occurred to James that he had never seen Caernervon's troops wearing white burrel mantles. He dismounted and waded in to retrieve one of the robes. Below it, he found the body of a tonsured priest. He leapt on his horse and raced back toward Myton Bridge. As the fog and smoke lifted, painted savages came running at him dragging bundles filled with gold plates and chalices. A black-faced gargoyle prodded up a prisoner with an archbishop's staff. Across the river, the surviving canons ran toward York clad only in their undergarments.

The backtracking Scot raiders howled with joy at discovering Sweenie's victory. They leapt down from their mounts and raised the little monk on their shoulders to parade him across the smoking field.

Randolph marched the procession toward James, who sat slack-jawed watching the bizarre scene. "I'd say you owe the Wee-Kneed a ballad, Jamie."

James recognized their prisoner. "You've hooked a rare fish, Sweenie! This is William Ayreminne! Caernervon's Keeper of the Rolls!"

The English captive grimaced at hearing his identity revealed.

James lifted the man's lowered chin with his blade. "Where is your queen, Roll Keeper?" Refused an answer, James nodded for McKie to noose the Englishman's neck and lift him by leveraging the rope across a saddle pommel.

The gagging prisoner squealed, "The river!"

James ordered him dropped. "Your next flight will be to your Maker."

Clutching at the rope under his chin, the prisoner gasped, "The archbishop sent her by barge to York!"

James rushed his raiders south along the banks of the Swale, desperate to catch Isabella before she could be sailed to safety. Dusk was falling when he climbed the last hill and caught glimpse of York's impressive ramparts. A barge lit by torches was being rowed feverishly toward the city's river gate. He counted no more than ten men defending the tower. Just as he had predicted, Caernervon had siphoned off the garrison to be used in the attack on Berwick.

He galloped along the banks in search of a ford, calculating that the precious cargo would reach the portcullis within the hour. Then, he saw a lady emerge from a pavilion on the barge. Surrounded by armed guards, she turned toward him with a look of desperation. He squinted to increase his sight. It had been ten years since he had last seen her. Could *that* woman truly be Isabella? She appeared fuller in figure than he remembered, but her azure blue eyes still burned bright in her face. He began removing his boots.

Randolph tried to restrain him. "Even if you could swim it, we're already a day behind. If we don't turn north now, we'll not make it back."

Shaking off his hand, James leapt from his saddle and dived into the water.

The gallows atop York's keep been set high enough for the draw and quartering to be seen from afar. On this morning, after attending a celebratory Mass in the minster, Caernervon led the finest procession held in England since the celebration of his father's victory in Wales. Behind him, his prize prisoner was dragged from the tower and marched down the street in chains while the crowds roared and threw garlands of black roses in mocking tribute.

Caernervon finally reached the execution site and took his viewing seat. Isabella, at his side, turned away, unwilling to watch the grisly ordeal. As the throngs chanted "Edward" and offered up grateful hosannas to him for capturing the Black Douglas, the executioner waited for his signal to commence.

Smiling, he milked the grand moment, for he knew that these recalcitrant barons below him would now be required to give back all the rights that he had been forced to relinquish in their damnable Ordinances. When the cheers reached their crescendo, he stood from his throne to accept the accolades. One flick of his hand and the man who had so plagued him—

"My lord! A force approaches!"

In the saddle, Caernervon roused from his drowsy revelry. He looked toward the blackened Northumbrian valley and saw a fast-moving band of horsemen coming at him amid a cloud of dust.

Was that not the three-starred shield of robin's egg blue on the herald?

"Douglas!" the king shouted. "At once, upon him before he escapes!"

As his knights galloped hell-bent toward the trapped Scots, Caernervon joined them in the lead, glancing back at Despenser with a toothy grin of anticipation. All was falling into place, just as he had planned. When Douglas and his raiders had been reported rushing north from York, he had convinced

Lancaster to abandon the Berwick siege and move west to cut the Scots off before they reached the border. Of course, some credit went to his vapid French wife, who had unwittingly forwarded a piece of invaluable intelligence. Her last letter mentioned that a captured spy had revealed under torture that Douglas intended to return along the coast to the Solway Firth. Armed with that timely gift, he had sent Lancaster to encircle Douglas and drive him into their pincers.

At last, the stain of Bannockburn would be erased.

The cloud of dust came closer, and Caernervon, drawing his sword, spurred to the glorious confrontation. The dust settled and the banners became more distinct. Those were not silver stars, but red roses. Baffled, he slowed to a halt as the two converging forces came into sight of each other.

The lead knight in the oncoming van removed his helmet. "Well?"

Lancaster?

Caernervon lurched up in the saddle. "Where is Douglas?"

Thomas Lancaster searched the grassy environs around them. "You were to chase him to me."

"No, you were to chase him to *me!* Tell me you have not lost him."

Lancaster narrowed his beady eyes. "I never *had* him!"

An officer in the king's guard pointed toward the far scarp of the Pennines, nearly a league away. There a line of horsemen rode rapidly along the horizon, heading north. Above the fleeing column flew a banner with a blue shield and three silver stars.

Caernervon circled Lancaster in an apoplectic fit. "Treasonous scapegrace! You have allowed Douglas to escape!"

Lancaster's face pinched with affront. "Had you heeded my counsel, we would have Berwick fully defended and impregnable by now!"

A courier galloped up from the south. "My lord! The queen!"

Caernervon stood in his stirrups, frantically scanning the distant column of escaping Scots. "My God! Has she been captured?"

"She is safe behind York's walls, my lord," the courier assured him.

Caernervon closed his eyes in relief. Although he would gladly be rid of Isabella, a Scot ransom for her return would have ruined him.

"She sent me to find you, Sire," the courier explained.

"What in Hell's name does she want now?"

"She begs you weigh with due skepticism the surveillance that she mentioned in her previous correspondence. She fears that the Scot prisoner may have been lying to throw you off Douglas's true route back to the Borders."

Caernervon sat stupefied. "She tells me this ... *now?*"

As the last of the Scots disappeared over the horizon, Lancaster turned a glare of unchecked disgust on the purported son of Edward Longshanks.

Thirty-Five

The lairds rushed from their seats in Newbattle Abbey and welcomed James and Randolph home with thunderous applause and hearty backslaps. Although the two raiders had failed, by mere minutes, to capture the English queen, their plunge deep into Yorkshire had so shaken the Plantagenet court in London that Caernervon had sent envoys to Dunfermline to negotiate a two-year truce to the war, the first in twenty-four years.

Hobbled by his injuries suffered in prison, Bishop Lamberton carved a path through his colleagues with his cane and escorted the two heroes to the dais, where Robert stood waiting. The bishop had another reason to feel heartened this eve. He had arranged this celebration as a pretext to call the Privy Council into session, during which he intended to put forth a profound proposal that he had long nurtured in secret.

Robert met his two favorite officers with a smirk, delighted that his decision to harness them had worked so splendidly. His nephew was forever striving to match exploits with James, who in turn was constantly irritated by Randolph's acerbic tongue and dashing verve. The two rivals were so similar in features and temperament that neither could long abide the other without falling into some argument or a contest of wits. Nothing entertained Robert more than the steady stream of correspondence from James complaining of Randolph's insubordination. Robert longed to be rid of his own administrative responsibilities and return to the field to arbitrate their disputes while at the same time needling them on, as he had in the old days. Their return had even reinvigorated his health; the mysterious lesions had receded, and the passing of time had even eased his grief over the Ireland disaster and his brother Edward's death.

Robert winked at Lamberton, setting in motion a prearranged surprise. The bishop retracted the curtain covering the sacristy, and Sweenie, armed with the English archbishop's staff captured at Myton, came bounding out from stage left onto the dais.

Robert spun James by the shoulders to face the monk. "I'm told you owe the Wee-Kneed a song."

The barons roared with laughter as Sweenie tapped his new episcopal staff against the boards to speed a payment of the debt.

Nodding with a grin of concession, James accepted a mandolin from an attendant and, strumming a chord, sang:

"On the misty plains of York,
Scotland's own wee David marched
Across the Bridge of Death
To fight the Bishop Arched.
He conjured up Hell's fires
To fright King Edward's priest.
And painted his face darkly
To mock an evil beast.
When the white-robed monks turned tail,
The Wee-Kneed fell to fightin'
And the River Swale gobbled up
The Chapter of the Myton."

Sweenie held a protracted bow, milking the acclamation as the barons whistled and stomped.

Lamberton waved the little monk off the dais. "Now begone with you, Weekneed, before I defrock you for wallowing in the sin of pride."

When those of lesser rank had finally cleared the nave, the bishop commanded the doors be bolted and, bringing the chamber to order, waved the privy councilors back to their seats. He brought forth from his parchments folio a document sealed with the Holy See's waxed imprint. After a hesitation, he delivered the correspondence to Robert with a chilling announcement: "The new pope has reaffirmed your excommunication, my lord."

Robert's good cheer vanished. He hung his head and retreated to his chair, slumping in bitter disappointment.

To ease the blow, Lamberton had delayed revealing the ecclesiastical decision until James returned from Yorkshire. He had hoped that Clement's death would bring an impartial successor to St. Peter's throne, but the craven cardinals had elected Jacques Diese to become Pope John XXII. The seventy-year-old former confidante of Clement had been born in Guenne, an English fiefdom, and this, his latest nuncio, made clear that he intended to continue the Curia's pro-English policy in the expectation that Caernervon would reciprocate by financing a new crusade to Palestine.

Several of the barons traded uneasy glances, most notably the Seneschal of the Realm, William Soules, and his allies, Robert Mowbray and David Brechin, all former Comyn supporters who had come grudgingly to Robert's cause after Bannockburn.

Lamberton closely monitored their reaction, particularly the uneasy shifting of Brechin, the young knight who years ago had been discovered carrying the letter with Red Comyn's plan to steal the crown. Handsome and dashing, Brechin only recently had returned from the Holy Land, where he had gained fame with the appellation, "The Flower of Knighthood." Over the years, Robert had made no attempt to hide his jealousy of Brechin's crusading deeds, accomplished while he and James had been at home fighting England.

After a troubled contemplation, Robert raised his distraught eyes and asked the bishop, "Do you see in this nuncio an invitation to negotiate?"

"I do not, Sire. The document is addressed to your council only. The new pope has refused to recognize you as our rightful king."

Robert dropped his chin to his chest again. These past sixteen years spent under the edict of excommunication had weighed heavily on him and the kingdom. Most of the priests in the abbeys and kirks still refused to say Mass or dispense the sacraments to his subjects. The commoners understood neither the nuances of the theological debate nor the power struggles between the Holy See and the royal courts, only that they were being condemned to Hell because he was their king. After a heavy sigh, he ordered the bishop, "You must sail to Avignon at once and renew our petition in person. You were clever enough to goad me into taking this crown. I expect you to apply those skills of persuasion to sway the Holy Father to our cause."

Lamberton hesitated, waiting for the murmurs across the nave to dissipate. Then, he took his bold gamble. "I would propose another course."

"A new monastery, perhaps?" Robert suggested hopefully. "Dedicated to the Holy Father's patron saint?"

Lamberton answered so softly that the barons were required to crane their necks to hear him. "The Curia's decision to reaffirm your excommunication, Your Grace, was instigated by the Dominican inquisitors. We have repeatedly offered sops and obsequies to the papacy, only to be spat upon. I pray you send a declaration instead. An ultimatum signed by all nobles warning that we shall no longer suffer the Church to dictate our fate."

Robert erupted to his feet. "I'll not allow your bickering with the Black Friars to threaten my kingdom! I cannot rule without holy sanction!"

Lamberton maintained a serene demeanor, hoping to hold Robert's temper in check. With head still lowered, the cleric said, "This new pope abuses his authority for crass political advantage. No nation should be required to relinquish its rightful sovereignty under the threat of God's retribution."

Robert reddened. "I forbid you to speak heresy in my presence."

"Do you believe the war we wage is just?" Lamberton asked him.

"Of course."

"Then either you are the heretic, or the pope is."

The chamber stirred uneasily at hearing that self-evident truth spoken so directly. Yet Lamberton did not flinch at the shocked reaction. He had warned Robert during the earliest days of the war that they would not prevail against England until they first won this standoff with the papacy. This two-year truce proposed by Caernervon offered a rare, and perhaps last, opportunity to capitalize on Robert's victories in the field. The Dominicans in Avignon were testing Scotland, and if they perceived Robert as weak and indecisive, they would continue to advise the pope to withhold recognition of his legitimacy and wait for Caernervon to renew the war, when they would come north with the English army and bring Scotland to heel under their spiritual reign of terror, just as they had done to the Occitan nobles in southern France.

With these myriad diplomatic undercurrents in mind, the bishop now debated the wisdom of pressing his controversial proposal, particularly in light of Robert's fragile confidence. But he felt such a declaration was so critical to Scotland's survival that he decided to take the risk. "What I would next divulge," he told Robert, "must be for your ears only, and those of your most trusted advisors."

Robert held an incredulous glare on his old confessor. After mulling the strange request for a private audience, he curtly dismissed the assembly and, in a pique, marched from the nave while beckoning James, Randolph, and Lamberton to follow him to his private quarters.

Inside his chambers, Robert found the leaders of the refugee Knights Templar—including Jeanne de Rouen, William Sinclair, and Peter d'Aumont—waiting for him.

Jeanne stole a questioning glance at James, having not spoken to him in months. After Marjorie's death, she had remained with Robert's infant grandson at Renfrew rather than return to Lintalee, and now James's cold manner confirmed that he was still rankled by what he perceived as her abandonment.

Robert was livid at the Templars for taking the risk of being seen in his court. "Did I not order you to remain in the Isles?"

"You did, my lord," d'Aumont conceded, but offering no explanation for the disobedience.

Robert's mood was not improved by the Auvergene Templar's reticence to be more forthcoming. "You came to my aid at Bannockburn. For that, I granted you sanctuary. But I cannot have you openly traveling the country. The Church will never remove the edict of excommunication—"

"I ordered them here," Lamberton revealed.

Robert's jaw fell open. "I see your thinking, Bishop. You intend to coax the Church by surrounding me with hunted heretics and felons."

Undeterred by the biting sarcasm, Lamberton nodded to d'Aumont.

The Templar retrieved a Bible from a small altar and extended it to Robert. "I must ask you to swear that what I tell you will never leave this room."

Robert bristled. "This is how I am repaid for saving your necks? Questioning the looseness of my tongue?"

D'Aumont did not waver from his insistence on the condition. "What the bishop now asks of me requires the breach of my own vows of secrecy."

Intrigued, Robert reluctantly gave the oath, as did James and Randolph.

Having gained their compliance, D'Aumont stared at the Bible, debating how best to preface his revelation. "This war you wage with England was fore-ordained many years ago."

"Well then," Robert quipped nastily. "We are wasting our time worrying about its outcome. That was certainly worth an oath."

D'Aumont did not rise to take the bait. "When our Order held Jerusalem, our brothers there found certain scrolls near the Temple Mount. They also captured inhabitants of the city who kept apart from the Moslems." He looked directly at Robert to drive home the significance of his next revelation. "Native Arabs who did not worship Allah."

"Jews?" Robert inquired, perplexed.

The Templar shook his head. "These prisoners claimed to be descendants of Our Lord's first followers. Yet they denied the authority of Rome. The sect was neither Roman Christian nor infidel. They called themselves Nasoreans."

James reminded the Templars, "Our Lord was called a Nasorean."

When d'Aumont did not deny the significance of that observation, which seemed more than coincidence, Robert moved to put a stop to all of the coyness. "What does any of this have to do with me?"

D'Aumont walked nearer to the crackling fire, to avoid being heard by possible lurkers beyond the door. Finally, he revealed in a subdued voice, "We had the scrolls translated and were told they contained several passages identical to those in Holy Scripture. But there were other teachings and verses."

"And?" pressed Robert.

D'Aumont's eyes shifted off. "Verses ... not in the Gospels."

Robert and James leaned closer, trying to comprehend that discovery.

"These Nasoreans proved to our satisfaction that the saints were not the true authors of the New Testament."

"How could that possibly be?" Robert demanded.

"The holy Gospels were copied from earlier accounts," d'Aumont said. "More *complete* accounts."

James asked d'Aumont, "Are you saying that certain passages were left out of Scriptures on purpose?" When the Templar did not deny it, James kept pressing him. "But why?"

D'Aumont wiped a bed of sweat from his brow, clearly uncomfortable with this line of inquiry. "After Our Lord's death, there arose a dispute between two factions of His disciples. One schemed to destroy the evidence proving that Christ never intended to allow one man spiritual dominion over another."

James took a step closer. "Which faction prevailed?"

"The followers of St. Paul. Those disciples who remained loyal to Our Lord's brother, James the Just, were cast aside as unbelievers." The Templar glared at James to drive home his point. "These banished followers of James were the same Nasoreans who authored the first written accounts of Christ's teachings."

James and Robert turned looks of disbelief upon Lamberton, who nodded a sheepish admission that he had not previously divulged all that he knew of Scotland's history.

"The Culdees were descendants of these Nasoreans," the bishop confessed. "The successors of St. Paul ordered all writings of this brother of Christ be destroyed. But a few survivors of the purge escaped Jerusalem and brought their copies here to Britain."

"During our defense of the Holy City," d'Aumont added, "my Templar brothers discovered a second set of copies hidden by these Nasoreans."

Lamberton waited for James and Robert to wrap their understanding around the implication of these connections. The Dominicans in the Holy See had cleverly manipulated the French king to suppress the Templars. In truth, both the Temple and the Culdees had been persecuted for a more sinister reason: They possessed evidence of the papacy's machinations to subvert the teachings of Christ.

"What then *was* Our Lord's true mission?" Robert asked.

D'Aumont was reluctant to finish, but their insistent glares drove him to the task. "Christ taught that each of us is responsible for our own soul. Salvation can be attained only by searching for truth, not by blind belief."

"That is the Gnostic deviancy!" Robert protested.

D'Aumont glanced toward the door, as if fearful that the Dominicans may have infiltrated agents into the court here. Raising his hands in a plea for the king to lower his voice, he explained, "Our Lord warned that priests would try to twist his words. The scrolls speak of a cosmic war fought again and again by souls who reincarnate into this world. The Nasoreans called it a war between the forces of Darkness and Light. The Cathari of Occitania also possessed copies of these scrolls."

"The Cathari were exterminated as heretics," James reminded him.

"For good reason," d'Aumont said. "The Occitan martyrs were spiritual descendants of these same Nasoreans. And hence they knew the truth."

Robert shot his councilors a questioning glance, as if convinced they had all fallen into the company of the deranged.

But James had already connected the strands: The Templars, Culdees, and Cathari were striplings nurtured from the same seed, all eliminated by the Church for the same crime: knowledge of the truth. He turned back to d'Aumont and asked, "Did these scrolls say who will prevail in this war?"

"The forces of the Light. But only if a New Jerusalem is first built."

James bored in on the Templar. "Built *where*?"

Jeanne stepped forward to answer for her reticent comrade. "Across the sea, beyond Ireland. In a land protected by a goddess and her star."

A stunned silence extended across the chamber, until Robert snorted with disbelief. "That's nothing more than a bard's fable. Any fool knows the world drops off beyond Ireland."

Jeanne retreated to rolled blanket that had been placed on a table. She opened it and brought forth what appeared to be some form of exotic vegetation. She pealed the husks on one of the plants and displayed rows of what appeared to be yellow teeth.

Robert examined the odd kernels. "This grows in Palestine?"

D'Aumont impaled the oblong plant on the tip of his sword and held its core over the fire. After roasting its teeth brown, he carved off a row of the kernels for the Scots to taste. "Five years ago, we sent a fleet west from the Orkneys. Navigating under the constellation of the Virgin, we came upon a new land that resembles your Isle in both climate and landscape. The natives there, dark-skinned as Arabs, call this plant 'maize.' The other they call 'aloe.' Its juice provides a healing balm for wounds. Our brothers brought back planting seeds from the vegetation."

"These scrolls you discovered," James said. "Where are they now?"

D'Aumont maintained a stony glare. "*That* we cannot reveal."

Robert flushed at the curt refusal. "Do you forget that you address a king?"

"Not *our* king," d'Aumont insisted with steeled defiance. "We serve only the Blessed Virgin, the Queen who rules over all kings."

James suspected these Templars were revealing just enough of their mysterious arcana to serve their ulterior designs. He studied Jeanne, wondering what other secrets she had withheld from him. If the monks *had* discovered a new land of bounty, why had they returned to Scotland? There was nothing here but strife and barren moors. And then it came to him: Why had the papal missionaries rowed across the Channel to conquer the Culdees? Why had England nearly bankrupted its treasury to conquer the North? Why did any foreigner with designs of subjugation ever come to Scotland? With a knowing glare, he challenged d'Aumont with a theory, "You came back for the Stone of Destiny."

The Scots tightened their circle, finally driving the monk to an answer. "We came back to see your war won. ... And to insure the safety of your Stone."

"What possible purpose could the Stone serve for you?" James asked.

Jeanne shook her head, exasperated at his persistence in delving into such esoteric matters. Knowing that he would not be dissuaded from an answer, she reluctantly revealed, "Your coronation Stone held the Ark of the Covenant in Solomon's Temple. The New Jerusalem cannot be built until all of the relics from the Israelite tabernacle are reunited."

"If you seek the foundation Stone," James said in a sharp cross-examination, "then you have already found the Ark."

When the Templars did not deny that charge, Robert turned to the man responsible for bringing these French heretic monks to Scotland. "Do you believe this wild tale, Bishop?"

"I do. You know that I have always believed that we Scots were given a great task in God's plan. The angels were with us at Bannockburn. Our freedom, and the freedom of those who will follow us, depends upon our refusal to bend to papist calumny. If we stand defiant, others may gain courage to do the same."

James watched Robert closely as he walked a few steps away to weigh the bishop's proposal to defy the pope. The wrangling of churchmen always left Robert enervated; he had never understood why all Christians could not accept the teachings of the Church without striving to twist them into some worldly advantage. He was no doubt also worried that his grandfather now languished in Purgatory because he had failed to fulfill their vow to go to Jerusalem. If he brazenly rejected the spiritual legitimacy of the excommunication as the bishop now counseled, they would never be permitted to take up the Cross and make good on their boyhood oath.

Either you are the heretic, or the pope is.

There was harsh truth in that cold assessment of their situation. These Templars, not the pope, had stood with them at Bannockburn, and if he and Robert had to throw their lots with Satan's legions, at least they would stand with those who had demonstrated loyalty in the face of death. What Scotsman worth his salt would choose theological righteousness over steadfastness in battle? He nodded firmly at Robert to spur him to the right decision.

Prodded on despite his misgivings, Robert sighed and crossed his breast after finishing a silent prayer for guidance. "This declaration you seek, Bishop. You have some phrasing in mind?"

Lamberton quickened with hope. "Aye, my lord."

Robert shot a nettled glare at James, convinced that his old friend enjoyed watching him suffer under such dilemmas. "If I go to Hell's fires for this, you'll not be far behind me."

"When have I ever been behind you? I dragged your London-coddled ass up Ben Lomond to put it on that throne out there."

Robert shook his head in dismay. Was it any wonder the Church refused to recognize his kingship when his own subjects spoke to him so cavalierly? He walked toward the door and, without turning, ordered the bishop, "Draft your writ. If it moves me, I will consider its promulgation."

And so, during the weeks that followed, Bishop Lamberton labored day and night on Scotland's reply to the new pope. To assist him, he recruited an old comrade, Abbot Bernard of Arbroath Abbey, who had carried the relics of St. Columba at Bannockburn and was a renowned Latinist, more skilled than any Scotsman in the art of rhetoric. After many hours of heated debate over whether to take a strident or conciliatory tone, the two clerics finally reached an accord.

Lamberton acquiesced in the obsequious formalities that Bernard insisted should be included for diplomatic salve. He also accepted certain odious references that tacitly recognized the pope as the arbiter of the Faith, for Bernard had rightly calculated that their demand to choose their own king without interference by the Church was radical enough; an attack upon the pontiff's legitimacy in spiritual matters would be left for another day. In exchange for these concessions, he had extracted the one condition that he considered more crucial than all the legalities combined: Bernard promised not to lay down his quill until he had summoned language so poetic and powerful that it would hearken music from the angelic realm when read to John XXII and his Curia.

Thus, in April of that year, 1320, Robert stood before Parliament in Arbroath Abbey and watched as the barons filed by to press their clan seals to Lamberton's unprecedented document. Soules, Mowbray, and Brechin held back, but they too were finally driven to sign by the king's judging glare. Brechin appeared particularly agitated, his brow damped with perspiration and his eyes in constant motion. After the young knight finally committed the deed, Robert examined the relief of his seal and observed, "That is the imprint of your wife's clan, if I am not mistaken, Lord Brechin?"

Brechin glanced nervously at Soules. "Aye, my lord. I carelessly neglected to bring my signet."

"For a man who fought in Palestine, you seem a bit ajar," Robert observed dryly. "I trust you did not tremble so when you faced the Saracens?"

Brechin daubed sweat from his forehead. "I have not been well."

James waited at the rear of the line to be the last to lay his mark on what many were affectionately calling the Scottish Declaration of Freedom. As his turn came and he pressed his ring to the parchment wax with a flourish of his wrist, he smiled at Lamberton in congratulations. Finding one paragraph particularly to his liking, he dipped the quill and emboldened its words to emphasize to the Holy Father that he would personally see to its enforcement:

> *For so long as there shall but one hundred of us remain alive*
> *we will never give consent to subject ourselves to the dominion*
> *of the English. For it is not glory, it is not riches, neither is it*
> *honours, but it is liberty alone that we fight and contend for,*
> *which no honest man will lose but with his life.*

A week later, as James rode back north toward Dunfermline, he consulted Robert's baffling new order again. Only a few days after his return to Lintalee, he had been commanded to arrest David Brechin in Roxburgh and, engaging in no conversation with him, deliver the prisoner with all haste to the king's judiciary. Now, reaching the palace, he dismounted and escorted Brechin into the abbey where the Parliament was in session. He found Soules, Mowbray, and seven former Comyn allies standing chained in the docks.

Robert shot to his feet on seeing Brechin shuffle down the aisle in leg irons. "Traitor! Has he confessed, Lord Douglas?"

James was taken aback by the accusation. "My liege, confessed to what?"

"Are you not charged with the surveillance of my enemies?"

James was confounded by both the indictment of treason and Robert's implication that he had played a role in whatever had happened. He turned to Brechin for an explanation.

The former Comyn knight kept his eyes lowered. "I did not partake of the act."

"Did not *partake!*" Robert screamed. "You absolve yourself by sitting idle while these traitors thrust the knife?"

"They swore me to secrecy before revealing their plans," Brechin said. "I did nothing but abide by my vow to God."

"You would see the crown stolen from me!"

"Not stolen. Rightly placed on a legitimate head."

Robert shouted so vehemently that he doused Brechin with spittle. "What harm did I ever cause to be done to you?"

"I took the Cross," Brechin said. "I cannot give allegiance to an excommunicate without darkening my soul."

"Damn your base pride!" Robert shouted. "I have heard my fill of your exploits in foreign lands! You toured Palestine garnering laurels while I crawled on my belly in an Arran cave to keep your fiefs safe!"

"You ask me to turn against my faith," Brechin reminded him.

"You are a Scotsman!"

"I am a Christian first."

Robert flailed his arms as he strode fulminating before the other prisoners. "Soules, your rank saves you from the block! You can contemplate the fate you've brought down upon your fellow conspirators while you rot in Dumbarton prison! They are condemned to death because of your preening ambition!" He turned on Brechin and drove the young knight a step back with a punishing finger. "And you, *crusader!*"—he parsed that word with syllabic disdain—"you who twice swore a personal bond of loyalty to me! You shall be dragged through the streets of Perth, then drawn and quartered! That should satisfy your heated lust for Heaven's reward!"

James dared not question Robert's judgment in front of the barons. Instead, he came aside the king's ear and, with a tight-lipped whisper, begged, "Rob, a word alone with you."

Robert, shaking and sweating profusely, wheeled wild-eyed on him. "And you, Lord Douglas, shall henceforth address me as a king!" He marched out of the council session to gain the seclusion of his privy chamber.

Stunned by the outburst, James followed on Robert's heels and pushed his way inside before the door could be barred. When Robert had finally stopped throwing anything within his reach, James sought to douse the fit with calmness. "What has happened?"

Eyes bloodshot and darting, Robert paced in an ever-tightening circle. He picked up the stoker at the hearth and drove it against the stones on the wall. "Soules's jilted mistress came to Liz and revealed the plot! That snake was scheming my murder!"

"Then hang Soules. But Brechin has only followed his conscience."

"Are you in league with them?"

James was driven to his heels by the charge. "Have you gone mad?"

"Why do you oppose me on this?"

"Brechin is beloved by all," James reminded him. "You'll only blacken your good name by his execution. It is not worthy of you. Gain Brechin's fealty by earning it with mercy."

Robert clawed frantically at the weeping lesions on his arms. Only weeks ago, the sores had appeared healed, but now they had returned with these manic rages. "I will tell you what is not worthy of me! You sleeping with that French nun outside the bonds of matrimony! Bringing ridicule and divine curses down upon my rule! That is why the pope denies my petitions! You will marry that woman at once!"

"My dealings with Jeanne are none of your concern."

"They *are* my concern, by God! You are one of my councilors! Your sinfulness reflects poorly on me! I know why you avoid her! You've wallowed long enough in this unseemly pining for that dead Fife woman! I am sick of it!"

James came up face to face with him. "Since when did you become so pious? Have you forgotten your dalliance on Tioram with Christiana while your wife languished in England?"

Robert took a step back, as if expecting James to come at him with a dagger and finish the regicide. "That was an indiscretion of youth. I command you to take a wife and rid me of this divine punishment for your debauchery!"

"Leave off this, I warn you!"

"I am your king! And you will abide me on this!"

"Listen to you! You rant on like Caernervon!"

Robert lunged and swung wildly, but James blocked the blow. Robert taunted him to throw a punch in retaliation.

James turned and marched out.

chirty-six

eanne assisted Elizabeth Bruce from the royal barge, and together they waded through the chilly breakwaters of Dornoch Firth toward the windswept dunes below Tain. Reaching the shore, they found the ancient path that led to St. Duthac's sanctuary. The ground was pocked with frozen footprints, many formed by the bare feet of pilgrims who had come here over the centuries to petition divine intercessions. Hearing the queen breathing hard from the exertion, Jeanne slowed their approach up the treacherous trail. "Perhaps we should rest a bit before we attempt it."

Leaning down to wring the water from the hem of her traveling mantle, Elizabeth looked up to demand a retraction of the implication that she was not capable of making the climb. How many ladies of her age could touch their shoes without bending their knees? She had just celebrated—nay, mourned—her forty-fifth birthday, but she still became indignant when the younger ladies in her court made a fuss over her. True, she had put on weight, and her joints ached from the rheumatism, but she still slept only three hours a night and outlasted them all in attending to the duties in the new royal residence at Cardross. "I once ran to that kirk. You can wrap me in the burial shroud the day I can no longer walk to it."

"The king ordered me to keep tight rein on you. And the physicians—"

"My husband is a fine one to give lectures about physicians! Had we listened to those blood-sucking leeches, we'd both be in the grave."

Seeing Jeanne take refuge in hurt silence, Elizabeth intertwined an arm with her elbow in a plea for forgiveness. She often forgot how withering hot her Irish temper could run. As they ascended the uneven stone stairway that led to the wooded bluffs, she choked up with tears. Each step along this hallowed track brought back crushing memories. Robert had begged her to delay the arduous journey until summer, but she was determined to set out at the first thaw to fulfill the vow she had made twenty-one years ago. On the night that she had cowered here with Belle, near starvation and not knowing if their men were alive, she had promised the Almighty that she would return one day on pilgrimage to this Culdee sanctuary if her husband were kept safe and resurrected in his kingship.

Unlike Robert, who felt perpetually oppressed by the Malachy Curse, she now looked back on their lives together as a succession of miracles. The most recent had also been the most blessed: Six months ago, she had given birth to a son, David. Although she had provided Robert with two daughters after her return from captivity in England, she had all but given up hope of producing a male heir. The pregnancy prior to David's had been difficult, and most Scots had expected her to lose this latest child to a miscarriage. In a moment of despair, she had even consulted a famous seer from Strath Fillan, who had deepened her pessimism with a report that his scrying revealed an empty throne.

For all of these reasons and more, the news of David's birth had been greeted with great celebration across the realm. But the joy was tempered by concern about Robert's alarming decline in health. After the parliamentary session at Arbroath, the skin-eating disease had begun to infect his mind more frequently, and she had heard the whispered fears that by siring an heir so late in his life, he had doomed the kingdom to a regency and another clan war. There was also some sentiment that Marjorie's son, Robert Stewart, now nine years old, had been divinely destined for the throne because of his mother's travails in England and her martyr's death in childbirth.

These conflicts among his subjects were troubling to her husband, but his most painful tribulation was his estrangement from James Douglas. Robert's outburst during the Brechin inquest had fractured their already strained friendship, and during these past years, the two men had communicated only by official correspondence. Robert was too proud to ask forgiveness for his baseless accusations of disloyalty. And James, equally stubborn, had repulsed all attempts at reconciliation. She had even enlisted Jeanne as an unofficial intermediary between the two men, but to little effect.

Now, as she often had in the past, she tried to prime her younger companion for more news. "I should not have taken you away from Jamie. Who will keep him out of trouble?"

Jeanne smiled at the poorly disguised foray for gossip. "He won't miss me, I should think."

"Have you seen him recently?"

"Last month. For one night, was all."

Elizabeth shook her head at the utter stupidity of men. When the war against England was renewed after the expiration of the two-year truce, Jeanne had accompanied James on the campaigns, including his second daring raid into

Yorkshire, this time to Rievaulx Abbey, where they had come within a whisker of capturing Caernervon. And yet rumors were rampant that Jeanne shared only James's bed, not his heart. She suspected that her escort had volunteered to accompany her on this pilgrimage to fulfill a secret quest of her own: By retracing the steps that Belle had walked, she was trying to better understand the long-departed woman who still held James captive. Determined to smoke her out on the subject, Elizabeth stole a sideways glance at her and risked, "May I ask you a question of a personal nature?"

Jeanne gave her a wry look. "Only if I am afforded the same opportunity."

Elizabeth chortled at the hard-driven bargain. During their month-long sojourn together, they had come to know each other so well that they often conversed in an informal, even jesting, manner. "You should be the king's diplomat. ... Why do you stay with Jamie?"

"He has never deceived me."

"Neither has my cook, but I don't warm my nights with him. ... Do you love him?" When Jeanne nodded, unable to speak it, Elizabeth huffed, "Then for the sake of Finian's fasting, why have you two not taken the vows?"

"His heart remains bound to another."

Before Elizabeth could vent her exasperation, a flicker of golden light above the tree line startled her. Was her mind playing tricks, or had that been an elf spark? These old oaks looked so familiar. A shudder of nostalgia came over her. How strange. That horrid day when she had staggered up this same path with Belle, they had spoken of the same stubborn man. A bard in Ulster once told her that life does not progress in a straight line, as the Roman monks insist, but spirals through time, backtracking to the same places and moments with certain aspects of the experience altered. Had she come back to Tain of her own free will? Or had God led her here again for some deeper purpose? As she grew older, she found herself pondering such questions that she once dismissed as mystical nonsense. Returned to the present, she asked Jeanne, "Jamie doesn't love you?"

"I accepted from the beginning that I'd never have that part of him."

"Has he ever spoken to you about Belle?"

"No."

"Insufferable creatures! These men of ours will carry their heart wounds to their graves!"

Falling silent, they walked the rest of the way counseled by their own troubled thoughts and memories.

When, at last, they reached the crumbling sanctuary fence that still surrounded the kirk, Elizabeth braced against its ancient stones to regain her wind. It was here that she and Marjorie, frightened and weary, had crouched while Belle

ran to the door. As the mists now swirled and closed in, she shivered with a
foreboding. She had no reason to be frightened now, for their old enemies were
long gone, the Earl of Ross dead and the Comyns subdued. Yet she was haunted
by a dread whose source she could not locate. She turned to call for her guards,
having forgotten that she had ordered them to remain at the barge. To avoid
the admiring throngs, she had insisted that no announcement of her arrival be
sent ahead. Tightening her grip on Jeanne's arm, she approached the kirk with
trepidation and pounded the doorknocker, just as Belle had done years ago.

A pock-faced Culdee monk crowned with a mash of white hair slid open the
slot. "No room!" He slammed it shut, nearly pinching her fingers.

She nodded, having expected the rude greeting, and persisted with a second
knock. "We require sanctuary!"

This time, the crabby monk cracked the rusty door and poked out his head.
"Sanctuary? From whom?"

Elizabeth brought her sleeve to her tremoring mouth. Every remembrance
of that night long ago came flooding back to her. She repeated Belle's frantic
plea, as if by reenacting the event she might alter the past. "The English seek
to capture us. You are our last hope."

The hermit swung the door back wide to challenge that claim. "The English
haven't troubled these parts since King Robert chased them south."

She winked through tears at Jeanne in conspiracy at Jeanne, and like an
actress about to play out an important scene, gruffly reminded the monk, "I
was told that the Culdees were the true descendants of Christ! I see now that
I was misinformed!"

The monk's glare sharpened with suspicion. "Who told you such a thing?"

"A brother of yours. Sweenie the Wee-kneed."

The monk yelped with excitement. "You know the Wee-kneed? That rapscal-
lion! That little half-devil! Where is he? Is he with you?"

"He is in the South risking his life to save our King!" Elizabeth snapped. "But
I will tell him of the base hospitality you have showered upon us!"

His memory jolted, the monk squinted to better see the queen's features.
Slowly, he lowered to his cracking knees and cried, "God's mercy!"

Bemused by his astonishment, Elizabeth brought him back to his feet. "It is
reassuring to know, Brother Fergus, that you still offer the same warm welcome
to pilgrims."

The monk's baggy lids swelled with tears. "You remembered."

Elizabeth walked to the corner of the chapel where she had fallen asleep on
that night long ago. Running her hand across the charred walls, she saw that
the stones had not been altered by a single crack or tuft of moss. She beckoned
her bag from Jeanne and, withdrawing from it a large votive candle, lit the

wick and stood over the flame while offering a prayer. After several minutes of tearful contemplation, she placed a draw sack of coins into Fergus's hand. "Tend this flame for me until I die."

Brother Fergus bowed in obeisance. When he returned upright, he saw, for the first time, Jeanne's features clearly in the votive's flickering light. His leathery hands trembled as he brought her startled face to his failing eyes. "How can it be? They told me you were dead."

Unnerved, Jeanne tried to pull away, but the monk would not release her.

Sobbing, he clutched at her. "Not a day has passed that I've not done penance for allowing the traitors take you."

Elizabeth was stunned. The old hermit was a bit dotaged, but how could he now mistake Jeanne for the deceased Belle? She empathized with Jeanne's hurt feelings; to be plagued by the memory of Jamie's old love was torment enough, but to be mistaken for Belle in the flesh was beyond cruel. Seeing Jeanne about to disabuse the monk of his error, she grasped the French lass's arm to petition her forbearance.

Brother Fergus begged Jeanne, "I pray you forgive me."

Elizabeth nodded for her to play the part.

"There is nothing to for—" Jeanne doubled over from a sharp pang.

Elizabeth eased her to the floor. "Are you ill?

Jeanne stumbled outside and vomited.

Brother Fergus hurried to his cell. Moments later, he returned with the sanctuary's famous healing stones. Assisting Jeanne back inside the kirk, he lowered her to the floor and laid the stones around her. After nearly a minute of hovering his hands over her in spiritual diagnosis, he looked up and smiled at Elizabeth. "Do you remember the vision that so frightened her?"

Elizabeth blanched, thrust back to the moment forever seared into her memory: Before the Earl of Ross had captured them on that fateful night, Belle had told her of being awakened by a strange dream of James running toward her carrying an infant.

Brother Fergus kissed Jeanne's womb. "This day we have been twice blessed. The saint has brought you back to us … with the promised child."

Thirty-seven

Despite the late winter chill, Isabella's anger boiled as she sat waiting in her carriage outside the Lion's Gate of London Tower. After raising a rebellion army in France and marshaling the support of the fractious English barons, she had deposed Caernervon, rendering him the first monarch in England's history to suffer such ignominy. Yet because she was French, and a woman, these London quislings now refused her the privilege of witnessing her own son be knighted in preparation for his coronation that afternoon. Even the lowly scribes who stood at the wall slits to record the ritual were being accorded more access than her.

Oui, remember this day in your chronicles, you feckless monks! England will not soon forget the First of February in the Year 1327.

She looked up with bitter regret at the cruciform window high above her. Four bloody years had passed since her ambitious paramour, Roger Mortimer, an accomplice in the *coup*, cheated Caernervon's execution ax by escaping through that aperture. She had finally surrendered to Mortimer's persistent advances, but only to enlist his aid in chasing her husband and his rapacious favourite, Hugh Despenser the Younger, off to Wales. Yet she soon learned to her dismay that she had merely replaced one inconstant lout with another: Mortimer was now pitting young Edward against her, puffing her son with flattery and stoking him to invade Scotland as the first act of his reign.

As the royal herald rode past her window, she conjured unheard curses at the new crest that Mortimer had commissioned to celebrate his rise to power.

Roger, you trumpet your escape from that Tower as if the Almighty Himself had reached down and plucked you from the block. But it was I, not God, who saved you. Do you forget the soporifics that I secreted into your cell that night? The gaolers who fell asleep on your watch paid dearly enough with their heads. You would be rotting in the grave had I not sent the galley to take you to Paris. I warm your bed, but do not think me blinded to your schemes. You will not shunt me from the governance of my son!

At last, the prince appeared on the ramparts to accept the dull acclamation of the throngs, whose loyalty had been purchased with coin that the realm's treasury could ill afford. Shod in sandals and dressed in a kirtle of velvet opened at the breast, young Edward could barely crane his narrow head and dark brown curls above the merlons. When the smattering of cheers dissipated, the boy descended the steps, followed by John of Hainault, a mercenary officer from the Continent hired for his protection. Escorted to a white stallion caparisoned in gold and black, Edward mounted and, offering his mother not even a nod of acknowledgment, rode off for Westminster with Mortimer at his side.

Her eyes welled up. *Child, you promised I would rule with you.*

All around her, the Tower grounds echoed with ghostly screams. Incensed that she had been left behind, she ordered her *postilion* to catch up with the royal procession. Her nerves, already frayed by the upheavals of the past months, were now shaken to the bone by the rattling clops over the cobblestones of Lower Thames Street. The city was strangely quite for this hour, a rare occurrence that she found blessed, until she realized that the crowds had merely become tense and surly on spying her approach. Even the weather had turned traitorous, seducing her with a glint of morning sun, only to give way to a lacerating mix of sleet and rain. Mortimer had tried to cower her to remain in her quarters, ostensibly for her safety, but she would not allow him to flaunt himself as the boy's prime counselor. These English ingrates needed reminding that the daughter of a French king had saved them from a hapless monarch bred of their own bloodlines.

She risked a glance past the crack in the curtains. Thrice she had traveled this gloomy ceremonial route. How frightened she had been on her first arrival in London, at the tender age of thirteen. Transported up from Margate on a galley under heavy guard, she had fallen green with seasickness. This morning was balmy compared to that horrid day, when the river had frozen over for the first time in thirty years. Caernervon had met her on Westminster's steps with a manner more frigid than the icicles hanging from the gargoyles. She had feared she would not survive a year in this mirthless land, but she had outlasted them all: Longshanks, Gaveston, Clifford, Despenser.

And now, her worthless husband.

Her second procession down these same treacherous warrens had taken place only three years ago, during her triumphant return from Paris. After escaping Caernervon's clutches, she had sailed across the Channel to the protection of her brother, Charles IV, now King of France. Her cousins, overjoyed at her return, had begged her to remain in Paris, but she was determined to see *her* Edward installed on the English throne. Now these fickle Londoners, who had once welcomed her back as their liberator, cast aspersions on her honor and slandered her with the epithet, the She-Wolf of France. Had she made an ill-fated choice by leaving Paris? No, she would yet bring these English back to her side. She cared not a whit for their love; it was their fear she desired.

The blast of a foghorn above London Bridge startled her from her scheming thoughts. That molding monstrosity never failed to thrust her into a despond. Only Norman dullards would cobble a veritable city of houses and shops atop a bridge. Unlike the elegant Parisian spans designed to enhance the beauty of the Seine, this squat traverse poisoned the Thames with sulfurous miasmas coughed up from hundreds of chimneys. Over the decades, so many buildings had been haphazardly encrusted upon the buttresses that the bridge now resembled a giant beaver's tunnel on the verge of collapse.

At the tollhouse, where William Wallace's severed head had once been nailed on display, a shriveled penis and testicles now hung from a stanchion.

She snorted a vengeful puff of air at the macabre sight.

There is the last of you, Despenser. You did not learn from Gaveston's folly, did you? He too underestimated me. You thought you could steal my estates and cast me away in some hole, but you did not count on the troubles with France. If there was one thing besides buggery that I could rely upon from my husband, it was his whimpering insecurity. He refused to cross the Channel and pay homage to Paris, so I offered to serve as his envoy and take the babe with me as a gesture of good will. What fools you were to let us go! But I kept my promise to return, no? When I marched across that bridge out there with an army reinforced with every man you ever insulted, the two of you scampered off to the wilds without raising a sword.

The royal procession doubled its pace across Fleet Street. Mobs from the outlying shires still loyal to Caernervon lined the way, no doubt drawn by the rumors that he would return at the eleventh hour with an army of thousands to abort the coronation. When the Abbey's spires finally broke through the low clouds, she felt safe enough to retract the curtain fully.

Across the way stood the Temple, once the most hallowed of confines in England, but now used as an armoury. Her thoughts returned to the Feast of the Swans, when Caernervon had pissed his breeches inside that sanctuary and his new knights had nearly drowned themselves in wine. Months later, most of them *did* drown, in Bannockburn's quagmire. The young knights who rode with her son this day now blustered that *they* were the generation destined to bring Robert Bruce and James Douglas to the Tower.

Several minutes later, they arrived at Westminster. Pelted by the strengthening rain, the Archbishop of Canterbury stood waiting on the portico with his drenched forehead braced against the biting wind. She thought he looked more like a duck with its bill tucked into its breast than the country's most venerated churchman. Young Edward dismounted and, without waiting for the rest of his entourage to arrive, nodded impatiently for the traditional entry to commence. The acolytes hurried ahead of their future king and the archbishop while unrolling a carpet of red vermilion toward the coronation chair.

Her carriage was diverted into a wynd adjacent to the south cloister. She angled her head through the window and discovered that a contingent of mounted guards had converged on her. "I must enter from the front!" When the sergeant of the detail ignored her protest and halted the carriage at a rear portal used by the monks to load foodstuffs, she threw open the door and clambered out in a rage. "Damn you! Did you not hear me?"

"Orders, my lady," the sergeant said coldly.

"Whose orders?"

"The King's."

"The King is no longer—" She only then understood that he was speaking of her son, not her deposed husband. Indignant, she flung off her cloak and tried to retreat through the cloister's garth, but the guards blocked her path. The sergeant pointed her toward a hallway that led into the chapter house.

Her heart pounded from terror. The cloister was deserted. Where were the monks? Conniving bastard! Mortimer had waited until this final hour to have her murdered. He knew the canons would be in the minster to witness the ceremony. As the guards drove her into the bowels of the cloister, she searched the colonnades for a path of escape. Finding none, she whispered to the sergeant, "Whatever you have been paid, I will double it for your forbearance."

The officer said nothing as he forced her pace with a hand at her elbow. The tapers along the narrow hall had been extinguished. She gasped at the evil cleverness of Mortimer's plan.

This is why he tried to convince me to remain here.

They were taking her to the abbot's private chapel to commit the deed. Roger and the other barons would make a great show of lamentation and insist that she had been waylaid by one of Caernervon's henchmen while praying alone to petition God's blessing on their new king. It would be the garrote under sheepskin, or perhaps a poison. No marks would be found.

She whispered a fervent prayer to the Virgin as the sergeant led her around a corner. When he refused to acknowledge her plaintive glance, she crossed her breast and begged, "I pray you, make it painless." She pressed her eyes closed and waited for the cord against her neck.

The door creaked open—a resounding chant stole her breath.

She was escorted into the south transept, and the sergeant released her to a chair in the first row facing the raised platform on the high altar. Had the officer lost his resolve? The archbishop and clergy turned on her from their elevated seats. Their faces were cast in surprise, or was it disappointment?

They did not expect to see me alive again.

The sergeant waited to be dismissed while she tried to compose herself.

Had this man risked his life to save hers? She accepted his kerchief to muffle her sobs. The barons and clerics were still staring at her, but the angle of their arched eyes revealed that they were shocked not by her continued existence, but her attire. For weeks she had debated what to wear. A gown too gaudy would have been seen as frivolous, particularly given the penurious state of the treasury. Parliament had criticized her taste as too risqué—too French, they really meant. When she had commissioned a ruby-studded girdle of silk for the wedding of her handmaiden, there had been talk of convening a trial for her dissipation of royal assets. On this day, she had overcompensated with a black satin dress, edged with *grise* fur and brightened only by a necklace of rubies encased in silver. These congenitally suspicious English no doubt saw in its somberness some omen of disaster or an occult message for Capetian spies to come to her aid. To the depths of Hell with them! If they persisted in calling her a wolf, then she would dress the part and—

"My lady?" the sergeant whispered to her ear. "Are you not well?"

She glanced down at her hands. They were shaking from her fury.

Across the nave, young Edward sat on the coronation chair, his feet dangling from the throne in yet another reminder of the perverse nature of the proceeding. He stared reverentially at Longshanks's black marble crypt, as if expecting the old man's ghost to rise up and crown him. On a crimson pillow lay arrayed the regalia of the realm: The cross, the scepter, the royal mace, the black Rood of St. Margaret stolen from the Scots, and the infidel dagger that had wounded Longshanks at Acre. A ripple of whispers roused Edward from his trance. Only then made aware that his mother had arrived, the boy greeted her with an indifferent glance, a coldness that stung.

She looked across the pews and studied the faces of John, Eleanor, and Joan. Those children had been the result of a miracle only slightly less astounding than divine intervention. The arrival of an heir had given Caernervon such a potent respite from his self-loathing that his nature had become altered. Although he continued to prefer the company of men, her husband would thereafter on occasion appear at her bedchamber, usually during some crisis in the realm, and he would endure the sexual act with her as if it were an expiation of his sins and a reaffirmation that he was truly king.

As the chanting monks raised the pitch of their *Te Deums*, she sank into the soothing Latin intonations. She had often found refuge in this abbey, sitting for hours under its ribbed vaulting while writing letters to her father that never made it across the Channel. This was the only place in England where she felt at peace. The flying buttresses and polished Caen stone, brightly painted in reds and greens, reminded her of Notre Dame, as did the arcades hung with tapestries of vermilion and gold and the thick haze from the censing angels that swirled around the lime-washed pillars. The nave almost danced with the streams of diffused light reflected from the rose window.

The chant ceased abruptly as the archbishop raised the jeweled crown of St. Edward the Confessor and called upon the prince to recite the concession that had been required of every king since William the Conqueror.

"He seizes not," Edward announced, "but receives."

Isabella heard snickering behind her. She knew what these English curs were thinking: Edward receives only because *his mother* has seized. Her eyes fell upon the Stone of Destiny resting on an exposed shelf under the coronation chair. She interrogated that imprisoned block of limestone in silence.

What black magic do you dispense, Stone? You claim to recognize true monarchs. Have I rid myself of a useless husband only to be tormented by a recalcitrant son? Caernervon was the first English king to be anointed in your presence. Yet you stood silent while the crown was ripped from his grasp. He swooned during the deposition, they said. Fell upon his knees begging for a second chance like a child found guilty of some petty transgression. If you were true, as the Scots say, you would have screamed the day he ascended this throne. Screamed not in recognition, but in protest. What prophecy will you now shout upon my son?

The archbishop tapped his toe in annoyance at being forced to wait for the distracted prince to strip to his shirt and breeches. When Edward, red-nosed and sniveling, finally acceded to the prostration to accept the anointments, the cleric betrayed a note of tonal dissonance in his pronouncement of the ordo's next demand: "You, Edward III of England, shall keep full peace and accord in God and to the Church, to the people and to the clergy?"

"I shall."

"Grant thou all rightful laws and customs and defend and strengthen them in accordance to the will of God?"

Edward flushed with pride as the archbishop raised the hallowed sword once carried by the Hammer of the Scots. So fervently did the boy despise his deposed father that he often fantasized of having been sired by Longshanks. Denied the characteristic Plantagenet ruddy complexion, prodigious height, and reddish hair, he never tired of searching for ways to alter his appearance, even wearing his locks long and wild in the fashion of that mad warrior. His hands quivered as he took the sword framed with gold-gilt quillons and darkened by Welsh, Scot, and French blood. With teeth set, he heaved the point of the heavy blade toward the heavens and looked down at his mother in accusation that she deemed him incapable of the task. Then, as if directing the warning at her, he spoke the final verse of the ordo, "I shall defend and strengthen."

She brought a hand to her mouth, stifling a gasp at that brazen act of insolence. Her worst fears were now confirmed: She had not used her son to gain power, as the lords suspected; no, he had used *her*. She had seen that cruel glare before. By sheer force of will, the boy was bent on transforming himself into the man he believed to be his grandfather.

As the lords and clerics filed up to give homage to their new king, she remembered the warning that she had confided to James years ago. Its terrible truth, she feared, was about to be proven again.

Men make oaths. Women suffer the consequences.

Caernervon peered out through the narrow air hole of his second-floor cell in Berkeley Castle. He finally turned aside, his bleary eyes no longer able to withstand the strain. He had been confined to this miserable keep on the Welsh frontier for more than a year, forced to keep a constant watch for billowing sails above the Severen estuary that fed to the Bristol Channel. Mortimer's henchmen had furthered his humiliation by banishing him to this keep, one of the domains once held by the Earl of Gloucester, the baron who had shamed him with the martyr's death at Bannockburn.

Yet each recession of the tide brought him only renewed despair. He had to keep faith that Archbishop Melton would come to release him. But what if his messages had not reached his old ally in York? No, he must not contemplate such a horrid thing. The archbishop was merely waiting until spring to bring a force. Once rescued, he would march with the cleric against that London mob with an army of fifty thousand and reclaim his crown. Melton would not fail him, for he had promised to elevate the cleric to the seat at Canterbury when Isabella and Mortimer were captured and exiled. Those two nesting vipers had cornered him in a fit of weakness. Driven nearly insane by the fear of losing another lover, he had relinquished the throne after being falsely promised that he would be reunited with Despenser on a well-appointed estate.

He resolved not to dwell on that horrid debasement. Yet his own mind persisted in betraying him; at times he wished never to be king again, then an hour would pass, and he would be consumed by the shame. The memories of that wretched day blinded him with raw grief. Two weeks after giving up the crown, he received the news that Despenser had been executed in the same brutal manner in which he himself had ordered Lancaster dispatched: Before being drawn and quartered, his favourite had been kept alive long enough to witness his genitals be hacked off and burned.

Oh, Hugh! My cowardice doomed you! As it doomed Piers!

Soon he would avenge them both. In the Almighty's eyes, he was still king. That was his only comfort. But time was running out. The terrors visited on him during the past months had caused his hair to fall out and his gums to inflame. He bled profusely from the nose and his skin had turned the shade of an overripe peach. Worst of all, he was plagued at night by visions of Lancaster's ghost coming to murder him.

That scheming French whore did this to me!

Isabella had bewitched him into believing he had seeded the whelp that now wore his stolen crown. How had he failed to see through her plotting? And who *was* the father of that brat? Lancaster? Gloucester? Piers had warned him about the Satanic mark on Isabella's back. That Frenchwoman had seduced him to her bed to disgorge the other three brats to make Parliament believe that Edward had also been his progeny. No doubt she had whispered her treacherous plans to the little bastard before he was even severed from her cord.

The mongrel pup would not wait his turn, as *he* had been required to do! When he got his hands on him, that boy will wish—a flash of swift movement came from the corner. Were the shades attacking him again?

Filthy devils! Away from me!

A dim light filtered through the air hole and illuminated a carving on the wall. Why had he not seen this before? He ran his hand across the etching.

A pentagram.

Piers has come back in spirit to save me!

Fifteen years had passed since his first lover had fled from their bed in a desperate exodus to escape Lancaster's ax. Piers had vowed to return to him in spirit. The Gascon's mother, an Albigensee, had taught her son the black art of demonic travel, and this symbol of that heresy was to accompany Piers's specter.

He retraced the pentagram's outlines to speed the manifestation.

The cell door creaked opened.

"Piers, is that you? I knew you'd not abandon me."

"Turn away!" a muffled voice commanded.

He pressed his forehead into the cot to shield his eyes. "I remember! The Devil's Pact! Not until the light of sun!"

Hands braced his shoulders from behind, and he pressed back into Piers's reassuring strength. *Oh Lord, this is powerful magic.* His limbs trembled as Piers reached for the drawstrings on his leggings and untied them seductively. His lover's smooth hands, so expert, reached to his waist and lowered his breeches. Caernervon arched his buttocks to receive Piers, and he felt a tremor of heat. The tip of Piers's cock slid down his back and toward his anus. He was being teased beyond endurance.

"This is for Thomas Lancaster," the voice behind him whispered.

He is acting out the part! God's confirmation!

Only Piers had known of their private games.

He begged for the penetration by thrusting his buttocks higher, remembering how Piers had bragged during their intimacies of wanting to introduce the hated Lancaster to this particular form of the joust. Piers was now mimicking the dead earl being taken in such a cruel manner, just as his lover had done so many times when they had been in bed together. "Shall I play him this time, Poppy?" He imitated Lancaster's high-pitched voice. "Don't despoil me, I pray you!"

Piers rammed his phallus into him, nearly caused him to faint. A voice came to his ear. "I watched him bleed to death on the gallows."

Who is Piers playing now? He tried to turn, but two sets of hands held him down. "Piers! I do not find this—"

The same voice whispered from the darkness, "Lancaster was still alive when they castrated him and burned their butchery before his eyes. You will now learn what it means to bear such agony."

"Damn you! Who are you?" He struggled to escape, but the weight of two men now pressed against his back. This was not Piers in the spirit, but intruders all too real. A sharp sizzle was followed by the acrid stench of smoke.

An excruciating bolt of heat shot through his bowels, incapacitating his legs. "God's mercy!"

"You'll have a lavish funeral."

"Christ save me!"

"Thousands will file by your corpse and offer prayers in gratitude that you were blessed with such a peaceful crossing. Not a scratch upon you. The Almighty commanded your removal from the throne. Why? Because you were taken to your Day of Judgment so soon after being deposed. A divine affirmation of your son's rightful accession."

"I am dying!"

"Yes, you *are* dying. And even a sodomite bent for Hell is entitled to know the method by which he is to leave this world. Yours will be apt in irony."

"Cut my throat! I beg you!"

"This ass that once disgraced the throne is now home to the hollowed femur," the assassin whispered. "About the size you fancy, I should think. The change in temperature is a scalded iron weaving through the bone."

Caernervon gagged on his own vomit. "Kill me! God, make haste!"

"Nay, we would not have you excelled by Lancaster in the pace of your martyrdom. Did they tell you his last words? He vowed to escort you to Hell to join Gaveston and Despenser."

Caernervon screamed until his throat gave out.

He fell to the floor, dead.

thirty-eight

Another Edward.

When news of the Westminster coronation reached Lintalee, James had groused that the Plantagenets were no more imaginative in choosing christening names than they were in adapting their military tactics. Now, as he led his veteran hobelars through the Kiedler Pass into Northumbria, he felt the ache of every wound he had suffered during the past forty-five years. Robert had ordered him to invade England again, this time to instruct the new babe-king in London on the consequences of abandoning a truce. He had lost count of how many times he had passed through this narrow Borders cleft that funneled between the two forks of the Tyne River. On this morning, however, unlike during raids past, the warm June sun did not brighten his spirits.

Sweenie rode alongside him, gnawing on a green apple to loosen his balky bowels. Age had shrunk the elfin monk to an even more diminutive stature, but his mind was as sharp as on that first day he had joined up with the Scot rebels at Glen Dochart. He had served as the army's chaplain for so long that he had developed the keen skill of reading his commander's thoughts and fashioning just the right taunt to provoke him to action. He found the art of the jestering akin to spiritual ministering; the Almighty, after all, surely possessed a skewed sense of humor, else why would He have brought this motley collection of ill-tempered Scots together if not for the sheer amusement? He threw the core at the hinds of James's horse and observed, "Randolph will have crossed Carter Bar by now. If he reaches Durham before us, we'll suffer his boasts without cease."

James measured the span his hand would have to travel to thump the monk's gourd-sized head. "He has a ten league head start with a thousand less men."

Sweenie nodded in mock agreement. "Aye, and he's not nearly as long in the tooth."

"I should have left you to roast on the spit at Myton."

"I was just making a point," Sweenie said.

"And what point might that be?"

"From what I hear, that fifteen-year-old lad on the English crib throne intends to run you about like an old hare until you drop from exhaustion."

"Does he now?"

"It's not too late to turn back to Lintalee and spend the rest of your dotage tending your garden. Randolph could take the command. He reminds me of you in the old days."

Instead of rising to the challenge, James remained silent.

Sweenie was concerned about his refusal to engage in the banter. Robert had always been the one to suffer the bouts of melancholy, not him. Turning serious, the monk kicked his hobbin closer and asked, "What troubles you?"

James spurred ahead to be alone. The knot in his stomach warned that this campaign would not be like the others. Could Isabella not control her own son? The boy king was raising an army rumored to be twice the size of the force his father brought north in 1314. Reportedly, young Edward had also employed crack mercenaries from the Continent and was releasing hundreds of felons from jails with the promise of a pardon as bounty in exchange for ten dead Scots. If Isabella's wee troublemaker so desperately wished a taste of war, he would be accommodated—not in Scotland, but deep in the heart of his own kingdom, where the fat Yorkshire burghers who replenished the brat's treasury could watch their own towns go up in flames for a change.

In such low moments, he actually longed for those desperate days when he and Robert scurried across the Highlands on foot, starving but firm in the conviction of their cause. Half of the men who fought with them at Bannockburn were now dead or crippled. In these past few years, he had communicated with the royal court at Cardross only by courier. He still nursed the insults suffered over Brechin's execution and Robert's demand that he take a wife. Robert's dementia had worsened after Elizabeth's death from injuries suffered in a fall down the stairs at Cullen Castle, and the entire kingdom now feared that the clans would renew their feuds before three-year-old David reached his majority.

He also missed Jeanne's calming touch. He hadn't heard from her in over a year, not since her terse message advising that she would be staying north to attend to the king's household and nurse his senile stepmother, who had passed away a few months later. Lintalee had grown cold with the French lass's absence. He had treated her poorly, that he could not deny. He had hoped he might grow to love her over time, but his longing for Belle had only increased with the years. He understood why she could no longer endure his companionship. Perhaps he *should* allow his memory of Belle to fade into oblivion. No one else remembered her sacrifice, and it had brought Scotland no closer to peace. He hung his head and muttered, "What use all this?"

Sweenie risked suffering a harangue by riding closer. "The great Irish chieftain Culchullan also suffered from heartsickness. So forlorn was he with the memory of a banshee from the netherworld that he could not force his limbs to move. It is the bane of all warriors of our race."

"Did he ever gain release from his cares?"

"Aye," Sweenie said, "but at a steep price."

"What healed him?"

"His charioteer rode to Anglesey and asked the Druids for a cure. The holy men sent the charioteer back to his master with the Elixir of Forgetfulness."

"The potion worked?"

Sweenie nodded. "But to seal the magic, Culchullan was required to forget all he had experienced in his life. All glories and deeds, even his comrades."

James pondered the strange tale. "Culchullan's lass must have been responsible for his acts of valor. Why else would he have been required to forget them to chase her memory?"

Sweenie shrugged. "I have never been in the thrall of a woman, so I possess no knowledge of such things."

A commotion to the rear disrupted their column, suddenly lifting James's spirits. McClurg and McKie drove up a band of fifty Welsh archers shackled at the wrists. James grinned at the haul; a wagon laden with captured gold would have been less precious, for longbowmen were such a bane to his troop that a Welshman's quiver was said to carry twenty-four Scot souls.

"We found them wandering near Hartbottle," McKie reported.

James marveled at the prodigious height of the captives and their thick fingers calloused from years of drawing the bowstrings. Many in this fearsome Welsh troop were much older than he had expected, but all had sunburnt faces and quick eyes. They had known no other employment since childhood, having been drafted into the royal service after demonstrating their skills on local archery fields following Sunday Mass. He rode through their ranks and demanded, "Where is your swaddled king?"

None of the Welsh would answer him, until a frightened young squire blurted out: "North of Durham. Looking for you."

"How many men does he bring?" James asked the boy.

The captured squire felt his comrades tried to silence him with scowls, but his nerves finally got the better of his honor. "Twenty thousand."

James turned to hide his dismay. Young Edward's boast of running him to death like an old hare now seemed more credible. With such an advantage in odds, the English could come at him in every direction. He and Randolph would need to move fast to combine forces with the Earl of Mar, who commanded a third Scot column moving farther south. He turned back to the two Trinity brothers and ordered, "Find Randolph and tell him to meet us south of Hexam on the quick."

"What about the Welsh?" McKie asked.

James studied the captives. "Hang them."

The condemned archers fell to their knees, praying in despair—all but their officer, who stepped forward with an air of noble resignation. "Do what you will with me. But I ask Christ's mercy for my men."

James was impressed by the officer's selfless courage. "If I spared any, it would be you."

"We are conscripts. We despise the English more than you do."

"You showed little of that hatred at Falkirk. I cannot risk your return to Edward's army. Fifty of you could turn a battle."

"These men have families."

He had no time to debate the merits of leniency. So many prisoners on foot would severely hinder his speed, and he could not spare the troops required to escort them to the border. The English scouts would be searching for their lost herce of archers, and if he and his Scots were discovered, they would lose the advantage of surprise. He led the Welsh officer a few steps away from the others. "You and your men wish to live at any cost?"

The officer silently interrogated his homesick conscripts. Then, after a moment's hesitation, he nodded grimly.

The young English king had been counseled to pack away his battle gear to keep it from rusting, but despite having ridden nonstop for three days in a cold downpour, he insisted on remaining in the ponderous armour crafted for him by London's finest silver workers. Freed at last from the chafing control of his mother, he was determined to imitate the stories he had heard of his famous grandfather living in the saddle.

John of Hainault, the military advisor retained by Isabella, sighed wearily as he wiped the water from his visor and surveyed their undisciplined, squabbling mash of untested knights and conscripts. Nothing about them remotely resembled Longshanks's old army of conquerors. This headstrong boy seemed unconcerned that half of his baggage wagons had been abandoned to the mud and that he had somehow lost an entire bataille of archers. Riots were breaking out between the Welsh and Yorkshiremen over gambling disputes. Worst of all, Edward had no clue where he was, let alone the Scots he was chasing.

Fearful that the inexperienced king was losing control of the army, Hainault tried a more forceful persuasion. "My lord, the horses must be rested, or we shall all soon be waist-deep in mud."

Edward stretched up in stirrups that had been fashioned to fit his short legs. He pointed toward the black smoke that billowed up over the distant horizon. "They are just over that ridge! We are within reach of them!"

"We have been within reach of them for two weeks. This Douglas—"

"I forbade you to speak that name!"

Unaccustomed to being addressed in such a churlish manner, by a teething cub no less, Hainault was beginning to question the wisdom of having placed his mercenaries at the command of Isabella's headstrong son. Yet now, trapped in the middle of this slogging nightmare, he could not transport them back across the Channel without first being paid. With muted voice, so as not to rile the boy any more than necessary, the officer observed, "The Scotsman appears to be leading us in circles."

"He is running from us!"

"If he *were* running from us, would he not be running home?"

Edward's face twisted in confusion. "What do you mean?"

"We have been chasing him south. If he feels endangered, why does he not retreat north?"

Edward felt the judging glares of his officers. "Speak plainly, damn you!"

Hainault tried to find an example to simplify his point. "If you cornered a rat in your room, Sire, would you leave the door open?"

"Of course not! You think me a fool?"

"No, my lord. You are a master strategist. But what would you do to rid yourself of the rat?" Hainault knew very well what the boy would say, having heard him repeatedly vow that he would never commit the mistakes of his dimwitted father, who had allowed the Scots to seduce him through a corridor of destruction to the humiliating defeat at Bannockburn.

"I'd close the door," Edward said, "and let the vermin starve!"

"Then I suggest you close the door."

Hainault watched with hope as Edward, inspired anew, looked north across the vast stretch of Northumbria that had been denuded of trees. Here there was no Ettrick Forest to protect Douglas and his Scots, only barren lengths of windswept plateaux crisscrossed by stone fences and hedgerows. If the boy took this army north to Haydon Bridge, he would have Douglas trapped below—

Anguished screams came from the rear.

The Welsh rushed from the column to greet what appeared to be a band of beggars staggering down the ridge.

Edward was furious. "I gave no order to break ranks!"

Ignoring the young king, the Welsh conscripts ran to embrace their lost countrymen and found their right hands wrapped with bloodied bandages. The officer leading these returned archers uncovered a stump on his right arm and held it up for Edward's observation. The others in his charge followed his example and displayed their drawing hands—all missing the thumb and first two fingers.

Edward brought a sleeve to his mouth. "Who did this?"

The mutilated officer pulled three blackened fingers from his belt pouch and threw them to the ground in an indictment of the young king's incompetence in allowing them to be captured. "It was our choice."

"*Your* choice?" Edward screamed. "An entire herce ruined! Do you know how much of my treasury I spent to equip you Welsh ingrates?"

"Douglas offered us our lives. That is more than your grandfather offered my kinsmen. We are no longer of use to you. I am taking my men home to their families."

Edward sat stupefied as the disabled archers walked off, heading south.

Hainault captured the king's reins and led him away from the troops, afraid they would lose even more confidence in him if they witnessed another of his raging fits. "Keep your wits about you. We must cross the Tyne and wait for Douglas to turn north."

Despite his inexperience, Edward possessed the remarkable ability to swiftly alter his emotions. Retreating into the steely mien that he had so often practiced, he shook off Hainault's paternal hold on his arm. "Call a council of my knights."

"For what purpose?"

Edward studied the black smoke swirling above the distant villages burned by the Scots. "Why should I wait for the rat to starve when I can send in the dogs?"

James kept his gaze fixed on the bleak purple horizon that seemed to roll on without end. Eight days had passed since his scouts last saw the English army, and he feared young Edward had finally tired of their game of hide-and-seek. He had driven his Scot raiders deeper into the heart of Northumbria and had crossed the Tyne and Wear rivers to wreak havoc in the Gaunless valley, dangerously stretching their escape route back to the Borders. So long as he had held the English in his sights, he had been confident he could outrun them.

But Isabella's babe-king had somehow managed to vanish.

Now, with the sun falling fast, James hurried his small army back up the Weardale, keeping south of the river. The local villages were abandoned, and the few farmers they had ferreted out from the cellars had known they were coming. For the first time on this campaign, he was worried. "Where is the wee bastard, Tom?"

Randolph tried to put up an insouciant front. "The lad isn't clever enough to go north."

"Hainault is at his side."

Randolph kept looking over his shoulder. "Should we try for the Tyne?"

Undecided, James rode ahead to reconnoiter the slanting moors. This vale north of the River Wear was wider than its southern counterpart, but still narrow enough to force the English army to crowd together in discomfort. South of the river arose a jagged ridge of sharp rocks and outcroppings. That spot offered as good a defensive position as any he had seen within a day's ride. Yet if he took shelter up there, the river would deny him a quick retreat back to Scotland. The horses were exhausted, and he had burned every burgh within reach. He had no choice but to make camp and wait for wee Edward the Slow to find him.

J ames and his raiders sat mired in the rain for another week. Although their supplies and fodder had become dangerously low, he took heart in the knowledge that they had survived worse privations. He had trained them to carry iron grilles, a provision that allowed them to stop at any time on their raids, cook oatcakes, and be back in the saddle within the hour, and when they came upon cattle or venison, they would roast steaks inside skinned hides while remaining on the run. Unaccustomed to eating meat, they found that the oats offered the additional advantage of settling their stomachs, and thus, unlike the English, they were never tied to a commissary train or held to the mercy of local burghers.

Then, on the eighth day of this torturous vigil, the mud-caked Scots were awakened by shouts. Returning from a scouting sortie, McKie and McClurg dragged up a captured English squire. St. Finian carrying sheaves of heavenly manna could not have offered a more welcome sight.

James pulled the dazed prisoner to his feet and greeted him with a clamping grip to the nape of his neck. "We thought you and your friends had all high-tailed it back to London. Where is your army?"

The squire buckled on seeing the dark face of his interrogator. He managed a tremulous reply through his constricted throat: "I don't know."

James honed his dagger on a rock. "I am not a patient man by nature. Today you have the misfortune of encountering me wet and hungry."

The squire collapsed to his knees, certain he was about to receive the same treatment meted out to the Welsh archers, or worse. "I left it a week ago. The king was as lost as I am now. He has offered an earldom to any man who finds you. There are fifty others out there looking for you, too."

"We've been sitting in this quagmire because that pipsqueak can't find his way around his own kingdom?" James counted off his steps in his usual method of calculating the days it would take to return to the border. "What is the condition of his troops?"

"The corn trains are rain-sotted. Most of the lads have taken ill."

James dragged the frightened squire to a horse. "You've been saved by the inanity of your new king. Go collect your reward." He drew a map on a scrap of sheepskin and armed the squire with it. "Advise wee Eddie that if he doesn't come soon, I'm going to go tell his mother how poorly he has behaved."

Stunned by the reprieve, the squire stabbed at the stirrups, mounting as fast as his shaking legs would allow.

"Wait!" James turned to Sweenie. "How much grain do we have left?"

The monk shook his head. "Not enough to do what you're thinking."

James ignored Sweenie's protest and motioned for him to deliver a small sack of oatmeal to the squire and tie it to his saddle. "To your king with my compliments. I'd not have him starve before he finds us."

T wo days later, James watched with relief as Edward led his bedraggled columns into the Weardale as if on parade down the Strand. The babe-king and his knights wore helmets crowned with the latest fad: Heraldic crests forged in the shapes of beasts such as lions, wolves, and dragons. And just as he had hoped, the boy was marching his battalions into the narrow ribbon between the steep moors and the river's banks. With a sharp whistle, he deployed his outnumbered Scots behind the rocks, keeping the swollen river between them and the English. Satisfied with their concealment, he saddled a horse and mounted.

Randolph tried to hold him back. "You're not going down there?"

James abandoned the safety of the boulders and trotted for the river.

On the northern bank, Edward struggled to remove his bascinet that featured a gold-gilt leopard reared on its hinds. After nearly a minute of this ineptitude, Hainault came up to assist him. Finally unhelmed, Edward chased his officer back with a punishing glare, and then turned with a puffed chest to accept the capitulation of the Scot felon who had defied his forefathers. Yet on the far side of the river, James merely sat in the saddle with an insufferable smirk. Unable to endure this insolent stare-down, Edward blurted, "I demand your surrender!"

"Is that gratitude?" James asked. "I trust the oats were nourishing. I enjoy mine with a sprinkle of sugar. Some of my men prefer them soaked in goat's milk, but we've had no luck finding a decent cannery here in England. Might you offer a recommendation?"

Edward edged closer to the water. "Did you not hear me?"

The boy's features came into sharper focus. James had expected the gaunt frame of Longshanks or the vapid grin of Caernervon, not the overwhelming beauty of his mother. In this short time he had observed him, he suspected that his young foe had also inherited Isabella's mercurial temper and insurmountable will. Time would tell if he had been blessed with her stout heart, as well. *This is your first test, lad. Don't let your mother down. Let's play the game out.*

"Did you not hear me!" Edward shouted again.

"Did you not hear *me?*"

Confused, Edward cupped his ear. "What say you?"

"I said, 'I demand your surrender!'"

"*My* surrender? No, I said I demand *your* surrender!"

James pointed at the nervous English soldiers waiting in ranks behind Edward. "Would you kindly order your men to strip naked, Eddie? You may keep those swaddling wraps on your loins. I wouldn't want you to soil yourself in front of your subjects."

Edward's voice cracked with utter incredulity. "Strip?"

"It took us a week to remove the armour from your father's rotting knights on the fields around Stirling. It will save us a great deal of needless work if you remove your shirts and leggings before the battle."

Edward's lips quivered with rage. Finally, he managed to sputter, "Knave! I will see your head hung from the Tower!"

"That's what your old man used to say! You remind me of him!"

Apoplectic, Edward spun toward Hainault and ordered, "Bring it up!"

James watched as the English conscripts rolled forward a giant iron tube that rested on a wooden frame with wheels. The yeomen lifted the hollowed end of the contraption toward the sky with ropes and drove wedges to fix its elevation, then they poured a bag of dark powder down the its gullet and ignited a dangling cord. A whistling cut the air, followed by an explosion in the sky.

The concussion nearly threw James from his horse. Recovering his balance finally, he reined around in a circle and found the English laughing at him.

Edward sported an impudent grin. "How do you like my new toy?"

Witnessing that marvel, James knew that his world had changed forever. If Caernervon had possessed such a weapon at Bannockburn, he and Robert would never have prevailed. He was determined not to reveal his concern as he waited for another explosion from the sky, but a rain cloud swept up the river from the west, spurring the gunnery yeomen to scramble and cover their magical tube with skins. Apparently whatever alchemy was used to conjure the explosion could not be summoned in rain.

Betrayed now by the weather, Edward slammed his fist to his thigh and called forward the next option in his arsenal, shouting, "Archers!"

Hainault was reluctant to relay the order, but he deemed it best not to question the young king in front of the Scots. On his signal, officers shoved the remaining bataille of long bowmen to the front.

The Welsh staggered up, some falling, others bending over to retch.

Their erratic behavior confounded Edward. "What in God's name is wrong with them? Have they caught the fever shivers?"

Hainault whispered to the king, "Triple rations of ale. It was the only way I could keep them from deserting. They are deathly afraid of that Scotsman."

Disgusted at their loss of fortitude, Edward rode through the Welsh ranks pummeling the cowering archers with the flat of his blade. "You *will* cross the river and kill that Scot! Or I will order the Hainaulters on you!"

The Welsh bowmen confronted a cruel choice: Attack the Black Douglas, or suffer the mayhem that the German mercenaries were itching to inflict on them. One by one, the archers waded into the water holding their bows aloft to keep them dry.

On the far bank, James restrained his skittish horse, silently begging the archers deeper into the water. *Come on, you poor wretches. Give your new cradle king another lullaby to cry himself asleep.* The first van of the three hundred archers swam across the river, and he slowly backed up the ridge, remaining just within their range. Many of their arrow fletches had been crushed and soaked by the rains, which he knew would severely hamper their accuracy. He pranced his horse in a taunt to draw them up the ridge.

The archers were so eager to take advantage of his proximity that they strung their bows without driving stakes into the ground to fend off a counterattack. They tweaked their strings, notched arrows, and—

Behind James, Randolph and his mounted raiders appeared over the ridge. They galloped toward the river, taking dead aim at the archers.

Edward could only watch as his frightened Welsh ran back for the protection of the water, too late to avoid being slain by the dozens. Those few who managed to avoid the first onslaught dived into the river, but Randolph and his cavalry rode along the banks, picking them off as if they were spearing salmon.

Only twenty survivors made it across to the English side.

Stricken by the costly butchery, Edward screamed at James, "Coward! Come fight me on an open field!"

James blew him a kiss. "That would not be honorable of me, lad! You have no archers!"

For another week, the two shivering armies sat staring at each other from across the river, each wondering which side the soupy mud would swallow up first. To frazzle Edward's nerves, James had ordered his men to slink along the banks at night and blow their horns, and the English, penned in like hogs in muck, could not sleep for fear of an ambush.

Yet James and his raiders were also trapped, down to one portion of watery porridge a day. That night, as the rain picked up again, Randolph laid down aside

James on the sloping ridge and watched the English camp. "We'll have to fight them eventually. If the lad is smart enough to wait us out, we're finished."

James looked up at the clearing night sky and found Columba's star for reassurance. He had been wondering how long it would take the old Randolph of the "straight-at-them" to return. His friendly rival had never fully accepted his tactics of the burn and run. He, on the other hand, had decided long ago that another bloody battle would never gain their freedom. They had won at Bannockburn, but the English still refused to leave them alone. There would always be a new generation of London knights seeking glory in Scotland. The only way to be rid of these people was to turn them against each other, tire them of paying ransoms and seeing their towns go up in flames, convince them that it was more likely that Scotland would annex Northumbria and Yorkshire. No, he had no intention of wasting another thirty years fighting *this* Edward. He had to teach the lad so painful a lesson that he would never again think of setting foot north of the border. He turned again to Randolph and asked, "Did I ever tell you the story of the fisherman and the fox?"

Randolph sat up and wrung the rainwater from his bedroll. "If you did, I managed to forget it, as I have all of your tedious yarns."

He continued telling his tale as if Randolph had begged to hear it. "A fisherman comes home to his cabin one night and finds a fox eating a roasted fish at the hearth. The fisherman draws his blade to kill the trapped fox. You're the fox. What do you do?"

Randolph snorted at the simplistic riddle. "What else can I do? I lunge at his throat. Trust I'm quicker than him."

"Aye, that's what I thought you'd say." James pulled up his cloak and feigned drowsing off.

Randolph levered to his elbows. "What? That's it?"

"You're dead. Tale over."

"What would *you* have done?"

"Steal the man's bed quilt."

Randolph rolled his eyes. "You make less sense with each passing day."

"I'd throw his bedding into the fire. When the fisherman lunges to save his precious quilt, out the door I'd go."

Randolph kicked and cursed his tattered roll, forced to choose between covering his sodden feet or his drenched neck. "Where are you going to find a quilt out here?"

James whistled. "Sweenie!"

The monk erupted from his slumber spewing curses. "If a man is to be denied a decent meal, is it asking too much to let him sleep?"

"Are the English well-bedded?" James asked the monk.

"Aye, you've given them time to build boards under their tents and set their wine casks nicely upon stilts. They're a Moor's tongue drier than we are."

Smiling at the little monk's cantankerousness, James rested the back of his head on his hands and studied the clouds, which looked to augur more rain. "A few days ago, I spied a lovely spot a short jaunt up the river. The Bishop of Durham's hunting park. It sports a stone wall that must be the envy of every baron in England."

"You woke me to tell me that?" Sweenie growled.

While counting the fires in the English encampment, James heard the faint voice of a minstrel singing a love ballad. He bounced his hand to the music's beat and mused, "Wee Eddie, I fear, is getting a bit too comfortable."

Before dawn, Edward arose from his knees after prayers, certain that the Almighty would finally bless him with victory after his all-night vigil under the crucifix. Refusing food, he strapped on his armour, which had been wiped with oil to prevent rusting, and walked from his tent to join his sleep-deprived army mustered in battle formation along the river. He was determined to crush these maddening Scots with a surprise attack. The fog remained low and thick, but the saints had granted him one intercession: the rains had finally abated. He ordered his knights to cross the river on the barges first, with the infantry to follow. When his army had finally reassembled in stealth on the far side, he drove his steed up the rocky embankment and broke the dawn's silence with a war cry to signal the assault.

Only a few jackdaws cackled in reply as the mists swirled and cleared over the abandoned Scot encampment. A half-league to the east, the sun crept over the horizon, revealing the banners with the Cross of St. Andrew.

Edward bit off a flurry of curses. The damnable Scots had moved their camp farther up the river on even more impregnable ground. Stomping the mud from his boots, he ordered Hainault to cross back over the river, tear down their own tents, and carry them along the banks to again face off against the enemy.

The work was backbreaking for the hungry, demoralized troops. Forced into even closer quarters, the Hainaulters scrapped with the Yorkshire conscripts, and not a night passed without one of the sleep-starved wretches waking from hallucinations that the Scots were upon them. The false alarms became so frequent that even Edward began to ignore them.

On the tenth night in his new camp, Edward donned a clean nightshirt and, after giving orders that under no circumstances was he to be disturbed, settled into his bed. Desperate to catch up on his lost sleep, he covered his eyes with shades and plugged his ears with wads of lint to drown out the incessant horn blaring of the Scots. He had even taken an extra goblet of wine, vowing aloud—as if his own mind could not possibly disobey a royal command—that he would no longer be plagued by the recurring nightmare of his father arising from the grave and wresting back the crown. Rumors were rampant in the camp that Caernervon had been seen alive in a monastery in France, and mutinous whispers blamed the army's predicament on divine retribution for the illegal deposition.

The wine soon worked its effect, and he drifted into drowsiness.

But after an hour of fitful tossing, the same smirking face that had plagued him for weeks reappeared in his dream. He mumbled and tossed. *God's curse upon these nights! How dare that felon treat me as a laughingstock! What a repugnant man! Dark as a Moor! And that lisp syrupy and thick! I will have him dragged to the Tower in the very footsteps of his father. They said Wallace did not cry out, but I will see to it that the executioner slows the—*

"Lords of England! You shall all die!"

Damn that infernal man!

Edward stuffed the earplugs deeper to chase the phantom alarums rattling in his brain.

"The Scots! Douglas! The Douglas is on us!"

Edward pounded his forehead against the matting, desperate to chase the visions. "Enough! Leave me be!"

"Then leave us be."

The infuriating voice now sounded so real that his ears buzzed. He ripped off his eyes shades, searching for the bottle to numb his nerves with more wine.

The Black Douglas—this time in the flesh—stared down at him.

Edward nearly pissed himself as he crawled from the bed and scrambled for the flaps. He saw through the crack that his guards were slain and the camp was filled with the din of a desperate fight. This time the Scots had not feigned the ambush. Trapped, he lunged for a dagger hanging in a scabbard from the tent post. "I won't be taken. You'll have to kill me."

The lad's foolish courage took James by surprise. He had planned to throw the royal brat over his shoulder and be off before the English learned what had hit them. Now, with only seconds before the guards came rushing in, he brought his blade to Edward's slender throat to finish him.

Isabella's limpid eyes stared back at him.

"Do it, damn you!" cried Edward. "I'll die a martyr! And all England will chase you to the gates of Hell!"

James could not run the boy through. "I knew your mother."

"My mother is a French whore!"

James was about to chastise the insolent pip when a blow from behind drove him to his knees. Dazed, he looked up at an English guard raising a blade.

Sweenie split the flaps and pounced on the guard's back.

James tried to stand, but the grogginess dropped him to his knees again.

Edward watched from the corner in frozen terror as his guard threw Sweenie to the ground and lunged for James. Sweenie dug his teeth into the attacker's arm. The guard wheeled and drove his dagger into Sweenie's gut. The monk clung tight to prevent the guard from retracting the blade and use it against James. They wrestled and knocked the taper from its stand, killing the light.

"Here!"

Blinded by the darkness, James swung his blade at that shout. He felt blood splatter across his face. Wiping his eyes, he came over the fallen guard and stared down in horror. His blow had also wounded Sweenie. The monk lay unconscious and bleeding, the dagger still in his gut.

Sweenie had sacrificed himself to warn of the guard's approach.

Still concussed, James didn't have the strength to drag both Sweenie and Edward away. He glared a promise of revenge at the boy as he threw Sweenie over his good shoulder. He kicked the supports and rushed out, letting the tent fall on Edward with a crash. Caught under the canvas, the boy screamed and thrashed, thinking he was being smothered to death.

Staggering for the river with Sweenie on his shoulder, James shouted at his men in the darkness, "To Douglas!"

The next morning, Edward marched through his camp surveying the damage inflicted by the Scot ambush. Two hundred of his soldiers had been killed and his cannon spiked with packed mud. But even in this wretched panorama of butchery, he found hope. "Douglas is desperate."

"They lost only three men," Hainault said. "I fear we are more desperate."

"I stared him down! He would not take me on! He is not the demigod you make him out to be. He is old and tired. Assemble the ranks."

"Our troops have not slept or eaten for days."

"At once!" Edward demanded.

Hainault did as ordered, and when the weary troops were finally loaded on the rafts, the young king rode before them and shouted the speech that he had rehearsed for weeks.

"Men of England!" he screeched in his high-pitched voice. "This is your hour of glory! The Scots have no crafts to cross the river! We outnumber them! God is on our side! To victory!"

Hainault reluctantly signaled for the assault.

Fueled only by the hope that their torment would soon be over, the forlorn English soldiers silently rowed the rafts across the river while keeping their eyes trained on the smoke wafting above the Scot encampment.

When the last of his army had crossed, Edward listened for the sounds of battle on the ridge above. Minutes later, he saw his infantry coming back down from the rocks with their pikes on their shoulders. He screamed at them, "What in God's name are you doing?"

"They are gone, my lord," an officer reported.

"That is impossible!" Edward ordered himself and Hainault ferried over to the Scot side, and together they clambered up the slope. Reaching the heights, they looked down below the ridge and found the Scot fires still burning. Yet all that remained in Douglas's camp was a pyramid of stones hung with a placard:

> *Brother Ned Sween of the True Culdee Church of Christ*
> *Friar, Patriot, Comrade*
> *The Best of Scotland Shall Forever Here Stand Watch*

Edward followed a trail of hoof prints in the mud to a second ridge, where the river angled back. The few trees that had stood behind that rise had been hacked away, out of view from his English encampment. The Scots had bundled the logs and laid them across the shallowest part of the river, then had ferried their horses across the water tethered to the flotsam. He slowly realized that the Scots had used their incessant raids and horn blowing to drown out the sounds of the timbering, which must have taken more than a week. The hardness of the horse chips confirmed that the Scots had gained a half-day's head start north. He fell to his knees and burst into tears. "No! No!"

Hainault shook his head as he stood over the sobbing king. This expedition had cost him five hundred men and had nearly drained England's treasury. Convinced now that he would never be paid, the continental officer began walking toward the river, forced to find another way to get his survivors back across the Channel.

"You cannot leave me!" Edward shouted.

Hainault turned back with a look of empathy. "Take heart, my lord. You have been outfoxed by the most cunning warrior alive. Learn from this experience. Perhaps it will one day serve you."

"But what am I to do now?"

"Sue for peace. So long as James Douglas commands Scotland's borders, you will never subdue that kingdom."

thirty-nine

ames squeezed David Bruce's shaking hand to reassure the frightened lad as they climbed the rampart steps leading to the great hall of Berwick Castle. Following instructions from Cardross, he had not revealed to the king's four-year-old heir the momentous nature of the ceremony that they were about to attend. Ten months after his Weardale campaign, another peace proposal arrived from London, this one accompanied by a marital agreement that would conjoin the royal families of the two warring realms.

He felt certain that had Elizabeth Bruce been alive, the wedding preparations would have been handled with more tact. But Robert, embittered by his wife's death from the fall and the ravages of his disease, had become so withdrawn that he had never gotten to know his son. Despite the continued rift in their personal relations, he had received orders from Robert tasking him with the delicate mission of bonding this perilous union between Scotland and England. The king's paramount concern, his council had advised, was that the boy not be allowed to mar this long-awaited day with a display of childish weakness.

During their weeklong journey south, he had grown fond of the precocious David, who was small of stature, sensitive, and keenly observant, as he had been at that age. The lad had inherited Robert's dark hair and chiseled features, but his puckish Irish grin and natural optimism clearly came from his mother. He wondered if the boy would thrive or suffer under the burden of the crown. No doubt a little of both, as had been the experience of his father.

Halfway up their ascent, David stopped to search the column of Scot nobles that stood in procession behind them. "Why is Papa not with us?"

Uncertain how to address that question, James finally explained, "Your father is still not feeling well."

"Is he going away like Mama?"

James lowered to a knee. "Let's hope he'll be better when we go home."

"But why must I be married now?"

Impressed by the lad's perceptiveness, he decided it was time to put an end to the cruel policy of isolating him from the truth. "To make certain the English stay at peace with us, your father has arranged for you to wed the sister of their king."

"What if I don't fancy her?"

He had no good answer for that valid question. This condition of the new Treaty of Edinburgh troubled him, too, but he took some consolation in knowing that both children would be allowed to live in their respective domiciles until they attained the age of majority. Before he could explain the situation further, the tower's iron-framed doors screeched open. He shuddered with a start, just as he had thirty-one years ago when he had climbed these same steps for the signing of the ignominious Ragman Rolls. Few of the Scots present on that shameful day were alive now to witness this triumphant return.

A gruff chamberlain marched out, driving David into James's arms. James looked up at the impatient Englishman and gestured for a moment's delay. The chamberlain slammed the doors, sneering a silent threat at the boy. James brought David, trembling, out of earshot of their countrymen who were watching with concern from the balustrade. "I once knew a lass in Paris who was not much older than you. To gain peace for her country, her father asked her to cross the Channel and marry the son of the King of England."

"Did she go?"

"Aye, she did. And you will meet her this afternoon. Perhaps she will tell you how she managed to be so brave. She will be watching to see if you have the mettle to be a king."

When David, blinking tears, nodded his readiness, James pounded on the door again. This time, it was *his* legs that nearly buckled. Here he was lecturing the boy on duty while his own nerves were threatening to betray him. He gazed across the river toward the spot where Gibbie had leapt to his death in the noose. And over there, beyond the bailey, stood the dungeon that once held his father. Every sorrow in his life seemed to have traveled through this city. He prayed this day would not add to that litany of grief. David tugged at his hand to indicate that the chamberlain was waiting, and he roused from the dark memories. "Aye, lad, let's go do Scotland proud."

They entered the hall hand-in-hand and found the rafters decked with ivy and rhododendrons, just as they had been on the night of the Ragman fete. The tapers cast dancing shadows—or were those the ghosts of comrades past?

On their approach, the English barons fell silent. Most were too young to have fought at Bannockburn; this was their first glimpse of England's legendary nemesis. He straightened to hide the slump from the shoulder wound he had suffered at Weardale. His eyesight had weakened in recent years, but he could just make out two gowned figures on a dais at the far end of the hall.

Isabella stood from her chair with a soft smile of anticipation lightening her still-slender face. She wore no powder to ease the lines of age, and her once-blonde hair was streaked with grey. Yet in this, their moment of mutual recognition, time seemed to turn retrograde; her cheeks filled with color and the old bounce came back to her step as she escorted her seven-year-old daughter to the floor with too much eagerness for propriety. Only the swish of her glittering russet gown broke the hush of astonishment that descended upon the English nobles, who had no choice but to stand aside and watch their queen mother meet their most hated enemy halfway.

James heard murmurs of protest, followed by the rustling of scabbards. He turned to survey the chamber. Where was Isabella's son? This treaty, he now saw, was her doing alone. Young Edward had no doubt insisted on staying in London, still pouting over his spanking at Weardale.

Isabella offered him her hand to receive homage.

He stifled a smile at her brazenness. *You were forced to petition for peace, Isabella, but you are still the clever negotiator.* He bowed and kissed her wrist, refusing to rub her nose in the defeat. Arising, he was met by the same seductive eyes that had accosted him years ago in Paris. His glance fell for a fleeting moment on her breasts, still lifted in a fashion that only the French could perfect. He had never chased from memory those persuasive agents of high diplomacy whose credentials she had first presented when he was still a sixteen-year-old virgin.

Finding him at a rare loss for words, Isabella turned to the boy at his side and inquired: "Your scribe here. Is he mute, or merely rude?"

James could not suppress a grin, remembering the question that she had asked of Bishop Lamberton during their first encounter in Paris years ago.

Robert's son, not understanding their private jest, tried to explain, "He is the Good Sir James, ma'am."

Smirking at that lofty moniker, Isabella pressed the boy's small hand in welcome. "You must be David."

The boy straightened to meet her inspection. "Aye."

Isabella shot a conspiratorial look at his chaperone. "Yes, I have heard about this hero of yours. In our kingdom, he is called the Black Douglas. He has demonstrated a nasty habit of launching costly intrusions across our borders. Did you know he twice nearly captured me?" Her pointed glance was clearly meant to remind James of his failure in holding up his end of her plan in the Myton raid. She gave a barely perceptible sigh of regret and, with little conviction, added, "Fortunately, he was too slow."

David came to James's defense. "He tells everyone that was Lord Randolph's fault."

The lad's unintended jest broke the tension in the hall, and the Scot nobles smiled and eased their rigid stances.

Isabella brought forward her shy daughter, who curtsied awkwardly, unable to look directly at David. "This is Joan," the queen mother said. "She is learning the *Pas*. Do you know it?"

David cast his gaze down in shame. "No, ma'am."

"That's a pity, for our custom is to dance at a betrothal." Isabella glanced across the chamber at every Scotsman except James. "Is there none in your court who might demonstrate the steps for you?"

Melted by David's pleading puppy eyes, James surrendered to Isabella's ploy. He signaled for the musicians to start a tune, and amid muffled gasps, led her to the center of the floor, just as he had done here so many years ago.

"If I stumble," he whispered to her, "I intend to reveal my teacher."

Isabella's eyes welled up. While waiting for the noble men and ladies of both countries to pair off, she intertwined her fingers with his under the cover of her long sleeve.

At the first note, James led her through the gauntlet of lifted arms. He had wrested many a trophy from these English——cities, bounties of gold, caches of weapons—but none was more prized than this marvelous creature. None present missed the irony of the moment: A Scotsman and a Frenchwoman had joined hands to decide the fate of England.

After a false start, he eventually remembered the steps that she had long ago taught him. He felt her drawing nearer, and if he closed his eyes, he could swear that Belle was now at his side. He sank into the soothing notes. Was this not the composition the minstrels played during his first dance with her in Paris? After all of these years, she still remembered.

With the swirling *Pas* providing cover, she whispered to his ear, "It seems, Lord Douglas, that we have returned to the place from which we started."

He pulsed her hand with affection. "Quite a dance it's been."

"You *were* worthy."

He gave her a quizzical look.

"You don't remember the question I once posed to you on this very floor?"

"At my age, I tend to forget more than I remember."

"That night, you had just treated the Countess of Buchan in a most unchivalrous manner. At the time, I thought you were quite unworthy of her. You have since redeemed yourself."

He turned away, nearly undone.

"You still grieve for her?"

"The years should have healed me, but ..."

"She loved you dearly."

"And how would *you* know *that?*"

"She once told me—"

The musical arrangement finished abruptly, interrupting her revelation. Isabella clung to his arm, desperate to say more. But the hall had become dangerously silent, with all eyes fixed on them. *Damn them to Hell!* She had bowed all her life to the demands of these sniveling English. No more would she suffer their insolent gossip. If she wished to speak of private matters, what could they do to her now? She stopped him and searched his eyes.

"*That* look I do remember," he whispered.

The dancers fled the floor, and Isabella had no choice but to allow him to escort her back to the dais. Both knew that this would be the last time they would ever speak. When out of earshot of the others, he slowed their return to her chair and asked under his breath, "Will your son deal with you in good faith?"

She shook her head, too choked up to answer him directly.

He took her up the three steps to the platform and held his bow to hide a whisper, "Should you ever find yourself in harm's way, send word."

Isabella drew a shallow breath near his ear that died with a sigh.

He looked one last time into her eyes, and then turned away. The wedding and the festivities to follow would extend through the week, but he had no wish to celebrate with those he had fought for thirty years. He had fulfilled his duty to Robert. Never had he so longed to return home.

He descended the dais and passed the parting dancers. On his way out, he stopped aside young David and patted him on the head. "You did well, lad. I'll be proud to serve you when you are king."

As he limped across the hall toward the doors, his thoughts returned to that night his father had been forced to surrender this city. At last, he had avenged that humiliation. But there was little satisfaction in it. These Englishmen on either side of him followed his halting progress with smirks and judging glares. Did they think him too old to box their ears again?

The ceremonial English guards, grizzled veterans of the old wars, frowned at the disrespect being shown him. They clashed the butts of their pikes to the stones in a grudging recognition of his deeds.

He acknowledged the gesture with a slight nod. At the portal, he paused, silently vowing never again to step foot in this godforsaken place.

"Douglas!"

He turned at that shout.

A knight with a brooding face marred by hooked nose had uttered that demand. The man's harsh features stung James's memory. Was his mind playing tricks, or had a ghost just risen from the grave? He stole a glance at Isabella. She shook her head at him in warning.

"You murdered my father."

James blinked hard, at a loss.

"Robert Clifford. ... the Second."

James felt the old blood lust rushing back through his veins. "We have that in common, then. Your father murdered mine."

"I demand justice. On the field."

Nothing would have given him more pleasure than to cut this branch of that wicked family's lineage.

Clifford tried to move a step closer in threat, but he staggered, his breath reeking of ale.

James looked beyond the man's shoulders and saw the English lords sniggering with anticipation. They had evidently plied him with drink to incite a confrontation. He debated his next move. If he allowed himself to be drawn into this duel, the English enemies of Isabella would have their pretext to declare her treaty breached.

Clifford swung at his jaw but he missed wildly. James pushed him aside and, staring down the English barons, walked toward the doors.

"We still have your bloody Stone!" Clifford shouted from his knees.

James marched back across the floor and grasped the drunken Englishman by the collar. Pulling him to his feet, he replied to the taunt in a voice loud enough for all in the hall to hear: "You may keep the block that sits in under your king's diapered ass in Westminster. It is the only speck of Scotland you English have managed to hold still under my watch."

The English lords lost their haughty smirks.

On the dais, Isabella sat stunned, only then divining from James's indifference that the stone stolen by Longshanks was not genuine.

James released the inebriated man and strode through the arched entry, slamming the heavy doors behind him.

In the bailey outside, he found McKie, McClurg, and his veterans mounted and waiting for him. He strode down the stairs and was about to raise his boot to the stirrup of his Arabian horse when he discovered a second saddlebag hanging from his pommel. He looked at his men for an indication of how the small rucksack had been placed there, but they sat mute and unforthcoming.

He raised the bag and, sniffing a familiar perfume, unwrapped its straps. From its folds he brought forth a sealed letter that was frayed and stained with what looked like drops of tears. He carefully broke the wax imprint and unfolded the letter's torn creases. As he read the cursive script written in French, his heart nearly stopped:

> *14 June in the Year of Our Lord, 1314*
> *Dearest Jamie,*
> *The English queen has offered to take down my words. She tells me you are reported near Stirling, where a great battle approaches. She has promised to do all in her power to see that this letter reaches you. She has shown great kindness to me. I regret the jealousy I once nurtured against her.*
> *Jamie, you must not hold Robert responsible for my fate. I chose the path to Scone willingly. We are all placed in this world by God for a purpose we cannot know until the end is near. Freedom is an empty prize if it costs the loss of treasured friendship.*
> *I have dreamt each night of being in your arms again. The wee monk at Glen Dochart promised me that we are not doomed to one fleeting life, but that we shall all return to this world to reunite with those who have shared our joys and tribulations.*
> *Keep watch on Columba's star. I will find you.*
> *Love, Belle*

The afternoon light began to fade as he read the last line again. Through filming eyes, he looked up at a tower window and saw Isabella lurking behind the curtains. Dipping his head to her in gratitude, he folded the letter and placed it under his vest. He mounted, fighting the weakness in his legs, and rode toward the bridge over the Tweed with his entourage.

He was nearly through the city's gate when a spider hurdled down on a thread and spooked his horse. The creature could have been the twin to the one he had found in the Arran cave years ago. The spider twirled and climbed the thread to lead his gaze skyward.

Above him hung a creaking cage.

Hundreds of townsfolk had rushed from their market shops to enjoy his discovery, a small revenge for the humiliating defeat that he had dealt them. When he reached behind his back, the gawkers recoiled, certain that he was drawing his ax in a fit of rage.

Instead, he brought to his chest a mandolin that he carried on his backpack. He had promised Belle that he would sing the last verse of her favourite ballad on their wedding day. After her death, he had not found the strength to even utter those words again. Could he remember them? His voice cracked as he strummed a chord and sang:

"On quiet glen where old ghosts meet
I see her walking now
Away from me so hurriedly
My reason must allow
That I have loved not as I should
A creature made of clay
When the angel woos the clay she'll lose
Her wings at the dawn of day."

Its vigil finished, the spider sprang from the thread and landed on the mane of the horse to be taken home.

Fighting to hold his emotions in check, James pulled the heart-stone from under his shirt and hung it on the bottom rung of the cage. He found a torch on the wall and, yanking it from its bolting, heaved it into the cage. The flames quickly erupted, and within just minutes the cage crumbled, dropping the elf-stone into the currents of the Tweed that flowed toward Scotland.

With his face glowing from the heat of the now-raging fire, he turned away from Berwick for the last time. As he rode off for Scotland, the English inhabitants who had abused Belle for seven years stood aside to form a path, lowering their heads in shame.

FORTY

No longer willing to stand aside and watch the king struggle to rise from his litter, Jeanne rushed up to assist him. "My lord, you have not been off a bed in months. Allow us to carry you to the shore."

Wrapped in linen strips greased with comfrey balm, Robert winced to his unsteady feet, gripping the French lass's wrist in gratitude for her courage. It had not passed his notice that even his physicians now hesitated to approach him for fear of contracting his flesh-eating disease. Tremoring from just that small effort, he removed her hand from his scabbed elbow and renewed his excruciating attempt to accomplish this last duty by his own power.

Word had spread across Galloway that he was making his long-delayed pilgrimage to Whithorn, and hundreds of men, women, and children, some from as far away as his birth land of Ayrshire, had hurried to this desolate peninsula on the southwest coast to join him on his last quest. On the eve of Bannockburn, kneeling in the saint's kirk overlooking that battlefield, he had vowed one day to pray in the cave where St. Ninian had sought seclusion a thousand years ago. The nine-day journey in the gurney from Cardross had been torturous, but he had suffered it without complaint.

The end, he knew, was drawing near.

Bishop Lamberton and the lords of the Privy Council followed him as he made halting progress down a wooded path toward the arch of rocks that marked the final descent on the Pilgrim's Way. The common folk formed a gauntlet along the track and fell to their knees as he passed, some reaching to touch his velvet cloak, others shouting the names of his victories. Overwhelmed by their outpouring of affection, he stumbled and nearly fell.

The royal guards tried to push back the adoring throngs, but he put a stop to their effort to shield him, and beckoned his subjects to his side. On this day, his entourage would be formed by the children and grandchildren of those who had served him in the schiltrons.

At last, he emerged from the tunnel of overhanging oaks. The briny gusts howling inland off the sea nearly blew him over. Steadying against the shoulder of one of his guards, he peered through the mists and found the saint's cave carved on a scarp overlooking the Irish Sea. His spirit sagged, for he saw that to reach those heights would require a climb strenuous even for a young man. He had not felt so weak since he had crawled half-dead into the Arran cave twenty-three years ago. This dune-mottled beach reminded him of that desolate isle, where he had survived those desperate days on hope alone. But there is no hope in old age. No angel of mercy like Christiana would appear to save him now. Elizabeth, Edward, Angus, Fraser ... all were gone.

His cherishing subjects mobbed him, and yet he had never felt so alone.

Ah, Jamie, I miss you.

Fighting the grip in his throat, he resolved not to reveal how womanly in emotion he had become during these past months. He squared his jaw in defiance of cruel fate, as he had done at Loudon Hill and Bannockburn and Scawton Moor, and called up the bishop to his side.

Lamberton, relying on his cane, hurried forward as swiftly as his crippled legs would allow.

Robert threaded arms with his confessor to accomplish these last steps together. He meant the gesture as a declaration: The Protector of St. Andrews had played an equal role in gaining their nation's freedom. As the two old comrades shuffled with bated steps across the wet sand, only the crash of waves could be heard above the muted coughs and muffled sobs around them.

After an hour of agonizing effort, they finally reached the hermit's lair.

Robert crumpled down against a boulder, and motioned the bishop to rest aside him. No larger than a servant's room, the dank chamber had been charred black from thousands of fires set by pilgrims who had come there to petition miracles. Respectful of their privacy, the commoners held back at the cave's entrance while Jeanne covered the two men with blankets. She lit a fire for their warmth and then retired to the beach.

Robert gazed out at the fading light across Ireland. His brother Edward's headless corpse lay over there in some unmarked hole. Andrew, Nigel, and Thomas languished in potter's fields somewhere in England, denied shriven burials. If the pope's churchmen spoke true, his brothers had forfeited their excommunicated souls for him. No, for Scotland. He had to believe that, else he could not bear the burden. He muttered in anguish, "Will it last?"

Lamberton cupped his ear to aid his failing hearing. "My lord?"

"This peace. When we are gone, what will prevent the English from waging war on us anew? The lad on their throne reminds me of Longshanks. Full of the blood lust."

Lamberton squinted toward the shore, trying to make out the weathered faces of their fellow countrymen pressing shoulder-to-shoulder to stay warm. Many of them he had baptized as babes. "Look upon your proud subjects. You have given them a legacy more precious than a fleeting truce. For the first time, they know that they can defeat the English. Will there be more wars? Aye, the world has known nothing else. But our struggle will not have been in vain. Never has so wee a nation subdued such a haught oppressor."

Robert sighed wearily, haunted by the same questions that had dogged him for years. Had that oracle spider on Arran been a figment of his fevered mind? How had Christiana discovered him so close to death's door? Did an angel light that fire on Turnberry's coast to bring him home?

It all seemed a shadowy dream now. In recent months, the border between reality and phantasmagoria had become more difficult for him to discern, and during the early morning hours in particular, he would become entrapped in visions so vivid that they dredged up more emotion than did waking life. He would fight the battles again, giving different orders and this time suffering defeats. The worst was a recurring nightmare in which he was captured and executed while all three Edward Plantagenets watched. When snared in these nightly struggles within his own mind, he was visited with a gnawing sense that he was being shown how his life might have played out had it not been directed by the hand of God. As he pondered these vexing mysteries, he became groggy, and slowly he slipped into a fitful sleep.

As dusk approached, Thomas Randolph risked a cautious approach into the cave. He gently jostled the slumbering king's shoulder. "My liege, the light recedes. We must return you to the priory soon."

Roused from his troubled slumber, Robert wiped the sleep from his eyes and struggled to his knees. "A moment more, Tom."

Recovering from his own nap, Lamberton understood what the king now wished. The bishop brought forth the holy water from his sacramental pouch and wrapped his shoulders with the frayed penitential stole that he had carried in every campaign since Methven. He had long ago sidestepped the papal nuncio forbidding the sacraments in Scotland by offering his own Culdee rites. This hour, he would do so again. "Shall I order the others away?"

Robert shook his head. "Beckon them closer."

The bishop hesitated. "If you are to give your confession—"

"What I say to God, I will say to them."

Lamberton motioned the barons into the cave, and the commoners on the beach surged nearer and knelt near the mouth.

Robert signed his breast. "I have placed the salvation of us all in doubt."

"No, my lord!" the Scots on the beach shouted. "No pope rules us!"

Robert raised a quivering hand to acknowledge their fealty. "I have made two sacred vows in my life. This day, by the grace of the Almighty, I have fulfilled one. The second I will not live long enough to accomplish. I must petition the aid of others to assist me in seeing that task finished. … When I die, I wish my heart taken to Jerusalem."

A mournful silence met that astounding request.

The Scots could not bear the thought of the heart that won Bannockburn resting forever in a foreign land. Yet not even Lamberton could dissuade the king from the conviction that the Curse of Malachy would continue to blacken his clan and the realm if he did not fulfill his grandfather's dying request: That he go to Jerusalem in penance for their forefather's hanging of the thief in violation of the saint's plea for mercy.

After a hesitation, Randolph stepped forward. "Sire, tell us who you wish to perform the deed, and it will be done."

"I would have my council choose."

These noblemen charged with the momentous decision shared uncertain glances. Randolph was clearly the most capable of accomplishing such an arduous and dangerous journey. But others exceeded him in rank, including Duncan of Fife, Patrick of Dunbar, Hugh of Ross, and Donald of Mar. The Culdee monks also had a claim to the honor, and although Lamberton was too feeble, the younger clerics attached to his office would argue their prerogative. As the men huddled and debated the best candidate, word of the king's request was passed, whisper to whisper, through the crowds below the cave.

A distant voice from the shoreline shouted, "Douglas!"

The commoners took up the chant, until not even the roar of the sea could drown out their pleas. "Douglas! Douglas!"

Lamberton smiled with pride as he palmed Robert's forehead to seal the sacrament. "Your subjects have chosen for you."

Robert enlivened on hearing their preference, but just as swiftly, he turned aside, full of despair. "I could not ask another such sacrifice of Lord Douglas."

"No one deserves the honor more," Randolph said.

Robert could not bring himself to look at those around him. "He holds me in ill esteem, for I have cost him dearly. Nothing could sway him to accept."

Lamberton knew the hard truth in that assessment. During the passage of years, he had repeatedly failed to persuade James to abandon his bitterness and reconcile with Robert. The bishop shook his head, and both lords and commoners, denied in their hope, slumped in disappointment.

Prisoner to a dilemma, Jeanne had stood on the periphery, listening to the debate. She threaded the ranks of noblemen and came before the king. "Lord Douglas will perform this deed."

The men waited to hear an explanation for that unlikely prediction, but Jeanne merely drew the cloak over her head and walked out of the cave.

j ames wandered through the graveyard of St. Bride's kirk, studying the faded headstones and contemplating their dark irony. He had fought for decades to gain freedom from England, and now, with the peace treaty finally signed, he found himself without a purpose. Ever since joining Robert's cause that fateful day outside Dumfries, he had dreamed of retiring to the life of a gentleman in leisure. But having attained it, he had no one to share in the bounty of victory. He often rode here from Lintalee to while away the days, even though all that remained of Douglasdale were this kirk and the ruins of his father's tower. He picked two handfuls of goldenrod and placed them on the graves of his stepmother and his father's servant, Dickson. Then, he entered the chapel and knelt at the front pew.

This is where I wish to rest.

Alas, he would rest there alone. Resisting Robert's petulant demands, he had never taken a wife. Jeanne had not returned to Lintalee after Elizabeth's death. He had been too proud to send for her. It was during low times like this that Sweenie would have raised his spirits with a taunt. He wondered what the little monk was up to in the spirit world. No doubt looping a snare of trouble for some unsuspecting Weardale shepherd.

He heard his dog, Mungo, whining below the window of the kirk. The old hound, bred from Chullan's bloodline, was as old as the twin mastiffs had been at Bannockburn. Chullan had died soon after that battle, his destiny fulfilled after sending Robert Clifford to a muddy grave. Mungo had been out of sorts lately. The dog still chased Northumbrian rabbits that treaded across the border, but at night it whimpered and pined for the men in the army, who were now long gone. He had considered finding a new companion for the mastiff, but he feared a pup would just run them both to death and—

"Are you the Black Douglas?"

He turned on the kneeler with his dagger drawn. How many times in his life had he heard *that* challenge? Every knave in England seemed bent on hunting him down to earn fame in a duel. Were they now stalking him even to his clan's kirk? He squinted in the dim light, and at the chapel's entrance saw a dark-skinned boy with agate eyes bathed in sadness.

He took a step closer to the intruder. "What is it you want?"

"I bring a message from the king."

"Toy with me, whelp, and I'll cut out that lying tongue." He stole a glance through the window and saw a dappled hobbin tied to a tree. How had this lad come upon him so easily? "Has Robert Bruce turned so skinflint that he refuses to pay couriers now? Does he wish me to win another battle for him? Arrest another of his subjects so he can enjoy watching him drawn and quartered?"

"The king is dying."

He braced on the pew and steeled his emotions, refusing to give Robert the comfort of a report detailing his grief. "What do I care? Leave me be!"

The boy retreated to the door, then turned back. "I was told to say something more." When James marched down the aisle to speed him away, the boy pressed his eyes closed and braced for the blow. As the shadow of a punishing arm came over him, he sputtered the words that he had memorized, "There be nothing stronger than a man's bond with his comrade in battle."

James held back his raised hand, stunned to hear the admonition that had been spoken years ago by his father on the morning he had left this very ground to go fight with Wallace. "Who told you that?"

"My mother."

"And she would be?"

"Her name is Jeanne."

James angled closer for the light streaming through the slit window. Only then did he see a younger version of his own face staring back at him.

"**B**ring up the light horse! The Welsh are on our flank!" As the king ranted orders, the barons stood around his bed, helpless to ease his delirium. He had fallen into another abyss of dementia, this one lasting three days, and his fevered rages were now so violent that the physicians had ordered his wrists tethered to the posts. Those who had been with him at Methven remembered how the disease first struck him on the field against the Comyns. Now, with the ink barely dried on their new treaty with England, the fragile peace was already imperiled. The king's heir, David, was too young to rule, and if the English learned of this approaching death, Edward III would declare the treaty invalid and rush his army across the border again.

Randolph pleaded, "My lord, you must calm yourself."

Robert fought against the restraints, his manic eyes darting at imaginary enemies. "Clifford masses! Where is Jamie?"

Randolph pressed a compress to the king's scabbed face. "Sire, Lord Douglas is not—"

"Douglas is on the field," said a voice at the door.

The men turned in shock.

Randolph rushed to grasp James's hand in gratitude for coming.

Robert, hearing the report to duty, cried, "Jamie! Your schiltrons to the fore, else we are turned!"

As the barons and clerics filed out to leave James alone with the dying king, the wind slammed the door shut, and the window shutters rattled with a report as loud as the first clash of pikes at Bannockburn.

Robert thrashed at blows being landed on him in battle.

James untied his wrists and jangled a sword near his old friend's ear to mimic the receding clash of arms. "The English break."

Robert eased his agitation. "Don't leave me."

"I am here, my lord."

Robert dragged the compress from his suddenly lucid eyes. "Lord? Must it be that, Jamie? Am I nothing but a king to you now?" He reached for his wrist to bring him nearer. "As always, you arrive at the battle's climax."

"And, as always, you have positioned me there."

Robert sank into the bed, reassured. He swallowed hard to muster the strength to speak. This rare gift of sanity, he knew, would not last long. "The Templars must be afforded perpetual refuge. Order them to keep the Stone hidden until David is rid of his regency."

"The monks are safe in the Isles. Sinclair commands them under the guise of a new guild. The Dominicans will not lay hands on them."

"This lad on England's throne will come at you when I'm gone."

"Let him come." James pressed a hand against Robert's chest to aid his breathing. Could this faint beat truly be driven by the lion's heart that had led them through so many travails?

"Do you remember our vow?"

"Aye, but that matters nothing——"

"Last night, I had a dream." Robert heaved with shallowing pants. "We were riding together again … in a foreign land … Columba's star led us to Our Lord's tomb … Jamie, will you …" He turned away, unable to finish the request.

"I will take you, Rob."

Robert lay staring into the distance as if locked upon the star.

James tested Robert's wrist for a pulse, and found the hand cold. He pressed a finger to close the king's lips in death and stood to go report his death to the waiting councilors.

"Roland."

At the door, James turned. Had his imagination conjured that whispered name? But it was true—Robert was still breathing, and his half-lidded eyes angled toward the bed table. On it sat the volume of chansons recounting the adventures of their favorite French knights, Roland and Oliver. He had long ago forgotten both the book and their promise to save the last chapter for their final victory. He turned to the first page and studied the inscription that Belle had written during their last moments together. "Where did you find this?"

Even in his weakened state, Robert managed a slight smile.

"You stole it *again*?"

"Read."

James pulled up a chair and thumbed through the fragile pages. Each chapter had marked a turning point in their conjoined destinies, inspiring them to carry on when all had seemed hopeless. The book had been with them on their miraculous crossing at Loch Lomond, in the cave on Arran, at their near-disastrous invasion at Turnberry, on the heights of Loudon Hill, and at their glorious victory at Bannockburn. Now, it had miraculously reappeared.

"Where did we stop?" Robert asked, his voice but a faint whisper.

James coughed to clear the clutch from his throat. "The Saracens had the Franks surrounded in Spain."

"Aye, the Vale of Thorns. Roland is searching for Oliver."

James found the place he had marked with a fir needle. "No, Roland has already found him."

"Found him?" Robert protested. "That is not as I remember it."

"Would you have me tell it, or not?"

Robert smiled through tears; even in this final hour, they could not avoid a quarrel.

Mollified with that concession, James returned to the story. "Oliver is mortally wounded in the eyes. But he fights on, blinded. He strikes Roland upon the head by mistake."

Robert begged, barely audible, "Not Roland."

James hesitated as he turned to the last page; it was stained with the mud of Bannockburn. Now it all came flooding back to him. In a fit of despairing rage, he had cast the book aside on the night that he had learned of Belle's death. Robert must have recovered it in Cambuskenneth Abbey and saved it for him.

He looked down at Robert. "You did not read ahead?"

Robert's eyes remained closed. "I waited ... for you."

James opened the buttons on Robert's sweat-drenched shirt. There, on his chest, was the scar from Clifford's sword at Methven. And on his forearm, the gnarled fracture from the blow at Moss Raploch. Beneath his proud, intractable bearing had walked a broken body. Why had he allowed their last years to be wasted? They should have been spent together, enjoying their victories over a warm fire and good drink. It all seemed faded now, the nursed wounds and perceived slights. He had failed to heed Belle's dying request, and had let down the two persons he most loved in the world. Now, all that was left to finish was this foolish tale. He drew a reluctant breath and began:

"Roland looks at Oliver's face
Which is pale, discoloured and grayish;
Blood runs down his body, clots
Form on the ground. Roland says: 'God!
I do not know what I shall do,
Old comrade, if I must lose you.'
Roland looks at Oliver with much
Affection and says tranquilly:
'Surely, that was not meant for me?
It is I, Roland, your old friend
Who wants only to make amends.'
Oliver says: "Now I hear you speak.
I cannot see you. I am too weak.
May God see you. I am sorry,
When I struck you I struck blindly.'
Roland answers: 'No harm done,
And before God, I wish you none.'
They bow to one another and so
Part with great love between the two."

"I'm sorry," Robert gasped.

"No matter. I would have just lost the book again if you had——"

"Your lass." Robert opened his swollen eyes for a brief moment. "I'm sorry I took her from you."

Before James could regain his composure, Robert stopped breathing.

That last act of contrition had released him. Even in death, he had insisted on the last word. Thinking the chanson finished, he had given up his spirit without allowing the forgiveness to be reciprocated.

Ah, Rob, you have charged on without me.

Fighting for his voice, James read the last chanson verses aloud, for he would never let it be said that he had left any task assigned by his king undone:

"Roland sees his friend in death,
Face down and with dust in his teeth.
Very gently he says good-bye:
'Oliver, so there you lie!
We have been days and years together
And never either harmed the other;
With you dead, there is nothing in life.'"

hat evening, James escorted Robert's body to Cambuskenneth Abbey, where it rested for three days on a bier overlooking the battlefield of Bannockburn. The funeral entourage then passed to the south of Loch Lomond and lingered at the banks where Sweenie had ferried them to safety from the MacDougall hounds. An honor guard composed of McKie, McClurg, and the Templars rode behind the gurney, with the mastiff Mungo bringing up the rear. The thousands who lined the route threw garlands and rushed forward to touch the casket. At Dunfermline, the king's heart was sealed in a silver reliquary and his body buried in the Abbey next to Elizabeth. During the solemn ceremony, Walter Stewart, the nation's new Regent, hung Robert's encased heart, threaded with cowhide cords, around James's neck.

In the bay at St. Andrews, a galley sent by the MacDonalds waited to take James and the royal honor guard to the Holy Land. On this last night before his departure, James walked into the country's hallowed cathedral there to pay his last respects at Lamberton's tomb. The beloved bishop had passed away a few days after Robert's death. Only weeks before, the cleric had returned from Avignon, where he had renewed his demand that the spiritual interdiction against Scotland be lifted. Resigned at last to England's defeat, Pope John XXII had reluctantly rescinded the bull of excommunication against Scotland. The Church had finally been forced to recognize a king crowned by a Pictish princess, anointed by Culdee monks, and protected by heretical Templars.

The bishop had finally won his holy war for the old Celtic Church.

At midnight, the mourners carried torches to the beaches below the cathedral so that Scotland might watch her king's heart sail away. As his small currach was pushed off from the rocks, James saw Jeanne and her son standing on the bluffs. Ordering the oars held, he waded back to the dunes and stood before the boy who had brought him the news of Robert's impending death.

"I never asked your name."

The boy pawed at the sand with his foot, afraid to look up. "Archibald."

James whistled Mungo from the boat, and when the old hound bounded through the water toward them, he told the boy, "Take care of Mungo for me, will you, Archie? We'll all go hunting when I get back." He hugged his son goodbye and repeated the last words that his own father had spoken to him before being led away to London Tower. "Remember that you are a Douglas. You bend to none but God and your—"

A collective gasp of alarm interrupted his instruction to his son.

He looked up at the watery horizon and saw two warships slicing the fog and sailing up alongside the waiting MacDonald galley. Their masts had hoisted banners bearing the Plantagenet leopards. The Scots began retreating to the bluffs to prepare for an English attack, and he was about to climb the sea wall to muster the defenses when Jeanne grasped his arm to stop him.

She pointed to a white banner being raised on the foremast of the lead ship. "They have been sent as safe escort."

Had Isabella arranged this? He could not believe that she would risk such a gesture, even though the two kingdoms had suspended hostilities. Given her precarious position with the English parliament in London, the offer was as dangerous as it was magnanimous.

He gazed across the moorlands one last time and gave thanks for the many lasses who had appeared with aid for him at pivotal moments in his life. Christiana's prophecy in the Arran cave had indeed come to pass: Belle, Eleanor, Idonea, Christiana, Elizabeth, Jeanne, Marjorie, the Galloway crone—all had proven stronger than the men of England. History would not remember their sacrifices, for the cold-blooded monks who recorded the deeds of kings and warriors gave scant credit to the lasses who stood with them. But Christiana's clairvoyance had proven all too true: Without these women, he and Robert would never have prevailed in their war for independence.

He filled his lungs with the fresh air of his homeland, recalling that day years ago when he had sailed off with Lamberton for France. On his return from Paris, he had vowed never to leave this Isle again.

So much for oaths.

What was it that Isabella had once told him? Aye, never allow yourself to be drawn into the orbit of a king.

He walked with Jeanne to the water's edge, and whispered to her, "Take care of Lintalee. When I am back in two years, I'll make things right between us." He kissed her and pushed the currach into the sea.

As he was rowed away, the haze cleared, and he looked toward the sky. His heart ached with an inexplicable dread.

He could not find Columba's star.

FORTY-ONE

A rush of alien sensations assaulted James as he led his nine men up the marble steps of Sevilla's palace. Castilian tongues clattered around him while pungent aromas from the *murakkaba* breads leavening in the market kilns flared his nostrils. He began to feel light-headed, blinded by the glare of the harsh Spanish sun that refracted off a towering minaret left by the Moors who had once governed here.

The Templar d'Aumont did not hide his disgust at being subjected to such insidious infidel influences. "We should have continued on to Majorca."

"The galley requires provisioning," James reminded the monk. "And Keith's broken arm must be tended. What harm can come of enjoying the Castilian king's hospitality for a few days?"

D'Aumont and his two Templar brothers, including William Sinclair, hid their necklaces with the outlawed Beausant insignia. The court of Alfonso XI would be thick with Dominican inquisitors, they knew, and if their affiliation were to be discovered, these rabidly devout Castilians would not hesitate to enforce the papacy's call for their arrests, given the Temple's history in this country. Decades ago, the French grand master had abandoned Castile to the Moors, a betrayal that gave rise to the formation of a rival Spanish order, the Knights of Calatrava, whose monks were still embroiled in a crusade to wrest the borderland of Al Andalus from Muslim Granada.

A turbaned functionary led the Scots into the royal hall, and the swarthy Calatravans turned and greeted them with cold silence.

King Alfonso, alone of all the Castilians present, appeared delighted by their arrival. The twenty-year-old monarch with sparkling black eyes and aquiline nose leapt from his chair to greet his famous guest. There was an excessive gracefulness in his manner, the flowing sleeves of his white silk robe tumbling with each flourish of his slender hands. James had expected to find an ascetic warrior-king in the mold of the heroic Cid, but this boy resembled more an

Arab caliph or a Greek potentate. Was that a hint of eye lining, or were his lashes naturally prominent?

At Alfonso's signal, a troubadour knelt before James and sang:

"Two hearts, noble, stout;
One beating, one mute;
Two realms, fierce, redoubt;
One free, one resolute;
The great Alfonso remembers Bruce
And welcomes Douglas, warrior yet
Who on the English did fiercely loose
A sharp defeat they shan't forget."

Cupping the heart cask that hung from James's neck, Alfonso studied it as if he were touching a holy relic. "Is it true, Lord Douglas, that you and your king were once hunted by dogs?"

James was surprised that the reports of his Loch Lomond escape had made it all the way to Espagna. He shrugged off the feat, quipping with self-deprecation, "Even starving hounds would not have bothered with our fleshless bones."

Alfonso smiled at his humility. "Do you not believe that the Almighty has a purpose for all events, even those seemingly random?"

"I am a man of arms, Sire. I leave theology to the clerics."

"What about your famous spider? Was it not sent at the moment of your direst need?"

"Aye, I believe it was."

"And your biblical Stone. Miraculously unearthed for King Bruce."

"God's hand was upon us then, as well."

"So you *do* delve into theology." Alfonso retreated into prayer as he walked before the ranks of his Calatravans. He stopped under a high balustrade that held a life-sized Christ on a cross twice the size of any crucifix extant in Scotland. He glanced up, leading his guest's attention toward the icon.

James marveled at the realistic carving of Our Lord in His travails. He could not shake the feeling that Christ's bleeding face and liquiscent glass eyes were focused directly on him alone.

Alfonso waited for the crucifix to work its power. "I too am a pious servant of God. And I believe the Almighty's grace has been visited on me this day. He has brought me the greatest warrior alive. At the moment of my darkest peril."

D'Aumont checked James with a forearm to his chest. "Lord Douglas is sworn to an oath."

Alfonso ignored that remonstrance and closed in on his famous guest. "Your King Bruce fervently desired to take the Cross, no?"

"How did you learn of this?" James asked.

Alfonso's eyes shaded with sadness. "A pity the Bruce did not see his dream fulfilled." The king delayed as if wishing to say something more, but then thought better of it. "My seneschal will see to it that you are well supplied. I will commission our Cistercians at San Clemente to pray for your safe journey on to Palestine." He folded his hands in preparation to take his leave.

James glared at d'Aumont for having insulted their royal host. Clearly, the Castilian monarch had sought only the honor of their companionship.

Walking from the hall, Alfonso stopped below the crucifix. Visited with a revelation, he turned back to James. "Perhaps it can yet be accomplished."

"My lord?"

"Your King Bruce's wish. The Holy Land is now open only to pilgrims, so you will see no battle there. But here, on the plains of Al Andalus, the great Douglas could win eternal salvation for the valiant Bruce. And you and your knights could be off to the Holy Sepulcher before winter sets in."

"The Bruce asked for Jerusalem only," d'Aumont insisted.

James stood mesmerized by the possibility. For thirty years he had prayed for the chance to take up the Cross and fulfill the boyhood vow he had made with Robert. Yet the Templar spoke true; he was compelled to decline the invitation to join the Iberian crusade, for it would require contravening the dictates of Parliament. "You do me great honor, Highness. But I am constrained by the mission set upon me by my country."

A ravishing lady with dark Egyptian features appeared from the shadowed periphery and came slithering to Alfonso's side. She had ringlets of chestnut hair and enchanting green eyes; a wide gold belt hung low on her jewel-studded gown of crimson velvet and fell in a chevron to the valley below her waist, allowing her comely hips to lead each step. Announced by the ambrosial scent of cassia perfume, she stood before James and studied his dark features. "You have the look of an Iberian. Pray tell, why is this?"

"I can answer only to my deeds," James said. "Not to the color of my skin."

The lady's alluring smile suddenly gave way to a glare of disdain. She turned from him dismissively and announced to the Calatravans, "This man cannot be the Douglas of Scotland."

Alfonso admonished her harshly in Castilian. Then, the king begged forgiveness from James. "Our women speak too freely. I pray you take no offense."

James saw that his stunning accuser seemed unfazed by the scolding. In truth, she utterly entranced him. "It is I who owes the apology. I seem to have disappointed the lady."

"Allow me to introduce Dona Leonor de Guzman," the king said.

James nodded knowingly, having heard the bards in La Rochelle sing of the beautiful mistress who had scandalously replaced the older Queen Dona Maria of Portugal in Alfonso's bed. Yet their flattering descriptions had not done her justice. Why was he quivering like a schoolboy? He had not felt such stirrings since … He bowed and kissed the back of her wrist.

She abruptly withdrew her hand, grazing his upper lip with the bevel of her garnet ring. She paraded before the celibate Calatravans, whose marred cheeks and jagged noses gave evidence of their past wounds. With a half-lidded look of derision, she turned back and found James's eyes still watering from the sting of her ring's scrape. "Your face bears no scars. No warrior who fought as many battles as the Douglas would be so unscathed."

Sinclair bristled at the slander. "You see no marks because Lord Douglas was too quick for any Englishman."

Dona Leonor drew a kerchief from her sleeve and staunched a thin seep of blood on James's lip. "I fear I have given him his first." She lowered her eyes to his hands, as if expecting a demonstration of their prowess. She slid her fingers down his forearm to test its strength.

His hand was quivering.

Greeting that discovery with a seductive smile, the lady called for a goblet of wine from an attendant. She brought the cup to James's lips, coupling her fingers over his.

He tried to pull away, fearful that Alfonso would take offense to such a bold display of intimacy.

Amused by his modesty, the Dona savored another sip under his admiring yet disconcerted gaze—and dropped the goblet.

James lunged to catch it, too late.

The goblet clanged to the floor, spilling the wine and coming to rest near the boots of the smirking Calatravans.

The Dona released his wrist with a flick of contempt and shot a haughty sneer at Sinclair. "Perhaps it is for the best that Scotland's champion does not challenge the Moors. The infidels are much quicker than Englishmen with the sword." With a sweep of her flared sleeve, she turned away and lamented, "Alas, there are no Roland and Oliver for our time."

James had bent to one knee to retrieve the goblet. Hearing her muttered aside, he looked up at her with a start. "What did you just say, my lady?"

She turned back, appearing surprised by his interest. "Roland and Oliver. You would never have heard of them. They were gallant knights who came to our land years ago to defend God's cause. The story is a mere fable, I fear. I see now that such chivalry is practiced only by Castilians." She whipped her train to the crease of her elbow, lashing his face lightly in a taunt, and continued her exit. As she passed, the men watched her ravishing form, revealed and hidden with each flow of her clinging gown.

At the portal, she glanced at Alfonso and shared a private smile with him before disappearing into the darkness of the stairwell.

S hielding his dry eyes from the brutal Andalusian sun, James searched the mountain range behind him to the north. Nearly ten leagues away, on the barren horizon, stood the besieged Castillo della Estrella—the Castle of the Stars—a formidable keep that reached so high on its rocky outcropping that the Moors believed it had once touched Heaven.

"The Calatravans should have come up by now," d'Aumont warned him. "We had best turn back for Sevilla."

James ignored the Templar's advice and drove his contingent of nine knights deeper into another arid *barranco* whose burnt scape was broken only by a few patches of olive trees. Convinced that Dona Leonor's invocation of Roland and Oliver was a divine sign, he had agreed to command a wing of Alfonso's army. But the Castilians maneuvered so methodically that, after a week of campaigning, he had decided to press ahead, intent upon seducing the Moors and their leader Osmin into a trap, just as he had done to Clifford at Glen Trool.

If only the infidel coward would stop and fight.

The Saracen scouting party they had been chasing for two days had disappeared again into the blazing Spanish haze.

His throat was so parched that he could barely swallow. Their water skins were dry and the heat was so unrelenting that steam rose from the buckles of their hauberks. Through all of the hardships in the English campaigns, he had never experienced sunstroke. He felt as if his soul was being flayed. He prayed the frothing horses would make it to the next plateau, and reaching the thistle-plagued crest, he looked down into a hull-shaped vale rimmed by rows of dying pomegranate striplings. At its lowest point, three Moslem women stood shading themselves under a smattering of palm trees. Draped in black robes and hoods, they drew a bucket from an oasis well.

Black ravens circled above them—a certain sign of water.

He licked his cracked lips. Muttering a prayer of thanks to God, he led his men on their staggering mounts down the ridge toward the blessed discovery.

Seeing their approach, the women hurried away—all but one, the tallest. She peered through her gossamer veil, and held her jar aloft in an offer.

He removed his helmet in anticipation of wetting his swollen tongue.

The woman walked toward him with her black robes whipping in the hot wind. A few steps away, she dropped her veil and hood.

My God ... can it truly be?

He thought there could be no fluid left in his body, but tears streamed down his cheeks. Had the Almighty granted him the miracle he had long petitioned? Many of the returned crusaders had said their most fervent prayers were answered in reward for the torments they endured for Christ.

Belle wept as she offered him the jar. "Drink, my love."

He reached to caress her blessed cheek. Her hair smelled of fresh rose water and her light copper skin was as smooth and unblemished as on that first day she had hovered over him during his boyhood race. How had she escaped the Berwick cage? He tried to clear his mind, but the blinding throbs kept attacking his temples. Had Caernervon concocted the false report of her death? Had the knave somehow deceived Isabella into unwittingly abetting the plot? Fighting faintness, he pressed his palms to his burning cheeks.

God damn these headaches!

A cascade of fractured thoughts flooded his brain. Rather than surrender Belle after Bannockburn, Caernervon must have secreted her here from England and ordered her nursed back to health to be used as a pawn in future negotiations. But why had he hidden her in this outback? Of course! The treacherous Dominicans had confined her in some desolate Spanish nunnery in exchange for being allowed to install the Inquisition on the Isles. After Caernervon was deposed, the monks must have abandoned her rather than reveal their role in the nefarious deed.

Belle dipped her sleeve into the water to cool his grimed face. "It is all in the past now, Jamie. If we're to fill that manor with those children, we'd best head home and get started."

He gasped with joy. Heaven-sent proof!

Only she knew of the plans they had discussed on the eve of the Methven ambush. He accepted the jar with trembling hands and poured its soothing water down his throat and across his seared face. Replenished, he moistened his lips and leaned down to receive the kiss he had been denied for half his life. The jar fell from his grasp—shards shattered across the sun-cracked ground.

Morgainne stood grinning up at him.

Distant shouts in a foreign tongue rang out from the ridgelines.

Disoriented, he turned to search for Belle again, but she had vanished. He looked up to the horizon. Surrounding him were five hundred mounted Moors flying banners with the Red Crescent. Their leader, Osmin, smiled down at him and, seeing no sign of the Calatravans, raised his hands skyward to thank Allah for the good fortune.

The shape-shifting goddess drew a sickle from under her robe and honed its edge with a sharpening stone. "Did ye think I'd forgotten?"

He swallowed painfully and tasted blood on his cracked tongue. Not a drop of water had touched it. The death hag, he realized, had deceived him with her glamourie. He clutched his breast, reassured at least that the heart cask still hung from his neck. "I gave Robert my word on Jerusalem."

"Aye, ye did make that promise, didn't ye? But your fate was writ in the stars long before. Comes round all life, biting its tail in the eternal jig." She smiled at him one last time, then sank into her hood and disappeared in a whirlwind of sand. Moments later, a raven flew from the vortex and fluttered away.

"Jamie!" Sinclair called out. "Are you heatstruck?"

Roused, James blinked hard. There was no spring well before him, only more dust-choked plains. He drew a wheezing breath and hung his head in despair.

Ah Rob, I have failed you.

Alfonso's lady had spoken true. He *had* grown too old for the fighting. His gut instincts for sensing a trap had failed him.

As McKie, McClurg, and the Templars formed up in a mounted schiltron around him, he nodded in grim acceptance of his fate, and then rode aside d'Aumont. "There is something I have long wished to ask you."

D'Aumont girded his breastplate. "Then you had best ask it quickly."

"Those scrolls of the saints you found in Jerusalem. Did they affirm Our Lord's promise of Heaven's reward?"

With an admonishing glare, D'Aumont repulsed that question born from a crisis of faith. "You know I have taken an oath of secrecy."

"Aye, and was that oath made to the same God of the Roman Church who abandoned your Order to the torture chambers of Paris?"

D'Aumont paled at that reminder of the Church's betrayal.

"Have we Scots not been more brother to you than those tonsured sheep in Avignon?"

The Templar sighed, nodding to confirm the truth of that point. Driven to the revelation, he said in a near whisper, "There will be no Day of Judgment. No bodily escape from the grave."

Shaken, James watched as the Moors on the ridges drew their scimitars and made a great show of forming up and contending over which squadron would take the honor of leading the assault. "And the Resurrection?"

D'Aumont shook his head at the futility of it all. "Our Lord reappeared to the Apostles in spirit only. He never sought to be nailed to the Cross. Only a fool, or worse, a priest, would claim that needless suffering leads to salvation. Christ begged his disciples to follow His teaching, not to worship His untimely death. His brother James and the Magdalene understood this. Most did not."

"If Christ did not overcome the flesh for our sins, how then are we to be redeemed?"

"Not by blind belief in the dictates of murderous popes."

"Then these crusades against the infidel have been for naught?"

D'Aumont nodded bitterly. "There have been many creeds. But none have ever been superior to one's own truth. Our war is not fought between faiths. It is fought by the legions of Light against the archons of Darkness."

James dropped his chin to his chest. Why had he asked such a blasphemous question at this last hour of his life? Thousands of crusaders before him had gone to their deaths fortified at least with the certainty of Heaven's approach. Now he understood why certain conspirators in the Church had goaded the French king and his puppet pope to eradicate these Templars. If the contents of their Jerusalem scrolls were ever widely revealed, the reason for the Church's wars against the Albigensee heretics and these Saracens would be exposed: The suppression of Christ's true mission.

He thought he had come to know these Templars, but the more he learned about them, the more shrouded in mystery they seemed. "If you do not revere Our Lord's Tomb, why then did you accompany me on this journey?"

D'Aumont and his two monks reached into their packs and unfurled their old mantles emblazoned with the splayed red crosses, just as they had done at the climax of the charge at Bannockburn. Theirs would be the last Templar blood shed in battle. Unlike the beams of the Roman cross of mortification, the traverses of their *cross pattée* did not end disconnected, but flared until their tips nearly merged, an esoteric promise that those who fought against the slavery of Darkness would one day reunite to defend the Light of Truth again.

On the ridges around them, the Moors saw the red crosses. They reined back, daunted by the reappearance of an old enemy they thought long vanquished.

D'Aumont straightened in the saddle and glared defiantly against what Fate had brought him in his final hour. Finding James still waiting for an answer to his question, the Templar finally admitted, "We came because you Scots gave us refuge."

James turned aside in shame, disgusted at having pitied his own misfortune. At least he would die on a mission for his country. These men were about to sacrifice themselves for a mere debt of honor.

Devoid of a plan for the first time in his life, he could think of nothing more to do but ride forward and mark off those fighting at his side, an old habit. He reached the end of his line of mounted warriors and rubbed his bleared eyes. Was his roasted mind betraying him again? He circled and again counted ten knights—one more than he had brought here, with Keith back in Seville tending his broken arm.

A ruddy-faced newcomer spat a maw of chewed root at the hooves of James's horse. "Another bonnie scrape you've led us into, Douglas."

James blinked hard, confounded. Where had he seen that deft arc of spittle before? *No, it couldn't be.* The death goddess had to be playing another one of her perverse tricks on him. "Gib?"

"I'm still of the opinion that you're touched in the head."

"Where did you come from?" James asked, questioning his own sanity.

"I never left you."

James glanced at the Templars to test if they too saw Gibbie Duncan, his boyhood mate who had jumped to death on the gallows at Berwick. Had these monks applied their occult craft to tear away the veil separating this world from the next? Did this prove the Culdee claim that existence is a circle, spiraling from flesh to shade and back to flesh?

"A lass is waiting for you over that ben," Gibbie reported, gnawing casually on a root. "She said to tell you to look up."

James lifted his pained eyes to the sky, now cast in that liminal golden light of a late Spanish afternoon, when the constellations could be seen without the aid of darkness. Above the Castle of the Stars, he found the tail of Sirius, trailed by a lone silvery orb, pulsing and bright.

Keep watch on Columba's star. I will find you.

Drawing strength from that reminder of Belle's promise, he reined forward, and as he straightened in the saddle, he felt Robert's heart cask bouncing against his breastbone. Its weight felt the same as the elf-stone he had abandoned on the burning cage at Berwick. He had become so accustomed to carrying Belle's talisman over these many years that he had all but forgotten its burden. Had she clairvoyantly given him the stone that day in Douglasdale to prepare him for this final task?

The Moors screamed their battle cry, signaling the attack.

He offered up a silent prayer to Columba's star, just as the saint had done centuries ago from his lonely perch atop Iona's grassy hillocks. Death's approach was not what brought the ache of anguish to his breast now. No, it was the realization that he, like Columba, would never see home again. He closed his eyes and tried to imagine Loch Lomond on an autumn day. The purple heather was ablaze and the oaks turned orange and red. A mizzling rain began to dimple the glittering surface that danced with trout and fireflies, and a bracing breeze wafted down the blue-green slopes of Glen Falloch to cool his burning forehead. He would have stayed there forever had the distant shouts not transformed from the high-pitched Arabic into the guttural yelps of Yorkshire English.

Morgainne had granted him a last miracle.

Before him lay the Dryfield scarp at Bannockburn. Not the infidels, but Caernervon's thousands, were coming at him now.

He would die in Scotland, after all.

He drew the Dun Eadainn ax from behind his back.

As the enemy closed in from all sides, McKie, McClurg, and the Templars slammed down their visors to meet the onslaught.

Bemused by it all, Gibbie leaned an elbow against his pommel and spat the last of his root mash in a jet that grazed James's nose. "So, what would the famous Black Douglas of Lanark who never suffered a scratch upon his pretty face have us do now?"

James sat lost in the center of the storm. As the ring of dust quickened and closed in on him, the ground quaked from the pounding of a thousand hooves. He removed the cask from his neck and stared at it wistfully. Robert's heart would be lost, left to languish here …

They got us in fists, but we got them in wits.

He laughed aloud, braced by those words of bravado that Robert had quipped to him when the Comyns had ambushed them as lads. If Gibbie *were* with him now, could Robert, Sweenie, and the others be far behind, spouting their taunts and jests? A balm of lightness swept over him, and then another thought struck: Had Robert arranged this doomed journey to speed his reunion with Belle?

"Jamie!" Gibbie cried over the rising din. "What do we do now?

James leaned across the saddle and thumped his boyhood friend on the chest. "We do what we've always done." He whipped Robert's heart cask by the cord above his head and heaved it forward at the infidels like a slingshot. Spurring to his last charge, he grinned at Gibbie and shouted, "We follow our king!"

EPILOGUE

NORFOLK, ENGLAND
FEBRUARY, 1358

As the queen mother came to the end of her account, William Douglas sat in stunned silence. He remembered, as a lad, having heard that one of the Scots in the honor entourage, a knight named Keith, had been left in Seville to mend his broken arm. When Keith learned of the disastrous battle on the Al Andalus plains, he had rushed to the field and found James's riddled body near the thrown heart cask. Keith had brought both back to Scotland. Sighing from weariness with the world, he stood to take his leave, unable to comprehend why God had denied King Robert and his uncle their dream of reaching the Holy Land.

Isabella, daubing her eyes with a kerchief, placed a hand on his forearm to delay him a moment more. "The Bruce's heart, I was told, now lies at Melrose Abbey?" When Douglas confirmed that report, she hesitated before risking the one question she had withheld for too many years. "I was never told where your uncle was laid to rest."

"In the Douglasdale kirk of St. Bride." The earl displayed his clan's crest on his brooch to her. "The guardians of my kingdom ordered a heart be added to our herald in honor of his sacrifice."

She studied the crest, then looked up at him. "You fought at Poiters?"

The earl nodded bitterly. More than a year had passed since that disastrous defeat in France, but his memory of it was still raw.

"Do you know who lost that battle for you?"

The earl glared at her, unable to fathom why she would punish him with such a cruel question.

"Your uncle taught my son how to fight at Weardale. Edward in turn imparted those lessons to my grandson, the Black Prince. So, as I see it, you Scots have only yourselves to blame for your predicament."

He smiled grimly at the irony. "One heart has yet to return home to Scotland, my lady. I would be grateful to know where the Countess of Buchan rests."

Isabella turned aside to muffle a cough of emotion. "I was never told, but I fear she was abandoned to the pauper's pit at Berwick."

Seeing that she too had grown fatigued, William made another move to depart. At the door, he heard her call him back.

"The last time your uncle and I spoke," she said, "he told me something else in confidence. The night that he and Robert Bruce looked death in the face on Arran Isle, there was more to the spider's prophecy."

Intrigued, William glanced at his squire.

Isabella stared into the fire. "The clairvoyant Isleswoman promised him that your Stone of Destiny would remain hidden until its scream is again required. She also said that the Templars charged with its protection would one day resurrect themselves in the guise of another brotherhood and fulfill their quest for tolerance of faith and conscience in a land far across the sea."

William did not know what to make of the strange revelation.

"Now," Isabella insisted. "There is a secret *you* must surrender to *me*. ... This man with you is not your second."

"Madam, I assure you that—"

When Isabella stood abruptly to repulse that lie, William finally nodded his accomplice forward and gestured him to an admission.

"My mother was ..."

Isabella confirmed the confession for him. "Jeanne de Rouen."

Archibald Douglas glanced at the door, worried that the guards would discover his true identity as the bastard son of the Black Douglas. "I escaped your grandson's prison in Poiters by passing myself off as a commoner who could bring no ransom. None of the officers in your army would believe that a Scot nobleman could have skin as dark as a Moor's. Your pale English made the same mistake when they underestimated my father."

Isabella warmed her hands over the last of the flickering embers, debating if she should reveal this deception to the castellan, who reported all of her activities to her son. She asked Archibald, "Do you believe, sir, that a lone abiding love can change the world?"

Archibald's face tightened. "I swear on the Holy Rood that I have seen only war and bloodshed bend the will of men. And I swear on my father's memory that I will not rest until England suffers what we Scots have long endured."

Smiling sadly, Isabella stared beyond his shoulders, as if speaking to a specter behind him. "Men swear such oaths. Women suffer the consequences."

"My lady?"

Drawn back to the present, Isabella promised Archibald, "My influence in London court has waned, but I will attempt to find you safe passage to Scotland. In return, you must do me two favors."

The generous offer astonished Archibald. "Anything within my power."

Isabella shuffled with bated steps toward the altar and opened the Bible that sat on its lintel. She took out a pressed red poppy she had picked on her last walk along the Seine in Paris. "Place this in the kirk at Douglasdale."

Archibald accepted custody of the remembrance. "And the second?"

The queen mother retreated to the small lancet window that offered her only view of the outside world. She had stood there often over the years wondering how the Countess of Buchan had survived her confinement under much worse conditions. "If you are unfortunate enough to live to be my age, you will encounter many a doubter who will gainsay what I have just told you about the triumph of love. Argue not with them like a rabid churchman. Was a heart ever swayed by cold logic or a hot pyre?"

The two Scotsmen shrugged, unable to offer a contradicting example.

She grasped Archibald's hand, as if to summon a distant memory from the ancient blood pulsing in his touch. "Rather, sit them down in one of your storied castles above a moonlit loch, and pour them a horn of your finest spirit, one that musters the ghosts and curls the tongue with the taste of history. Then, tell them, as I have you, of your father and his brave Lass of Scone, and how they gave all to crown a king and set a nation free."

AUTHOR'S NOTE

The poet who could do justice to the exploits of
Douglas would win himself great and enduring fame.
— John Barbour, *The Brus*

William Douglas, the nephew of James Douglas, visited Isabella of France shortly before her death in 1358, but nothing was recorded of their conversation. Nor is it known if Archibald Douglas, who escaped prison after the Battle of Poiters, was present at this meeting, although he accompanied his cousin on the campaigns in France.

Primary sources for Scotland's wars of independence during the 14th century are limited, and they have suffered the accusation, levied against many medieval accounts, that legend intrudes. The most comprehensive source is *The Brus*, an epic written in 1375 by John Barbour, Archdeacon of Aberdeen. Barbour relied on first-hand reports of participants who spoke several years after the events. The cleric vowed to tell the truth as best he could find it, and most historians believe that, in large measure, he succeeded. An unabashed admirer of James Douglas, Barbour depicted him as Bruce's equal in skill, cunning, and courage.

In his *Tales of a Grandfather*, Sir Walter Scott described Robert Bruce as the first to see the spider in the cave. Yet researchers have confirmed that Scott's version was based on an account in Hume of Godcroft's history of the Douglas clan, written two hundred years earlier. In Godcroft, it is Douglas who sees the spider and convinces Bruce of its significance.

To my knowledge, I am the first author to suggest the possibility that James Douglas and Isabelle MacDuff were lovers. Baffled by Isabelle's decision to turn against her husband and clan, chroniclers in England at the time spread rumors that she was Robert Bruce's mistress. Yet I contend that it was more likely her love for Douglas that drove the Countess of Buchan to risk her life by placing the crown on Bruce's head.

Barbour offered a tantalizing hint of this in his description of the escape from Methven. Elizabeth Bruce, Isabelle MacDuff, and the king's sisters accompanied their husbands on that desperate retreat after the English ambush. The archdeacon revealed with a euphemistic wink that among those harried Scot warriors trying to get Robert Bruce and his family to safety, "not one among them there that to the ladies' profit was more than James of Douglas." The modern biographer I.M. Davis was more direct; without hazarding a guess as to the woman in question, he wrote that Douglas "may have been running a love affair" during the Methven campaign.

It seems implausible that Douglas would have carried on such an affair with Elizabeth Bruce or the married Bruce sisters during the retreat, particularly while their husbands—his comrades—were in danger and in such close proximity. Isabelle MacDuff, however, was estranged from John Comyn, an enemy of the Bruces. Falling in love with Douglas would explain her decision to risk her life and abscond west with the Bruces. Moreover, Davis found no record indicating that Douglas had ever married. The late Caroline Bingham observed in her biography of Robert Bruce that the king would have expected his councilors to take wives for the sake of propriety and the smooth devolution of titles and domains. Barbour described Douglas's life in great detail, but the cleric inexplicably failed to explain this mystery. The most likely explanation is one that the chroniclers of the time would have failed to know, or would have deemed too private to record: A broken heart.

This story is historical fiction, not academic history, and aspects of it are, by necessity, speculative. I took liberties with, and filled gaps in, traditional accounts of the period with my portrayal of: 1) James Douglas's boyhood, of which little is known except that he came under the tutelage of Bishop Lamberton and accompanied the cleric to Paris; 2) Douglas's relationship with Jeanne de Rouen, a character that I created because nothing is known about the identity of the woman who gave birth to his son Archibald out of wedlock; and 3) the fascinating and controversial Isabella of France. Twice Douglas narrowly missed capturing the English queen, and they came together for the last time in Berwick to formalize the peace agreement and forge the marriage between David Bruce and Isabella's daughter. Beyond that, their interactions must be left to the imagination.

Finally, historians continue to debate the factual basis for the legend that a small band of Knights Templar escaped the persecutions in France and, after being given refuge in Scotland, came to Robert Bruce's aid at Bannockburn. To defend that possibility, I would remind readers of what M. Louis Charpentier, the French author and researcher of medieval Gothic cathedrals, once cautioned: "When history and tradition are not in agreement, it is safe to bet, almost as a certainty, that it is the historians, makers of history, who are deceived."

SOURCES
AND
ACKNOLWEGEMENTS

The ballad *Raglan Road* was written by the late Irish poet Patrick Kavanaugh. Quotations from John Barbour's epic, *The Brus*, are from Tom Scott's translations in his *Tales of King Robert the Bruce*. The song on the galleys during the Turnberry invasion was based upon Robert Burns's poem, *March to Bannockburn*, which was likely based on verses sung during the Bruce wars. Belle's ballad in the cage is from the old Celtic song, *The Braes O'Balquiddher*. Excerpts describing the adventures of Roland and Oliver are from *The Story of Roland* by James Baldwin.

A special thanks goes to Alyssa Rasley and John Jeter for their superb editing; to John Rechy and the members of his writing workshop for their guidance and support; and to David Martin, Michelle Millar, and Stewart Matthew.

The definitive biography of James Douglas is I.M. Davis's *The Black Douglas*. Biographies of Robert Bruce are numerous, but my favorite is the late Caroline Bingham's *Robert the Bruce*. Pat Gerber's *Stone of Destiny* offers theories about the relic, and Michael Prestwich's *The Three Edwards* explores the lives of those Plantagenet monarchs. Several books have been written about Bannockburn and the disputed location of the second day's battle; Peter Reese's *Bannockburn* provides a good overview. Yet the most valuable and memorable account of the battle that I had the privilege to receive came from a private tour generously conducted by the late Bob McCutcheon, a Stirling bookseller and local expert on the Bruce years. After walking the battlefield with Mr. McCutcheon one memorable afternoon, I came to understand not only the tactics, but also the proud Scottish temperament that helped win that unlikely victory.

About the Author

A graduate of Indiana University School of Law and Columbia University Graduate School of Journalism, **Glen Craney** practiced trial law before joining the Washington press corps to cover national politics and the Iran-contra trial for *Congressional Quarterly* magazine. The Academy of Motion Pictures, Arts and Sciences awarded him the Nicholl Fellowship prize for best new screenwriting. He is also a Chaucer Award First-Place Winner, a two-time indieBRAG Medallion Honoree, and a three-time *Foreword Reviews* Book-of-the-Year Award Finalist. His debut historical novel, *The Fire and the Light,* was named Best New Fiction by the National Indie Excellence Awards and a Finalist/Honorable Mention winner for *Foreword's* BOYTA in historical fiction. His novels have taken readers to Occitania during the Albigensian Crusade, to the Scotland of Robert Bruce, to Portugal during the Age of Discovery, to the trenches of France during World War I, and to the American Hoovervilles of the Great Depression. He lives in Malibu, California.

Dear Reader: Please visit my website at **www.glencraney.com** and join my **mailing list** to be the first to received special offers and news of upcoming titles. And if you enjoyed this book and feel it worthy, I would be grateful for honest reviews on Amazon and Goodreads. Thank you.